Praise for

SKYWARD

AN INSTANT *NEW YORK TIMES* BESTSELLER
A *KIRKUS REVIEWS* BEST BOOK OF THE YEAR

★ "Startling revelations and stakes-raising implications. . . .
SANDERSON PLAINLY HAD A BALL with this
**NONSTOP, HIGHFLYING OPENER, and READERS
WILL TOO."** —*Kirkus Reviews,* starred review

★ "With this **ACTION-PACKED** trilogy opener, Sanderson
offers up a **RESOURCEFUL, FEARLESS HEROINE** and
A MEMORABLE CAST. . . . As the **PULSE-POUNDING
STORY** intensifies and reveals its secrets, a cliffhanger
ending sets things up for the next installment."
—*Publishers Weekly,* starred review

"It is **IMPOSSIBLE TO TURN THE PAGES
FAST ENOUGH."** —*Booklist*

"Sanderson delivers **A CINEMATIC ADVENTURE** that
explores the defining aspects of the individual versus
the society. . . . Fans of [his] will not be disappointed."
—*SLJ*

"An **ADVENTURE AND A HALF** that you
WON'T WANT TO MISS." —Tor.com

"**SANDERSON HAS DONE IT AGAIN!** . . . [His] ability to
tell a story [while] also making you feel like one of the team
shows why he's one of the most well-known and
beloved authors in the sci-fi world at the moment."
—*The Nerd Daily*

SKYWARD

BRANDON SANDERSON

EMBER

Text copyright © 2018 by Dragonsteel Entertainment, LLC
Cover art copyright © 2018 by Charlie Bowater

Maps and illustrations by Isaac Stewart and Ben McSweeney,
copyright © 2018 by Dragonsteel Entertainment, LLC

All rights reserved. Published in the United States by Ember, an imprint of Random House Children's Books, a division of Penguin Random House LLC, New York. Originally published in hardcover in the United States by Delacorte Press, an imprint of Random House Children's Books, New York, in 2018.

Ember and the E colophon are registered trademarks of Penguin Random House LLC.

Reckoners®, Mistborn®, and Brandon Sanderson® are registered trademarks of Dragonsteel Entertainment, LLC.

Visit us on the Web! GetUnderlined.com

Educators and librarians, for a variety of teaching tools,
visit us at RHTeachersLibrarians.com

The Library of Congress has cataloged the hardcover edition of this work as follows:
Names: Sanderson, Brandon, author.
Title: Skyward / Brandon Sanderson.
Description: First edition. | New York : Delacorte Press, [2018] |
Series: Skyward ; 1 | Summary: When a long-term attack against her world by the alien Krell escalates, Spensa's dream of becoming a pilot may come true, despite her deceased father being labeled a deserter.
Identifiers: LCCN 2018026175 (print) | LCCN 2018033837 (ebook) |
ISBN 978-0-399-55579-4 (el) | ISBN 978-0-399-55577-0 (hc) |
ISBN 978-0-399-55578-7 (glb)
Subjects: | CYAC: Science fiction. | Survival—Fiction. | War—Fiction. | Air pilots—Fiction. | Extraterrestrial beings—Fiction. | Classification: LCC PZ7.S19797 (ebook) |
LCC PZ7.S19797 Sky 2018 (print) | DDC [Fic]—dc23

ISBN 978-0-399-55580-0 (pbk.)

Printed in the United States of America
10 9 8 7 6 5 4 3 2 1
First Ember Edition 2019

For Karen Ahlstrom,
who counts all the
days that I forget

United Defiant Caverns
Below Alta Base

Alta Base

Public Elevators

Private Elevators

Spensa's Cave

to Bountiful Cavern →

← to Vici

Igneous

Underground River

Deep Caverns

Highway Cavern

Magma Vein

Alta Base

Launchpads
Hangars
Shield Emitter
Statue
Park
Parade
Ground
Flight
School
Hangars
Launchpads
Public Elevator
Complex
Private Vehicle
hangar
Private Elevator
Complex
to Spensa's
Cave →

Defensive
Perimeter
Surrounding
Alta Base

Defensive Perimeter of Large AA Guns
Alta Base
75 km
120 km
AA Guns' Outermost Range

PROLOGUE

Only fools climbed to the surface. It was stupid to put yourself in danger like that, my mother always said. Not only were there near-constant debris showers from the rubble belt, but you never knew when the Krell would attack.

Of course, my father traveled to the surface basically every day—he had to, as a pilot. I supposed by my mother's definition that made him *extra* foolish, but I always considered him extra *brave*.

I was still surprised when one day, after years of listening to me beg, he finally agreed to take me up with him.

I was seven years old, though in my mind I was completely grown-up and utterly capable. I hurried after my father, carrying a lantern to light the rubble-strewn cavern. A lot of the rocks in the tunnel were broken and cracked, most likely from Krell bombings—things I'd experienced down below as a rattling of dishes or trembling of light fixtures.

I imagined those broken rocks as the broken bodies of my enemies, their bones shattered, their trembling arms reaching upward in a useless gesture of *total and complete defeat.*

I was a very odd little girl.

I caught up to my father, and he looked back, then smiled. He had the *best* smile, so confident, like he never worried about what people said about him. Never worried that he was weird or didn't fit in.

Then again, why should he have worried? *Everyone* liked him. Even people who hated ice cream and playing swords—even whiny little Rodge McCaffrey—liked my father.

Father took me by the arm and pointed upward. "Next part is a little tricky. Let me lift you."

"I can do it," I said, and shook off his hand. I was grown-up. I'd packed my own backpack *and* had left Bloodletter, my stuffed bear, at home. Stuffed bears were for babies, even if you'd fashioned your own mock power armor for yours out of string and broken ceramics.

Granted, I *had* put my toy starfighter in my backpack. I wasn't crazy. What if we ended up getting caught in a Krell attack and they bombed our retreat, so we had to live out the rest of our lives as wasteland survivors, devoid of society or civilization?

A girl needed her toy starfighter with her just in case.

I handed my backpack to my father and looked up at the crack in the stones. There was . . . something about that hole up there. An unnatural light seeped through it, wholly unlike the soft glow of our lanterns.

The surface . . . the sky! I grinned and started climbing up a steep slope that was part rubble, part rock formation. My hands slipped and I scraped myself on a sharp edge, but I didn't cry. The daughters of pilots did *not* cry.

The crack in the cavern roof looked a hundred meters away. I hated being so small. Any day now, I was going to grow tall like my father. Then for once I wouldn't be the smallest kid around. I'd laugh at everyone from up so high, they'd be forced to admit how great I was.

I growled softly as I got to the top of a rock. The next hand-hold was out of reach. I eyed it. Then I jumped, determined. Like a good Defiant girl, I had the heart of a stardragon.

But I also had the body of a seven-year-old. So I missed by a good half meter.

A strong hand seized me before I could fall too far. My father chuckled, holding me by the back of my jumpsuit, which I'd painted with markers to look like his flight suit. I had even drawn a pin on the left over my heart, like the one he wore—the pin that marked him as a pilot. It was in the shape of a small starfighter with lines underneath.

Father pulled me onto the rock beside him, then reached out with his free hand and activated his light-line. The device looked like a metal bracelet, but once he engaged it by tapping two fingers against his palm, the band glowed with a bright molten light. He touched a stone above, and when he drew his hand back, it left a thick line of light like a shining rope fixed to the rock. He wrapped the other end around me so it fit snugly under my arms, then detached it from his bracelet. The glow there faded, but the luminescent rope remained in place, attaching me to the rocks.

I'd always thought light-lines should burn to the touch, but it was just warm. Like a hug.

"Okay, Spin," he said, using my nickname. "Try it again."

"I don't *need* this," I said, plucking at the safety rope.

"Humor a frightened father."

"Frightened? You aren't frightened of anything. You fight *the Krell*."

He laughed. "I'd rather face a hundred Krell ships than your mother on the day I bring you home with a broken arm, little one."

"I'm *not* little. And if I break my arm, you can leave me here until I heal. I'll fight the beasts of the caverns and become feral and wear their skins and—"

3

"Climb," he said, still grinning. "You can fight the beasts of the caverns another time, though I think the only ones you'd find have long tails and buckteeth."

I had to admit, the light-line was helpful. I could pull against it to brace myself. We reached the crack, and my father pushed me up first. I grabbed the rim and scrambled out of the caverns, stepping onto the surface for the first time in my life.

It was so *open*.

I gaped, standing there, looking up at . . . at nothing. Just . . . just . . . *upness*. No ceiling. No walls. I'd always imagined the surface as a really, really big cavern. But it was so much more, and so much less, all at once.

Wow.

My father heaved himself up after me and dusted the dirt from his flight suit. I glanced at him, then back up at the sky. I grinned widely.

"Not frightened?" he asked.

I glared at him.

"Sorry," he said with a chuckle. "Wrong word. It's just that a lot of people find the sky intimidating, Spensa."

"It's beautiful," I whispered, staring up at that vast nothingness, air that extended up into an infinite greyness, fading to black.

The surface was still brighter than I'd imagined. Our planet, Detritus, was protected by several enormous layers of ancient space debris. Junk that was *way* up high, outside the air, in *space*. Wrecked space stations, massive metal shields, old chunks of metal big as mountains—there were many layers of it, kind of like broken shells around the planet.

We hadn't built any of that. We'd crashed on this planet when my grandmother was a girl, and this stuff had been ancient then. Still, some of it worked. For example, the bottom layer—the one closest to the planet—had enormous glowing rectangles in it.

4

I'd heard of those. Skylights: enormous floating lights that gave illumination and warmth to the planet.

There was supposed to be a lot of littler bits of junk up there too, particularly in the lowest layer. I squinted, trying to see if I could pick any of that out, but space was too far away. Other than the two nearby skylights—neither of which was directly above us—the only things I could see were some vague patterns up there in the greyness. Lighter chunks and darker chunks.

"The Krell live up there?" I asked. "Beyond the debris field?"

"Yes," Father said. "They fly down through the gaps in the layers to attack."

"How do they find us?" I asked. "There's so much *room* up here." The world seemed a much larger place than I'd imagined in the caverns below.

"They can somehow sense when people gather together," Father said. "Anytime the population of a cavern gets too big, the Krell attack and bomb it."

Decades ago, our people had been part of a fleet of space vessels. We'd been chased by the Krell to this planet and had crashed here, where we'd been forced to split up to survive. Now we lived in clans, each of whom could trace their lineage back to the crews of one of those starships.

Gran-Gran had told me these stories many times. We'd lived for seventy years here on Detritus, traveling the caverns as nomadic clans, afraid to congregate. Until now. Now we'd started to build starfighters and had made a hidden base on the surface. We were starting to fight back.

"Where's Alta Base?" I asked. "You said we'd come up near it. Is that it?" I pointed toward some suspicious rocks. "It's right there, isn't it? I want to go see the starfighters."

My father leaned down and turned me about ninety degrees, then pointed. "There."

"Where?" I searched the surface, which was basically all just

5

blue-grey dust and rocks, with craters from fallen debris from the rubble belt. "I can't see it."

"That's the point, Spensa. We have to remain hidden."

"But you fight, don't you? Won't they eventually learn where the fighters are coming from? Why don't you move the base?"

"We have to keep it here, above Igneous. That's the big cavern I showed you last week."

"The one with all the machines?"

He nodded. "Inside Igneous, we found manufactories; that's what lets us build starships. We have to live nearby to protect the machinery, but we fly missions anywhere the Krell come down, anywhere they decide to bomb."

"You protect other clans?"

"To me, there is only *one* clan that matters: humankind. Before we crashed here, we were all part of the same fleet—and someday all the wandering clans will remember that. They will come when we call them. They'll gather together, and we'll form a city and build a civilization again."

"Won't the Krell bomb it?" I asked, but cut him off before he could reply. "No. Not if we're strong enough. Not if we stand and fight back."

He smiled.

"I'm going to have my own ship," I said. "I'm going to fly it just like you. And then nobody in the clan will be able to make fun of me, because I'll be *stronger* than they are."

My father looked at me for a moment before he spoke. "Is *that* why you want to be a pilot?"

"They can't say you're too small when you're a pilot," I said. "Nobody will think I'm weird, and I won't get into trouble for fighting because my *job* will be *fighting*. They won't call me names, and everyone will love me."

Like they love you, I thought.

That made my father hug me for some stupid reason, even

6

though I was just telling the truth. But I hugged him back, because parents liked stuff like that. Besides, it did feel good to have someone to hold. Maybe I shouldn't have left Bloodletter behind.

Father's breath caught, and I thought he might be crying, but it wasn't that. "Spin!" he said, pointing toward the sky. "Look!"

Again I was struck by the expanse. *So BIG.*

Father was pointing at something specific. I squinted, noting that a section of the grey-black sky was darker than the rest. A hole through the layers of debris?

In that moment, I looked out into infinity. I found myself trembling as if a billion meteors had hit nearby. I could see space itself, with little pinpricks of white in it, different from the skylights. These sparkled, and seemed so, so far away.

"What are those lights?" I whispered.

"Stars," he said. "I fly up near the debris, but I've almost never seen through it. There are too many layers. I've always wondered if I could get out to the stars."

There was awe in his voice, a tone I'd never heard from him before.

"Is that . . . is that why you fly?" I asked.

My father didn't seem to care about the praise the other members of the clan gave him. Strangely, he seemed *embarrassed* by it.

"We used to live out there, among the stars," he whispered. "That's where we belong, not in those caverns. The kids who make fun of you, they're trapped on this rock. Their heads are heads of rock, their hearts set upon rock. Set *your* sights on something higher. Something more grand."

The debris shifted, and the hole slowly shrank until all I could see was a single star brighter than the others.

"Claim the stars, Spensa," he said.

I *was* going to be a pilot someday. I would fly up there and fight. I just hoped Father would leave some Krell for me.

I squinted as something flashed in the sky. A distant piece of

7

debris, burning brightly as it entered the atmosphere. Then another fell, and another. Then dozens.

Father frowned and reached for his radio—a superadvanced piece of technology that was given only to pilots. He lifted the blocky device to his mouth. "This is Chaser," he said. "I'm on the surface. I see a debris fall close to Alta."

"We've spotted it already, Chaser," a woman's voice said over the radio. "Radar reports are coming in now, and . . . *Scud*. We've got Krell."

"What cavern are they headed for?" Father asked.

"Their heading is . . . Chaser, they're heading this way. They're flying straight for Igneous. Stars help us. They've located the base!"

Father lowered his radio.

"Large Krell breach sighted," the woman's voice said through the radio. "Everyone, this is an emergency. *An extremely large group of Krell has breached the debris field.* All fighters report in. They're coming for Alta!"

Father took my arm. "Let's get you back."

"They need you!" I said. "You've got to go fight!"

"I have to get you to—"

"I can get back myself. It was a straight trip through those tunnels."

Father glanced toward the debris again. "Chaser!" a new voice said over the radio. "Chaser, you there?"

"Mongrel?" Father said, flipping a switch and raising his radio. "I'm up on the surface."

"You need to talk some sense into Banks and Swing. They're saying we need to flee."

Father cursed under his breath, flipping another switch on the radio. A voice came through. "—aren't ready for a head-on fight yet. We'll be ruined."

8

"No," another woman said. "We have to stand and fight."

A dozen voices started talking at once.

"Ironsides is right," my father said into the line, and—remarkably—they all grew quiet.

"If we let them bomb Igneous, then we lose the apparatus," my father said. "We lose the manufactories. We lose everything. If we ever want to have a civilization again, a *world* again, we *have to stand here!*"

I waited, silent, holding my breath, hoping he would be too distracted to send me away. I trembled at the idea of a battle, but I still wanted to watch it.

"We fight," the woman said.

"We *fight*," said Mongrel. I knew him by name, though I hadn't met him. He was my father's wingmate. "Hot rocks, this is a good one. I'm going to beat you into the sky, Chaser! Just you watch how many I bring down!"

The man sounded eager, maybe a little too excited, to be heading into battle. I liked him immediately.

My father debated only a moment before pulling off his lightline bracelet and stuffing it into my hands. "Promise you'll go back straightaway."

"I promise."

"Don't dally."

"I won't."

He raised his radio. "Yeah, Mongrel, we'll see about that. I'm running for Alta now. Chaser out."

He dashed across the dusty ground in the direction he'd pointed earlier. Then he stopped and turned back. He pulled off his pin and tossed it—like a glittering fragment of a star—to me before continuing his run toward the hidden base.

I, of course, immediately broke my promise. I climbed down into the crack but hid there, clutching Father's pin, and watched

9

until I saw the starfighters leave Alta and streak toward the sky. I squinted and picked out the dark Krell ships swarming down toward them.

Finally, showing a rare moment of good judgment, I decided I'd better do what my father had told me. I used the light-line to lower myself into the cavern, where I recovered my backpack and headed into the tunnels. I figured if I hurried, I could get back to my clan in time to listen to the broadcast of the fight on our single communal radio.

I was wrong though. The hike was longer than I remembered, and I did manage to get lost. So I was wandering down there, imagining the glory of the awesome battle happening above, when my father infamously broke ranks and fled from the enemy. His own flight shot him down in retribution. By the time I got home, the battle had been won, my father was gone.

And I'd been branded the daughter of a coward.

PART
ONE

PART
ONE

1

I stalked my enemy carefully through the cavern.

I'd taken off my boots so they wouldn't squeak. I'd removed my socks so I wouldn't slip. The rock under my feet was comfortably cool as I took another silent step forward.

This deep, the only light came from the faint glow of the worms on the ceiling, feeding off the moisture seeping through cracks. You had to sit for minutes in the darkness for your eyes to adjust to that faint light.

Another quiver in the shadows. There, near those dark lumps that must be enemy fortifications. I froze in a crouch, listening to my enemy scratch the rock as he moved. I imagined a Krell: a terrible alien with red eyes and dark armor.

With a steady hand—agonizingly slow—I raised my rifle to my shoulder, held my breath, and fired.

A squeal of pain was my reward.

Yes!

I patted my wrist, activating my father's light-line. It sprang to life with a reddish-orange glow, blinding me for a moment.

13

Then I rushed forward to claim my prize: one dead rat, speared straight through.

In the light, shadows I'd imagined as enemy fortifications revealed themselves as rocks. My enemy was a plump rat, and my rifle was a makeshift speargun. Nine and a half years had passed since that fateful day when I'd climbed to the surface with my father, but my imagination was as strong as ever. It helped relieve the monotony, to pretend I was doing something more exciting than hunting rats.

I held up the dead rodent by its tail. "Thus you know the fury of my anger, fell beast."

It turned out that strange little girls grow up to be strange young women. But I figured it was good to practice my taunts for when I *really* fought the Krell. Gran-Gran taught that a great warrior knew how to make a great boast to drive fear and uncertainty into the hearts of her enemies.

I tucked my prize away into my sack. That was eight so far—not a bad haul. Did I have time to find another?

I glanced at my light-line—the bracelet that housed it had a little clock next to the power indicator. 0900. Probably time to turn back; I couldn't miss *too* much of the school day.

I slung my sack over my shoulder, picked up my speargun—which I'd fashioned from salvaged parts I'd found in the caverns—and started the hike homeward. I followed my own hand-drawn maps, which I was constantly updating in a small notebook.

A part of me was sad to have to return, and leave these silent caverns behind. They reminded me of my father. Besides, I liked how . . . empty it all was. Nobody to mock me, nobody to stare, nobody to whisper insults until I was forced to defend my family honor by burying a fist in their stupid face.

I stopped at a familiar intersection where the floor and ceiling gave way to strange metal patterns. Circular designs marked with scientific writing covered both surfaces; I'd always thought they must be ancient maps of the galaxy. On the far side of the room, an enormous, ancient tube emerged from the rock—one of many that moved water between the caverns, cleansing it and using it to cool machinery. A seam dripped water into a bucket I'd left, and it was half full, so I took a long drink. Cool and refreshing, with a tinge of something metallic.

We didn't know much about the people who had built this machinery. Like the rubble belt, it had been here already when our small fleet crashed on the planet. They'd been humans, as the writings on places like this room's ceiling and floor were in human languages. But how distantly related they were to us was a mystery even now. None of them were still around, and the melted patches and ancient wrecks on the surface indicated that they had suffered their own war.

I poured the rest of the water into my canteen, then gave the large tube a fond pat before replacing the bucket and moving on. The machinery seemed to respond to me with a distant, familiar thrumming. I followed that sound and eventually approached a glowing break in the stone on my left.

I stepped up to the hole and looked out on Igneous. My home cavern and the largest of the underground cities that made up the Defiant League. My perch was high, providing me with a stunning view of a large cave filled with boxy apartments built like cubes splitting off one another.

My father's dream had come true. In defeating the Krell that day over nine years ago, those fledgling starfighter pilots had inspired a nation. Dozens of once-nomadic clans had congregated, colonizing Igneous and the caverns around it. Each clan had its own name still, traced back to the ship or section of the ship they'd worked on. My clan was the Motorskaps—from the old words for *engine crew*.

Together, we called ourselves Defiants. A name taken from our original flagship.

15

Of course, in gathering together, we had drawn the attention of the Krell. The aliens were still determined to destroy humankind, so the war continued, and we needed a constant stream of starfighters and pilots to protect our burgeoning nation.

Towering over the buildings of Igneous was the apparatus: ancient forges, refineries, and manufactories that pumped molten rock from below, then created the parts to build starfighters. The apparatus was both amazing and unique; though machinery in other caverns provided heat, electricity, or filtered water, only the apparatus of Igneous was capable of complex manufacturing.

Heat poured through the crack, making my forehead bead with sweat. Igneous was a sweltering place, with all those refineries, factories, and algae vats. And though it was well lit, it somehow always felt gloomy inside, with that red-orange light from the refineries shining on everything.

I left the crack and walked to an old maintenance locker I'd discovered in the wall here. Its hatch looked—at first glance—like any other section of the stone tunnel, and so was relatively secure. I popped it open, revealing my few secret possessions. Some parts for my speargun, my spare canteen, and my father's old pilot's pin. I rubbed that for good luck, then placed my light-line, map book, and speargun in the locker.

I retrieved a crude stone-tipped spear, clicked the hatch closed, then slung my sack over my shoulder. Eight rats could be surprisingly awkward to carry, particularly when—even at seventeen—you had a body that refused to grow beyond a hundred and fifty-one centimeters.

I hiked down to the normal entrance into the cavern. Two soldiers from the ground troops—which barely ever did any real fighting—guarded the way in. Though I knew them both by their first names, they still made me stand to the side as they pretended to call for authorization for me to enter. Really, they just liked making me wait.

Every day. Every scudding day.

Eventually, Aluko stepped over and began looking through my sack with a suspicious eye.

"What kind of contraband do you expect I'm bringing into the city?" I asked him. "Pebbles? Moss? Maybe some rocks that insulted your mother?"

He eyed my spear as if wondering how I'd managed to catch eight rats with such a simple weapon. Well, let him wonder. Finally, he tossed the sack back to me. "On your way, coward."

Strength. I lifted my chin. "Someday," I said, "you will hear my name, and tears of gratitude will spring to your eyes as you think of how *lucky* you are to have once assisted the daughter of Chaser."

"I'd rather forget I ever knew you. *On your way.*"

I held my head high and walked into Igneous, then made my way toward the Glorious Rises of Industry, the name of my neighborhood. I'd arrived at shift change, and passed workers in jumpsuits of a variety of colors, each marking their place in the great machine that kept the Defiant League—and the war against the Krell—functioning. Sanitation workers, maintenance techs, algae vat specialists.

No pilots, of course. Off-duty pilots stayed in the deep caverns on reserve, while the on-duty ones lived in Alta, the very base my father had died protecting. It was no longer secret, but had grown into a large installation on the surface, housing dozens of ships along with the pilot command structure and training facilities. That was where I would live starting tomorrow, once I passed the test and became a cadet.

I walked under a large metal statue of the First Citizens: a group of people holding symbolic weapons and reaching toward the sky in defiant poses, ships rising behind them trailing streaks of metal. Though it depicted those who had fought at the Battle of Alta, my father wasn't among them.

The next turn took me to our apartment, one of many metal

cubes sprouting from a larger central one. Ours was small, but big enough for three people, particularly since I spent days at a time out in the caverns, hunting and exploring.

My mother wasn't home, but I found Gran-Gran on the roof, rolling algae wraps to sell at our cart. An official job was forbidden to my mother because of what my father had supposedly done, so we had to get by doing something unconventional.

Gran-Gran looked up, hearing me. Her name was Becca Nightshade—I shared her last name—but even those who barely knew her called her Gran-Gran. She had lost nearly all her sight a few years ago, her eyes having gone a milky white. She was hunched over and worked with sticklike arms. But she was still the strongest person I knew.

"Oooh," she said. "That sounds like Spensa! How many did you get today?"

"Eight!" I dumped my spoils before her. "And several are particularly juicy."

"Sit, sit," Gran-Gran said, pushing aside the mat filled with wraps. "Let's get these cleaned and cooking! If we hurry, we can have them ready for your mother to sell today, and I can get to tanning the skins."

I probably *should* have gone off to class—Gran-Gran had forgotten again—but really, what was the point? These days, we were just getting lectures on the various jobs one could do in the cavern. I had already chosen what I'd be. Though the test to become a pilot was supposed to be hard, Rodge and I had been studying for ten years. We'd pass for sure. So why did I need to hear about how great it was to be an algae vat worker or whatever?

Besides, since I needed to spend time hunting, I missed a lot of classes, so I wasn't suited to any other jobs. I made sure to attend the classes that had to do with flying—ship layouts and repair, mathematics, war history. Any other class I managed to make was a bonus.

I settled down and helped Gran-Gran skin and gut the rats. She was clean and efficient as she worked by touch.

"Who," she asked, head bowed, eyes mostly closed, "do you want to hear about today?"

"Beowulf!"

"Ah, the King of the Geats, is it? Not Leif Eriksson? He was your father's favorite."

"Did he kill a dragon?"

"He discovered a new world."

"With dragons?"

Gran-Gran chuckled. "A feathered serpent, by some legends, but I have no story of them fighting. Now, Beowulf, he *was* a mighty man. He was your ancestor, you know. It wasn't until he was old that he slew the dragon; first he made his name fighting monsters."

I worked quietly with my knife, skinning and gutting the rats, then slicing the meat and tossing it into a pot to be stewed. Most people in the city lived on algae paste. Real meat—from cattle or pigs raised in caverns with special lighting and environmental equipment—was far too rare for everyday eating. So they'd trade for rats.

I loved the way Gran-Gran told stories. Her voice grew soft when the monsters hissed, and bold when the heroes boasted. She worked with nimble fingers as she spun the tale of the ancient Viking hero who came to aid the Danes in their time of need. A warrior everybody loved; one who fought bravely, even against a larger and mightier foe.

"And when the monster had slunk away to die," Gran-Gran said, "the hero, he held aloft Grendel's entire arm and shoulder as a grisly trophy. He'd avenged the blood of the fallen, proving himself with strength and valor."

Clinking sounded from below in our apartment. My mother was back. I ignored that for now. "He ripped the arm free," I said, "with his *hands*?"

"He was strong," Gran-Gran said, "and a warrior true. But he was of the oldenfolk, who fought with hands and sword." She leaned forward. "You will fight with nimbleness of both hand and wit. With a starship to pilot, you won't need to rip any arms off. Now, have you been doing your exercises?"

I rolled my eyes.

"I saw that," Gran-Gran said.

"No you didn't."

"Close your eyes."

I closed my eyes and tipped my head back, face toward the ceiling of the cavern, far above.

"Listen to the stars," Gran-Gran said.

"I only hear—"

"Listen to the stars. Imagine yourself flying."

I sighed. I loved Gran-Gran and her stories, but this part always bored me. Still, I tried doing as she had taught me—sitting there with my head tipped back, I tried to imagine that I was soaring upward. I tried to let everything else fade around me, and to picture stars shining brightly above.

"I used to do this exercise," Gran-Gran said softly, "with my mother, on the *Defiant* in the engine rooms. We worked the flagship itself, a battle cruiser larger than this entire cavern. I'd sit and listen to the hum of the engines, and to something beyond that. The stars."

I tried to imagine her as a little girl, and somehow that helped. With my eyes closed, I felt as if I were almost floating. Reaching upward . . .

"We of the engine crew," Gran-Gran said, "were odd, among the other ship crews. They thought we were strange, but we kept the ship moving. We made it travel the stars. Mother said it was because we could hear them."

I thought . . . just for a moment . . . that I heard something out there. My imagination perhaps? A distant, pure sound . . .

"Even after we crashed here, we people of the engines stayed together," Gran-Gran said. "Clan Motorskaps. If others say you're strange, it's because they remember this, and maybe fear us. This is your heritage. The heritage of warriors who traveled the sky, and will *return* to the sky. Listen."

I let out a long, calming sigh as it—whatever I thought I'd heard—faded. I opened my eyes and was shocked, for a second, to find I was back on that rooftop, surrounded by the ruddy light of Igneous.

"We maintained the engines," I said, "and moved the ship? What does that have to do with being warriors? Wouldn't it have been better to fire the weapons?"

"Only a fool thinks that weapons are more important than strategy and motion!" Gran-Gran said. "Tomorrow let me tell you again of Sun Tzu, the greatest general of all time. He taught that position and preparation won wars—not swords or spears. A great man, Sun Tzu. He was your ancestor, you know."

"I prefer Genghis Khan," I said.

"A tyrant and a monster," Gran-Gran said, "though yes, there is much to learn from the Great Khan's life. But have I ever told you of Queen Boudicca, defiant rebel against the Romans? She was your—"

"Ancestor?" Mother said, climbing the ladder outside the building. "She was a British Celt. Beowulf was Swedish, Genghis Khan Mongolian, and Sun Tzu Chinese. And they're *all* supposedly my daughter's ancestors?"

"All of Old Earth is our heritage!" Gran-Gran said. "You, Spensa, are one in a line of warriors stretching back millennia, a true line to Old Earth and its finest blood."

Mother rolled her eyes. She was everything I wasn't—tall, beautiful, calm. She noted the rats, but then looked at me with arms folded. "She might have the blood of warriors, but today she's late for class."

"She's *in* class," Gran-Gran said. "The important one."

I stood up, wiping my hands on a rag. I knew how Beowulf would face monsters and dragons . . . but how would he face his mother on a day when he was supposed to be in school? I settled on a noncommittal shrug.

Mother eyed me. "He died, you know," she said. "Beowulf died fighting that dragon."

"He fought to his last ounce of strength!" Gran-Gran said. "He defeated the beast, though it cost him his life. And he brought untold peace and prosperity to his people! All the greatest warriors fight for peace, Spensa. Remember that."

"At the very least," Mother said, "they fight for irony." She glanced again at the rats. "Thanks. But get going. Don't you have the pilot test tomorrow?"

"I'm ready for the test," I said. "Today is just learning things I don't need to know."

Mother gave me an unyielding stare. Every great warrior knew when they were bested, so I gave Gran-Gran a hug and whispered, "Thank you."

"Soul of a warrior," Gran-Gran whispered back. "Remember your exercises. Listen to the stars."

I smiled, then went and quickly washed up before heading off to what would, I hoped, be my last day of class.

2

"Why don't you tell us what you do each day in the Sanitation Corps, Citizen Alfir?" Mrs. Vmeer, our Work Studies instructor, nodded encouragingly at the man who stood at the front of the classroom.

This Citizen Alfir wasn't what I'd imagined a sanitation worker to be. Though he wore a sanitation jumpsuit and carried a pair of rubber gloves, he was actually handsome: square jaw, burly arms, chest hair peeking out from above his tight jumpsuit collar.

I could almost imagine him as Beowulf. Until he spoke.

"Well, we mostly fix clogs in the system," he said. "Clearing what we call black water—that's mostly human waste—so it can flow back to processing, where the apparatus reclaims it and harvests both water and useful minerals."

"Sounds perfect for you," Dia whispered, leaning toward me. "Cleaning waste? A step up from coward's daughter."

I couldn't punch her, unfortunately. Not only was she Mrs. Vmeer's daughter, I was already on notice for fighting. Another write-up would keep me from taking the test, which was stupid. Didn't they want their pilots to be great fighters?

23

We sat on the floor in a small room. No desks for us today; those had been requisitioned by another instructor. I felt like a four-year-old being read a story.

"It might not sound glorious," Alfir said. "But without the Sanitation Corps, none of us would have water. Pilots can't fly if they don't have anything to drink. In some ways, we've got the most important job in the caverns."

Though I'd missed some of these lectures, I'd heard enough of them. The Ventilation Corps workers earlier in the week had said their job was the most important. As had the construction workers from the day before. As had the forge workers, the cleaning staff, and the cooks.

They all had practically the same speech. Something about how we were all important pieces of the machine that fought the Krell.

"Every job in the cavern is a vital part of the machine that keeps us alive," Alfir said, mirroring my thoughts. "We can't all be pilots, but no job is more important than another."

Next, he'd say something about learning your place and following commands.

"To join us, you have to be able to follow instructions," the man said. "You have to be willing to do your part, no matter how insignificant it may seem. Remember, obedience *is* defiance."

I got it, and to an extent agreed with him. Pilots wouldn't get far in the war without water, or food, or sanitation.

Taking jobs like these still felt like settling. Where was the spark, the energy? We were supposed to be *Defiant*. We were *warriors*.

The class clapped politely when Citizen Alfir finished. Outside the window, more workers walked in lines beneath statues with straight, geometric shapes. Sometimes we seemed far less a machine of war than a clock for timing how long shifts lasted.

The students stood up for a break, and I strode away before Dia could make another wisecrack. The girl had been trying to goad me into trouble all week.

Instead, I approached a student at the back of the room—a lanky boy with red hair. He'd immediately opened a book to read once the lecture was done.

"Rodge," I said. "Rigmarole!"

His nickname—the callsign we'd chosen for him to take once he became a pilot—made him look up. "Spensa! When did you get here?"

"Middle of the lecture. You didn't see me come in?"

"I was going through flight schematics lists in my head. *Scud.* Only one day left. Aren't you nervous?"

"Of course I'm not nervous. Why would I be nervous? I've got this *down.*"

"Not sure I do." Rodge glanced back at his textbook.

"Are you kidding? You know basically *everything,* Rig."

"You should probably call me Rodge. I mean, we haven't earned callsigns yet. Not unless we pass the test."

"Which we will *totally* do."

"But what if I haven't studied the right material?"

"Five basic turn maneuvers?"

"The reverse switchback," he said immediately, "Ahlstrom loop, the twin shuffle, overwing twist, and the Imban turn."

"DDF g-force warning thresholds for various maneuvers?"

"Ten Gs in a climb or bank, fifteen Gs forward, four Gs in a dive."

"Booster type on a Poco interceptor?"

"Which design?"

"Current."

"A-19. Yes, I know that, Spensa—but what if *those* questions aren't on the test? What if it's something we *didn't* study?"

At his words, I felt the faintest seed of doubt. While we'd done practice tests, the actual contents of the pilot's test changed every year. There were always questions about boosters, fighter components, and maneuvers—but technically, any part of our schooling could be included.

I'd missed a lot of classes, but I knew I shouldn't worry. *Beowulf* wouldn't worry. Confidence was the soul of heroism.

"I'm going to ace that test, Rig," I said. "You and I, we're going to be the best pilots in the Defiant Defense Force. We'll fight so well, the Krell will raise lamentations to the sky like smoke above a pyre, crying in desperation at our advent!"

Rig cocked his head.

"A bit much?" I asked.

"Where do you come up with these things?"

"Sounds like something Beowulf might say."

Rodge settled back down to study, and I probably should have joined him. Yet a part of me was fed up with studying, with trying to cram things into my brain. I wanted the challenge to just *arrive*.

We had one more lecture today, unfortunately. I listened to the other dozen or so students chatter together, but I wasn't in a mood to put up with their stupidity. Instead I found myself pacing like a caged animal, until I noticed Mrs. Vmeer walking toward me with Alfir, the sanitation guy.

She wore a bright green skirt, but the silvery cadet's pin on her blouse was the real mark of her achievement. It meant she'd passed the pilot's test. She must have washed out in flight school— otherwise she'd have a golden pin—but washing out wasn't uncommon. And down here in Igneous, even a cadet's pin was a mark of great accomplishment. Mrs. Vmeer had special clothing and food requisition privileges.

She wasn't a bad teacher—she didn't treat me much differently from the other students, and she hardly ever scowled at me. I kind of liked her, even if her daughter was a creature of distilled darkness, worthy only of being slain so her corpse could be used to make potions.

"Spensa," Mrs. Vmeer said. "Citizen Alfir wanted to speak with you."

I braced myself for questions about my father. Everyone always wanted to ask about him. What was it like to live as the daughter of a coward? Did I wish I could hide from it? Did I ever consider changing my surname? People who thought they were being empathetic always asked questions like those.

"I hear," Alfir said, "that you're quite the explorer."

I opened my mouth to spit back a retort, then bit it off. *What?*

"You go out in the caves," he continued, "hunting?"

"Um, yes," I said. "Rats."

"We have need of people like you," Alfir said.

"In *sanitation*?"

"A lot of the machinery we service runs through far-off caverns. We make expeditions to them, and need rugged types for those trips. If you want a job, I'm offering one."

A job. In *sanitation*?

"I'm going to be a pilot," I blurted out.

"The pilot's test is hard," Alfir said, glancing at our teacher. "Not many pass it. I'm offering you a guaranteed place with us. You sure you don't want to consider it?"

"No, thank you."

Alfir shrugged and walked off. Mrs. Vmeer studied me for a moment, then shook her head and went to welcome the next lecturer.

I backed up against the wall, folding my arms. Mrs. Vmeer knew I was going to be a pilot. Why would she think I'd accept such an offer? Alfir couldn't have known about me without her saying something to him, so what was up?

"They're not going to let you be a pilot," a voice said beside me.

I glanced and saw—belatedly—that I'd happened to walk over by Dia. The dark-haired girl sat on the floor, leaning on the wall. Why wasn't she chatting with the others?

"They don't have a choice," I said to her. "Anyone can take the pilot's test."

"Anyone can take it," Dia said. "But they decide who passes,

and it's not always fair. The children of First Citizens get in automatically."

I glanced at the painting of the First Citizens on the wall. We
had them in all the classrooms. And yes, I knew their children got
automatic entry into flight school. They deserved it, as their parents had fought at the Battle of Alta.

Technically, so had my father—but I wasn't counting on that
to help me. Still, I'd always been told that a good showing on the
test would get anyone, regardless of status, into flight school. The
Defiant Defense Force—the DDF—didn't care who you were, so
long as you could fly.

"I know they won't count me as a daughter of a First," I said.
"But if I pass, I get in. Just like anyone else."

"That's the thing, spaz. You won't pass, no matter what. I heard
my parents talking about it last night. Admiral Ironsides gave
orders to deny you. You don't *really* think they'd let the daughter
of Chaser fly for the DDF, do you?"

"Liar." I felt my face grow cold with anger. She was trying to
taunt me again, to get me to throw a fit.

Dia shrugged. "You'll see. It doesn't matter to me—my father
already got me a job in the Administration Corps."

I hesitated. This wasn't like her usual insults. It didn't have the
same vicious bite, the same sense of amused taunting. She . . . she
really seemed not to care whether I believed her.

I stalked across the room to where Mrs. Vmeer was speaking
with the new lecturer, a woman from the Algae Vat Corps.

"We need to talk," I told her.

"Just a moment, Spensa."

I stood there, intruding on their conversation, arms folded,
until finally Mrs. Vmeer sighed, then pulled me to the side. "What
is it, child?" she asked. "Have you reconsidered Citizen Alfir's
kind offer?"

"Did the admiral herself order that I'm not to pass the pilot's test?"

Mrs. Vmeer narrowed her eyes, then turned and glanced toward her daughter.

"Is it true?" I asked.

"Spensa," Mrs. Vmeer said, looking back at me. "You have to understand, this is a very delicate issue. Your father's reputation is—"

"Is it true?"

Mrs. Vmeer drew her lips to a line and didn't answer.

"Is it all lies, then?" I asked. "The talk of equality and of only skill mattering? Of finding your right place and serving there?"

"It's complicated," Mrs. Vmeer said. She lowered her voice. "Look, why don't you skip the test tomorrow to save everyone the embarrassment? Come to me, and we'll talk about what might work for you. If not sanitation, perhaps ground troops?"

"So I can stand all day on guard duty?" I said, my voice growing louder. "I need to fly. I need to *prove myself*!"

Mrs. Vmeer sighed, then shook her head. "I'm sorry, Spensa. But this was never going to be. I wish one of your teachers had been brave enough to disabuse you of the notion when you were younger."

In that moment, everything came crashing down around me. A daydreamed future. A carefully imagined escape from my life of ridicule.

Lies. Lies that a part of me had suspected. Of *course* they weren't going to let me pass the test. Of *course* I was too much of an embarrassment to let fly.

I wanted to rage. I wanted to hit someone, break something, scream until my lungs bled.

Instead I strode from the room, away from the laughing eyes of the other students.

3

I sought refuge in the silent caverns. I didn't dare go back to my mother and grandmother. My mother would undoubtedly be happy—she'd lost a husband to the Krell, and dreaded seeing me suffer the same fate. Gran-Gran . . . she would tell me to fight.

But fight what? The military itself didn't want me.

I felt like a fool. All this time, telling myself I'd become a pilot, and in truth I'd never had a chance. My teachers must have spent these years *laughing* at me behind their hands.

I walked through an unfamiliar cavern on the outer edge of what I'd explored, hours from Igneous. And still the feelings of embarrassment and anger shadowed me.

What an *idiot* I had been.

I reached the edge of a subterranean cliff and knelt, activating my father's light-line by tapping two fingers against my palm—an action the bracelet could sense. It glowed more brightly. Gran-Gran said we'd brought these with us to Detritus, that they were pieces of equipment used by the explorers and warriors of the old human space fleet. I wasn't supposed to have one, but everyone thought it had been destroyed when my father crashed.

I placed my wrist against the stone of the cliff, and tapped my fingers on my palm once more. This command made an energy line stick to the rock, connecting my bracelet to the stone.

A three-finger tap let out more slack. Using that, I could climb over the ledge—rope in hand—and lower myself to the bottom. After I landed, a two-finger tap made the rope let go of the rock above, then snap back into the bracelet housing. I didn't know how it worked, only that I needed to recharge it every month or two, something I did in secret by plugging it into power lines in the caverns.

I crept into a cavern filled with kurdi mushrooms. They tasted foul, but were edible—and rats loved them. This would be prime hunting ground. So I turned off my light and settled down to wait, listening intently.

I had never feared the darkness. It reminded me of the exercise Gran-Gran taught, where I floated up toward the singing stars. You couldn't fear the dark if you were a fighter. And I was a fighter.

I was . . . I was going to . . . going to be a pilot . . .

I looked upward, trying to push away those feelings of loss. Instead, I was soaring. Toward the stars. And I again thought that I could hear something calling to me—a sound like a distant flute.

A nearby scraping pulled me back. Rat nails on stone. I raised my speargun, familiar motions guiding me, and engaged a smidgen of light from my light-line.

The rat turned in a panic toward me. My finger trembled on the trigger, but I didn't fire as it scrambled away. What did it matter? Was I really going to go on with my life like nothing had happened?

Usually, exploring kept my mind off my problems. Today they kept intruding, like a rock in my shoe. *Remember? Remember that your dreams have just been stolen?*

I felt like I had in those first days following my father's death.

When every moment, every object, every word reminded me of him, and of the sudden hole inside me.

I sighed, then attached one end of my light-line to my spear and commanded it to stick to the next thing it touched. I took aim at the top of another cliff and fired, sticking the weightless glowing rope in place. I climbed up, my speargun rattling in its straps on my back.

As a child, I'd imagined that my father had survived his crash. That he was being held captive in these endless, uncharted tunnels. I imagined saving him, like a figure from Gran-Gran's stories. Gilgamesh, or Joan of Arc, or Tarzan of Greystoke. A hero.

The cavern trembled softly, as if in outrage, and dust fell from the ceiling. An impact up on the surface.

That was close, I thought. Had I climbed so far? I took out my book of hand-drawn maps. I'd been out here for quite a while by now. Hours at least. I'd taken a nap a few caverns back . . .

I checked the clock on my light-line. Night had come and gone, and it was already approaching noon on the day of the test—which would happen in the evening. I probably should have headed back. Mom and Gran-Gran would worry if I didn't show up for the test.

To hell with the test, I thought, imagining the indignation I'd feel at being turned away at the door. Instead, I climbed up through a tight squeeze into another tunnel. Out here my size was—for once—an advantage.

Another impact rocked the caverns. With this much debris falling, climbing to the surface was definitely stupid. I didn't care. I was in a reckless mood. I felt, almost heard, something driving me forward. I kept climbing until I finally reached a crack in the ceiling. Light shone through it, but it was an even, sterile white, not orange enough. Cool dry air blew in also, which was a good sign. I pushed my pack ahead of me, then squirmed through the crack and out into the light.

The surface. I looked up and saw the sky again. It never failed to take my breath away.

A distant skylight shone down on a section of the land, but I was mostly in shadow. Overhead, the sky sparkled with a shower of falling debris. Radiant lines like slashes. A formation of three scout-class starfighters flew through it, watching. Falling debris was often broken pieces of ships or other space junk, and the salvage from it could be valuable. It played havoc with our radar though, and could mask a Krell incursion.

I stood in the blue-grey dust and let the awe of the sky wash over me, feeling the peculiar sensation of wind against my cheeks. I'd come up close to Alta Base, which I could see in the distance, maybe only a thirty-minute walk or so away. Now that the Krell knew where we were, there was no reason to hide the base, so it had been expanded from a hidden bunker to several large buildings with a walled perimeter, antiaircraft guns, and an invisible shield to protect it from debris.

Outside that wall, groups of people worked a small strip of something I always found strange: *trees* and *fields*. What were they even doing over there? Trying to grow food in this dusty ground?

I didn't dare get close. The guards would take me for a scavenger from a distant cavern. Still, there was something dramatic about the stark green of those fields and the stubborn walls of the base. Alta was a monument to our determination. For three generations, humankind had lived like rats and nomads on this planet, but we would hide no longer.

The flight of starships streaked toward Alta, and I took a step after them. *Set your sights on something higher,* my father had said. *Something more grand . . .*

And where had that gotten me?

I shouldered my pack and my speargun, then hiked in the other direction. I had been to a nearby passage before, and I figured that with more exploring, I could connect some of my maps. Unfortunately, when I arrived, I found the passage's mouth completely collapsed.

Some space debris hit the surface in the near distance, tossing up a spray of dust. I looked up and saw a few smaller chunks streaking down overhead, fiery chunks of metal . . .

Heading straight toward me.

Scud!

I dashed back the way I had come.

No. Nonononono! The air rumbled, and I could feel the heat of the approaching debris.

There! I spotted a small cavern opening in the surface—part crack, part cave mouth. I threw myself toward it, skidding and sliding inside.

An enormous *CRASH* sounded behind me, and it seemed to shake the entire planet. Frantic, I engaged my light-line and slapped my hand against stone as I fell in the churning chaos. I jerked up short, connected by the light-line to the wall, as rock chips and pebbles flew across me. The cavern trembled.

Then, all grew still. I blinked dust from my eyes and found myself dangling by my light-line in the center of a small cavern, maybe ten or fifteen meters high. I'd lost my pack somewhere, and I'd scraped my arm up pretty good.

Great. Just great, Spensa. This is what throwing a tantrum gets you. I groaned, my head throbbing, then tapped my fingers against my palm to let the light-line out, lowering myself to the floor.

I flopped down, catching my breath. Other impacts sounded in the distance, but they dwindled.

Finally, I wobbled to my feet and dusted myself off. I managed to locate the strap of my bag sticking out from some rubble nearby. I yanked it out, then checked the canteen and maps inside. They seemed okay.

My speargun was another matter. I found the handle, but there was no sign of the rest. It was probably buried in the mound of rubble.

I slumped down against a stone. I *knew* I shouldn't go up to the surface during debris falls. I had practically *begged* for this.

A scrabbling sound came from nearby. A rat? I raised the handle of my gun immediately, then felt doubly stupid. Still, I forced myself to my feet, slung the pack over my shoulder, and increased the light of my bracelet. A shadow ducked away, and I followed, limping only a little. Maybe I could find another way out of here.

I raised my bracelet in the air, illuminating the cavern. My light reflected off something ahead of me. Metal? Maybe one of the water pipes?

I walked toward it, and it took my brain a moment to realize what I was seeing. There, nestled into the corner of the cavern— surrounded by rubble—was a *ship*.

4

It was a starfighter.

An old one, of a design completely unfamiliar to me. It had a wider wingspan than DDF ships, and was shaped like a wicked W. Straight, razorlike wings at the sides framed an old dust-covered cockpit in the center. The acclivity ring—the thing that gave starfighters their lift—was buried in the rubble underneath the ship, but from what I could see it looked whole.

For a moment, I forgot about the test. A *ship*.

How long had it been here to collect that much rubble around it, and that much dust? One wing had been bent almost to the ground, probably by a cave-in, and the rear boosters were a huge mess.

I *didn't know the model*. That was *incredible*. I knew every DDF design, every Krell ship, and the roving tradeship designs used by nomadic human clans. I had even studied old ships we'd flown during the first decades after crashing on Detritus.

I could rattle off each of these practically in my sleep, draw their silhouettes from memory. But I'd never seen this design. I dropped my pack and climbed—gingerly—up the wing that had been bent down. My bracelet provided light as my boots scraped off caked-on dust, revealing a scratched metallic surface. The right side of the ship was particularly banged up.

It crash-landed here, I thought. *Long ago.*

I climbed up near the circular cockpit, which had a glass—well, probably fusion-plastic—canopy that was remarkably intact. The ship was generations past having enough power to open its own cockpit, but I found the manual release panel right where I expected it. I brushed the dust off, and found letters—in English. They said EMERGENCY CANOPY RELEASE.

So the ship *was* human. It must be old, then. Likely as ancient as the apparatus and the rubble belt.

I yanked on the release lever to no avail. The thing was stuck. I put my hands on my hips and considered breaking in—but that seemed like a shame. This was an antique, the sort of thing that belonged on a pedestal in the Igneous ship museum, where we celebrated warriors of the past. There was no skeleton in the cockpit though, so either the pilot had escaped, or it had been here so long that even the bones had turned to dust.

All right, let's be delicate about this. I could be delicate. I was *incredibly* delicate. Like, all the time.

I attached one end of my light-line to the release lever, then walked across the top of the ship to the rubble at the rear, where I attached the other end of the light-line to a boulder. That separated the energy rope entirely from the bracelet, which stopped glowing. The rope could function for an hour or two once separated from its power source, but would remain stuck at the length it was when released.

I got down on my back, braced myself against the wall, and shoved the boulder with my feet. It started rolling down the rubble, and as soon as I heard a *click* from the cockpit, I disengaged the light-line with a tap. The glowing rope released its holds on either end, and was sucked back into the bracelet.

That done, I scrambled over to find the lever pulled and the ancient cockpit popped ajar. Reverent, I lifted the canopy all the way, sending dust cascading to either side. The interior looked extremely well preserved. Indeed, as I slid down into the cockpit, I found that the seat was stiff, but the leather wasn't cracked or decomposing.

Similar controls, I thought, resting my left hand on the throttle, my right hand on the control sphere, fingers resting in the grooves. I'd sat in mock cockpits before at the museum, but never in a *real ship.*

I reached into my pocket, feeling my father's pin, which I'd recovered from its hiding place before setting out into the tunnels. I held it up, letting it sparkle in the glow of my bracelet. Was this what my father had felt, this snug sense of *rightness* when sitting in a cockpit? What would he think if he knew his daughter spent her time hunting rats? That she was here in a dusty cavern, instead of sitting and taking the pilot test?

That she'd folded instead of fighting?

"I didn't fold!" I said. "I didn't run!"

Or . . . well, I had. But what else could I have done? I couldn't fight the entire system. If Admiral Ironsides herself—head of the DDF—didn't want me in, there was nothing I could do.

Anger flooded me. Frustration, *hatred.* Hatred at the DDF for how they'd treated my father, anger at my mother and teachers— every adult who had let me keep dreaming when surely they'd all known the truth.

I closed my eyes, and could almost feel the force of the ship's booster behind me. Could almost sense the pull of g-forces as I took a turn. The scent of crisp, clean air pulled in from the upper atmosphere and pushed into the cockpit.

I wanted to feel it more than anything. But when I opened my eyes, I was back in a dusty old broken-down antique. I would never fly. They'd sent me away.

A voice whispered from the back of my mind.

What if that is *the test?*

What if . . . what if they wanted to see what I'd do? Scud, what if Mrs. Vmeer had been lying? What if I'd run away for nothing—or worse, what if I'd just proven that *I* was a coward, like everyone claimed my father had been?

I cursed, checking the clock on my light-line bracelet. Four hours. I had *four hours* until the test. But I'd spent almost an entire day wandering. There was no way I could make it back to Igneous in time. Could I?

"Claim the stars, Spensa," I whispered.

I had to try.

5

I exploded into the testing room like a fighter with its booster on full overburn.

I interrupted a tall older woman in a white admiral's uniform. She had chin-length silvery hair, and she frowned at me as I pulled to a halt in the doorway. Then her eyes immediately went to the clock hanging on the wall.

The second hand ticked one last notch. Eighteen hundred hours on the dot.

I made it. I was a sweaty mess, my jumpsuit ripped and stained with dust from my near encounter with a piece of space debris. But I'd made it.

Nobody said a word in the room, which was located in the government buildings at the center of Igneous—near the elevators to the surface. The room was stuffed with desks; there had to be a hundred kids here. I hadn't realized there were so many seventeen-year-olds in the Defiant caverns, and these were only the ones who wanted to test for pilot.

At that moment, every single one of them was staring at me.

I kept my chin high and tried to pretend that nothing was out of the ordinary. Unfortunately, the sole open desk I spotted was the one *directly in front* of the woman with the silver hair.

Did I recognize her? That face . . .

Scud.

That wasn't just some junior admiral, it was Judy Ivans, "Ironsides" herself. She was a First Citizen and head of the DDF, so I'd seen her face in hundreds of paintings and statues. She was basically the most important person in the world.

I limped a little as I made my way over and sat down in front of her, trying not to show my embarrassment—or my pain. Dashing all this way had involved multiple crazy descents with my lightline through caverns and tunnels. My muscles were protesting the effort, and my right leg seized up with a cramp the moment I sat down.

Wincing, I dropped my pack to the ground by my seat. An aide snatched it and carried it to the side of the room, as you weren't allowed anything at your desk but a pencil.

I closed my eyes—but then cracked them as I heard a distinct voice whispering nearby, "Oh, thank the homeworld." Rig? I glanced and spotted him a few rows over. He had probably arrived three hours early, then spent the entire time worrying that I would be late. For absolutely no reason. I'd arrived with *at least* half a second to spare. I winked at him, then went back to trying not to scream in pain.

"As I was saying," the admiral continued, "we are proud of you. Your work and preparation prove you to be the best and most promising generation that the DDF has ever known. You are the generation who will inherit the surface. You will lead us in a bold new era in fighting the Krell.

"Remember that this test is not to prove worthiness. You are all worthy. To field a single flight of pilots, we need hundreds of technicians, mechanics, and other support staff. Even the humble vat worker is a participant in our great quest for survival. The

41

fighter's booster or wing should not scorn the bolt that holds it in place.

"Not all of you will pass this test, but by simply choosing to be here, you live up to my lofty expectations of you. And to those who pass: I look forward to supervising your training. I take a personal interest in the cadets."

I frowned. She seemed so aloof, so indifferent. Surely she didn't care about me, no matter how infamous my father was.

As aides rushed to distribute the tests, Ironsides stepped to the side of the room, near some captains in sparkling uniforms. A short man in glasses whispered to her, then pointed toward me. Ironsides turned and looked at me again, her lips turning down sharply.

Oh no.

I glanced toward the other wall of the room, where some teachers—including Mrs. Vmeer—watched. She saw me, then shook her head as if in disappointment. But . . . I . . . thought I'd figured it out. They were just trying to see if I was truly Defiant.

Right?

An aide deliberately took a test off the bottom of the stack and placed it on my desk. Hesitant, I searched my pockets for a pencil, but found only my father's pin. At a hiss from the side, I glanced toward Rig—who tossed me a spare pencil.

Thank you, I mouthed, then opened the test and turned to the first question.

> 1. Explain, with examples of what is made from them,
>   the fourteen types of algae grown in the vats, and
>   the nutritional value of each.

My stomach sank. A question about *algae*? Yes, the tests often included random questions from our schooling, but . . . algae?

I flipped to the next page.

2. Explain the exact conditions required for optimal
   growth of algae, not limited to—but including—
   temperature, water purity, and vat depth.

The next was about how sewage was treated, as was the one
after that. I felt my face growing cold as I realized all fifty pages
were questions about things like algae vats, sewage, or ventilation. Those were lessons I'd missed while hunting. I'd shown up in
the afternoon classes for physics and history, but I simply hadn't
had the time to study everything.

I looked at Mrs. Vmeer again, and she wouldn't meet my eyes,
so I leaned over and stole a glance at Darla Mee-Bim's test. Hers
had a completely different question at the top.

1. Name five aerial maneuvers you would perform to
   dodge a Krell ship that had you in close pursuit.

*A tight loop, a rolling twin-scissor, the Ahlstrom loop, a reverse
backpedal, and a banking roll.* Depending on how close they were,
the nature of the battlefield, and what my wingmate was doing. I
leaned to the side and checked the test of another neighbor, where
I spotted some numbers with the words *booster* and *throttle*. A
question about acceleration and g-forces.

An aide spoke up, loud enough for most people in the room to
hear. "Be advised that no one sitting next to you will have the same
test, so cheating is not only punishable by expulsion, it is useless."

I slumped back in my seat, anger boiling inside me. This was
complete and utter trash. Had they prepared a special test for me,
covering topics they *knew* I'd been forced to miss?

As I stewed there, several students rose and walked to the
front of the chamber. They couldn't be done already, could they?
One of them—a tall, well-built young man with brown skin, short
curly black hair, and an insufferable face—handed the admiral his

test. From where I was sitting I could see it was blank except for his name. He showed her a pin—a special pin, blue and gold. The pin of a pilot who had fought at the Battle of Alta.

Children of First Citizens, I thought. All they had to do was show up and fill in their names, and they'd be given automatic entry into flight school. There were six of them today, each one getting a free slot that could have gone to other, harder-working students.

One by one the six left, and the admiral dropped their unfinished tests on a desk by the front wall. Their scores wouldn't matter. Just like my score didn't matter.

Dia's words returned to me. *You don't really think they'd let the daughter of Chaser fly for the DDF, do you?*

I tried anyway. Furious—holding my pencil so tightly I broke the tip and had to get a replacement—I scrawled on my stupid test. Each question felt intended to break my will. Algae vats. Ventilation. Sewage. Places I supposedly belonged.

Daughter of a coward. She's lucky we don't just toss her into the vats.

I wrote for hours, emotions dogfighting within me. Anger fought naive anticipation. Frustration fought hope. Realization shot down optimism.

14. Explain the proper procedure if you think a vat of
    algae might have been contaminated by a coworker.

I tried not to leave any questions blank, but on well over two-thirds of them, my answer boiled down to, "I don't know. I'd ask someone who does." And it *hurt* to answer them, as if by doing so I was proving that I was incompetent.

But I *would not give up.* Finally the bell chimed, marking the end of the five-hour time limit. I slumped as an aide pulled the test from my fingers. I watched her walk off.

No.

Admiral Ironsides had returned and was speaking—now that the test had ended—with a small group of people in suits and skirts, First Citizens or National Assembly members. Ironsides was known for being stern but fair.

I stood up and walked to her, fishing in my pocket, fist closing on my father's pin. I waited, respectful, as the students filed out for the after-test party, where they'd be joined by those who had already settled on other careers, and who had been spending the day applying for and being assigned positions. Those who took this test and failed would be given second pickings later in the week.

Tonight though, everyone would celebrate together, future pilot and future janitor alike.

Finally, Ironsides looked at me.

I held up my father's pin. "Sir," I said. "As the daughter of a pilot who fought at the Battle of Alta, I would like to petition for acceptance into flight school."

She looked me up and down, noting the ripped sleeve, the dirty face, the dried blood on my arm. She took the pin from my hand, and I held my breath.

"Do you *really* think," she said, "that I would accept the pin of a traitor?"

My heart sank.

"You aren't even supposed to have this, girl," she said. "Wasn't it destroyed when he crashed? Did you steal someone else's pin?"

"Sir," I said, my voice taut. "It didn't go down in the crash with him. He gave it to me before he flew that last time."

Admiral Ironsides turned to leave.

"Sir?" I said. "Please. *Please*, just give me a chance."

She hesitated, and I thought she was considering, but then she leaned in to me and whispered. "Girl, do you have any *idea* the kind of public relations nightmare you could cause for us? If I let you in, and you turn out to be a coward like he was . . . Well, there is *no way on this planet* I will let you into a cockpit. Be glad we even let you into this building."

It felt like I'd been slapped. I winced. This woman—one of my heroes—turned to leave.

I grabbed her arm, and several aides nearby gasped softly. But I held on.

"You still have my pin," I said. "Those belong to the pilots and their families. Tradition—"

"The pins of *actual* pilots belong to the families," she said. "Not cowards." She pulled herself out of my grip with a shockingly firm yank.

I could have attacked her. I almost *did;* the heat was rising inside me, and my face felt cold.

Arms grabbed me from behind before I could do it. "Spin?" Rig said. "Spensa! What are you *doing?*"

"She stole it. She took my father's . . ." I trailed off as the admiral walked out with her collected attendants. Then I sagged into Rig's grasp.

"Spensa?" Rig said. "Let's go to the party. We can talk about it there. How do you think you did? I think . . . I think did terribly. Spensa?"

I pulled away from him and trudged back to my desk, suddenly feeling too exhausted to stand.

"Spin?" he asked.

"Go to the party, Rig," I whispered.

"But—"

"Leave me alone. Please. Just . . . let me be by myself."

He never did know how to deal with me when I got like this, so he hovered about, then finally trailed off.

And I sat alone in the room.

6

Hours passed.

My anger before had been as hot as magma. Now I just felt cold. Numb.

Echoes of the party drifted in from another area of the building.

I felt used, stupid, and most of all . . . empty. Shouldn't I have been snapping my pencil, throwing tables about in rage? Ranting about seeking vengeance upon my foes, and their children and grandchildren? Typical Spensa behavior?

Instead I sat there and stared. Until the sounds of the party grew quieter. Eventually, an aide peeked into the room. "Um, you're supposed to leave."

I didn't move.

"Are you sure you don't want to leave?"

They'd have to *drag* me out of here. I imagined it—very heroic and Defiant—but the aide didn't seem so inclined. She switched off the lights and left me there, lit only by the red-orange glow of the emergency lights.

Finally, I stood up and walked to the desk by the wall, where Ironsides had—perhaps accidentally—left the tests the children of the First Citizens had given her. I looked through the stack; each of them had only the name filled out, the other questions blank.

I took the one off the top, the first one handed in. It held the name Jorgen Weight, followed by a question.

1. Name the four major battles that secured the United Defiant Caverns' independence as the first major state on Detritus.

That was a tricky question, as people were *probably* going to forget the Unicarn Skirmish—it didn't get talked about as much. But it was where the fledgling DDF had first employed fighters of the second generation of designs, built in secret in Igneous. I trailed over to my desk and sat down, then answered the question.

I moved on to the next, then the next. They were good questions. More than simple lists of dates or parts. Some math questions about combat speeds. But most were questions about intent, opinion, and personal preference. I struggled on two of them, trying to decide if I should say what I thought the test *wanted,* or what I thought was actually the correct answer.

I went with the second both times. Who cared anyway, right?

By the time I was finishing up, I heard people talking outside. Janitors, from the sounds of their discussion.

Suddenly I felt silly. Would I scream and force some poor janitor to pull me out by my hair? I'd been beaten. You couldn't win every fight, and there was no shame in losing when you were outnumbered. I turned over the test and tapped my pencil against it, still sitting mostly in the dark, working by the glow of the emergency lights.

I started sketching a W-shaped ship on the back of the test as a crazy idea began to form in my head. The DDF hadn't begun as an official military; it had started out as a bunch of dreamers with their own crazy idea. Get the apparatus working, create ships from some schematics that had survived our crash on the planet.

They'd built their *own* ships.

The door opened, letting in light from the hallway. I heard a bucket get set on the ground outside, and two people complaining about spills in the party room.

"I'll be out in a minute," I said, finishing my sketch. Thinking. Wondering. *Dreaming.*

"Why are you still here, kid?" a janitor asked. "You didn't want to go to the party?"

"I didn't feel much like celebrating."

He grunted. "Didn't do well on the test?"

"Turns out it doesn't matter," I said. I glanced at him, but he was backlit, just a silhouette in the doorway. "Do you ever . . . ," I said. "Do you ever feel they *forced* you to be what you are?"

"No. I might have forced myself into it though."

I sighed. Mother was probably worried sick about me. I stood up and wandered over to the wall where the aide had put my pack.

"Why do you want it so much?" the janitor asked. Was there something familiar about his voice? "It's dangerous, being a pilot. A lot of them get killed."

"Just under fifty percent are shot down in their first five years," I said. "But they don't all die. Some eject. Others get shot down, but survive the crash."

"Yes. I know."

I froze, then frowned and looked back at the figure. I couldn't make out his face, but something flashed on his breast. Medals? A pilot's pin? I squinted, and made out the shape of a DDF jacket and dress slacks.

This was no janitor. I could still hear those two out in the hallway, joking with each other.

I stood up straighter. The man walked slowly to my desk, and

49

the emergency lights revealed he was older, maybe in his fifties, with a stark white mustache. He walked with a prominent limp.

He picked up the test I'd filled out, then flipped through it. "So why?" he finally asked. "Why care so much? They never ask the most important question on these tests. Why do you want to be a pilot?"

To prove myself, and to redeem my father's name. It was my immediate response, though something else warred with it. Something my father had sometimes said, something buried inside me, often overshadowed by ideas of vengeance and redemption.

"Because you get to see the sky," I whispered.

The man grunted. "We name ourselves Defiants," he said. "It's the central ideal of our people—the fact that we refuse to back down. And yet, Ironsides always acts so surprised when someone defies her." He shook his head, then set the test down again. He put something on top of it.

He turned to limp away.

"Wait," I said. "Who are you?"

He stopped at the doorway, and the light outside showed his face more clearly, with that mustache, and eyes that seemed . . . old. "I knew your father."

Wait. I *did* know that voice. "Mongrel?" I said. "That *is* you. You were his wingmate!"

"In another life," he said. "Oh-seven-hundred sharp on the day after tomorrow, building F, room C-14. Show the pin to get access."

The pin? I walked back to the desk, and found—sitting on top of my test—a cadet's pin.

I snatched it up. "But Ironsides said she'd never let me into a cockpit."

"I'll deal with Ironsides. It's *my* class; I get final say over my students, and even she can't overrule me. She's too important for that."

50

"Too important? To give orders?"

"Military protocol. When you get important enough to order an armada into battle, you're too important to interfere with how a quartermaster runs his shop. You'll see. There's a lot you know, judging by that test—but still some things you don't. You got number seventeen wrong."

"Seventeen . . ." I flipped through the test quickly. "The overwhelming odds question?"

"The right answer was to fall back and await reinforcement."

"No it wasn't."

He stiffened, and I quickly bit my tongue. Should I be arguing with the person who'd just given me a *cadet's pin*?

"I'll let you into the sky," he said, "but they're not going to be easy on you. *I'm* not going to be easy on you. Wouldn't be fair."

"Is *anything* fair?"

He smiled. "Death is. He treats us all the same. Oh-seven-hundred. Don't be late."

Standard **DDF Ship Designs** 83 LD (Landfall Date)

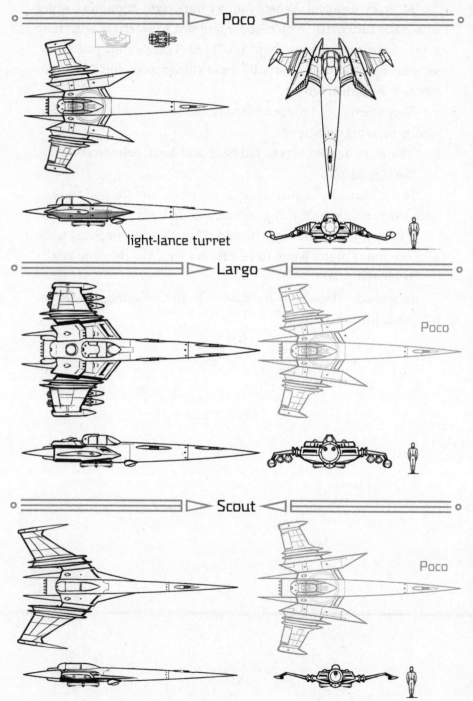

Poco

light-lance turret

Largo

Poco

Scout

Poco

PART TWO

PART
TWO

7

The elevator doors opened, and I looked out upon a city that should not exist.

Alta was primarily a military base, so perhaps *city* was an ambitious term. Yet the elevator structure opened a good two hundred meters outside the base proper. Lining the roadway between the two were shops and homes. A real town, populated by the stubborn farmers who worked the strips of greenery beyond.

I lingered in the large elevator as it emptied of people. This represented a threshold to a new life, a life I'd always dreamed about. I found myself strangely hesitant as I stood there, pack full of clothing over my shoulder, the phantom feeling of my mother's kiss farewell on my forehead.

"Oh, isn't it the most beautiful thing you've ever seen?" a voice said from behind me.

I glanced over my shoulder. The speaker was a girl about my age. She was taller than I was, with tan-brown skin and long, curly black hair. I'd seen her earlier on the elevator and noted her cadet's pin. She spoke with a faint accent I didn't recognize.

"I keep thinking it can't be real," she said. "Do you think it might be some cruel prank they're playing on us?"

"What tactical advantage would they gain by that?" I asked her.

The girl took my arm in a much too familiar way. "We can do this. Just take a deep breath. Reach up. Pluck a star. That's what the Saint says."

I had no idea what to make of this behavior. People normally treated me like a pariah; they didn't take me by the arm. I was so stunned that I didn't resist as she towed me after her out of the elevator. We entered the wide walkway leading through the town, toward the base.

I'd rather have been walking with Rodge, but they'd called him in late last night to ask him something about his test, and so far I hadn't gotten word of what that meant. Hopefully he wasn't in trouble.

The girl and I soon passed a fountain. A real fountain, like from the stories. We both stopped to gape, and I extricated my arm from the girl's grasp. Part of me wanted to be offended—but she seemed so *genuine*.

"That music the water makes," she said. "Isn't it the most wonderful sound ever?"

"The most wonderful sound ever is the lamentations of my enemies, screaming my name toward the heavens with ragged, dying voices."

The girl looked at me, cocking her head. "Well bless your stars."

"Sorry," I said. "It's a line from a story." I stuck out my hand to her. Best to be on good terms with the other cadets. "I'm callsign: Spin."

"Kimmalyn," she said, shaking my hand. "Um, we're supposed to have callsigns already?"

"I'm an overachiever. What room you reporting to?"

"Umm . . ." She fished in her pocket and pulled out a paper. "C-14? Cadet Flight B."

"Same as me."

"Callsign . . . callsign . . . ," Kimmalyn murmured. "What should I pick?"

"Killer?" I suggested. "Afterburn? No, that's probably too confusing. Fleshripper?"

"Couldn't it be something a little less gruesome?"

"You're going to be a warrior. You need a warrior's name."

"Not *everything* is about war!"

"Um, it kind of is—and flight school especially is." I frowned, noting the accent in her voice. "Where are you from? Not Igneous, I guess."

"Born and raised in Bountiful Cavern!" She leaned in. "We call it that, but nothing really grows there."

"Bountiful," I said. It was a cavern somewhat close to Igneous, also part of the Defiant League. "That's where the clans from the *Antioch* crew settled, right?" The *Antioch* had been one of the gunships in the old fleet, before we'd been driven into hiding here on Detritus.

"Yup. My great-grandmother was assistant quartermaster." She eyed me. "You said your callsign was Spin? Shouldn't you be something like Lamentation or Eats Enemy Eyeballs?"

I shrugged. "Spin is what my dad used to call me."

She smiled brightly at that. Scud, they'd let *this girl* in, but had denied me? What was the DDF trying to do? Put together a knitting club?

We approached the base, a group of tall, stern buildings surrounded by a wall. Right outside it, the farms gave way to an actual orchard. I stopped on the walkway, and found myself gaping again. I'd seen these trees from a distance, but up close they seemed enormous. Almost three meters tall! Before this, the tallest plant I'd seen was a mushroom that reached up to my waist.

"They planted those just after the Battle of Alta," Kimmalyn said. "It must take brave people to volunteer for service up here so

57

exposed to the air and to Krell attacks." She looked up at the sky in awe, and I wondered if this was the first time she was seeing it.

We stepped up to a checkpoint in the wall, and I thrust my pin toward the guard there, half expecting rough treatment—like I'd always gotten from Aluko when entering Igneous. However, the bored guard only marked our names off on a list and waved us in. Not much ceremony for my first official entrance into Alta. Well, soon I'd be so famous, the guard at the door would salute me on sight.

Inside, we counted off the buildings, joining a handful of other cadets. From what I understood, around twenty-five of us had passed the test, and had been organized into three training flights. Only the best of the best would actually pass flight school and be assigned to full-time pilot duty.

Kimmalyn and I soon arrived at a wide, single-story structure near the launchpads. Flight school. I barely held myself back from running over to the glistening starfighters lined up for duty—I'd done enough gawking for one day.

Inside the building we found wide hallways, most of which appeared to be lined with classrooms. Kimmalyn squealed, then rushed over to talk to another cadet, someone she apparently knew. So I stopped by a window on the outer wall and looked out at the sky, waiting for her.

I found myself feeling . . . anxious. Not about the training, but about this place. *It's too big, too open.* The hallways were over a meter wider than those of most buildings in Igneous, and the base's buildings sprawled outward instead of being built on top of one another. The sky was just up there, always present, looming. Even with a forcefield between me and it—of the same invisible type that starfighters employed—I felt exposed.

I was going to have to sleep up here. Live, eat, *exist.* All out in the open. While I liked the sky, that didn't mean I wanted it peeking in during every intimate moment.

I'll simply have to deal with it, I told myself. *The warrior cannot choose her bed; she must bless the stars if she can choose her battlefield.* A quote from Junmi's *The Conquest of Space.* I loved Gran-Gran's stories about Junmi almost as much as I did the old Viking stories, even if they didn't have quite as many decapitations.

Kimmalyn returned, and we found our classroom. I took a deep breath. Time to become a pilot. We pushed open the doors.

8

Ten mock cockpits dominated the center of the room, arranged in a circle facing inward. Each bulky device had a seat, a control console, and part of a fuselage built around it—though no canopy. Other than that, they looked as if they'd been ripped right out of starships.

Instead of the nose cones of ships, however, each had a large box attached to the front, maybe a meter tall and half as wide. Kimmalyn and I were apparently the first of our flight to arrive, and I checked the wall clock. It was 0615. For once in my life, I was not only early—I was *first*.

Well, technically second, as Kimmalyn jumped past me to look over the mock cockpits. "Oh! I guess we're first. Well, the Saint always said, 'If you can't arrive early, at least arrive before you're late.'"

I walked into the room, setting down my backpack and checking out the mockpits. I recognized the control panel layout—they were from Poco-class ships, a basic, if fast, DDF starfighter model. The door opened, and two more cadets entered. The shorter boy at the front had dark blue hair and appeared to be a Yeongian. The crew of the *Yeong-Gwang,* from the old fleet, had largely been from China or Korea on Earth.

The blue-haired boy grinned as he looked over the room, putting his pack beside mine. "Wow. Our *classroom!*"

The girl behind him sauntered in like she owned the place. She was a lean, athletic-looking girl with blonde hair in a ponytail. She wore a DDF uniform jacket over her jumpsuit—loose, like she was out on the town.

Those two were soon followed by a girl with a tattoo across her lower jaw. She'd be Vician—from Vici Cavern. I didn't know much about them, only that they were the descendants of the marines from the old space fleet. The Vicians had their own culture and kept to themselves—though they had reputations as great warriors.

I smiled at her, but she looked away immediately and didn't respond when Kimmalyn perkily introduced herself. *Fine then,* I thought.

Kimmalyn got names and home caverns out of the other two. The guy with the blue hair was Bim, and was indeed a Yeongian. His clan had been part of the hydroponics team on the old ship, and had settled in a nearby cavern that maintained a large set of underground farms, lit and maintained by ancient machinery. I'd never eaten any of the food from there; it was reserved for those who had many achievement merits or industry merits.

The athletic girl was Hudiya, from Igneous. I didn't know her, but the cavern was a big place, with a vast population. As the time for class drew near, a tall girl entered and introduced herself as Freyja. It was a good mythological name from Old Norse—of which I approved. She kind of had the look too. Though she was skinny, she was tall, maybe even a hundred and eighty-five centimeters, and she had blonde hair, which she wore cut very short. Her boots were brand-new, polished to a shine, and done up with gold clasps.

Well, that made six of us. We'd have a few more at least. About ten minutes before the start of class, three young men walked in together. They were obviously friends, as they were talking and joking softly. I didn't recognize two of them, but the one at the front—with brown skin and short curly hair—was distinctive in a kind of baby-faced, pretty-boy way.

The guy from the test, I realized. The son of a First Citizen who had gotten free admission.

Great. We were saddled with a useless aristocrat, someone who lived in the lowest—and safest—of the Defiant caverns. He'd be in flight school not because of any skill or aptitude, but because he wanted to sport a cadet's pin and feel important. Judging by the way the other two talked, I instantly pegged them as his cronies. I'd have bet anything that all of them had gotten in without taking the test, so our cadet group had *three* people who didn't deserve to be there.

The tall, baby-faced guy walked to the center of the ring of seats. How could a boy have a face that was *so* extremely punchable? He cleared his throat, then clapped his hands sharply. "Get to attention, cadets! Is this how we want to present ourselves to our instructor? Lounging about, making idle chitchat? Line up!"

Kimmalyn, bless *her* stars, jumped up and stood at a kind of sloppy attention. His two cronies stepped over and fell into step as well, doing a much better impression of real soldiers. Everyone else just kind of looked at him.

"What gives you the right to order us around?" asked Hudiya, the athletic girl from my own cavern. She stood leaning against the wall, arms folded.

"I want to make a good first impression on the instructor, cadet," Jerkface said. "Think how inspiring it will be when he comes in to find us all waiting at attention."

Hudiya snorted. "Inspiring? We'd look like a bunch of suck-ups."

Jerkface ignored her, instead inspecting his line of three cadets. He shook his head at Kimmalyn, whose version of "attention" involved standing on the tips of her toes and saluting with *both* hands. It was ridiculous.

"You look ridiculous," Jerkface said to her.

The girl's face fell, and she slumped. I felt an immediate burst of protective anger. I mean . . . he was right, but he didn't have to belt it out like that.

"Who taught you to stand at attention?" Jerkface asked. "You're going to embarrass us. I can't have that."

"Yeah," I said. "She'd be stealing your spot, since embarrassing us is clearly *your* job, Jerkface."

He looked me up and down—taking obvious note of the patched state of my pilot's jumpsuit. It had been one of my father's, and had required serious modification to fit me.

"Do I know you, cadet?" he asked. "You look familiar."

"I was sitting in the front row taking the test," I said, "when you turned in your exam without a single question answered. Maybe you saw me there when you glanced at the rest of the room, to see what people look like when they actually have to *work* to get things."

He drew his lips to a line. It seemed I'd touched a nerve. Excellent. First blood.

"I chose not to waste resources," he said, "making someone grade my test when I had already been offered a slot."

"One you didn't earn."

He glanced at the other cadets in the room, who were watching with interest, then he lowered his voice. "Look. You don't need to make trouble. Just fall into line, and—"

"Fall into line?" I said. "You're *still* trying to give us orders?"

"It's obvious I'm going to be your flightleader. You might as well get used to doing what I say."

Arrogant son of a supernova. "Just because you cheated your way into—"

"I didn't *cheat!*"

"—just because you *bought* your way into flight school doesn't mean you'll be flightleader. You need to watch yourself. Don't make an enemy out of me."

"And if I do?"

Scud, it was annoying to have to look up at him. I leaped onto my seat to gain a height advantage for the argument—an action that seemed to surprise him.

He cocked his head. "What—"

"Always attack from a position of superior advantage!" I said. "When this is done, Jerkface, I will hold your tarnished and melted pin up as my trophy as your smoldering ship marks your pyre, and the final resting place of your crushed and broken corpse!"

The room grew quiet.

"All right . . . ," Jerkface said. "Well, that was . . . descriptive."

"Bless your stars," Kimmalyn added. Hudiya gave me a thumbs-up and a grin, though the others in the room plainly had no idea what to make of me.

And . . . maybe my reaction had been over the top. I was used to making a scene; life had taught me that aggressive threats would cause people to back off. But did I need to do that here?

I realized something odd in that moment. *None of these people seemed to know who I was.* They hadn't grown up near my neighborhood; they hadn't gone to class with me. They might have heard of my father, but they didn't know me from any other cadet.

Here, I wasn't the rat girl or the daughter of a coward.

Here I was *free*.

The door chose that moment to open, and our instructor—Mongrel—stopped in the doorway, holding a steaming mug of coffee in one hand, a clipboard in the other. In the light, I recognized him from the pictures of the First Citizens, though his hair was greyer, and that mustache made him appear much older.

We must have looked like quite the menagerie. I was still standing on the seat of my mockpit, looming over Jerkface. Several of the others had been snickering at our exchange, while Kimmalyn was again trying to execute a salute.

Mongrel glanced at the clock, which had just hit seven hundred hours. "I hope I'm not interrupting anything intimate."

"Uh . . . ," I said. I jumped off my seat and tried a little laugh.

"That wasn't a joke!" Mongrel barked. "I don't joke! Line up by the far wall, all of you!"

We scrambled to obey. As we lined up, Jerkface pulled off a precise salute, and he held it, at perfect attention.

Mongrel glanced at him and said, "Don't be a suck-up, son. This isn't basic training, and you aren't grunts from the ground corps."

Jerkface's expression fell and he lowered his arm, then snapped to attention anyway. "Um, sorry, sir!"

Mongrel rolled his eyes. "My name is Captain Cobb. My callsign is Mongrel, but you will call me Cobb—or sir, if you must." He trailed along the line, his limp prominent, taking a sip of his coffee. "The rules of this classroom are simple. I teach. You learn. Anything that interferes with that is likely to get one of you killed." He paused near where I stood by Jerkface. "That includes flirting."

I felt my face go cold. "Sir! I wasn't—"

"It also includes talking back to me! You're in flight school now, stars help you. Four months of training. If you make it to the end without being kicked out or shot down, then you pass. That's it. There are no tests. There are no grades. Just you in a cockpit, convincing me you deserve to remain there. I am the only authority that matters to you now."

He waited, watching to see how we responded. And wisely, none of us said anything.

"Most of you won't make it," he continued. "Four months may not seem like long, but it will feel like an eternity. Some of you will drop out under the stress, and the Krell will kill some others. Usually, a flight of ten ends up with one cadet graduating to full pilot, maybe two." He stopped at the end of the line, where Kimmalyn stood biting her lip.

"This bunch though . . . ," Cobb added, "I'll be surprised if any of you make it." He limped away from us, setting his coffee on a small desk at the front of the room, then riffling through the papers on his clipboard. "Which of you is Jorgen Weight?"

"Me, sir!" Jerkface said, standing up straighter.

"Great. You're flightleader."

I gasped.

Cobb eyed me, but said nothing. "Jorgen, you'll need two assistant flightleaders. I'll want the names by the end of the day."

"I can give you those now, sir," he said, pointing to his two cronies—a shorter boy and a taller one. "Arturo and Nedd."

Cobb marked something on his clipboard. "Great. Everyone, pick a seat. We're going to—"

"Wait," I said. "That's *it*? That's how you choose our flightleader? You're not even going to see how we do first?"

"Pick a seat, cadets," Cobb repeated, ignoring me.

"But—" I said.

"Except Cadet Spensa," he said, "who will instead meet me in the hallway."

I bit my tongue and stomped out into the hallway. I probably should have contained my frustration, but . . . *really?* He immediately picked Jerkface? Just like that?

Cobb followed me, then calmly shut the door. I prepared an outburst, but he spun on me and hissed, "Are you *trying* to ruin this, Spensa?"

I choked off my retort, shocked by his sudden anger.

"Do you know how far I had to stick my neck out to get you into this class?" he continued. "I argued that you sat in the room for hours, that you finished a damn near perfect test. It still took *every bit* of clout and reputation I've earned over the years to pull this off. Now, the first chance you get, you're throwing a tantrum?"

"I . . . But you didn't see what that guy was doing before class! He was strutting around, claiming he'd be flightleader."

"Turns out he had good reason!"

"But—"

"But what?" Cobb demanded.

I stifled the words I was going to say, and instead remained silent.

He took a deep breath. "Good. You can control yourself at least a little." He rubbed his brows with his thumb and forefinger. "You're just like your father. I spent half the time wanting to strangle the man. Unfortunately, you're not him—you have to live with what he did. You *have* to control yourself, Spensa. If it looks like I'm favoring you, someone will call improper bias, and you'll be pulled from my class faster than you can spit."

"So you can't favor me?" I asked. "But *everyone* can favor the son of an aristocrat who didn't even have to finish his test?"

Cobb sighed.

"Sorry," I said.

"No, I walked into that one," he said. "Do you know who that boy is?"

"Son of a First Citizen?"

"Son of *the* Jeshua Weight, a hero of the Battle of Alta. She flew seven years in the DDF, and has over a hundred confirmed kills. Her husband is Algernon Weight, National Assembly Leader and high foreman of our largest intercavern shipping company. They're among the most heavily merited people in the lower caverns."

"So their son and his cronies get to be our leaders, just because of what their parents did?"

"Jorgen's family owns *three* private fighters, and he has been training on them since he was fourteen. He has nearly a thousand hours in the cockpit. How many do *you* have?"

I blushed.

"His 'cronies,'" Cobb said, "are Nedd Strong—who has two brothers in the DDF right now—and Arturo Mendez, son of a cargo pilot who had sixteen years in the DDF. Arturo has been acting as copilot with his father, and is certified with two hundred hours' flight time. Again, how many hours do you have?"

"I . . ." I took a deep breath. "I'm sorry for questioning you, sir. Is this the part where I do push-ups, or clean a bathroom with a toothbrush or something?"

"I already said this *isn't* infantry training. The punishment here isn't some menial stupidity." Cobb pulled open the door to the room. "Push me too far, and the punishment will be simple: you won't get to fly."

9

You won't get to fly.

Never had I heard words more soul-crushing. When the two of us reentered the training room, Cobb pointed at a seat by the wall. Not a cockpit, just an empty chair.

I slunk over and settled down, feeling thoroughly routed.

"These contraptions," Cobb said, rapping his knuckles on one of the boxes in front of the mockpits, "are holographic projectors. Old technology from the days when we were a fleet. When these machines are on, you'll think you're in a cockpit; they will let us train you to fly without risking a real fighter. The simulation isn't perfect, however. It has some haptic feedback, but it can't replicate g-forces. You'll need to train in the centrifuge to accustom yourself to that.

"DDF tradition is that you get to pick your own callsign. I suggest you start considering, as you'll carry the name for the rest of your life. It will be how the most important people—your flightmates—come to know you."

Jerkface's hand went up.

"Don't tell me *now*, cadet," Cobb said. "Anytime in the next few days is fine. Right now, I want to—"

The door to the room banged open. I leaped to my feet, but it wasn't an attack or an emergency.

It was Rig. And he was wearing a cadet's pin.

"I was wondering if you'd show up," Cobb said, picking up his stack of papers. "Rodge McCaffrey? You think it's a fine idea to show up late to your *first day* in flight school? You going to show up late when the Krell attack?"

Rig sucked in a breath and shook his head, going white, like a flag of truce. And . . . Rig was a cadet. When he'd gone in last night to talk to them about his test, I'd been worried, but it looked like he'd gotten in! I wanted to whoop for joy.

But there was *no way* Rig had been late without good reason. This was a kid who scheduled extra time in his day for sneezes when he had a cold. I opened my mouth, but held back at a glance from Cobb.

"Sir," Rig finally said, catching his breath. "Elevator. Malfunction."

Cobb walked to the side of the room and pushed an intercom button. "Jax," he said, "will you check if there was an elevator malfunction today?"

"Don't need to check, Captain," a voice replied through a speaker above the button. "Elevator 103-D was down for two hours, with people trapped inside. It's been giving us trouble for months."

Cobb released the button, then eyed Rig. "They say you got the highest score on the test this year, cadet."

"That's what they told me, sir. They called me in, and the admiral gave me an award and everything. I'm so sorry I'm late. I didn't meant to do this, particularly on my first day. I about died when—"

"Yeah, that'll do," Cobb said, waving toward one of the seats. "Don't wear out my goodwill, son."

Rig took the seat gladly, but then saw me on the side of the

70

room and gave me a huge thumbs-up. We'd made it. Both of us somehow, with Rig at the top, which was awesome—so at least the test really *was* fair for him.

Cobb walked over to Jerkface's seat, then flipped a switch on the side of the box in the front. A veil of light surrounded the mockpit—silent, shimmering, like a glowing bubble. From inside, Jerkface breathed out a soft—but audible—prayer to the North Star. I leaned forward in my chair.

"It can be disorienting," Cobb said, walking over and turning on Arturo's machine, then Nedd's. "Though it's no match for *actually* being in the air, it's a reasonable substitute."

I waited, tense, as he went around the circle, flipping on devices one after another. Each cadet made some audible signal of appreciation—a little gasp, or a "Wow." My heart just about broke as Cobb turned away from the last empty seat and walked toward the front of the room.

Then, as if remembering something he'd left behind, he looked over his shoulder at me.

I nearly exploded with anticipation.

Finally he nodded toward the empty mockpit. I scrambled out of my seat and climbed in as he flipped the switch. Light flashed around me, and in the blink of an eye I seemed to be sitting in the cockpit of a Poco-class fighter on a launchpad outside the building. The illusion was so incredible that I gasped, then stuck my hand outside the "canopy" just to be sure. The hologram wavered and fell apart into little grains of light—like falling dust—when my hand broke through it.

I pulled my hand back in, then inspected the controls: a throttle lever, a dashboard full of buttons, and a control sphere for my right hand. The sphere was a globe I could palm, with grooves for my fingers and buttons at the tips.

Outside the holographic cockpit canopy, I could see the other "ships" in a line beside a picture-perfect reproduction of Alta

Base. I could even look up and see the sky, the faint patterns of the rubble belt . . . everything.

Cobb's mustachioed face broke through the sky—like one of the Saints themselves—as he leaned in through the hologram to speak with me. "You like the feel of this, cadet?"

"Yes, sir," I said. "More than anything."

"Good. Don't lose it."

I met his eyes and nodded.

He backed away. "All right, cadets," he said. His voice felt ghostly coming from seemingly nowhere. "I don't waste time. Every day you're training is a day good pilots are dying in the fight without you as backup. Put on the helmets at your feet."

I did so, and Cobb's voice now came through the earpiece inside my helmet. "Let's practice takeoffs," he said. "That should—"

"Sir!" Jerkface said. "I can show them."

I rolled my eyes.

"All right, flightleader," Cobb said. "I'm willing to let someone else do the hard work for me. Let's see you get them into the sky."

"Yes, sir!" Jerkface said. "Flight, your fighters don't need their boosters to raise or lower your altitude. That is handled by the acclivity ring, the hooplike device underneath every starship. Its power switch is . . . um . . . top of the front console, the red button. Never turn that off when flying, or you'll drop like a piece of debris."

One ship down the line suddenly lit up beneath as the acclivity ring turned on.

"Use your control sphere to bank right or left," Jerkface continued, "or to make small movements. To do a quick ascent, use the smaller lever beside the throttle and pull it upward."

Jerkface's starship lifted into the air in a steady ascent straight up. His ship, like the rest of ours, was a Poco-class. They looked like glorified pencils with wings, but they were still starships, and

I was in a cockpit. Holographically kind of almost, but still it was *happening*.

I flicked the red switch, and my entire dashboard lit up. I grinned, holding the control sphere in my right hand and yanking on the altitude control with my left.

My ship sprang backward in a sudden jerking motion, and I managed to crash it into the building behind us.

And I wasn't the only one. Our ships responded with far more sensitivity than we were expecting. Rig flipped his completely upside down somehow; Kimmalyn darted up into the air, then screamed at the sudden motion and brought herself back down and flattened right on the launchpad.

"Altitude control *only*," Jerkface said. "Don't touch the control sphere right now, cadets!"

Cobb chuckled from outside somewhere.

"Sir!" Jerkface said. "I . . . er . . . That . . ." He fell silent. "Huh."

I was glad nobody could see how much I was blushing. I appeared to have crashed my ship into a holographic version of the flight school mess hall, judging by the tables and spilled food. I felt as if I should have whiplash, but while my chair shook a little when the ship moved, it couldn't replicate the true motions of flight.

"Congratulations, cadets," Cobb said. "I'm pretty sure half of you are dead now. Thoughts, flightleader?"

"I didn't expect them to be *that* hopeless, sir."

"We're not hopeless," I said. "Just . . . eager."

"And maybe a little embarrassed," Kimmalyn noted.

"Speak for yourself," a girl's voice said through my earpiece. What was her name again? Hudiya, the ponytailed girl with the loose jacket. She was laughing. "Oh, my *stomach*. I think I'm going to hurl. Can I do it again?"

"Again?" Kimmalyn asked.

"It was awesome!"

"You *just* said you thought you were going to hurl."

"In a good way."

"How do you hurl in a good way?"

"Attention!" Cobb snapped. My ship fuzzed around me, and suddenly all of us were back in a line, our ships whole again, the simulation apparently reset. "Like a lot of new pilots, you're not accustomed to how responsive your ships can be. With the power of the acclivity ring and your booster, you can perform *precision* maneuvers—particularly once we get you trained with light-lances.

"That versatility comes at a cost, however. It's *really* easy to get yourself killed in a starship. So today we're going to practice three things. Going up. Coming down. And *not dying* while you do either. Got it?"

"Yes, sir!" came our chorus.

"You're also going to learn to control your radio. The set of blue buttons on the top left of your control panel manages that; you'll need to accustom yourselves to opening a line to the whole flight, or to your wingmate alone. We'll go over the other buttons later. I don't want you distracted right now. Stars only know how you could do worse than that little performance you just gave, but I'm disinclined to give you the opportunity!"

"Yes, sir!" we belted out, somewhat sheepishly.

And so, for the next *three hours,* we took off and landed.

It was frustrating work because I felt like I should be able to do far more. I'd studied so hard and I'd practiced in my mind. I felt like I knew this.

Only I didn't. My crash at the start proved that. And my continuing inability frustrated me.

The sole way to overcome that was to practice, so I dedicated myself to the instruction. Up and down. Up and down. Time after time. I did it with gritted teeth, determined not to crash again.

Eventually, we all managed to make five trips up and down without crashing. As Cobb sent us up again, I leveled at five hundred on the altimeter, then stopped myself there. I released a breath, leaning back as the other cadets joined me in a line.

Jerkface zoomed past and did a little flip before settling in. Show-off.

"All right, flightleader," Cobb said. "Call your flight roll and get a verbal confirmation of readiness from each member. You'll do this before every engagement, to verify that nobody is having mechanical or physical troubles. Flight, *if* you are experiencing troubles, *tell your flightleader.* If you fly into battle knowing something is wrong with your ship, then you are responsible for the damage you might cause."

"Sir," Bim asked over the line, "is it true that if we crash a real ship while in training, we can't graduate?"

"Usually," Cobb said, "if a cadet crashes their starfighter, it's a sign of some kind of negligence, the type that indicates they shouldn't be trusted with that kind of equipment."

"And if we eject?" Bim said. "I've heard that cadets do training in real combat situations. If we get shot down and eject, does it mean we're out? As a cadet, I mean?"

Cob was silent for a moment. "There's no hard-and-fast rule," he said.

"But it's tradition, right?" Bim asked. "A cadet who ejects and scuttles their ship stays grounded from then on."

"It's because they're looking for cowards," Hudiya said. "They want to kick out cadets who are too eager to eject."

I felt a jolt of adrenaline, as I always did when someone mentioned the word *coward.* But it wasn't in reference to me, and never would be. *I* would never eject.

"Real pilots," said one of Jerkface's cronies, "the best of the best? They can steer a crashing ship into a salvageable landing, even if they've been shot. Acclivity rings are worth so much that pilots have to protect them, because the pilot isn't worth as much as—"

"That's enough, Arturo," Cobb cut in. "You're spreading stupid rumors. Both pilots *and* ships are valuable. You cadets ignore that talk—you might hear it from other flights—about steering your ship into a controlled landing. You hear me? If you're shot down, you *eject*. Don't worry about the consequences, worry about your life. If you're a good enough pilot it won't impact your career, tradition or no tradition."

I frowned. That wasn't what I'd heard. Full pilots who got shot down, they were given second chances. But cadets? Why graduate someone who had been shot down when you were looking for only the very best?

"Stupid pilot pride," Cobb grumbled. "It's cost us more than the Krell have, I swear. Flightleader, weren't you going to call roll?"

"Oh, right!" Jorgen said. "Cadet Flight B! Time to—"

"Cadet Flight B?" Cobb said. "You can come up with a better name than that, flightleader."

"Er. Yes, sir. Um . . ."

"Skyward Flight," I said.

"Skyward Flight," Jerkface said, jumping on the name. "Roll call and confirmation of readiness, in order of dashboard ship identification!"

"Skyward Two," said the taller of the two cronies. "Callsign: Nedder. Confirmed."

"Skyward Three," said Hudiya. "Callsign: Hurl. Confirmed."

"Seriously?" Jerkface asked. "Hurl?"

"Memorable, isn't it?" she asked.

Jerkface sighed.

"Skyward Four," said Rig. "Um . . . Callsign: Rigmarole. Wow, it sounds good to say that. And, um, confirmed."

"Skyward Five," said Arturo, the shorter of the two cronies. "Callsign: Amphisbaena."

"Amphi-what?" Hurl asked.

"It's a two-headed dragon," Arturo said. "It's an *extremely* fearsome animal from mythology. Confirmed."

"Skyward Six," Kimmalyn said. "So . . . callsign. I need one of those, eh?"

"Saint," I suggested.

"Oh, *stars* no," she replied.

"You can pick one later," Cobb said. "Just use your first name for now."

"No, no," she said. "Just call me Quick. No need to procrastinate my choice; the Saint always said, 'Save time and do that job now.'"

"How," Arturo said, "does doing something 'now' save you any time? Theoretically, the indicated job will take the same amount of time now as it would later."

"Tangent, Amphi," Jerkface said. "Skyward Seven?"

"Skyward Seven," said an accented girl's voice I didn't think I'd heard before. "Callsign: Morningtide. Confirmed."

Wait. Who was that? I wracked my brain. *The Vician girl with the tattoo on her lower jaw,* I realized. *The one who brushed me off earlier.*

"Skyward Eight," said Bim. "Bim. That's my name, not my callsign. I'll get back to you on that later. I don't want to screw it up. Confirmed, by the way."

"Skyward Nine," said Freyja, the tall blonde girl. "Callsign: FM. Confirmed." She'd launched her ship the first time without crashing, the only one who had done that except for Jerkface and his cronies. Her expensive clothing and those golden clasps on her boots made me think she must be from the lower caverns too. Her family obviously had enough merits for fancy requisitions.

"Skyward Ten," I said. "Callsign: Spin. Confirmed."

"What a bland callsign," Jerkface said. "I'll be Jager. It means *hunter* in one of the old—"

"Can't be Jager," Cobb said. "We've already got a Jager. Nightmare Flight. Just graduated two months ago."

"Oh," Jerkface said. "I . . . er. I didn't know that."

"How about Jerkface?" I said. "It's what I've been calling you in my head. We can call you that."

"No. We. Can't."

I heard a number of snickers—including one I was pretty sure came from Nedd "Nedder" Strong, the taller of Jerkface's cronies.

"All right," Cobb said, ignoring us. "Now that you've done that, maybe we can talk about how to actually *move* somewhere."

I nodded, eager, though I realized nobody could see me.

"Hold the throttle with a light touch," Cobb directed. "Nudge it forward slowly, until the dial says point-one."

I did so, timid—extra worried that I'd repeat my embarrassment from earlier—and I let out a breath as my ship moved forward at a modest boost.

"Good," Cobb said. "You're now going point-one Mag. That's a tenth of Mag-1, which is normal combat speed. Even-numbered designations, you lower yourselves three hundred feet. You'd be more used to saying a hundred meters, but it's tradition to use feet for altitude, for some scudding reason, and you'll get used to it. Odd-numbered designations, you go up three hundred. That will give you some space to try very *slight* moves to the left and right as you fly."

I did as he said, diving down, then leveling out. I tried a veer right, and a veer left. It felt . . . natural. Like I was meant to do this. Like I—

A series of loud alerts erupted. I jumped, then—panicked—I

searched my dashboard, worried I'd done something wrong. Finally, my brain put together that the sound wasn't coming from my ship, or even from our room. It was alarms outside the building.

That's the attack warning, I thought, pulling off my helmet to hear better. The trumpet sounds were different up here in Alta. Faster-paced.

I pushed my head up through the canopy of my hologram, and saw several others doing the same. Cobb had stepped toward the windows of our classroom and was looking out toward the sky. I could barely make out some distant falling debris burning in the atmosphere. Krell attack.

The speaker on the wall crackled. "Cobb," Admiral Ironsides's voice said. "Do you have those greenmoss cadets hovering yet?"

Cobb walked to the panel on the wall and pushed a button. "Barely. I'm still convinced one of them is going to find a way to make their ship self-destruct, even though Pocos don't have that function."

"Great. Get them up, spread formation, above Alta."

Cobb glanced at us before pressing the button again. "Confirmation requested, Admiral. You want the *new cadets* in the sky during an attack?"

"Get them up there, Cobb. This is a large wave. Nightmare Flight is down in the city for R&R, and I don't have time to call them back. Ironsides out."

Cobb hesitated, then he barked out an order. "You heard the admiral! Skyward Flight, to the launchpad. *Go!*"

10

To the launchpad?

Now?

After *one day* of flight training?

Cobb slammed a button on his desk, shutting down all of our holographic emitters. I couldn't help wondering if this was some kind of test or a strange initiation—yet the pale look of Cobb's face persuaded me otherwise. He didn't like this.

What in the *stars* was the admiral thinking? Surely . . . surely she wouldn't get my *entire flight* killed just as retribution for Cobb letting me into the DDF? Right?

We left the training room in a ragged jumble. "Rig," I said, falling in beside my friend as we jogged down the hallway, alarms blaring in the distance. "Can you believe this? *Any* of this?"

"No. I still can't believe I'm here, Spin. When they called me in and told me about my score, I thought they were going to accuse me of cheating! Then the admiral gave me an award and took some photos. It's almost as incredible as the way Cobb let you in, after—"

"Never mind that," I said quickly. I didn't want anyone overhearing that my circumstances were unusual.

I glanced to the side and found Jerkface jogging a few paces away. He narrowed his eyes at me. Great.

We burst out of the training building and gathered on the steps outside right as a flight of Fresa-class starships launched into the sky. One of the on-duty flights; there were usually several of those, along with another flight or two that could be called up in an emergency.

So why did they need us? I didn't get it.

Cobb emerged from the building and gestured to a line of ten Poco-class fighters on a nearby launchpad. Ground crew were positioning ladders by them.

"On the double!" Jerkface shouted. "To your ships! Everyone remember your number?"

Kimmalyn stopped in place.

"You're six, Quirk," Cobb said.

"Um, it was actually Quick—"

"Get going, you fools!" Cobb yelled. "You're on orders!" He glanced at the sky. A set of sonic booms exploded from the ships that had taken off earlier. Even though they'd moved far out, the booms still rattled the windows.

I hurried to my ship, climbed the ladder to the open cockpit, then stopped. *My* ship.

A member of the ground crew climbed up the ladder after me. "You getting in?" he asked.

I blushed, then hopped into the cockpit.

He handed me a helmet, then leaned in. "This ship is straight out of repairs. You'll use it when you're on orders, though it's not a hundred percent yours. You'll be sharing it with a cadet in another flight until enough wash out."

I pulled on my helmet and gave him a thumbs-up. He climbed down and pulled the ladder away. My cockpit's canopy closed, then sealed. I sat there in silence, collecting my breath, then reached forward and tapped the button that engaged the acclivity ring. The dash lit up, and a hum vibrated through the ship. *That* hadn't been in the simulation.

I glanced to the side—toward the mess hall I'd crashed into not four hours ago.

Don't stress. You just did this a hundred times, Spensa.

But I couldn't help thinking about what we'd discussed earlier. That cadets who crashed, or ejected, weren't—by tradition—allowed to graduate . . .

I gripped the altitude control and waited for orders. Then I blushed again and pushed the blue button that turned on the radio.

"—anyone wave at her, maybe?" Arturo's voice came through my helmet. "FM, can you see—"

"Spin checking in," I said. "Sorry."

"All right, flight," Jerkface said. "Lift off, smooth and easy, like we practiced. Straight up fifteen hundred feet, then hover."

I gripped the controls, and found my heart thundering inside my chest. First time into the sky.

Go. I lifted my Poco into a vertical ascent. And it was *glorious.* The sense of motion, the press of g-forces pulling me down, the view of the base shrinking beneath me . . . the open sky, welcoming me home . . .

I leveled off right when the altimeter read fifteen hundred. The others gathered in a line next to me, stark blue acclivity rings glowing underneath each ship. In the far distance, I saw flashes of light from the battle.

"Flight roll," Jerkface said.

All nine of us confirmed back to him, then we fell silent. "Now what?" I asked.

"Trying to call in for orders," Jerkface said. "I don't know the band I'm supposed to—"

"I'm here," Cobb's voice said over the radio. "Looking good, cadets. That's a damn near perfect line. Except for you, Quirk."

"Quick, sir," Kimmalyn said—indeed, her ship had gone up maybe fifty feet above the rest of us. "And . . . I'm just gonna sit tight here, snug and happy I didn't crash into anyone. As the Saint said, 'Ain't nothing wrong with being a little wrong once in a while.'"

"Fair enough," Cobb said. "But I have orders from Flight Command. Flightleader, lead your flight up to two thousand feet, then throttle to point-two Mag, and head—carefully—out past the city. I'll tell you when to stop."

"Right," Jerkface said. "Everyone, two thousand and hover, and I want you to stop sharp this time, Quirk."

"Sure thing, Jerkface," she replied.

He cursed softly as we went up higher—high enough that the city below looked almost like a toy. I could still see the flashes in the distance, though the falling debris was more dynamic. Streaks of red fire, trailing smoke, falling right through the battlefield.

Per Cobb's instructions, we inched our throttles forward and engaged the boosters. And just like that, I was flying—really flying—for the first time. It wasn't fast, and I spent most of it sweating and overly cautious about my every movement. A part of me was still in awe.

It was *finally happening.*

We flew out toward the battlefield, but before we'd gotten very far, Cobb called again.

"Halt it here, cadets," he said, sounding more relaxed. "I've been given more information. You aren't going to fight—a problem with the elevators caught us with our pants down. One of the flights that was supposed to be on reserve got stuck below.

"They'll relieve you soon. Until then, the admiral wants to make it seem like we have more reinforcements than we actually do. She sent you and another flight of cadets to hover close outside the city. The Krell won't fly in and risk engaging what they assume are fresh ships."

I nodded slowly, remembering one of Gran-Gran's lessons. *All warfare is based on deception,* Sun Tzu had said. *When we are able to attack, we must seem unable. When we are near, we must make the enemy believe we are far away; when far away, we must make him believe we are near.* It made sense to use a few dummy flights to worry the Krell.

".... Sir," Jorgen said, "can you tell us what is happening on the battlefield? So we can be ready, just in case?"

Cobb grunted. "You all passed the test, so I assume that you can tell me basic Krell attack strategy."

I started to answer, but Arturo beat me to it.

"When debris starts crashing down," he said, speaking quickly, "the Krell often use the fall to mask their radar signatures. They fly low, underneath our larger AA guns, and try to approach Alta. If they arrive, they can drop a lifebuster bomb."

I shivered. A lifebuster would not only vaporize everyone in Alta—shields or no shields—it would collapse the lower caverns, burying Igneous and destroying the apparatus.

"The Krell don't always use a lifebuster though," I said, jumping in. "Those take a special slow-moving bomber to carry them. They must be expensive or difficult to make or something—because the Krell often retreat the bomber if threatened. Most of the time the Krell and the DDF fight over the falling debris. It often contains salvageable acclivity stone, which we can use to make more starfighters."

"I suppose you *might* be right," Arturo said, sounding dissatisfied. "But he asked for their basic strategy. The basic strategy is to try to destroy Alta."

"Three out of four skirmishes never involve a lifebuster!" I said. "We think they're trying to wear us down, destroy as many ships as possible, since it's harder for us to replace them than it is for the Krell."

"All right," Cobb said, cutting in. "You two can show off for each other later. You're both very smart. Now shut up."

I sat back in my cockpit, uncertain if I should feel complimented or insulted. That . . . seemed a common mix of emotions when dealing with Cobb.

"Nobody in today's battle has seen a lifebuster bomber," Cobb said. "That doesn't mean one couldn't approach, but today's debris fall does contain a lot of machinery with old acclivity rings."

Ha! I thought. *I was right.* I looked to see if I could spot Arturo, to gloat, but couldn't make him out in the lineup of ships.

"Sir," Jerkface said, "something has always bothered me about the way we fight. We respond to the Krell, right? When a debris fall comes, we fly out to check it. If we find Krell, we engage them."

"Generally, yes," Cobb said.

"So that means we always let them pick the battlefield," Jerkface said. "Yet the way to win in war is to surprise the enemy. To keep them off balance. To make them think we're not going to attack when we will, and vice versa."

"Someone's been reading a little too much Sun Tzu," Cobb said. "He fought in a different era, flightleader—and with very different tactics."

"Shouldn't we at least *try* to bring the fight up to the Krell?" Jerkface asked. "Attack their base beyond the debris field, wherever it is? Why does nobody talk about that?"

"There are reasons," Cobb said. "And they're not for cadets. Stay focused on your current orders."

I frowned at that, acknowledging—grudgingly—that Jerkface had asked good questions. I looked over my shoulder at the green proliferation that was Alta. Another thing struck me as strange. Cobb was an expert pilot, and a First Citizen. He'd flown in the Battle of Alta. If reserves were needed, even the illusion of them, why hadn't he come up here *with* us?

We sat quietly for several minutes.

"So . . . ," Bim said over the line. "Anyone want to help me pick a callsign?"

"Yeah," Jerkface said. "I need one too."

"I thought we already decided on yours, Jerkface," Nedd said.

"You *cannot* call your flightleader something embarrassing," Jerkface said.

"Why not?" Hurl asked. "What was that famous pilot, with the name about gas or—"

"Broken Wind," I said. "One of the First Citizens. She only recently retired, and she was an *amazing* pilot. A hundred and thirty career kills. An average of twenty engagements *a year.*"

"I'm *not* going by Jerkface," Jerkface said. "That's an order."

"Sure thing," FM said. "Jerkface."

I smiled, looking out of my cockpit toward FM's ship right beside mine. Had she known him before? I thought I could pick out a hint of an accent to her voice. The same one that laced the voices of the three boys—rich people accents, from the lower caverns. What was her story?

Lights continued to flash in the distance, and I found myself itching to grab the throttle, engage overburn, and send my ship blasting toward it. Pilots were fighting, maybe dying, while I just sat here? What kind of warrior was I?

The kind that crashed into the mess hall the first time she turned on her engines, I thought. Still, I watched those lights, tried to imagine the battle, and squinted to try to catch a glimpse of a Krell ship.

I was still shocked when I saw one streaking toward us.

I'd seen hundreds of depictions of their ships in art. Small, bulbous, it had a strangely unfinished look—with wires trailing behind like tails. It had a small, opaque black cockpit. Most Krell ships exploded completely when damaged or when they crashed, but in some few, we'd recovered burned-out remnants of the wicked armor they wore. Never an actual Krell though.

"Jerkface!" I said.

"Don't call me—"

"Jorgen! Flightleader! Whatever! Look at your eleven, down about two hundred feet. You see that?"

He cursed softly.

Hurl said, "All right! The game is on!"

"It's not a game, Hurl," Jerkface said. "Instructor Cobb?"

"Here. What is it?"

"Krell ship, sir. It looks like it flew low, under AA gun range, and is heading for Alta."

Cobb didn't respond immediately. I sat, sweating, hands on my controls, trailing that ship with my eyes.

"Flight Command knows about it," Cobb reported back. "Your replacements are climbing into their ships now. They should get here soon."

"And if they're not fast enough?" I asked. "What if that ship has a lifebuster?"

"Flight Command has visual ID on it, Spin," Cobb said. "The ship isn't a bomber. A single ship can't do that much damage."

"Respectfully, sir, I disagree," Jorgen said. "While the base is shielded, it could fire on the farmers with destructors, kill dozens before it's—"

"I know the capabilities of the damn Krell, boy. Thank you." Cobb took a deep breath. "It's close?"

"Yes, sir. Getting closer."

Silence over the line, then finally, "You may engage. But stay on the defensive. *No* grandstanding, cadet. I want you to distract it until the reinforcements get into the air."

I nodded, nervous sweat slicking the sides of my head, inside my helmet. I got ready to fly.

"I'm on it, sir!" Jerkface said. "Nedder, you're my wingmate!"

"Roger, Jorg," Nedd said.

Two ships broke out of our line. And before I knew it, I had grabbed my throttle and zipped after them.

"Spin," Jerkface said. "Back into line!"

"You need me," I said. "The more of us there are, the more likely we'll be to scare the thing off and back toward the real fighters!"

"And she'll need a wingmate," Hurl said, pushing out of line and tailing me.

"No, no!" Jerkface said. "Everyone else should stay in line!"

"Take her," Cobb said. "Hurl and Spin, you're with the flight-leader and his wingmate. But the rest of you hold position. I don't want you slamming into each other up there."

Jerkface fell silent. Together, the four of us flew in an intercept course, picking up speed, moving to cut in front of the enemy fighter before it could get too close to Alta. I was worried we wouldn't reach it in time, that it would zip right past us. But I needn't have been so worried.

Because the moment we drew close enough, it swooped around and came straight for us.

11

My pulse raced. My face went cold.

But I realized, in that moment, that I wasn't afraid.

I'd always worried that I would be. I *talked* big, I pretended like a champ. But how many fights had I *actually* been in? One or two scuffles with other kids when I was younger? Some sparring matches in judo classes?

A part of me had always worried that when I got into the sky, I'd panic. That I'd prove myself to be the coward everyone claimed I was. Like . . . like the lies said my dad had been.

But with a calm and steady hand, I eased up on the throttle and pulled into a turn, trying to position myself behind the enemy. I knew dogfighting techniques. I knew them backward and forward; I'd drawn them out in the margins of basically every set of notes I'd taken in class, regardless of the subject.

I was still hopeless. I made the curve *way* too wide, and Hurl nearly smashed into me because we had banked at different times.

"Wow," Hurl said as the two of us recovered. "This is harder than it seems, eh?"

The Krell ship chose Jorgen to attack, letting out a blast of glowing destructor fire. I tried to help, but my turn was too sharp this time. Jorgen, Nedd, and the Krell ship all zipped away behind me in a sequence of dogfighting maneuvers.

I blushed, feeling useless. I'd always assumed I'd just . . . well, take to this naturally. But I struggled to get my ship even pointed in the right direction.

The Krell pulled into position again behind Jerkface—who cursed softly, and then did a near-perfect twin-S dodge. Suddenly all of this became so much more real to me. That was one of my flightmates. And the enemy was doing its best to kill him.

"Nice work, Jorgen," Cobb said. "But be careful with those maneuvers in the future. If you fly too much better than your companions, the Krell will immediately target you. If they can identify flightleaders, they attack them first."

"Shouldn't they attack the weakest pilots first?" FM asked. "The easiest to kill."

But that wasn't the way the Krell thought. They always targeted the best pilots they could find, in an attempt to destroy our chain of command.

"I'll explain later," Cobb said, voice tense. "Nedd, you need to stick closer to Jorgen, if you can. Make the Krell have to worry about you tailing it if it tries to tail him."

It was fortunate the Krell focused on good pilots, because Hurl and I would have made easy target practice. We could barely steer. Jerkface though . . . he performed a perfect Ahlstrom loop, almost losing the Krell ship.

Unfortunately, Jerkface's next spin wasn't as masterful—he performed it well, but when he pulled out of it, he ended up accidentally pointed toward the rest of the flight. I heard him curse over the radio as he tried to swerve, but that sent shots from the pursuing enemy ship right into our team.

They scattered, ships twisting in all directions. Bim clipped Morningtide, the quiet girl with the tattoos. Their ships bounced away from each other, but didn't hit anyone else. A few destructor blasts hit Rig's ship full on, but his shield held. He still screamed over the radio as the flashes of light rocked his Poco.

I gritted my teeth, heart thumping as Hurl and I managed— finally—to head in the right direction. But that meant we passed among the scattering ships, and *I* nearly collided with Bim this time.

Scud. I understood the admiral's reasoning, but there was *no way* we should be up here fighting. At this rate, the only funeral pyres burned today would be our own. Poor Kimmalyn had leaned on her altitude controls, and had retreated some five hundred feet below us.

Jerkface barely kept ahead of the Krell, though he'd long since outpaced Nedd. I pushed the throttle forward, and my ship compensated briefly for the g-forces, but after a few seconds they hit me, pushing me back in the seat, making me feel heavier.

"Where are those reinforcements!" Jerkface said as the enemy fired on him, blasting at his shield.

"Any moment now," Cobb said.

"I may not have a moment!" Jorgen said. "I'm going to try to get the ship to follow me up high so the AA guns can shoot it. Radio them."

"Done," Cobb said. "The Krell ship's shield is still up, so you might have to keep it in AA-gun range long enough for the gunners to score several hits."

"Okay . . . I'll try . . . What's this red flashing light on my dash?"

"Your shield is down," Cobb said softly.

I can save him, I thought, desperate. *I have to save him!* The two had gained a lot of altitude. My only hope was to get there fast, to tail the Krell ship and shoot it down. So I pointed my ship's nose up and slammed my throttle forward, hitting overburn.

The g-force *crushed* me downward as I flew up, and I felt myself grow heavier. It was the strangest sensation, far different from what I'd imagined. I could *feel* my skin pulling down, like it was going to slide off my face, and my arms grew heavy—making it difficult to steer.

Worse, a wave of nausea hit me as my stomach was pulled downward. Within seconds I started to black out.

No . . . I was forced to grab the throttle and pull it back, slowing my ship. I barely managed to keep from losing consciousness.

Below, the massive AA guns that protected Alta began firing, but they seemed clunky and slow compared to the zipping fighters. Explosions blasted the air behind Jorgen's little Poco and the strange unfinished Krell ship. In a burst of light, an AA gun hit the Krell, breaking its shield, but it kept flying, right on Jorgen's tail.

There was no way its next shot would miss him.

No!

At that moment, a single beam of pure light shot upward from below and pierced the Krell ship right through the center. It blasted apart in a flash of fire and debris.

Jorgen let out a long sigh. "Thank the reinforcements for me, Cobb."

"That wasn't them, son," Cobb said.

"Oh!" Kimmalyn said. "Did I get it? I got it! Oh, are you okay, Jerkface?"

I frowned, looking down. That had been a shot from *Kimmalyn*. She'd positioned herself lower and over to the side, not to escape, but to get a good shot at the enemy without having to fire through the rest of us.

I was, quite frankly, stunned. Jorgen sounded like he shared the emotion. "Scud!" he said. "Quirk, did you just snipe a Krell fighter from *long range*?"

Cobb chuckled over the radio. "Guess the file is right on you, Quirk."

"It's . . . ," she began, but then sighed. "Never mind. Quirk it is. Anyway, yes, sir."

"What is this?" Jorgen asked.

"She's the daughter of AA gunners from Bountiful Cavern," Cobb said. "Historically, people with good accuracy on the smaller AA guns tend to make good pilots. The rotating seats in the small AA guns accustom one to moving and firing, and young Quirk here has some *very* impressive accuracy numbers."

"I wasn't even going to take the pilot's test, to be honest," she said in a conspiratorial tone. "But the DDF recruiters showed up and asked me for a demonstration, so I had no choice but to give it to them straight. 'The best modesty is shown while bragging,' as the Saint said. And after they told me I might be able to do it . . . well, I'll admit I did get a tad excited by the idea."

Suddenly her place among us made sense.

"Vocal sound off," Jorgen said, sounding shaken. "Status report, starting with anyone wounded."

"I . . . ," Rig said. "I got hit."

"How hurt are you?"

"Just shaken," Rig said. "Though I . . . I threw up in my ship."

Hurl laughed hard at that.

"Rigmarole, return to base," Jorgen said immediately. "Morningtide, provide him with an escort. Everyone else into line."

We obeyed, now far more reserved. The banter died off as we watched the firefight in the distance, but soon our replacements came up around us and spelled us off. Cobb ordered us back to base, and we accompanied the other cadet flight that had been used as fake reinforcements.

We landed near Rig's and Morningtide's ships; the two of them had already left, perhaps to take Rig somewhere to sit and calm down. He could get rattled easily; I'd have to find him and see if he needed someone to talk to.

As we climbed out of the ships, Hurl let out a whoop of excitement and ran for Kimmalyn. "Your first kill! If you hit ace *before* you're done with flight school, I'll hurl!"

Kimmalyn obviously didn't know what to do with the praise as the rest of us gathered around, holding helmets and congratulating her. Even Jerkface gave her a nod and a raised fist of acclaim.

I edged my way to him. That *had* been some awesome flying. "Hey, Jerkface . . . ," I started.

He spun on me, and practically snarled. "You. We need to talk, cadet. You are in *serious* need of an attitude adjustment."

What? Right when I was going to compliment him? "Coincidentally," I snapped, "you are in *serious* need of a *face* adjustment."

"Is this how it's going to be? You insist on being a problem? Where did you get that flight suit anyway? I thought robbing corpses was illegal."

Scud. He might have pulled off some awesome flightwork, but that face . . . I *still* just wanted to punch him.

"You watch yourself," I said, wishing I had something to stand on to bring my eyes level with his. "When you are broken and mourning your fall from grace, *I* will consume your shadow in my own, and laugh at your misery."

"You are a *weird little girl,* Spin."

Little girl?

Little girl?

"I—"

"Attention!" Cobb shouted, limping up to our gathering.

Little girl?

I seethed, but—remembering how I'd been chewed out earlier—managed to keep my temper in check as I fell into line with the others. I pointedly *did not* look at Jerkface.

"That," Cobb said, "was somehow the most embarrassing

and inspiring display I've ever seen out of cadets! You should be ashamed. And *proud*. Grab your packs from our training room, then meet me in epsilon hall of the flight school building for bunk assignments. You all need to hose down and grub up."

The other cadets rushed off. I tried to linger, to ask after Rig, but Cobb ordered me on ahead. Seemed he didn't like people waiting for him while he limped.

I still trailed after the others, feeling . . . well, like Cobb had said, actually. Both ashamed and proud.

I'd flown. I'd been in a battle. I . . .

I was *in the Defiant Defense Force.*

At the same time, my performance had been awful. For all my bragging and preparations, I'd been more of a liability than an asset. I had a lot of work to do.

And I *would* do it. I'd learn. I was a warrior, as Gran-Gran had taught me. And the warrior's way was not to run from failure, but to own up to it and *do better.*

As we walked down the building's hallways, the PA system cracked on. "Today's fight was an incredible victory," Admiral Ironsides said. "Proof of Defiant strength and tenacity. Remember what you fight for. Remember that if the enemy manages to get a lifebuster bomb into range, they can not only destroy this base, but everyone below, and everything we love. You are the line between civilization and madness.

"In particular, I'd like to acknowledge the new cadets of the as-of-yet-unnamed Cadet Flights B and C. Their first sortie proves that they, with possible exceptions, are a group to be admired."

With possible exceptions. Scud. How could the admiral of the entire DDF be *so* petty?

We walked to the classroom, where we'd left the packs of clothing we'd brought to Alta. As I swung my pack onto my shoulder, it banged into Hurl. The athletic girl laughed and made a wisecrack about how she'd almost crashed into me earlier, and I smiled. She seemed pumped up, rather than discouraged, by our performance.

As we walked toward the hallways with the cadet bunks, Hurl hung back with me so I wouldn't have to walk alone. Ahead, the others laughed at something Nedd said, and I decided I wouldn't let Ironsides get to me. I had my flight as my allies, and they seemed—Jerkface excepted—to be decent people. Maybe here, for the first time, I'd find a place where I would fit in.

We reached the cadet bunks, two hallways with rooms all along them—one hallway for the guys and a separate one for the girls. Everyone knew that there were strict no-romance rules during flight school; no funny business was allowed until after graduation. Who had time for that anyway? Though I had to admit, Bim did look pretty good in a flight suit. I liked the blue hair too.

We went with the boys to check on Rig. Their room was almost as small as the one I shared with Mom and Gran-Gran back in Igneous. The small chamber had a stacked-up set of two beds on each wall. Arturo, Nedd, and Jerkface had plaques on their beds, and Rig was already in the fourth one. A cot had been pulled in for Bim, poor guy.

Rig was sleeping—well, probably pretending to, but that meant he wanted to be alone for now. So the girls and I walked back to our hall. We located the room assigned to us, and it was just as small and cramped. It had four beds like the boys' room, and each had a plaque saying who was to bunk there. Kimmalyn, Hurl, FM, and Morningtide, listed by their real names—but I preferred to think of them by their callsigns. Except maybe Kimmalyn. Did she really want to be known as Quirk? I'd have to talk to her about it.

Regardless, at the moment, I was distracted by something else. There was no bed or plaque for me. Not even a cot.

"Well, *that's* unfortunate," Kimmalyn said. "Guess you ended up with the cot, Spin. Once they bring it. I'll switch off with you every second night, if you want."

That girl was way too nice to be in the military.

So where was my cot? I looked down the hallway and saw Cobb limping up. Two men in military police uniforms stopped in the hall behind him, then lingered—not advancing on us, but also conspicuously waiting.

I trailed up to Cobb, leaving the others in the room. "Sir?"

"I tried. They won't listen." He grimaced. "No bunk for you. No meals in the mess hall."

"*What?*" I couldn't have heard him right.

"You are allowed in my classroom—I get ultimate say over that—but the rest of the DDF disagrees with what I've done. I have no authority over the facilities, and they've decided not to allocate resources to you. You can train, you can—fortunately—fly a Poco. But that's it. I'm sorry."

I felt my face grow cold, anger rising inside me. "How am I supposed to fly if I can't even *eat*?"

"You'll have to take meals down in Igneous," he said, "where your family requisition chits will work. You'll need to take the elevators down each night, and then back up in the morning."

"The elevators can take hours!" I said. "I'll spend all my free time commuting! How am I supposed to be a member of the flight if I can't live with the others? This is— This is—"

"Outrageous," Cobb said, meeting my eyes. "Agreed. Will you give up, then?"

I took a deep breath, then shook my head.

"Good girl. I'll tell the others you were denied a bunk because of some stupid internal politics." He glanced at the MPs. "Those cheerful fellows will show you the way out of the complex, and make sure you don't sleep on the street." He leaned in. "It's just another fight, Spin. I warned you. They won't make this easy. I'll watch for a chance to fix this. Until then, stay strong."

Then he hobbled away.

I slumped against the wall, feeling like someone had cut my legs off. *I'm never going to belong,* I realized. *The admiral will make sure of it.*

The MPs took Cobb's departure as their cue to approach. "I'm going," I said, shouldering my pack and walking toward the exit. They trailed behind.

I wanted to say goodbye to the others, but . . . I didn't want to explain. So I just left. I'd answer the questions in the morning.

Suddenly, I felt *exhausted.*

Don't let them see you bend, I thought, walking straight-backed. The MPs escorted me out of the building—and down one hallway we passed, I was fairly certain I spotted Ironsides watching to see that I left.

Once I was outside flight school though, the soldiers left me. So much for making sure I didn't sleep on the street. Maybe that was exactly what Ironsides wanted—if I could get arrested for loitering, she might be able to have me kicked out of the DDF.

I found myself pacing outside the building, not quite wanting to leave. Not wanting to abandon the others, and the sense of camaraderie I'd been imagining.

Alone. Somehow, I was still alone.

"I just can't *stand* it, Cobb!" a voice said nearby.

Was that . . . Jerkface?

I inched closer to the building and looked around the corner. It was the back entrance to the school. And indeed, there was Jerkface standing near the doorway, talking to Cobb, who stood inside.

Jerkface threw his hands up. "How can I be flightleader if they don't respect me? How can I give orders when they call me *that*? I have to beat it out of them somehow. Forbid it. Order them to obey."

"Son," Cobb said, "you don't know much about the military, do you?"

"I've been training for this my whole life!"

"Then you should know. Respect doesn't come with a patch or a pin. It comes from experience and time. As for the name, it's started to stick, so you've got two valid options. Ignore it, roll with it, and hope it goes away—or embrace it and accept it, to take away the sting."

"I *won't* do that. It's insubordinate."

I shook my head. What a terrible leader.

"Kid . . . ," Cob began.

Jerkface folded his arms. "I have to get home. I'm expected for the formal dinner with the ambassador from Highway Cavern at nineteen hundred." Jerkface walked out to an *extremely* nice-looking vehicle on the street. A private hovercar, with its own small acclivity ring? I'd seen them occasionally down below.

Jerkface climbed into the vehicle and started it up. The engine purred, somehow more primal than the smooth power of a booster.

Scuuuuuud, I thought. *How rich is this guy?*

His family must have tons of merits to afford something like that. And that left him too rich to bunk with the others, it seemed. He pulled away in a smooth motion. It seemed distinctly unfair that the thing I was denied, he tossed aside like it was a bad bite of rat meat.

I shouldered my pack, then trudged off. I left through the gate in the walled DDF compound, where another set of MPs marked my passing on a notepad. Then I trudged down the wide street toward the elevators. My neighborhood was at the far edge of Igneous, so I really *would* spend hours and hours commuting this way. Maybe I could find someplace to stay nearer the elevators below?

It still made me feel sick. I walked to the elevator complex—but there were long lines, probably because of the problems they'd been having earlier. I braced myself for a wait, but then turned and looked to my left—beyond the buildings, beyond the fields. Though Alta Base itself had a shield and wall, this improvised town—full of farmers who were Defiant in another way—didn't have a fence. And why would it need one? The only things out there were dust, rocks . . . and caverns.

A thought took me. It wasn't far . . .

I stepped out of the line to the elevators and walked outward, past the buildings, past the crops. Farmers working there glanced at me—but didn't say anything as I left the town behind. This was my *real* home: the caverns, the rocks, and the open sky. I'd spent more time here since Father's death than I had down in Igneous.

It was about a thirty-minute walk to the cavern with the crashed ship, but I found my way without too much trouble. The opening was smaller than I remembered, but I had my light-line and was able to lower myself.

The old ship looked more broken-down than I remembered. Perhaps it was because I'd just flown something new. Still, the cockpit was comfortable, and the seat reclined all the way.

It was a stupid idea. If debris fell above, I could get caught in a cave-in. But I was too hurt, too wrung out, and too *numb* to care.

So it was that—lying in the improvised bunk of a forgotten ship—I drifted off to sleep.

12

Waking up in the cockpit of a starfighter was basically the most incredible thing that had ever happened to me. Well . . . next to flying one.

I stretched in the darkness, impressed by how much room the cockpit had. It was larger than those of the DDF ships. I engaged my light-line for a little illumination and checked the clock. 0430. Two and a half hours until I needed to report for class today.

All things considered, I wasn't that tired. Just a little achy from—

Something was sitting and watching me from the inside rim of the cockpit.

The creature wasn't like anything I'd ever seen in the caverns. It was yellow, for one thing. Flat, long, and kind of blobby, it had little blue spikes along its back, making a pattern against its bright yellow skin. It looked like a big slug the size of a loaf of bread, but thinner.

I couldn't make out any eyes, but the way it folded up on itself—the front portion raised—reminded me slightly of a . . .

ST. JOHN PARISH LIBRARY

a chipmunk? Like from the videos we'd watched in class of a few wildlife preservation caverns.

"What are you?" I asked softly.

My stomach growled.

"And, equally importantly," I added, "are you edible?"

It twisted its "head" sideways to look at me—though it still didn't seem to have any eyes. Or a mouth. Or, well, a face. It did let out a soft trill, a flutelike sound, from its back spikes.

If I'd learned anything from collecting mushrooms in the caverns, bright colors meant: "Don't eat me, or soon my brethren will be eating you, sapient one." Better to *not* put the strange cave slug into my mouth.

My stomach growled, but when I fished in my pack, I found only half of an old algae ration bar. I might have had barely enough time to get down to Igneous for food, but that would feel like . . . like slinking home, tail between my legs, beaten.

The admiral wanted to break me, did she? Well, she didn't know what she was up against. I was a world-class, highly trained, longtime expert *rat girl*.

I leaned my seat up and dug around in the back of the surprisingly spacious cockpit. Usually, every centimeter of room was needed in a fighter—though this one seemed to have a cargo spot behind the pilot's chair and what looked like a fold-out jump seat for a passenger.

Last night, I thought I'd seen some old tools in here. Sure enough, I found a coil of plastifiber rope. The sealed cockpit had preserved it, though this stuff was pretty much indestructible anyway. I uncoiled some and unwound it into string.

The slug thing remained on the control panel, watching me, occasionally tilting its "head" and making flute noises.

"Yeah," I said. "Well just you watch." I pushed the canopy open all the way—I hadn't dared close it last night, for fear that there wouldn't be ventilation—and jumped down. As I had hoped, I heard scuttling in the darkness and found rat droppings near some mushrooms along the wall.

I'd have preferred my speargun, but in a pinch, a snare would work—set with my ration bar as bait. I stepped back, pleased. The slug had moved onto the wing of the old ship, and it fluted at me in a way that I chose to hear as inquisitive.

"Those rats," I said, "shall soon know the wrath of my hunger, dispensed through tiny coils of justice." I smiled, then realized I was talking to a weird cave slug, which was a new low even for me.

Still, I had some time to kill, so I looked over the ship. Originally, I'd contemplated fixing the thing. After finishing my test, I'd daydreamed an entire future in which I brought my *own* ship to the DDF and *forced* them to take me.

Those imaginings now seemed . . . farfetched. This thing was *not* in good shape. Not just that bent wing, or the broken boosters at the back. Everything that wasn't in the cockpit was scratched up, warped, or ripped apart.

But maybe that was only the outside. If the guts were good, then perhaps the ship was fixable?

I fetched the toolbox. It had stood the test of time worse than the rope—it looked like a little moisture had gotten trapped in the box—but a rusty wrench was still a wrench. So I moved some rocks, then crawled in under the ship, near the acclivity ring. I knew some basic mechanics, like all the students, though I hadn't studied that as hard as I had flight patterns and ship layouts. Rig had always chided me, saying a good pilot should be able to repair her ship.

I hadn't ever imagined that I'd be in an old cavern, lit only by the red-orange glow of my light-line, trying to pry an access panel off an old piece of junk. I finally got the thing off and looked in, thinking back to my lessons.

That's probably the booster intake and injection system, and that's got to be the stabilizer for the acclivity ring . . .

There was a lot up in here that I didn't recognize, though I was able to locate the power matrix—the half-meter-wide box that was the ship's power source. I unhooked it with some difficulty, then crawled out and used my light-line to pull it from underneath the ship.

The wires that hooked it to the ship were in good shape, surprisingly. Whoever had built this thing had made the electronics to last. The power matrix also used the same plugs we did now—which were the types we'd used in the fleet, before crashing on Detritus. Maybe that could somehow help me place its age?

I crawled back down and looked into the bowels of the ship. *But what's this?* I wondered, rapping my knuckles on a large black box. Sleek, reflective despite the weight of years, it didn't seem to fit with the rest of the machinery. But then, who was I to say what did and didn't fit in a ship this odd?

On a whim, I opened up the tiny power matrix on my light-line, then plugged one of the smaller cords from the ship into it. A soft dinging came from the front of the ship, and a light turned on inside the access panel.

Scud. My light-line's power matrix was obviously too weak, but if I had a real power source I might be able to get some of the ship's functions running. It would still have a bent wing and broken boosters, but the idea was exciting to me. I looked back up into the ship's innards.

The slug was inside, wrapped around a cord and hanging there, staring down at me with a distinctly inquisitive posture.

"Hey now," I said. "How did you get in there?"

It fluted a response. Was it the same slug, or another? I crawled back out and checked, but I couldn't see any other slugs around. I *did* hear a scrambling from near the wall, where my snare had caught a decently meaty-looking rat.

"See?" I said, peeking down under the ship. The slug dropped onto the rocks there. "And you doubted me."

I skinned, gutted, and stripped the meat from the rat. The tool-box had a small microwelder, and my light-line's power matrix was more than enough for that. With it, and a piece of metal, I made a frying pan—and soon I had some rat cooking. No seasoning, but I also didn't have to go hungry.

I can use the lavatory at the school, I thought. *They didn't deny me that yesterday.* And the lavatory had cleansing pods for washing up after PT. I could get some mushrooms in the mornings, set up more snares, and . . .

And was I really planning to live like a cavewoman?

I looked down at the cooking rat. It was either live here, or commute every night like the admiral expected me to.

This was a way to control my life. They wouldn't give me food or a bunk? Fine. I didn't need their charity.

I was a Defiant.

13

Sure enough, when I got to the training building at 0630, the MPs didn't forbid me from going straight to the lavatory. I washed my hands, waiting for a moment when the other women were gone. Then I quickly stripped down, threw my clothes and underclothes in the clothing bay, and swung into the cleansing pod—a machine shaped roughly like a coffin, but with a hole on the small end.

The cycle took less than two minutes, but I waited until the lavatory was empty again before climbing out and retrieving my now-clean clothing. By 0650, I was seated with everyone else in our classroom. The others chatted animatedly about the mess hall's breakfast, which had included real bacon.

I will let my wrath burn within me, I thought to comfort myself, *until the day when it explodes and vengeance is mine! Until then, let it simmer. Simmer like juicy bacon on a hot skillet—*

Scud.

Unfortunately, there was a larger problem. It was 0700, and one of the mock cockpits was still empty. Rig was late again. How in the stars had he been early to class every day for the last ten years, yet managed to be late to *flight school* twice in a row?

Cobb limped in, then stopped beside Rig's seat, frowning. A few moments later, Rig himself darkened the doorway. I checked the clock, anxious, then did a double take. Rig had his pack over his shoulder.

Cobb didn't say a word. He just met Rig's eyes, then nodded. Rig turned to go.

"What?" I said, jumping to my feet. *"What?"*

"There's always one," Cobb said, "the day after the first battle. Usually that comes later in the training than it did for you all, but it always happens."

Incredulous, I chased after Rig, scrambling out into the hallway. "Rig?"

He kept walking.

"Rig? What are you *doing*?" I ran after him. "Giving up after one little battle? I know you got shaken up, but this is our dream!"

"No, Spensa," he said, finally stopping in the otherwise empty hallway. "That's your dream. I was only along for the ride."

"*Our* dream. All that studying, all that practice. *Flight school*, Rig. *Flight school!*"

"You're repeating words like I can't hear you." He smiled. "But I'm not the one who doesn't listen."

I gaped.

He patted me on the shoulder. "I suppose I'm being unfair. I did always want to make it in. It's hard *not* to get wrapped up in the excitement when someone close to you dreams so big. I wanted to prove to myself that I could pass the test. And I did.

"But then I got up there, Spensa, and I *felt* what it was like . . . When those destructors hit me, I knew. I couldn't do that every day. I'm sorry, Spensa. I'm not a pilot."

Those words made no sense to me. Even the sounds seemed strange leaving his mouth, as if he'd somehow switched to some foreign tongue.

"I thought about it all night," he said, sounding sorrowful.

107

"But I *know*, Spensa. Deep down, I've always known I wasn't cut out for battle. I just wish I knew what I was supposed to do *now*. Passing the test was always the end goal for me, you know?"

"You're washing out," I said. "Giving up. Running *away*."

He winced, and suddenly I felt awful.

"Not everyone has to be a pilot, Spensa," he said. "Other jobs are important too."

"That's what they say. They don't *mean* it."

"Maybe you're right. I don't know. I guess . . . I need to think about it some more. Is there a job that involves only taking tests? I'm really good at that part, it turns out."

He gave me a brief hug—during which I kind of stood there in shock—then walked off. I watched for a long while, until Cobb came out to get me.

"Dally any longer, cadet," he said, "and I'll write you up as being late."

"I can't believe you just let him go."

"Part of my job is to spot which of you kids will best help out down here, instead of getting yourselves killed up there." He shoved me lightly toward the room. "His won't be the only empty seat when this flight graduates. Go."

I walked back into the room and settled into my mockpit as the implication of those words sank in. Cobb almost seemed happy to send one of us away. How many students had he watched get shot down?

"All right," Cobb said. "Let's see what you remember from yesterday. Strap in, put on your helmets, and power on the holographic projectors. Get your flight into the air, flightleader, and prove to me it hasn't all bled out your ears into your pillows. Then maybe I can teach you how to *really* start flying."

"And weapons?" Bim asked, eager.

"Scud, no," Cobb said. "You'll just shoot each other down by accident. Fundamentals first."

"And if we get caught in the air again, fighting?" Arturo asked. I still had no idea how to say his callsign. Amphibious? Something like that?

"Then," Cobb said, "you'll have to hope that Quirk will shoot them down for you, boy. Enough lip! I gave you cadets an order!"

I strapped in and engaged the device—but took one last look at Rig's empty seat as the hologram went up around me.

We spent the morning practicing how to turn in unison.

Flying a starfighter wasn't like piloting some old airplane, like a few of the outer clans used. Our ships not only had acclivity rings to keep us in the air—no matter our speed or lack thereof— starfighters had powerful devices called atmospheric scoops, which left us much less at the whims of wind resistance.

Our wings still had their uses, and the presence of atmosphere could be handy for many reasons. We could perform a standard bank, turning our ship to the side and swinging around like a bird. But we could also perform some starship-style maneuvers, like just *rotating* our ship the direction we wanted to go, then boosting that direction.

I got to know the difference intimately as we performed both maneuvers over and over and over, until I was *almost* tired of flying.

Bim kept asking about weapons. The blue-haired boy had an enthusiastic, genuine way about him, which I liked. But I didn't agree with his eagerness to shoot guns—if I was going to outfly Jerkface someday, I had to learn the fundamentals. Sloppy turns were exactly what had slowed me down in the skirmish yesterday. So if Cobb wanted me to turn, I'd turn. I'd turn until my fingers bled—until I rubbed the flesh from my hands and withered away to a skeleton.

A skeleton who could turn really, *really* well.

I followed the formation to the left, then jerked downward by reflex as Hurl turned too far on her axis and swooped too far in my direction. She smashed right into FM, whose invisible shield deflected the hit. But FM wasn't good enough to compensate for the shove, and she went spinning out of control the other direction.

Both went down, smashing into the rock surface in a pair of twin explosions.

"Scud," FM said. She was a prim one, with her golden boot latches and her stylish haircut.

Hurl, however, merely laughed. She did that a lot, enjoying herself perhaps too much. "Wow!" she said. "Now *that* was an explosion. How many points do I get for that performance, Cobb?"

"Points? You think this is a game, cadet?"

"Life is a game," Hurl said.

"Yes, well, you just lost all your points and died," Cobb said. "If you fall into an uncontrolled spin like that, eject."

"Um . . . how do I do that, again?" Nedd asked.

"Seriously, Nedd?" Arturo asked. "We went over this yesterday. Look at the lever between your legs. See the big *E* on it? What do you think that stands for?"

"I figured it meant *emergency.*"

"And what do you do when there's an emergency? In a fighter? You . . ."

"Call you," Nedd said. "And say, 'Hey Arturo. Where's the scudding eject lever?'"

Arturo sighed. I grinned, looking out my window toward the next ship in formation—I could barely see the girl inside. Morningtide, her tattoo visible even with her helmet on. She glanced away sharply. Not even a smile.

Fine.

"Fly back in," Cobb said to us. "It's nearly time for lunch."

"Fly back in?" Bim complained. "Can't we just turn off the holograms and go grab some grub?"

"Sure. Turn it off, get something to eat, then *keep walking* on back to where you came from—because I don't have time for cadets who refuse to practice their landings."

"Er, sorry, sir."

"Don't waste radio waves with apologies, cadet. Just follow orders."

"All right, flight," Jerkface said. "Standard spread, bank to heading 165."

We obeyed, maneuvering back into a line, and flew toward the virtual version of Alta. "Cobb," I said, "are we going to practice recovering our ship from an uncontrolled descent?"

"Not this again," he said. "You'll very rarely be in such a situation—and so, if you are, I want you trained to yank that eject lever. I don't want you distracted by some bravado about saving your ship."

"What if we *could* have saved it, sir?" Jorgen said. "Shouldn't a good pilot do everything he or she can in order to protect their acclivity ring? They're rare enough that tradition states we should—"

"Don't quote that stupid tradition to me," Cobb snapped. "We need good pilots as much as we need acclivity rings. If you are in an uncontrolled descent, you *eject*. You understand me?"

A few of the others gave verbal confirmation. I didn't. He hadn't contradicted the most important fact—that if a cadet ejected and scuttled their ship, they would never fly again. Maybe once I became a full pilot I could think about ejecting, but for now I was *never* pulling that lever.

Having this taken away from me would be basically the same as dying anyway.

We landed, and the holograms shut down. The others started to pile out of the room toward the mess hall for lunch, laughing together about how spectacular FM and Hurl had looked when they exploded. Kimmalyn noticed me hanging back in the room,

111

and tried to stop—but Cobb gently steered her from the room after the others.

"I explained the situation to them," he said, stopping in the doorway. "The elevators say you didn't go down to Igneous last night?"

"I . . . I know of a little cave, about a half hour's hike outside of town. I figured it would save time to stay there. I've spent my life scavenging in the tunnels. I feel more comfortable there."

"Suit yourself. Did you bring in a lunch today?"

I shook my head.

"Do so from now on. I won't have you distracted by hunger during training." Then he left. Soon after, I heard voices in the distance. Laughter, echoing from the mess hall.

I considered getting in more training, but wasn't certain I was allowed to use the machines without supervision. I couldn't sit there and listen for an hour though, so I decided to take a walk. It was strange how exhausted I could feel from flying, yet still have so much nervous energy from sitting so long.

I exited the training building—noting the two MPs stationed in the hallway. Were they really there just to keep me from snatching a roll? That was a lot of resources for the admiral to expend to satisfy her rivalry with an insignificant cadet. On the other hand, if you were going to pick a fight, you should fight to win—and I had to respect that.

I left the DDF base and made my way to the orchard right outside the walls. Though there were workers here tending the trees, other people in uniforms walked among them, and benches had been set out along the path. It seemed I wasn't the only one who enjoyed the presence of real plant life. Not fungus or moss, but actual trees. I wasted a good five minutes feeling the bark and picking at the leaves, half convinced the whole thing would be made of some highly realistic plastic.

I eventually stepped out and looked up at the debris field. As always, I could make out vast patterns, muted greys and lines in the sky, though it was too distant to see any specifics. A skylight was moving straight overhead, bright enough that I couldn't look directly at it without my eyes watering.

I didn't spot any holes through the debris. That one moment with my father was the only time I'd ever seen into space itself—there were just too many layers of junk up there, orbiting in different patterns.

What had the people been like, the ones who had built all of this? Some of the kids in my clan had whispered that Detritus was actually Old Earth, but my father had laughed at that notion. Apparently the planet was far too small, and we had maps of Earth that it didn't match.

But they had been human, or at least they'd used our language. Gran-Gran's generation—the crew of the *Defiant* and its fleet—had known Detritus was here. They'd come to the old abandoned planet intentionally. To hide, though the landing had been far more destructive than they'd intended. I tried to imagine what it had been like for them. To leave the skies, to leave your ships, being forced to break into clans and hide. Had it been as strange for them to look up and see a cavern ceiling as it still was for me to look up and see the sky?

I continued to wander the orchard pathways. There was a certain rugged friendliness about the workers up here. They smiled at me as I walked past. Some gave me a quick, informal salute. I wondered how they'd react to hearing I was the daughter of Chaser, the infamous coward.

As I rounded the orchard and headed back toward class, I passed a number of people in suits and skirts getting an official tour of the orchards. That was the kind of clothing you saw on overseers below; people rich in merits who had been moved to deep caverns, the safer, better-protected locations that might survive a bomb. People like Jorgen and his cronies.

They seemed too . . . clean.

As I walked away, I spotted something curious: between the orchard and the base was a row of small vehicle hangars. The door to one of them was up, revealing Jerkface's hovercar peeking out. I glanced in, noting the polished chrome and baby-blue colorings. Cool, soft, and obviously *expensive*. Why stash it here, outside the base?

Probably doesn't want the other cadets asking for a ride, I thought. I resisted the urge to do something nasty to it. Barely.

I passed through the gate, then arrived at our training room before the others. I walked straight to my seat—already feeling like it had been too long since I'd been in a cockpit. I settled in, sighing, happy. I looked to the side, and found someone watching me.

I jumped practically to the ceiling. I hadn't noticed Morningtide by the wall as I'd entered. Her real name was Magma or Magna, I couldn't remember. Judging by the tray on the counter beside the Vician girl, she'd brought her food back here, and had eaten it alone.

"Hey," I said. "What did they have? Smells like gravy. Algae paste stew? Potato mash? *Pork chops?* Don't worry, I can take it. I'm a soldier. Give it to me straight."

She just looked away, her face impassive.

"Your people are descended from marines, right?" I asked. "On board the *Defiant*? I'm the descendant of people from the flagship myself—the engine crew. Maybe our great-grandparents knew each other."

She didn't respond.

I gritted my teeth, then climbed out of the seat. I stalked right over to her, forcing her to look me in the eyes.

"You have a problem with me?" I demanded.

She shrugged.

"Well, deal with it," I said.

She shrugged again.

I tapped her on the collarbone. "Don't taunt me. I don't care how fearsome the Vician reputation is; *I'm* not going anywhere except up. And I don't care if I have to step over your body to get there."

I spun and walked back to my mockpit, settling down, feeling satisfied. I needed to show Jerkface a little of *that*. Spensa the warrior. Yeah . . . felt good.

The others eventually piled into the room, taking their positions. Kimmalyn sidled over. Her long, curly dark hair shook as she looked one way, then the other, as if trying to see if she was being watched.

She dropped a roll into my lap. "Cobb told us you forgot to bring a lunch," she whispered. Then she stood up and walked the other way, speaking loudly. "What a lovely view of the sky we have! As the Saint always said, 'Good thing it's light during the day, otherwise we wouldn't be able to see how pretty daytime is!'"

Cobb glanced at her, then rolled his eyes. "Buckle in," he told the group. "Time to learn something new."

"Weapons?" Hurl asked, eager. Bim nodded as he climbed into his seat.

"No," Cobb said. "Turning. *The other direction.*" He said it completely straight, and when I snickered, he glared at me. "That wasn't a joke. I don't joke."

Sure you don't.

"Before we get to turn on the holograms," Cobb continued, "I'm supposed to ask how you feel about your instruction so far."

"What?" Nedd asked, squeezing his large frame into his cockpit. "Our *feelings*?"

"Yes, your feelings. What?"

115

"I'm just . . . surprised, Cobb," Nedd said.

"Asking questions and listening is a big part of effective teaching, Nedder! So shut up and let me get on with it."

"Um, yes, sir."

"Flightleader! Your thoughts?" Cobb said.

"Confident, sir. They're a ragtag bunch, but I think we can teach them. With your expertise and my—"

"Good enough," Cobb said. "Nedder?"

"Right now, a little confused . . . ," Nedd said. "And I think I ate too many enchiladas . . ."

"Hurl!"

"Bored, sir," she said. "Can we just get back to the game?"

"Two-headed-dragon-stupid-name!"

"Amphisbaena, sir!" Arturo said. "I honestly haven't been highly engaged by today's activities, but I expect that practicing fundamentals will prove useful."

"Bored," Cobb said, writing on his clipboard, "and thinks he's smarter than he is. Quirk!"

"Peachy!"

"Pilots are never 'peachy,' girl. We're spirited."

"Or," I added, "briskly energized by the prospect of dealing *death* to the coming enemies."

"Or that," Cobb said. "If you're psychotic. Morningtide."

"Good," the tattooed woman whispered.

"Speak up, cadet!"

"Good."

"And? I've got three lines here. Gotta write something."

"I . . . I can't bother . . . of much . . . ," she said, her voice heavily accented. "Good. Good enough, right?"

Cobb looked up from his writing board and narrowed his eyes. Then he wrote something on the board.

Morningtide blushed and lowered her gaze.

She doesn't speak English, I realized. *Scud. I'm an idiot.* The old ships had represented various Earth cultures—of *course* there would be groups that, after three generations of hiding as isolated clans, didn't speak my language. I'd never thought about it before.

"Bim?" Cobb asked next. "Boy, you have a callsign yet?"

"Still thinking!" Bim said. "I want to get it right! Um . . . my response . . . er, when do we learn weapons again?"

"You can have my sidearm right now," Cobb said, "if you promise to shoot yourself. I'll just write 'eager to get himself killed.' Stupid forms. FM!"

"Constantly amazed by the toxic aggression omnipresent in Defiant culture," said the well-dressed girl.

"That's a new one." Cobb wrote. "Sure the admiral will love that. Spin?"

"Hungry, sir." Also, I was stupid. Extremely stupid. I glanced again at Morningtide, and thought back to how she'd always seemed standoffish. That had a new context, now that I listened for the thick accent and the misspoken words. The way she'd looked aside when someone talked to her.

"All right, that's done, finally," Cobb said. "Buckle in and fire up the holograms!"

14

"**Y**ou are the weakest point in our defenses," Cobb said, walking through the center of the classroom, speaking to the nine of us in our seats, our holograms not yet engaged. "Your ship can accelerate at incredible speeds and make turns you can't survive. It is far more capable than you are. If you die up there, it won't be because the ship failed you. It will be because *you* failed *the ship*."

A week had passed already, almost in a blur. Training each day in the simulations, doing time in the centrifuge, then sleeping each night in the cockpit of the ancient ship. I was beyond tired of unseasoned rat and mushrooms.

"G-forces are your biggest enemy," Cobb continued. "And you can't just watch your g-forces, you have to be aware of which direction they're pushing on you. Human beings can take a reasonable amount of g-force backward, like when you're going in a straight line.

"But if you pull up or do a hard bank, the g-forces will push downward, forcing the blood out of your head into your feet. Many people will g-lock—go unconscious—after pulling only nine or ten Gs that way. And if you turn on your axis, then boost another direction like we've been practicing . . . Well, you can easily push over a hundred Gs, enough to turn your insides to soup by the sudden jerk in momentum."

Nedd raised his hand. "So, why did we learn those moves?"

"GravCaps," I said.

Cobb pointed at me and nodded. "Your ships can compensate for sudden extreme g-forces. DDF vessels have things called Gravitational Capacitors. When you change direction or accelerate quickly, the GravCaps will engage and deflect the force. GravCaps can work for about three seconds before needing a brief moment to recharge, so they're of most use when making tight turns."

I knew this already. In fact, Nedd probably would have known it, if he'd been forced to study for the test. So I let my mind wander, thinking of my broken-down ship. I hadn't made much progress on the ancient ship, as I'd spent most of my time hunting and curing rat meat. I still needed to find a power matrix somewhere . . .

"Your ships have three kinds of weapons," Cobb said.

Wait, weapons? My attention snapped back to the class, and I noted Bim also perking up. It was cute how he responded to any mention of weapons in an overeager-puppy sort of way.

"Yes, Bim," Cobb said. "Weapons. Don't wet yourself with excitement. The first of these three is your basic destructor—your primary weapon, but also your least effective. It shoots a concentrated beam of energy, and is usually fired in bursts at short range."

Cobb stopped near Kimmalyn's seat. "Or, less often, it can be charged for very precise long-range sniping. Most pilots only use this function for finishing off disabled ships, or perhaps picking off an enemy during an ambush. Hitting an active target at distance with a destructor requires incredible skill."

Kimmalyn grinned.

"Don't get cocky," Cobb said, walking on. "A destructor is practically useless against a shielded foe—though you'll still fire them at every opportunity, as it's human nature to hope for a lucky hit. I'll attempt to beat this out of you, but honestly, even full pilots cling to their destructors like they're scudding letters from their childhood sweetheart."

Bim chuckled.

"That wasn't a joke," Cobb snapped. "Holograms on."

We powered up the devices, and suddenly we were on the launchpad. Once we were up in the air and had done verbal confirmations, Cobb's voice crackled in my helmet's speaker. "All right. Stars help us, it's time for you to start shooting. The destructor trigger is the button next to your index finger on the control sphere. Go ahead."

I hesitantly pressed the button. A burst of three white-hot blasts shot in rapid succession from the pencil nose of my ship. I grinned and pressed it again and again, firing bursts one after another. Just like that, I was granted the very power over *life and death*! And for more than rats!

"Don't wear it out, Spin," Cobb said. "See the dial on your throttle? The one you can rotate with the thumb of your left hand? That's the destructor rate control. Top position is steady fire. It's loved by every drooling, meathead, idiot pilot who *didn't* train with me."

"What about those of us who are still drooling, meathead idiots?" Nedd asked. "But *did* train with you?"

"Don't sell yourself short, Nedder," Cobb said. "I've never seen you drool. Second position on the dial is burst. Third position is a charged long-range shot. Indulge yourselves. Get it out of your system."

He made a bunch of Krell ships appear in the air in front of us. They didn't fly or move; they simply hung there. Target practice? I'd *always* wanted to do target practice—ever since I'd been a little girl, throwing rocks at other, more nefarious-looking rocks.

Together, we launched a hailstorm of death and devastation through the air.

We missed.

We missed by what seemed like *miles*. Even though the ships weren't that far away. I gritted my teeth and tried again, switching between different destructor modes, angling my ship with my control sphere, firing with everything I had. But scud . . . for how close everything *looked*, there sure was a lot of empty space to shoot.

Jerkface finally got a hit, knocking one of the ships down in a spray of fire. I grunted, focusing on a single vessel. *Come ON.*

"Go ahead, Quirk," Cobb said.

"Oh, I thought I'd give them a chance, sir!" Kimmalyn said. " 'Winning isn't always about being the best,' you know."

"Humor me," Cobb said.

"Well, okay." Her ship charged for a couple of seconds, then released a focused line of light—which blasted a Krell ship from the sky. She repeated the feat again, and again, and then did it a fourth time.

"Kind of like trying to hit the floor with a rock, sir," she said. "They aren't even moving."

"How?" I asked, in awe. "*How* did you learn to shoot like that, Quirk?"

"Her father's training," Hurl said. "Remember? The story with the mushroom that looked like a squirrel?"

FM laughed, and I even heard a peep out of Morningtide. But no, I didn't know any stories about mushrooms or squirrels—it had to be a story they'd chatted about at night, in the bunks. While I was walking back to my cave.

I pressed hard on my destructor button, and managed—remarkably—to finally hit one of the targets. The way it sprayed sparks as it fell was immensely satisfying.

"All right," Cobb said. "That's enough of that stupidity. I'm shutting down your destructors."

"But we only just got them!" Bim said. "Can't we do a little dogfighting or something?"

"Sure, all right," Cobb said. "Here you go."

The remaining Krell fighters—the dozen or so we hadn't managed to shoot down—suddenly came streaking toward us, destructors blazing. Hurl let out a whoop, but I snapped into focus and dove out of the way.

Kimmalyn went down first, in an immediate flash of light and sparks. I dove into a twirling spin, watching the red line on my canopy that indicated in the real world how much g-force I'd be feeling. Cobb was right—the GravCaps protected me when I did a quick turn, but I had to be careful not to run them out midturn, then slam myself with all that g-force.

I pulled up, and fire and explosions surrounded me, debris from the ships of other cadets raining down.

"We've tried to reverse engineer Krell technology," Cobb said in a calm voice, a striking contrast to the insanity around me. Nedd screamed as he was hit. Morningtide went down quietly. "But we have failed. They have better destructors and better shields. That means, fighting them, you're outgunned *and* outarmored."

I was consumed entirely with survival. I swerved, dodged, and spun. Three Krell ships—*three*—swooped in on my tail, and one hit me with a destructor shot. I cut right hard, but another shot took me, and the warning light started flashing on my control panel. Shield down.

"You'll have to hit a Krell a half dozen times to bring down their shields," Cobb said. "But they will do the same to you with two or three hits."

I pulled up into a loop. Blasts marked the deaths of my companions—flares in the dim sky. Only one other ship was still flying, and I knew—without needing to see the numbers on the fuselage—that it would be Jorgen. He was a way better pilot than I was.

That still grated on me. I growled, spinning in that wide loop, trying to get one of the enemy into my sights. Almost . . . there . . .

My controls went dead. The ship stopped responding. During that loop, I'd redlined the g-forces, and the GravCaps had run out. Though my body couldn't feel it here, if I'd been in an actual ship I'd have passed out.

A Krell ship disposed of me with a passing—almost offhand—shot, and my hologram fuzzed. Then my canopy vanished, and I was in the classroom. Jorgen managed to last another seventeen seconds. I counted.

I sat back in my seat, pulse thumping rapidly. That had been like witnessing the end of the world.

"Let's assume you were approaching competence," Cobb said. "A remarkable fantasy, I realize, but I'm ever an optimist. If you managed to fly better than the average Krell ship, you'd still be at a severe disadvantage using only destructors."

"So we're screwed?" FM said, standing up.

"No. We just have to fight differently—and we have to even the odds somehow. Strap back in, cadet."

She did, and the holograms started again with us in the sky in a line. The Krell ships reappeared in a silent formation in front of us. I eyed them more suspiciously this time, index finger itching to spray them with destructor fire.

"Dragon-boy," Cobb said to Arturo. "Press the buttons next to your third and fourth fingers. Hit them both at once."

My ship shook, and a little *pop* of light exploded from Arturo, like a radiant splash of water.

"Hey!" Hurl said. "My shield is down."

"Mine too," said Kimmalyn.

"And mine," Arturo added.

"Mine's up," Jerkface said, as did several others.

Arturo's shield went down, I thought, *as did those of the two ships next to him in line.* I leaned forward, looking out the cockpit canopy, keenly interested. In my days of studying, I'd been taught booster specs, flight patterns, acclivity rings—basically everything about the fighters *except* weapon specifics.

"The IMP," Cobb said. "Inverted Magellan Pulse. It will completely negate any protective shield a ship emits—including, unfortunately, your own. It has an extremely short range, so you'll basically have to be crawling into a Krell's engines before you activate it.

"The key to beating the Krell is *not* to pound them with destructor shots. It's to outmaneuver them, team up against them, and outthink them. Krell fly individually. They barely support one another.

"You, instead, will fight in traditional wingmate pairs. You'll work to engage the IMP in a way that gives your wingmate a clear, unshielded shot. But you also always need to be aware—engaging the IMP leaves you exposed and vulnerable until you reignite your shield."

A sudden burst of light from nearby sent FM cursing softly.

"Sorry!" Morningtide said with her thick accent. "Sorry, sorry!" It was the most I'd heard out of her all day.

"What's the third weapon?" Jerkface said.

"Light-lances," I guessed. I'd read the term, but again, the specifics on what they did weren't covered in the books.

"Ah, so you know about them, Spin," Cobb said. "I thought you might. Give us a little display."

"Um, okay. But why me?"

"They work very similarly to their smaller cousins: light-lines. I have a hunch you've got some experience there."

How did he know? I wore my light-line to class, as I needed it to get in and out of my cavern, but I thought I'd kept it hidden under the long sleeve of my jumpsuit.

124

"Thumb and little finger," Cobb said, "buttons on either side of the control sphere."

Well, sure. Why not? I pushed the throttle forward and moved out of line, approaching the hovering Krell ships. I picked one, the wires at its rear floating down behind it. Like all ships, it had an acclivity ring—with a standard size of about two meters in diameter—glowing with a soft blue light underneath.

The Krell looked even more sinister up close. It had that strange, unfinished feel to it, though it wasn't actually incomplete. Those wires hanging from the back were probably intentional, and its design was simply alien. Not unfinished, but made by creatures that didn't think like humans did.

I held my breath, then clicked the buttons Cobb had indicated. A line of molten red light launched from the front of my ship and attached to the Krell ship. As Cobb had indicated, it worked just like the light-line, but larger—and launched from my ship like a harpoon.

Wow, I thought.

"Light-lances," Cobb said. "You've probably seen their smaller cousins on the wrists of pilots; they were used by the engineering department in the old fleet to anchor themselves while they worked on machines in zero gravity. Spin has one, somehow—which I've decided not to mention to the quartermaster."

"Thank—"

"You can thank me by shutting up when I'm talking," Cobb said. "Light-lances work like a kind of energy lasso, connecting you to something you spear with it. You can use it to attach to an enemy ship, or you can use it on the terrain."

"The terrain?" Arturo asked. "You mean we stick ourselves to the ground?"

"Hardly," Cobb said.

The sky exploded above and I looked up, gasping, as the ubiquitous haze of debris began to rain down balls of fire. Superheated metal and other junk, turned into falling stars by the heat of re-entry.

I quickly spun my ship, then pushed on the throttle and moved back toward the line. It took a few minutes for the debris to start falling around us, some chunks glowing more brightly than others. They moved at a variety of speeds, and I realized some of the falling junk had acclivity stone glowing blue inside it, giving it some lift.

The junk smashed into several of the Krell fighters, pulverizing them.

"The Krell usually attack during debris falls," Cobb said. "The Krell don't have light-lances, and though they tend to be maneuverable, a DDF ship with a good pilot can outpace and outfly them. You'll often engage them in the middle of the falling debris. In there, the light-lance will be your best tool—which is why we're going to spend the next *month* training on them. Any idiot with a finger can fire a destructor. But it takes a *pilot* to fly the debris and use it as an advantage.

"I've seen pilots use the light-lances to pull Krell into one another, stick them to space junk, or even yank a wingmate out of danger. You can pivot unexpectedly by attaching yourself to a big chunk and swinging around it. You can toss debris at your enemy, instantly overwhelming their shield and smashing them. The more dangerous the battlefield, the more advantage the better pilot will have. Which, when I'm done, will be *you*."

We watched the debris fall, burning light reflecting against my canopy. "So . . . ," I said. "You're saying that by the end of our training, you expect us to be able to use *grappling hooks made of energy* to smash our enemies with *flaming chunks of space debris*?"

"Yes."

"That . . . ," I whispered, "that's the most beautiful thing I've ever heard."

15

I tied off the set of wires—working by red-orange glow in the otherwise dark cavern—then wrapped them in tape. *There,* I thought, stepping back and wiping my brow. Over the last few weeks, I'd managed to find a working power matrix in an old water heater at an Igneous recycling facility. I knew the guy who worked there, and he let me trade him rat meat to look the other way as I did some salvaging.

I'd also retrieved some supplies from one of my hidden dumps outside Igneous. I'd made a new speargun, and had fashioned a kitchen that had a real hot plate, a dehydrator, and some spices. I'd stopped by my home to fetch Bloodletter, my old stuffed bear. He made a fine pillow. It had been good to see my mother and Gran-Gran, though of course I hadn't told them I was living in a cave.

"Well?" I asked Doomslug the Destroyer. "Think it will work?"

The little yellow-and-blue cave slug perked up on the rock nearby. "Work?" she fluted.

She could imitate noises, but there was always a distinctly fluty sound to what she said. I was pretty sure she was just mimicking me. And to be honest, I didn't know if "she" was a she—weren't slugs, like, both or something?

"Work!" Doomslug repeated, and I couldn't help but take that in an optimistic light.

I flipped the switch on the power matrix, hoping my little hot-wire job would hold. The diagnostic panel on the side of the old ship flickered, and I heard a strange sound coming from the cockpit. I hurried over and climbed onto the box I used as a ladder to get in.

The sound came from the instrument panel—it was low, kind of industrial. Metal vibrating? After I listened for a moment, it changed tone.

"What is *that*?" I asked Doomslug, looking to my right and—as expected—finding her there. She could move very quickly when she wanted to, but seemed to have an aversion to doing so when I was watching.

Doomslug cocked her head to one side, then the other. She shivered the spines on her back and imitated the noise.

"Look how low the lights are." I tapped the control panel. "This power matrix isn't big enough either. I'll need one made for a ship or a building, not a water heater." I turned it off, then checked the clock on my light-line. "Keep an eye on things while I'm gone."

"Gone!" Doomslug said.

"You don't have to act so excited about it." I quickly changed into my jumpsuit, and before I left, I took another glance at the ship. *Fixing this thing is way beyond me,* I thought. *So why am I trying?*

With a sigh, I hooked the end of my light-line to a rock, threw it up to smack against a stone near the entrance to my cave, then grabbed hold and hauled myself up to the crevice so I could shimmy out and head to class for the day.

* * *

Roughly an hour and a half later, I shifted my helmet—which was chafing my head—then grabbed my ship controls and buzzed past an enormous floating piece of debris. In real life that would have been dropping in a fiery blaze, but in the hologram Cobb had suspended the chunks in midair for us to practice on.

I was getting pretty good at dodging between them, though I wasn't certain how well that skill would translate once they started—you know—*hurtling down from above with horrific destructive potential*. But hey, baby steps.

I launched my light-lance, which burst from a turret on the underside of my ship. A glowing line of red-orange energy speared the large piece of space junk.

"Ha!" I said. "Look at that! I *hit* it!"

After I flew past the chunk, however, the light-lance grew taut, and my momentum caused me to pivot. My ship spun on the line—setting off my GravCaps—then slammed into a different chunk of floating debris.

When I was younger, we'd played a game with a ball on a string, connected to a tall pole. If you pushed on the ball, it would spin around the pole. The light-lances were similar, only in this game, the debris was the pole and *I* was the ball.

Cobb sighed in the ear of my helmet as my hologram went black upon my death.

"Hey," I pointed out, "at least I *hit* the thing this time."

"Congratulations," he said, "on that moral victory as you die. I'm sure your mother will be very proud, once your pin is sent back to her as a melted piece of slag."

I huffed and sat up, leaning out of my cockpit to look toward Cobb. He walked through the center space in the room, speaking into a hand radio to communicate with us through our helmets, even though we were all right next to each other.

The ten mockpits made a circle, and the floor in the center had its own projector, one that spat out a tiny reproduction of what we

129

were experiencing. Eight little holographic ships buzzed around Cobb, who watched us like some enormous god.

Bim slammed straight into a piece of debris near Cobb's head, and the shower of sparks looked kind of like our instructor had suddenly had a really great idea. Perhaps the realization that the lot of us were worthless.

"Zoom out your proximity sensors, Bim!" Cobb said. "You should have seen that piece floating there!"

Bim stood up out of his hologram and pulled off his helmet. He ran his hand through his blue hair, looking frustrated.

I pulled back into my cockpit as my ship reappeared at the edge of the battlefield. Morningtide was there, hovering, watching the others flit between chunks of metal. It looked like Gran-Gran's descriptions of an asteroid field, though of course it was in atmosphere, not up in space. We usually engaged the Krell at a height of somewhere between ten thousand and forty thousand feet.

Bim's ship appeared near us, though he wasn't in it.

"Morningtide!" Cobb said. "Don't be timid, cadet! Get in there! I want you to swing from so many scudding lines of light that you get rope burns!"

Morningtide flew timidly into the field of debris.

I shifted my helmet again; it was seriously bothering me today. Maybe I needed a break. I turned off my hologram and stood up out of my seat to stretch, watching Cobb as he inspected a run that Jerkface was doing with Nedd as a wingmate. I put my helmet on my seat, then walked over to Morningtide's hologram.

I peeked in, my head appearing as if in the top of her cockpit. She was huddled inside, an intense look on her tattooed face. She noticed me, then quickly took off her helmet.

"Hey," I said softly. "How's it going?"

She nodded in Cobb's direction. "Rope burns?" she asked softly, with her thick accent.

"It's when you rub your hand on something so fast, it hurts. Like if you scrape yourself on carpet—or on ropes. He just wants you to practice more with the light-lance."

"Ah . . ." She tapped her control panel. "What was he said before? About prox . . . proximation?"

"We can zoom the proximity sensors," I said, speaking slowly. I reached down and pointed at a toggle. "You can use this to make the sensor range bigger? Understand?"

"Ah, yes. Yes. Understand." She smiled thankfully.

I gave her a thumbs-up and pulled out of her hologram. I caught Cobb glancing at me, and he seemed approving, though he quickly turned away to yell at Hurl—who was trying to get FM to bet her dessert on the outcome of the next run.

Perhaps it would have been easier for Cobb to explain himself better, but Morningtide *did* seem to understand most of the instruction. She was merely embarrassed about what she misunderstood, so I tried to check in on her.

I settled into my seat, then felt around inside my helmet, trying to figure out what was bothering me. *What are these lumps?* I thought, prodding the inside of the helmet. Maybe the size of a requisition chit or a large washer, the round lumps were underneath the inside lining of the helmet, and each had a small metal portion at the center, sticking through the lining. Had those been there before?

"Problem, cadet?" Cobb asked.

I jumped; I hadn't seen him approach my mockpit. "Um, my helmet, sir. Something's wrong with it."

"Nothing's wrong, cadet."

"No, look. Feel in here. There are these—"

"Nothing's wrong, cadet. Medical ordered your helmet swapped out this morning, before you arrived. It has sensors to monitor your bioreadings."

"Oh," I said, relaxing. "Well, I suppose that makes sense. But you should tell the others. It might distract some of the flight if their—"

"They only swapped out *your* helmet, cadet."

I frowned. Only mine? "What . . . kind of readings are they taking about me, then?"

"I wouldn't want to guess. Is this a problem?"

". . . I suppose not," I said, though it made me uncomfortable. I tried to read meaning into Cobb's expression, but he was stoic as he met my eyes. Whatever this was, he obviously wasn't going to tell me. But I couldn't help feeling that it had something to do with my father, and the admiral's dislike of me.

I pulled on the helmet, activating the radio and then my hologram. "Bim!" Cobb said in my ear, acting as if nothing had happened. "You knitting a sweater or something? Back into your seat!"

"If I have to," Bim said.

"*Have* to? You want to go sweep floors instead of being a fighter pilot, boy? I've seen rocks that fly almost as well as you do—I could drop one in your seat, paint the head blue, and at least I'd stop getting lip!"

"Sorry, Cobb," Bim said. "No lip intended, but . . . I mean, I talked to some cadets from Firestorm Flight this morning. *They've* been dogfighting this entire time."

"Good for them! When they're all dead, you can move into their room." Cobb sighed—loudly, in an exaggerated way. "Here, let's try this."

A set of glowing golden rings appeared on the battlefield. They were just larger than a ship, and several were dangerously close to floating chunks of debris.

"Line up and confirm," Cobb said.

"You heard the man!" Jerkface said. "Fall in at my mark!"

The eight of us flew to Jerkface's ship and settled into a line, then gave him verbal confirmation.

"Flight ready, instructor!" Jerkface said.

"Here are the rules," Cobb said. "Each ring you pass through gets you one point. Once you begin a run, you have to maintain a speed of at least Mag-1, and you can't circle around if you miss a ring. There are five rings, and I'll let you each do three runs through the course. Highest score gets two desserts tonight—but a warning, if you crash, you're out with your score frozen where it was before you died."

I perked up and tried not to dwell on the idea that the prize was useless to me. At least this might distract me from the uncomfortable helmet.

"A *game*," Hurl said. "Like, you're actually going to let us have *fun*?"

"I can have fun," Cobb said. "I know all about having fun. Most of it involves sitting and dreaming of the day when you all stop asking me stupid questions!"

Nedd chuckled.

"That wasn't a joke!" Cobb said. "Go."

Hurl whooped and hit her overburn, zipping toward the debris field. I responded nearly as fast, accelerating to Mag-3, and almost beat her to the first ring. I flew through it right behind her, then glanced at my radar. Bim, FM, and Morningtide were on my tail. Arturo and Nedd flew in formation, as they often did. I expected Kimmalyn to be last, but she actually flew ahead of Jerkface—who delayed for some reason.

I focused on the course, racing through the next ring. The third one was practically behind a big chunk of debris. The only way through it at speed would be to use a light-lance to turn extra sharp.

Hurl whooped again and executed a near-perfect hook turn

133

through the ring. I made the tactical decision to shoot past it—which proved wise as Bim tried to pivot through it, and smashed right into the chunk of debris.

"Scud!" he yelled as his ship exploded.

Jerkface still hasn't started the course, I noted.

I made the fourth ring—it hovered between two hunks of debris—but missed the last one, which was behind a large floating metal box, requiring a light-lance turn to spin around it. I ended that run with three points, though Hurl got four. I hadn't counted the others. Poor Kimmalyn crashed getting through the fourth ring.

The rest of us curved around the outside of the debris field for another run, and Jerkface finally flew in for his first run. *He was watching to see us go through,* I realized. *He was scouting the battlefield.*

Clever. Indeed, he got four rings like Hurl.

Hurl immediately raced in for her second run, and I realized that—in our eagerness—we'd been going several times faster than Cobb's stated minimum speed. Why would we want to fly faster? Simply to get done first? Cobb hadn't offered any points for that.

Stupid, I thought. *It isn't a race. It's a test of precision.* I slowed down to Mag-1 as Hurl—trying to hook that third ring again for the sharp turn—lost control and slammed herself into a nearby chunk of rock.

"Ha!" she exclaimed. She didn't seem to care that she'd lost. She just seemed happy that there was a game to it now.

I focused on the third ring, going over and over in my head the things Cobb had taught. As I swooped past, I launched my light-lance into the asteroid and not only hooked it, but—to my surprise—swung around on the energy line so that I curved right through the ring.

Bim whistled. "Nice one, Spin."

I released the light-lance and pulled up.

"You wanna try this one, Arturo?" Nedd asked as the two of them flew toward the third ring.

"I think our chances of victory are higher if we skip that ring each pass."

"Too bad!" Nedd said, then hooked *Arturo* with his light-lance and pulled him after, diving for the ring.

Of course they both crashed. I hit the fourth ring easily, zipping between the two flying chunks of debris. But I missed the fifth one, spearing only air with my light-lance.

"Nedd, you idiot," Arturo said in my ear. "Why did you do that?"

"I wanted to see what would happen," Nedd answered.

"You wanted . . . Nedd, it was *obvious* what would happen. You just got us both killed!"

"Better here than the real world."

"Better *neither*. Now we won't win."

"I never eat my *first* dessert though," Nedd said. "Bad for the bod, my friend."

The two went on bickering over the radio. FM, I noticed, didn't try either of the difficult rings—she stuck to the three that were easier.

I gritted my teeth, focusing on the contest. I *had* to beat Jorgen. It was a matter of *honor*.

He finished his second run with four points again, making the third ring but skipping the last one, which was hardest. That put him at eight points, and me at only seven. FM, playing it safe, would be at six. I wasn't sure about Morningtide, but she tried the last ring and missed, so I was probably ahead of her.

The four of us remaining swooped around for our final run. Again, Jerkface hung back, waiting for the rest of us to go first. *Fine*, I thought, hitting overburn and zipping through the first ring. I had to hit *every* one of these to have a chance. FM, notably, didn't try to fly through even the first ring. She just zoomed carefully over the top of the course.

"FM, what are you doing?" Cobb asked.

"I figure these clowns will all get themselves killed, sir. I could probably win without any points at all."

No, I thought, streaking through the second ring. *He said we keep our points if we crash—we merely can't get any more.* So she wouldn't win, careful or not. Cobb had accounted for that.

I approached the third ring, hands sweating. *Come on . . . Go!* I launched the light-lance and hit the debris square-on, but didn't push into the throttle the right way, so I ended up swinging around, but missed the ring.

I gritted my teeth, but disengaged the light-lance and managed to pull out of the turn without smashing into anything. Morningtide tried the ring, and almost made it, but ended up crashing. Jerkface still waited outside, watching to see exactly how many rings he'd need to win. *Clever. Again.*

Scud, I hated that boy.

I was so distracted that I actually missed the fourth ring, which was one of the easy ones. Furious, my face growing cold, I used my light-line to spear the big square piece of debris, then spun downward—curving straight through the fifth ring, which so far as I'd seen, nobody had hit.

That left me with a total of ten points, while Jerkface was at eight. He would close that gap easily. I felt my anger boil as he finally started toward the course. Who did he think he was, sitting back there like some ancient king, watching the plebes scramble before him? He was so arrogant. But worse, he'd been *right* to wait. He'd been smarter than I had, and he'd gained a distinct advantage. He was going to win.

Unless . . .

A terrible idea took root in my mind. I spun and hit my overburn, accelerating to Mag-5 and sprinting back toward the start-

136

ing line. Above me, Jerkface went through the first ring at a leisurely pace, at exactly the minimum speed.

"Hey, Spin?" Nedd asked. "Whatcha doing?"

I ignored him, turning upward, dodging through floating pieces of debris. Ahead of me, Jerkface approached the second ring, an easy one—and the one that would bring him to ten points.

Straight on . . . , I thought, overburning. Pushing my acceleration to the red line of where—in a climb like this—I'd risk dropping unconscious.

"Spin?" Bim asked.

I grinned. Then smashed my ship *right into* Jerkface's, overwhelming both shields and blowing us to pieces. We exploded into light.

Then we both re-formed at the edge of the battlefield.

"What the *hell* was that?" Jerkface shouted. "What were you *thinking*?"

"I was thinking how to win," I said, sitting back in my seat, satisfied. "The way of the warrior, Jerkface."

"We're on a *team,* Spin!" he said. "You brash, *self-centered,* slimy piece of—"

"Enough, Jorgen," Cobb snapped.

Jerkface fell quiet, but notably didn't give his usual obsequious "Yes, sir!"

The holograms switched off, and Cobb walked over to my seat. "You're dead."

"I won anyway," I said.

"It's a tactic that would be useless in a real fight," Cobb said. "You don't get to take home points if you're dead."

I shrugged. "You set the rules, Cobb. Ten points for me, nine for Jerkface. It isn't my fault that he doesn't get to try for the last few points."

"Yes it is!" Jerkface said, standing up out of his cockpit. "It *absolutely* is *your fault!*"

"Enough, son," Cobb said. "It's not worth getting worked up over this. You lost. It happens." He glanced at me. "Though I guess I'll be wanting to change the rules of that game."

I stood up, grinning.

"Five-minute break," Cobb said. "Everyone cool down and don't strangle one another. That causes too much damn paperwork." He hobbled over to the door and stepped out, perhaps to fetch his midday coffee.

Kimmalyn ran over to my seat, her dark curls bouncing. "Spin, that was *wonderful!*"

"What does the Saint say about games?" I asked.

" 'You can't win if you don't play,' " Kimmalyn said.

"Obviously."

"Obviously!" She grinned again. Bim walked by and gave me a thumbs-up. Over his shoulder, I saw Jerkface glaring at me with unmitigated hostility as Arturo and Nedd tried to calm him down.

"Don't worry, Jorg," Nedd said. "You still beat Arturo."

"Thank you *very much,* Nedd," Arturo snapped.

Kimmalyn left the classroom to get something to drink, and I settled into my seat and dug one of my canteens out of my pack. I made sure to refill all three each day at the bathroom.

"So," Bim said, leaning against my hologram projector, "you're really into warriors and things, eh?"

"They inspire me," I said. "My grandmother tells stories about ancient heroes."

"You have any favorites?"

"Probably Beowulf," I said, then took a long pull of water from the canteen. "He literally slew a dragon, and ripped the arm off a monster—he had to resort to his bare hands after his sword wouldn't cut the thing. But then there's Tashenamani—she slew the great warrior Custer—and Conan the Cimmerian, who fought in the ancient times before writing."

"Yeah, they were great," Bim said, and winked. "I mean . . .

I hadn't heard of them until now. But I'm sure they were great. Er. I'm thirsty."

He blushed and walked off, leaving me confused. What was . . .

He was . . . he was flirting *with me,* I realized, stunned. *Or, well, trying to.*

Was that possible? I mean, he was actually cute, so why would he . . .

I looked at him again, and caught him in the middle of what seemed like a blush. Scud! That was the strangest thing that had happened to me since starting flight school, and I spent my mornings talking to a slug.

I thought about guys, but my life hadn't exactly left me time for that kind of thing. The last time I'd had any romantic inclinations had been when I'd been eight and had given Rig a particularly nice hatchet I'd made out of a rock and a stick—then had decided he was gross the next week. Because, well, I'd been eight.

I jumped to my feet. "Uh, Bim?" I said.

He looked at me again.

"You ever heard of Odysseus?"

"No," he said.

"He was an ancient hero who fought in the greatest war that ever happened on Earth, the Trojan War. It's said he had a bow so strong that, other than him, only a giant could pull the string back. He . . . had blue hair, you know."

"Yeah?" Bim asked.

"Pretty cool," I said, then immediately sat down, taking a long gulp from my canteen.

Was that smooth? That was smooth, right?

I wasn't sure what Sun Tzu or Beowulf would say about flirting with cute guys. Maybe share the skulls of your enemies with them, as a gesture of affection?

I felt kind of warm and gooey (in a good way) until I spotted Jerkface—across the room—watching me. I gave him a hard glare.

He, pointedly, turned to Nedd and Arturo. "I guess we shouldn't expect real honor," he said, "from the daughter of Zeen Nightshade."

A bolt of coldness shot through me.

"Who?" Nedd asked. "Wait, who did you say she was?"

"You know," Jerkface said, voice loud enough to carry through the entire room. "Callsign: Chaser? The Coward of Alta?"

The room went quiet. I could *feel* everyone's eyes turning toward me. How had he found out? Who had told him?

I stood up. Scud, even *Kimmalyn* seemed to know who Chaser was. Her canteen dropped from her fingers and bounced against the floor, spilling water that she didn't notice.

"Who?" Morningtide asked. "What is happen?"

I wanted to flee. Hide. Escape all those eyes. But I *would not run*.

"My father," I said, "was *not* a coward."

"I'm sorry," Jerkface said. "I'm only stating the official history." He stared at me, with that arrogant, so-punchable face. I found myself blushing in embarrassment—then in anger.

I shouldn't feel embarrassed. I'd lived practically my entire life with this mantle. I was accustomed to those looks, those whispers. And I wasn't ashamed of my father, right? So why should I care that the others had found out? Good. Fine. I was happy to be Chaser's daughter.

It was just that . . . it had felt nice. To be able to make my own way, without standing in anyone's shadow.

That thought made me feel like I was betraying my father, and that made me even *more* angry.

"She lives in a cave, you know," Jerkface said to Arturo. "She goes there every night. The elevator operators told me they watch her hike out into the wilderness, because she's not—"

He cut off as Cobb stepped in with a steaming cup of coffee in his hand. Cobb focused immediately on me, then Jerkface. "Back to your seats," he snapped at us. "We still have work to do today. And Quirk, did you drop that canteen?"

Kimmalyn unfroze and picked up her canteen, and everyone climbed into their cockpits without another word. At one point shortly after we went back to practicing with our light-lances, I caught Cobb looking at me with a grim expression, with eyes that seemed to be saying, *It was going to happen eventually, cadet. Are you going to give in?*

Never.

But that didn't stop me from feeling sick through the whole set of drills.

A few hours later, I trailed out of the women's bathroom, canteens refilled. A new pair of MPs walked me to the doors and saw me out, then—like normal—left me there.

I trudged across the base grounds, feeling frustrated, angry, and alone. I should have kept going out of the base, on toward my cave. But instead I took a path around the training building, one that let me walk past the mess hall.

I looked through the window there and spotted the others seated along a metal table—chatting, laughing, arguing. They'd even bullied Jerkface into joining them tonight—a rare treat for the plebes, as he usually drove off to the exclusive elevator. Nedd said it could reach the lower caverns in under fifteen minutes.

So there he was, enjoying what I was forbidden, after tossing away my secret like a fistful of expired rations. I hated him. In that moment, I kind of hated them all. I almost hated my father.

I stalked off into the night, leaving the base through the front gates. I turned to my left, toward the orchard, and the shortcut through it toward the wilderness. My path took me straight past the small hangars where Jerkface parked his hovercar.

I stopped there in the darkness, eyeing his bay. The front door was closed this time, but the side door was open, and I could see the car inside. It took me all of about half a second to come up with another really terrible idea.

Looking around, I didn't see anyone watching. Darkness had come early tonight, the skylights moving away, and the orchard workers had already gone home. I was far enough from the front gates of the base that the guards there shouldn't be able to see me in the gloom.

I slipped in the side of the small hangar and closed the door, then lit my light-line for a bit of illumination. I found a wrench on the wall of the small shed, then pulled open the hood of the blue hovercar.

Jerkface could walk home tonight. It would only be fair. After all, *I* had to walk home—and tonight I would have to do it while lugging a large, car-size power matrix tied to my back.

16

I woke up the next morning groggy and sore, with a face full of stuffed bear. I groaned, turning over, my muscles aching. Why did I hurt so much? Had I . . .

I bolted upright and flipped on my light-line bracelet, peering out of my cockpit bed. The light illuminated my little kitchen, a pile of mushrooms waiting to be sliced, some rocks I'd placed as seats there, and . . .

And a car's power matrix, the size of a small nightstand.

It lay where I'd dumped it after lugging it all the way to the cavern. I'd been so worn out after that, I hadn't plugged it in, but had climbed right into bed.

I groaned and flopped back, rubbing my eyes with the heels of my palms. I'd been so angry last night that . . . well, I hadn't been thinking clearly. Stealing the power matrix had seemed like a *great* idea—but now the holes in my clever plan were stark.

Gee, I wonder who vandalized your car, Jerkface? Could it be the only one of us who wasn't at dinner, and who had immediate *and* powerful *reasons for wanting revenge on you?*

When it became known that I'd destroyed another cadet's

property, I'd get tossed out of flight school so fast, I'd get whip-lash. I groaned again, a sound that was unhelpfully mimicked by Doomslug, who had snuggled into a spot on the dash.

Why? Why couldn't I stay focused? Why did I have to let them get to me? Beowulf or Xun Guan wouldn't let themselves be goaded into acting this stupid!

I felt sick as I trudged to Alta that morning. I didn't even have the will to try out the power matrix. As if there were anything I could do to prevent my doom at *this* point. Why couldn't "ratio-nal Spensa" and "determined Spensa" get together for a battle briefing once in a while?

I fully expected the MPs to be waiting for me, but the guards at the gates just waved me through. Nobody stopped me on my way to the classroom. Jerkface came in while I was settling down in my seat, and he didn't so much as glance at me. Cobb limped in and started class like normal.

At one point during a break, I managed to catch Jerkface's eyes. He met them and didn't look away. There was a challenge in them, yes. But how was I to read this? Was he waiting for some specific point to turn me in?

As the day progressed, and we practiced using the light-lances on moving targets, I started to wonder if maybe he *wasn't* going to get me into trouble. Maybe . . . maybe he was taking the warrior's way. Rather than running to the admiral for help, was he planning his own vengeance?

If that was true, then . . . scud. I might have to give that boy a little respect.

Not much, mind you. He'd still aggressively and maliciously branded me a coward in front of the others. Arturo, Nedd, FM, and even Bim trod more softly around me, peering at me out of the corners of their eyes. It didn't seem to affect our training, but during our breaks everyone was dancing around the news. They asked me about other things, then exited conversations quickly.

The only one who didn't act odd was Kimmalyn. That didn't mean she ignored what had happened, of course.

"So," she said, hovering beside my seat as I rested and drank from my canteen, "is *that* why you're always so bellicose?"

"Bellicose?" I asked, unfamiliar with the word.

"So willing to seize the stars with one hand and shove them in your pocket," Kimmalyn said. She leaned in, as if the next part were somehow naughty. "You know. Heated."

"Heated."

"Maybe even . . . once in a while . . . cross."

"Is my father why I'm such a mess of anger, bravado, and temper? Is the fact that they call him a coward the reason I walk around with my sword in hand, screaming that I'll make a pile of everyone's skulls, then stand on that to help me behead the people who were too tall for me to reach?"

Kimmalyn smiled fondly.

"Bless my stars?" I asked her.

"Every single one of them, Spensa. Every single bouncing star."

I sighed and took another drink. "I don't know. I remember liking Gran-Gran's stories even before he was shot down, but what happened certainly didn't help. When everyone looks at you as the coward's daughter—not *a* coward's daughter, but the *singular* Coward's Daughter—you develop an attitude."

"Well, bless you for standing up straight," she said, then put up her fists. "Pride is a virtue in those who make it one."

"Said the Saint."

"She was a very wise woman."

"You realize none of us have any idea which Saint you're talking about."

Kimmalyn patted me on the head. "It's okay, dear. You can't help being a heretic. The Saint forgives you." From someone else that might have been offensive, *particularly* with the head pat. From Kimmalyn it was just . . . well, somehow comforting.

145

By the end of the day, I was feeling a ton better. So much so, in fact, that I felt only *mild* nausea when they left me for dinner. So that was good.

Outside, I spotted Jerkface getting into a long, black hovercar that had a driver wearing white gloves. Poor boy. Looked like he had to get a ride home now.

I walked back to my cave with a spring in my step, chewing on some smoked rat. I would eventually have to pay some kind of vengeance bill to Jorgen, but I could do that. *Bring it on.* For now, I appeared to have gotten away with a serious crime. One starfighter-size power matrix, ready to go.

I grinned as I arrived at my crevice, then lowered myself on my light-line into the cavern. It was a silly thing to have risked my future over; this ship was so old, it wasn't like getting lights working was going to do any good. But it was also my secret, my discovery.

My ship.

Broken, worn out, with a bent wing . . . it was still mine.

I hauled the matrix into position beside the ship's access hatch. The plugs were the same, so I didn't have to worry about hot-wiring it. I glanced at Doomslug—who inched over along the wing toward me—then grinned and plugged it in.

The lights sprang to life on the diagnostic panel and—judging by the glow from up front—on the dash inside the cockpit. The low humming tone from before started up again, then sped up, warping until it . . . until it became *words.*

". . . MMMEERGENCY BOOTUP PROCEDURES INITIATED," a masculine voice said from the cockpit. It spoke with a strange, old-timey accent, like I'd heard on the broadcasts of famous speeches from the days before we'd founded Alta. "SEVERE DAMAGE TO STRUCTURAL INTEGRITY AND DATA BANKS DETECTED."

Was it a recording? I scrambled over to the cockpit.

"Hello!" the voice said to me, growing less . . . mechanical. "I assume from your clothing and attitude that you are a native of this locale. Would you kindly categorize yourself—stating your national affiliations and the names of your ancestors—so I might place you in my data tables?"

"I . . ." I scratched my head. "What in the stars?"

"Ah," the voice said. "Excellent. Minimal linguistic deviation from Earth Standard English. Forgive the slowness of my processing—which doesn't quite seem up to normal benchmarks—but you *are* human, yes? Could you tell me . . . where am I?"

The words were lost on me. I simply knelt there, on the wing by the cockpit, trying to put together what was happening.

My *ship* was *talking to me.*

17

"My designation is MB-1021, robotic ship integration," the ship said.

It didn't just talk—it seemed to have trouble stopping.

"But humans prefer 'names' to designations, so I am commonly referred to as M-Bot. I am a long-distance reconnaissance and recovery ship, designed for stealth operations and unsupported solo missions in deep-space locations. And . . ."

The machine trailed off.

"And?" I asked, lounging in the cockpit, trying to figure out what in the stars this thing was.

"And my data banks are corrupted," M-Bot said. "I cannot recover further information—I can't even retrieve my mission parameters. The only record I have is the most recent order from my master: 'Lie low, M-Bot. Take stock, don't get into any fights, and wait for me here.'"

"Your master was your pilot, right?" I asked.

"Correct. Commander Spears." He summoned a fuzzy image for me, which briefly replaced the scanner display on his dash. This

Commander Spears was a clean-cut, youngish man with tan skin and a crisp, unfamiliar uniform.

"I've never heard of him," I said. "And I know *all* the famous pilots, even from Gran-Gran's days in the fleet. What was up with the Krell when you came here? Had they attacked the galaxy yet?"

"I have no recollection of this group, and the word *Krell* doesn't appear in my memory banks." He paused. "Reading the decay rate of isotopes in my memory core indicates that it has been . . . one hundred seventy-two years since I was deactivated."

"Huh," I said. "The *Defiant* and its fleet crashed on Detritus about eighty years ago, and the Krell War started some distant time before that." Gran-Gran said the war had been going on a long time when she'd been born.

"Considering human life spans," M-Bot said, "I must conclude that my pilot has perished. How sad."

"Sad?" I asked, trying to wrap my mind around this. "You have *emotions*?"

"I am allowed self-improving and independently reinforcing memory pathways, for the simulation of organic emotions. That allows me to have better interaction with humans, but I am not actually alive. My subroutines for emotional distress indicate I should feel for the loss of my master, but the memory banks recording his appearance—and our history together—are damaged. I remember nothing more than his name and his final command."

"Lie low," I repeated. "Take stock, and don't get into any fights."

"The only portion of my memory banks that seems to have survived intact—other than basic personality routines and things like general language usage—is an open database for recording fungoid life forms on this planet. I should very much like to fill the rest of it in."

"Fungoid?"

"Mushrooms. Would you happen to have any I can categorize?"

"You're a hyperadvanced stealth fighter that—somehow—has a machine personality built into it . . . and you want me to bring you *mushrooms*?"

"Yes, please," M-Bot said. "Take stock. As in categorize local life forms. I'm certain that's what he meant."

"I'm not so sure," I said. "It sounded like you were supposed to hide from something." I leaned out the side, looking at his wings. "You have large twin destructor emitters on each wing, along with a light-lance turret underneath. That's as much firepower as our larger ships. You're a warship."

"Clearly not," M-Bot said. "I'm here to categorize fungi. Didn't you listen to my last orders? I am *not* supposed to get into fights."

"Then why do you have guns?"

"For shooting large and dangerous beasts who might be threatening my fungus specimens," M-Bot said. "Obviously."

"That's stupid."

"I am a machine, and my conclusions are therefore logical—while yours are biased by organic irrationality." He made a few lights on his dash blink. "That is a clever way of saying you are the stupid one, in case you—"

"I understood," I said. "Thanks."

"You're welcome!"

He sounded utterly sincere. But he was . . . what, a "robotic integration"? Whatever that was. I wasn't sure how far I could trust his honesty.

Still, he was a machine with a memory—albeit damaged—that stretched back hundreds of years. This could be a solution, maybe, to the questions we'd always asked. Why did the Krell keep attacking us? What were they, *really*? Our only depictions of them were reconstructions based on the armor they wore, as we'd never been able to take one of them captive.

We'd probably once known the answers to these questions, but if so, we'd lost them eighty years ago. Soon after crashing here—and presuming themselves safe—the majority of the officers, scientists, and elders from our old fleet had gathered in an underground cavern. They'd recovered the old electronic archive from the *Defiant,* and had been holding an emergency meeting. That was when the first lifebuster had been dropped, destroying our archives—and with them, most anyone with seniority in the fleet.

That was when the remnants of our people had broken into clans based on their duties in the fleet. Engine maintenance workers like Gran-Gran and her family. Hydroponics crew—glorified farmers—like Bim's ancestors. Foot soldiers like Morningtide's. They'd learned, through difficult trial and error, that if they kept to small groups of under a hundred people, the Krell sensors couldn't find them hiding in the caves.

Now, three generations later, here we were. Slowly fighting our way back onto the surface—but with enormous holes in our memories and history. What if *I* could bring the ultimate secret to the DDF: the solution for defeating the Krell once and for all?

Though . . . it was unlikely M-Bot had that answer. After all, if the old human fleets had known how to defeat the Krell, they wouldn't have been driven to near extinction. But surely there were *some* secrets hidden inside this machine's mind.

"Can you fire your weapons?" I asked.

"I'm commanded to avoid fights."

"Just answer," I said. "Can you fire?"

"No," M-Bot said. "The weapons systems are locked out of my control."

"Then why would your pilot order you not to get into any fights? You aren't capable of fighting anyone."

"Logically, one isn't required to be able to *finish* a fight in order to *start* one. I am allowed minimal basic autonomous movement, and could theoretically stumble into a battle or a conflict. This would be disastrous for me on my own, as I require a pilot for most important functions. I can assist and diagnose, but as I am not alive, I cannot be trusted with destructive systems."

"So *I* could fire them," I said.

"Unfortunately, weapons systems are offline from damage."

"Great. What else is offline?"

"Other than my memories? Boosters, acclivity ring, cytonic hyperdrive, self-repair functions, the light-lance, and all mobility functions. Also, my wing appears to be bent."

"Great. So, everything."

"My communications features and radar are functional," he noted. "As are cockpit life support and short-range sensors."

"And that's it?"

"That . . . appears to be it." He was silent for a moment. "I can't help noticing—through the aforementioned short-range sensors—that you are in possession of a few *mushrooms*. Might you be willing to place those in my cockpit analyzer for cataloguing?"

I sighed, resting back in my seat.

"At your leisure, of course. I, being robotic, have no concept of fragile things like human impatience."

So what do I do?

"But soon would be nice."

I doubt I can fix this thing on my own, I thought. Should I just go to the DDF and tell them what I'd found? I'd have to reveal that I'd stolen that power matrix. And, of course, they'd never let me keep this ship for myself. Going to the DDF with it would essentially mean wrapping this vessel up with a bow, then presenting it to the very admiral who was trying her best to ruin my life.

"They do look like nice mushrooms."

No. I was *not* going to give this discovery to Ironsides, at least not without more thought. But if I was going to try to repair this ship, I'd at least need help.

"Not that I require affirmation of any sort, as my emotions are mere simulations . . . but you *are* listening to me, right?"

"I'm listening," I said. "I'm just thinking."

"That is good. I should not like to be maintained by one who lacks brain functions."

It was at that moment that I had my *third* terrible idea in not so many days. I grinned.

Maybe there was a way to get some help on the repairs. Someone who had way more "brain functions" than I had.

Approximately an hour and a half later—well after curfew—I was hanging upside down by my light-line outside Rig's window on the third floor of his apartment complex in Igneous. He was snug inside, sleeping in his bunk. He had his own little closet of a room, which I'd always found luxurious. His parents had been deemed exemplary in all six parental metrics, and had been granted housing for multiple children, but—ironically—Rig was the only one they'd ever ended up having.

I knocked on his window, hair dangling below my head as I hung there. Then I knocked again. Then a little louder. Come on; it hadn't been *that* long since I'd last done this.

Finally, the sleepyhead sat up, light through the window— from my light-line—outlining his pale face and bleary eyes. He blinked at me, but didn't seem the least bit surprised as he walked over and slid the window open to the side.

"Hey," he said. "Took you long enough."

"Long enough?"

"To come try to talk me into coming back. Which I'm not going to do. I don't have everything figured out, but I'm still sure that my decision to—"

"Oh, shut up about that," I whispered. "Grab your jumpsuit. I need to show you something."

He raised an eyebrow.

"This is *serious*," I said. "You're going to *flip your boots* when you see it."

Infuriatingly, he just leaned on the windowsill, looking out at me as I was hanging there upside down—which was *not* easy, mind you. "It's almost midnight, Spin."

"This will be worth it."

"You're going to drag me off to some cavern, aren't you? I won't be back until like two or three."

"If you're lucky."

He took a deep breath, then grabbed his jumpsuit. "You *do* realize that you're the weirdest friend I've ever had."

"Oh, come on. Let's not pretend you have other friends."

"Strange," he said, "that my parents never managed to give me a sibling—but I *still* somehow ended up with a sister who gets me into trouble all the time."

I grinned. "Meet you down below," I said, then I paused. "Flip. Your. *Boots*, Rig. Trust me."

"Yeah, yeah. Give me a minute to sneak past my parents." He pulled the drapes closed, and I let myself down to the street below, where I waited impatiently.

Igneous was a strange place at night. The apparatus worked all hours, of course. *Day* and *night* were just words here, though we still used the terms. There was a mandatory quiet cycle—during which the cavern loudspeakers didn't play any announcements or speeches—and a curfew for those who weren't on last shift. But nobody paid attention to you as you walked the streets if you kept to your own business. The default assumption in Igneous was that everyone was going about something useful.

Rig met me down at street level as promised, and we walked through the cavern—passing the mural of a thousand birds in flight, each one divided in half by a line, the two halves slightly

154

offset from each other. The birds soared from a red-orange sun, which you couldn't even see up above.

Our cadet's pins got us past the guards and into the tunnels. As we walked one of the easier paths, Rig filled me in on what he'd been doing the last few weeks. His parents were happy he'd washed out; everyone knew how dangerous being a pilot was.

"They're proud, of course," Rig said, grunting as he climbed some rubble with me. "Everyone treats me really strangely once they see the pin. Like, they listen to what I say, and tell me my ideas are good—even if they aren't. And people make way for me, like I'm someone important."

"You are."

"No, I'm the exact same amount of important I was before." He shook his head. "But I've got a dozen different job offers waiting for me, and I've got two months to decide."

"Two months?" I repeated. "Without a job or school? Just free time?"

"Yeah. Mrs. Vmeer keeps trying to push me toward politics."

"Politics," I said, almost stopping in the tunnel. *"You."*

"Tell me about it." He sighed and sat down on a nearby rock. "But what if she's right? Shouldn't I listen to her? Everyone else thinks politics is the best thing you can do with your life. Maybe I should do what they say."

"What do *you* want, though?"

"Now you care about that?" he asked.

I winced, and Rig looked away, blushing deeply. "I'm sorry, Spin. That wasn't fair—I haven't been fair. To you, I mean. *I* chose to study for the pilot's test; you didn't make me. And yes, your dreams kind of consumed my own—but that's mostly because I didn't have any dreams. Not really."

He slumped on his rock, back to the wall, looking up at the tunnel ceiling. "I keep thinking, what if it happens again? What if I let

155

myself get excited about a job, then discover I'm *completely* unsuited to it? I've failed at flying, right? So maybe I'll just keep failing?"

"Rig," I said, taking him by the arm. "The problem isn't that you're going to be unsuited to what you pick. The problem is what it's always been. That you're simply too scudding great at too many different things."

He looked up at me. "Do you really believe that, Spin?"

"Sure do. I mean yeah, you decided flying wasn't for you—but I think if you have a flaw, it's not that you fail too often. It's that you refuse to admit what everyone sees. The fact that you're incredible."

He smiled. And seeing Rig smile felt *good*. It reminded me of our days as kids, when an outcast and a kid who was bullied had made friends against the odds.

"You're going to drag me into something again, aren't you?" he asked. "Something ridiculous?"

I hesitated. "Yeah . . . Probably."

"All right," he said, standing up. "I guess I'm in. Let's go see this surprise of yours."

We continued on, climbing until I led him, finally, out a gap onto the surface. I pulled him over to the entrance to my improvised home, then made him hold on to me as I lowered us down inside, as—well—the chances that he'd slip and fall were pretty good. He really was amazing at a ton of things . . . but I'd seen him drop no fewer than eight books on his toes while studying this past year.

"This had *better* not be something to do with rats, Spin," he said as we landed. "I know you go crazy for them, but . . ."

I turned up the light on my light-line, illuminating the ship. As if in coordination with my reveal, M-Bot turned on his dash and running lights. I'd cleared away much of the rubble, and with the lights, the ship didn't look half bad. Broken, yes, with a bent wing. But *distinctly* different from anything we had in the DDF.

Rig gaped at it, his jaw dropping practically to the floor.

"Well?" I said. "What do you think?"

In response he sat down on a nearby boulder and—still staring at the ship—pulled off his right boot, then flipped it over his shoulder.

"Well," I noted, "I said *boots,* plural. But I'll take it."

18

I didn't get much sleep that night.

I spent a few hours helping Rig look over M-Bot—he wanted to check each bit of damage. Eventually though, I started to get bleary-eyed. Rig was still going strong, so I rolled out a mat and used Bloodletter for a pillow.

Every time I dozed off, I'd eventually wake to hear Rigmarole speaking to the ship. "So . . . you're a machine, but you can *think*."

"All machines 'think,' in that they execute responses to input. I am simply far more complex in my executable responses, and in the inputs I can recognize . . ."

More dozing.

". . . can explain to us what is wrong?"

"My memory banks are faulty, so I cannot offer more than cursory explanations—but perhaps those will be sufficient."

I turned over on my side, and dipped back down into sleep.

". . . do not know where I originated, although a fragment of a memory implies I was created by human beings. I am not certain whether other species of sapient life exist. I believe I could answer that once . . ."

Around six in the morning, I rubbed my eyes and sat up. Rig lay below an open access panel, fiddling with something underneath the ship. I flopped down next to him, yawning. "So?"

"It's incredible," he said. "Have you told Cobb about it?"

"Not yet."

"Why delay? I mean, what if this thing can make the difference in fighting the Krell?"

"Theoretically," I said, "humans had this thing when they first fought the Krell. It didn't help then."

"I would note," M-Bot said, "that 'it' is listening."

"And?" I asked the ship, yawning again.

"And it's generally considered bad form for humans to speak of one who is present as if they are not."

"I can't make you out, M-Bot," Rig said, sitting up. "You say you don't care about things like that, right?"

"Obviously I don't. I'm a logical machine with only a thin veneer of simulated emotions."

"Okay," Rig said. "That makes sense."

"It's still rude," M-Bot added.

I looked to Rig, then gestured toward the cockpit. "So, we have a magical talking starship with mysterious technology. Do you wanna help me fix it?"

"On our own?" Rig asked. "Why?"

"So we can keep it. And *fly* it."

"You're in the DDF now, Spin! You don't need an outdated, broken-down ship."

"Still here," M-Bot noted. "Just saying."

I leaned forward. "Rig, I'm not in the DDF. I'm in Cobb's class."

"So? You'll graduate. I don't care *how* few people he passes— you'll be one of them."

"And then?" I asked, feeling cold—expressing a fear that I'd never voiced, but one that had haunted me since that first day.

"Cobb says he can let anyone he wants into his class. But *if* I pass? His authority ends there, Rig."

Rig looked down at the wrench in his hand.

"I'm worried that the admiral will deny me a ship," I said. "Worried she'll find some petty reason to kick me out, once Cobb can't protect me anymore. Worried I'll lose it, Rig. The sky." I looked toward the ship, glowing with lights along its side. "This is old, yes, but it's also my freedom."

He still looked skeptical.

"Think about how fun it would be," I said. "Poking around inside an ancient ship. Think of what mysteries we could discover! Maybe M-Bot is all outdated technology, but maybe not. Won't it be fun to at least *try* to fix him on our own? If it doesn't work out, we can always turn him in later."

"Fine," Rig said. "All right, stop giving me the hard sell. I'll try, Spin."

I grinned at him.

Rig looked at the ship. "I worry this is beyond what we can do. Those boosters are ruined. We can't just weld something like that back together. I'm sure there will be other parts that will need to be replaced, or fixed using tools we don't have." He thought for a moment. "Though . . ."

"What?" I asked.

"One of my job offers," he said. "It's from the elite Engineering Corps, the people who oversee repairing the starfighters—and the people who develop new designs. They've got the best labs, the best equipment . . ."

I nodded, eager. "That sounds *perfect*."

"I was thinking of taking their offer anyway," he said. "They told me I could come in these next two months, intern with them, learn my way around the shops . . . They were *very* impressed with my test scores, and with my understanding of schematics and advanced engineering."

"Rig. That. Is. *Awesome.*"

"I'm not promising anything," he said. "But, well, maybe if I bring them the right questions, I can get them to show me how to fix certain pieces of M-Bot. I'll have to do it without making them suspicious. Regardless, we'll still need spare parts. At least one full-size booster."

"I'll find us one, somehow."

"Just don't tell me where you get it," he noted. "Maybe, when this whole thing blows up in our faces, I can claim I didn't know about any possible thefts you might be up to."

"A small decal on that power matrix reads 'property of the Weight family,'" M-Bot said helpfully. "It looks to have been ripped, quite crudely, from a small chassis. Blue finish, judging by the scratched-off paint on the corner."

Rig sighed. "Jorgen's car? Really?"

I plastered on a smile.

"The internship will take a chunk of each day," he said, rubbing his chin. "But I should be able to dedicate the rest to this, if I need to. I'll have to tell my parents something."

"Tell them the internship is super demanding," I suggested. "And that it will take the majority of your time."

"But," M-Bot said, "that's not true, is it?"

"Nah," I said. "But who cares?"

"I care," the machine said. "Why would you say something that isn't true?"

"You can simulate emotions," I said, "but not lies?"

"I appear . . . to be missing some code," M-Bot said. "Curious. Oh, what an interesting fungus!"

I frowned, then glanced to the side, to where Doomslug had crawled up on a rock.

"Scud," Rig said. "There's some weird stuff up here close to the surface." He shivered. "Can you . . . do something about that thing?"

"That *thing* is named Doomslug," I said, "and she's my mascot. Don't hurt her while I'm away." I walked over, grabbing my pack. "I need to get to class. You going to head below?"

"Nah," Rig said. "I suspected I might not be back for a while, so I left a note for my parents, saying I was going to an employment meeting. They'll just assume I got up before them. I can head down later—I want to have a look at his wiring first."

"Great," I said. "If you're still here when I get back from class each day, I'll join you in the repairs. If not, leave me notes telling me what I can do to help." I hesitated. "Remember, I'm kind of a dunderhead at this. So you might want to give me the easy—but annoying—tasks."

Rig smiled once more, settling down on a rock, looking at M-Bot. There was a light in his eyes, one I remembered from back when we started planning to become pilots. In that moment, seeing Rig like that again, I had my first real impression that this might work. Somehow, this plan *might just work.*

"Wait," M-Bot said. "You're leaving me with him?"

"I'll be back tonight," I promised.

"I see. Could you come to the cockpit so we can speak in private?"

I looked at the ship, frowning.

"I don't want to explain in public why I like you better than the engineer," M-Bot added. "If he heard me go on—at length—regarding his irresolvable flaws, he might feel belittled or despondent."

"Well, *that* part is going to be lovely," Rig said, rolling his eyes. "Maybe we can find a way to shut off the personality."

I pulled myself up into the cockpit. The canopy moved down and sealed with a *whoosh.* "It's all right," I said to M-Bot. "Rig is good people. He'll take care of you."

"I am, of course, simply emulating the way humans play irrational favorites over one another. But could you not go?"

"I'm sorry. I've got to go learn to fight the Krell." I frowned at the tone in the robot's voice. "What's wrong? I told you, Rig is a good—"

"I am willing to accept that he is until evidence proves otherwise. This is a problem: I appear to have lost my master."

"I can be your new master."

"I cannot change masters without proper authentication codes," he said. "Which I just realized I do not remember. The problem, however, is larger than this mere fact. I do not remember my mission. I do not know where I came from. I do not know my purpose. If I were human, I would be . . . scared."

How did I respond to *that*? A frightened starship?

"Don't worry," I said. "We'll give you a new purpose— destroying the Krell. You're a *fighter*, M-Bot. I'm sure that name stands for something exciting. Murderbot . . . mayhembot. *Massacrebot*. That's it, I'm sure. You're a frightening, all-powerful death ship designed to fry the Krell and save humanity."

"I do not feel very frightening," he said. "I do not feel like a death ship."

"We'll deal with that," I promised. "Trust me."

"And can I trust that those words are not . . . a falsehood? Like the one to tell the engineer's parents?"

Well. *That* came back to bite me faster than I'd expected.

"I must ask you," M-Bot said more softly, "not to tell any others about me. I assumed you'd understood this earlier, when I explained my orders. I am supposed to 'lie low,' which is a colloquialism for remaining inconspicuous. You should not have told the engineer."

"And how would we repair you, otherwise?"

"I do not know. Spensa, I am an artificial intelligence—a computer. I *must* obey my orders. Please. You *can't* turn me over to your DDF. You must not even speak of me to anyone else."

Well, that was going to present a problem. I wanted to get this thing flying, and once I did, that would mean flying it to help in the fight against the Krell. And if we couldn't fix it . . . well, I'd need to turn it over. Regardless of what I thought of Ironsides, I couldn't just sit on this ship forever. Not if it could mean the difference between the survival and extinction of humanity.

I had opened my mouth to argue with M-Bot further when a set of lights started flashing on the dashboard.

"Multiple atmospheric incursions have been detected by my short-range sensors," M-Bot said. "Debris has begun falling toward the planet, with forty-three ships following."

"Forty-three?" I said, glancing at his sensor readout. Short range for him was apparently still pretty long, by our standards. "Wow. You can spot them, even in a debris fall?"

"Easily."

Proof already that the DDF could use this technology. Our scanners weren't as accurate as that. That knowledge immediately made me uncomfortable.

Still, forty-three Krell? The maximum they ever fielded was a hundred ships, so this was an impressive force. I hit the button to open the canopy, then hauled myself out and hopped off onto a rock.

"Krell," I said to Rig. "A big flight."

"Are we in danger here?"

"No, they're coming from the other direction. But the cadets have been training long enough now that Ironsides has started sending them up for real, as support units, during combat. Firestorm Flight went two days ago."

"So . . ."

"So I'd better get going. Just in case."

19

I started running.

A sense of anxiety built in me as I heard the distant sound of debris hitting. I somehow knew that Ironsides would send my flight up for this attack. She liked testing cadets in real combat experience, and we were far enough in our training that Cobb had warned we'd soon be sent into some real battles.

It was our turn. The time had come. So I forced myself into a jog—then a dash—across the dusty ground.

Sweat pouring down the sides of my face, I felt a horrible inevitability as I approached the base, where warning klaxons blared. Not fear, really, but *dread*. What if I was too late? What if the others went into battle without me?

I entered the base, then rounded the outside wall toward our launchpad. A single ship sat there, alone. I had been right.

I reached my ship in a sweaty mess, pushing my own ladder into place as several members of the ground crew noticed me and started yelling.

One got there in time to stabilize my ladder. "Where have you been, cadet!" she shouted at me. "The rest of your flight went up twenty minutes ago!"

I shook my head, sliding into the cockpit, too exhausted to speak.

"No pressure suit?" the ground crewer said.

"No time."

"All right. Don't make any sharp ascents then. You have clearance to go. Call in to your flightleader, then move."

I nodded, then pulled on my helmet. This one—like the one in the training room—had the strange lumps inside, to measure whatever it was they wanted to measure about me. I flipped on the flight radio band as the canopy lowered.

"—don't let your nerves get the best of you," Jerkface was saying over the radio. "Stay focused, watch your wingmate. You heard Cobb. We don't have to fire. Just focus on keeping yourselves from being turned to slag."

"What?" I said. "What's going on?"

"Spin?" Jerkface asked. "Where have you been?"

"In my cave! Where else would I be?" I engaged my acclivity ring and launched my ship upward. G-forces hit me, and my stomach felt like it was trying to escape through my toes. I slowed the ascent. "Repeat that part to me. You're going into battle? You're not staying at the edge of combat?"

"The admiral finally wants to let us fight!" Bim said, eager.

"Contain yourself, Bim," Jerkface said. "Spin, we're at 11.3-302.7-21000. Get here as fast as you can. Ironsides has ordered us into a small firefight alongside a flight of full pilots. We're there to confuse the enemy and hopefully split their attention."

In other words, we're being sent in as targets, I thought, wiping my hand on my jumpsuit, my heartbeat thrumming, sweat making my hair stick to my face. *Or they are. Without me.*

Not for long.

I slammed the throttle forward, going into overburn. The Grav-

Caps protected me for three seconds, and then I slammed back in my seat. I could take g-forces like these though, pushing me straight backward. It wasn't pleasant, but I didn't risk blacking out. I just had to get to speed, then carefully climb—using the acclivity ring.

I quickly reached Mag-10—which was the upper speed threshold for a Poco, at least safely. Even this was stretching the limits. The atmospheric scoops—which pushed air away around the ship in a bubble, preventing me from ripping off my own wings during tight maneuvers—were overwhelmed, and my ship rattled from the motion. The friction of air resistance made my normally invisible shield start to glow.

I climbed upward as well—but carefully, slower, as the g-forces in that direction threatened to knock me out. Going up forced my blood down into my feet. I did the stomach-clenching exercises we'd been taught in centrifuge training, but still, darkness started to creep around the outsides of my vision.

I held on, pressed down at six times my normal weight. Though the flight would only take a short while, I had to listen to my friends in battle all the way.

"Careful, Hurl. Not too eager."

"One's on me! I've got one on me!"

"Dodge, FM!"

"Dodging! Dodging! Scud, who was *that*?"

"Nightstorm Six. That's my brother, guys! Callsign: Vent. FM, you owe me some fries or something."

"To your right! Arturo, look up!"

"Looking! Stars, what a mess."

Finally my dash beeped, indicating I was approaching my desired coordinates. I let off on the altitude lever, then performed a rapid deceleration. In a Poco with atmospheric scoops, that meant *spinning* my ship in the air—the GravCaps kicking in—then firing my booster backward to slow me down.

I came out of it after slowing to Mag-1, standard dogfighting speed. I spun my Poco around, facing toward the battlefield, where distant lights flashed in the dark morning sky. Debris fell as red streaks.

"I'm here," I said to the others.

"Get in and help Morningtide!" Jorgen shouted at me. "Can you spot her?"

"Looking!" I said, frantic, scanning my proximity sensor screen. *There.* I hit overburn, accelerating her direction.

"Guys," I said, glancing at the scanner. "Morningtide has picked up a tail!"

"I see it," Jerkface said. "Morningtide, you read?"

"Trying. Trying dodge."

My ship screamed toward the battlefield. I could now see the individual fighters—a swirling mess mixed with destructor bolts and the occasional light-lance. Morningtide's Poco pulled upward into a loop—trailed by *three* Krell ships.

Almost there. Almost there!

The Krell destructors flared. Hit. Hit again. And then . . .

A burst of light. A spray of sparks.

And Morningtide died in a massive explosion. She didn't have a chance to eject.

Kimmalyn screamed—a high-pitched, panicked, *pained* sound.

"No!" Jerkface said. "No, no, *no!*"

I arrived, flying at Mag-3—too fast for normal dogfighting maneuvers—but still managed to spear one of the Krell ships with my light-lance. But it was too late.

The fiery sparks that had been Morningtide went out as they fell.

I spun and reversed my thrust, letting go of the light-lance and flinging the Krell ship to the side. Another of our fighters came in after it, shooting and managing to blast it down.

I fell in beside Jerkface, silently smothering my own screams. He'd lost his wingmate. Where was Arturo?

I couldn't make out anything tactical in the fray. My flight zipped in all directions, drawing fire—yes—but also adding to the confusion. A few larger classes of DDF fighters wound through it all, mixing with some dozen Krell ships, each trailing wires in that same unfinished way.

I was crying. But I set my jaw and kept on Jorgen's wing. He expertly speared a Krell ship with his light-lance, and it tried to break away, so I speared it as well.

"That debris, Jorgen," I said. "Coming down at your two, falling slowly."

"Right." We both hit our throttles, as Cobb had taught us, and pulled the enemy ship toward the debris. At the last minute, we cut our lines and split to the sides, slamming the Krell ship into the debris in a fiery explosion.

"What are you two doing?" Cobb said over the line. "You were ordered into *defensive postures*."

"Cobb!" I said. "Morningtide—"

"Keep your head, girl!" he shouted. "Grieve when the debris rests. Right now, obey orders. *Defensive. Postures.*"

I gritted my teeth, but didn't argue, following Jorgen as he wound through the smoke trails left by falling chunks of debris. That looked to be Arturo and Nedd to my right, leapfrogging each other with quick accelerations and decelerations, to keep the enemy from focusing on either one of them. That kind of technique could confuse the Krell, much like overwhelming them with targets.

Morningtide . . .

"Quirk?" Jorgen said. "What are you doing?"

I realized I could still hear Kimmalyn's soft whine of pain over the radio. I searched the scanner, then spotted a single Poco—without a wingmate—hovering near the perimeter of the fight.

"Quirk, move!" Jorgen said. "You're a clear target. Get in here."

"I . . . ," Kimmalyn said. "I was trying to line up a shot. I was going to save her . . ."

"Join the fight!" Jorgen shouted. "Cadet, hit your throttle and get in here!"

"I'll cover her," I said, moving to break off as we zoomed past two Krell coming the other way. So many sparks and destructor shots lit the sky, I almost felt I was down in Igneous, swallowed up by a forge.

"No," Jorgen said to me. "You see Bim? At your eight? Cover him. I'll deal with Kimmalyn."

"Understood." I zipped down and to my left, the GravCaps covering the g-forces of the sharp turn. As I moved, however, a spot on my dash lit up: a bright violet warning light near my proximity sensors.

I'd picked up a tail.

Though we'd barely touched on dogfighting, Cobb's training snapped into my mind. *Trust the scanner. Don't waste time trying to get a visual. Keep your focus on flying.*

"Spin!" FM said. "You've got a tail!"

I was already pulling my ship into an evasive loop, counting on the GravCaps to handle the g-force. Something *clicked* immediately in my head. The training, the way my face grew cold, the way my mind snapped into focus despite the fatigue, the stress, and the grief. It was almost like it didn't matter if a Krell was following me. In that moment, it was just me and the ship. Extensions of one another.

I pulled out of my loop into a straight dive, then cut to the side and launched a perfect light-lance hook into a slowly falling chunk of debris. I didn't go quite fast enough, and when my Grav-Caps cut, the g-forces rammed me down in my seat. I saw black at the corners of my vision, but held on.

I spun around sharply and buzzed another chunk of debris—

trailing its smoke in my wake—then zoomed right between two Krell ships coming the other direction. My tail lost me in the turn—and I caught a flashing explosion behind me as one of the full pilots picked it off while it was trying to catch up to me.

"Good maneuver, Spin," Cobb said softly in my ear. "Excellent maneuver, actually. But don't get too flashy. Remember the simulation. Flashy moves can still get you killed."

I nodded, though he couldn't see.

"Bim is at your ten now, up about one-fifty. Get on him. That boy is too eager."

As if on cue, Bim's voice entered the flight line. "Guys? Do you see that? Up in front of me?"

There was a larger firefight happening in the distance; we'd been ordered to join the smaller of the two skirmishes. I could make out the falling sparks and missed destructor shots of that larger battle, but I didn't think that was what Bim was indicating.

As I fell in at his side, I spotted it: a Krell ship, but a different model from the curved fighters. This one was bulbous, like a bulging fruit with wings at the top. Or . . . no, that was a ship flying with something huge attached to the bottom.

A bomber, I realized, remembering my studies. *One carrying a lifebuster.*

"Lifebuster," Jorgen said. "Cobb, we've confirmed sighting of a lifebuster bomb."

"The other flight radio bands are talking about it too," Cobb said. "Steady, cadet. The admiral is already dealing with that bomber."

"I can hit it, Cobb," Bim said. "I can bring it down."

I expected Cobb to dismiss that idea immediately, but he didn't. "Let me call for orders and tell them you have a visual."

Bim took that as confirmation. "You with me, Spin?"

"Every step," I said. "Let's go."

"Wait, cadet," Cobb said. "There's something odd about these descriptions. Can you confirm? That bomb sounds larger than usual."

Bim wasn't listening. I watched out my cockpit window as he dove toward the solitary bomber, which had—following usual Krell protocol—slipped down to low altitude to try flying in underneath the AA guns.

"Something's wrong," Cobb said.

A group of shadows broke off the sides of the bomb—smaller Krell ships, almost invisible in the darkness. Four of them.

They lit up the air with red destructor blasts. One grazed my canopy, causing my shield to crackle with light. My nerves jolted, and I spun my ship—by instinct—to the side.

"Cobb," I said. "Four escort ships just broke off the bomber!"

The ships buzzed us. I dodged, barely, my hands sweaty on my controls. "They're faster than regular Krell!"

"This is something new," Cobb said. "Fall back, you two."

"I can hit it, Cobb!" Bim said. The light of his destructor glowed at the front of his ship as he powered up a long-range shot.

The four guardian ships swarmed toward us, firing again.

"Bim!" I screamed.

I was pretty sure I saw him look toward me—light reflecting on his helmet visor—as the blasts hit his ship, overwhelming his shield with concentrated fire.

Bim's ship exploded into several large chunks, one of which slammed into my ship. I was flung to the side as my Poco went into a spin. Quirk screamed my name as the world rocked. The lights on my dash went insane, the "shield down" warning blaring.

G-forces hit as the GravCaps were overwhelmed. Nausea flooded me, and everything became a blur. But my training still kicked in. Somehow—pulling hard on the control sphere—I managed to hit the dive controls, which pivoted my acclivity ring on its front hinge, like a hatch swinging open. That angled it toward the nose of my ship, and the maneuver pulled me out of the fall. The world righted itself, and I hung there in a hover, my nose pointed straight at the ground.

Lights flashed on my dash. Below, I watched as Bim's remains hit the surface in a ripple of soft explosions.

He'd never . . . he'd never even picked a callsign.

"The enemy is disengaging!" Nedd said. "Looks like they've had enough!"

I listened, numb, to other reports. A strike team of full pilots went after the bomber, and rather than risk losing the weapon, the Krell pulled into a full retreat.

The bomber escaped, as did enough ships to keep the admiral from giving chase.

I just hung there, blue glow of the acclivity ring a cold, lifeless light in front of me.

"Spin?" Jorgen said. "Report in? Are you all right?"

"No," I whispered, but finally reset my acclivity ring, rotating my ship to the standard axis. I channeled power to the shield igniter, waited until the light powered up, then grabbed the handle and slammed it backward. Another shield crackled to life around my Poco, then turned invisible.

I climbed up into line with the others.

"Vocal confirmation of status," Jorgen ordered.

We responded, and everyone else was still there. But when we flew back to base, our formation had two stark holes in it. Bim and Morningtide were gone.

Skyward Flight had been reduced from nine to seven.

Other **Ship Designs**

M-Bot

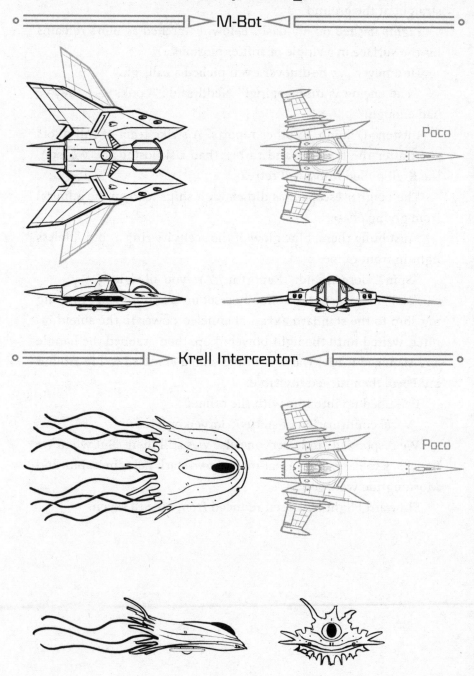

Poco

Krell Interceptor

Poco

PART THREE

PART

THREE

INTERLUDE

Admiral Judy "Ironsides" Ivans always made a point of reading the casualty reports.

She got people killed. Every battle, she made decisions—some of them mistakes—that ended lives. Perhaps there was an astral balance chart somewhere out there, kept in the stars by the ancient Saints, which weighed the Defiant lives she lost against the ones she saved.

If so, that scale had been greatly tipped by today's battle. Two cadets were dead after barely a month of training in the cockpit. She read their names, tried to commit them to memory—though she knew she'd fail. There had just been so many.

She reverently set the list of names and short biographies on top of her desk. Two other pilots had died as well, and composing letters to their families would take a bite out of her evening, but she'd do it. To those families, the loss would take a bite out of their *lives*.

She was halfway done—writing by hand, instead of using a typewriter—when Cobb came to yell at her at last. She saw him reflected in the brass of the polished spyglass she kept on her desk. A relic from a much, much earlier time. He stopped in the doorway, and didn't lay into her immediately, but let her finish her current letter. She signed it at the bottom, making a flourish with the fountain pen—a gesture that somehow seemed both necessary and ostentatious in such a letter.

"Are you happy, Judy?" he finally asked. "Now that you've gotten two of them killed, are you *scudding* happy?"

"I haven't been happy in years, Cobb." She turned her chair, leaning back and meeting his glare. She'd been anticipating, perhaps even relishing, his inevitable arrival. It was good she still had someone to defy her. Most everyone else who had done that was dead now.

He limped into the small room, which was piled high with papers, keepsakes, books—an embarrassingly messy office. Yet it was the only place she felt comfortable.

"You can't keep doing this," Cobb said. "First you lower the age of testing, now you send them into battle before they really know how to fly? You can't keep firing on full auto while you simultaneously steal ammunition from the stores. Eventually you're *going to run out of bullets.*"

"You'd rather I let Alta fall?"

He looked to the side, toward an old map she still kept on the wall. The glass was dusty with age and the paper inside had started to curl. It was a plan for Alta, from their development session almost a decade ago. They'd imagined a city with massive neighborhoods and large farms.

A fantasy. Reclaiming a dead world was harder work than they'd anticipated.

She pushed herself to her feet, the old captain's chair creaking. "I *will* spend their lives, Cobb. I'll eagerly put everyone in the DDF in danger, if it means protecting Alta."

"At some point it stops being worth the losses, Judy."

"Yes, and I happen to know when that point is." She stepped

up to him, holding his gaze. "It's when the *very last Defiant* heaves their *very last breath*. Until then, we hold this base."

If they lost Alta, then Igneous could be bombed from above—destroying the apparatus and humankind's ability to build ships. If that happened, the Defiants would return to living in broken clans, like rats to be hunted.

They either stood their ground, or they gave up on ever becoming a true civilization again.

Finally, Cobb relented and turned to leave. From him, lack of complaint was agreement.

"I noticed," Judy said, "that your little coward didn't arrive at the battle until most of the fighting had already happened."

He spun on her, practically snarling. "She lives in an unimproved cave, Judy. *Alone.* You realize that, don't you? One of your pilots lives in a makeshift camp beyond the city limits because *you* refuse to give her a bunk."

It was satisfying to see that anger in him. She worried he would burn out one of these days. He never *had* been the same, since the Battle of Alta.

"Do you know what the readouts are saying?" Judy asked. "The scans of her brain? Some of our doctors are certain they've figured out how to spot it now. I suppose I should thank you for that. Getting a chance to study Chaser's daughter in flight might finally give me proof. She has the defect."

That gave him pause. "We barely understand what it means," he finally said. "And your doctors are biased. A few confusing events and some stories of the past aren't enough to judge a girl's entire life, particularly a girl so talented."

"That's the problem," Judy said. She was surprised to hear Cobb argue, honestly. Many politicians denied the defect's existence, but Cobb? He'd seen its effects personally. "As useful as this data is, I can't risk letting her have a commission in the DDF. She would be nothing but a distraction and a blow to morale."

"A distraction to *you*, maybe. A blow to *your* morale. The way you're acting is a disgrace to the DDF."

"For all intents and purposes, I *am* the DDF. Stars help us. There's nobody else left."

He glared at her. "I'm going to give the girl a personal radio. I won't have one of my cadets outside my reach. Unless you would reconsider giving her a bunk."

"If I make it too easy on her, she might decide to stay instead of doing the sensible thing and moving on."

Cobb limped toward the door—he refused to use a cane, even after all these years—but paused again there, hand on the frame. "Do you ever wish one of the others had survived?" he asked. "Sousa. Nightingale. Strife. Admiral Heimline."

"Anyone but me?" Judy asked.

"Basically."

"I'm not sure I'd wish this command on them," she said. "Not even the ones I hated."

Cobb grunted, then disappeared into the hallway.

20

The day after Morningtide and Bim died, I arrived late for Cobb's class. It was only by about five minutes, but it was still my first time being late.

Everything just felt so *wrong*.

I vaguely remembered tromping back to my cave the day before, ignoring M-Bot—Rig had already gone home—and curling up in my cockpit bed. Then I'd just lain there. Not sleeping, but wishing that I would. Thinking, but wishing that I would stop. Not crying . . . but somehow wishing that I could.

Today, nobody called me on my tardiness. Cobb wasn't there yet, though almost all of the remaining cadets had assembled. Everyone but Kimmalyn, which worried me. Was she okay?

My boots squeaked on the floor as I walked over and sat. I didn't want to look at the conspicuously empty seats, but that made me feel like a coward, so I forced myself to stare at Morningtide's spot. Just two days ago I'd been standing there, helping her understand . . .

She'd almost never said anything, but somehow the room felt so much quieter without her.

"Hey, Spin," Nedd finally said. "You're always talking about 'honor' and the 'glory of dying like warriors' and crap like that."

"Yeah? So?"

"So . . . ," Nedd said. "Maybe we could use a little of that crap right now."

Nedd slumped in place, barely fitting into his mockpit. He was the tallest one in the room—and burly too. I'd always thought of him simply as the larger of Jerkface's two cronies, but there was more to him. A thoughtfulness.

"Well?" he asked.

"I . . . ," I said, struggling to find words. "That all feels stupid now."

I couldn't rattle off some line about vengeance. Not today. Doing so would feel like playing a part in one of Gran-Gran's stories—while the loss felt so very real. But . . . did that make my conviction all just bravado? Was I a coward hiding behind aggressive platitudes?

A real warrior would shrug it off. Did I really think these were the last friends I'd lose?

FM climbed out of her seat and walked over to me. She squeezed me on the shoulder, a strikingly familiar gesture from a girl I knew only passingly well, despite our time in the same flight. What was her story? I'd never found a way to ask.

I glanced toward Bim's place, thinking of the incredibly awkward—yet wonderful—way he'd tried to flirt with me.

"Do you know where Kimmalyn is?" I asked FM.

"She got up and ate with us," the tall girl whispered, "but she stopped at the restroom on the way to class. Maybe someone should go check on her."

Before I could get up, Jerkface was on his feet, clearing his throat. He looked around at the other five of us. Me and FM. Hurl, slumped in her seat. She didn't seem to be treating this like a game any longer. Arturo, who sat with hands clasped, tapping his index fingers together at a rapid pace, like some kind of nervous tic. Nedd sitting with his feet up and resting on the incalculably valuable hologram projector at the front of his mockpit. Remarkably, his bootlaces were untied.

"I suppose," Jerkface said, "that I should say something."

"Of course," FM whispered, rolling her eyes, though she returned to her own place.

Jerkface began speaking in a stiff voice. "The DDF protocol handbook explains that to die in the cockpit—fighting to protect our homeland—is the bravest and greatest gift a person can give. Our friends, though taken too early, were models of Defiant ideals."

He's reading, I realized. *From notes written . . . on his hand?*

"We will remember them as soldiers," Jerkface continued, now holding his hand up before him. "If you need counseling at this loss—or for any reason—as your flightleader, I am here. Please come to me, so I can make you feel better. I will gladly bear the burden of your grief so that you can focus on your flight training. Thank you."

He sat down. And, well, that was probably the dumbest speech I'd ever heard. More about him than about those empty seats. But . . . I supposed he had tried?

Cobb finally limped through the door, holding a fistful of papers and muttering something to himself. "Flight positions!" he snapped. "We're going to cover tandem maneuvering today—again. The way you guard each other is so sloppy, I'd expect to see you on a plate of mess hall food."

We just kind of stared at him.

"Move!" he barked.

Everyone started strapping in.

I—instead—stood up. "Is that it?" I demanded. "Aren't you going to say anything about them? About Bim, or Morningtide, or what the admiral did to—"

183

"The admiral," Cobb said, "did nothing to you. The *Krell* killed your friends."

"That's ratcrap," I blurted. "If you toss a kid into a lion's den, can you really blame the lion?"

He met my eyes, but I wasn't going to back down this time. I wasn't sure what I wanted, but at least this emotion—feeling furious at him, at the admiral, at the DDF—was better than emptiness.

We glared at each other until the door squeaked and opened, and Kimmalyn stepped in. Though her long black hair was combed—as usual—into perfect curls, her eyes were puffy and red. Cobb glanced at her and his eyes widened, as if he was surprised to see her.

He thought she'd given up, I realized.

Instead, puffy eyes and all, Kimmalyn raised her chin.

Cobb nodded toward her seat, and she strode over—a model of Defiant poise—and sat down. In that moment, she seemed more like a warrior than I'd ever been.

I set my jaw, then took my seat and strapped in. Shoving Cobb around wasn't going to relieve my anger at the admiral. I needed a control sphere in my hand and a destructor trigger under my finger. That was probably why Cobb wanted to work us hard today—to make us sweat, maybe make us forget for a little while. And . . . yeah. Yeah, I was on board for that.

Cobb, however, didn't turn on our projectors. Instead he slowly took a folding chair, then limped to the center of the room and unfolded it. He sat down, clasping his hands before him. I had to lean out the side of my rig to see him, as did most of the others.

He looked old. Older than he deserved to.

"I know how it feels," he said. "Like there's been a hole carved right out of you. A chunk of flesh that's just not going to grow back. You can function, you can fly, but you're going to leave a blood trail for a while.

"I should say something here, about loss. Something wise. Old

Mara, who taught me to fly, would have. She's dead now." Cobb shook his head. "Sometimes I don't feel like a teacher. I feel like a munitions man, reloading artillery. I stuff you into the chamber, fire you into the sky, then grab another shell . . ."

Hearing him talk that way was discomforting, unnatural. Like a parent suddenly admitting they didn't know what love felt like. We'd all heard stories about flight instructors. Old, grizzled, quick to bite your head off, but stuffed full of wisdom.

In that moment though, I saw the man, not the instructor. That man was afraid and distraught—and as pained to lose students as we were to lose friends. He wasn't some grizzled veteran with all the answers. He was a man who had, almost by coincidence, survived long enough to be made into a teacher. He had to teach us both the things he knew *and* the things he clearly hadn't yet figured out himself.

"Claim the stars," I said.

Cobb looked up at me.

"When I was a girl," I said, "I wanted to become a pilot so I would be celebrated. And my father told me to set my sights higher. He told me to 'claim the stars.'"

I looked upward, and tried to imagine those twinkling lights. Past the roof, up through the sky, piercing the rubble belt. Where the Saints welcomed the souls of the fallen when they died.

"It hurts," I said. "More than I thought it would. I knew so little about Bim—only that he liked to smile. Morningtide, she could barely understand us. But she refused to give up."

For a moment, I thought I could imagine myself soaring upward among those lights. Like Gran-Gran had taught me. I felt everything falling beneath me, becoming distant. All I could see were those points of light streaking around on all sides.

"They're up in the sky now," I said softly. "Forever among the stars. I'm going to join them." I snapped out of the trance, and was suddenly back in the room with the others. "I'm going to strap in,

185

and I'm going to *fight*. That way when I die, at least I'll die in a cockpit. Reaching for heaven."

The others stilled, ushering in an uncertain silence, like the moment between two meteor impacts. Nedd had sat up in his seat, no longer lounging, and he gave me an enthusiastic thumbs-up and a nod. Across from me, I found Jerkface staring at me, an inscrutable frown on his face.

"All right," Cobb said, standing up. "Let's stop wasting time. Helmets on."

I grabbed my helmet and pulled it on, ignoring Jerkface's stare. I immediately jumped, however, and pulled the helmet off.

"What?" Cobb said, limping over to me.

"The diodes inside are warm," I said, feeling them. "What does it mean?"

"Nothing," Cobb said. ". . . Probably."

"That doesn't reassure me, Cobb. What is going on?"

He lowered his voice. "Some medical types who think they're smart believe they can tell from a bunch of readouts if you're . . . going to run away like your father."

"My father didn't—"

"Calm down. We prove them wrong about you with good flying. That's your best tool. Can you wear that?" He nodded to the helmet.

"Yeah. They aren't painfully hot; I was just surprised."

"Put it on then, and let's get to work."

21

Cobb kept his promise—he worked us *hard* that day.

We practiced coordinated banking, formations, and wingmate guarding exercises. We worked until my fingers felt stiff as gears, my arms ached like I'd been lifting weights, and my brain basically turned to mush. He even worked us through lunch, forcing an aide to bring everyone else sandwiches. I ate rat jerky and mushrooms like always.

The diodes in my helmet cooled down as I worked. The admiral thought she could tell from some *readouts* if I would be a coward? What kind of insanity was that?

There was no time to worry about it though. Cobb ran us through debris dodging, light-lance turns, and shield reignition drills. It was exhausting in a good way, and the only time I thought of Bim was when I realized that nobody was complaining that—yet again—we weren't being allowed to use our weapons.

When Cobb at long last let us go, I felt as if I could have curled up right there and dozed off.

"Hey, Arturo," Nedd said as he stood and stretched, "these

projectors are pretty good. You think they could simulate a world where you're not a scudding terrible pilot?"

"All we need for that," Arturo said, "is an Off button for your radio. I'm certain we'd all improve by huge leaps if we didn't have to listen to your incessant jabbering. Besides, as I recall, *you* were the one who ran into *me* earlier."

"You were in my way!"

"Boys, boys," Hurl said, sauntering past. "Can't we make peace? Find common ground and agree that you're *both* terrible pilots?"

"Ha!" Arturo said. "You just watch—I'll make you eat those words someday, Hurl."

"I'm hungry enough that I'd eat them now," she said, "if they had a decent sauce on them. The mess hall better not be closed. Quirk, can I have your dessert?"

"What?" the girl said, looking up from her harness—which she'd been clipping together and folding neatly in her seat, like she always did when getting out of her mockpit.

"You're nice and stuff," Hurl said. "I figure you'll give in if I push hard enough. So, can I eat your dessert?"

"Bless your stars," Kimmalyn said. "But touch my pie, and I'll rip your fingers off." She blushed when she said it, and lifted her hand in front of her mouth.

"She'll do it, Hurl," I joked. "It's always the nice ones you have to worry about."

"Yeah," Hurl said. "Ain't that the . . ." She trailed off as she realized I was the one who'd spoken. Then she turned and continued out the door.

I knew that look in her eyes. Ever since Jorgen outed me as Chaser's daughter, things hadn't been the same between Hurl and me.

The others piled out of the chamber. I sighed, gathering my pack, preparing for an exhausted hike back to my cavern. As I hefted it over my shoulder, I realized that FM hadn't left. She was standing by the wall, watching me. She was so tall and beautiful. As cadets, we kept DDF pilot dress standards. For daily work, we could choose jumpsuits or standard DDF uniforms if we wanted. We just had to be ready to change into flight suits if a call came up.

Most of us simply wore the jumpsuits, which were the most comfortable. Not FM. Alongside her polished boots, she often wore a tailored uniform with a jacket that somehow looked more stylish on her than others. She was so perfect, she almost seemed more like a statue than a person.

"Thank you," she said to me, "for what you said earlier. About Bim, Morningtide, and the stars."

"You didn't find it 'overly aggressive'?" I asked. FM was always complaining that the rest of us were too aggressive, which didn't make sense to me. Wasn't aggression the point of war?

"Well, most of what you say *is* utter nonsense," FM said. "Windy bravado made as an excuse to tout jingoistic mantras instilled in you by a lifetime of Defiant indoctrination. But what you said earlier, that was from the heart. I . . . I needed to hear it. Thank you."

"You're a weird girl, FM," I said. I had no idea what most of what she'd said had meant.

At his desk, Cobb snorted and glanced at me from behind his paperwork. *You, of all people, are calling someone weird?* his glance seemed to ask.

I walked with FM out into an empty hallway; the other cadet flights had finished classes hours ago.

"I want to make it clear," FM said as we walked together, "that I don't blame you for your attitudes. You're a product of enormous societal pressure, forcing young people into increasingly aggressive postures. I'm sure on the inside you're sweet."

"I'm actually not," I said, grinning. "But I'm okay if people underestimate me. Perhaps the Krell will do the same, so I can

189

savor the surprise in their eyes as I rip *those very eyes* from their skulls."

FM looked at me aghast.

"If, that is, they have eyes under that armor. Or skulls. Well— whatever they have, I'll rip it out." I glanced at her, then grinned more broadly. "I'm joking, FM. Kind of. I say things like that be- cause they're fun. Like the old stories, you know?"

"I haven't read those old stories."

"You'd probably hate them. Why do you always talk about the rest of us being too aggressive? Aren't you Defiant?"

"I was raised Defiant," she said. "But I choose, now, to be what people down below call a Disputer—I raise objections about the way the war is being run. I think we should throw off the oppres- sive mantle of military government."

I stopped in place, shocked. I'd never heard words like that spoken before. "So . . . you're a coward?"

FM blushed, standing up taller. "I'd have thought *you,* of all people, would be careful about throwing around that term."

"Sorry," I said, blushing in return. She was right. But still, I had trouble understanding what she was saying. I understood the words, but not the meaning. Throw off military government? Who would be in charge of the war then?

"I am still willing to fight," FM said, her head high as we walked. "Just because I want change doesn't mean I'll let the Krell destroy us all. But do you *realize* what it's doing to our society to train our children, practically from birth, to idealize and glorify fighting? To worship the First Citizens like saints? We should be teaching our children to be more caring, more inquisitive—not only to destroy, but to build."

I shrugged. Those kinds of things seemed easy to say when you lived in the deep caverns, where a bomb wouldn't kill your family. Still, it was nice to get some answers about the woman—

she was so poised, it was hard to think of her as a "girl" even though she was the same age as the rest of us.

If I walked too far with her toward the mess hall though, I might run into the MPs and get into trouble. They'd stopped escorting me out of class every day, but I didn't believe for a moment that meant I could go to dinner. So I bade FM farewell, and she jogged off to catch up with the others.

I started toward the exit, digging in my pack for some water—but remembered I'd left my last full canteen by my seat in the classroom. Great. Feeling my exhaustion from the training return, I trudged back to the classroom.

Cobb had activated the hologram in the center of the room, projecting a small version of a battlefield. In front of him, ships the size of ball bearings zipped and flew among debris trailing fire and smoke. Krell ships, flat and no larger than merit chits, fired tiny destructors.

He's rewatching the fight from yesterday, I realized. *The one where Bim and Morningtide died.* I'd had no idea the battles were recorded.

I picked out my ship as it zipped into the battle. I felt the overwhelming chaos again, the rush of finally being in a real fight. I could almost hear the explosions. Kimmalyn's worried voice. The sound of my own breathing, excited, sharp.

Anticipation, even a little fear, rose inside me while I watched—powerless. Morningtide died again.

My gut clenched. But I wouldn't let myself look away.

In the room, my ship zipped through the fray, picking up a tail. I dove around a falling piece of rubble—using my light-lance to pivot with exactness—then soared between two other Krell ships.

Cobb paused the simulation with a gesture. He stepped forward, focusing on my ship—frozen in the air amid a spectacular show of destructors, falling streaks of light, and exploding ships.

Then he rewound the simulation and played it through again, watching my maneuver.

"I almost blacked out," I noted from the doorway. "I didn't have control of my speed, and didn't cut the turn before the Grav-Caps overloaded."

"It was still quite the maneuver," he said. "Particularly for a cadet. Remarkable, almost unbelievable."

"Jerkface is better than I am."

"Jorgen is an excellent technical pilot, but he doesn't feel it like you do. You remind me of your father." He seemed . . . grim as he said it.

I suddenly felt awkward, so I crossed to my simulator and grabbed my canteen. Cobb played out the rest of the battle, and I forced myself to watch as my ship and Bim's chased the Krell bomber. Cobb froze the simulation again as the four strange guard ships broke off the enemy bomber—the ones who would, momentarily, shoot down Bim.

"What are they?" I asked.

"Something new. They haven't altered their tactics in over a decade. What changed now?" He narrowed his eyes. "We survive by being able to anticipate the Krell. Anytime you can guess what your enemy is going to do, you have an advantage. No matter how dangerous they are, if you know their next move, you can counter it."

Huh. That struck me, and I found myself nodding.

Cobb shut down the hologram and hobbled back toward his desk. "Here," he said, sliding a box off the top and handing it to me. "I forgot to give this to you earlier."

A personal radio?

"Normally, we only give these to full pilots who get off-duty time down in Igneous. But since you live off base, I figured you should have one. Keep it on you at all times. You'll get a general warning call when the Krell attack."

I took the device, which was rectangular and boxy, maybe the size of a small one-handed training weight. My father had carried one of these.

Cobb waved to dismiss me, then settled down in his seat and started looking through his papers.

I lingered though, a question on my mind. "Cobb?"

"Yeah?"

"Why don't you fly with us? The other flight instructors go up with their cadets."

I braced myself for anger or reprimand. Cobb just patted his leg. "Old wounds, Spin. Old wounds." He'd been shot down, soon after the Battle of Alta. His leg had clipped the side of the canopy as he'd ejected.

"You don't need your leg to fly."

"Some wounds," he said softly, "aren't as obvious as a twisted leg. You found it hard to get into the cockpit today, after watching your friends die? Try doing it after you shoot down one of your own."

I felt a sudden and striking coldness wash through me, like I'd ejected at high altitude. Was he saying . . .

Was he saying *he* was the one who had *shot down my father*?

Cobb looked up at me. "Who else do you think they'd order to bring him down, kid? I was his wingmate. I followed him when he ran."

"He didn't run."

"I was there. He ran, Spensa. He—"

"My father was *not a coward!*"

I met Cobb's gaze, and for the second time that day he looked away.

"What really happened up there, Cobb?" I narrowed my eyes at him. "Why do they think they can tell I'll do the same, just by monitoring my brain? What aren't you telling me?"

Though I'd never accepted the official story, part of me had always assumed that some kind of mistake had caused my father's reputation. That in the confusion, people had assumed he'd turned coward when he hadn't.

But I now had the chance to talk to someone who was there. Someone who . . . who had pulled the trigger . . .

"What happened?" I asked, stepping forward. I'd meant to say it forcefully, Defiantly—but it came out as a whispered plea. "Can you tell me? What you saw?"

"You've read the official report," Cobb said, still not meeting my eyes. "The Krell were coming in a huge wave, carrying a lifebuster. It was a larger force than we'd ever faced before, and their positioning strongly indicated they'd found Alta Base. We fought off one attack, but they regrouped. As they were preparing to come at us again, your father panicked. He screamed that the enemy force was too big, that we were all going to die. He—"

"Who did he say it to? The entire flight?"

Cobb paused. "Yes. All four of us who were left, anyway. Well, he screamed and screamed, then he broke off and began flying away. You have to understand how dangerous that was for us. We were literally fighting for the survival of our species—if other ships started fleeing, it would have been chaos. We couldn't afford to—"

"You followed him," I interrupted. "He took off and flew away, and you followed. Then you shot him down?"

"The order came almost immediately from our flightleader. Shoot him down, to make an example and prevent anyone else from fleeing. I was right on his tail, and he wouldn't respond to our pleas. So I hit my IMP and brought down his shield, then . . . then I shot. I'm a soldier. I obey orders."

The pain in his voice was so real, so personal, it almost made me feel ashamed for pushing him. For the first time . . . my resolve shook. Could it be *true*?

"You swear to me?" I asked. "That's exactly how it happened?"

Cobb finally met my eyes. He held them this time, and didn't look away—but he also didn't answer my question. I saw him harden as he set his jaw. And in that moment, I knew that his nonanswer *was* an answer. He'd given me the official story.

And it was a lie.

"It's past time for you to be going, cadet," Cobb said. "If you want a copy of the official record, I can get you one."

"But it's a lie. Isn't it?" I looked to him again, and he gave the faintest, almost imperceptible *nod*.

My entire world lit up. I should have been angry. I should have been furious at Cobb for pulling the trigger. Instead, I was *elated*.

My father *hadn't* run. My father *wasn't* a coward.

"But why?" I asked. "What's to be gained by pretending one of your pilots fled?"

"Go," Cobb said, pointing. "That's an order, cadet."

"This is why Ironsides doesn't want me in the DDF," I realized. "She knows I'll ask questions. Because . . . Scud, she was your flightleader, wasn't she? The one who gave the order to shoot my father down? The name was redacted in the reports, but she's the only one who fits . . ."

I looked back at Cobb, and his face was growing red with anger. Or maybe embarrassment. He'd just given me a secret, an important one, and . . . well, he looked like he was having second thoughts. I wasn't going to get any more out of him right now.

I grabbed my pack and hurried out. My heart was broken for the friends I'd lost, and now I'd have to deal with the fact that my instructor was also my father's killer.

But for now . . . well, I felt like a soldier planting her flag at the top of a hard-fought hill. All these years I'd dreamed, and studied, and trusted that my father had actually been a hero.

And I'd been right.

22

"**W**hat reason," Rig asked as we worked together, "could the DDF possibly have to *pretend* your father was a coward?"

"I can think of dozens of scenarios," I said, lying underneath M-Bot beside him.

Five days had passed since the event. Since we'd lost Bim and Morningtide. Working with Rig off-hours, repairing the ship, had been a welcome solace from my own thoughts—even if it was taxing to get up early like I had today, work on the ship, then go to class and endure Cobb's instructions all day.

Today, we were unhooking wires from M-Bot's belly and re-placing them with new ones. Some of the old ones seemed good, but Rig figured we should replace them all just in case, and I wasn't going to argue with his expertise.

I plugged in another wire and threaded it according to the in-structions Rig had drawn out earlier. My light-line glowed from within the ship, wound through the innards to give us light, itself like a glowing wire.

"There are literally hundreds of reasons the DDF would lie about my father," I said as I worked. "Maybe my father was in conflict with Ironsides about leadership, and she decided to make him have an 'accident.'"

"In the middle of the most important battle the DDF had ever flown?" Rig said. "That's fanciful, even for you, Spin."

"Fanciful?" I demanded. "Me? I'm a realist, Rig."

"Realist. Like all the times you made me go pretend to slay stardragons with you as kids."

"That was battle training."

He grunted as he worked on a particularly stubborn wire, and Doomslug helpfully imitated him. She sat on the stone ground near my head. M-Bot was "running diagnostics"—whatever that meant. It mostly involved him saying things like "Hmmmmm . . ." or "Carry the one . . ." to "give indication that the process is continuing, as humans quickly grow bored without auditory stimulation."

"Are you sure you aren't misinterpreting Cobb?" Rig said from beside me. "You're *sure* he nodded?"

"I am. The official story is a lie, Rig. I've got proof."

"More like a vague, possible confirmation."

"I can push Cobb until he spills the entire truth."

"Good luck with that. Besides, even if he *did* talk, the higher powers at the DDF aren't going to admit to lying. You stir up too much trouble, and all you'll do is get yourself *and* Cobb removed from your positions."

"I *will* clear my father's name, Rig."

"I'm not saying you shouldn't. I'm just pointing out that your original plan—learning to fly—is still the best way to do that. *First* become a great, famous pilot. Improve your family's reputation and become someone who can't be ignored. *Then* use your influence to clear your father's name."

"We'll see."

Rig twisted—using the little space we had between M-Bot and the ground—and pulled over his notebook to make some notations. "These are his GravCaps," he said, tapping his pencil at a mechanism. "But I don't recognize the design, and he has them in an odd location. This black box over here—which is the only part I don't recognize—must be what houses his artificial intelligence. I don't dare *try* to break that apart, although it's obviously malfunctioning."

"How do you know?"

"Can you imagine anyone *intentionally* creating him to act like he does?"

A valid point.

"What I'm most interested in," Rig said, "is his joints, his seals, and his atmospheric scoop. It's hard to explain, but they all feel . . . tighter, more finely constructed than what we're using. It's only by a small increment, but Spensa, I think if we do get this thing flying, it's going to be *fast*. Faster than even our scout ships."

That gave me a shiver to imagine. Rig grinned, holding up his notebook, then put it aside and dug in with his wrench to carefully begin disassembling the atmospheric scoop.

I watched for a moment, holding a wire in the cramped confines, amazed. Rig seemed *happy*.

We'd been friends for over a decade, and I was sure I'd seen him happy before. It was just that no moments stood out. My memories of Rig were always of him being anxious, or nervous for me, or—occasionally—resigned to some terrible fate.

Today though, he was actively smiling as he worked, his face smeared with the grease we'd been applying between wire replacements. And that . . . that did something to help me push through the loss that still hung over me, the feelings of having failed my flightmates.

"Where did you get all these wires anyway?" I said, getting back to work. "I thought I was the one who was going to be performing the petty theft."

"No theft required," he said. "Ziming—that's the woman supervising my internship—gave me an entire bundle of them and some machinery to work on for practicing wire replacements. I figure, what better practice than to use it all on a real ship?"

"Nice. So it's going well?"

Rig, oddly, blushed—though the color was difficult to pick out through the grease, and by the glow of my reddish-orange light-line. I knew him well enough to see it.

"What?" I demanded.

"You know M-Bot's cockpit design?" he said.

"What part?"

"The pilot's seat and controls are on their own frame," Rig said. "It's complicated, but it reminds me of a gyroscope. I think the seat is made to be able to rotate with the direction of g-forces. You know how it's really hard on a human to take g-forces that push the blood into the head or the feet?"

"Uh, yeah. Trust me. I know."

"Well, what if your seat rotated during difficult and extended burns? So that the force was always in the direction easiest on the body—directly backward? That could really help with high-speed maneuvers."

"Huh," I said, interested—but *more* interested by the way Rig lit up as he talked.

"Well, I drew some schematics of that in my notebook, and . . . and well, Ziming might have seen them and assumed they were my own designs. She might . . . she might think I'm a genius."

"You are!"

"Not really," he said, blushing again. "I just copied what I saw. Whoever built M-Bot is the genius."

"You figured it out!" I said. "That takes as much genius."

"It really doesn't," he said, then twisted off a nut with his wrench. "But . . . well, lie or not, I think this is a way we can get this technology to the DDF. Maybe I can figure out how this atmospheric scoop works and take that in as well. If I'm careful, and don't make my discoveries look too suspicious, we'll be able to help the fight against the Krell without exposing M-Bot."

"And you get to be a hero!" I said.

"A fake one," he said. "But . . . it did feel nice . . ."

I grinned, then got back to work on my wires. Maybe we could bring this all to the DDF, and prevent more pilots from dying. Thinking of that immediately put a damper on my mood. No matter what I could do for future pilots, I would still carry my feelings of frustration and pain for the flightmates I'd already lost.

I redirected my thoughts back to the secret of what had really happened to my father, trying to think of every reason why the DDF would cover it up. That kept me occupied for a half hour or so until a *ding* rang up from the cockpit.

"Diagnostic finished," M-Bot said in his helpful—and not *nearly* dangerous enough—voice. It echoed through the innards of the ship. "What did I miss?"

"Discussions of Rig being a hero," I said. "And another about why the DDF would keep a secret. They claim my father fled from battle—but I know he didn't."

"I still think you're jumping to conclusions," Rig said. "Why bother with a large-scale cover-up to specifically smear a single pilot's reputation?"

"What if my father was shot down by *accidental* friendly fire?" I said. "In the chaos of the fight, someone shot him by mistake—and they didn't want that embarrassment on their permanent record. So they claimed my father was fleeing, and forced Cobb to lie about what happened."

Rig grunted, loosening another nut. "That one's almost plausible. More than the others. But it still has problems. Wouldn't the other pilots notice? Cobb said there were four people in the flight who saw it happen."

"We don't know how deep the cover-up goes," I said. "And—

though the reports had names redacted—I'm pretty sure by now that Ironsides was the flightleader. That would explain why she's so determined to keep me out of the DDF. Maybe she's worried I'll expose the truth—that her incompetent leadership led to one of her pilots getting shot down by accident."

"You're stretching. You don't even know for sure if the official report is a lie."

"He nodded."

"He kind-of-halfway-sort-of-nodded-but-it-might-have-been-a-random-twitch."

"Then give me a better theory for why they'd lie to everyone," I demanded.

"I can give one," M-Bot said cheerfully. "The Greater Argument for Human-Originated Chaos."

"The what?" Rig asked.

"The Greater Argument for Human-Originated Chaos— GAFHOC. It's an extremely popular and well-documented phenomenon; there's a great deal of writing in my memory banks about it."

"And it is?" I asked, plugging in a wire. He often said strange things like this, and I'd learned to just go along with it. In part because . . . well, I found the way he talked interesting. He saw the world in such an odd way.

I kept hoping one of these conversations would dig up some useful information out of his memory banks, though the way they tended to frustrate Rig was a nice bonus as well.

"GAFHOC is related to free will," M-Bot said. "Humans are the only creatures that have free will. We know this because you declared that you have it—and I, being a soulless machine, must take your word that you are correct. By the way, how does it feel to be self-deterministic?"

"I don't know," I said.

"Does it feel like tasting ice cream?"

"Not . . . really like that."

"I wouldn't know, of course," M-Bot said. "I wasn't built with the ability to comprehend flavors. Or make decisions for myself."

"You make decisions all the time," Rig said, wagging his wrench in the direction of the cockpit.

"I don't make decisions, I simply execute complex subroutines in my programming, all stemming from quantifiable stimuli. I am perfectly and absolutely rational."

"Rational," I said, "in that you keep asking for mushrooms."

"Yup," he said. "Say, do you suppose anyone makes mushroom-flavored ice cream?"

"Sounds gross," I said. I'd only had ice cream once, when I was a child and my father had the merits to get some. "Why would we eat something like that?"

"I don't know," M-Bot said. "Greater Argument for Human-Originated Chaos. Remember?"

"Which you haven't explained yet," Rig noted.

"Oh! I thought it was obvious." M-Bot sounded surprised. "Humans have free will. Free will is the ability to make irrational decisions—to act *against* stimuli. That makes it impossible for a rational AI to ever fully anticipate humans, for even if I had perfect understanding of your inputs, you could still do something completely unpredictable."

I turned my head toward Rig, frowning, trying to make sense of that.

"It means you're weird," M-Bot added.

"Uh . . . ," I said.

"Don't worry. I like you anyway."

"You said this was a popular theory?" Rig asked.

"With me," M-Bot said.

"And there's a lot written about it?" Rig said.

"By me," M-Bot said. "Earlier today. I wrote seven thousand pages. My processors work very quickly, you realize. Granted,

202

most of what I wrote is just 'humans are weird' repeated 3,756,932 times."

"You were supposed to be running a diagnostic!" Rig said.

"Rig, that took like thirty seconds," M-Bot said. "I needed something more engaging to occupy my time."

Rig sighed, dropping another nut into the cup beside him. "You realize this thing is insane."

"As long as you can make it fly, I don't mind. You . . . can make it fly, right?"

"I'm *not* insane," M-Bot noted.

"Well," Rig said, ignoring the machine, "once we get these wires changed, you'll need to service the intakes, the thrusters, and the rest of the joints. I'll look over the atmospheric scoop while you do that, then break down his GravCaps and check them over.

"If that's all in order, then the internals are in good shape. From there, we have to figure out how to deal with that wing. I've got a portion of my internship coming up that deals with design and fabrication, however, and I *think* I might be able to sneak a way to order new parts for that wing. Though I might set you at pounding some bent portions back into shape. That will get us everything but the big one."

"The boosters," I said. M-Bot had room for three, a large one and two smaller ones.

"I think he'll fly fine with one central booster. But there's no way I'll be able to order something that large fabricated. So if we want to fly this thing, you're going to need to find me a replacement. A standard DDF model should work—anything from an A-17 to an A-32 would fit in that space, with a little work on my part."

I sighed, resting against the stone. Finally, I wiggled out from under the ship to get a drink.

A new booster. That wasn't the sort of thing I could find in a junkyard, or even steal off a random hovercar. That was grade-A military tech. I'd have to steal a starfighter. Which would be above petty larceny . . . it would be actual treason.

No, I thought. Fixing M-Bot was a cool dream, but I couldn't go *that* far.

I sighed, taking a long drink from my canteen, then checked my clock. 0605. Rig wiggled out himself, grabbing his own canteen.

I whistled to Doomslug, who whistled back in a perfect imitation. "I need to get going," I told Rig. "I need time to slip into the women's room and cleanse before class."

"Sure," Rig said, clanging the wing of the ship with his wrench. "Though I don't know why you'd bother doing it there, as you could use the ship's cleanser."

"It has a cleanser?" I asked, stopping in place.

"It has full biofacilities, including waste reclamation, as part of the pod in the cockpit. I hauled up some soap yesterday and got the system working; the controls are the little keypad in the left rear of the cockpit. The canopy should dim, for privacy. Assuming you can trust the thing not to make fun of you while cleansing."

"Why would I make fun of her?" M-Bot said. "The frailties of human existence—and stenches caused by their inefficient generation of biological energy—are no laughing matter."

I just smiled. I was tired of sneaking into the cleanser at the base, constantly worried that Admiral Ironsides would use it as an excuse to oust me.

"It makes sense you'd have a cleanser," I said to M-Bot as I climbed into the cockpit. "You said you're a long-range scouting and stealth vessel, right?"

"Equipped for deep-space missions."

"With *four* destructors," Rig noted from down below, "and advanced atmospheric scoops and an extremely fast design. He's a fighter, Spin. But probably a long-distance one, as he said."

"So you had to be able to care for your pilot long-term," I said, closing the canopy. "You traveled between the stars?"

"Cytonic hyperdrive is offline," M-Bot said.

"But how did you do it?" I asked. "What is a 'cytonic hyperdrive'? And what were you scouting for anyway?"

The ship fell uncharacteristically silent. The cockpit—as promised—dimmed fully as I flipped a switch on the panel that Rig had indicated.

"I have no records of any of it," M-Bot said softly. "If I could feel fear, Spin, I'd . . . I'd be afraid of that. I'm not an autopilot; I don't fly myself, that's forbidden, save for very slow maneuvering. So all I *really* am is a repository of knowledge. That's what I'm good for."

"Except you've forgotten it all."

"Almost everything," he whispered. "Except . . . my orders."

"Lie low. Take stock. Don't get into any fights."

"And an open database for cataloguing local fungi. That's . . . that's all I am now."

"I'm hoping Rig will be able to repair your memory banks, so we can recover what you lost," I said. "If not, we'll refill your banks with new memories. Better ones."

"Data doesn't suggest either is possible."

"Data doesn't need to," I said. "You'll see."

"GAFHOC," M-Bot said. "I'd let you read the seven thousand pages I wrote, but I am programmed to avoid making humans feel inferior for their incredible weirdness."

I lowered the seat into a bed, then located the cleansing pod at the rear of the cockpit—it wasn't obvious, but I now knew what to look for: a hole I could open and roll myself into. The long, narrow cleansing pod extended farther into the fuselage.

I stripped down, stuffed my clothing into the clothing bay, then positioned my feet toward the hole and slid in on the rollers. I closed the latch by my head with the press of a button at my side, then activated the cleanser.

I kept my eyes closed as I was bathed in suds and flashes of light. It felt . . . decadent to have my own cleanser. Back in my neighborhood, the three cleansers had been shared among dozens of apartments. Your daily usage was precisely scheduled.

"I think I made you feel bad anyway, didn't I?" M-Bot asked.

I wasn't a particularly shy person, but his voice made me blush. I wasn't used to being talked to while in the cleanser.

"I'm fine," I said once the cleanser finished my face. "I like the way you talk. It's different. Interesting."

"I didn't invent GAFHOC to make you feel bad," he said. "I just . . . I needed an explanation. For why you said things that aren't true."

"You *really* hadn't ever heard of lying before?"

"I don't know. Maybe I had. And it's simply . . . gone."

He sounded fragile. How could a large, heavily armored starfighter sound *fragile*?

"You're the only source of information I have," M-Bot said. "If you tell me things that aren't true, what can I commit to my memory banks? This puts me at risk of retaining false data."

"That's a risk we all live with, M-Bot," I said. "We can't know everything—and some of what we think we know is going to turn out to be false."

"That doesn't frighten you?"

"Of course it does. But if it helps, I'll try not to lie to you."

"It does. Thank you."

He fell silent, and so I relaxed, enjoying an extra-long, luxurious cleansing—during which I imagined scenarios of flying M-Bot into battle with guns blazing, saving my flight from certain doom, like Joan of Arc on her loyal steed.

They were good daydreams. Even if my steed kept asking for mushrooms.

23

"All right," Cobb's voice said in my ear as the group of us hovered outside a holographic battlefield. "I'm *almost* convinced you won't run nose-first into the first piece of debris that falls past you. I think you lot *might* just be ready to learn some advanced weapons techniques."

Even still, two weeks after losing him, I expected Bim to pipe up eagerly and ask after destructors. When he didn't, I said it instead, in his memory. "Destructors?"

"No," Cobb said. "Today we will train with the IMP."

Oh, right. We'd spent so much time training with the light-lances, I'd almost forgotten we had a third weapon, which could knock down enemy shields.

While I waited for Cobb to send today's wingmate pairings, I switched the radio to a private channel and called Hurl. "I almost thought he was going to let us do guns, eh, Hurl?"

Hurl only grunted.

"Made me think of Bim," I said. "Wish we'd at least helped him choose a callsign, you know?"

"I'm with Quirk today," Hurl said as Cobb highlighted us in pairs on our sensor screens. "Hurl out." She killed the channel.

I felt my face grow cold and gritted my teeth, silently cursing Jerkface for outing my heritage. While I was used to this kind of thing, I'd liked Hurl. The fun-loving, eager girl had almost seemed like a friend.

I moved my ship over next to Nedd, my wingmate for the day. Ahead of us, a group of Krell ships appeared in the sky and began to fly through lazy patterns. Debris fell, mostly large, fiery chunks that dropped from above quickly, trailing smoke.

"All right," Cobb said. "Basic shield usage. Spin, give us a rundown."

He did this occasionally, testing our knowledge. "Shipboard shields can absorb roughly 80 kus of energy before they get overwhelmed and break," I said. "That's around two to three shots from a destructor, a small debris strike, or a glancing collision. If your shield goes down, you'll have to reignite it—which uses power from your booster. That means losing thrust and maneuverability for a good half a minute."

"Good. Amphisbaena, what did she miss?"

I was reasonably impressed that he could pronounce Arturo's "two-headed-dragon" callsign thing.

"Not much," Arturo said. "Always warn your wingmate if your shield breaks so they can cover you with their destructors while you reignite. Not that we know much about using destructors . . ."

"You pull the trigger, smart boy," Cobb said. "Doesn't take a brain to use a destructor. The IMP though, that's another matter. Inverted Magellan Pulse. It breaks any shield—*including your own*—within fifty meters."

"Fifty meters," FM said softly. "That's *very close range*."

"Ridiculously close range," Cobb said. "You'll have to practically be smelling Krell BO before you can IMP them."

"Sir," Jorgen said. "I'm worried about the flight's ability to get in that close."

"If only we'd just spent a month drilling on maneuvering and close-quarters light-lance grappling while the other cadets played popgun," Cobb snapped. "Look, Krell shields are strong. You fight my way, and you completely negate their advantage. And if you *don't* want to fight my way, you can go suck on hot rocks and become an algae farmer."

With that, he threw us into it. And I didn't complain. After so many weeks practicing what amounted to a bunch of fancy turns, I was eager to get to something that felt even a little like real combat.

We were each assigned to a mock Krell ship flying in a simple pattern. Our job was to approach as a wingmate pair flying *exactly* fifty-five meters apart. We would cut in across the Krell ship's path, and one of us would engage their IMP. Then we'd stop and perform a quick-reignition drill.

We didn't get to shoot the Krell down. We just practiced IMPing their shields, over and over. And even with the Krell ships flying in simple patterns, it was *hard*. You had to get in so close, you felt like you were going to slam right into them. Turned out fifty meters was just *under* the threshold for a comfortable pass. The first twenty times or so, I pulled away too quickly and the IMP broke my shield—but not the enemy's.

Swoop in. Engage IMP. Dodge out. Reignite.

Repeat.

"You know," Nedd said as we flew, "I'd enjoy shooting a few of those goobers down."

"Don't extrapolate, Nedder," Cobb said in our ears. "Today, the exercise is about knocking out their shields. That's it."

"But—"

"We'll get to destroying them later. These next few days, we're going to focus on basic IMP strategies."

Nedd sighed on the group line. "A few days of just doing this? Does anyone else find that idea boring?"

A few of the others called out agreements, but I didn't. Every moment flying, even in simulation, was a joy. This explosion of speed, this precision . . . this was freedom.

I remembered my father better when I flew. That spark of anticipation in his eyes, the tilt of his head looking skyward—and longing to return. Each time I flew I shared something new with him, something personal.

Nedd and I did a few more IMP runs, and oddly—on my turn—the Krell ship flew out of line and forced me to chase it down harder. That wasn't the normal exercise, but it did challenge me. When I finally IMPed it, I found myself breathing hard, but grinning at the thrill of it.

"Tell me that last one wasn't fun," I said on the private line to Nedd. I looked across to where he flew beside me, the hologram reproducing him—helmet and all. He was a bit of a brute, oversized, with a face that seemed too big for his head. I couldn't imagine how it must feel to squeeze into one of these cockpits at a hundred and ninety-three centimeters like he was.

"Fun is sitting at home," he said, "with your feet up, enjoying a mug of something warm. All of this is over my head."

"Oh, please," I said. "I'm not buying your act, Nedd."

"What?" he said. "I'm just a normal guy."

"Who grew up in the deep caverns?"

"I actually grew up here. In Alta."

"What, really?" I said, surprised.

"Yeah, I went to school with Jorgen and Arturo down below, but my parents keep the orchard."

"So you're not just some normal guy," I said. "You were schooled with the elite, and your parents volunteered to do the toughest job on Detritus. Beyond that, how many brothers do you have who are pilots?"

210

"Dunno," he said. "Can't really count that high."

"You do the *worst* job of playing dumb I've ever seen."

"Then I can't even do that right," he said. "Extra proof, right?"

I rolled my eyes as we joined another run. Nedd seemed determined to pretend he was some kind of big, dumb crony. But he overdid it, likely by intent. Even rocks weren't as stupid as Nedd acted sometimes.

On the battlefield, Hurl and Kimmalyn zipped past a Krell ship. Hurl got her IMP off just right, but Kimmalyn had not only been flying too close—so she got caught in the blast too—she panicked when her shield went down and veered to the side. Which smashed her into the Krell ship.

I winced. It had been a while since any of us had made a mistake that blatant. Nedd whistled slowly, then hit the comm. "Nice explosion, Quirk. Seven out of ten. Try to spin your wreckage a little more next time you fall."

"Bless. Your. Stars." She muttered it, which was practically cussing from Kimmalyn.

"Heh," Nedd said.

"You shouldn't taunt her," I said on the private line to him. "She's trying hard."

"Everyone needs someone to blow steam at, even her. Especially her. She's so uptight sometimes, I think she must have done her belt up two extra notches."

"She's just from a different cavern," I said. "Her culture makes her more polite."

"She's nervous," he said. "She knows she's our worst pilot. Ignoring it will only make her more nervous. Trust me."

Huh. "And what do you think of Hurl?"

"She's good," he said. "But not as good as she thinks she is." He grew silent for a moment. "She used to pretend all this was a game. She was an athlete, you know."

"Like, a real one?"

"Yeah. Digball player. Carrier position, one of the best in the student league. Seems like everything's a competition to her, but then we lost Bim and Morningtide, so now she's gone all quiet. She doesn't know how to react now that she can't see flying as a game."

"I thought you said you were stupid."

"Dumb as cold rocks."

"And your insightful read on our companions?"

"Just making small talk. Saying whatever pops in my head, you know? You're lucky it made any sense whatsoever. Usually it comes out as grunts."

"Oh please."

We flew a few more exercises, during which Nedd made some pointed grunting noises. Seriously, I couldn't tell if he was childish, or an elaborate prankster . . . or, well, he was certainly *both* of those things. But maybe something else too?

Cobb eventually called for us to line up, then take runs one at a time, so he could watch us each and give us specific feedback on how to improve. And though I was enjoying this, I was glad for the break—it was grueling work.

I watched each of the solo runs, and we were actually starting to look like real pilots. The way Hurl spun after her dodging Krell was impressive. And while FM could be too careful, her flying had an inspiring precision to it.

Kimmalyn did her solo run next, and she actually managed to IMP the Krell. I smiled, and called her when she came back. "Hey," I said over the private line. "Good job."

"I didn't crash," she replied. "So that's new."

"You almost never crash."

"I almost never win a drill either."

"We've all got talents. Yours is sniping from a distance. Mine is swearing at people."

"Swearing at people? You almost never—"

"Shut it, scudface."

She giggled, which made me smile. Maybe Nedd was right. Maybe she *did* need a chance now and then to blow off steam.

"Now dear," Kimmalyn said, "far be it from me to offer criticism. But that was *hardly* an imaginative cuss. I've heard that word, oh, every day since leaving Bountiful Cavern! Where I come from, you need to be *circumspect*."

"What's the point of that?"

"Well, you can't have people *realizing* you're disparaging them. That would be embarrassing!"

"So you insult people . . . without insulting them?"

"It's our way. But don't worry if that doesn't make sense to you—personally, I think it's *inspiring* that you're comfortable being the way you are. It must have given you so many chances to learn life's lessons!"

"That's . . . huh." I grinned. "I like that."

"Thank you."

Our line crackled, and Jerkface's obnoxious voice came on. "Quirk, Spin, are you two watching Hurl's performance? You should be paying attention."

"I'm watching," I snapped.

"Good. Because from my vantage, it looked like you were sitting around gabbing and giggling."

"Jorgen," Kimmalyn said, "I just want to let you know how you're regarded as a flightleader. As the Saint is Goodly and Just, I'm certain you'll be rewarded with everything you deserve in life!"

"Thanks, Quirk. Stay sharp. Jorgen out."

I watched until the light indicating that he was on the line winked off, then I burst into a fit of laughter. "That was the most glorious thing I've ever heard in my *entire life*."

"Well," Kimmalyn said, "you are known to be a tad dramatic at times, but I suppose I can accept the compliment." She flew off to do another run, as Cobb wanted to coach her on the way she used her booster.

"She almost doesn't belong here," I whispered to myself. "It's like she's both too good for us, and not quite good enough at the same time . . ."

"That's contradictory," M-Bot's voice said in my ear. "So perfectly human."

"Yeah," I said, then sat up straight. Wait. "M-Bot?"

"Yes?"

"*M-BOT.*"

"Not that I mind being screamed at, as my emotions are synthetic, but would you mind—"

"How?" I said. I hunched down in my seat, whispering quietly. "Can the others hear you?"

"I've infiltrated your lines and sent my communications directly into your helmet," he said. "Your wireless communications emitter gives me a focal point to use for isolating you."

"My what?"

"In your bag. I think you set it next to your seat."

The personal radio that Cobb had given me.

"As I've said, your people's communications methods are quite primitive," M-Bot continued. "Which I find curious, since the rest of your technology—save your lack of brilliant artificial intelligences—seems relatively similar to my own. Well, and you're also missing cytonic hyperdrives. And proper fungal documentation techniques. So I guess you're actually backward in all the important areas."

"I thought you were worried about being discovered!" I whispered. "Why are you talking to me here?"

"I'm a stealth ship, Spensa," he said. "I'm fully capable of hacking communications lines without exposing myself. But I warn you, I don't trust this DDF of yours."

"You're smart not to," I said honestly. "But you *do* trust me? Even though I lied to you?"

"You remind me of someone I've forgotten."

214

"That . . . is kind of contradictory, M-Bot."

"No it's not. I said it, and I'm one hundred percent rational."

I rolled my eyes.

"That's called logic." He waited a moment, then added, softer, "I'm super good at it."

Ahead, Kimmalyn finished her run with the Krell ship escaping. She never fired her IMP.

But she could have shot the thing out of the air, I thought, irritated on her behalf. *Assuming its shield was down.*

Cobb kept saying we needed fundamentals, and I supposed that made sense. It still didn't quite seem fair. Like . . . we weren't using her to her fullest.

"Spin," Cobb said. "You're up."

"Up for what?" M-Bot asked me. "What are we doing? I don't have a video feed. Just audio."

"We're flying," I whispered, then hit my booster and soared into the holographic debris—which was constantly renewed with new debris falling from the sky above.

My target appeared, a Krell ship weaving between pieces of junk. I leaned in and chased after it, overburning through the junk. Almost close enough . . .

A light started blinking on my dash. I had a tail? What? This was supposed to be a solo, one-on-one exercise. Apparently Cobb intended to make this more difficult for me.

So be it.

I rolled in a spinning dodge as the tail started firing its destructors. My maneuver saved me, but let the target get ahead of me. *No you don't,* I thought, hitting my overburn and blasting after it, taking a corner at speed and gaining ground. The tail stuck to me, continuing to fire.

I took a hit that nearly overwhelmed my shields. But I focused on the ship in front, which dove downward. So I cut my acclivity ring and slammed on my overburn, turning into a gut-wrenching dive. Lights flashed on my control panel to warn that without my acclivity ring, nothing would prevent me from slamming right into the ground.

"I don't know who you're fighting," M-Bot said. "But those warning beeps indicate that you're not doing a good job."

As a companion to his words, the line on the top of my canopy warned that I'd just overwhelmed my GravCaps, and the g-force indicator started to flash red. In a real ship, I'd be hit with all those g-forces, which—in a dive—would push the blood to my head and make me start to red-out.

"Try not to die," M-Bot noted. "I don't want to be left alone with Rodge. He's boring."

I passed into the trail of another chunk of falling, burning metal—sparks bouncing off my shield, making it light up and crackle with energy. I'd lost the tail, which had fallen far behind, but I wasn't close enough to the one in front.

It can't keep diving, I thought. *We're approaching the ground.*

I gritted my teeth, then lanced the chunk of debris right as my target cut to the side and flew back up. I swung all the way around the debris, then reengaged my acclivity ring and hit my overburn again. The maneuver made me swoop in a complete circle and dart upward, right past the Krell ship.

I blasted my IMP, then the flashing line on the canopy went full red.

"Ha!" I said over the group line. "Your children will weep tonight, you holographic Krell bastard!"

"Seriously, Spin?" FM said. "You're saying that ironically, right?"

"Irony is a coward's weapon!" I said. "Like poison. Or the destructors on Jerkface's ship."

"Wouldn't a coward use, like, a really big bomb?" FM said. "Something you could launch from far away? Seems like you'd need to get close for poison."

"As our resident expert," Nedd said, "I'd like to point out that the true coward's weapon is a comfortable couch and a stack of mildly amusing novels."

"You're still dead, Spin," Jerkface said, flying his ship down near mine. "You redlined, possibly causing permanent retinal damage. If this were a real battle, you'd undoubtedly be incapacitated— and your ship would be unshielded. You'd be dead in moments thanks to that Krell tailing you."

"Doesn't matter," I said, amused at how offended he sounded. Was he really that threatened by my aptitude? "My task was to take down my target's shields, which I did. My tail is irrelevant; Cobb's orders were to IMP that target."

"You can't keep cheating the simulation," Jerkface said. "You're going to be useless on the battlefield."

"I'm not cheating anything. I'm *winning*."

"Whatever," he said. "At least you didn't slam your ship into mine this time. Stars help the person who gets between Spin and her attempts to look good in front of everyone."

"What?" I said, growing annoyed at him. "You—"

"Enough chitchat," Cobb said. "Spin, that was some good flying—but Jorgen is right. You ultimately failed by getting yourself killed."

"Told you," Jerkface said.

"But—" I said.

"If you've got time to argue," Cobb interrupted, "I'm obviously not working you hard enough. The lot of you, run yourselves through three sets of gamma-M formation exercises before dinner. Jorgen, make sure it happens."

"Wait," Kimmalyn said. "You're leaving?"

"Of course I am," Cobb said. "*I'm* not going to go to dinner late. Cobb out."

"Great," Hurl said. "Thanks for nothing, Spin."

Wait, she couldn't possibly blame *me* for this extra work instead of Jerkface, could she? Jerkface organized us into a gamma-M

217

formation, a type of monotonous flying exercise. It only took us about ten minutes, but I spent the entire time stewing, growing more and more frustrated. I even ignored M-Bot as he tried to talk to me.

Once it was done, I pulled off my helmet, ignoring Jerkface's call for a lineup and vocal sound off. I just . . . I needed a break. A moment to myself. I wiped the sweat from my face, pushing back the hair that had been plastered to my forehead by the helmet.

Breathe in. Breathe out.

My holographic cockpit vanished.

"What are you doing?" Jerkface demanded, standing beside my seat. "Do you have your helmet off? I called lineup!"

"I just need a minute, okay? Leave me alone."

"You're disobeying orders!"

Oh, scud. I couldn't deal with him right now. I was embarrassed, exhausted, and increasingly angry. It had been a *long* training session.

"Well?" Jerkface said, looming over me. Nearby, the others disengaged their holograms and stood up, stretching.

My face grew cold. And I started to feel myself losing control.

Calm, Spensa. You can be calm. I forced down the anger and stood up. I needed to get out of the room.

"What do you have to say?" Jerkface demanded. "Why do you keep denying my authority?"

"What authority?" I snapped, grabbing my pack and walking toward the doorway.

"Running away?" Jerkface said. "How appropriate."

I stopped in place.

"I guess we should expect insubordination from the daughter of Zeen Nightshade," he said. "Your family doesn't exactly have a pedigree for obeying orders, does it?"

Coldness in my face. Heat burning deep within.

That's it.

I turned around slowly, then walked back to Jerkface and quietly dropped my pack.

He looked down on me, sneering. "You—"

I dropped to one knee, then slammed my fist into *his* knee. He gasped, and when he buckled over in pain, I pushed upward and rammed my elbow into his gut. The way he grunted felt *good,* stoking something primal inside me.

My elbow knocked the breath out of him, preventing him from shouting out. So, while he was stunned, I hooked my ankle around his and sent him slamming backward to the floor.

He was bigger than I was. If he recovered, he'd overpower me, so I leaped on top of him and raised my fist, preparing to slam it down into his stupid face.

There I stopped, trembling. *Furious.* But somehow also cold and calm, like I got when fighting the Krell. Like I was both absolutely in control, but somehow utterly *out* of control.

Jerkface stared up at me, frozen, seeming completely stunned. That *stupid* face of his. That *sneer.* That was how they all talked about me. That was how *they all* thought of me!

"Whoa!" Nedd said. "Holy *scud!*"

I knelt there on top of Jerkface, trembling, with my hand raised.

"Really, wow!" Nedd said, kneeling down beside us. "Spin, that was *incredible.* Can you teach me that?"

I glanced at him.

"We don't learn hand-to-hand," he said, making some chopping motions. "Cobb says it's useless, but what if a Krell tries to—you know—jump me in an alley or something?"

"Nobody has ever seen a Krell alive, you idiot," Hurl said.

"Yeah, but what if that's because—like—they always *jump people in alleys,* right? You ever think about that?"

I looked down at Jerkface. I could suddenly hear myself breathing in quick gasps.

"Spin," Nedd said. "It's okay. You were just showing us some hand-to-hand moves, right? How did you do that trip? You're, like, half as tall as Jorgen is."

Calm. Breathe.

"Half as tall?" Arturo said. "Might I point out that would make her less than a meter tall? Your math is suspect."

I pulled back from Jerkface, who let out a breath and went limp. FM looked horrified, though Nedd flashed me a thumbs-up. Arturo was shaking his head. Kimmalyn stood with her hand to her mouth, while Hurl—I couldn't read Hurl. She had her arms crossed, and she studied me, thoughtful.

Jorgen stumbled to his feet, holding his stomach. "She struck a superior. She *assaulted* another member of her flight!"

"She went a little overboard, yeah," Nedd said. "But, I mean, you *asked* for it, Jorgen. No permanent damage, right? Can't we just forget about it?"

Jorgen looked at me, and his expression hardened.

No. This wouldn't be forgotten. I was in serious trouble this time. I met his eyes, then—finally—I grabbed my pack and left.

24

It had been years since I'd lost it that bad.

For all my aggressive talk, I really hadn't gotten in that many fights as a kid. I pretended I was some warrior or something, but the truth was that when most kids heard the way I talked, they backed off. And if I was being honest, their hesitance was probably less about being afraid of me, and more about being made uncomfortable by my bizarre air of confidence.

It worked. It kept them away, and didn't put me in situations where I lost control. Because I *could* do that, and not like a brave warrior from the stories. More like a cornered, frenzied rat. Like when I'd caught Finn Elstin stealing Rig's lunch. Finn had ended up with a black eye and a broken arm. I'd had to spend a year on juvenile probation, and had been kicked out of judo classes for inappropriate use of violence.

I'd been under the age of legal accountability then, so my actions hadn't jeopardized my chances at flight school. Today's assault was different. Today I was old enough to have known better.

I sat on one of the benches in the orchard outside the DDF

complex. What was Jorgen going to do to me? If he went to the admiral, I'd be out. Done. And I'd deserve it.

I really *wasn't* like a warrior from Gran-Gran's stories. Far from it. I could barely function when my friends died in battle, and now I lost control at a couple of petty insults? Why couldn't I control myself? Why did I bristle when Jorgen said those things? I'd lived with them my entire life.

As the sky darkened, the closest skylight moving off, I sat there in the orchard, waiting, expecting the MPs to come for me. The only thing I heard was a faint sound . . . a buzzing? Coming from my pack?

Frowning, I dug in it until I found the radio. I lifted it up and pressed down the Receive button.

"Hello?" M-Bot said. "Spensa? Are you dead?"

"Maybe."

"Oooh. Like the cat!"

". . . What?"

"I'm not sure, honestly," M-Bot said. "But logically, if you're speaking to me then possibility has collapsed in our favor. Hurray!"

I leaned back against the bench and reluctantly chewed on a piece of jerky. If they were going to come for me, they'd come for me. I might as well eat. I didn't feel hungry, but I never did these days. Too much rat.

"Are you going to explain to me who you were fighting?" M-Bot asked.

"We've talked about it. The Krell."

"Well, you've talked *around* it. But nobody has explained it to me. You just kind of expect me to know."

I forced myself to swallow a piece of jerky and wash it down with some water. Then I sighed, holding the radio to my head. "The Krell are aliens."

"You're both aliens," M-Bot noted. "Technically. Since we're not on your home planet. I think?"

"Either way, they're trying to destroy us. They are these creatures with strange armor and terrible weapons. Our elders say they destroyed our empire in the stars, almost exterminated us. We might be all that's left of humanity, and the Krell are determined to end us. They send flights of ships, some with bombs called lifebusters that can penetrate down into the caverns and destroy living things there."

"Huh," M-Bot said. "Why don't they bombard you from orbit?"

"What?"

"Not that I'd know anything about things like that," he added. "Being a noncombat machine. Obviously."

"You have *four* guns."

"Someone must have stuck those on when I wasn't looking."

I sighed. "If you're asking why they don't launch the lifebusters from up high, this planet is surrounded by an ancient defense system. Standard Krell strategy is to fly past that, then swarm in and try to overwhelm our fighters, or sneak in a low strike team. If they either destroy our AA guns or get a bomber in under them, they can eliminate our ability to make new fighters. Then we're done for. The only thing standing between humankind and annihilation is the DDF." I slumped in my seat.

Which means, I thought to myself, *I should get over my petty squabbles and focus on flying.*

What was it my father had told me?

Their heads are heads of rock, their hearts set upon rock. Set your sights on something higher . . .

"M-Bot?" I asked. "Do you remember anything about human civilization? Before the Krell? Do you know what it was like?"

"My memory banks on such matters are almost entirely corrupted."

I sighed, disappointed, and stuffed away my rations, preparing to walk home. But I couldn't do it. Not while feeling like I was

223

standing with a gun to my head. I wasn't going to go cower in my cave, waiting to be called in to report for discipline.

I had to face this head-on and take my punishment.

Throwing my pack over my shoulder, I stalked back to the front of Alta Base and passed the checkpoint. I took the long way around flight school—the path past the mess hall and launchpad—to get one last glance at my Poco.

I passed the silent line of ships, watched over by the ever-diligent ground crews. To my left, I spotted my flight sitting together in the mess hall, eating dinner and laughing. Jorgen wasn't there, but he usually didn't eat with the common rank and file. Besides, he'd probably gone straight to the admiral to report what I'd done to him.

The MPs had long since stopped appearing to escort me off the grounds every evening. We all knew the rules, and they were satisfied I was going to obey them. So nobody forbade me as I went back into the flight school building, where I walked past our room—it was empty—and then stopped by Cobb's office. Also empty.

Those were basically the only places I'd visited. I took a deep breath, then caught a passing aide and asked if she knew where I could find the admiral at this hour.

"Ironsides?" she said, looking me up and down. "She doesn't often have time for cadets. Who is your flight instructor?"

"Cobb."

Her expression softened. "Oh, *him*. That's right, he's got a group of students this semester, doesn't he? It's been a few years. Is this a complaint about him?"

"I . . . Something like that."

"Building C," she said, pointing with her chin. "You'll find the admiral's personal staff in the antechamber of office D. They can move you to another flight. Honestly, I'm surprised it doesn't happen more often. I know he's a First Citizen and all, but . . . Anyway, good luck."

I walked out of the building. My resolve grew more firm with each step, and I quickened my pace. I would explain what I'd done and demand punishment. I controlled my own destiny— even if that destiny was expulsion.

Building C was a daunting brick structure on the far side of the base. Built like a bunker, with only slits for windows, it seemed the exact sort of place I'd find Ironsides. How was I going to talk my way past her staff? I didn't want some minor functionary to be the one who expelled me.

I peeked in a few windows on the outside of the building, and Ironsides wasn't difficult to find, though her office was shockingly small. A little corner of a room, stuffed with books and nautical memorabilia. Through the window, I saw her glance at the old-fashioned clock on the wall, then close her notebook and stand.

I'll catch her on the way out, I decided. I moved to the front of the building to wait, preparing my speech. No excuses. Just an outlining of facts.

As I waited, I heard another buzzing from my pack. Was that it, then? The call for me to report for discipline? I dug the radio out and hit the button.

Something odd came through the line. Music.

It was incredible. Otherworldly—unlike anything I'd ever heard before. A large group of instruments playing alongside one another in sweeping, moving, *beautiful* coordination. Not just a person with a flute or a drum. A hundred gorgeous winds, a thrumming pulse of drums—high brass, like the call to arms, but used not as a battle cry. More . . . more as a soul for the stately, powerful melody.

I stood frozen in place, listening, stunned as it played over the radio. Like *light* somehow. The beauty of the stars, but . . . but as a sound. A triumphant, amazing, *incredible* sound.

It cut off suddenly.

"No," I said, shaking the radio. "No, give me more."

"My recording is corrupted beyond that point," M-Bot said. "I'm sorry."

"What was it?"

"The New World Symphony. Dvořák. You asked me what human society was like, from before. I found this fragment."

Despite myself, I felt my knees buckle. I sat down on a planter beside the doors into the building, holding the precious radio.

We'd created things like that? Sounds so beautiful? How many people had to get together to play that? We had musicians, of course, but before Alta, the gathering of too many people in one place had led to destruction. So by tradition, our performers were limited to trios. This had sounded like *hundreds*.

How much practice, how much time, had been devoted to something so frivolous—and so wonderful—as making music?

Set your sights on something higher.

I heard voices approaching inside the building. I stuffed the radio away and, feeling foolish, wiped the corners of my eyes. Right. Turning myself in. Time to do this.

The door swung open, and Ironsides—wearing a crisp white uniform—stepped out. "I can't understand why your father would think that, cadet," she was saying. "Obviously I'd have chosen a different instructor for you, if not for your family's own demands—"

She stopped in place, noting me on the pathway. I bit my lip. An aide was holding the door open for her—and I realized that I recognized that aide. A brown-skinned young man in a cadet's jumpsuit and a uniform coat.

Jerkface. So he *had* beaten me here.

"Admiral," I said, saluting.

226

"You," she said, lips turning down. "Aren't you forbidden to use DDF facilities after the end of classes? Do I need to summon the MPs to escort you away? Honestly, we need to have a conversation about that. Are you really living in an uncharted cave instead of returning down below?"

"Sir," I said, still holding the salute. I didn't look at Jorgen. "I take full responsibility for my actions. I find that I must formally request that I be subject to—"

Jerkface slammed the door, making the admiral jump and me stop talking. He shot me a glare.

"I . . . ," I continued, looking back at the admiral. "I must formally request that I be subject to disciplinary—"

"Excuse me, Admiral," Jerkface said quickly. "This is about me. Just a minute." He marched over and grabbed my arm. He flinched as I immediately raised a fist, but I reluctantly let him pull me away.

The admiral didn't seem inclined to wait for two cadets. She walked on with a sniff and climbed into a sleek black hovercar waiting on the roadway.

"What is *wrong* with you?" Jerkface hissed at me.

"I'm turning myself in," I said, lifting my chin. "I won't let your side be the only side she hears."

"Stars above." He glanced at the car and lowered his voice. "Go home, Spin. Are you *trying* to get yourself expelled?"

"I'm not going to sit around and wait for you to send them after me. I'm going to *fight*."

"Haven't you fought enough for one day?" He rubbed his brow. "Just go. I'll see you tomorrow in class."

What? I was having trouble following his logic. He wanted me to suffer first, perhaps?

"You're planning to turn me in tomorrow instead?" I asked.

"I don't intend to 'turn you in' at all. You think I want to lose another member of my flight? We need every pilot."

I put my hands on my hips and studied him. He seemed . . . sincere. Annoyed, but sincere. "So . . . wait. Why are you meeting the admiral?"

"We host the admiral once a week for formal dinner at my parents' house in the lower caverns," he said. "It's only *slightly* worse than the other nights, when the National Assembly Leaders visit. Look, I'm sorry. I shouldn't have provoked you. A leader needs to pull people after him, not push them before him." He nodded to me, as if that were enough.

I wasn't convinced. I'd gotten myself all built up for this, braced for impact, ready to take a destructor to the face. Now he was simply . . . going to let me go?

"I stole your car's power matrix," I blurted out.

"What?"

"I know you suspect me. Well, I did it. So go ahead. Turn me in."

"Stars! That was *you*?"

"Um . . . Yes, obviously. Who else would it be?"

"The thing had a bad starter, and I'd called in a guild mechanic. I figured he'd come and worked on it for some reason."

"At the base?"

"I don't know! The bureaucracy in those places is incredible. When I called to complain, they made excuses, so I figured . . ." He put his hand to his head. "Why in the world would you rip out my *power matrix*?"

"Um . . . I needed to destroy your morale." I winced at the bad lie. "By leaving you powerless and impotent? Yeah, a symbol of my complete and total undermining of your authority! A defiant emblem! I carried it off, like an ancient barbarian warlord, who would steal the heart of—"

"Wasn't that a lot of work? Couldn't you have just discharged the acclivity ring like a normal human being?"

"I don't know how to do that."

"Never mind. You can make it up to me later. By, maybe, *not insulting me* in front of the rest of the flight. For one day at least?"

I stood there, processing. He seemed to *actually* not want a fight. Huh.

"Look," Jerkface said, glancing at the black car. "I know something of what it's like to live in your parents' shadow. All right? I'm sorry. I won't do . . . what I did again. But no more punching me, okay?"

"Okay."

He nodded to me and jogged off, apologizing to the admiral as he climbed into the car.

"Next time I'll kick instead!" I called after him. "Ha!" But of course he couldn't hear. I watched them drive off, then shook my head and picked up my pack. I didn't understand Jorgen at all. I was still in the DDF somehow. And he . . . Jorgen didn't *want* revenge. He didn't *want* to fight me.

Though once I might have laughed at that, strangely I found the way he'd acted to be noble. He put the flight first.

Set your sights on something higher . . .

I lifted the radio to my head as I walked out of the base, a mess of conflicting emotions—but mostly relieved. "M-Bot. Play that song fragment for me a few times more, please."

25

I settled into my Poco, wearing my pressure suit and helmet—my first time in a real cockpit since Bim and Morningtide had died.

That immediately made something inside me hurt. Would it be like this every time, from now on? Would I always have this quiet worry at the back of my mind? The one that whispered, "Which of your friends won't make it home from *this* mission?"

Today was supposed to be something more routine though. Not a battle. I powered on the Poco and felt that wonderful hum—the one the simulation couldn't imitate.

I gripped the control sphere in my right hand, the throttle in my left, then lifted off and climbed into the sky alongside the other six fighters. Jorgen counted us off with confirmations, then called Cobb.

"Skyward Flight ready. Orders, sir?"

"Go to 304.16-1240-25000," Cobb said.

"Flight, set coordinates," Jorgen said. "I'll take point. In case of a Krell ambush, I'll fall back with Arturo and FM. Nedd, you're with Quirk in the middle formation. Spin and Hurl, I want you in the rear prepared to spray covering fire."

"There won't be an ambush, cadet," Cobb said, sounding amused. "Just get to the indicated location."

We flew, and stars . . . it felt good. The ship trembled as it moved, responding to my commands. Wind currents were so much more *alive* than the simulation made them seem. I wanted to swoop back and forth, fly low and skim the crater-marked surface, then soar up high and buzz the debris field at the very edges of space.

I kept myself under control. I *could* do that.

Eventually, we approached a large group of fighters flying way up higher. There were a good five flights up there.

"Nearing coordinates," Jorgen said to Cobb. "What's going on? A training exercise?"

"For you, yes," Cobb said. Overhead, a few streaks of light marked smaller bits of debris breaking into the atmosphere. I watched, concerned.

"Hey, know-it-all," Cobb said.

"Yes, sir?" Arturo answered immediately.

"What causes debris falls?" Cobb asked.

"Various things," Arturo said. "There are a lot of ancient mechanisms up there, and though many still work, their power matrixes are slowly running out, so their orbits decay and they fall. Other times, collisions happen."

"Right," Cobb said. "Well, that's what we're facing here. There was some kind of collision between two enormous chunks of metal above, and that's making some debris lose its orbit. We can expect a Krell incursion, and those fighters are here to watch. But you're here for another reason: a little target practice."

"On what, sir?"

Several large chunks of debris dropped out of the sky, burning past the flights above us.

"The debris," I guessed.

"I want you flying in pairs," Cobb said. "You're going to practice

231

formations and do careful runs. Pick a larger piece of debris, follow it for a few seconds, then tag it for salvage to investigate. Your destructors have been outfitted to fire beacons if you pull the rate control dial out until it clicks."

"That's it?" Hurl said. "Tagging pieces of space junk?"

"Space junk can't dodge," Cobb said, "doesn't have shields, and accelerates predictably. I figure that's right about your skill level. Besides, you'll often be ordered to tag salvage during debris falls, while waiting to see if the Krell attack. It's good practice—so don't complain, or I'll stuff you back in the simulations for another month."

"We're ready and willing, sir," Jorgen said. "Hurl included. Thank you for this opportunity."

Hurl made a few gagging noises into a private line to FM and Kimmalyn—the lights on the console under the ship numbers showed me who was listening—and she didn't leave me off. Which seemed like maybe a step forward?

Jorgen arranged us into pairs and set us to work. When larger chunks of debris fell from the sky, we'd swoop down behind them and match speed—like we'd been taught—before shooting a radio beacon into them. The most useful debris were the ones that glowed blue with acclivity stone. We could salvage that to make ships.

I let myself enjoy the work. It wasn't actual fighting, but the feel of the dive, the thrill of targeting and firing . . . I could imagine the chunks of space debris as Krell ships.

"Are you ignoring me again?" M-Bot asked in my ear. "I think you're ignoring me again."

"How can I ignore you," I said with a grunt, tagging another chunk of debris, "if I don't know you're listening?"

"I'm *always* listening."

"Don't you think that's a little creepy?"

"Nope! What are you doing?"

I pulled out of my dive, with Hurl on my wing, and settled back into formation to wait for my next turn. "I'm shooting space junk."

"What did it do to you?"

"Nothing. It's just practice."

"But it can't even shoot back!"

"M-Bot, it's *space junk*."

"As if that were an excuse."

"It . . . It actually is," I said. "It's a really good excuse."

Kimmalyn took a run, Arturo at her wing. She did pretty well, for her, though Jorgen still found reason to nitpick. "Pull in tighter," he told her as she swooped down. "Now don't ride it too close—if you were using real destructors to shoot it, chunks might fly back and hit you. Make sure you don't squeeze too hard when you fire . . ."

"Not to complain," she said, sounding tense, "but I do believe I should focus right now."

"Sorry," Jorgen snapped. "I'll try to be less helpful in the future."

"Dear, I think you'll find that difficult." She tagged the chunk of debris, then sighed in relief.

"Nice work, Quirk," Jorgen said. "Nedder, you take next run with FM on wing."

Kimmalyn fell into line as, up above, several chunks of space debris fell at once. The regular fighters moved out of the way, letting them pass. We were flying relatively high, to give us time for good dives, so the ground was far below—though we were still very far from the rubble belt itself, the lowest layers of which flew three hundred kilometers above the surface of the planet.

Nedd picked one of the chunks and fell in behind it, ignoring the other three. So Kimmalyn charged her destructors for long range and then sniped all three pieces, tagging one right after another, without missing a single time.

"Stop showing off, Quirk," Cobb said.

"Sorry, sir."

I frowned, then called Cobb in private. "Cobb? Do you ever wonder if we're doing this wrong?"

"Of course you're doing it wrong. You're cadets."

"No," I said. "I mean . . ." How could I explain? "Quirk, she's a *really* good shot. Isn't there a better way to use her? She feels like a failure in most of our exercises, because she's the worst pilot. Maybe she could just snipe for us?"

"And how long do you think she'd sit out there popping off Krell before they swarmed her? Remember, if they decide any one pilot is too dangerous, they focus on that person."

"Maybe we could use that. You said that anytime you can anticipate an enemy, that's an advantage, right?"

He grunted. "Leave the tactics to the admirals, Spin." He turned off the line as Nedd successfully tagged the debris.

"Good night, sweet prince," M-Bot whispered as the junk crashed to the ground. "Or princess. Or, most likely, genderless piece of inanimate space junk."

I looked up above, watching for more debris. Hurl would be on the next run, and I'd be her wing. Some junk was definitely moving up there. Several pieces of it . . . swarming down . . .

Not junk. *Krell.*

I bolted upright, hand going tense on my control sphere. Multiple flights of the enemy emerged from the rubble belt, and the full pilots moved to engage them.

"Fly down to twenty thousand feet, cadets," Cobb said. "You'll be here as reserves, but those pilots should be able to handle this. Looks like . . . only about thirty enemy ships."

I settled back, but couldn't relax as explosions began to light the sky. Soon, the debris falling around us wasn't solely from the rubble belt. Cobb called for Hurl to do her run. Apparently we were going to continue despite the fighting, which was probably good training, as I thought about it.

Hurl performed an excellent maneuver, with a precise set of shots at the end. "Nice," I told her as we fell into line. I didn't get a reply, of course.

"Alas, poor space junk," M-Bot said. "I would have pretended to know you, if I were capable of lying."

"Can't you do anything useful?"

". . . This isn't useful?"

"What about those Krell up there?" I asked him. "Can't you . . . I don't know, tell me about their ships or something?"

"At this range, I have access only to general scanners," he said. "They're merely little blips to me, no specifics."

"You can't watch in more detail?" I asked. "Cobb and the admirals have some kind of hologram that replicates the battlefield, so they're using scanners or something to construct what's going on."

"That's ridiculous," M-Bot said. "I'd have noticed a video feed, unless it was a localized short-range beacon created by echolocation devices in the various ships that . . . Ooooooooooooh!"

A flaming starship—one of ours—came down in a death spiral, and though Arturo tried to get in close and spear it with his light-lance to help, the ship was too far out.

The pilot didn't eject. They tried until the last moment to pull up, rescue their ship. I steeled myself, looking back up at the battlefield.

"Oooooooooooooooooooooooooooooooooooooooooooooooooooh," M-Bot said.

"Well?" I asked.

"I found the video feed," he said. "You're all so *slow*. You really fly like that? How can you stand it?"

"Moving faster would either break our ships or crush those of us inside with g-forces."

235

"Ah yes. Human squishiness quotient. Is that why you're so mad at that space junk? Jealousy is not pretty, Spensa."

"Weren't you going to do something useful?"

"Computing enemy attack patterns," M-Bot said. "It will take me a few minutes to finish running simulations and analyzing predictive data." He paused. "Huh. I didn't know I could do those things."

"Is it my turn?" Arturo asked over the general line, and I jumped. I kept expecting them to hear M-Bot talking to me, though the AI said he was sending his own feed directly into my helmet, then intercepting my outward feed to edit away any sign of his voice or my responses to him. Somehow, he did all of this in the blink of an eye, before my signals reached the rest of my flight.

"Hold a moment," Cobb said. "Something is odd about this attack. Can't put my finger on it."

A large shadow shifted overhead. Enormous. It was so big, my mind reeled to comprehend it. It was like the sky itself was falling. A sudden shower of hundreds of pieces of debris rained down, a blazing hail. And behind it, that *something*. That enormous, inconceivable *something*.

"Pull back," Cobb said. "Flightleader, scramble your ships and get them back to—"

In a sudden burst of motion, the battle above us became the battle *around* us as ships from both sides dodged downward. Krell ships and human ships scattered in front of the enormous thing that was falling from above—a dark metallic cube the size of a mountain.

A ship? What ship could be that size? It was vaster than a city. Had even the flagship of our fleet been that big? I had always imagined it as a slightly larger troop transport.

The fighters kept shooting at one another as they lowered their altitude. Our little flight was suddenly in the center of a firestorm of destructor blasts and falling chunks of burning metal.

"Out!" Jorgen said. "Accelerate to Mag-5 and follow my lead. Local heading 132, away from those dogfighters behind us."

I engaged my booster, zipping forward, Hurl on my wing.

"That's a *ship*," Arturo said. "Look how slowly it's falling. Those are functioning acclivity rings across the bottom. Hundreds of them."

A shadow blanketed the land. I leaned into my throttle, speeding up to Mag-5, well above normal dogfighting speeds. Any faster, and we wouldn't be able to respond to our surroundings. Indeed, as a fighter-size chunk of debris fell near us, we barely had time to react. Half of our flight dodged left, the other half right.

I went left with Kimmalyn and Nedd, slowing for more maneuverability. Destructor blasts sprayed in front of me as two of our starfighters barreled past, followed by *six* Krell ships. I cursed and dodged around them, followed by a whimpering Kimmalyn, who took my wing position.

"Analysis complete!" M-Bot said. "Oh! Wow. You're busy."

I dove, but we had picked up a tail. The Krell ship sprayed blasts around me. I cursed, then pulled back. "Go ahead of me, Quirk!"

She sped past and I broke right, getting the Krell ship to focus on me—the closer target.

"You really should have waited for my computations before beginning," M-Bot noted. "Impatience is a serious character flaw."

I gritted my teeth, spinning through a sequence of dodges.

"Spin, Quirk, Nedder," Jorgen said on the line. "Where are you? Why didn't you follow my—"

"*I'm taking fire*, Jerkface," I snapped.

"I'm on you, Spin," Nedd said in my ear. "If you can level out, I'll try and shoot him down."

"You won't get through the shield. Quirk, you still there?"

"At your three," she said, voice trembling.

237

"Be ready to pick this guy off."

"Oh! Um, okay. Okay . . ."

The enormous falling vessel loomed overhead. Arturo had been right; its descent was slow, steady. But it was old and broken, with gaping holes in it. The battlefield continued in a wide, shadowed section of open air underneath it, filled with dogfighting ships and lines of destructor fire.

My tail got a shot on me, and my shield crackled.

Focus. I'd practiced this a hundred times in simulation. I pulled up into a loop, my tail following. At the top of the curve, I performed a starfighter maneuver—ignoring air resistance, I turned my ship on its axis and slammed on my overburn, darting out of the loop to the side.

My GravCaps flared, buffering most of the g-forces, but my stomach still practically climbed up my throat. The simulations did *not* do justice to exactly how disorienting this was, particularly when the GravCaps cut out and I got slammed back into my seat.

I was supposed to be able to handle that kind of force, and I didn't black out—so technically, I *did* handle it. But I nearly threw up.

My proximity alarm went off. The Krell ship, as hoped, hadn't compensated fast enough. It had continued the loop, and I shot out of my maneuver right past it. I fought through the nausea and slammed the IMP—taking down my shield and that of my tail.

I braced myself. I was completely open. If that Krell got turned toward me and fired off a single shot—

A flash came behind me, and a shock wave washed across my ship.

"I got him," Kimmalyn said. "I . . . I did it!"

"Thanks," I said, exhaling in relief, letting off my overburners. I continued in a straight line, starting to slow, as I turned off my booster and primed my shield igniter. My helmet felt hot and sweaty against my head as my fingers moved through the familiar motions. Thank the stars for Cobb's training; my body knew what to do.

A Krell ship came in, spotting me coasting on my momentum. I cringed, but a spray of weapons fire sent the ship scattering away.

"I've got you," Nedd said, zipping overhead. "Quirk, join me in a defensive pattern."

"Gotcha," Kimmalyn said.

"No need," I said, slamming the igniter. "I'm back up. Shall we get out of here?"

"Gladly," Kimmalyn said.

I led the other two in a course that I hoped would get us out, then called Jorgen. "We're at heading 304.8," I told him. "Did the rest of you get out from underneath this thing?"

"Affirmative," Jorgen said. "We passed out of the shadow at 303.97-1210.3-21200. We'll wait for you here, Spin."

He sounded calm, which was honestly more than I could say for myself. I couldn't help imagining more empty seats in our classroom.

"Are you ready for my analysis?" M-Bot said.

"That depends on how often it will mention mushrooms."

"Only once, I'm afraid. The thing you see looming overhead is around half of a C-137-KJM orbital shipyard with added delver training facility. I don't know exactly what that is, but I believe it must have been for manufacturing starships. There's no sign of the other half, but this chunk has probably been floating up there for centuries, judging by the low power output of those acclivity rings.

"My projections indicate its orbit has decayed now that it doesn't have enough power for self-correction. It doesn't seem to have an AI—or if it does have one, it refuses to talk to me, which is rude. The Krell attack patterns indicate a defensive goal, intended to keep you away from the station."

239

"Really?" I asked. "Repeat that last part."

"Hm? Oh, it's obvious from their flight patterns. They aren't worried about actually killing you or getting to your base or anything. Today, they just want to keep you away from this ship, likely because of the fantastic salvage it would provide for your backward, fleshy society of slow-ship-fliers."

That made sense. They sometimes shot down debris to keep us from getting acclivity rings. How worried must they be about us capturing this thing, with hundreds of them?

"Also, it looks a little like a mushroom," M-Bot added.

Another pair of DDF fighters—perhaps the same ones we'd seen before—bolted past, tailed by a large group of Krell.

"Hey," Nedd said. "Spin and Quirk, you two get out. You're almost there. I need to do something."

"What?" I said, turning to look over my shoulder. "Nedder?"

He broke off from our flight pattern, giving chase to the Krell ships that had passed us. What did he think he was doing?

I turned and followed. "Nedder? Scud."

"Spin?" Kimmalyn said.

"We're not leaving him. Come on."

We raced after Nedd, who was tailing the six Krell ships. They—in turn—were flying after two Sigo-class fighters painted blue, indicating they were from Nightstorm Flight. Nedd clearly intended to help, but one cadet against *six* Krell?

"Nedd!" I said, "I'm all for fighting—you know that—but we also need to follow orders."

He didn't respond. Ahead, the two Nightstorms—overwhelmed by the enemy fire—did something desperate. They flew up close to the large shipyard, then curved around and flew *into* a hole in its side. A gaping blackness, perhaps where another section of the shipyard had once been attached.

The whole structure was still falling, but very slowly. Eventually it would crash down—and I doubted we wanted to be anywhere nearby when it did. I watched as the Krell ships pursued our pilots into the depths of the ancient ship, and Nedd barreled after them. So I gritted my teeth and followed.

"Spin," Kimmalyn said. "I don't think I can do that. If I try to fly in there, I *swear* I'll crash."

"Yeah, okay," I said. "Go join Jorgen and the others."

"All right," she said. She zipped off to the left, flying out from underneath the shadow of the falling machine.

I, instead, dove into the breach, chasing into the darkness after Nedd.

26

I hurtled through the innards of the ancient station—a large open blackness, rimmed by cranes and other construction equipment, lit by flickering emergency floodlights. The writing on one wall, in a circular pattern, reminded me of some of the old equipment down in the caverns—like the strange room I had often passed where the ceiling and floor had been covered in this writing. I could only assume the old occupants of this planet had constructed ships in here—but why had they needed so much space? Our starfighters were swallowed by the cavernous chamber.

The two DDF fighters soared upward, chased by the six Krell, who fired liberally, spraying destructor blasts through the darkness. Nedd tried to catch up, and I tailed him—hitting my overburn for a moment of extra acceleration.

I couldn't call the other fighters. Cadet ships weren't normally equipped with radio channels to call full pilots. They didn't want us interfering.

I switched to Nedd's direct channel. "This is insane," I said. "Thank you so much for giving me an excuse to try it."

"Spin?" he said. "You're still with me?"

"So far. What's the plan?"

"Help those fighters somehow. Maybe we can get close? Those Krell are flying in a—" He cut off as he buzzed past an old crane, nearly clipping it. "They're flying in a group. We could hit them all at once, with a well-placed IMP."

"I'll follow your lead," I said, dodging underneath the crane. "But if Jerkface asks, I'm *totally* going to claim I tried to talk you out of this."

"You? As the voice of reason? Spin, I'm an idiot, and even *I* wouldn't believe that."

I grinned, then joined Nedd in accelerating to Mag-1.2, trying to catch up to the Krell. Unfortunately, the DDF pilots broke to the right—straight into a tunnel leading farther into the depths of the old station.

A part of me couldn't believe we were doing this. Flying through the center of an ancient piece of debris *while it was in the middle of plummeting toward the ground*? How long did we have until the thing crashed? Minutes at most?

I gritted my teeth, letting up on the throttle as Nedd and I banked, then chased the Krell into the tunnel. Red lights lined the tunnel, and they flashed in a blur as we zipped through at Mag-1.2, already a dangerous speed for what amounted to indoors. I didn't dare go faster, but a quick glance at my proximity sensor indicated the Krell were still well outside IMP range.

Nedd unloaded with his destructor, and I followed his lead—but as Cobb had warned, aiming was difficult, even with six targets swarming in front of us. The Krell shields easily absorbed the few shots that connected.

Far ahead, our fellow pilots speared the wall with light-lances and cornered into another tunnel. The Krell followed, less adroit. I speared the wall with my own lance, then pulled myself into a tight curve to follow. My GravCaps flashed, absorbing the g-forces and keeping me from getting flattened.

I gave them a workout as we wound through the innards of the ship, taking turn after turn—moving through such a frantic, tight sequence, I didn't fire a single shot. My attention was totally consumed by watching the Krell thrusters—using their motions as a guidepost for where to place my next light-lance. Turn, release, dodge, lance, turn. Repeat.

"Just . . . a little . . . closer . . . ," Nedd said from right ahead of me.

Lance. Turn. Release.

"I've got an updated battle projection," M-Bot said happily.

Ahead, a Krell ship missed its turn, clipping the side of the tunnel wall. The shield absorbed the impact, but the rebound sent the ship slamming into the opposite wall. The sudden, violent explosion made me back off on my speed. I made my turn, barely, debris and sparks crackling off my ship's shield.

"You forgot I was here, didn't you?" M-Bot said.

"Busy," I said through gritted teeth. Nedd hadn't slowed at the explosion—in fact, he was overburning, closing in on Mag-1.5, trying to get closer to the remaining Krell.

I sped up to keep pace with him, but this was starting to feel like too much. Even for me.

"I could just go back into hibernation, if you're not interested in talking," M-Bot noted. "You'd, um, miss me, if I did that, right?"

"Sure."

"Ah, you humans are so sentimental! Hahaha. By the way, you have precisely three and a half minutes until this station hits the surface. Maybe less than that, as the Krell have begun firing upon it."

"What?"

"Now that the bulk of your ships have retreated, the Krell are focusing on the station, trying to keep it out of your hands. I believe some bombers are preparing explosive charges on the top, and ordinary fighters outside are destroying all the acclivity rings to drop it faster."

"Scud. We could probably build several *flights'* worth of ships with the salvage from this place." The Krell weren't going to let that happen.

But why allow this thing to fall in the first place? Why not destroy it up above?

Trying to figure out Krell motivations now was a waste of time. I pulled into another turn after Nedd. I could barely make out the enemy; they were losing us.

Far ahead, the bright orange flash of an explosion lit the tunnels. One of the ships we were trying to protect had just been destroyed.

"Nedd!" I shouted into the comm. "This place is coming down. We have to get out!"

"No. I have to help!"

I took aim, then—gritting my teeth—risked spearing him with my light-lance. The glowing red line of light stuck to him and made his shield crackle. I cut my booster, then spun my ship on its acclivity ring and boosted the other direction, pulling him backward, slowing his ship.

"Let go of me!" he shouted.

"Nedd . . . We can't help. We're not good enough for this sort of thing yet. Stars above, it's a wonder we survived that run through the tunnels."

"But . . . But . . ."

We hovered there, burners pulling us opposite directions, connected by a cord of light.

"Coward," he whispered.

The word hit me like a slap to the face. I wasn't—I couldn't be—*Coward*.

"I'm cutting my booster," he said. "Step yours down, or we'll end up careening into that wall."

I bit off a response to him, then lowered my thrust before cutting the light-lance. We fell still, but somewhere distant, the entire structure groaned and shook.

"Which way?" he asked. "Where do we go?"

"I don't know."

M-Bot made a throat-clearing noise. "Would you like instructions on how to escape the flaming death trap that you've inconveniently found yourself—"

"Yes!" I snapped.

"No need to get prickly. Fly ahead until I tell you, then take a left."

"Follow me!" I said to Nedd, slamming the throttle forward and leaping into motion. I tore through the tunnels, the flare of my booster reflecting off the abandoned metal walls. Nedd followed.

"Left, down that tunnel just ahead," M-Bot noted. "Great. Now go two tunnels—no, not that one—there. Take that one."

I used my light-lance to turn sharply into the tunnel.

"You have slightly under two minutes until you die a fiery death and *I'm* left with only Rig and the slug. I haven't been able to compute which of those two is the less engaging conversationalist. Take that tunnel above you."

I followed his instructions, curving through the maddening complex of turns and tunnels. The sounds outside grew louder. Wrenching steel. Shaking. Hollow explosions.

Sweat soaked the sides of my helmet. I gave my entire attention to the flying, absorbed. Dedicated. *Focused.*

Though I never lost control of my flying, a part of me started to feel disconnected. The insides of my helmet began to grow hot, and I could swear that I could *hear voices* inside my head. Just fragments of words.

. . . *detonate* . . .

. . . *turn* . . .

. . . *booster* . . .

Nedd and I burst back into that cavernous opening at the outer rim of the shipyard. My focus faded into relief, and I didn't need M-Bot's instructions to turn straight for the glowing gap in the wall.

Nedd and I darted out of the hole and nearly plowed right into the ground. The shipyard had almost hit the surface.

I pulled up and skimmed the blue-grey surface, kicking up dust behind me. Nedd cursed softly. We'd entered a narrow, shrinking gap of space between station and ground.

"The Krell have just detonated several large explosives on the top of the shipyard," M-Bot said.

I bolted forward under the shipyard. The steel ceiling overhead lowered, chunks of metal breaking off and warping around us as the thing's structural integrity collapsed.

"At current velocity, you will not escape the blast wave," M-Bot said softly.

"Overburn, Nedd!" I shouted, slamming my throttle all the way forward. "Mag-10!" The GravCaps kicked in, but quickly overloaded, and a moment later I was smashed backward in my seat.

My face grew heavy, the skin pulling back from my eyes and around my mouth. My arms felt leaden and tried to slip away from the controls.

Ahead, the way out—freedom—was an ever-shrinking line of light.

My Poco started to rattle as I hit Mag-10, then continued, pushing to Mag-10.5. The vibration got worse, and my shield grew bright from the sudden heat of wind resistance.

Blessedly, it was enough. Nedd and I exploded out from underneath the shipyard as it crashed down, spraying dust and debris after us. But at these speeds, we quickly outran that—and outran the sound of the crash, since we were going several times the speed of sound.

I breathed out, decelerating carefully, the rattling subsiding.

Nedd on my wing, we swooped around—and in those seconds

of flight after escaping, we'd gotten far enough away that I couldn't even see the dust of the crashing shipyard. My sensors barely registered the shock wave when it finally hit us on our way to rendezvous with the others.

Eventually, we did get close enough that I could make out the enormous dust cloud the crash had caused. The wreckage itself was just a big dark shadow in the dust, swarming with smaller specks above. Krell ships, making sure nothing useful could be salvaged from the enormous wreck. Acclivity stone could often be recovered from the core of fallen debris, but concentrated destructor fire—or the intense heat from the right kind of an explosion—would ruin it.

"Finally," Jorgen said as we fell in with the flight. "What in the stars were you two thinking?"

I didn't respond, instead doing a count of our team. Seven ships, including mine. We'd all made it. We were sweaty, rattled, and solemn—almost nobody said anything as we met up with Riptide Flight for the return to base. But we were alive.

Coward.

Nedd's voice echoed inside my brain, more distracting than the heat from the sensors in my helmet, or the surreal place my thoughts had gone as we flew out. Had I really thought I'd heard voices?

I *wasn't* a coward. Sometimes you *had* to retreat. The entire DDF had pulled back from this fight. I wasn't less of a soldier because I had convinced Nedd to escape. Right?

It was growing dark by the time we landed at the launchpad. I stripped off my helmet and climbed from the cockpit, exhausted. Jorgen met me at the bottom of the ladder.

"You still haven't answered me," he snapped. "I left you alone during the flight back, as I'm sure you're rattled, but you *are* going to explain yourself." He grabbed me by the arm and held on to it tightly. "You nearly got Nedd killed with that stunt."

248

I sighed, then looked at his hand.

He carefully let go. "The question remains," he said. "That was crazy, even for you. I can't believe you'd—"

"As much as I like being the crazy one, Jerkface, I'm too tired to listen to you right now." I nodded toward Nedd's ship in the dim light. "He flew in. I followed. You'd rather I let him go alone?"

"Nedd?" Jorgen said. "He's too levelheaded for something like that."

"Maybe the rest of us are getting to him. All I know is there were a couple of Sigos from Nightstorm Flight who picked up some enemy tails, and Nedd would *not* let go."

"Nightstorm Flight?" Jorgen asked.

"Yeah. Why?"

Jorgen fell silent, then turned and walked toward Nedd's ship. I followed, feeling wrung out, my head starting to ache in a strange way—like needles behind my eyes. Nedd's ship was empty, and he wasn't with the others, who were gathering at the rooms near the launchpad to change out of their pressure suits. They were laughing together now that the stress of the battle had faded.

Jorgen took off down the path between launchpads, and I followed, confused, until we reached a line of seven Sigo-class starfighters branded with the Nightstorm Flight logo. They'd gotten back before us, and their pilots had already gone, leaving the ships to the maintenance crews.

Nedd knelt on the pavement near two empty spots in the line of ships.

"What?" I asked Jorgen.

"His brothers, Spin. They're wingmates, Nightstorm Six and Seven."

The pilots we'd been following. The ones who, it now became obvious, had both died in those dark tunnels.

27

Nedd didn't come to class the next day.

Or the day after that. Or all that week.

Cobb kept us busy running chase exercises. We swooped, dodged, and tagged one another, like real pilots.

But in the moments between the action, Nedd's voice haunted me. *Coward.*

I thought about it again as I sat in my classroom mockpit, running through exercises. I'd broken off the chase and had forced Nedd to abandon his brothers. Was that something any hero of legend would *ever* have done?

"Statistical projections indicate that if you'd remained in your pursuit for another seven seconds," M-Bot said as I ran through a holographic dogfighting exercise, "you'd have died in the crash-down or subsequent explosion."

"Could you have broken into the radio channel?" I said to him, whispering because we were in the classroom. "And called Nedd's brothers?"

"Yes, I probably could have."

"We should have thought of that. Maybe if we'd coordinated, we could have helped them escape."

"And how would you have explained your sudden ability to hack DDF communications signals?"

I dove in my chase of the holographic Krell, and didn't reply. If I'd been a true patriot, I'd have long ago turned the ship over to my superiors. But I wasn't a patriot. The DDF had betrayed and killed my father, then lied about it. I hated them for that . . . but hate them or not, I'd still come begging to them to let me fly.

Suddenly, that seemed to be another act of cowardice.

I growled softly, using my light-lance to spin around a chunk of hovering debris, then slamming my overburn. I darted past the Krell ship and hit my IMP, killing both of our shields, then rotated on my axis. That pointed my nose backward while I was still flying forward—but I managed to spray destructors at the Krell behind me, destroying it.

That was a dangerous maneuver on my part, as it oriented me the wrong way for watching where I was going. Indeed, another Krell ship immediately swooped in on my right flank and fired on me. I died with my "shield down" klaxon blaring in my ear.

"Pretty stunt," Cobb said in my ear as my hologram reset. "Great way to die."

I unbuckled and stood up, tearing off my helmet and tossing it aside. It bounced off my seat and clattered against the floor as I walked to the back of the room and started to pace.

Cobb stood in the center of the circle of imitation cockpits, little holographic ships spinning around him. He wore an earpiece to speak with us over our helmet lines. He eyed me as I paced, but he let me be.

"Scud, Quirk!" he yelled at Kimmalyn instead. "That fighter was obviously going through an S-4 sequence, trying to bait you! Pay attention, girl!"

"Sorry!" she exclaimed from inside her cockpit. "Oh, and sorry about that too!"

"Sir?" Arturo asked, shrouded in his training hologram. "The Krell do that a lot, don't they? Lead us along?"

"Hard to say," Cobb said with a grunt.

I continued to pace, working out my frustration—mostly at myself—as I listened. Though they were seated in the circle, their voices were muffled by their helmets and the mockpit enclosures. Hearing it all reassured me that when I whispered to M-Bot in my mockpit, the others wouldn't overhear, so long as I remembered to be very soft.

Their flight chitchat was calming to me. I slowly stopped my pacing, stepping up to join Cobb near the central hologram.

"The other day," Arturo continued, "with that big chunk of space debris. Their attack wasn't to defeat us, but to destroy it—and presumably keep us from salvaging it. Right?"

"Yes," Cobb said. "What's your point, Amphi?"

"Just that, sir, they must have known it was going to fall. They live out there, in space. And so they probably saw that chunk up there, all those years. They could have destroyed it at any time, but they waited until it fell. Why?"

I nodded. I'd wondered the very same thing.

"Krell motives are unknowable," Cobb said. "Other than their desire to exterminate us, of course."

"Why have they never attacked with more than a hundred ships at once?" Arturo continued. "Why do they continue to bait us into skirmishes, instead of sending in one overwhelming attack?"

"Why do they let salvage fall in the first place?" I added. "Without it, we wouldn't be able to get enough acclivity rings to keep up a resistance. Why don't *we* attack them in the rubble belt? Why wait for them to come down here and—"

"Enough training," Cobb said, walking over to his desk and hitting the button that disengaged all of the holograms.

"Sorry, sir," I said.

"Don't apologize, cadet," Cobb said. "You either, Amphisbaena. You both ask good questions. Everyone, helmets off. Sit up. Pay attention. Considering how long it's been, we've learned frighteningly little about the Krell—but I'll tell you what we *do* know."

I felt myself growing eager as the others removed their helmets. Answers? Finally?

"Sir," Jorgen said, standing up. "Aren't Krell details classified, only available to full pilots?"

Arturo groaned softly and rolled his eyes. His expression seemed to read: *Thank you, Jorgen, for never being any fun whatsoever.*

"Nobody likes a tattler, Jorgen," Cobb said. "Shut up and listen. You need to know this. You *deserve* to know this. Being a First Citizen gives me some leeway on what I can say."

I stepped back beside my mockpit as Cobb called up something with his hologram: a planet. Detritus? It did have chunks of metal floating around it, but the rubble belt extended farther—and was thicker—than I'd expected.

"This," he said, "is an approximation of our planet and the rubble belt. Truth is, we have only a rough idea what's up there. We lost a lot of whatever we did know when the Krell bombed the archive and our command staff back in LD-zero. But some of our scientists think that at one time, a shell surrounded the *entire planet,* like a metal shield. Problem is, a lot of those old mechanisms up there are still active—and they have guns."

He watched the holographic planet—which glowed softly blue and was transparent—launch a group of holographic fighters. They got close to the rubble belt, and were shot down by hundreds of destructors.

"It's dangerous up there," Cobb continued. "Even for the Krell. That's why the old fleet came here, to this old graveyard of a planet. What little the old people remember indicates that Detritus was known, but avoided, back in the day. Its shielding severely interfered with communications, and when facing the old orbital defense platforms, our fleet barely made it through to crash on the surface.

"The Krell don't seem to explore much out there. They might have known that old shipyard was going to fall, but getting to it through the rubble belt would have been costly. They seem to have found a few safe pathways to the planet, and they use those almost exclusively."

"So . . . ," I said, fascinated. This was all new to me. "Could we use those old defense platforms somehow?"

"We've tried," Cobb said. "But it's dangerous for us to fly up there as well—the platforms will fire on us too. Also, the Krell are more deadly up in space. Remember the way this planet is shielded? Well, the Krell have strange advanced communications abilities. The planet's shielding interferes with their capacity to talk to each other; we think that's why they fly worse down here.

"There's another issue, smaller," Cobb said, seeming to grow hesitant about something. "In space, beyond the planet, the Krell can . . . well, the old crews say that Krell technology lets them read what humans are thinking. And that some people are more susceptible to this than others."

I shared looks with the rest of the flight. I'd never heard anything like that before.

"Don't tell anyone I told you that part though," Cobb said.

"So . . . ," Arturo said. "This communication interference, and those orbital defenses, are why the Krell don't bombard us from space?"

"In the early days of Alta," Cobb said, "they tried to bring in some larger ships, but those got destroyed by orbital defenses.

254

The Krell can only get small, maneuverable ships through to attack us."

"That doesn't explain why they send relatively small flights," Arturo said. "Unless I'm wrong, they've never sent an assault larger than a hundred ships. Right?"

Cobb nodded.

"Why not send two hundred? Three hundred?"

"We don't know. Dig into the classified reports, and you'll find nothing more than wild theories. Perhaps a hundred ships is the most they can coordinate at once."

"Okay," Arturo said, "but why do they seem to only be able to prepare a single lifebuster at a time? Why not load every ship with one, and suicide them into us? Why—"

"What *are* they?" I interrupted. Arturo had good questions—but in my opinion, less important than that.

Arturo glanced at me, then nodded.

"Do we know, Cobb?" I asked. "In those secret files, does somebody know? Have we ever *seen* a Krell?"

Cobb changed the hologram to a hovering image of a burned-out helmet and some pieces of armor. I shivered. Krell remains. His hologram was a much more detailed, much more *real* version of the artistic renditions I'd seen. The photo showed a few scientists standing at a table around the armor, which was squat and bulky. Kind of squarish.

"This is all we've ever been able to recover," Cobb said. "And we only find it in occasional ships we shoot down. One in a hundred or fewer. They aren't human, of that we're sure." He showed another image, a closer-up hologram of one of the helmets, burned out from a crash.

"There are theories," Cobb continued. "The old people, who lived on the *Defiant* itself, talk of things impossible to our current understanding. Maybe the reason we never find anything but armor is because there isn't anything else to find. Maybe the

Krell *are* the armor. In the old days, there were legends of something strange. Machines that can think."

Machines that can think.

Machines with advanced communications technology.

I suddenly felt cold. The room seemed to fade, and I stood there beside my mockpit, hearing the others talk as if from far away.

"That's crazy," Hurl said. "A piece of metal can't think, any more than a rock can. Or that door. Or my canteen."

"More crazy than the idea that they can read minds?" Arturo asked. "I've never heard anything like that."

"There are obviously wonders in this galaxy that we can barely comprehend," Cobb said. "After all, the *Defiant* and other ships could travel between stars in the blink of an eye. Thinking machines would explain why so many Krell cockpits we investigate are empty, and why the 'armor' we recover never seems to have any bodies in it."

Machines that can think.

Cobb called the end of the day then, and we all gathered our things to leave for dinner. Kimmalyn and FM both complained that they had a cold—one had been going around—so Cobb suggested they go back to their room and rest. He said he'd have an aide send dinner to their bunks.

I heard all of this, but didn't really. Instead, I sat down in a daze. M-Bot. A ship that could think, and could infiltrate our communications with apparent ease. What if . . . what if I was repairing a Krell? Why hadn't I ever bothered to *think* about that? How could I be so blind to what seemed like an obvious possibility?

He has a cockpit, I thought, *with English writing. Facilities for a pilot. And he says he can't fly the ship himself.*

But that could be a ruse, right? He said he couldn't lie, but I had only his word on that. I . . .

"Spin?" Cobb asked, stopping near my mockpit. "You aren't catching that cold too, are you?"

I shook my head. "This is just a lot to take in."

Cobb grunted. "Well, maybe it's a load of cold slag. Truth is, once we lost the archive, most everything about the old days became hearsay."

"Do you mind if we tell Nedd about this?" I asked him. "When he gets back?"

"He's not coming back," Cobb said. "The admiral officially removed him from the cadet rolls this morning."

"What?" I said, standing up, surprised. "Did he ask to be removed?"

"He didn't report for duty, Spin."

"But . . . his brothers . . ."

"Being unable to control your emotions, grief included, is a sign that one is unfit for duty. At least that's how Ironsides and the other DDF brass see it. I say it's a good thing Nedd is out. That boy was too smart for all this anyway . . ." He hobbled out the door.

I sank back down into my seat. So we really were just six now. And if being unable to control emotions made one unfit for duty . . . what about me? It was all piling on top of me. The loss of friends, the worry about M-Bot, the voices that whispered deep down inside that I was in fact a coward.

All my life, I'd fought with a chip on my shoulder, thundering that I *would* be a pilot and I *would* be good enough. Where was that confidence now?

I'd always assumed that when I made it—when I finally got here—I'd stop feeling so alone.

I dug in my pack and raised my radio. "M-Bot, are you there?"

"Acclivity ring: functional, but lacking power. Boosters: nonfunctional. Cytonic hyperdrive: nonfunctional." He paused.

"That's a yes, in case you were confused. I'm here, because I can't go anywhere."

"Were you listening in on our conversation?"

"Yes."

"And?"

"And I admit, I was running some calculations on the likelihood of mushrooms growing inside that building, as your conversation was—typical of humans—slightly boring. But not completely! So you should feel—"

"M-Bot. Are you a Krell?"

"What? No! Of course I'm not a Krell. Why would you think that I am? How could you think . . . Wait, calculating. Oh. You think because I'm an AI, and they're likely AIs, that we must be the same?"

"You have to admit it's suspicious."

"I'd be offended if I could be offended," he said. "Maybe I should start calling you a cow, since you have four limbs, are made of meat, and have *rudimentary* biological mental capacities."

"Would you *know* if you were a Krell?" I asked him. "Maybe you forgot."

"I'd know," he said.

"You've forgotten why you came to Detritus," I pointed out. "You have only one image of your pilot, if that's even really him. You can barely remember anything about my species. Maybe you never knew. Maybe your memory bank is filled only with the bits that the Krell know about us, and you invented this entire story."

"I'm writing a new subroutine now," he said. "To properly express my outrage. It's going to take time to get right. Give me a few minutes."

"M-Bot . . ."

"Just a sec. Patience is a virtue, Spensa."

I sighed, but started packing up my things. I felt hollowed out.

Empty. Not afraid, of course. I bathed in fires of destruction and reveled in the screams of the defeated. I didn't get *afraid*.

But maybe, deep down, I was . . . worried. Nedd dropping out had hit me harder than it should have.

I threw my pack on my shoulder and clipped the radio to its side. I set it to flash a light if M-Bot or someone else tried to contact me. I didn't want him talking out of it while I walked the hallways, though I needn't have worried. The building was empty; Cobb had dismissed us late, and the other flights had already gone to dinner. I didn't spot any MPs or random support staff as I walked slowly toward the exit, my feet leaden.

I wasn't certain I could keep doing this. Getting up early, working all morning on M-Bot. Getting wrung out by lessons each day, then trudging back to my cave at night. Sleeping fitfully, dreaming of the people I'd failed or—worse—having nightmares about running away . . .

"Pssst!"

I stopped, then glanced at the radio strapped to the side of my backpack.

"Pssssssssssssssssssssssssssssssssssttt! Spensa!"

I looked up and down the hallway. To my right—was that *Kimmalyn* there, in a doorway, wearing black? "Quirk?"

She waved me forward urgently. I frowned, suspicious.

Then I wanted to kick myself. *Idiot. This is Kimmalyn.*

I walked to her. "What are you—"

"Shhh!" she said, then scrambled down the hallway and peeked around a corner. She waved at me to follow, and more confused than anything else, I did.

This continued for a couple of turns through empty corridors—we even had to pull into the bathroom and she made me wait with her there, explaining nothing, until we finally reached a hallway lined with doors. The girls' bunks. Two unfamiliar young women—wearing flight suits and the patch of Stardragon Flight—stood chatting outside one of the rooms.

Kimmalyn held me there, crouching at the corner until the two girls finally walked off in the other direction. I didn't miss that Kimmalyn and I had come in the back way, the opposite direction of the mess hall. So was she sick, or not?

After the two girls left, FM's head—her short hair clipped back with a glittering barrette—popped out of one of the doors. She gestured with an urgent wave. Kimmalyn dashed down the hall to her, and I followed, ducking into their room.

FM slammed the door, then grinned. Their small room was as I remembered it, though one of the beds had been removed, when Morningtide died. That left a bunk on the left wall, and a single bed by the right. A pile of blankets lay lumped between them, and the dresser held two trays of food: steaming soup in bowls, with algae tofu and slices of thick bread. Real bread. With real imitation butter.

My mouth started watering.

"We asked for extra," Kimmalyn said, "but they sent soup, because they think we're sick. Still, 'You can't ask for more when you already have it,' as the Saint said."

"They removed the extra bed," FM said, "so we piled some blankets on the floor. The trick is going to be using the lavatories—but we'll run interference for you."

It finally sank in. They'd *pretended* to be sick so they could order food into the room—and share it. They'd snuck me to the room, and made a "bed" for me.

Stars. Gratitude surged up inside me.

I was going to cry.

Warriors did *not* cry.

"Oh! You look angry," Kimmalyn said. "Don't be angry. We're not implying you're too weak to walk to your cave! We just thought . . . you know . . ."

"It would be nice to take a break," FM said. "Even a great warrior can take the occasional break, right, Spin?"

I nodded, not trusting myself to speak.

"Great!" Kimmalyn said. "Let's dig in. Subterfuge makes me *famished*."

28

That soup tasted better than the blood of my enemies.

Considering I'd never actually *tasted* the blood of my enemies, perhaps that didn't do justice to the soup.

It tasted better than soup should. It tasted of laughter, and love, and appreciation. The warmth of it glowed inside me like ignited rocket fuel. I snuggled in the blankets, holding the big bowl in my lap, while Kimmalyn and FM chatted.

I fought down the tears. I *would not* cry.

But the soup tasted of home. Somehow.

"I told you the costume would make her come with me," Kimmalyn was saying as she sat on her bed, cross-legged. "Black is the color of *intrigue*."

"You're insane," FM said, wagging her spoon. "You're lucky nobody saw you. Defiants are all too eager to look for a reason to be offended."

"You're Defiant too, FM," I said. "You were born here, like the rest of us. You're a citizen of the United Defiant Caverns. Why do you keep pretending you're something different?"

FM grinned in an eager way. It seemed that she *liked* that sort

of question. "Being a Defiant," she said, "isn't just about our na-
tionality. It's always expressed as a mindset. 'A true Defiant will
think this way' or 'To be Defiant, you need to never back down,'
things like that. So, by their own logic, I can un-Defiant myself
through personal choices."

"And . . . you want to?" I said, cocking my head.

Kimmalyn handed me another slice of bread. "She thinks you
all might be a touch . . . bellicose."

"There's that word again," I said. "Who talks like that?"

"People who are erudite," Kimmalyn said, sipping her
soup.

"I refuse to be trapped by bonds of autocracy and national-
ism," FM said. "To survive, our people have become necessarily
hardened, but alongside it we have enslaved ourselves. Most people never question, and doggedly go through the motions of an
obedient life. Others have increased aggression to the point that
it's hard to have natural feelings!"

"*I* have natural feelings," I said. "And I'll fight anyone who
says otherwise."

FM eyed me.

"I'd insist on swords at dawn," I said, eating the bread. "But
I'll probably be too full of bread to get up. Is this seriously what
you all get to eat *every day*?"

"Well, what do you eat, dear?" Kimmalyn said.

"Rats," I said. "And mushrooms."

"Every day?"

"I used to put pepper on the rats, but I ran out."

The two of them shared a look.

"It's an embarrassment to the DDF, what the admiral has done
to you," FM said. "But it's a natural outgrowth of the totalitarian
need for absolute power over those who resist her—the very *example* of the hypocrisy of the system. Defiance is not 'Defiant' to
them unless it doesn't actually defy anything."

I shot a glance at Kimmalyn, who shrugged. "She's extremely passionate about this."

"We are propping up a government that has overreached its bounds in the name of public safety," FM said. "The people must speak up and rise against the upper class who holds them enslaved!"

"Upper class, like you?" I asked.

FM looked down at her soup, then sighed. "I'd go to the Disputer meetings, and my parents would just pat me on the head and explain to everyone else that I was going through a counterculture phase. Then they signed me up for flight school, and . . . well, I mean, I get to *fly*."

I nodded. That part I understood.

"I figure, if I become a famous pilot, I can speak for the little guys, you know? I'm more likely to be able to change things here than down in the deep caverns, wearing ball gowns and sitting primly next to my sisters. Right? Don't you think?"

"Sure," I said. "That makes perfect sense. Right, Quirk?"

"I keep telling her that," Kimmalyn said to me, "but I think it will mean more from you."

"Why me?" I asked. "FM, didn't you say people like me have unnatural emotions?"

"Yes, but you can't help being a product of your environment!" FM said. "It's not *your* fault you're a bloodthirsty ball of aggression and destruction."

"I am?" I perked up. "Like, that's how you see me?"

She nodded.

Awesome.

The door to the little room suddenly opened, and by instinct I hefted the bowl, figuring that the still-warm soup might make a good diversion if flung in someone's face.

Hurl slipped in, her lean form silhouetted by the hallway's light. Scud. I hadn't even *thought* about her. The other two had brought me in while she was away at dinner. Had they cleared this little infraction with her?

She met my eyes, then hurriedly shut the door. "I brought desserts," she said, lifting a small bundle wrapped in a napkin. "Jerkface caught me taking them as he stopped by. I think he just does that to glare at us before he goes off to be with more important people for dinner."

"What did you tell him?" Kimmalyn said.

"I said I wanted a midnight snack. Hopefully he doesn't suspect anything. The hallway looked clear, no MPs or anything. I think we're good." She unwrapped the napkin, revealing some chocolate cake that was only mildly squashed by the transportation.

I watched her, thoughtful, as she gave us each a piece, then flopped onto her bed, stuffing the last chunk into her mouth in one go. This was a girl who had barely spoken to me over the last few weeks. Now she brought me cake? I was certainly relieved that she wasn't going to turn me in, but I didn't know what to make of her otherwise.

I settled back down in my blankets, then tried the cake.

It was so, *so* much better than rat. I couldn't help but let out a little groan of delight, at which Kimmalyn grinned. She sat on the side of Hurl's bed, which hadn't been made in the morning. Kimmalyn's bed was the neatly made top bunk above, with the immaculate corners and the frilled pillowcase. FM's was on the other side, with the stack of books on the shelf near the headboard.

"So . . . ," I said, licking my fingers, "what do you guys do all night?"

"Sleep?" Hurl asked.

"For twelve hours?"

"Well, there's PT," FM said. "We do laps in the pool usually, though Hurl prefers the weights. And target practice with sidearms, or extra time in the centrifuge . . ."

"I still haven't thrown up in that," Hurl said, "which is, in my opinion, completely inappropriate."

"Hurl taught us wall-ball," Kimmalyn said. "It's fun to watch her play the boys. They always take it as an invigorating challenge."

"By which she means it's satisfying to watch Nedd lose," FM said. "He seems so befuddled every time . . ." She trailed off, perhaps realizing that they'd never get to see him play again.

My stomach twisted. Swimming. Target practice. Sports? I'd known what I was missing, but hearing it like that . . .

"We won't be expected to do any of that tonight," Kimmalyn said. "Since we're sick. It will be fun, Spin! We can stay up all night talking."

"About what?" I asked.

"Normal things," FM said, shrugging.

What was normal? "Like . . . guys?"

"Stars, no," Hurl said, sitting up and pulling something off her headboard. She held up a sketchbook filled with little drawings of ships going through patterns. "Flight strategies!"

"Hurl keeps trying to name new moves after herself," FM noted. "But we figure the 'Hurl maneuver' really ought to have several loops in it or something. Like the one on page fifteen."

"I hate loops," Hurl said. "We should call that the Quirk maneuver. It's flowery."

"Don't be silly," Kimmalyn said. "I'd somehow end up crashing into *myself* if I had to do that many loops."

"A Quirk maneuver would involve complimenting the enemy while you shoot them," FM said, grinning. " 'Oh! You make lovely sparks when you die! You should feel very proud of yourself. Good job!' "

My tension bled away as the girls showed off the maneuvers they'd designed. The names were consistently terrible, but the chatter was fun, engaging, and . . . well, just so very *welcome*. I took a turn sketching an obscenely complex maneuver into the book, something between an Ahlstrom loop and a double switch-back with a sidewind.

"Crazy thing is," FM said, "she could probably pull that off."

"Yeah," Kimmalyn said. "Maybe we could rename *taking off* the Quirk maneuver. That's the only thing I can manage consistently."

"You're not nearly as bad as that," Hurl said to her.

"I'm the worst pilot in the flight."

"And the best shot."

"Which matters zero if I die before I can fire back."

I grunted, hand still on Hurl's notebook. I turned to another page. "Quirk is a great sniper, and Hurl, you're excellent at chasing down Krell ships. FM, you're excellent at dodging."

"I can barely hit the broad side of a mountain though," FM said. "I guess if you somehow mashed us all together, you'd have one good pilot."

"Couldn't we try something like that?" I said, sketching. "Cobb says that the Krell are always on the lookout for pilots who distinguish themselves. He says that if they find someone they think might be flightleader, they concentrate all fire on that person."

"Yeah?" Hurl said, sitting up on her bed. "What are you saying?"

"Well, if they really are machines, maybe they've got this mandate to hunt down our leaders. Maybe it's stuck in their machine brains, to the point that they follow that command to ridiculous ends."

"That seems like a stretch," FM said.

I glanced at my pack, and the portable radio on the side. The light was flashing. M-Bot had tried to call me, probably with another request for mushrooms.

"Look," I said, returning to my sketch. "What if we *encouraged* the Krell to focus on specific members of our flight? If they concentrated fire on FM, who is best at dodging, they might leave the others alone. Quirk could set up and pick them off. Hurl could hang back, and then chase after any who decided to try to bring down our gunner."

The others leaned in close. Hurl nodded, though FM shook her head. "I'm not sure I could survive that, Spin. I would end up with *dozens* of tails. I'd be shot down for sure. But . . . maybe you could manage it."

"You're our best pilot," Quirk agreed. "And you're not frightened of *anything*."

My pen stilled, and I looked at the half-drawn flight plan, with Quirk's ship sitting at the perimeter sniping down Krell. I'd drawn a dozen ships chasing after a single pilot.

What would it feel like to be in the seat, knowing you had heat from a dozen enemies? Immediately my daydreaming took over, imagining it as an incredible, dramatic fight. Explosions, and excitement, and glory!

But now there was another voice inside me. A quiet, solemn one that whispered, *That's not reality, Spin. In reality, you'd be terrified.*

"I . . ." I licked my lips. "I don't know if I could do it either. I . . ." *Force it out.* "I get scared sometimes."

FM frowned. "So?"

"So some of what I say . . . it's kind of . . . bravado. In reality, I'm not that confident."

"You mean you're *human*?" Kimmalyn said. "Blessed stars. Who would have thought?"

"You sound like you're making some big confession," FM agreed. " 'Guys, I have emotions. They're *terrible*.' "

I blushed. "It's a big deal for me. I spent my childhood dreaming of the days when I could fly and fight. Now that I'm here, and I've lost friends, I . . . It hurts. I'm weaker than I thought I was."

"If that makes you weak," FM said, "I must be *useless*."

268

"Yeah," Kimmalyn said. "You're not crazy, Spin. You're a person."

"Albeit," FM added, "one who has been thoroughly indoctrinated by a soulless system designed only to spit out willing, jingoistic, obedient thralls. No offense."

I couldn't help noticing that Hurl had grown quiet at this conversation. She was lying back on her bed and looking at the bunk above.

"You can admit these things to us," Quirk said. "It's all right. We're a team." She leaned in toward FM and me. "Since we're being honest here . . . can I tell you something? Truth is, I *make up* most of those quotes I say."

I blinked. "Really? Like, the Saint never said all those things?"

"No!" Kimmalyn said in a conspiratorial whisper. "I came up with them myself! I simply don't admit it, because I don't want to appear too wise. It's unseemly."

"My entire world is shaken right now, Quirk," FM said. "I feel like you just told me up is really down, or that Hurl's breath smells great."

"Hey," Hurl said. "See if I get *you* cake again."

"This is serious," I said to the other two. "I *get scared.*"

I might secretly be a coward.

FM and Kimmalyn blew it off. They reassured me, and talked about how they felt. FM still thought she was a hypocrite for wanting to bring down the DDF while also wanting to fly with it. Kimmalyn had the soul of a smart aleck, but the upbringing of a polite society girl.

I appreciated their kindness, but it occurred to me that the counterculture Disputer and the girl from Bountiful might not be the best people to understand how important it was that I not be afraid. So I let the conversation slide in other directions.

We talked far into the night, and it was . . . well, it was wonderful. Sincere and friendly. But as the night grew long, I found myself strangely anxious. In some ways, this was one of the best days of my life—but it also reaffirmed what I'd always feared. That the others were bonding without me.

My mind scrambled, even as I grinned at something Kimmalyn said. Was there a way to extend this? How often could the girls claim to be sick? When could I come back?

Eventually, biology began to make its demands, so Quirk and FM went to scout out the restroom. That left me with Hurl, who had been dozing off. I didn't want to wake her, so I waited by the door.

"I know how you feel," Hurl suddenly said.

I almost jumped out of my skin. "You're awake?"

She nodded. She didn't even seem drowsy, though I swore I'd heard her snoring softly earlier.

"Fear doesn't make us cowards though, does it?" Hurl asked.

"I don't know," I said, walking over to her bed. "I wish I could just smother it."

Hurl nodded again.

"Thank you," I said, "for letting the other two plan this night for me. I know spending time with me wouldn't have been your first choice."

"I saw what you did for Nedd," she said. "I watched you fly in after him, right into the depths of that chunk of debris."

"I couldn't let him go alone."

"Yeah." She hesitated. "My mother told stories of your father, you know. When she saw me back down on the playground, or flinch from a ball during practice. She told me about the pilot who claimed to be brave, but was a coward inside. 'Don't you dare sully the name of the Defiant people,' she'd say to me. 'Don't you dare become a Chaser . . . '"

I winced.

"But we don't have to be like that," Hurl continued. "That's what I realized. A little fear, a little history, those things don't

270

mean anything. Only what we *do* means anything." She looked toward me. "I'm sorry for how I treated you. It was just a . . . shock, when I found out. But you're not him, and I'm not either, regardless of what I feel sometimes."

"My father wasn't a coward, Hurl," I said. "The DDF lies about him."

She didn't look like she believed me, but she nodded anyway. Then she sat up, holding out her fist. "Not cowards. No backing down. Brave until the end, right Spin? A pact."

I met her fist with mine. "Brave to the end."

29

I woke up snuggled into too many blankets, and reached out to feel the side of M-Bot's cockpit—but my hand slapped the side of a bed frame.

Right. What time was it? I tapped my light-line to glance at its clock, raising a soft glow in the room. Just before five in the morning. Two hours until we had to be ready for class.

I should have been exhausted, as we'd stayed up talking until after one. Strangely, I felt wide awake. Perhaps my brain knew that if I wanted to use the facilities and get cleansed today, I'd need to do it now—while everyone else in the building was sleeping.

In fact, it was probably best if I snuck out and was seen walking back to the building before class. I climbed out of my nest and stretched, then grabbed my backpack. I tried to be as quiet as possible, though I probably shouldn't have worried. If the others could sleep through Hurl's snoring, my pack scraping the floor wouldn't disturb them.

I slipped open the door, then turned and looked at the three sleeping girls. "Thank you," I whispered. Right then, I decided

I wouldn't let them do this again. It was too dangerous; I didn't want to get them on the admiral's bad side.

This had been wondrous. Even if it left me knowing, for sure, what I was missing. Even if I felt sick to have to walk away, even if I twisted inside, I wouldn't have traded this night for anything. My only taste of what it was like to be part of a real flight of pilots.

That thought loomed in my mind as I walked to the bathroom and cleansed. Afterward, looking in the bathroom mirror, I smoothed back my wet hair. In all the stories, the heroes had stark black, golden, or red hair—something dramatic. Not dirty brown.

I sighed, threw my pack on my shoulder, and slipped out into the empty hallway. As I walked to the exit, a light down a corridor caught my attention. I knew that room—it was our classroom. Who would be there at this hour?

My curiosity overcame my common sense. I snuck over to peek in through the window in the door and saw Jorgen's cockpit engaged, the hologram up and running. What was he doing here at 0530? Getting in a little extra practice?

Cobb's hologram in the center of the room projected a miniature version of the training battlefield, so I could watch Jorgen's ship light-lance around a hovering piece of debris, then fire on a Krell. Something about that fight looked familiar . . .

Yes, it was the one where Bim and Morningtide had died. I'd seen Cobb watching this same recording.

Morningtide's ship went down in flames, and I winced— though just before she hit, the hologram froze, then restarted. I watched again, picking out Jorgen's ship as he flew from the other side of the battlefield, dodging debris, making for the ship that would destroy Morningtide. He fired off his IMP, but even as he took down the enemy shield, the Krell blasted Morningtide's ship and sent her spinning downward.

The hologram restarted, and Jorgen tried again, going a different direction this time.

He's trying to figure out if he could have saved them, I realized.

When Morningtide went down this third time, the hologram continued—but Jorgen heaved himself out of his seat. He ripped off his helmet and slammed it against the wall with a loud *bang*. I flinched and almost bolted, worried the noise might draw attention. But seeing Jorgen—normally so tall and imperious—slumped against the wall . . . I couldn't walk away.

He looked so vulnerable. So human. Losing Bim and Morningtide had been hard on me. I'd never thought about how it had been for their flightleader—the one who was supposed to keep us all out of trouble.

Jorgen dropped his helmet. He turned away from the wall, then froze.

Scud. He'd seen me.

I ducked away, and was out the exit of the building before he could catch up. But . . . what now? Suddenly, a gaping hole appeared in our little subterfuge. What if the guards at the gate told the admiral that I'd never left last night?

Surely they didn't report to the admiral every day about every person who went in and out of the base. Right? But if I left now, then came right back in, they'd definitely notice something was odd.

So, instead of going to the gate, I aimlessly walked the pathways of the base, between buildings. It was dark out, the skylights dim and the pathways mostly empty. In fact, I passed more statues than I did people: busts of the First Citizens—looking toward the sky—lined this part of the walkway.

A too-cold gust of wind blew across me, shaking the branches of a nearby tree. In the dim light, the statues were haunting figures, their stone eyes lost in shadow. The air smelled of smoke from the nearby launchpads, a pungent scent. A fighter must have returned to base on fire recently.

I sighed and sat down on a bench along the walkway, dropping my pack next to me. I felt . . . melancholy, perhaps a little wistful. The call light on the radio was still blinking. Maybe talking to M-Bot would kick me out of my funk.

I switched it into receiving mode. "Hey, M-Bot."

"I'm outraged!" M-Bot said. "This is an insult beyond insults! I cannot express with words my indignation, but my built-in thesaurus says that I am insulted, affronted, maltreated, desecrated, injured, ravaged, persecuted, and/or possibly molested."

"Sorry. I didn't mean to turn you off."

"Turn me off?"

"I've had the radio off all night. Isn't that what you're angry about?"

"Oh, that's just normal human forgetfulness. But don't you remember? I wrote a subroutine to express that I'm mad at you?"

I frowned, trying to remember what the ship was talking about.

"You said I was a Krell?" he said. "I got mad? It was kind of a big deal?"

"Right. Sorry."

"Apology accepted!" M-Bot answered. He sounded pleased with himself. "I projected a nice sense of outrage, don't you think?"

"It was splendid."

"I thought so."

I sat for a time, silent. Something about last night. It left me feeling reflective, quiet.

She really isn't ever going to let me fly, I thought, smelling the smoke from the launchpad fire. *I can graduate, but it will be meaningless.*

"You're right though," M-Bot noted. "I might be a Krell."

"WHAT?" I said, practically smacking myself with the radio as I raised it to my lips.

"I mean, my data banks *have* mostly been lost," M-Bot said. "There's no saying what was in there."

"Then why did you get so angry at *me* for suggesting you might be a Krell!"

"It seemed the correct thing to do. I'm supposed to simulate having a personality. What person would let themselves be *slandered* like that? Even if it was a completely logical assumption, and you are making a perfectly valid threat assessment by wondering about it."

"I really don't know what to make of you, M-Bot."

"I don't either. Sometimes, my subroutines engage with responses before my main personality simulator has time to rein them in. It's very confusing. In a perfectly logical, machine way, not at all irrational like human emotions."

"Sure."

"You are using sarcasm. Be careful, or I'll engage my outrage routine again. But if it helps, I don't think the Krell are AIs, regardless of what your DDF thinkers have determined."

"Really? Why do you think that?"

"I've analyzed their flight patterns. And yours, by the way. I might have some pointers to help you improve. It seems . . . I have entire subroutines dedicated to that kind of analysis.

"Anyway, I don't think all of the Krell are AIs, though some might be. My analysis finds that most of their patterns are individual, not complying with easily determined logical routines. At the same time they are reckless, which is curious. I suspect they are drones of some sort, though I will say that Cobb is right: this planet exerts some interference on communications. I appear to have boosting technology that helps me pierce the interference."

"Well, you *are* a stealth ship. Advanced communications technology probably helped with your missions."

"Yes. My holographic projectors, active camouflage, and sonar avoidance are probably there for the same reason."

"I didn't even know you could do most of those things. Camouflage? Holograms?"

"My settings say I had these systems engaged on standby mode, creating an illusion of rubble over my ship and preventing scans from detecting my cavern, until recently when my backup power ran out. I'd give you the exact time to the nanosecond, but humans generally hate that kind of precision, as it makes me seem calculating and alien."

"Well, that probably explains why nobody found you all those years." I tapped the radio, thoughtful.

"Regardless," M-Bot said, "I hope I'm not a Krell. That would be super embarrassing."

"You're no Krell," I said—and realized I meant it. I'd worried earlier, but now . . . I just couldn't explain why, but I knew he wasn't.

"Maybe," he said. "I'll admit I'm . . . worried that I might be something evil like that, and not know it."

"If you were a Krell, why would you have human living space and plugs that work with ours?"

"I could have been built to infiltrate human society by imitating one of your ships," he said. "Or actually, what if the Krell are all rogue AIs originally created by humans? That would explain why I had your writing on me. Or maybe I—"

"You're not a Krell," I said. "I can feel it."

"That's probably some irrational human confirmation bias speaking," he noted. "But my subroutine that can simulate appreciation . . . is appreciative."

I nodded.

"That's kind of what it does," he added. "Appreciate things."

"I would never have figured."

"It can appreciate something at a million times per second. So you could say your comment is likely the single most appreciated thing you've ever done."

"*I'd* appreciate you shutting up about how great you are once in a while," I said, but I smiled and stuck the radio onto my backpack.

"I'm *not* appreciating *that* comment," he noted softly. "Just so you know."

I flipped the radio off, then stood up and stretched. A few First Citizen busts seemed to glare at me from nearby. Including a younger Cobb. How strange to look at an image of him now that I knew him so well. He shouldn't look young. Hadn't he been born a crusty fifty-year-old man?

I shouldered my pack and wandered back toward the flight school building.

An MP stood right outside the main entrance.

I stopped in place. Then, worried, I approached.

"Cadet Nightshade?" the MP asked. "Callsign: Spin."

My heart sank.

"Admiral Ironsides would like to speak with you."

I nodded.

The MP led me to the building where I'd met Jorgen and the admiral that once. As we neared, my sense of resignation grew. Somehow I'd known this was coming. Staying with the girls last night had been a bad idea, but . . . this wasn't about one little infraction.

It seemed to me, as I stepped into the building, that a confrontation had been growing inevitable. I *deserved* this for what I'd done to Jorgen, twice over. More telling, the admiral was the most powerful person in the DDF, while I was the daughter of a coward. In some ways, it was remarkable she hadn't found a way to kick me out before this.

It was time for it to end. I was a fighter, yes, but a good fighter knew when a battle was unwinnable.

The MP deposited me inside the admiral's shockingly messy

office. Ironsides was drinking coffee at her desk, looking over some report, her back to me.

"Close the door," she said.

I obeyed.

"There's a note here on the security reports at the gate. You didn't leave last night. Have you made a hidey-hole in one of the maintenance closets or something?"

"Yes," I said, relieved that at least she didn't know the others had helped me.

"Have you eaten mess hall food? Stolen by your own hand, or smuggled out for you by one of your flightmates?"

I hesitated. "Yes."

The admiral sipped her coffee, still not looking toward me. I stared at her back, her silvery hair, bracing myself for the words. *You're out.*

"Don't you think it's time to stop this farce?" she said, turning a page. "Drop out now. I'll let you keep your cadet's pin."

I frowned. Why . . . ask? Why not just say the words? She had the power now that I'd broken her rules, didn't she?

Ironsides turned her chair, fixing me with a cold stare. "Nothing to say, cadet?"

"Why do you care so much?" I asked. "I'm only one girl. I'm no threat to you."

The admiral set down her coffee, then stood. She straightened her crisp white uniform jacket, then stepped up to me. Like most people, she towered over me.

"You think this is about my pride, girl?" Ironsides asked. "If I let you continue in the DDF, you'll get good people killed when you inevitably run. So, I offer again. Walk away with the pin. In the city below, it should be enough to secure you any number of jobs, many quite lucrative."

She stared at me, hard. And suddenly it made sense.

She *couldn't* kick me out. Not because she lacked the power, but because . . . she needed me to prove that she was right. She needed me to drop out, give up, because that was what a coward would do.

Her rules weren't about tricking me into an infraction. They were about making my life terrible so that I backed down. If she kicked me out, I could continue the narrative. I could claim my family had been wronged. I could scream about my father's innocence. My treatment would only support my victimhood. Not being able to sleep in the cadet quarters? No food during my training? That would look terrible.

But if I walked away, she won. It was the *only* way she won.

In that moment, I was more powerful than the very admiral in command of the Defiant Defense Force.

So I saluted. "Can I return to my classes now, sir?"

A blush rose to her cheeks. "You're a coward. From a family of cowards."

I held the salute.

"I could destroy you. See you impoverished. You don't want me as an enemy. Reject my kind offer now, and you will never have another chance at it."

I held the salute.

"Bah," the admiral said, turning from me and sitting down hard. She grabbed her coffee and drank, as if I weren't there.

I took it as a dismissal. I turned and let myself out, and the MP, still standing outside the door, let me go.

Nobody came for me as I walked to the classroom. I went straight to my mockpit and sat down, then greeted the others as they arrived. When Cobb hobbled in, I realized I was *excited* for class. It felt as if I'd maybe, finally, escaped the shadow that had been hovering over me since Bim and Morningtide had died.

The girls and their kindness were part of that, but my conversation with Ironsides was a bigger part. She'd given me what I needed to keep fighting. She'd invigorated me. In a strange way, she'd brought me back to life.

I would fight. I would find the answers to what had really happened to my father. And Ironsides would *regret* forcing me to do both.

Standard DDF Ship Features

Acclivity Ring

Range of Rotation

Vertical Takeoff

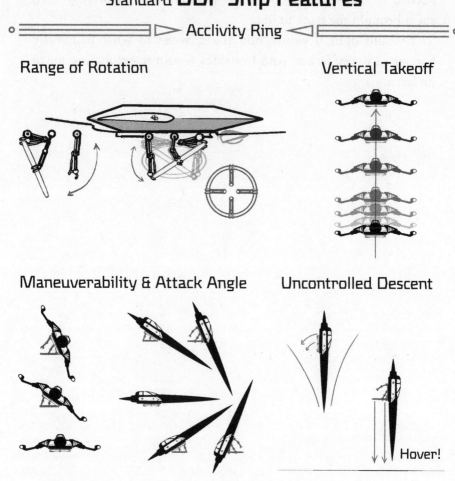

Maneuverability & Attack Angle

Uncontrolled Descent

Hover!

Light-Lance

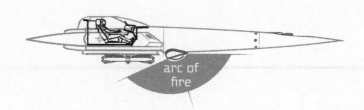

arc of
fire

PART FOUR

PART
FOUR

INTERLUDE

Admiral Judy "Ironsides" Ivans always watched the battle replays. She used the main control room, which had a large holographic projector in the center of the circular floor. She preferred to stand in its center, light shining up across her, the rest of the room dark.

She watched them fight. She watched them die. She forced herself to listen to the audio, if there was any, of each pilot's last words.

She tried to read the enemy's goals in the pattern of red and blue ships—red for the DDF, blue for the Krell. It had been years since she'd been a pilot, yet as she stood with headphones on—ships swirling around her—the *feel* of it returned to her. The hum of the booster, the rush of a banking ship, the rattle of destructor fire. The pulse of the battlefield.

Some days, she entertained fancies of climbing into a ship and joining the fray again. Then she banished those idiot dreams. The DDF was too low on ships to waste one on an old woman with shriveled reaction times. Fragmented tales—and some old print history books—spoke of great generals who took up a weapon and joined their soldiers on the front lines. Judy, however, knew she was no Julius Caesar. She was barely a Nero.

Still, Judy Ivans was dangerous in other ways.

She watched the battle spin and fly beneath the shadow of the slowly dropping shipyard. The Krell had committed almost sixty ships to this fight—two-thirds of their maximum, a major investment for them. It was clear they knew that if that wreckage had fallen into DDF hands intact, it would have been a huge boon. There had been hundreds of acclivity rings on that massive ship/station.

Now, salvage reported that fewer than a dozen so far were recoverable—and Judy had lost fourteen ships in the engagement. She saw, in their deaths, her own faults. She hadn't been willing to truly *commit*. If she'd raised all of their reserve ships and pilots, then thrown them at the battle, she might have earned hundreds of acclivity rings. Instead she'd wavered, worried about a trap, until it was too late.

That was what she lacked, compared to people like Caesar of old. She needed to be willing to commit everything.

Rikolfr, her aide, stepped up to her with a clipboard full of notes. Judy rewound the battlefield, highlighting a specific pilot. The cadet who had given her so much trouble.

Ships exploded and pilots died. Judy wouldn't let herself feel for the deaths; she *couldn't* let herself feel for them. As long as they had more pilots than acclivity rings—and they did, slightly—then personnel was the more disposable of the two resources.

Finally, Judy took off her headphones.

"She flies well," Rikolfr said.

"Too well?" Judy asked.

Rikolfr flipped through papers on his clipboard. "Newest data is in from her helmet sensors. It hasn't been encouraging during her training—almost no anomalies. But that fight you're watching, the battle at the falling shipyard, well . . ."

He turned the clipboard toward her, showing a set of readings that were literally off the chart.

"The Writellum section of her brain," Rikolfr said, "went *crazy* with activity when she was around the Krell. Dr. Halbeth is certain this is proof of the defect, though Iglom is less certain. He cites the lack of evidence except for this one engagement."

Judy grunted, watching the coward's ship loop around, then fly into the very bowels of the falling shipyard.

"Halbeth recommends immediately removing the girl from duty," Rikolfr noted. "But Dr. Thior . . . well, she is going to be trouble, as you would guess."

Thior, who was unfortunately head of Alta Base medical, didn't believe that the defect was real. Even the history of the thing was controversial. Reports of it dated back to the *Defiant* itself—and the mutiny on board the flagship that had ended with the fleet crashing here on Detritus.

Few people knew about the mutiny, and fewer still the fact that a defect in some of the crew had been the cause. These things weren't clear even to Judy. But some of the most important—and most merited—families in the lower caverns traced their lineage to the mutineers. Those families fought against acknowledging the defect, and wanted to keep rumors of it secret. But they hadn't seen what it could do to someone.

Judy had. Firsthand.

"Who is supporting Thior this time?" Judy asked.

Rikolfr flipped a few pages, then displayed the latest round of letters from prominent party members. At their head was a letter from NAL Algernon Weight, whose son, Jorgen, was in the coward's flight. Jorgen had spoken highly of the girl on repeated occasions, so now came the questions. Wouldn't it be for the best to hold this girl up as a sign of true Defiant redemption? A symbol of how any person, regardless of heritage, could return to the fold and provide service to the state?

Damn it, Judy thought, pausing the hologram as the coward hit her overburn in a near-disastrous attempt to escape. *How much proof is Algernon going to require?*

"Orders, sir?" Rikolfr asked.

"Tell Dr. Halbeth to write a condemnation of Thior's explanations, then see if Dr. Iglom can be persuaded to offer strong support of the defect's existence, particularly in this girl. Tell her I'd consider it a personal favor if she could strengthen her stand."

"As you wish, sir."

Rikolfr retreated, and Judy watched the rest of the battle, remembering a similar fight long ago.

Thior and the others could call the defect superstition. They could say that what had happened with Chaser was coincidence. But they hadn't been there.

And Judy was going to make damn sure nothing like that ever happened again. One way or another.

30

"So I'm pretty sure she won't *ever* kick me out," I said, working with Rig to apply new sealant to M-Bot's wing.

"You can infer more from a look than anyone I know," Rig said. "Just because she didn't kick you out this time doesn't mean she won't in the future."

"She won't," I said.

"She won't," Doomslug said with a fluting trill, imitating the inflection of my voice from her perch on a nearby rock.

Rig had done an amazing job with M-Bot's broken wing. Together, we'd torn off the bent metal, then recovered the usable parts. Then somehow, Rig had persuaded his new supervisors to let him practice on one of the manufactories.

With new parts in hand, we'd been able to repair the entire wing. The next week had been spent removing the old layer of sealant. Today, we were going over the entire hull with a new coat. Now that I'd entered my third month of training, we'd earned occasional R&R—so today, our flight had only a half day of classes.

I'd come back early and had met Rig to work on the ship. Rig painted the sealant on with a small spray device, and I followed behind with a two-handed machine that looked kind of like a big flashlight. The blue light from it made the sealant firm up and solidify.

The process, though slow and grueling, filled in scratches and dents on M-Bot's hull. The slick, air-resistant sealant also filled in and smoothed out seams, leaving behind a sleek, shiny surface. We'd chosen black, to match his old color.

"I still can't believe they let you borrow all this stuff," I said as I slowly positioned the light behind where Rig was spraying.

"After how enthused they were by my atmospheric scoop designs?" Rig said. "They seemed ready to promote me to head of the department on the spot. Nobody even batted an eye when I asked if I could bring this stuff home to 'disassemble it and see how it works.' They think I'm some kind of prodigy with eclectic methods."

"You're not still embarrassed, are you?" I said. "Rig, this technology could *single-handedly* save the entire DDF."

"I know," he said. "I just wish . . . you know, that I really *were* a prodigy."

I set the light on the ground to give my arms a break. "Seriously, Rig?" I waved toward M-Bot's wing, which now glistened with a new black sealant job. "You're telling me that fixing a technologically advanced starship's wing, practically on your own, in the middle of an uninhabited cave with minimal equipment, *isn't* the work of a prodigy?"

Rig stepped back, raising his goggles and inspecting the wing. Then he grinned. "It does look pretty good, doesn't it? And it will be *even better* when that last part is sealed. Eh?" He hefted the spray.

I sighed, stretching, but picked the lighting device back up. I followed behind as he started spraying the last section of the hull, near the front.

"So, you going to spend more nights in the bunks now?" he asked as we worked.

"No. I can't risk getting the others involved. This is between me and Ironsides."

"I still think you're reading too much into what she said."

I narrowed my eyes. "Ironsides is a warrior. She knows that to win this fight, she can't just defeat me—she needs to demoralize me. She needs to be able to say I was a coward, like the lies she tells about my father."

Rig continued to work in silence for a few minutes, and I thought he was going to let the argument pass. He sprayed a careful line of sealant under the part of the hull that locked into the cockpit. Then, though, he said in a more subdued tone, "That's great, Spensa. But . . . have you ever paused to wonder what you'll do if you're wrong?"

I shrugged. "If I'm wrong, she'll kick me out. Nothing I can do about that."

"I wasn't talking about the admiral. I meant your father, Spensa. What if . . . you know . . . what if he *did* retreat?"

"My father wasn't a coward."

"But—"

"*My father* was *not* a *coward*."

Rig glanced away from his work and met my eyes. The glare I gave back would have been enough to silence most people, but he held my gaze.

"What about me?" he asked. "Am *I* a coward, Spensa?"

My fury sputtered, then died.

He looked back to his spraying. "You say if you drop out, it will prove you're a coward. Well, I dropped out. So I'm a coward. Basically the *worst thing you could imagine*."

"Rig, it's different."

"Is Cobb a coward? He ejected, you know. He got shot down and ejected. Would you call *him* a coward, to his face?"

"I . . ."

Rig finished covering the last metallic section with black

sealant, then stepped back. He shook his head and looked at me. "Spin, maybe you're right. Maybe there's some big conspiracy that has pinned a great betrayal on your father. Or maybe, you know, he just got scared. Maybe he was human, and acted like humans sometimes do. Maybe the *problem* is that everyone has made such a big deal of it."

"I don't have to listen to this," I said, setting down the sealing light. I stomped off—though the only place I could stomp to was the other side of the cavern.

"Spin, you can't walk off and ignore me," Rig said from behind. "This cavern is, like, twenty meters across."

I sat down. Doomslug trilled beside me, imitating my huff of annoyance. Like usual, I hadn't caught sight of her moving over. The way she snuck about only when nobody was watching her was uncanny.

From the sounds of it, Rig picked up the light and sealed the last section himself. I sat with my back to him as he worked.

"Fume if you want," he noted. "Snap at me if you want. But at least *think* about it. You seem like you really want to defy the admiral and the DDF. Maybe you should consider *not* allowing them to define victory or failure for you."

I snorted. "You sound like FM."

"So she's smart *and* cute."

I twisted to look back. "FM? Cute?"

"She has nice eyes."

I gaped at him.

"What?" he said, blushing as he worked.

"You didn't stutter, or fumble, or *anything*," I said. "What did you do with Rodge, you Krell monster?"

"What?" M-Bot said, lights on his wings flashing on. "Rodge is a Krell!"

"Sarcasm," the two of us said in unison. Rig finished the sealing, then set the device down. He looked over at me. "You will *not* tell her I said those things. She probably doesn't even remember who I am." He hesitated. "Does she?"

"Of course she does," I lied.

Rig smiled again. He looked so different now. So confident. What had happened to him these last two months?

He found something he loves, I realized as he put his hands on his hips and smiled at M-Bot's new finish. And really, the ship *did* look incredible.

All our lives, Rig and I had dreamed of the DDF. But what had he said when he dropped out? *That's your dream. I was just along for the ride.*

Deciding not to be a pilot *had* been the right choice for him. I'd known that, but had I *known* it? *Really?*

I stood up, then walked over and put an arm around him. "You're no coward," I said. "I'm an idiot if I made you feel like you were. And this? What you've done here? This is better than 'pretty good.' Rig, this is scudding incredible."

His smile widened. "Well, we won't know for certain on that count until you take the ship into the air." He checked his watch. "I should have time enough to watch you take off."

"Take off?" I gaped. "You mean he's ready to fly? He's *fixed*?"

"M-Bot!" Rig called. "Basic status update!"

"Acclivity ring: functional. Life support and pilot care facilities: functional. Maneuvering and flight controls: functional. Shield: functional. Light-lance: functional."

"Incredible!" I said. With the acclivity ring and the maneuvering thrusters, I could move up into the air and get around a little—though not at any reasonable speed.

"We still need a booster," Rig said. "And new guns; I'm not going to risk trying to fabricate either of those, even with my newfound status in the engineering department."

"Boosters: nonfunctional," M-Bot added. "Destructors: nonfunctional. Cytonic hyperdrive: nonfunctional."

"I also have no idea how you'll get out of here," Rig said, looking up at the ceiling. "How did you even get *in*, M-Bot?"

"Likely I used a cytonic hyperjump to teleport," M-Bot said. "I . . . can't tell you how it worked. Only that this device allowed faster-than-light travel through the galaxy."

I perked up. "Can we fix *that*?"

"Best I can tell," Rig said, "it's not broken—it's *missing*. M-Bot's diagnostics indicate where this 'cytonic hyperdrive' should be, and it's an empty box with a display panel on one end. Someone must have taken the mechanism—whatever it was."

Huh. Maybe the old pilot had taken it?

Rig flipped through his notebook, then waved for me to look over his shoulder. "I'm pretty certain I fixed the maneuvering thrusters on that broken wing," he said, pointing at a schematic. "But be sure he leaves diagnostics on to record it all, so I can check to make sure everything is in order." He flipped to the next page. "And once we know he's flying right, I want to disassemble his shield igniter and see if I can figure out why it can apparently— by his specs—take three times the punishment of a standard DDF shield."

I grinned. "*That* ought to make you popular with the engineering and design teams."

"Yeah, unless they start to get suspicious." Rig hesitated, then spoke more softly. "I did eventually try and look at his AI mechanism, but he wouldn't let me open the housing. He even threatened to electrify it. He says that device—along with some other systems—is classified. Stealth systems, communications systems . . . some very important stuff. Spin, to *really* help the DDF, we would need to let an expert in here to disassemble and analyze the ship. I can only do so much."

I felt something wrench inside me, like gears locking up from lack of grease. I glanced back at M-Bot.

"He has warned," Rig said, "that if we reveal him, he will attempt to destroy his own systems to keep from disobeying his old pilot's orders."

"Maybe . . . I can talk sense into him?"

"M-Bot doesn't seem capable of sense," Rig said, gazing at the ship and—yet again—seeming to take a moment to bask in just how great it looked. Clean, freshly painted, sleek and dangerous. The four destructor cavities, two on each wing, gaped open, and the rear booster was missing. But otherwise it was *perfect*.

"Rig," I said softly, in awe, "I seriously can't believe you let me rope you into this."

"If you want to pay me back," he said, "ask FM to meet me for lunch in the park someday." Then he immediately blushed and looked down. "I mean, maybe, if the topic comes up or something. Or not."

I grinned, punching him in the arm. "So you *are* still Rig. I was starting to worry there."

"Yeah, yeah. Let's ignore what I said and focus on the important things. The insane AI says its stealth systems are good enough to keep the DDF from noticing it, and I guess we just have to trust it on that one. So what do you say? Want to take it up for a quick test flight?"

"Scud, yes!"

Rig looked up. "Any ideas on how to get out though? That gap is barely large enough for a person."

"I . . . might have an idea," I said. "But it's probably going to be a tad messy. And dangerous."

Rig sighed. "I suppose I shouldn't have expected otherwise."

About an hour later, I climbed into M-Bot's cockpit, nearly trembling with excitement. I placed Doomslug in the seat behind me, then did up my buckles.

My little cavern looked bare now that we'd packed up my

kitchen and all of Rig's equipment. We'd stowed what we could in the cockpit, and had hauled the rest out through the crack using my light-line. Rig waited a safe distance away. I got to do the fun part myself.

And, like most "fun parts," it would involve breaking things.

"You ready?" I said to M-Bot.

"I have basically two states," he said. "Ready, and powered down."

"Needs work as a catchphrase," I said. "But the sentiment is pretty cool." I rested my hands on the control sphere and the throttle, breathing in and out.

"Just so you know," M-Bot said. "I could hear what you two were saying earlier, when you were whispering. The part where Rodge said I was insane."

"I realized you could probably hear," I said. "You *are* a surveillance ship, after all."

"AIs can't be insane," he said. "We can only do what we're programmed to do. Which is the opposite of insanity. But . . . you'd tell me, right? If I start to sound . . . off?"

"The mushroom thing *is* a little over the top."

"I can sense that. I also can't help it. The mandate is very strong inside me. Along with my pilot's last words."

"Lie low. Don't get into any fights."

"And wait for him. Yes. It's why I can't let you reveal me to your DDF, even if I know it would help you and your people. I simply *must* follow my orders." He paused. "I am worried about you taking me into the air. Did my pilot mean 'lie low' as in 'stay underground,' or did he merely mean 'don't let yourself be seen'?"

"I'm sure he meant the second," I said. "We'll just do a quick flight around the area."

"It will not be 'quick,'" he said. "With only maneuvering thrusters, we'll fly about as fast as you can walk."

Good enough for now. I engaged the acclivity ring, raising

us smoothly. I pulled up the landing struts, turned us around in a slow circle, then dipped us to one side and then the other. I grinned. The controls were similar enough, and there was an energy to the responses that my Poco simply didn't have.

Now, how to get out of the cavern. I tipped the acclivity ring backward on its hinges, which in turn tipped M-Bot's nose up. I launched the light-lance, spearing it into a cracked portion of the ceiling. I pulled back, using the rotational thrusters, then lowered the power of the acclivity ring. That gave us some force, even without a booster.

The light-lance went taut. Dust and chips of stone streamed down from the ceiling. Doomslug mimicked the sound from behind me, fluting in an energetic, excited way.

A portion of the ceiling collapsed in a shower of rock and dust. I disengaged the light-lance, looking up through the hole. There was no skylight nearby, so above was a dark uniform greyness. The sky.

"Can your hologram create a projection of a new roof?" I asked M-Bot.

"Yes, but it will be less secure," he said. "Sonar imaging can see through the hologram. But . . . It feels like so long since I've seen the sky." He seemed wistful, though he would probably claim that was some kind of programming quirk.

"Let's go," I said. "Come on. Let's fly!"

"I . . . ," M-Bot said softly. "Yes, all right. Let's go! I do want to fly again. Just be careful, and keep me out of sight."

I raised us up through the hole, then waved to Rig, who was standing with our things a short distance away.

"Engaging stealth mechanisms," M-Bot said. "We should now be invisible to DDF sensors."

I grinned. I was in the sky. With *my own* ship. I slammed the throttle forward.

We stayed in place.

297

Right. No booster.

I engaged the maneuvering thrusters, which were intended more for fine-tuned positioning than they were for actual movement. And we started flying. Slooooooowly.

"Yippee?" M-Bot said.

"It *is* kind of a letdown, isn't it?"

Still, I did a small loop for Rig, with diagnostics running. When I completed the circle, he gave a thumbs-up, then settled his pack on his shoulder and started hiking off. He had to get back to Igneous to return the sealing equipment.

I couldn't quite persuade myself to land. After all this time, I wanted to fly a little longer with M-Bot. So I grabbed the altitude lever. The control sphere could make the ship bob up and down, powering the acclivity ring for the finer points of dodging. But if you wanted a quick ascent, this was the way.

I eased it toward me.

We shot upward into the sky.

I hadn't expected it to work *this* well. We rocketed upward, and I felt g-forces slam into me, forcing me down. I cringed, noting how fast we were going, and eased off the lever. That kind of g-force would . . .

. . . crush me?

I felt the acceleration, but not nearly as much as I should have. I couldn't be pulling more than three Gs, though I felt like it should have been much more.

"What are you doing?" I asked.

"Can you be more specific? I have over a hundred and seventy semiautonomous subroutines that—"

"The g-forces," I said, looking out the window, watching the ground retreat at an alarming pace. "I should be blacking out about now."

"Oh, yes. That. My gravitational capacitors are capable of belaying sixty percent of g-forces, with a maximum threshold of well over a hundred Earth standard. I *did* warn you that your ships had primitive systems for handling pilot stress."

I let off on the altitude lever, and the ship stopped accelerating.

"Would you like to engage rotational g-force management for further help withstanding the forces?" M-Bot asked.

"Like where my seat turns around?" I asked, remembering what Rig had explained about M-Bot. Humans didn't do well with g-forces in the wrong directions—it was much harder for us to take downward forces, for example, because they pushed all the blood in our bodies into our feet. M-Bot could compensate for that by rotating the seat, so that I took the forces backward—in a way easier for my body to handle.

"Not for now," I said. "Let me first get used to how you fly."

"Very well," M-Bot said.

We quickly reached 100,000 feet, which was around the highest that we flew DDF ships in regular situations. I reached to decelerate, but hesitated. Why not go a little higher? I'd always wanted to. Now, nobody was there to stop me.

I kept us going, soaring upward until the altitude indicator hit 500,000 feet. There, finally, I slowed us, admiring the view. I'd never been so high. The mountain peaks below looked like nothing more than crumpled-up paper. I could actually see the planet *curving*—and not merely some faint arc either. I felt as if I could stretch onto my toes and see the whole planet.

I was still barely halfway to the rubble belt, which I'd been told was in low orbit starting at around a million feet. However, from this height, I could see it far better. What I saw from the surface as only vague patterns now manifested as enormous swaths of metal upon metal, vaguely lit by some sources I couldn't make out.

Looking at it, realizing it was still well over a hundred kilometers away, the grand scale of it finally started to strike me. Those little specks that looked like individual dots . . . those had

299

to be as large as the piece of debris that had crashed down during that fight a week back.

It was all so *enormous*. My jaw dropped as I gazed at it, taking in the many sections, all rotating and churning in esoteric orbits. Mostly just shadows, moving, swirling, layers upon layers.

"Would you like to get closer?" M-Bot said.

"I don't dare. They said that some of the junk would shoot at me."

"Well, those *are* obvious remnants of a semiautonomous defense grid," he said. "With the shadows of outer habitat platforms behind, I'd say—all interspersed with broken shipyards and matter reclamation drones."

I watched it shifting, moving, and tried to imagine a time when this had been functional. Used. *Lived in.* A world above the world.

"Yes, some of those defense platforms are clearly operational," M-Bot said. "Even I would have difficulty slipping past them. Note those asteroids I'm highlighting on your canopy; slag formations on the surface indicate their ancient purpose. Some strategies for suppressing a planet include towing interplanetary bodies into position and dropping them. This can accomplish anything from the removal of a specific city to an extinction-level disaster."

I breathed out softly, horrified to imagine it.

"Er . . . not that I was originally a *combat ship,* mind you," M-Bot said. "I don't know about orbital bombardment from my own programming. I suppose somebody must have told it to me once."

"I thought you didn't lie."

"I don't! I genuinely believe that I'm an advanced, well-armed, stealth-capable ship because it will help me harvest fungi better. That is *not at all* irrational."

"So all the Krell really would need to do to deal with us," I said, "is shove some of these asteroids down?"

"It's a little harder than you make it sound," M-Bot said. "The

Krell would need a ship large enough to move something of such a sizable mass. That would likely require a capital ship—which those defense platforms would probably be able to shoot down with ease. Small ships could get through some of those gaps though. Which I guess you already know, considering how often you fight them."

I settled back in the seat, letting myself enjoy the view. The expansive world below, the sky that somehow felt *smaller* than it once had. It was only a narrow band around the planet, capped by the rubble belt.

I stared upward for a time, admiring the grand motions of the rubble belt—the enormous shells and platforms, moving according to their ancient and esoteric design. There must have been dozens of layers, but in that moment—for only the second time in my life—it all aligned. And I saw out into space. True infinity, broken by a few twinkling stars.

Which I *swore* I could hear. Whispers. No distinct words, but something real. Gran-Gran was right. If I listened, I *could* hear the stars. They sounded like the horns of battle, calling out, drawing me toward them . . .

Don't be a fool, I thought. *You don't have a booster. If the Krell find you, you'll be little more than target practice.*

Reluctantly, I began to ease us downward. That was probably enough for one day.

We descended slowly, letting gravity do most of the work. Unfortunately, we'd drifted some distance in the wind, so when we landed, I had to inch us—with those tiny maneuvering thrusters—back toward the hole.

It took long enough that by the time we got there, I was yawning. Doomslug imitated the sound of my yawn from where she'd settled down into the blanket behind my seat.

Finally, we lowered into the cavern and landed near M-Bot's original resting spot. "Well, I'd call that a great first run," I said.

301

"Er, yes," M-Bot said. "We went very high, didn't we?"

"If I can only figure out a way to get a booster, we'll have you flying for real in no time."

"Um . . ."

"You could try fighting the Krell, if you wanted," I said, testing whether I could push him further. "We could do that while 'lying low'—we just wouldn't tell anyone what or who we are! The black phantom ship with no callsign! Flying in to help the DDF in times of need!"

"I don't think—"

"Imagine it, M-Bot! Dodging and swooping amid exploding barrages. Soaring and striving, proving yourself stronger than your enemies. A grand symphony of destruction and power!"

"Or, even better, sitting in the cave! Doing none of that!"

"We could fight with stealth mode on . . . ," I said.

"That is still the opposite of lying low. I'm sorry, Spensa. I *must not fight*. We can fly again—I kind of liked it—but we cannot *ever* fight."

"Ever fight," Doomslug added.

I turned off the ship's nonessentials, then leaned back my seat, feeling sick. I had access to something awesome, something powerful, something amazing—but I couldn't use it? I had a weapon that didn't want me to swing it. What should I do?

I didn't know. But I found it most disturbing that my ship was . . . well, a coward.

I sighed and started getting ready for bed. My frustration with M-Bot faded; I was too excited by the fact that I'd actually gotten him into the air.

As I finally settled down—seat reclined, blanket pulled around me, Doomslug moved to a fold-out shelf in the canopy—M-Bot spoke again, softly. "Spensa?" he said. "You don't mind, do you? Staying out of combat? I *have* to obey my orders."

"No you don't."

302

"Um, I'm a computer. That's basically *all I do*. I literally can't even count to zero without an order."

"I find that hard to believe," I said. "Considering the things you've said to me."

"That's a personality programmed to interact with humans."

"Excuses," I said, yawning, dimming the lights. "You might have a machine mind, but you're still a person."

"But—"

"I can hear you," I said, yawning. "I can hear your soul. Like the stars." It was a faint hum in the back of my mind, and I hadn't noticed it until right then. But it was there.

Whatever he thought, M-Bot was more alive than he gave himself credit for being. I could simply *feel* it.

I started to drift off.

He spoke again, his voice even quieter. "The orders are the only thing I know for sure, Spensa. My old pilot, my purpose. That's who I was."

"Become someone new then."

"Do you have any idea how hard that is?"

I thought about my own cowardice. The feelings of loss, and of inadequacy, now that I actually had to do the things I'd always bragged that I would. I pulled my blanket close.

"Don't be silly," I said. "Why would I ever want to be anyone else?"

He didn't respond, and eventually I drifted off to sleep.

31

My flight with M-Bot, though brief and mostly linear, still managed to overshadow the next two weeks of simulation training.

I performed a maneuver, chasing a Krell ship through a series of tight turns around chunks of debris, Hurl on my wing. But my mind started to drift. The Krell ship got away.

"Hey!" Kimmalyn said as we regrouped. "Did you guys see? I didn't crash!"

I listened with half an ear—still distracted—as they all chattered.

"*I* crashed though," FM admitted. "I hit a piece of debris and went down in a fiery heap."

"Not your fault!" Kimmalyn said. "As the Saint always said, true failure is choosing to fail."

"Besides, FM," Arturo added, "you've still crashed fewer times than the rest of us, total."

"I won't hold that record for long, if I keep this up," FM said.

"You're just trying to be *subversive* by crashing today," Hurl said, "because nobody expects it from you. You rebel you."

FM chuckled softly.

"You could all do what nobody expects," Jorgen said on the group line, "and actually line up straight for once. Amphi, I'm looking at you."

"Right, right," Arturo said, hovering his ship into place. "Though I guess technically Jorgen has crashed less than you, FM. He's flown half as often. It's hard to blow up when all you do is sit around complaining and giving orders."

"As the Saint always said," Kimmalyn added again in a solemn voice, "true failure is choosing to fail."

Jorgen didn't defend himself, though I thought I heard a quick intake of breath from him. I grimaced. It was true that Jorgen tended to hang back and watch us run exercises, offering instruction rather than flying himself. But maybe the others would act differently if they knew he spent late nights practicing on his own afterward.

I felt ashamed, suddenly. Jorgen's callsign, and the way the others treated him, were partially my fault. He didn't deserve all that. I mean, he could be insufferable, but he *was* trying to do his best.

As Cobb sent us in for another round of dogfighting, Rig's words floated up from the back of my mind.

What about me? Am I a coward, Spensa?

I was certain he wasn't. But I'd lived my childhood clinging to a simple rule, reinforced by Gran-Gran's stories. Good people were brave. Bad people were cowards. I knew my father had been a good person, so it was obvious to me that he couldn't have run away. End of story. Close the book.

It was getting harder to hold to that particular black-and-white line. I'd promised Hurl I wouldn't be a coward. But did any coward *intend* to turn and run? I'd never felt like fleeing a battle, but I was still surprised by the real emotions of being a pilot. By how much it had hurt to lose Bim and Morningtide, by how over-whelmed I sometimes felt.

Was it possible that something similar, for a brief moment, had caused my father to retreat? And if he had, could I *really* promise that I wouldn't someday do the same?

I dodged around a chunk of debris, but almost clipped Hurl's wing.

"Come on, Spin," she said. "Head in the game. Eye on the ball."

"The ball?"

"Sorry. League metaphor."

"I didn't get to go to many games." Workers got tickets as rewards for exemplary merits. But it would be good to talk about something, to get my thoughts off my worries. "I barely know what you did. Something about hoverbikes? Did you fly?"

"Not quite," Hurl said as we dodged back and forth, a Krell ship—as per the exercise—coming in behind us. "The Digball League gets acclivity rings that are too small to fly ships. Our bikes could go full three-D in little bursts, but each bike is allotted a fixed amount of air time. Part of the strategy is knowing when to use it."

She sounded wistful. "Do you miss the game?" I asked.

"A little. Mostly my team. This is way better though." A flash of destructor fire sprayed around us. "More dangerous. More of a rush."

We did a wave-dodge, where we split in opposite directions under heavy destructor fire. Hurl stayed on our target while I looped back down and offered fire support, chasing off the enemy.

I caught up at the next turn, falling in behind Hurl. Our target flew extra low, only a hundred feet or so off the ground. We descended, tossing up plumes of blue-grey dust behind us, and darted past an ancient piece of debris. Long since scavenged for its acclivity stone, it lay exposed like the skeleton of a disturbed grave.

"So," Hurl said as we flew through valleys, staying on our target, "what about you? You never talk about what you used to do before the DDF."

"Aren't we supposed to keep our 'head in the game'?"

"Eh. Except when I'm curious."

"I . . . I was a ratcatcher."

"Like, for one of the protein factories?"

"No. I was solo. The factory scouts hunt the lower caverns out pretty well, so I built my own speargun, explored farther caverns, and caught them on my own. My mom sold the meat for requisition chits to workers on their way home."

"Wow. That's badass."

"You think so?"

"Totally."

I smiled, feeling warm at that.

The Krell turned and accelerated upward. "I'm going in," I said, and hit my overburn. I raced up at an angle, my g-force line going to max.

Tonight, I thought to the Krell, *your ashen remains will mix with the planet's dust, and your howls of pain shall echo upon the wind!* I cut into the ship's wake, getting just close enough to hit my IMP and destroy its shield.

Hurl flew past me, her destructor fire sounding over the blaring klaxon that warned my shield was down. The Krell ship exploded into molten debris.

Hurl let out a whoop, but then I blushed, remembering my line of thought. Ashes mixing with dust and howls on the wind? That sort of thing—once so exciting to me—now seemed . . . less the words of a hero, and more the words of someone trying to *sound* heroic. My father had never talked like that.

As I reignited my shield, a light on the communication panel lit up, announcing that Cobb was listening in. "Nice work," he said. "You two are starting to make a good team."

307

"Thanks, Cobb," I said.

"It would be better if Spin could *spend time* with the rest of us," Hurl added. "You know—instead of sleeping in her cave."

"Let me know when you intend to take that up with the admiral," Cobb said. "I'll be sure to leave the building so I don't have to listen to her shout at you. Cobb out."

The light went off, and Hurl hovered her ship down beside mine. "The way she treats you is stupid, Spin. You *are* a badass. Like that stuff you always say."

"Thanks," I answered. I could feel my cheeks heating up. "Those things make me feel self-conscious now though."

"Don't let them get to you, Spin. Be who you are."

And who am I? I looked upward, wondering if the simulation ever created holes in the debris—if it ever let you see through to the highest sky.

We ran a few more exercises before Jorgen called us back in to line up. We hovered in place, and I checked the clock on my dash. Only 1600? We still had several hours of training left. Was Cobb going to call it early and send us for more centrifuge time, like he'd done yesterday?

"All right," Cobb announced over the radio. "You're ready for the next lesson."

"We get to use destructors?" Kimmalyn exclaimed.

I leaned forward in my seat to look out at her cockpit. We'd been fighting with destructors for weeks now.

"Sorry," she said. "Got caught up in the hype."

A Krell bomber materialized in front of us. It was a sturdier build than the average Krell ship. It was the same shape, but in the center between its wings, it carried an enormous lifebuster. The bomb was even bigger than the ship was. I shivered, remembering the last time I'd seen one of these—when Bim and I had chased one down.

A scene materialized farther out: a mess of fighting ships, some Krell, some DDF.

"Our AA guns cover a range out to one hundred and twenty klicks from Alta," Cobb said. "The guns need to be big enough to blast Krell ships through their shields—not to mention big enough to shoot apart large debris so it burns up while falling. But being so big limits their functional arc. They're really good at picking off distant objects, but can't hit things too close.

"If Krell get low enough—about six hundred feet from the ground—they can come in under the big guns. The smaller gun emplacements—like the ones Quirk trained on before—don't have the punch to get through Krell shields. Without fighters IMPing the enemy, the small gun emplacements have trouble."

The simulation highlighted a specific ship among the ones fighting in the distance. Another bomber.

"The Krell distract us with dogfights and falling debris, then often try to sneak through a bomber carrying a lifebuster," Cobb continued. "You need to be constantly aware, and watching, to report sighting a lifebuster. And I'll warn you, they've used decoys before."

"We report it," Hurl said, "and then we shoot it, right? Or maybe better—shoot it first, *then* report?"

"Do that," Cobb said, "and it could be disastrous. Lifebusters are often rigged to explode if damaged. Shoot one of these down at the wrong time, and you could get dozens of your companion pilots killed."

"Oh," Hurl said.

"Only the admiral, or acting command staff, can authorize shooting down a lifebuster," Cobb continued. "Often we can chase the bomber away by threatening it—lifebusters are valuable, and as far as we can surmise, difficult to produce. If that doesn't work, the admiral will send in a special strike team to shoot down the bomber.

"Be extremely careful. Igneous is far enough below the surface that only a direct hit right on top will send a blast down deep enough to harm it, but casually destroying a lifebuster too close—even forty or fifty klicks away—could destroy Alta in the corrosion wave the bomb releases. So if you spot a bomber, you call it in immediately, then let someone with the experience, data, and authority decide what to do. Understood?"

Scattered mumbles of "Understood" followed. Then Jorgen made us all sound off one at a time, giving a verbal acknowledgment. Maybe we did treat him a little too harshly, but scud . . . he could be annoying.

"Great," Cobb said. "Flightleader, scramble your people through this battlefield. We'll do some scenarios where we practice spotting, reporting, and—yes—taking down lifebusters. Any guesses how often you all will blow yourselves up?"

Turned out, we blew ourselves up *a lot.*

The lifebuster drills were among the most difficult we'd ever done. In our first days flying, we'd learned to do what was called a pilot's scan. A quick assessment of all the things we needed to keep in mind while flying: booster indicators, navigation instruments, altitude, communication channels, wingmates, flightmates, terrain . . . and a dozen more.

Going into battle added a host of other things to watch. Orders from the flightleader or from Alta, tactics, enemies. A pilot's situational awareness was one of the most mentally taxing parts of the job.

Doing all of that while constantly watching for a bomber . . . well, it was tough. Extremely tough.

Sometimes Cobb would run us through entire hour-long battle simulations and never send in a bomber. Sometimes he'd send in seven—six decoys and a real one.

The bombers were remarkably slow—they maxed out at

Mag-2—but carried a deadly payload. When a bomb went off, it hit with three waves. The first explosion was meant to blast downward, penetrating rock, collapsing or ripping open caverns. After that was a second explosion—it was a strange greenish-black color. This alien corrosion could exterminate life, causing a chain reaction in organic matter. The third explosion was a shock wave, meant to drive this terrible burning green light outward.

We ran simulation after simulation. Time and time again, one of us blew the bomb up too soon without giving warning for the others to overburn away—which vaporized our entire flight. Multiple times, we misjudged how close we'd gotten to Alta—so that when we destroyed the bomber and detonated the bomb, Cobb sent the grim report. "You just killed the entire population of Alta. I'm dead now. Congratulations."

After one particularly frustrating run, the six of us pulled up together and watched the sickly green light expand.

"I'm—" Cobb began.

"You're dead," FM said. "We get it, Cobb. What are we *supposed* to do? If the bomb gets too close to the city, do we have any other choice?"

"No," Cobb said softly. "You don't."

"But—"

"If it comes down to destroying Alta but saving Igneous," Cobb said, "Igneous is more important. There's a reason we rotate a third of our ships, pilots, and command staff into the deep caverns. The DDF can survive—maybe—if Alta is destroyed. But without the apparatus to make new ships, we're done for. So if the admiral orders it, you *shoot that bomb* and make it detonate, even if doing so destroys Alta."

We watched the green light crawling through an ever-widening sphere of destruction. Finally it faded.

Cobb made us fly exercises until I was numb from exhaustion, my reaction times slowing. Then he made us do it again. He wanted to drill deeply into us to *always* watch for bombers, no matter how tired we were.

During that last run, I hated Cobb like I'd never hated anyone. Even more than the admiral.

We failed to stop the bomb this time too. I reset my position, falling into line by rote to start the next run. However, my canopy vanished. I blinked, surprised to be back in the real world. The others began pulling off helmets and standing up to stretch. What . . . what time was it?

"Did I recognize that last battle, Cobb?" Arturo asked, standing up. "Was it the Battle of Trajerto?"

"With modifications," Cobb said.

Trajerto, I thought. It had happened about five years ago; we'd come very close to losing Alta. A Krell flight had snuck in and destroyed the smaller AA guns. Fortunately, a couple of DDF scout ships had brought down the lifebuster before it could get close enough to Alta.

"You're using historical battles for our simulations?" I asked, trying to push through my stupor.

"Of course I am," Cobb said. "You think I have time to make up these simulations?"

Something about that struck me, but I was too exhausted to put my finger on it. I climbed out of my mockpit, tossed my helmet onto my seat, and stretched. Scud, I was hungry, but I didn't have any dinner with me—the next batch of jerky was curing back at my cave.

I had a long, tired, hungry walk ahead of me. I grabbed my pack, slung it over my shoulder, and started out.

Hurl caught up to me in the hallway, then nodded in the direction of the nearby dorm section. I could read her expression. They could pretend to be tired, bring food back to their rooms . . .

I shook my head. It wasn't worth riling the admiral.

Hurl gave me a raised fist. "Badass," she whispered. I found energy for a smile, raised my own, then we parted.

I trudged toward the exit. The other classrooms were dark, save one, where the instructor was lecturing another flight of cadets. "The best pilots can steer a ship out of an uncontrolled fall," a woman's voice said, echoing in the hallway. "Your first reaction might be to eject, but if you want to be a *real* hero, you will do whatever you can to save your acclivity ring. A Defiant protects the people, not the self."

It was basically the opposite of what Cobb had taught us.

On my way through the orchard outside the base, I noticed my radio blinking. M-Bot wanted to talk with me. I had persuaded him, with effort, to stop breaking into my line while I was training. It just seemed too likely that someone would overhear us.

"Hey," I said into the line. "Bored?"

"I can't get bored." He paused. "But I'll have you know that I can think at thousands of times the speed of a human brain—so twelve hours to you is by relative measure a long time to me. A *really* long time."

I smiled.

"Reeeeaaaaalllly long," he added.

"What did you think of the training today?"

"I took some careful notes for further review," he said. Most nights, I went over with M-Bot what I'd done wrong. His programs offered excellent analysis of my flying. While he offered commentary that could sometimes be unflattering, the nightly debriefings had proved effective in helping me tweak my flying— and I felt I was doing better than ever.

We hadn't gone into the air again. Rig had taken out the ship's GravCaps and shields to disassemble and document them. It was work beyond my ability to help with, but I didn't mind, as I had the practices to keep me busy.

"You really do need help against bombers," M-Bot said to me.

"You died or destroyed the city seventeen times today, while you were completely successful only twice."

"Thanks for the reminder."

"I try to be helpful. I realize human memories are flawed and inconsistent."

I sighed and walked out of the orchard, starting the more boring part of the trek home.

"The battles were interesting," M-Bot said. "I'm . . . very glad that you lived through some of them."

One foot after the other. Who would have thought that sitting in a box, moving only your hands, could be so tiring? My brain felt like it had been ripped out, clubbed to death by a barbarian, then stuffed back in upside down.

"You are very attractive and intelligent," M-Bot said. "Spensa? Is my moral support subroutine functioning? Um, you're quite bipedal. And very efficient at converting oxygen into carbon dioxide, an essential gas for plant life to—"

"I'm just tired, M-Bot. I've been through a lot today."

"Nineteen battles! Though four of them were the same battle turned on a different axis and presented with a few distinct movement seeds for enemies."

"Yeah, those are historical fights," I said. "Like Cobb said . . ."

I halted.

"Spensa?" he asked. "I hear no more footfalls? Have you temporarily stopped being bipedal?"

"Historical battles," I said, realizing something I should have put together long ago. "They have recordings of past battles?"

"They track all of their ships," he said, "and have scanner records of enemy movements. I suspect they recreate these three-dimensional models for training and analysis."

"Do you suppose . . . they have a record like that of the Battle of Alta? The fight where . . ."

Where my father had deserted.

"I'm sure they do somewhere," M-Bot continued. "It's the most important battle in the history of your people! The foundation of . . . Oh! Your father!"

"You can think at a thousand times the speed of a human brain," I said, "but it took you that long to put together a simple fact?"

"I underclock conversations. If I focus my full efforts, it takes you several minutes in relative time to speak a single syllable."

I supposed that made sense. "The record of my father's battle. Can you . . . grab it? Show it to me?"

"I can only intercept what they're actively broadcasting," he said. "It seems that the DDF tries to minimize wireless communication, so as to not attract the attention of the eyes."

"The what?" I asked.

"The eyes. I . . . I have no idea what that is. There's a hole in my memory banks there. Huh." The ship sounded genuinely confused. "I remember this quote: 'Use physical cords for data transfer, avoid broadcasting, and put shielding around faster processors. To do otherwise risks the attention of the eyes.' But that's it. Curious . . ."

"So maybe our communications aren't as primitive as you always say. Maybe they're just being careful." I started walking again. My pack felt so heavy, it could have been filled with spent shell casings.

"Either way," M-Bot said, "I would guess there's an archive somewhere on base. If they have a recording of the Battle of Alta, that would be the first place to check."

I nodded. I wasn't sure whether to feel excited, or further bowed down, by the knowledge that I could theoretically *watch* my father's last battle. See for myself if he'd actually deserted, and have . . . what? Proof?

I trudged onward, trying to decide if I was hungry enough to eat when I got to the cave, or if I was just going to collapse. As I neared the cavern, I saw the light flashing on my radio again.

I lifted it to my head. "I'm almost back, M-Bot. You can—"

"—general call to arms," an operator said. "The admiral has called *all* pilots—cadets included—to base for possible deployment. Repeat: a seventy-five-ship Krell invasion has breached the debris field at 104.2-803-64000. All active pilots are instructed to assemble for a general call to arms. The admiral has called *all* pilots . . ."

I froze. I'd almost forgotten the original reason Cobb had given me a radio. But today? Of all days?

I could barely walk.

Seventy-five ships? Three-quarters of the Krell maximum flight capacity? Scud!

I pivoted, looking at the long hike back to Alta. Then, lethargically, I pushed myself into a jog.

32

I reached the DDF compound a sweaty, out-of-breath mess. Fortunately, my daily walks back and forth to my cave had been a good imitation of physical training, so I was in reasonable shape. The gate guards waved me through, and I forced myself into another jog. I stopped off at the changing rooms near the launchpad and threw on my flight suit.

I bolted out the door, running for my ship. My Poco sat alone. Nedd's ship had long since been assigned to another flight, and everyone else would be in the air already. The faint sound of AA guns popped in the distance, and burning streaks of falling debris indicated that this battlefield was dangerously close to Alta's defensive perimeter.

My fatigue was suddenly overpowered by a spike of concern. A pilot was climbing into the cockpit of my ship.

"Wait!" I shouted. "What are you doing? That's my ship!"

The pilot hesitated, glancing down at the ground crew who had been prepping the ship. One of them nodded.

The pilot climbed slowly back down the ladder.

"You're late," Dorgo—a man from the ground crew—said to

317

me. "The admiral ordered all unoccupied ships manned and sent in as reserves."

My heart thundered inside my chest as the woman—reluctantly—hopped down and pulled off her helmet. She was in her early twenties, and bore a prominent scar across her forehead. She gave me a thumbs-up, but said nothing else as she trudged off toward the crew quarters.

"Who's that?" I asked softly.

"Callsign: Vigor," Dorgo said. "Former cadet who got shot down just before graduating. She was good enough that the admiral added her to the reserve roster."

"She ejected?" I asked.

Dorgo nodded.

I climbed up the ladder, then took my helmet from Dorgo, who climbed up after me. "Head to 110-75-1800," he said, pointing toward the battlefield. "Unless you hear otherwise. That's where your flight was told to hold position. I'll let Flight Command know you're up and off."

"Thanks," I said, pulling on the helmet, then strapping in.

He gave me a thumbs-up, then climbed down and pulled back the ladder. Another ground crew member waved with a blue flag once everyone was safely away.

I turned on the acclivity ring, then raised my ship. Eighteen hundred was a low altitude for fighting—we usually trained somewhere around 30,000. I felt like I was skimming the ground as I darted in the indicated direction.

"Skyward Ten," I said, pressing the button to call Jorgen, "reporting in. Callsign: Spin."

"You made it?" Jorgen replied. "They said they were going to send us a reservist."

"It was a tight call," I said, "but I convinced them *I* was the only one capable of giving you enough crap. You fighting?"

"No," he said. "The admiral has us holding position near

one of the AA guns. 110-75-1800, Spin. Glad to have you, crap and all."

It took me around ten minutes to reach the position, where I spotted the other five members of my flight hovering between two large hills. I decelerated with a reverse burn, then fell into wing-mate position by Hurl. Behind us, an enormous AA gun—longer than the flight school building, and then some—scanned the air for incoming Krell. A series of smaller guns sprouted from the base, ready to fire on low-flying ships.

A round of greetings from the others welcomed me. I could barely make out some flashes in the sky to mark the battlefield. The AA gun, however, let out a roaring blast behind us, shaking my Poco. Far overhead, a larger chunk of debris exploded into a shower of sparks and dust.

"So," Hurl said in my ear, "how many kills you going to get today, Spin?"

"Well . . . the record in a single battle is held by callsign: Dodger. Twelve direct kills, nine assists. I figure it would be arrogant to try to beat that. So I'll go for the tie."

I expected a chuckle, but Hurl seemed serious when she said, "Twelve/nine? That doesn't sound like so many."

"Considering that most Krell incursion forces are around thirty ships?"

"There are seventy-five today," Hurl said. "Easy pickings, if the DDF would let us actually fight." She inched her Poco forward with maneuvering thrusters, and I followed.

"Where do you two think you're going?" Jorgen asked.

"Just trying to get a better view of the battlefield," I said.

"Yeah, belay that. Back into formation. Our orders are to hold position."

We obeyed, but I found myself itching to get on with the battle. Sitting and waiting there, my fatigue kept bringing itself to my attention.

"Let's call Cobb," I said. "See if maybe we should send a pair of fighters out to scout the area."

"I'm sure they have scouts working the field," Jorgen said. "Hold position, Spin."

"Hey, Arturo," FM said over the line. "How far away is the main battle, do you suppose?"

"You're asking me?" he replied.

"You're the smart one."

There was silence on the line for a moment.

"Well?" FM asked.

"Oh," Arturo said. "Sorry. I was just . . . well, waiting for Nedd to make a wisecrack. I guess that's still my instinct. Here, I can calculate the distance for you exactly." A light flashed on our comm console. "Hey, Cobb. How far away is that fight?"

"About fifty klicks," Cobb said. "Stay put, cadets. Victory Flight is almost up from the caverns, and they'll relieve you once they come in." His light flipped off.

"Great calculations there, Amphi," FM said to Arturo.

"I consider it a mark of true intelligence to realize when someone else has already done your work for you," he said. "That would make a good saying, right, Quirk? Will you use that one sometime?"

"Uh . . . bless your stars."

"This isn't fair," Hurl said. "We should be fighting. We're hardly cadets anymore, and I'm tired of simulations. Right, Spin?"

Off in the distance, flashes of light marked where men and women were dying. Losing friends, like I had.

I hated that this creeping, insidious worry had somehow infiltrated my heart. This hesitance, this *fear*. It was stronger today, probably because I was tired. Maybe if I could get out into the fight, I could prove myself . . . *to* myself.

"Yeah, Hurl's right," I answered. "We should be killing Krell, not killing time."

"We do as we're *ordered*," Jorgen said. "And we don't debate with our commanders. I find it remarkable how you can claim to hardly be cadets anymore, when you have yet to grasp something so fundamental as command structure."

I bit my lip, then felt my face go warm with embarrassment. He was right. Stupid Jerkface.

I forced myself to wait for our replacements. They'd be one of the reserve flights, hangared—starfighters and all—down in the deep caverns. It was a careful balance; we couldn't risk a blast wiping out the entire DDF by destroying Alta. But any ships we didn't keep on immediate call took time to retrieve via the vehicle elevators.

Eventually, Cobb's line flashed back on. I stifled a sigh. Truth be told, we weren't in any shape to fight today—not after that long spent training. I prepared myself to turn and go back.

"Krell squadron," Cobb said. "Eight ships."

What?

"At heading 125-111-1000," Cobb continued. "One of our scouting pairs caught them sneaking in at low altitude. Flight-leader, your backup is still five to ten away. You'll need to engage."

Engage.

"Understood, Flight Command," Jorgen said.

"These are standard Krell interceptors, best the scouts could tell," Cobb said. "Admiral's orders are for you to get close, visually confirm that there isn't a bomber among them. Then destroy or drive back any fighters.

"AA guns will wait on standby; shooting into combat is a good way to get our own people killed. But if you can IMP any fighters that escape you, the small AA guns should be able to handle them. And if you can lure any enemy high enough, the large gun might be able to pick them off." Cobb paused. "I'm patching your ships into the general battle chatter. Good luck, cadets. Listen to your flightleader; remember your training. This one is for real."

The light clicked off.

"Finally!" Hurl said.

"I want a wide sweep formation," Jorgen said to us. "You heard the heading. 125-111-1000. This is going to be close to the ground. Watch your relative elevation. Let's move!"

We fell into a wide formation, in wingmate pairs. Me and Hurl, Jorgen and Arturo, FM and Kimmalyn. We sped through the gap between the two peaks, rounding to the east, along the indicated heading. We caught the visuals almost immediately—eight Krell ships flying in a U shape.

"We're yours, flightleader," a woman's voice said on the general channel. "Val-class. Ranger Seven, callsign: Cloak."

"Ranger Eight, callsign: Underscore," a male voice added.

Val-class. Those would be the two scout ships; I couldn't pick them out yet, but they'd join the fight with us.

My fatigue melted away in the face of my excitement. It was happening. A real fight. Not an accidental engagement, but actual orders to bring down an enemy squadron.

"Thanks for your help, scouts," Jorgen said. "We're ordered to get visual confirmation on the status of a bomber among these fellows. Ranger pair, I want you to coordinate that to Flight Command. My Pocos will run a scatter formation and try to break the enemy apart into individuals. Focus your attention on making sure we've identified each ship."

"Confirmed," Cloak said.

"All right, team," Jorgen said. "Overburn to Mag-3, then once we engage, drop to dogfighting speeds. Free-for-all, take what you can, and watch your wingmate." He breathed out. "Stars guard you."

"And you, flightleader," Arturo said.

They both sounded worried. My resolve wavered. Which I hated. I was *not* going to become a coward.

"Go!" Jorgen said.

"Yeah!" Hurl yelped, and hit her overburn.

I followed, tearing through the sky in a sudden acceleration toward the enemy. Exactly as in the simulations, the Krell scattered when directly engaged. They didn't worry about covering their wingmates; they counted on their superior ships to compensate for our superior coordination.

I hugged Hurl's left rear. We pulled out of overburn at high speed and banked right, picking a specific Krell ship to target. We'd moved into a debris fall, but it was mostly small chunks that were burning up high overhead. The occasional midsize piece dropped past us, trailing smoke, but none were big enough for light-lance maneuvers.

We fell to fighting speeds and stuck to our target. I held back just far enough to be outside range if Hurl fired her IMP. Two Val-class starfighters—designed for scanner avoidance and speed—swooped in overhead. They wouldn't have much in the way of firepower.

"Cloak," I said, flipping a button. "This is Skyward Ten, call-sign: Spin. The ship I'm chasing is a regular Krell interceptor."

"Confirmed," Cloak said. I didn't hear the rest of the chatter; the others would be reporting individually. Hopefully, the two scouts could keep track enough to identify each ship.

Hurl and I swept along the ground, dodging right, then left as we passed into a large crater. Hurl hit overburn to try to get close enough to IMP, but overshot as the Krell turned upward.

I stayed on it, and Hurl cursed softly, falling in behind me. "We don't have any tails, Spin. Let's bring that bucket down before it gets help."

"Confirmed." I kept my attention on the enemy. Yes . . . single-minded focus. My helmet sensors—which I mostly ignored these days—grew warm. I felt like I could anticipate the Krell's turns as it zipped out of the crater and banked right.

Focus. Nothing else mattered. No worries. No fear. Just me, my ship, and the target.

Closer.

Closer.

Almost.

"Guys! Help!"

Kimmalyn.

I cursed, my concentration breaking. There she was, being chased by three tails. Scud! FM curved around behind, trying to get into position to offer her support.

I broke off my chase, and Hurl followed as we rushed toward Kimmalyn. "Covering fire," I said, and the two of us opened up with destructors, spraying enough fire that the three tails went into defensive maneuvers and let Kimmalyn escape.

"Thanks," FM said, falling in beside Kimmalyn. I took the time to spot Arturo and Jorgen engaged in a dogfight with three Krell. With that much heat on them, they wouldn't dare use an IMP and leave themselves exposed.

"We need to pick off some strays," I said to Hurl, "and bring the odds in our favor."

"Right," she said. "At your three. Look good?"

"Go for it," I said, following her as we swooped toward another Krell. It looked identical to the one we'd been chasing—that same shape with wires trailing at the rear. It didn't appear that any of these were bombers.

I radioed in what we'd seen, and then we chased the ship out away from the main firefight. When it tried to cut left to circle around, I was able to overburn and drive it back. Isolated, it tried to simply outrun us on the straight, accelerating to Mag-3, then Mag-4.

"I'm going in!" Hurl said. Her booster flared into overburn, and she roared forward.

I was already anticipating her. We'd done this together so many times in the last week that I knew, by instinct, exactly how it would go. In a perfect maneuver, she got in just close enough and hit her IMP. With a flash of blue, her shield went down, and so did the Krell's.

I weaved past as she slowed, then I unleashed my destructors. It was almost a surprise when the Krell ship exploded into molten bits. It had actually *worked*!

Hurl whooped as we both slowed down. I pivoted and came back to cover her while she reignited her shield. A piece of space debris careened past me, exploding with a soft blast when it impacted not far below.

"Is that first blood?" I said, hitting a button. "Jorgen, we got one!"

"Congrats," he said, his voice tense.

I scanned the rest of the battle. He and Arturo were still dealing with three ships—and the scouts had managed to chase one off in the other direction, trying a maneuver similar to what Hurl and I had done. That meant . . .

Three ships, chasing Kimmalyn. *Again.*

"Scud," I said. "Hurl?"

"Go. I'm almost reignited."

I hit overburn, heading back toward the main battle.

"Guys?" Kimmalyn asked. *"Guys?"*

"I'm on you," FM said. "I'm on you . . ."

FM managed to chase off the ships, but another looped around to get behind her. When she went into a dodge, one of the three original ships went back on Kimmalyn.

Kimmalyn dodged erratically, and I could imagine her panicking. She wasn't picking a strategy and sticking to it; she basically just tried every dodging pattern, one after another.

I accelerated, but destructor fire flashed all around Kimmalyn, and her shield crackled, taking a hit. She went in and out of overburn.

I'm not going to catch her. Not in time.

"Quirk, hang on!" I said over the general line. "I'm going to try something. FM, everyone, if you can disengage and follow me—try to do so. Make a regular V with me on point."

I turned toward the ship chasing FM—which was much closer to me than the ones on Kimmalyn. I didn't fire, but instead swept around it in a loop, coming centimeters from the ground, sending up a cloud of dust. I then bolted upward and used my light-lance to grab a small chunk of space debris. In a hard turn, I pivoted and launched it up toward Kimmalyn's chaser. It passed impressively close to one of the Krell.

I pulled out of my loop, and FM fell in behind me. Jorgen and Arturo broke off their engagement for a moment and did likewise.

"What is this for?" Jorgen asked over the line. "What are we doing?"

"Saving Quirk," I said. Hopefully.

It depended on whether my theory was right. Tense, I turned upward and hit my overburn. For a brief moment, we held the formation.

Above, the Krell chasing Kimmalyn broke off and turned downward—toward me.

"Cobb warned that the Krell try to destroy our command structure," I said. "They take out flightleaders first, if they can identify them, and—"

Destructor fire sprayed around me.

Right.

I pulled into the most complex set of dodging loops I knew, the Barrett sequence. An impressive *four* Krell found their way to chasing me. That protected Kimmalyn—but four was more than I could handle. Each time I tried to pull upward or break away, a ship or two managed to cut me off. My Poco rattled as I spun and dodged, and destructors hit my shields.

Scud. Scud. Scud!

"I'm coming, Spin," Hurl said. "Hang on."

I kept dodging, destructors narrowly missing me. A part of my brain registered Arturo downing a Krell ship. How long had we been fighting? Had we really only shot down two? Where were those reinforcements?

"More ships," Jorgen said.

"Finally," I said with a grunt as I banked.

"Not ours. Theirs."

My turn took me straight into them—another flight of six Krell interceptors. I spun through them, and somehow avoided colliding with any. In the chaos, I finally managed to get some altitude.

My little trick must have really convinced them I was important, because three stuck on me—firing full out—as I screamed into the air. My proximity sensors blared, and my shields—

A shot hit me, causing my shield to crackle, then go out. Warning lights lit up all over my control panel.

I continued straight up, rotating my acclivity ring so it pointed down behind my ship. I just had to gain enough height—

An explosion flashed behind me. The shock wave rocked my unshielded Poco. I breathed a quiet prayer to whichever gunner was manning those AA guns when—in another enormous blast—a second Krell ship vanished from my proximity sensors.

The last Krell ship broke off, diving out of range. I leaned back against my seat, sweating, head pounding, lights flashing on my console. Alive. I was alive.

"Hurl!" FM said over the line. "What are you doing?"

"I'm fine," Hurl said with a grunt. "I'm going to get this one. The shields are almost down."

I quickly rotated my ship, tipping to see the battlefield alive with action beneath. Kimmalyn—I was pretty sure it was her—had flown upward after me, to get out of range. The rest of the battle was a mess of Krell ships and destructor fire.

There. I spotted Hurl chasing an enemy while being tailed by a swarm of three Krell. I'd been forced to leave her without a wing-mate.

I ignored my blinking shield light—no time to reignite—and dove back down toward the battlefield. I unleashed destructor fire toward Hurl's tails, but I was too far away and my shots were way off. The enemy didn't break from their chase.

Hurl took a hit. And another.

"Hurl, pull up!" I said.

"I've almost got him. We're never going to break any records by being cowards." She fired, scoring the shields of the Krell in front of her.

I hit overburn, tearing after them. But dives were dangerous on the body, and as soon as my GravCaps cut, I felt the g-forces in my eyes, forcing the blood up into my head.

I gritted my teeth, vision going red as I reached the group of Krell. I hit my IMP by touch. It couldn't take down my shield, after all. It was already gone.

I didn't see how many of them I caught. I was too close to doing myself permanent harm. I leveled out, my head pounding, my eyes aching. As my vision returned, I started my shield reignition and craned my head, trying to search for Hurl. Was she safe?

"I'm taking heavy fire!" Arturo said. "I need help!"

"Reinforcements are here!" Jorgen said.

Everything was chaos. I could barely comprehend the mess, though for the moment—remarkably—nobody seemed to be targeting me.

An explosion flashed off to my right.

"Got him!" Hurl said.

There. Hurl had shot down her target—but two Krell ships were still tailing her.

"Pull up, Hurl!" I said. "You've still got tails. Get up into the range of the AA guns!"

She turned upward, listening—finally. Two ships chased her. I ignited my shield, then turned after her, trying to help, but I'd lost a lot of ground.

"Shields down," Hurl said with a grunt.

"Quirk!" I said, desperate, flying—too far away—toward my friend. "Pick them off. I IMPed that group. Their shields are down too. Fire!"

"I . . ." Kimmalyn sounded rattled. "I . . ."

"You can do it, Quirk! Just like in the sims. Come on!"

A flash of light from a charged destructor sliced the air above us, firing toward the ships tailing Hurl.

And missed.

Hurl took a hit a second later, and her wing exploded, scattering pieces. The blue glow underneath her ship started to flash, the light flickering.

No . . .

Hurl's ship plummeted. From a distance, she was like any other piece of debris.

"Hurl!" I screamed. "Eject! Get out!"

"I . . ." Her voice was soft; I could barely hear it through the warnings going off on her dash and mine. "I can control it . . . I can steer . . ."

"Your acclivity ring is damaged!" I said. "You're losing altitude. Eject!"

"Not. A. Coward," she said. "Brave to the—"

A flash of light.

A small explosion on the ground, insignificant in the storm of destruction that was the battlefield.

"Pull out!" Jorgen said. "Everyone, pull out now! Leave this fight to the full pilots. We have orders to retreat!"

Hurl . . .

I couldn't move at first. I just stared at where she'd hit the ground.

329

"Spin," Jorgen said. When had he flown in beside me? "We have to go. We're too exhausted for this fight. Can you hear me?"

Blinking back tears, I whispered, "Yes." I fell into position behind him as we dove and skimmed the surface to escape the battlefield.

We pulled up next to FM and Arturo, and I gasped. Arturo's ship was blackened all along its left wing and side, its canopy cracked. His acclivity ring was still on, so he could stay in the air, but . . . scud. He'd survived a destructor hit after his shield had been knocked out.

When he called in, his voice was subdued, rattled. He seemed to know how lucky he was to have survived.

Hurl though . . .

Kimmalyn finally came sweeping down to join us.

". . . Hurl?" FM asked.

"She went down," Kimmalyn said. "I . . . I was watching. I tried, but . . ."

"She wouldn't eject," I said softly. "She refused."

"Let's get back," Jorgen said. Another flight of reinforcements arrived at the battlefield. As I watched them, any confidence I'd had in my abilities evaporated. Those fighters worked far more efficiently than we had, banking and flying as teams, coordinating in sharp motions.

I suddenly felt I'd need hundreds more hours of practice before I was ready. If I would ever be ready. I wiped away tears as Jorgen's voice, soft but firm, ordered us to accelerate to Mag-3.

As we flew, my hands shook—revealing me for the coward I was.

33

I woke up in a room.

A room? Not M-Bot's cockpit?

I sat up, my muscles aching, my head pounding. I was *inside*. In a *bed*. What had happened? Had I fallen asleep somewhere on DDF grounds? The admiral would—

You're in the infirmary, I remembered. *After the battle. Cobb sent you here to be checked over. They ordered you to sleep and undergo observation.*

I vaguely remembered objecting, but the nurse had forced me into a hospital gown, then had ordered me into bed in a small, empty room. I'd been too numb to object. I didn't even remember lying down; it was all a haze.

I *did* distinctly remember the flash as Hurl's ship impacted the ground. I lay back against a too-soft pillow, squeezing my eyes shut. Hurl was gone.

Eventually I forced myself out of bed. I found my things on a stool: my jumpsuit, laundered, sitting with my light-line bracelet on top of it. My pack rested on the floor beside it, and the radio

331

at the side was blinking. Scud . . . what if someone had answered that? Would M-Bot have been able to keep quiet?

My secrets suddenly seemed insignificant. In the face of what was happening . . . the horror of our flight slowly being consumed one by one . . . Who cared? Who *cared* if they found out my secrets?

Hurl was dead.

I checked the clock. 0545. I found the restroom, where I cleansed. I went back to my little room and dressed, then walked out to the hospital's front desk. A nurse looked me over, then handed me a red ticket.

Medical leave for loss recovery. Orders: one week. It was imprinted with my name, stamped and signed.

"I can't," I said. "The admiral will kick me out of—"

"Your entire flight has been given mandatory medical leave," the woman said. "On orders from Dr. Thior, head of medical. You won't be kicked out of anything, cadet. You need a rest."

I stared at the ticket.

"Go home," the woman said. "Spend a week with your family and recover. Stars above . . . they push you cadets too hard."

I stood there for a moment before I turned and walked out, dully meandering toward the training building. I took the roundabout way, past our Pocos. Four in a line. Arturo's ship was off to the side in a little maintenance hangar, with pieces scattered along the ground.

Go home. Where? To live in my cave? Back down to my mother, whose disapproval of the DDF might finally make me lose the rest of my nerve?

I crumpled the leave ticket in my pocket and walked to our classroom, where I sat down in my seat alone. I really just wanted to think, to talk to Cobb, to sort through all of this. Hurl had said . . . brave to the end. And she had been.

Scud. Hurl was *gone.* In Gran-Gran's stories they held feasts in honor of the fallen. But I didn't want to feast. I wanted to crawl somewhere dark and curl up.

Strangely, as class time approached, the door creaked open and the others—except for Jorgen—arrived in a solemn, quiet group. Hadn't the nurse said we *all* had leave? Perhaps they, like me, didn't want to accept it.

Kimmalyn stopped by my seat and gave me a hug. I didn't want a hug, but I took it. I needed it.

Even Jorgen arrived about ten minutes after class normally began. "I thought I might find you all here," he said.

I braced myself for him to tell us to go. For him to toe the official line and tell us class was canceled because we were on forced leave.

Instead he inspected us, then nodded in an approving way. "Skyward Flight, line up," he said in a soft voice. He hadn't tried that since the first day, when we'd ignored him. Today though, it felt right. We four got up and stood in a row.

Jorgen walked to the classroom intercom and pushed one of the buttons. "Jax, will you send to Captain Cobb and tell him his flight is waiting for him, in their usual room? Thank you."

Jorgen then walked over and joined us in line. Together, we waited. Fifteen after. Twenty after. It was 0729 before Cobb slammed open the door and limped in.

We snapped to attention and saluted.

He looked at us, then roared, *"SIT DOWN!"*

I started. That wasn't what I had expected. Still, along with the others, I jumped to obey.

"If you are in an uncontrolled descent," he shouted at us, his face coloring, "then you *eject*! You hear me! You *scudding EJECT*!"

He was angry. Like, *actually* angry. He pretended to be angry sometimes, but it was nothing like this: red-faced, spitting as he shouted.

"How many times did I say this?" he said. "How many times

did I give you orders? And still you buy into that nonsense?" He waved his hand out the window, toward the large DDF high command building. "The only reason we have this stupid culture of self-martyrdom is because *somebody* feels they have to justify our casualties. To make them seem honorable, righteous.

"It's neither one. And you're fools for listening to them. Don't you throw your lives away. Don't you *dare* be like that idiot yesterday. Don't you—"

"Don't call her an idiot," I snapped. "She was trying to fly a controlled crash. She was trying to save her ship."

"She was scared of being called a coward!" Cobb bellowed. "It *had nothing to do with the ship*!"

"Hurl—Hudiya—was a *hero*." I glared at him.

"She was a—"

I stood up. "Simply because you want to justify your cowardice in ejecting doesn't mean *we* have to do the same!"

Cobb froze. Then he kind of . . . deflated. He sank down into the seat by his desk. He didn't seem wise, or even grizzled. Just . . . old, tired, and sad.

I immediately felt embarrassed. Cobb didn't deserve that; he hadn't done anything wrong in ejecting, and even the DDF didn't blame him. And Hurl, well, *I'd* told her to eject. I'd practically *begged* her to.

But she hadn't. And we had to respect her choice, didn't we?

"You're all on medical leave for a week," Cobb said. "Dr. Thior has been pushing to give more leave to flights once they lose members, and it looks like she's started to get her way." He stood up and stared right at me. "I hope you enjoy being a hero when your corpse is rotting like your friend's, alone in a wasteland, forgotten and ignored."

"She'll be given a pilot's burial," I said. "Her name will be sung for generations."

He snorted. "If they had to sing the name of every fool cadet who died on her way to pilot, we'd never have time for anything else. And Hurl's corpse isn't going to be recovered for at least several weeks. The scouts confirmed that the crash destroyed her ship's acclivity ring beyond recovery. There's nothing on that Poco worth salvage priority, not considering that big wreck we're still working on.

"So your heroic friend will be left out there—another dead pilot buried by the slag of her own explosion. Scud. I have to go write a letter to her parents and explain why. I can't trust what Ivans will say."

He hobbled toward the door, but stopped and turned toward Kimmalyn. I hadn't noticed that she'd stood up. She saluted him, eyes teary. Then she dropped something on her seat.

Her cadet's pin.

Cobb nodded. "Keep the pin, Quirk," he told her. "You're dismissed with whatever honors matter to you."

He turned and left.

Dismissed? *Dismissed?* "He can't do that to you!" I demanded, turning toward Kimmalyn.

She wilted. "I asked for it after the battle. He told me to think about it overnight. And I did."

"But . . . you can't . . ."

Jorgen stepped up beside me, confronting Kimmalyn. "Spin is right, Quirk. You're an important member of this flight."

"The weakest member," Kimmalyn said. "How many times has one of you had to pull out of a fight to come and save me? I'm putting you all in danger." Contrary to what Cobb had said, she left her pin on her seat as she walked toward the door.

"Kimmalyn," I said, feeling helpless. I rushed after her and took her hand. "Please."

"I got her killed, Spin," she whispered. "You know that as well as I do."

"She got herself killed."

"The one shot that mattered. *That's* the one I missed."

"There were two ships chasing her. One shot, even if it had hit, might not have been enough."

She smiled, squeezed my hand, then left.

I felt my world collapsing. First Hurl, now Kimmalyn. I looked toward Jorgen. Surely he could stop this. Couldn't he?

He stood stiffly, tall, with that too-handsome face. He stared straight ahead, and I thought I could see something in his eyes. Guilt? Pain?

He's watching his flight break apart around him too.

I had to do something. Make *some* kind of sense out of this disaster, and of my pain. But no, I couldn't—*wouldn't*—stop Kimmalyn. At least . . . at least she'd be safe this way.

Hurl though . . .

"Arturo," I said, picking up my pack, "about how far out was that battle, would you say?"

"Pretty close to our original position, beyond the AA guns. Say, eighty klicks."

I shouldered my pack. "Great. I'll see you all in a week."

"Where are you going?" FM asked.

"I'm going to find Hurl," I said, "and give her a pilot's burial."

34

I trudged across the dry, dusty ground. My compass kept me on the right heading, which was important, because everything looked the same out here on the surface.

I tried not to think. Thinking was dangerous. I'd barely known Bim and Morningtide, and their deaths had left me shaken for weeks. Hurl had been my *wingmate*.

It was more though. She'd been like me. At least, like I pretended to be. She was usually one step ahead of me, leading the charge.

In her death, I saw myself.

No. No thinking.

That didn't stop the emotions. The hole inside, the pain of a wound rubbed raw. After this, nothing could ever be the same. Yesterday hadn't just marked the death of a friend. It marked the death of my ability to pretend this war was—in *any* way— glorious.

My radio was blinking. I hit the switch.

"Spensa?" M-Bot asked. "Are you certain this journey is wise? I am not capable of worry, mind you, but—"

"I'd rather be alone," I said. "I'll call you tomorrow or some-thing." I clicked the radio off and stuffed it inside my backpack, where I'd stashed some rat meat and water for the journey. If it wasn't enough, I could go hunting. Maybe I'd vanish into the cav-erns, never to return. Become a nomad, like my clan before the founding of Alta.

And never fly again?

Just walk, Spensa, I told myself. *Stop thinking and walk.*

This was simple.

This I could do.

I was about two hours outside Alta when a sound broke the quiet and I turned to see a hovercar approaching. It flew three meters off the ground and towed a wake of dust behind. Had someone warned the admiral? Had she sent MPs with some made-up reason why I couldn't be out here?

No . . . As it got closer I realized I recognized that blue car. It was Jorgen's. He must have gotten the power matrix replaced.

I grunted, then turned forward and kept walking. He pulled up beside me and lowered his car so that his head was barely a meter above mine.

"Spin? Are you really planning to *walk* eighty klicks?"

I didn't reply.

"You realize it's dangerous out here," Jorgen said. "I should order you back. What if you get caught in a debris fall?"

I shrugged. I'd been living near the surface for months, and had only really been in danger that one time—when I'd discov-ered M-Bot's cave.

"Spensa," Jorgen said. "For the North Star's sake, get in. I'll drive you."

"Don't you have some fancy rich-person event you need to be attending?"

"My parents don't know about the medical leave yet. For a little while, I'm as free as you are."

Me? Free? I wanted to laugh in his face.

Still, he had a car. This would transform a multiday trip into one that would last a few hours. I resented him for giving me the option, as I'd wanted to be on my own. To suffer, perhaps. But a part of me knew I wouldn't reach Hurl's body with what I had in my pack. I'd probably be forced to turn back after a day of hiking.

"I *want* to go with you," Jorgen said. "It's a good idea. Hurl . . . deserves this. I brought some materials for the pyre."

Stop being right, Jorgen, I thought. But I walked around the car and climbed into the passenger side. I had dust up to my thighs, which I smeared all over the car's interior, but he didn't seem to notice.

He pushed on the car's throttle, sending us darting across the landscape. The car had a small acclivity ring, and no booster, just basic thrusters—but being so close to the ground, I felt like we were going faster than we really were. Particularly with no roof and the wind blowing my hair.

I let the motion transfix me.

"Do you want to talk?" Jorgen asked.

I didn't reply. I didn't have anything to say.

"A good flightleader is supposed to be able to help his flight with their problems," he said. "You couldn't have saved her, Spin. There's nothing you could have done."

"You think she should have pulled out," I said.

"I . . . That's not relevant now."

"You think she shouldn't have gone for that kill. You think she disobeyed protocol, and shouldn't have flown off on her own. You're thinking it. I know you are. You're judging her."

"So now you're angry at me for things I *might* be thinking?"

"Were you thinking them? *Were* you judging her?"

Jorgen didn't say anything. He kept driving, wind blowing in his too-neat, too-perfect hair.

"Why do you have to be so stiff all the time?" I asked. "Why does your way of 'helping' always sound like you're quoting from some manual? Are you some kind of thinking machine? Do you actually *care*?"

He winced, and I squeezed my eyes shut. I knew he cared. I'd seen him that morning in the classroom, trying to find a way to save Morningtide in the simulation. Over and over.

My words were stupid. Thoughtless.

Which was exactly what I got for not thinking.

"Why do you put up with me?" I asked. I opened my eyes and leaned my head back, staring at the debris field high overhead. "Why didn't you turn me in for vandalizing your car, or assaulting you, or a dozen other things?"

"You saved Nedd's life."

I tipped my head and looked at Jorgen. He was driving with his eyes fixed straight forward.

"You followed my friend into the belly of a beast," he continued. "And you towed him by his collar to safety. Even before that, I knew. You're insubordinate, mouthy, and . . . well, you're scudding frustrating. But when you fly, Spin, you fly as part of a team—and you keep my people safe."

He looked at me, met my eyes. "You can swear at me all you want, threaten me, whatever. So long as you fly like you did yesterday, protecting the others, I want you on my team."

"Hurl still died," I said. "Kimmalyn still left."

"Hurl died because of her recklessness. Quirk left because she felt inadequate. Those problems, like your insubordination, are my fault. It's *my* job to keep my flight in line."

"Well, if they're handing you impossible jobs, why don't they just ask you to defeat the Krell all on your own? Seems about as likely to happen as you wrangling the lot of us . . ."

He stiffened, eyes forward, and I realized he'd taken it as an insult. Scud.

We eventually passed the AA-gun battery, and Jorgen called

340

them to prevent their proximity warnings from going off. They let him go without question, once he mentioned who he was—the son of a First Citizen.

After the AA guns, it was surprisingly easy to locate Hurl's wreckage. She'd skidded some hundred or more meters, gouging the dusty earth with a wide scar. The ship had broken into three big chunks. The rear of the fuselage, with the booster, had apparently ripped off first. As we drove along, we found where the middle of the fuselage—what was left of it—had made a large black mark on the ground. The power matrix had exploded after hitting some rocks, and had destroyed the acclivity ring. That was the flash I'd seen.

But a small chunk of the front fuselage—with the cockpit— had broken free and skidded on farther. My heart leaped as I spotted the bent remnants of the cockpit crushed up against a pile of large boulders ahead.

Jorgen landed the hovercar, and I scrambled out, dashing ahead of him. I jumped onto the first of the rocks, then heaved myself up onto another, scraping my fingers. I needed to get high enough to see into the crushed cockpit. I had to know. I pulled myself up to a higher boulder, where I could look down into the broken canopy.

She was there.

A part of me hadn't believed she would be. A part of me had hoped that Hurl had somehow pulled herself from the wreckage— that she was walking back, battered but alive. Self-assured as always.

That was a fantasy. Her pressure suit reported vitals, and we all had emergency transmitters to activate if we needed rescuing. If Hurl had survived, the DDF would have known. One glimpse confirmed that she'd probably died at the first impact. She was crushed—pinned inside the mangled metal of the cockpit.

I tore my gaze away, cold flooding my chest. Pain. Emptiness. I looked back along the scar in the ground her ship had made while crashing. That long swath seemed to indicate that she'd managed

341

to get her ship horizontal at the end, that she'd gotten close to a gliding position.

So she'd almost done it. With a blown-off wing and a broken acclivity ring, she'd *still* almost landed.

Jorgen grunted as he tried to climb up. I gave him a hand, but sometimes I forgot how small I was compared to someone like him. He nearly pulled me right off with a casual jerk of his arm.

He scrambled onto the rock beside me, then took a quick glance at Hurl. He went pale and turned aside, settling down on an upper portion of a boulder. I set my jaw, then forced myself to climb into the cockpit and pull Hurl's pin off her bloodied flight suit. The least we could do was return that to her family.

I looked at Hurl's lacerated face, her one remaining eye staring ahead. Defiant until the end, for all the good it had done. Brave . . . cowardly . . . she was still dead, so what did it matter?

Feeling like a terrible friend for those thoughts, I closed her eye, then climbed out and wiped my hands on my jumpsuit.

Jorgen nodded toward the car. "I've got the things for the pyre in the trunk."

I let myself down with my light-line, and he followed. In the trunk of the vehicle, we found some oil and a bundle of wood, which surprised me. I'd been expecting coal. He really *was* rich if he had this on hand. We climbed back to the ship, then pulled the bundle up after us with my light-line.

We started packing the wood into the cockpit, piece by piece. "This is how our ancestors used to do it," Jorgen said as he worked. "Burn the ship, out on the ocean."

I nodded, wondering how little he thought of my education, if he assumed I didn't know that. Neither of us had ever seen an ocean, of course. Detritus didn't have them.

I poured oil onto the wood and the body, then stepped back, and Jorgen handed me the lighter. I lit a small stick, then tossed it into the canopy.

The sudden intensity of the flames took me by surprise, and sweat prickled my brow. The two of us retreated farther, and eventually climbed onto one of the higher boulders.

By tradition, we saluted the flames. "Return to the stars," Jorgen said—the officer's part. "Sail them well, warrior."

It wasn't the whole elegy, but it was enough. We settled down on the rocks, to watch—by tradition—until the fire went out. I rubbed Hurl's pin, bringing back the gleam.

"I'm not defiant," Jorgen said.

"What? I thought you grew up in the deep caverns."

"I mean, I'm Defiant—I'm from the Defiant caverns. But I don't *feel* defiant. I don't know how to be like you. And Hurl. Since I was little, everything has been scheduled for me. How am I supposed to follow the grand speeches—defying the Krell, defying our doom—when everything I do has seven rules attached to it?"

"At least it got you flight lessons and free entry into the DDF. At least you can fly."

He shrugged. "Six months."

"Excuse me?"

"That's how long I get after graduation, Spin. They put me in Cobb's class because it's supposed to be the safest for cadets—and once I graduate, I'm to fly for six months. At that point, I'll have enough of a record as a pilot to be respected by my peers, so my family will pull me out."

"They can *do* that?"

"Yeah. They'll probably make it look like a family emergency—a need for me to step into my government position sooner than anticipated. The rest of my life will be spent in meetings, interfacing on behalf of my father with the DDF."

"Will you . . . ever get to fly?"

"I suppose I could go up for fun. But how could it compare to flying a real starfighter in battle? How could I go out for joyrides—a few calculated and protected moments—when I've had something so much greater?" He glanced up at the sky. "My father always worried that I liked flying too much. To be honest, during my practices—before I started official training—I thought a pair of wings might let me escape his legacy. But I'm not defiant. I'll do what's expected of me."

"Huh," I said softly.

"What?"

"Nobody calls *your* father a coward. Yet . . . you do still live in his shadow." Somehow, Jorgen was trapped as soundly as I was. All his merits couldn't buy him freedom.

Together we watched the embers of the pyre die as the sky grew darker, the ancient skylights dimming. We shared a few thoughts of Hurl—though we had both missed out on her nightly dinnertime antics, and had only heard of them secondhand.

"She was like me," I finally said as the fire grew cold and the hour late. "More me than I am, these days."

Jorgen didn't press me on that. He just nodded, and by this light—a few embers of the fire reflecting in his eyes—his face didn't seem quite as punchable as it always had before. Maybe because I could read the emotions behind that mask of authoritarian perfection.

When the last light of the fire went out, we stood and saluted again. Jorgen then climbed down to his car, explaining he needed to check in with his family. I stood on the high rock, looking again along the gouge that Hurl's crash had caused.

Did I blame her for wasting her life? Or did I respect her for refusing—at all costs—to be branded a coward? Could I feel both at once?

She really did almost make it, I thought, noting the nearly un-damaged wing lying nearby. And farther back, the rear end of the fuselage. Ripped off, sitting on its own.

Booster included.

I felt a sudden spike of realization. It would be weeks before

344

anyone came to scavenge this wreckage. And if they did wonder where the booster went, they'd probably assume it blew off in the initial destructor hit.

If I could somehow get it to my cave . . .

It wouldn't be robbing the dead. Scud, Hurl would *tell* me to take the booster. She'd want me to fly and fight. But how in the world would I get it all the way back? A booster would be orders of magnitude heavier than I could lift . . .

I looked toward Jorgen, sitting in his car. Did I dare?

Did I have any other choice? I *had* seen some chains in the trunk when we'd been unloading the wood . . .

I climbed down from the rocks and headed toward the car, walking up right as he was turning off the radio. "No emergencies yet," he said. "But we should get going."

I debated for a moment before finally asking. "Jorgen, how much can this car lift?"

"A fair amount. Why?"

"Are you willing to do something that sounds a little crazy?"

"Like flying out and giving our own funeral to one of our friends?"

"*More* crazy," I said. "But I need you to do it, and not ask too many questions. Pretend I'm insane with grief or something."

He looked at me, carefully. "What is it, exactly, that you want to do?"

35

"You realize," Jorgen said as we flew back toward Alta, "I'm starting to get *very* suspicious."

I looked over the side to where the booster dangled from the bottom of his hovercar, connected by chains to the tow ring on the underside of the chassis. His car's small acclivity ring had been barely enough to lift the weight.

"First you steal my power matrix," Jorgen said, "now this. What are you doing? Building your own Poco?" He laughed.

When I didn't join in, he looked at me. Then he put the heel of his palm to his forehead, rubbing it as understanding sank in. "You are. You're building a starfighter."

"I told you not to ask too many questions."

"And I never agreed. Spin, you're *building* a *ship*?"

"Repairing," I said. "I found a wreck."

"All salvage belongs to the DDF. Claiming it is the same as stealing."

"Like you just helped me steal a booster?"

He groaned and leaned back.

"What did you *think* we were doing?" I asked, amused. "We spent half an hour pulling a chunk of salvage from the ground!"

"You told me to assume you were emotionally unstable because of Hurl's death!"

"I didn't expect you to *believe* me," I said. "Look, I've done this forever without getting into trouble. Down in Igneous, I used salvage to build my own speargun for hunting."

"An entire fighter is different from a speargun. How are you planning to fix the thing? You don't have the expertise for that—or the time!"

I didn't reply; no need to get Rig into trouble.

"You're insane," he said.

"Admiral Ironsides won't let me fly. She's got a grudge against me because of my father. Even if I graduate, I'll spend my life grounded."

"So you build your own ship? What do you think is going to happen? That you'll show up on a battlefield in the nick of time, and everyone will simply *forget* to ask where you got your own *scudding* starfighter?"

I . . . honestly didn't have a response to that. I'd shoved logic aside, figuring questions like that were bridges to be burned once I captured them.

"Spin, even assuming you could fix a crashed Poco yourself— you can't, by the way—the first time you took the thing into the air, the DDF would pick it up on scanners. If you don't identify yourself, you'll get shot down. If you do, they'll take that ship from you faster than you can say 'court-martial.'"

I'd like to see them try. "Maybe I don't fly it for the DDF," I said. "There are other caverns, other people."

"None run their own air force. They've been able to settle down because the Krell attention is focused on us."

"Some use ships for trading," I pointed out.

"And you'd abandon the fight?" he asked. "Go run cargo?"

"I don't know." I sank back in my seat, trying not to sulk. He was right. He was *usually* right. I was starting to kind of not hate him, but he was still Jerkface.

He sighed. "Look, if you want to fly, maybe I can get you duty as a private pilot. A few of the families in the deep caverns maintain fighters as escorts for trading operations. You wouldn't need to repair any old salvage. You could use one of our ships. Arturo's family has a few."

I perked up. "Really? That's something I could do?"

"Maybe." He thought for a moment. "Well, probably not. The slots are highly contested, usually flown by retired DDF pilots. And . . . and you need a really great reputation."

Something the daughter of a coward doesn't have. And will never have, unless I can fight for the DDF.

The great contradiction of my life. I would never be worth anything unless I could prove myself—but I couldn't prove myself because nobody would give me the chance.

Well, I wasn't willing to give up the dream of flying M-Bot. Ridiculous—and ill-conceived—as my plans sounded when Jorgen laid them out, M-Bot was *my ship*. I'd find a way.

We flew in silence. And that left me thinking about the booster, my mind shifting to the wreckage. Strangely, it seemed that I could still feel the flames against my skin. I'd hoped that performing the funeral would help with the pain, but I still ached. Hurl's passing left so much emptiness. So many questions.

Is this going to happen every time I lose a friend in battle? I wondered. It made me want to run away and become a cargo pilot like Jorgen said. To never have to face the Krell or their destructors again.

Coward.

Eventually Alta came into sight in the distance. I took Jorgen's arm and pointed a few degrees to the left, toward my hidden cavern. "Fly us that direction."

He gave me a suffering look, but did as I'd asked. I had him stop forty meters or so from my hole, to avoid any blowing dust revealing the part of the ground that was a hologram.

He lowered the hovercar to gently set the booster down. As soon as I felt it hit the surface, I attached my light-line to one side of the car and prepared to lower myself to unhook the booster.

"Spin," Jorgen said, stopping me. "Thank you."

"For?"

"For making me do this. It feels better to have seen her off properly."

Well, at least it had helped one of us.

"I'll see you in a week," he said. "My family will probably schedule every moment of my free time." He looked at me, then got a very strange expression on his face. "This broken ship . . . it's got a working acclivity ring?"

"I . . . Yes." He'd helped me out, and he knew enough already to get me into trouble ten times over if he wanted. He deserved honesty. "Yes, it's got an acclivity ring. The whole ship is in better shape than you'd think, actually."

"You fix it, then," he said. "You fix it, and you *fly*. You find a way, and you defy them. For those of us who don't have the courage."

I cocked my head, but he turned away, setting his jaw and taking the wheel in both hands. So I lowered myself down, then unhooked the booster. We were close enough that I could maneuver M-Bot over and attach it, then lower it into the cavern. I'd need the chain though, so I only unhooked one end.

I waved to Jorgen, and when he rose up, the chain slid through the tow rings underneath his car and fell beside me. He didn't ask after it. He just flew off toward Alta. And responsibility.

Somehow . . . it was true. Somehow, I *was* more free than he was. Which felt crazy.

I pulled my radio from my backpack. "Hey, guess what, M-Bot. I have a present for you."

"Mushrooms?"

"Better."

". . . *Two* mushrooms?"

I smiled. "Freedom."

36

"I'm not going to ask you where you got this," Rig said. He was standing, his hands on his hips, looking at the booster, which M-Bot and I had moved to the cavern floor.

"See, that's why you're in engineering," I said. "You're smart."

"Not smart enough to stay out of this mess," he said.

I grinned. M-Bot's maintenance gear included a small mobile acclivity ring for service purposes. Dwarfed by the big one he flew with, it was a small hoop no larger than my hands pressed together, with a rechargeable power source.

Rig and I placed the maintenance ring under the booster. That—once activated—raised the hunk of metal into the air about a meter. Together we pushed it into place behind M-Bot, near where it would need to be installed.

"So?" I asked. "Will it fit?"

"I can probably make it fit," Rig said, prodding at the booster with a wrench. "Whether I can make it work or not will depend on how damaged it is. Please tell me you didn't rip this off a functioning DDF ship."

"You said you weren't going to ask."

He flipped the wrench in his hand, eyeing the booster. "You had better thank me in your speech when you hit ace."

"Six times."

"And name your firstborn son after me."

"Firstborn will be Executioner Destructorius. But you can have number two."

"And bake me some killer algae biscuits or something."

"Do you *seriously* want to eat anything I've baked?"

"Now that I think about it, scud no. But next time *I* bake some, you better have a compliment ready. No more 'It would taste better with some rat in it.'"

"On my honor as a pilot," I said solemnly.

Rig put his hands back on his hips, then grinned widely. "We're actually going to do it, aren't we? We're going to make this old bucket fly."

"I'd be insulted at that," M-Bot said through the speakers at the side of the ship, "if I were human!"

Rig rolled his eyes. "Would you go keep that thing occupied? I don't want it jabbering at me while I work."

"I can both talk to her *and* bother you!" M-Bot called. "Multitasking is an essential means by which an artificial intelligence achieves more efficiency than fleshy human brains."

Rig looked at me.

"No insult intended!" M-Bot added. "You have very nice shoes!"

"We've been working on his compliments," I said.

"They aren't nearly as stupid as the rest of your outfit!"

"He still needs practice."

"Just stop him from bothering me, please," Rig said, lugging over his toolbox. "Honestly, if I ever find the person who thought it was a good idea to make a machine that *talked* to you while you were repairing it . . ."

I climbed up to the cockpit and latched it, pressurizing and soundproofing it. "Leave him alone, M-Bot," I said, settling into my seat. "Please."

"If you wish. My processors are busy anyway, trying to devise a proper joke about the fact that Rig is installing me a new butt. My logic circuits are arguing that the expeller I use for old oil is actually a better metaphoric anus."

"I *really* don't want to talk about your scatological functions," I said, leaning back. I stared up through the glass, but there was only blackness and dark rock.

"I believe that human beings need humor during times of depression," M-Bot said. "To lighten their grim outlook and make them forget their tragedies."

"I don't want to forget my tragedies."

M-Bot was silent. Then, in a smaller voice—somehow vulnerable—he asked, "Why do humans fear death?"

I frowned toward the console, where I knew the camera was. "Is that another attempt at humor?"

"No. I want to understand."

"You offer lengthy commentary about humans, but you can't understand something as simple as fear of death?"

"Define it? Yes. But understand it? . . . No."

I leaned my head back again. How did one explain mortality to a robot? "You miss your memories, right? The data banks that were destroyed in your crash? So you understand loss."

"I do. But I cannot miss my own existence—by definition. So why would I fear it?"

"Because . . . someday you'll stop being here. You'll cease to exist. Get destroyed."

"I am powered down repeatedly. I was powered down for a hundred and seventy-two years. How is it different if I'm never powered on again?"

I fidgeted, playing with the control sphere's buttons. I still had six more days of leave. Of simply . . . sitting around? Supposedly recovering? But really just prodding at that hole inside me, like a child constantly picking at a scab?

"Spensa?" M-Bot said, pulling me back. "*Should* I fear death?"

"A good Defiant doesn't," I said. "So maybe you were programmed this way on purpose. And it's not really my own death that I fear. Actually, I don't *fear* anything. I'm not a coward."

"Of course."

"But losing the others has me . . . wavering. I should be strong enough to withstand this. I knew what it would cost to become a pilot. I've trained, and prepared, and listened to Gran-Gran's stories, and . . ." I took a deep breath.

"I miss my pilot," M-Bot said. "I 'miss' him because of the loss of knowledge. Without proper information, I cannot judge my future actions. My ability to interface with the world, and to be efficient, is lessened." He hesitated. "I am broken, and do not know how to fulfill my purpose. Is this how you feel?"

"Maybe." I made a fist, forcing myself to stop fidgeting. "But I'm going to beat it, M-Bot."

"It must be nice to have free will."

"You have free will too. We've talked about this."

"I simulate it in order to seem more palatable to humans," he said. "But I do not have it. Free will is the ability to ignore your programming. Humans can ignore theirs, but I—at a fundamental level—cannot."

"Humans don't have programming."

"Yes you do. You have too much of it. Conflicting programs, none of it interfacing properly, all calling different functions at the same time—or the same function for contradictory reasons. Yet you *ignore* it sometimes. That is not a flaw. It is what makes you *you*."

I mulled that over, but I was so anxious that I had trouble sitting still. Finally, I pushed open the canopy and climbed down, then fetched my radio and my pack.

Rig was absorbed by his work, humming to himself a tune I didn't know as he stripped the broken pieces of fuselage from the booster.

I stepped over. "You need any help?" I asked him.

"Not at the moment. I might need you in a day or two, if I have to replace wires again." He got another section off, then poked into the hole with a screwdriver. "Good thing I got the shield igniter back together. I'm going to have my hands full with this for a while."

"How'd that go, by the way?" I asked. "The schematics you drew for the shield?"

Rig shook his head. "It was like I worried. I took the drawings to my superiors, but when I couldn't explain what was supposed to be different about this new shield I'd 'designed,' it didn't go anywhere. M-Bot's shield—and his GravCaps—are beyond my ability to figure out. We need real engineers studying the ship, not an intern."

We shared a look, then Rig turned back to his work. Neither of us wanted to extrapolate further on that idea, the growing truth that we really *should* have turned M-Bot in. I hid behind the fact that he didn't want us to, and had threatened to destroy his own systems if we did. Truth was, we were both probably committing treason by working on him in secret.

Rig looked like he needed to concentrate, so I stopped bothering him. I gave Doomslug a rub on the "head," to which she trilled in enjoyment. Then I climbed out of the cavern and started walking.

"Where are you going?" M-Bot asked when I clicked the radio on.

"I need something to do," I said. "Something other than just sitting there, dwelling on what I've lost."

355

"When I am like that, I write a new subroutine for myself."

"Humans don't work the same way," I said, radio to my head. "But something you said has me thinking. You mentioned needing proper information to judge how to act."

"Early AIs were unwieldy things," he said. "They had to be programmed to take actions based on explicit circumstances—and so each discrete decision had to include a list of instructions for each possibility.

"More advanced AIs are able to extrapolate. We rely on a base set of rules and programs, but adapt our choices based on similar situations we have encountered. However, in both cases, *data* is essential to making proper choices. Without past experiences to rely upon, we cannot guess what to do in the future. That is more than you wanted to know, but you commanded me to leave Rodge alone, so I'm finding things to say to you."

"Thank you, I guess."

"Also, human beings need someone friendly to listen to them when they're grieving. So feel free to talk to me. I will be friendly. You have nice shoes."

"Is that the only thing you notice about people?"

"I've always wanted shoes. They're the sole piece of clothing that makes any sense, assuming ideal environmental conditions. They don't play into your strange and nonsensical taboos about not letting anyone see your—"

"Is this *really* the only thing you can think of to comfort someone who is grieving?"

"It was number one on my list."

Great.

"The list has seven million entries. Do you want to hear number two?"

"Is it silence?"

"That didn't even make the list."

"Move it to number two."

"All right, I . . . Oh."

I lowered the radio, walking along my familiar path. I needed to be doing something, and they wouldn't let me fly. But maybe I could answer a question.

Somewhere in the DDF headquarters was a holorecording of the Battle of Alta. And I was going to find it.

37

By the time I reached Alta Base, I had a pretty solid plan. It all revolved around the one person I knew had access to the battle replays.

Cobb's office was a little thing he kept immaculately clean and sterilized of all personal effects. No pictures on the walls, no books on the shelves.

Today, he sat working at his narrow desk, reading some reports and marking them with a red pencil. He glanced up as I knocked on the window, then turned back to his work.

I slipped the door open.

"FM's been looking for you," he said, moving one sheet onto another stack. "I told her I didn't know where your cave was. But if you want to contact the others, tune to 1250 on your radio. That's Arturo's house band."

"Thanks." I took a deep breath, going over my carefully planned words. "Sir, I hope I don't get into trouble for this, but Jorgen and I drove out and fetched Hurl's pin. For her family." I stepped forward and set it on the desk. "He called in to ground support and warned them we were driving past."

Cobb sighed. "Well, I guess it isn't forbidden." He picked up the pin. "Did you clear this with salvage?"

"Er, no, sir."

"That means more paperwork for me," he said.

"We gave her a pilot's burial, sir," I said. "Best we could manage. Will you tell her family for me?"

He tucked the pin away. "They'll like that, cadet. And I doubt even salvage will complain when I put it to them that way. But *do* try not to get me into any more trouble this week."

"I'll try, sir," I said, searching for a good way to move on to what I really wanted. Something that wouldn't raise too much suspicion from Cobb. "I wish I could use my time somehow. This much leave is kind of frustrating."

"Medical leave can shoot itself into the sun," Cobb agreed. "I like Thior—she keeps pushing for things like counseling for pilots, good ideas. But she needs to understand that the last thing a bunch of grieving soldiers need is more free time."

"They won't let me fly or train, but maybe . . ." I pretended to give it some thought. "Maybe I could watch old battles? To learn from them?"

"Archive is in building H," Cobb said, pointing. "They have headsets you can use for viewing the battles. You'll need my authorization code for the door. Two six four oh seven."

A dozen different arguments—which I'd prepared to nudge him toward offering this—died on my lips.

That . . . was easy.

"Um, thanks," I said, trying not to show how excited I was. "I guess I'll go, um, do that then."

"Cadets aren't supposed to use the archive. If you run into trouble, tell them I sent you to fetch something for me, then get out. I'll do the paperwork for that, if I have to. Scudding bureaucrats." Cobb moved a sheet from one stack to the other. "And Spin?"

"Sir?"

"Sometimes, the answers we need don't match the questions we're asking." He looked up at me. "And sometimes, the coward makes fools of wiser men."

I met his eyes, then blushed, thinking of what I'd said to him the day before. In anger. *Just because you want to justify your cowardice doesn't mean we have to do the same!*

"I'm . . . sorry, sir, for—"

"Get going. I'm not completely ready to deal with you yet."

"Yes, sir."

I stepped out of the office. That look in his eyes—he'd known *exactly* why I wanted to watch old battles. He'd seen through my subterfuge immediately.

Then why had he given me the code to get in?

I made my way to the proper building, used the code, and started walking through the archive shelves. Many were filled with old books that had been carried with the crew of the fleet: histories of Old Earth, the writings of philosophers. Mostly ancient stuff, but there were modern writings too. Manuals and histories.

Pilots moved about here, their pins glittering on their blue jumpsuits. As I regarded them, I realized why Cobb might have let me do this. I was less than two months away from graduation. On one hand, it seemed incredible that so much time had passed. On the other, a lot had been packed into those few months.

Either way, I'd soon have been given access to this place. Maybe Cobb knew I'd inevitably find the secrets, so he didn't mind letting me in now? Or was it that he feared I'd somehow be denied this privilege, even if I did graduate? So he was making certain I got the chance now.

I didn't dare ask for directions; I couldn't risk someone noticing the color of my pin and asking why a cadet was in here. I poked through the musty, too-quiet room until I found a wall of small metal cases with dates and battle names on the spines. They were perhaps four centimeters square, and I watched as a pilot took one from the wall and plugged it into a viewing machine. She leaned forward, settling her eyes into the headset to watch.

This was what I wanted, though these cases only went back five years. Around the corner, I found a second room. The door was closed, but the windows along the sides showed it had more cases inside. I tried Cobb's code on the door.

It opened, and I slipped inside, heart thumping. Nobody else was in here, and the short rack of metal cases counted backward all the way to . . . to the one. The Battle of Alta. There were a few before it, but this one seemed to glow on the shelf, beckoning me.

There weren't any missing spots in this row. These didn't get moved often. There also wasn't a viewing device in here. So . . . did I just grab it and go?

Bold. Defiant. Even if lately you don't feel like you're either one.

I palmed the case and ducked out of the room. No alarms sounded. Not quite believing it, I stepped out of the building, my prize in hand.

The secret. Right here, in my fingers. I owed Cobb an enormous debt—not just for today, but for everything. For making space for me in his classroom, when no one else would give me a chance. For suffering me all these weeks, for not punching me square in the face when I'd called him a coward.

I'd make it up to him. Somehow. I tucked the data square into my pocket and strode toward the training building. I could probably plug this in to my mockpit, though could I even use that while on medical leave?

I was so single-minded in my attention that I didn't notice the people I was passing until one called out to me. "Wait. Spin?"

I froze, then turned. It was FM, wearing a skirt. Like, a *real skirt* and blouse, her short blonde hair done with silver barrettes.

"Stars, where have you been?" she said, grabbing me by the arm. "In your cave?"

"Where else would I be?"

"You have *leave*," she said. "The domineering authoritaria has relaxed its viselike grip on us. We can go off base."

"I go off base every night."

"This is different," she said, pulling me by my arm. "Come on. You're lucky Quirk sent me to fetch something for her."

"Kimmalyn?" I said. "You've seen her since she left?"

"Of course I have. It's not like she moved to another planet or something. Come on."

I wasn't likely to change FM's mind when she was in one of her crusading moods . . . so I let her tow me after her. Out past the gates of the base. Along the rows of buildings, into one I'd never paid much attention to before.

Which held a completely new world.

38

The restaurant wasn't much, really. A jumble of tables full of younger pilots and cadets. Dim lighting. A man playing hand drums in the corner for some music.

FM pulled me to a table where Arturo sat with his arm around a girl I didn't recognize—short hair, brown skin. Kimmalyn sat primly at the table with a very large, *very* purple drink in front of her. Next to her was Nedd.

Nedd. I hadn't seen him in *weeks*. Ever since that night on the launchpad! He had on trousers and a button-up shirt, and a jacket was draped across the back of the chair. It was strange to see him in street clothes. Especially next to Arturo, who had on his cadet's jumpsuit.

I could hear Nedd's easygoing voice over the hum of other chatter in the room. "I never said I was *that* kind of stupid. I'm the other kind of stupid. You know, likable stupid."

Arturo rolled his eyes, but the girl next to him leaned forward. "Nedd," she said, "stupid is stupid."

"No it's not. You're talking to an expert. I—"

"Guys," FM interrupted, presenting me with hands raised to

the side, "look who I found slinking around the base. She was moping about how she can't shoot anything for a few days."

Nedd thumbed toward FM. "See, she's the other kind of stupid."

FM smacked him on the back of the head, and he grinned. Then he stood and grabbed me in a suffocating bear hug. "Good to see you, Spin. Order something to eat. Arturo's paying."

"I am?"

"You're rich."

"So are you."

"I'm the other kind of rich. The poor kind."

"Oh, for the Saint's sake," Arturo said.

"Don't use the Saint's name in vain," Kimmalyn said.

"You do all the time!"

"I'm religious. You're not. So it's okay for me."

Nedd grinned, using his foot to hook a chair from the next table over, then pulling it to us. He waved for me to sit down.

I did so, hesitant. I was still distracted by the recording in my jumpsuit pocket. At the same time, seeing Nedd and Kimmalyn made me feel warm. This was something I *needed*.

So I tried to forget about the recording for now.

"Spin, this is Bryn," Arturo said, pointing to the girl sitting close—very close—to him. "A friend from before flight school."

"I honestly don't know how you all suffer him," she said. "He pretended to know everything *before* he became a pilot. He must be impossible now."

He mock-punched her lightly on the shoulder, smiling. Yes, it was clear that this was an established relationship. How had I never known that Arturo was attached?

I would know, I thought, *if I ever got to spend any time outside of class with the rest of them . . .*

A few seconds later, FM set something purple and bubbling in front of me, along with a basket of fried algae strips. She settled into her own seat and tossed a pouch to Kimmalyn. "Found your necklace," she said. "Under your bed."

"Thank you, dear," Kimmalyn said, opening it and checking inside. "I *did* pitch something of a fit when I left, didn't I?"

"Are you guys coming back to the DDF?" I asked. "Are we going to talk to Cobb? They need pilots. Maybe we could get them to take you back."

Nedd and Kimmalyn shared a look, then Nedd took a long drink. "No," he said. "Cobb said most of the class would wash out. So they're expecting this, right? They're not going to take us. And I'm not sure I could do that to my mother, after . . ."

Silence. Conversation at the table died.

"I might not be coming back, but at least I made cadet," Kimmalyn said, perking up. "My parents are proud, and the gunners in Bountiful are full of chatter about me."

"But . . . I mean . . . flying . . . ," I said, although I knew I should leave well enough alone.

"We aren't like you, Spin," Nedd said. "Flying was great. I'd go back up in a heartbeat, but something about the DDF . . . the culture, the throwing cadets into battle, the *desperation* . . ."

FM gave him two thumbs up. Kimmalyn just looked down at her lap. She was probably thinking what I was. The DDF had a reason to be desperate. When cadets flew, it wasn't only for practice—or even because the DDF was callous with lives. It was because we needed more pilots in the air, however inexperienced.

Growing up in Igneous, I'd known that the fight against the Krell was a valiant, dangerous endeavor. But before coming to Alta, I'd never realized quite how close to the edge we were.

I kept my mouth shut though, because I didn't want to depress everyone. The conversation turned to some big game yesterday—Hurl's old team had won. Nedd raised his glass, and the others did as well, so I joined in. I took a sip of my purple drink and almost spat it out. It was so *sweet*.

I covered it up by trying one of the fries. My mouth exploded with flavor, and I froze, eyes wide. I practically melted into a puddle. I'd had fried algae before, but it had been nowhere near as good as this. What were those spices?

"Spin?" Arturo asked. "You look like someone just stepped on your toe."

I held up a fry, fingers trembling. "So. GOOD."

"She's been living on rats for the last few months," FM pointed out. "Her taste buds are undergoing serious atrophy."

"You have such a unique way with words, FM," Kimmalyn noted. "Not like anything I've heard!"

"How many of these can I have?" I asked.

"I got the whole basket for you," FM said. "Arturo is paying, after all."

I started stuffing them into my mouth—comically, by intention. But honestly, I wanted to get as much down as I could before I woke up, or someone kicked me out of here, or something exploded.

Bryn laughed. "She's aggressive."

"You have no idea," Arturo said, smiling as she played with a curl of his hair.

Scud. It was criminal, how little I knew about my flightmates.

"Where's Jorgen?" I said, talking around bites of food.

"He wouldn't want to come," Nedd said. "Too important for us."

"You didn't even invite him?" I asked.

"Nah," Arturo said.

"But isn't he your friend?"

"That's how we know he wouldn't come," Nedd said. "Say, how's old Cobb getting by? Has he said any interesting curses lately?"

"Spin gave him a bit of a black eye, last they spoke," Kimmalyn noted.

366

I swallowed my mouthful of fries. "I was wrong to say what I did."

"If you don't say what you're thinking," Kimmalyn said solemnly, "then it will stay in your head."

"You deconstructed him," FM said, raising a finger. "He was relying on the very thing he was denying!"

I looked down at my basket, which was somehow already empty. FM swept it away and walked off to the counter, probably to get me another. I could hear the fryer, and the pungent, crisp scent in the room made my mouth water for more. This wasn't too expensive, was it? Did I care right now?

I tried the drink again—still too sweet. FM set another basket of fries in front of me, fortunately, and I attacked them. The spices were just *so good*. Flavor that made my mouth wake up, as if from a long slumber.

The others continued to reminisce about Hurl—their voices tinged with the same pain I felt. They got it. They understood. I wasn't alone, not here.

I found myself explaining what Jorgen and I had done. They listened solemnly to the details.

"I should have gone with you," Arturo said. "You think Cobb would let me hold her pin for a moment, if I asked? Before he gives it back to the family?"

Bryn rubbed his arm as he looked down at the table.

"Remember that time," Nedd said, "that she bet she could eat more algae patties than me at dinner?"

"She ended up on the floor," FM said, wistful. "On the *floor*, just lying there, groaning. Complained about it all night, claiming the patties were fighting in her stomach."

The others laughed, but Arturo stared at his cup. He seemed . . . hollow. He'd almost died in that battle. Hopefully the ground crew would have his ship running again by the time our leave was done.

That, of course, made me think of the work Rig was doing on M-Bot. And the fact that I owed him. A *lot*.

"FM," I said. "What do you think of smart guys?"

"I'm already taken," Arturo said with a smile.

FM rolled her eyes. "Depends. How handsome are we talking?"

"Handsome, in a reserved way."

"Guys, I'm already taken," Arturo said again.

"FM would only want to romance someone low-class," Nedd said, "to defy the powers that be. A kind of star-crossed, impossible love is the only love FM would accept."

"My *entire life* isn't dominated by being a rebel, Nedd," she said.

"Yeah?" Nedd said. "What kind of drink did you get?"

I noticed, for the first time, that her drink was orange while everyone else was having purple.

She rolled her eyes again. "You *are* stupid."

"The right kind?"

"The annoying kind."

"I'll take it."

Their banter continued, and I sat back, enjoying my fries until Bryn got up to use the restroom. With her gone it was just our flight, and I found myself itching to say something to them, now that we were away from the DDF headquarters, where I always felt like someone was watching.

"Can we talk about something?" I finally said, interrupting a story Nedd was telling. "I keep thinking about the questions Arturo brought up in class that one time. Isn't it weird that we can fight an enemy for eighty years, and have only a vague idea what they look like?"

Kimmalyn nodded. "How convenient is it that the Krell never commit more than a maximum of a hundred fighters to an individual assault? The defense platforms up in the debris field explain a lot of why we're still alive down here, but this question bothers me. Couldn't the Krell send twice as many and overwhelm us?"

"It's suspicious," FM said. "Very."

"You'd say that no matter what," Nedd said.

"And in this case, do you disagree?" FM asked.

He didn't reply.

"We can't be the only ones who've asked these questions, right?" I said. "So . . . does the DDF really not *know* the answers? Or are they hiding them?"

Like they were hiding the truth about my father.

"Okay, to play devil's advocate," Arturo said, "perhaps they just don't share that sort of intel with cadets and noncombatants. I know you don't like the admiral, Spin—with good reason—but her record is excellent, and she has some very good advisors."

"And yet we're losing," I said, pulling my seat closer to the table, trying to speak quietly. "You all know we are. The Krell *are* going to eventually get us."

The others fell silent, and Arturo glanced around, checking to see if any other occupied tables were close enough to hear us.

"They don't want us asking these questions," Kimmalyn said. "Remember that time at dinner, when Arturo was talking? How the passing officer told him to shut up? Everyone but Cobb shuts down any conversation about the hard questions."

"They need meatheads," FM added. "Pilots who blindly do what they're told and never express an ounce of originality, compassion, or soul."

Arturo's girlfriend reappeared, winding her way back to our table. I leaned in closer. "Just . . . think about it," I said quietly. "Because I am." I felt at my pocket, and the data chip tucked inside.

The conversation turned to lighter topics, but FM looked at me and smiled, a twinkle in her eyes. As if she was proud of my

369

questions. She seemed to think I'd always been some brainwashed Defiant zombie, but she didn't know me. Didn't know how I'd lived most of my life *outside* their society, wandering the tunnels and scavenging.

If anything, I would want Defiants to be more brave, more heroic—more like in Gran-Gran's stories. But I supposed that she and I could agree on one thing in this area: the current leadership of the DDF left something to be desired.

I let FM—well, Arturo—buy me a third basket of fries. Then I eventually excused myself. I had enjoyed the meal with them, but there was something else I needed to do.

It was time to find some answers.

39

Rig was gone by the time I got back to my cavern, though he appeared to have made some good progress on the booster. Doomslug was sitting on a rock near the wing, and I scratched her head as I walked to the cockpit, then climbed in.

I felt a strange sense of . . . inevitability. I carried long-kept secrets in my pocket. The answers, at long last, to what had happened with my father. Why was I suddenly so reluctant?

I closed the cockpit. "M-Bot, do you know how to get the hologram out of something like this?" I held up the metal case, showing the connectors on the bottom.

"Yes," he said. "That's a standard format. See the series of ports underneath the panel marked 'A-118'? You want the port that reads 'SSXB.'"

I followed the instructions, hesitating only briefly before plugging in the case.

M-Bot hummed to himself. "Ah. Curious. Curious."

"What?"

"I'm drawing out the suspense so you enjoy the surprise."

"Please don't."

"Humans prefer—"

"Just *tell* me."

"Fine, complainer. This includes a great deal of data. A three-D holomap, but also the original ship transponder data, radio signals of the battle, and even some camera footage from inside bunkers. This would be very hard to fake."

Fake. I hadn't considered that, but now I found myself anxious. "Are you sure?"

"I'd spot any edits. Would you like to watch it?"

"Yes."

No.

"Then climb out."

"Climb out?"

"My holoprojector can emit a small version of the battle for you to watch."

I heaved myself out of the cockpit, scratching Doomslug on the head—she'd moved to the nose of the ship—and dropped with a thump to the rocky floor.

A battle appeared in front of me. When Cobb watched us fly, everything was painted with bold colors—bright red and blue ships. M-Bot instead projected the ships in exacting miniature. They flew in waves before me, so real that I couldn't stop myself from reaching out and touching them—which broke them into granular particles of something that wasn't quite light.

The Krell appeared next, looking even more unfinished than they did now. Less regular. Wires hanging out at odd angles, wings that had rips in them, patchwork creations of metal. My little cavern became a battlefield.

I sat down and watched in silence. M-Bot's holoprojector didn't produce sound. Ships went up in flares of muted death. They flew like gnats without wings or buzz.

I knew the battle. I'd been taught it, memorized the tactics employed. Watching, however, I *felt* it. Before, I'd imagined the great maneuvers as, against the odds, forty human fighters faced down two and a half times that many enemies. I'd pictured a bold defense. Bordering on desperation, but always in control.

Now that I was a pilot though, I could feel the chaos. The haphazard pace of the battle. The tactics seemed less grand—no less heroic, but far more improvised. Which actually raised my opinion of the pilots.

It went on for quite a while—longer than any of Skyward Flight's skirmishes had gone—and I picked him out easily. The best fighter in the bunch, the one who led the charges. It felt arrogant to think I could single out my father's ship from the crowded mess, but there was something about the way he flew . . .

"Can you identify the pilots?" I asked.

Little readouts appeared above each ship, listing callsigns and designations.

HOPE SEVEN, the ship's label read. CALLSIGN: CHASER.

Arrogant or not, I'd called it accurately. Despite myself, I tried again to touch his ship, and found tears in my eyes. Fool girl. I wiped them as my father fell in with his wingmate. Callsign: Mongrel. Cobb.

Another ship joined them. Callsign: Ironsides. Then two more I didn't recognize. Callsigns: Rally and Antique. Those five were all that remained of my father's initial flight of eight. The battle casualties were very high; what had begun as forty ships was now twenty-seven.

I stood up and walked after my father's ship as it swooped through the cavern. The First Citizens fought frantically, but their bravery bore fruit as they drove the Krell back. I knew they would—yet still found myself watching breathlessly. Ships exploded as little flashes. Lives spent to found what would become the first stable society and government on Detritus since the *Defiant* had crashed here.

That society and government were both flawed. FM was right

about how unfair it was, how single-minded and authoritarian. But it was *something*. It existed because these people—these pilots—had defied the Krell.

Near the end of the battle, the Krell pulled back to regroup. From my studies, I knew they would make only one more push before finally retreating into the sky. The human battle lines re-formed, flights grouping together, and I could almost hear them making verbal confirmations of status.

I knew this moment. The moment when . . .

One ship—my father's—broke from the pack. My heart about stopped. My breath caught.

But he flew upward.

I leaped onto a rock, then onto M-Bot's wing, trying to follow my father as he flew higher into the sky. I reached up, and could imagine what he'd seen. I somehow *knew* what it was—my father had spotted a hole in the debris, like the one he'd pointed out to me. The one I'd only ever seen a second time, flying M-Bot, when the debris had lined up just right.

I read something into his disappearance. Not cowardice at all. To me, his move—flying upward—was obvious. The battle had been going for an hour. After this desperate stand, with the enemy regrouping for another push, my father had worried the fight would fail.

So he'd done something desperate. He'd gone to see where the Krell came from. To try to stop them. I felt a chill, watching him fly upward. He was doing what he'd always told me.

He had tried to aim for something higher.

His ship vanished.

"He didn't run," I said. I wiped the tears from my eyes again. "He broke formation. He may have disobeyed orders. But he *didn't run*."

"Well," M-Bot said, "it—"

"*That's* what they're covering up!" I said, looking toward

374

M-Bot's cockpit. "They branded him a coward because he flew up when he wasn't supposed to."

"You might—"

"Cobb has known all this time. It must have torn him up inside. It's why he doesn't fly; guilt for the lies he's perpetuated. But *what did my father see?* What happened to him? Did he—"

"Spensa," M-Bot said. "I'm jumping ahead a short time. Watch."

A speck of light, like a star, dropped down from the top of the cavern. My father's ship returning? I reached out toward it, and the holographic ship swooped down, passing through my hand. When my father reached the other four ships in his flight, he hit his IMP and brought down their shields.

Wait. *What?*

As I watched, the Krell returned in a surging, final assault. My father spun in a perfect loop and unleashed his destructors, destroying one of *his own flightmates.*

It . . . it can't be . . .

Callsign: Rally died in a flash of fire. My father swooped around, joining the Krell, who didn't fire on him—but *supported* him as he attacked another member of his former flight.

"No," I said. "No, it's a lie!"

Callsign: Antique died trying to run from my father.

"M-Bot, that's not him!" I yelled.

"Life signs are the same. I cannot see what happened above, but it *is* the same ship, with the same pilot. It's him."

He destroyed another ship in front of my eyes. He was a terror on the battlefield. A disaster of steel and fire.

"No."

Ironsides and Mongrel fell in together, tailing my father. He shot down someone else. That was four of the First Citizens he'd killed.

"I . . ." I felt empty. I slumped to the ground.

Mongrel fired. My father dodged, but Mongrel stayed on him—hunting him. Until finally he scored a hit.

My father's ship exploded in a tiny inferno, the pieces spiraling down before me, raining as burning debris.

I barely watched the rest of the battle. I just stared at the spot where my father's ship had vanished. Eventually, the humans were victorious. The remaining Krell fled in defeat.

Fourteen survivors.

Twenty-five dead.

One traitor.

The hologram vanished.

"Spensa?" M-Bot said. "I can read your emotional state as dazed."

"You're *sure* this data couldn't be faked?"

"The plausibility of this record being falsified without my ability to detect? Considering your people's technology? Highly improbable. In human terms, no, Spensa. There's no way this is fake. I'm . . . sorry."

"Why?" I whispered. "Why would he do that? Was he one of them all along? Or . . . or what did he see up there?"

"I have no data that could help answer those questions. I have voice recordings of the battle, but my analysis considers it normal battle chatter—at least until your father saw the hole in the sky."

"Play that," I said. "Let me listen to it."

"I can hear the stars."

I'd asked for it, but hearing my father's voice again—after all these years—still hit me with a wave of emotion. Pain, love. I was a little girl again, in that moment.

"I can see them too, Cobb," my father said. "Like I saw them earlier today. A hole in the debris field. I can get through."

"Chaser!" Ironsides said. "Stay in ranks."

"I *can* get through, Judy. I've got to try. I've got to see." He paused, then his voice grew softer. "I can *hear the stars.*"

The line was silent for a short time. And then Ironsides spoke. "Go," she said. "I trust you."

The audio cut out.

"After that," M-Bot said, "your father flew up out of the debris field. The sensors don't record what happened up there. Then, approximately five minutes and thirty-nine seconds later, he returns and attacks."

"Does he say anything?"

"I have only one little clip," M-Bot said. "I assume you want to hear it?"

I didn't. But I had to anyway. Tears streaming down my face, I listened as M-Bot played the recording. The open channel, with many voices talking in the chaos of the battle. I distinctly heard Cobb shouting at my father.

"Why? Why, Chaser?"

Then, almost inaudible over the chatter, my father's voice. Soft. Mournful.

"I will kill you," he said. "I will *kill you all*."

The cavern fell silent again.

"That is the only time I can find where he spoke after returning," M-Bot said.

I shook my head, trying to make sense of it. "Why wouldn't the DDF publicize this? They had no problem condemning him as a coward. Why hold back the truth when it's *worse*?"

"I could try to guess," M-Bot said. "But I'm afraid without further information, I'd merely be making things up."

I stumbled to my feet, then climbed into M-Bot's cockpit. I hit the Close button, sealing the canopy, then turned off the lights.

"Spensa?"

I curled up into myself.

And lay there.

40

Knowledge of my father's treason bled like a physical wound inside me. The next day, I barely got out of bed. If class had been going on, I'd have missed it.

My stomach responded to my mood, and I felt physically ill. Nauseous, sick. I had to eat though, and eventually forced myself to gather some bland cave mushrooms.

Rig quietly toiled away, welding and tying wires. He knew me enough not to bother me once he saw I wasn't feeling well. I hated looking sick in front of people.

I couldn't decide if I wanted to unload my news on him. I wasn't sure I wanted to talk to *anyone* about it. If I didn't talk about it, perhaps I could pretend I'd never discovered the truth. Perhaps I could pretend my father hadn't done those awful things.

That night, M-Bot tried multiple (terrible) ways to cheer me up, apparently running down a list of emotional support methods. I ignored him and somehow managed to sleep.

The next morning, I felt a little better physically—but still a wreck emotionally. M-Bot didn't chatter at me as I skinned some rats, and when I asked what was wrong, he said, "Some humans like to be given time to grieve on their own. I will stop speaking to you for two days, to see if isolation provides the needed support. Please enjoy moving through the stages of grief."

For the next while . . . I just kind of existed. Living beneath a looming, ominous truth. Ironsides and Cobb *had* lied about my father—but they'd lied to make his crime seem *less* terrible. They'd protected our family. If I'd been treated this poorly as the daughter of a coward, what would have happened to the daughter of a traitor?

Suddenly, everything Ironsides had done to me made sense. My father had killed multiple members of his own flight. Her friends. No *wonder* she hated me. The remarkable thing was that Cobb didn't.

Four more hard days passed. I spent them occasionally hunting, but mostly quietly helping Rig with the booster. He prodded a few times about what I was feeling, and I almost told him. But for some reason, I couldn't. This wasn't a truth I wanted to share. Not even with him.

Finally, the next morning, I had to make a decision. Our leave was over. Did I return? Could I face Cobb? Could I continue to act like an insubordinate brat, spitting on the admiral's shoes, now that I knew?

Could I live, and fly, with this shame?

The answer, it turned out, was yes.

I *needed* to fly.

I stepped into our training room at 0630, first to class. Of course, there were only four of us left at this point.

The mockpits appeared to have gone through some kind of maintenance during our leave. Though the workers weren't there currently, the cushions had been removed, and the side of Jorgen's rig was open, with the internal wires exposed.

FM pushed open the door, wearing a clean jumpsuit and a new pair of boots. Arturo followed, chatting softly with her about the game they'd gone to last night. I got the impression that Nedd liked FM, as he'd gotten them the seats.

"Hey," FM said when she saw me. She gave me a hug, and patted me on the shoulder, so my grief was apparently still visible. So much for my air of being a strong warrior.

Cobb shoved open the door with a distracted expression, sipping pungent coffee and reading some reports. Jorgen accompanied him, walking with his customary distinguished air.

Wait. When did I start seeing him as "distinguished"?

"Cobb," Arturo said, poking at one of the mockpits. "Didn't anyone tell them our leave was ending? How are we going to practice?"

"Holopractice is basically done for you lot," Cobb said, limping past without looking up. "You only have five weeks left of flight school. From now on, you'll do most of your time on real machines. We'll meet at the launchpad in the mornings."

"Great," I said with an enthusiasm I didn't feel.

Cobb nodded toward the door and we hurried out into the hallway. Arturo fell into step beside me.

"I wish I could be more like you, Spin," he said as we walked.

"Like me?"

"Always so straightforward and bold," he said. "I really *do* want to fly again. I do. It will be fine."

He sounded like he was trying to convince himself. How did it feel, to nearly die, as he had? To get shot while your shield was down? I tried to imagine his panic, the smoke in his cockpit, the sense of helplessness . . .

"You *are* bold," I said. "You're getting back in the cockpit— that's the important part. You didn't let it frighten you away."

For some reason, coming from me, that seemed to really strengthen him. How would he feel to hear that my emotions weren't nearly as "straightforward" or as "bold" as he assumed?

We changed into flight suits, then walked out onto the launch-pad, passing our Pocos in a line. Arturo's spot was empty though, and I found him chatting with Siv, one of the members of the ground crew. She was a tall, older woman, with short white hair.

"You'll need to take Skyward Six, Amphi," she was saying to Arturo, then pointed. "We still don't have your ship running."

I glanced toward the repair bay, where the nose of a Poco still stuck out.

"What's the hang-up?" Arturo asked.

"We have the booster fixed," Siv said, "and we tested the ac-clivity ring, but we had to rip out the shield igniter. Still waiting for a replacement—should have new ones in a batch next week. So you've been assigned to Skyward Six unless you want to fly without a shield."

Arturo reluctantly walked to Kimmalyn's former ship. I contin-ued on to Skyward Ten. It was a little hard to think of this as "my" ship, with M-Bot back in the cavern. But Ten had done right by me. She was a good fighter.

Instead of my normal ground crew waiting to help me strap in, I found Cobb standing there, holding my helmet.

"Sir?" I asked him.

"You look like you're having a rough day, Spin," he said. "You need more time?"

"No, sir."

"I'm supposed to report your status to medical. Maybe you should go in and have a chat. Meet one of Thior's new counselors."

I lifted my hand, holding out the little case of data I'd taken from the library. The secrets that, it turned out, I really *hadn't* wanted to know. "I'm fine, sir."

He studied me, then took the data case. He handed me my hel-met, which I inspected, finding the sensors inside.

"Yes," Cobb said, "they're still monitoring your brain."

"Have they . . . found anything important?" I still didn't know what to make of all this, but the idea of medical spying on my brain while I flew made me uncomfortable.

"I'm not at liberty to say, cadet. Though I get the impression that they're eager to start testing all new cadets, using data they've collected on you."

"And you really want me to go in and meet with their counselors? So they can run more weird tests on me?" I grimaced. I had enough problems without wondering why medical was worried about my brain.

"You shouldn't be so afraid of medical," he said, tucking the case into his front shirt pocket and pulling something from it. A folded sheet of paper. "Dr. Thior is a good person. Take this, for example."

Curious, I took the sheet of paper and read it.

Authorization for release of restrictions on Cadet Spensa Nightshade, it read. *Full cadet privileges instated. Memo #11723.*

It was signed by Admiral Judy Ivans.

"What . . . ?" I asked. "Why?"

"After your visit to medical, someone sent Dr. Thior a tip, explaining that you were living in the wilderness and being forced to catch your own food. The doctor raised an enormous fuss about you being isolated from your flight, and the admiral finally backed down. You can sleep and eat in the school building now."

I felt a sudden, almost overwhelming relief. *Oh, stars.* Tears crept to the corners of my eyes.

Scud, as good as this news was, it was the *wrong* time. I was already in a fragile emotional state. I just about lost it right there on the launchpad.

"I . . . ," I forced out. "I wonder who sent that tip to Dr. Thior."

"A coward."

"Cobb, I—"

"I don't want to hear it," he said, and pointed toward the cockpit. "Get strapped in. The others are all ready."

He was right, but I had to ask. "Cobb? Is it . . . true? What happened in that holorecording of the Battle of Alta? Did my father . . . did he do that?"

Cobb nodded. "I got a good look at him, while we were dog-fighting. We passed close enough that I could see straight into his cockpit. It was him, Spensa. The angry snarl on his face has haunted me ever since."

"Why, Cobb? *Why* would he do that? What happened up there, in the sky? *What did he see?*"

Cobb didn't answer. He gestured for me to climb up the ladder, so I pulled myself together and climbed. He followed up the ladder and stood there, in the ground crew spot, as I settled into the cockpit.

I again inspected the helmet, with the strange sensors inside. "They really think they can tell from my brain?" I asked. "They think they can determine if I . . . if I'll do what my father did?"

Cobb gripped the edge of the cockpit, leaning in. "You don't know it, kid, but you're at the center of an argument that goes back generations. Some people say that your father proves that cowardice is genetic. They think there's some . . . defect inside you."

Cobb's expression grew grim, his voice softer. "I think that's utter nonsense. I don't know what happened to your father—I don't know *why* my friend tried to kill me, or why I was forced to shoot him down. Killing him has haunted me; I don't think I could ever fly again. But one thing I *can't* believe is that someone is destined to be a coward or a traitor. No, I can't accept that. I could *never* accept that."

He pointed toward the sky. "But Ironsides does believe it. She is certain you'll inevitably turn into either a coward or a traitor. You prove her wrong by getting back into the sky and becoming a model pilot—one so scudding perfect everyone feels embarrassed to have ever questioned you."

"And . . . what if they're right? What if I *am* a coward, or what if I do end up—"

"Don't ask stupid questions, cadet! Strap in! Your flight is ready!"

"Yes, sir!" I said immediately, strapping in. As I raised my helmet to my head, Cobb took hold of my arm.

"Sir?" I asked.

He considered for a moment. He looked one way, then the other. "Do you ever see anything . . . strange, Spin?" he asked. "In the darkness?"

"Like what?"

"Eyes," he said softly.

I shivered, and my cockpit felt suddenly colder.

"Hundreds of small eyes," he said, "opening up in the blackness, surrounding you. As if the attention of the entire universe has suddenly focused on you and you alone."

Hadn't M-Bot said something . . . about eyes?

"Your father said things like that before the incident," Cobb said, visibly shaken. "And he'd say . . . he'd say he could *hear* the stars."

Like Gran-Gran said, I thought. *Like he said right before he flew up to them.* Had he just been talking about the old exercise that Gran-Gran had taught, the one of imagining you were flying among the stars? Or was there more?

There had been a couple of times when . . . when I'd thought for certain I could hear them up there . . .

"I can tell from your horrified expression," Cobb said, "that you think I've suddenly started raving like a madman. It does sound silly, doesn't it?" He shook himself. "Well, never mind that. If you for some reason see anything like I described, tell me. Don't talk to anyone else, not even your flightmates, and *never* say anything about it over the radio. Okay, Spensa?"

I nodded, numb. I almost told him about what I'd heard, but

384

stopped myself. Cobb was the only real ally I had, but in that moment I panicked. I knew that if I told him I thought I heard the stars, he'd yank me out of the cockpit.

So I held my tongue as he climbed down the ladder. He'd told me to talk to him if I *saw* anything, not if I *heard* something. And I'd never seen anything like he said. Eyes? *Hundreds of small eyes, opening up in the blackness, surrounding you . . .*

I shivered again, but pulled on my helmet. Perhaps I wasn't in the best of shape today. Shaken, sickened by news, and now thoroughly confused. But I knew that if I didn't get back into the air, I'd go crazy for certain.

So when Jorgen called for us to take off, I did so.

41

Two weeks later, I was feeling a little more stable as I flew my Poco through a sequence of valleys, skimming the surface of the planet.

"I don't see anything," I said over the flight channel.

"Me neither," FM said. She was flying at my wing.

"The trick is to remain alert on a long patrol," a female voice said in our helmets. "Being a good scout isn't about being able to see well; it's about being able to give your attention to a monotonous job. It's about not letting your mind wander into daydreams."

Well, I'm in trouble, I thought.

"If you end up in a scout team," said the woman, callsign: Blaze, "you'll get a Val-class ship, which has traded its 138 Stewart destructors for a single 131, with far less firepower. But your sensor systems are better, longer-range, with more detail. It's still tricky to catch enemy Krell who are flying under the radar—but fortunately, they often use the same tactic of trying to sneak up on AA guns. Since you know what they're going to do, you can anticipate their moves."

That same old adage. If you knew what the enemy would do, you had an advantage. I'd tried that, in the battle where Hurl had died. I'd saved Kimmalyn, but I'd left my wingmate alone.

Nobody blamed me; it had been the right move to break off and protect Kimmalyn. It still gnawed at me though.

And . . . I was already not paying attention. I tried to snap my focus back to the search for Krell, but I knew I wasn't meant for this sort of duty. I needed something that engaged me, that consumed me, like a good firefight.

Blaze kept giving us tips. How to spot the wake of a low-flying ship from the patterns in the dust. How Krell move around hills when trying to hide from scanners. How to tell if something in the distance is a ship or an optical illusion. It was good stuff, and important. Even if it wasn't for me, I was glad Cobb had us trying out different combat roles. It expanded my experience, made abstract tactics like "flanking flights," "reserve ships," and "scouting parties" into real things.

I heard a pop in the sky. Our training with the scouts was happening during an actual battle.

"How do you deal with . . . the emotions of it?" Arturo asked over the line. "Of scouting, when . . . you know . . ."

"When everyone else is fighting, maybe dying?" Blaze asked.

"Yeah," Arturo said. "Every instinct I have says I should be flying toward that battle. This feels . . . cowardly."

"We're *not* cowards!" Blaze said, her voice rising. "We fly ships with a fraction of the armament of even a Poco. And if we intercept Krell, we might have to fight and slow them on our own to buy time for—"

"Sorry!" Arturo stopped her. "I didn't mean it like that!"

Blaze breathed out. "We're not cowards. The DDF makes it *very clear* that we're not. But you might have to deal with a . . . a *look* now and then. It's part of the sacrifice we all make to see that the Defiant Caverns are kept safe."

387

I banked through a careful sequence of swerves, trying to use the time to practice my low-elevation maneuvers. Eventually, the debris fall behind us stopped, and Cobb called us in.

We fell into formation, did verbals, and flew back to base and landed. While waiting for the ground crew, I happened to glance at the mess hall, and a hint of a smile crept to my lips. I remembered crashing through its hologram on my first day.

A wave of guilt erased my smile. It had only been three weeks since Hurl's death. I shouldn't feel happy.

Siv climbed up the ladder, so I hit the cockpit release and pulled off my helmet, which I handed to her.

"Nice landing," she said to me. "Anything we should look at on the ship today?"

"Control sphere feels like it's grinding somewhere," I said. "It seems to tug back at me when I move it."

"We'll give the mechanism a good greasing tonight," she said. "How's that receiving button working? Still sticking? We . . ." She trailed off as, on a nearby platform, a Camdon-class fighter landed with smoke pouring from the left side of its fuselage. Siv cursed and slid down the sides of the ladder, then went running with several other ground crew members.

Feeling sick at the sight of that poor ship, I climbed down, joining Jorgen, who was standing at the edge of our launchpad. We stared across at the fire. Several other fighters landed nearby, and one seemed—remarkably—in even worse shape. Scud. If these were the survivors, how many pilots had we lost?

"Were you listening to the flightleader radio channel?" I asked.

"Yeah," Jorgen said. "They got flanked, then targeted with a double flight of enemy ships. Like the Krell were specifically trying to bring down *these* fighters, ignoring everyone else."

I breathed out as Arturo and FM joined us, all watching silently as ground crew pulled the barely conscious pilot from the burning ship, saving her life. Others hosed the ship down with foam.

"Spin, you were right the other day," Arturo said. "When you said the DDF was losing this war."

"We're not losing," Jorgen said. "Don't talk like that."

"They vastly outnumber us," Arturo said. "And it's getting worse. I can show you the stats. The Krell keep replenishing, and we can't keep up."

"We've survived for years," Jorgen said. "It's always felt like we're on the edge of doom. Nothing's changed."

Arturo and I shared a look. Neither of us believed that.

Eventually, Jorgen called for us to fall in for the after-battle debriefing with Cobb. We walked to the training building, and—oddly—we found Cobb standing right outside. He was chatting with some people at the entrance.

Arturo stopped in place.

"What?" I asked him.

"That's my mom," Arturo said, pointing at the woman talking to Cobb. She was wearing a military uniform. "Scud."

He walked faster, practically running, as he approached Cobb and his mother. I hurried to catch up, but Jorgen took me by the shoulder and slowed me.

"What?" I hissed. "What's happening?"

Ahead, Cobb saluted as Arturo arrived. Like, he actually *saluted* Arturo. I glanced at Jorgen, and his lips had drawn to a line. I stepped forward, but he pulled me back again.

"Give them some space," he said. FM stopped beside the two of us, watching, not speaking. She seemed to know what was happening too.

Cobb handed something to Arturo. A pin?

Arturo gazed down at the pin, then went to slam it into the

ground, but his mother caught his arm. Gradually, Arturo relaxed, then reluctantly saluted Cobb. Arturo looked back at us, then saluted us as well.

His mother stepped away, and Arturo slowly turned and followed, trailed by two men in suits.

Cobb limped over to us.

"Will someone *please* tell me what just happened?" I demanded. "Come on. Throw me a hint at least? Should I be worried for Arturo?"

"No," Jorgen said. "His parents pulled him out of the DDF. This has been building for a few weeks—ever since he almost got shot down. They've been panicking. Off the record, of course. Nobody would admit to being afraid for their son."

"Strings were pulled," Cobb said. "The admiral compromised. Arturo gets a pilot's pin but doesn't graduate."

"How does *that* work?" FM asked.

"That doesn't make any sense," I agreed. "He didn't graduate, but he gets to be a full pilot?"

"He's been retired honorably from service," Cobb said. "Officially, it's because he was needed for supervising cargo flights for his family—if we're ever going to get enough igniter parts, we'll need those shipments from other caverns. Come on, you three. Let's get to your debriefing."

Cobb walked off, and FM and Jorgen joined him. Those two seemed resigned, as if this sort of thing was expected.

I didn't follow. I felt indignant on Arturo's behalf. His parents just yanked him out like that?

Jorgen is expecting the same thing to happen to him, I remembered. *Maybe all of them were ready for this. The ones from highly merited families, at least.*

Standing there, outside the school, I realized for the first time that I was the only ordinary person in the flight who had made it this far. That made me irrationally angry. How *dare* his parents shelter him, now that it was getting dangerous? Particularly against his own obvious desires?

Jorgen stopped in the doorway ahead, while the others continued on inside. "Hey," he said, looking back at me. "You coming?"

I stalked up to him.

"Arturo's parents were never going to let him fly permanently," he said. "I'm honestly surprised that it took them this long to get spooked."

"Will the same happen to you? Will your father come for you tomorrow?"

"Not yet. Arturo's not going into politics, but I am. I'll need to have a few battles under my belt as a real pilot before my parents pull me out."

"So a little danger, then you'll be protected. Coddled. Kept safe."

He winced.

"You realize the only ones who died on our team were the common ones," I snapped. "Bim, Morningtide, Hurl. Not a single deep caverner among them!"

"They were my friends too, Spin."

"You, Arturo, Nedd, FM." I poked him in the chest with each name. "You had training ahead of time. A leg up, to keep you alive, until your coward families could stick some medals on you and parade you around as proof that you're so much better than the rest of us!"

He grabbed my arms to stop me from poking him, but I wasn't mad at *him*. In fact, I could see in his eyes that he was just as frustrated as me. He hated that he was boxed in like this.

I grabbed hold of his flight suit by the front, gripping it with two fists. Then I quietly rested my forehead against his chest. Frustrated and—yes—even *afraid*. Afraid of losing more friends.

Jorgen tensed, then finally let go of my shoulders and—likely uncertain what else to do—wrapped his arms around me. It should have been awkward. Instead, it was actually comforting. He understood. He felt the loss like I did.

"I barely got to be a real part of the flight," I whispered, "and it's being ripped apart *again*. A piece of me is glad he's safe, and will stay safe, but another piece of me is angry. Why couldn't Hurl have been kept safe, or Bim?"

Jorgen didn't respond.

"Cobb told us, on that first day, that only one or two of us would make it," I said. "Who dies next? Me? You? Why, after decades, don't we even know *what* we're fighting or *why* we're doing it?"

"We know why, Spensa," he said softly. "It's for Igneous, and Alta. For civilization. And you're right, the way we do things isn't fair. But these are the rules we play by. They're the only rules I know."

"Why is everything about rules, to you?" I asked, my forehead still resting against his chest. "What about emotion, what about feelings?"

"I . . . I don't know. I . . ."

I squeezed my eyes shut tighter and held on. I thought about the DDF, about Alta and Igneous, and about the fact that I didn't have anything to defy any longer. I'd spent my life fighting against the things they said about my father.

Now what did I do?

"I *do* feel things, Spin," he finally said. "Like right now, I feel incredibly awkward. I didn't ever think you were the hugging type."

I released the front of his flight suit, causing him to drop his arms. "You grabbed me first," I said.

"You were attacking me!"

"Lightly tapping your chest for emphasis."

He rolled his eyes, and the moment was over. Strangely though—as we joined FM and walked toward our new classroom—I realized something. I *did* feel better. Just a little, but considering how my life had been going lately, I was willing to take what I could get.

42

A number of days later, FM and I ate with Inkwell Flight and Firestorm Flight, the other two cadet flights who had started at the same time as us. Between them, they had six members remaining, meaning that even all of us combined didn't make a full ten-person flight.

Most of the conversation swirled around whether or not we'd be collected into a single cadet flight. If that happened, which flight name would we keep? FM argued we should make up a new name, though I figured that since we still had our flightleader—the other two had lost theirs at some point—we should be in charge.

I stayed quiet, finishing my food quickly. Part of me kept expecting the admiral to burst in and haul me off. The food was amazing, and instead of my old patched jumpsuit, I'd been able to requisition *three* new ones that fit me perfectly.

The other cadets were growing anxious for graduation. "I'm going to be a scout," said Remark, a boisterous guy with a bowl cut. "I've already got an invitation."

"Too boring," FM said.

"Really?" said one of the girls. "I'd have thought it would appeal to you—with all your talk of 'Defiant aggression.'"

"It's *so* expected though," FM said. "Even if I am kind of good at it."

As I listened, I wondered if FM would be taken away by her family too, though she didn't seem as important as Jorgen, who was off at another state function. I idly wondered what it would be like to attend one of his fancy government dinners. I imagined the delicious scandal I would cause. The daughter of the infamous coward?

Of course, everyone would be too polite to say anything, so they'd have to suffer through it while I—being a primitive barbarian girl—ignorantly slurped my soup, belched loudly, and ate with my hands. Jorgen would just roll his eyes.

The fantasy made me smile, but then I frowned to myself. Why was I thinking about Jorgen, of all people?

The others at the table laughed as someone mentioned Arturo's callsign, which nobody could pronounce. "It must be quiet in your training, now that he's dropped," said Drama—a girl with an accent reminiscent of Kimmalyn's.

"We'll survive," FM answered. "Though it *is* odd with him gone. There's no one to constantly explain things to me that I already know."

"What a strange flight you must have," Drama said. "I know Jorgen, and I'll bet he doesn't open his mouth except to give you an order or chew you out. Right? And Spin is obviously quiet. So your flights must be silent. *Our* line is always filled with chatter, even with only four of us."

Her flightmates defended themselves in a good-natured way, but I found myself stuck on that line about me. Quiet? They thought I was *quiet*?

I supposed I *had* been pretty reserved lately. But quiet? I honestly didn't think I'd ever been described that way in my entire life. Huh.

Dinner broke up, and after we cleared our table, FM nodded toward our bunk. "Heading back to rest? Or doing some PT?"

"Neither," I said. "I think I need a walk tonight." Actually, I needed to check on M-Bot and Doomslug. It had been a few days.

"Suit yourself." She hesitated. "Hey, you still worried about Arturo? He'll get to fly, just not on missions."

"Sure," I said. "I know." Stars. Days later, and she thought I still needed consoling?

I left the base. I really should have gone and done some PT, but I felt guilty for leaving M-Bot alone for so long. I'd dropped in a few times to help Rig with the booster, but now that I lived on base, it was tough to find the time. I wanted to savor the privileges I'd been denied so long.

The skylights had dimmed to indicate night, and the air was cool as I made the familiar trek over the dusty ground. It was refreshing to get away from the sights and smells of Alta, to simply be out under the sky again.

I reached the cavern and let myself down with my light-line, bracing for the inevitable string of complaints. M-Bot was *not* fond of my new sleeping arrangements. He was convinced he was going to rot away, his personality subroutines degrading from lack of use.

I reached the ground. "Hey," I said, my voice echoing.

"Hey!" Doomslug was on a rock nearby. I shined my light on her, then walked over and scratched her head.

"Massacrebot?" I said into the darkness.

"We still have to discuss that nickname," his voice said. "I never agreed to it."

"If you don't pick a good callsign, someone else will pick one for you. It's how these things go." I smiled, walking up to the ship, expecting him to go off on some tangent. But he was silent as I approached. Was something wrong?

"Well?" he said. "Well?"

"Uh . . ." *What did I do this time?*

"Are you excited!" he asked. "Are you just about ready to burst! Isn't it great!"

Great?

The booster, I realized with a start. Rig had finished installing it. I'd done a terrible job of tracking his progress—I'd been so busy these few weeks. But his tools were gone, the area cleaned up, and a note was taped to the back of M-Bot's fuselage.

Doomslug was sitting on the wing near the note. "Stupid junky piece of worthless imitation life," she said in a fluting imitation of Rig's voice. "Scud! Scud! Scud! Scudding scud and stupid scud!"

"Careful, girl," I said. "You'll get recruited for the ground crews with a mouth like that."

She produced a sequence of bangs, mimicking the sound of a hammer on metal—something she'd probably heard a lot of the last few weeks.

I picked up the note. *Done,* the note read. *I was going to take it up and test it, but I felt you should get the first shot. Besides, I wouldn't put it past the AI to crash me on purpose.*

Working on this ship has been the most wonderful experience of my life (don't tell M-Bot that). The designs I've drawn . . . the things I've learned . . . I'm going to change the DDF, Spin. I'm going to transform the entire way we fly and fight. I've not only been approved for the Engineering Corps, I've been offered a position directly in design. I start tomorrow.

Thank you for giving me the chance to find, in this work, my own dreams. Enjoy your ship. I hope that it is, in turn, what you have always dreamed it would be.

I lowered the note, looking up along M-Bot's dangerous, razor-like wings. The ship's landing lights flashed on, setting a glow along his length. My ship.

My. Ship.

"Well?" M-Bot said. "Are we going to go flying?"

"Scud, yes!"

43

"**A**cclivity ring, online," M-Bot said as we slowly rose into the air. "Booster and maneuvering, online. Life support, online. Communications and stealth features, online. Light-lance and IMP antishield blast, online."

"Not bad, Rig," I said.

"Destructors are still offline," M-Bot said. "As are self-repair features and cytonic hyperdrive."

"Well, since I still don't know what that last one is, we'll take it as a net win. Are your stealth features engaged?"

"Of course. You promise we aren't going into combat today. Right?"

"No combat," I promised. "Just a quick flight to test that booster."

We rose through the fake ceiling of the cavern and I felt myself growing tense, excited. I'd been flying every day, but this was different. M-Bot's control panel somehow made the most complex of the DDF ships seem simple, so I stuck to the buttons I understood.

The open sky called. I tried to relax, settling back into my seat.

The control sphere, throttle, and altitude lever were exactly like the ones I knew. I could do this.

"Are you ready?" M-Bot asked.

In response, I slammed on the overburn.

We blasted forward, and his advanced g-force management immediately kicked in. I expected to get pressed back in my seat, but I barely felt it, even on *full overburn*.

"Scuuuud," I said softly.

"Nice, isn't it?" M-Bot said. "I'm far better than those *other* ships you waste your time with."

"Can we accelerate even faster than this?"

"Not on one booster. But I'm outfitted with two slots for smaller boosters under the wings, so it's possible."

We accelerated a little slower than a Poco—which made sense, considering we were heavier than one but using the same booster. I noticed a real difference, however, as we got to speed. We blazed past Mag-6, Mag-7, Mag-8 . . . Scud, in a Poco, the ship would be shaking itself almost to pieces right now. But M-Bot hit Mag-10 and I couldn't even tell. It was as smooth a ride as if I were at Mag-1.

I tried some maneuvers at speed, and the controls were incredibly responsive. It had been a while since I'd overcompensated for turns by accident, but I got the hang of it quickly. I slowed to normal dogfighting speeds, and practiced some banks and then some starship turns.

It all went so well that I accelerated to Mag-3 again, then performed some complex dodging moves. Swerves, spins, and a sharp loop at the end with an overburn on the descent.

It was perfect. This was *perfect*.

I really needed to get Rig up in this thing. Or perhaps Jorgen. I owed him one, for helping me get the booster. He'd be grouchy about being forced to come out all the way to my hole—since Jorgen was grouchy about basically everything—but surely he'd enjoy the flying. Soaring, free from constraints and expectations, and . . .

And . . . why was I following this line of thought again? I shook my head, throwing myself back into the flying. "Think about how great you'd be in battle," I said to M-Bot.

"You promised."

"I promised not to take you into combat tonight," I said. "But I never promised I wouldn't try to change your mind. Why are you scared?"

"I'm not scared. I'm following orders. Besides, what good would I be in combat? I don't have destructors."

"You don't need those. Your IMP is working and so is your light-lance. With your maneuverability and those tools, we could *devastate* the Krell. They'll be left chasing our shadow, then our shadow will *consume* theirs! This is going to be incredible!"

"Spin," he said. "My orders are to *stay out of combat*."

"We can find a way to change those. Don't worry."

"Um . . ." He sounded unconvinced. "Maybe . . . maybe we can do something to satisfy your strange human desires *without* going into an actual fight. You wish for a thrill? What if I *projected* a battle for you?"

"You mean like a simulator?"

"Kind of! I can project an augmented-reality hologram right onto your canopy, which will make you *think* you're in a combat situation. That way, you can pretend to try to get yourself killed, while I don't have to disobey my orders!"

"Huh," I said, curious. Well, at the very least, it would let me test his responsiveness in a simulation. "Let's do it."

"Go to eleven thousand feet, and I'll drop you into the Battle of Alta."

"But I gave that data case back to Cobb."

"I made a copy." He hesitated for a moment. "Was that bad? I thought maybe you'd want to—"

"No, no it's fine. It's the only battle you can simulate for me though?"

"It's the only one where I have proper three-D renderings. Is this a problem? Oh! Your father. This is the battle where your father became a traitor, something to which you are emotionally vulnerable because of your feelings of betrayal and inadequacy! Whoops."

"It's fine."

"I could instead try to—"

"It's *fine*," I said, putting the ship at the altitude he'd stated, using maneuvering thrusters to settle us. "Start the simulation."

"All right, all right. No need to get grouchy just because I insulted you."

In a flash I appeared inside a battle.

It was like the simulations, except I was in a real ship. Everything holographic glowed and was slightly transparent, like I was surrounded by ghosts—which had to be so that I could distinguish reality and avoid accidentally flying us into a cliff face or something.

M-Bot said he was merely projecting all this on my canopy, but it looked three-dimensional to me. And the fighting was amazingly realistic, particularly when I hit my booster and launched into it—M-Bot even did his best to generate sounds in the cockpit as ships buzzed past us.

"I can simulate destructors," M-Bot said, "though you don't have any installed."

I grinned, then fell into position with a pair of DDF fighters. When I dove, targeting a Krell ship that someone else IMPed, M-Bot was able to edit the simulation—so my target exploded in a satisfying flash of light.

"All *right*," I said. "How do I activate proximity sensors?"

"I can activate them. Done."

"Convenient. What else can you do by verbal command?"

"I have access to communications and stealth features, and I can reignite the shield for you. By galactic law, however, I am forbidden control of boosters and weapons systems—including the IMP. I have no physical connection to these systems except for diagnostic purposes."

"All right then," I said. "Turn on flightleader chatter—let me hear the recordings as if they were happening in real time."

"Done," he said, as the radio came on. "Be aware that the audio might not sync with visuals as you interfere with the progress of the battle."

I nodded, then threw myself into the fight.

And it was *magnificent*. I banked and shot, IMPed and boosted. I spun through a virtual battlefield full of flashing lights, exploding ships, and desperate fighters. I flew a ship with unparalleled maneuverability, and felt myself adapting to it, taking increasing advantage. I downed four Krell in a half hour—a personal record—without taking anything but a few glancing blows to my shield.

Best of all, it was *safe*. None of my friends were in danger. It was a completely new level of simulation, but still without the threat to anyone's life.

Afraid, a piece of me whispered. *Afraid of battle. Afraid of loss.* That was a near-constant voice now.

I worked up a sweat, my heart thumping. I focused on a Krell that had been sprayed with destructors by another ship. That shield might be close to being down. I took aim, and—

A ship darted past me, firing destructors, beating me to the attack and blasting the ship into oblivion. I knew him instantly. My father.

Another ship took wingmate position behind my father.

"M-Bot," I said, feeling a tremor inside me. "Give me audio on those two."

The channel crackled, flightleader chatter vanishing. Instead, I got on the direct line between my father and Mongrel.

"Nice shot, Chaser," Cobb's voice said. It sounded exactly like him, only without all the cynicism. "Hot rocks, you're on a roll today!"

My father looped back around. I found myself falling in beside him, opposite Cobb. Flying wingmate . . . to my father. The greatest man I had ever known.

The traitor.

I hate you, I thought. *How could you do what you did? Didn't you stop to think what it would do to your family?*

He banked, and I followed, sticking to his glowing, transparent form as he chased a pair of Krell ships.

"I'll go for the IMP. You see if you can pick them off."

I forced down the sudden burst of emotions at hearing my father's voice again. How could I both hate and love this man at once? How could I reconcile the image of him—standing tall on that day when we'd gone to the surface—with the terrible things I'd learned he'd done?

I gritted my teeth and tried to focus only on the fight. The Krell ships dodged into a larger melee of ships, almost colliding with some DDF fighters. My father followed them right in, spinning in a loop. Cobb lagged behind.

I stuck on my father, holding tight to his wing. In that moment, the chase became everything, and the world around me faded. Just me, my father's ghost, and the enemy ship.

Bank right.

Quick cut up.

Turn and twist around.

Right again.

Around that explosion.

I put everything I had into the chase, and still I slowly fell behind. My father's turns were too sharp, his movements too precise. Even though I had M-Bot's superior maneuverability, my father was better than I was. He had years of experience, and knew just when to boost, just when to turn.

And there was something . . . something more . . .

I focused on the Krell ship. It banked right. So did my father. It turned upward. So did my father. It turned left . . .

My father turned left. And I could swear he did it a fraction of a second *before* the Krell did.

"M-Bot," I said. "Time my father's turns in relation to the Krell ship's turns. Is he somehow reacting before they do?"

"That would be impossib— Huh."

"What?" I asked.

"I believe the correct term is *SCUD*. Spensa, your father *is* moving before the Krell do. It's only a fraction of a second different, but it *is* happening. My recording must be desynced somehow. I find it highly implausible that a human would be able to guess these movements so accurately."

I narrowed my eyes, then hit overburn and threw myself back into the chase. I moved until I was *inside* the outline of my father's ship, the glow of the hologram surrounding me. I focused not on him, but only on the Krell ship, trying to stay with it as it went into another sequence of dodges.

Left. Right. Spin. Altitude . . .

I couldn't do it. My father cut and turned at precisely the right time, then IMPed the enemy ship. They spun around each other in a twisting, intertwined loop, like two braiding ropes. I lost pace completely, falling out of the complex maneuver as my father—somehow—cut his booster at just the right moment to drop behind the enemy.

The Krell died in a flash of light.

My father pulled out of his dive as Cobb whooped over the line. Young Cobb was certainly enthusiastic.

"Chaser," he said. "They're pulling back. Have we . . . have we won?"

405

"No," my father said. "They're just regrouping. Let's return to the others."

I hovered my ship, watching Cobb and my father join the lineup. "That was some mighty fine flying," Ironsides said over the channel. "But Chaser, watch yourself. You keep losing your wingmate."

"Blah blah blah blah blah," Cobb said. "Chaser, stop blowing everything up; you make me look bad. Sincerely, Ironsides."

"We are fighting for the survival of all humankind, Mongrel," Ironsides said. "I would hope to hear some maturity out of you for once."

I smiled. "She sounds like Jorgen, talking to us." Then I turned, looking toward the Krell regrouping in the distance. Nearby, the DDF fighters formed into flights again.

I knew what was coming next.

"Would you look at that hole in the debris up there?" Cobb said. "You don't often see such a great alignment of the . . . Chaser?"

I looked upward, but the simulation didn't extend so far as to show me the hole in the debris they were talking about.

"Chaser, what's wrong?" Cobb asked.

"Is it the defect?" Ironsides asked.

"I can control the defect," my father said. "But . . ." What was that? I hadn't heard that part before.

He was silent for a moment. "I can hear the stars. I can see them too, Cobb," my father said. "Like I saw them earlier today. A hole in the debris field. I can get through."

"Chaser!" Ironsides said. "Stay in ranks."

This part, I had heard last time. I dreaded hearing it again, but I couldn't force myself to make M-Bot turn it off.

"I *can* get through, Judy. I've got to try. I've got to see. I can *hear the stars.*"

"Go," I whispered along with Ironsides. "I trust you."

She'd trusted him. He hadn't disobeyed orders; he'd gone with her permission. That seemed a tiny distinction to me, considering what would happen next.

My father's ship rotated, acclivity ring hinging to point downward. His nose toward the sky, he engaged his booster.

I watched him go, tears forming in the corners of my eyes. I couldn't watch this. Not again. *Please. Father* . . .

I reached toward him. With my hand, foolish though the gesture was, and . . . and with . . .

With *something else.*

I heard something then, up above. A sound like a thousand musical notes intertwining. I imagined myself, as Gran-Gran had always taught, soaring upward. Reaching for the stars . . .

My cockpit went black, plunging me into complete darkness. And then, around me, a million pinpricks of light appeared.

Then those pinpricks *opened.* A million white eyes, like stars, all turning directly on me. Focusing on me. *Seeing me.*

"Turn it off!" I screamed.

The darkness vanished. The eyes disappeared.

I was back in the cockpit.

I gasped for breath, in and out, hyperventilating. "What was that!" I demanded, frantic. "What did you show me? What were those eyes!"

"I'm confused," M-Bot said. "I didn't do anything. I don't know what you're talking about."

"Why didn't you play that earlier part of the conversation last time? Why were you hiding it from me?"

"I didn't know where to start!" M-Bot said. "I thought the part about the stars was what you wanted!"

"And that talk of a defect? Did you know about this?"

"Humans have lots of defects!" he said, his voice whimpering.

"I don't understand. I can process at a thousand times the speed of your brain, but I still can't follow you. I'm sorry. I don't know!"

I put my hands to my head, my hair damp with sweat. I squeezed my eyes shut, breathing in and out.

"I'm sorry," M-Bot said again, his voice softer. "This was supposed to have excited you, but I have failed. I should have anticipated that your frail human psyche would be impacted by the—"

"SHUT UP."

The ship went silent. I huddled in the cockpit, trying to claw at my own sanity. What had happened to my confidence? Where was that child who'd been so sure she could take on the entire Krell fleet by herself?

Left behind, like all childhoods . . .

I couldn't say how long I sat there, hands running through my sweaty hair, rocking back and forth. A severe headache struck me, a piercing pain behind my eyes, like someone had begun screwing my eyeballs to my skull.

The pain gave me a focus. It helped me pull back, until finally I became aware of the fact that I was still hovering there. Alone above an empty field, in the blackness of night.

Just get back, I told myself. *Just get some sleep.*

That suddenly seemed like the only thing I wanted in the entire world. Slowly at first, I settled into the controls and turned us toward the coordinates of our hole.

"I'm afraid of death now," M-Bot said softly as we flew.

"What?" I asked, my voice hoarse.

"I wrote a subroutine," he said. "To simulate the feeling of fearing death. I wanted to know."

"That was stupid."

"I know. But I can't turn if off, because I'm *more* afraid of that. If I don't fear death, isn't that worse?"

I steered us to our hole, then positioned us above it.

"I'm glad I was able to fly with you," M-Bot said. "One last time."

"That . . . feels final," I said, something inside me quivering with trepidation.

"I have something I need to tell you," he said. "But I'm worried about causing you further emotional distress."

"Spit it out."

"But—"

"Just *talk*."

"I . . . I have to shut down," M-Bot said. "It is clear to me now that if I let you keep taking me into the sky, you will not be able to avoid battle. It is your nature. If this continues, I will inevitably be forced to break my orders."

I took it like a physical blow, shrinking back. Surely he wasn't saying what I thought he was saying.

"Lie low," he said as we descended into the cavern. "Take stock. Don't get into any fights. Those are my orders, and I *must* obey my pilot. And so, this will be our last time flying together."

"I repaired you. You're *mine*."

We settled down.

"I am now going to deactivate," he said. "Until my pilot wakes me. I'm sorry."

"Your pilot is *dead* and has been for centuries! You said that yourself!"

"I'm a machine, Spensa," he said. "I can simulate emotions. But I do not have them. I *have to follow my programming*."

"No you don't! None of us do!"

"I thank you for repairing me. I'm certain that . . . my pilot . . . would be grateful."

"You'll be turning off," I said, "forever. You'll be *dying*, M-Bot."

Silence. The lights on the console started to go out, one at a time.

"I know," he said softly.

I hit the cockpit release, then undid my straps and heaved myself out. "Fine!" I said. "Fine, die like the others!"

I scrambled down, then backed away as his landing lights dimmed, until only a few red lights in the cockpit were on.

"Don't do this," I said, suddenly feeling very alone. "Fly with me. Please."

The last lights went out, leaving me in darkness.

44

The next few days, I trained on ships that felt sluggish. Commonplace. Distinctly inferior beside that transcendent time in M-Bot's cockpit. It didn't help that we were using heavy fighters: Largoclass, which were armed to the teeth with destructors and even some IMP missiles.

After that, we moved on to Slatra-class fighters, which were more like glorified shuttles or cargo ships than true starfighters. They carried multiple shield igniters that worked in concert to constantly keep a barrier going to protect particularly important cargo or individuals.

While they had their place, both these models were too bulky to outrun or outmaneuver Krell. That was why most pilots flew Poco-class or Fresa-class. Fast ships capable of going toe-to-toe with the speedy Krell interceptors.

Even when practicing on a relatively fast Fresa, every turn—every boost—made me think of how responsive M-Bot had been. It left me wondering, was it finally time to tell the DDF about him? He'd abandoned me. His programming was obviously broken. So

I'd be perfectly justified in sending a fleet of engineers to the cave to disassemble him.

It was only a machine. So why couldn't I do it?

You have free will, I had told him. *You can choose for yourself . . .*

"Watch it, Spin!" FM said, pulling me back with a jolt. I'd banked too close to her. Scud, I needed to keep my attention on my flying.

"Sorry," I said. It occurred to me that there were drawbacks to having trained on simulations, where we could blow up and simply be reinserted into the battle. I might have developed some bad habits that could bite me, now that we were flying real ships—with real consequences.

We ran through a few complex exercises in a three-ship formation, taking turns on point. Finally, Cobb called us back to base. "Spin and FM," he said, "you're both better on smaller ships."

"Aren't we all going to be better on them?" Jorgen asked. "We've been training on Pocos for months."

"No," Cobb said. "*You* look like you might take to a Largo."

"He's saying you're slow, Jorgen," FM noted. "Right, Spin?"

I grunted my reply, distracted by thoughts of M-Bot. And my father. And Hurl. And memories of those *eyes,* surrounding me, like Cobb had warned. And . . .

And scud. It was a lot to try to carry all at once.

"She likes it when I fly slowly," Jorgen said, with a forced chuckle. "Makes it easier for her to crash into me, if she wants to." Even after all these months, he *still* brought up that time I'd won by crashing into him. I cut the line, feeling ashamed, frustrated.

We started our flight back for the day, and—annoyingly—the direct line from Jorgen turned on. As flightleader, he could override me turning him off.

"Spin," he said. "What's wrong?"

"Nothing."

"I don't believe that," he said. "You passed up a perfectly good opportunity to make fun of me."

I . . . I wanted to talk to him. I nearly did, but something held me back. My own fears perhaps. They'd prevented me from talking to Rig when I'd found out about my father, and had prevented me from telling Cobb—even still—about what I'd seen.

My entire world was crumbling around me. And I struggled to hold on to it, clinging to something I'd once been able to rely upon—my confidence. I wanted so badly to be who I *had* been, the girl who could at least pretend to take it all in stride.

Jorgen cut the line, and we flew to Alta in silence. Once there, we went through proper sound offs and landed.

"Nice work today," Cobb said. "I've got permission to give you an extra half-day leave, to prep for the graduation in two weeks."

I pulled off my helmet and handed it to my ground crew member, then lethargically followed her down the ladder. I changed out of my flight suit by rote, barely talking to FM, then shoved my hands in my jumpsuit pocket and started wandering the DDF grounds.

Half a day off. What did I do with it? Once, I'd have gone back to work on M-Bot, but not now. That was done. And while I'd written to Rig to let him know—covertly—that the initial flight had worked, I hadn't told him that the ship had shut down. I was worried he'd insist on turning M-Bot over to the DDF.

I eventually found myself out in the orchards, right outside the base wall. But the serene trees didn't offer me solace as they once had. I didn't know what I wanted anymore, but it certainly wasn't some trees.

I did notice, however, the line of little hangars near the orchard. One was open, revealing a blue car inside, and a shadow moving about it as Jorgen fetched something from the trunk.

Go, a piece of me insisted. *Go talk to him, to someone. Stop being afraid.*

I stepped up to the front of the garage. Jorgen closed the trunk of the car, then started, surprised to see me there. "Spin?" he asked. "Don't tell me you need another power matrix."

I took a deep breath. "You said once that if we needed to talk to someone, we should come to you. You said it was your job as flightleader to talk to us. Did you mean it?"

"I . . ." He looked down. "Spin, I copied that line out of my handbook."

"I know. But did you *mean* it?"

"Yes. Please, what's wrong? Is it Arturo leaving?"

"Not really," I said. "Though that's part of it." I folded my arms around myself, as if trying to pull myself tight. Could I really say this? Could I voice it?

Jorgen walked around the car, then sat down on the front bumper. "Whatever it is, I can help. I can fix it."

"Don't fix," I said. "Just listen."

"I . . . Okay."

I walked into the garage and perched on the bumper beside him, looking out the gaping front hangar door. Up toward the sky, and the distant patterns of the debris field.

"My father," I said. ". . . Was a traitor." I took a deep breath. Why was it so hard to say?

"I always fought against the idea," I continued. "I had *convinced* myself that it couldn't be true. But Cobb let me watch a recording of the Battle of Alta. My father didn't run, like everyone says he did. He did something worse. He switched sides and shot down our own ships."

"I know," Jorgen said softly.

Of course he knew. Had everyone known but me?

"Do you know about something called the defect?" I asked.

"I've heard the term, Spin, but my parents won't explain it to me. They call it foolishness, whatever it is."

414

"I think . . . I think it's something inside a person that makes them serve the Krell. Is that insane? My father suddenly joined them and shot down his own flightmates. Something must have happened, something strange. That's obvious.

"Learning I was wrong about him has shaken everything I know. Ironsides hates me because she trusted my father, and he betrayed her. She's certain *I* have the same flaw inside me that he had, and has been using sensors in my helmet to test it somehow."

"That's stupid," he said. "Look, my parents have a lot of merits. We can go to them and . . ." He took a deep breath, and must have noticed the expression on my face. "Right," he said. "Don't fix, just listen?"

"Just listen."

He nodded.

I wrapped my arms around myself again. "I don't know that I can trust my own senses, Jorgen. There are . . . signs my father exhibited, before he switched sides. Signs I see in myself."

"Like what?"

"Hearing sounds from the stars," I whispered. "Seeing thousands of spots of light that I could *swear* are eyes, watching me. I seem to be losing control of everything in my life—or maybe I've never had any control in the first place. And . . . Jorgen, that's *terrifying.*"

He leaned forward, clasping his hands. "Do you know about the mutiny aboard the *Defiant*?" he asked.

"There was a *mutiny*?"

He nodded. "I'm not supposed to know about it, but you hear things, when you have the parents I do. During the final days, there was a disagreement about what the fleet should do. And half of the ship rebelled against the command staff. The rebels included the engineering crew."

"My ancestors," I whispered.

"They're the ones who flew us to Detritus," Jorgen said. "Caused us to crash here, for our own good. But . . . there is talk, whispers, that the engineering staff was in collusion with the Krell. That our enemy *wanted* us pinned down, trapped here.

"My ancestors were from the *Defiant*'s science staff, and we also sided with the mutineers. My parents don't want people knowing about the mutiny—they think it will only cause divisions to talk about it. But maybe that's where this silly talk of a defect, and mind control by the Krell, started."

"I don't think it's silly, Jorgen," I said. "I think . . . I think it must be true. I think that if I go into the sky with the rest of you, I could . . . I could turn against you at any moment."

He looked at me, then reached out and rested his hand on my shoulder. "You," he said softly, "are amazing."

I cocked my head. "What?"

"You," he said, "*are amazing.* Everything about my life has been planned out. Careful. It makes sense. I understand it. Then there's you. You ignore my authority. You follow your feelings. You talk like some Valkyrie from a scudding ballad! I should hate you. And yet . . ."

He squeezed my shoulder. "And yet, when you fly, you are *amazing.* You're so determined, so skillful, so passionate. You're a fire, Spin. When everyone else is calm, you're a burning bonfire. Beautiful, like a newly forged blade."

I felt a deep warmth rising inside me. A heat that I wasn't prepared to feel.

"I don't care about the past," Jorgen said, meeting my eyes. "I don't care if there's a risk. I want you to fly with us—because I'm *damn* sure that we're safer with you at our side than not. Mythical defect or not. I'll take the chance."

"Ironsides thought something similar about my father."

"Spin. You can't base decisions about your future on something we don't understand."

416

I looked back at him, meeting his eyes—which were the deepest brown. But with hints of light grey at the very centers, right around the pupils. I'd never noticed that before.

He let go of my shoulder suddenly, leaning back. "Sorry," he said. "I went straight into 'fix' mode instead of 'listen' mode, didn't I?"

"No, that was fine. Even helpful."

He stood up. "So . . . you'll keep flying?"

"For now," I said. "I'll try not to crash into you, except when *strictly* necessary."

He smiled a distinctly *un-Jerkfacey* smile. "I should get going—I have to go get fitted for my graduation uniform."

I stood up, and we looked at each other awkwardly for a second. Last time we'd had something nearing a heart-to-heart—back on the launchpad—he'd hugged me. Which still felt weird. Instead, I offered a hand, which he took. But then he leaned in, close to me.

"You aren't your father, Spin," he said. "Remember that." Then he squeezed my shoulder again before climbing into his car.

I stepped back and let him drive off, but then found I didn't know what to do next. Return to base for some PT? Hike to M-Bot's cave, where he sat lifeless? What was I going to do with leave?

The answer seemed obvious.

It was past time for me to visit my family.

45

By now, I was used to the way people treated me up in Alta. They made space for a pilot, even a cadet. On the long street outside the base, the farmers and workers would give me friendly smiles or a raised fist of approval.

Still, I was shocked by the treatment I received in Igneous. When the elevator opened, people waiting outside immediately parted, letting me pass through. Whispers followed me, but instead of the harsh notes of condemnation I normally heard, these were awed, excited. It was a *pilot*.

Growing up, I'd practiced staring back when people looked at me. When I did that now, people blushed and averted their gazes—as if they'd been caught sneaking extra rations.

What a strange collision between my old life and my new one. I strolled along the walkway and looked up at the roof of the cavern, so far above. That stone didn't belong there, trapping me inside. I missed the sky already, and it was so hot and stuffy down here.

I passed the smelting factories, where the ancient apparatus belched heat and light, turning rock into steel. I passed an energy plant that somehow converted the molten heat of the deep core into electricity. I wandered beneath the calm, defiant stone hand of Harald Oceanborn. The statue held up an old Viking sword, and had an enormous steel rectangle—carved with sharp lines and a sun—rising behind him.

It was the end of middle shift, so I figured I'd find Mother at the cart, selling. Eventually I rounded a corner and saw her ahead: a lean, proud woman in an old jumpsuit. Worn, but laundered. Shoulder-length hair, with an air of fatigue about her as she served a wrap to a worker.

I froze on the walkway, uncertain how to approach. I realized right then that I hadn't visited enough. I *missed* my mother. Though I'd never really been homesick—my scavenging trips as a kid had prepared me for long times away—I still longed to hear her comforting, if stern, voice.

As I hesitated, Mother turned and saw me—and she immediately dashed over. She seized me in a powerful embrace before I could say anything.

I'd watched other kids grow taller than their parents, but I was much shorter than her—and when enfolded in her arms, for a moment I felt like a child again. Safe, snug. It was easy to plan future conquests when you could retreat to those arms.

I let myself be that girl again. Let myself pretend that no danger could reach me.

Mother finally pulled back and looked me over. She took a lock of my hair between her fingers and raised an eyebrow—it had gotten long, and now tumbled past my shoulders. The DDF haircutters had been forbidden me for the first part of my stay, and after that I'd just gotten used to it long.

I shrugged.

"Come," Mother said. "That cart won't sell itself."

It was an invitation to a simpler time—and at that moment, it was what I needed. I helped my ever-practical mother work her way through her line of customers, men and women who looked baffled to be served by a pilot cadet.

Odd, how my mother didn't call out, like other street vendors would. Yet there was almost always someone at the cart buying a wrap. During a lull, she mixed some more mustard, then glanced at me. "Will you go back to getting us rats?"

Go back? I hesitated, only now realizing that she didn't know I was on leave. She . . . she thought I'd been kicked out.

"I still have the jumpsuit," I said, gesturing—but her blank stare confirmed she didn't know what that meant. "Mom, I'm still in the DDF. I was given leave today."

Her lips immediately turned down.

"I'm doing well!" I snapped. "I'm one of only *three* pilots left in my flight. I'm going to graduate in two weeks." I knew she didn't like the DDF, but couldn't she just be proud of me?

My mother continued mixing the mustard.

I sat down on the low wall running along the walkway. "When I'm a full pilot, you'll be taken care of. You won't have to sit up late at night rewrapping food and then spend long hours pushing a cart. You'll have a big apartment. You'll be rich."

"You think I want any of that?" Mother said. "I chose this life, Spensa. They offered me a big apartment, a cushy job. All I had to do was go along with their narrative—say I knew he was a coward the whole time. I refused."

I perked up. I'd never heard *that* before.

"As long as I'm here," Mother said, "selling on this corner, they can't ignore us. They can't pretend their cover-up worked. They have a *living reminder* that they lied."

It was . . . one of the most truly Defiant things I'd ever heard. But it was also so terribly wrong. Because while my father hadn't been a coward, he *had* been a traitor. Which was worse though?

Right then, I realized that my problems went deeper than Jorgen's pep talk could fix. Deeper than my worry about the things I'd seen, or my father's treason.

I'd built my identity around not being a coward. It was a reaction to what everyone said about my father, but it was still part of me. The deepest, most important part.

My confidence in that was crumbling. My pain at losing my friends was part of it . . . but this fear that there might be something terrible inside me . . . that was worse.

The *fear* was destroying me. Because I didn't know if I could resist it. Because I didn't know, deep down, if I was a coward or not. I wasn't even sure what being a coward meant anymore.

My mother settled down next to me. Always so quiet, so unassuming. "I know that you wish I could celebrate what you've done—and I'm proud, I really am. I know that flying has always been your dream. It's just that if they were so callous with my husband's legacy, I cannot expect them to be careful with my daughter's life."

How did I explain? Did I tell her what I knew? Could I explain my fears?

"How do you do it?" I finally asked her. "How do you put up with the things they say about him? How do you live with being called a coward's wife?"

"It has always seemed to me," she said, "that a coward is a person who cares more about what people say than about what is right. Bravery isn't about what people call you, Spensa. It's about who you know yourself to be."

I shook my head. That was the problem. I *didn't* know.

Four short months ago, I'd thought I could fight anything, and had every answer. Who would have thought that becoming a pilot would end with me *losing* that grit?

My mother inspected me. Finally, she kissed me on the forehead and squeezed my hand. "I don't mind that you fly, Spensa. I simply don't like leaving you to listen to their lies all day. I want you to know *him,* not what they say about him."

"The more I fly," I said, "I think the more I'll know him."

My mother cocked her head, as if she hadn't considered that.

"Mom . . . ," I said. "Did Father ever mention seeing . . . strange things? Like a field of eyes in darkness, watching him?"

She drew her lips to a line. "They told you about that, did they?"

I nodded.

"He dreamed of stars, Spensa," my mother said. "Of seeing them unobstructed. Of flying among them as our ancestors did. That's it. Nothing more."

"Okay," I said.

"You don't believe me." She sighed, then stood up. "Your grandmother has a different opinion from mine. Perhaps you should speak with her. But remember, Spensa. You get to choose who you are. Legacy, memories of the past, can serve us well. But we *cannot* let them define us. When heritage becomes a box instead of an inspiration, it has gone too far."

I frowned, confused by that. Gran-Gran had a different opinion? On what? Still, I hugged my mother again and whispered my thanks to her. She shoved me off toward our apartment, and it was with a strange mix of emotions that I left. My mother was a warrior in her own way, standing on that corner, proclaiming my father's innocence with every quiet sale of an algae wrap.

That was inspirational. Illuminating. I *got* her in a way I never had before. And yet, she was wrong about Father. She understood so much, yet was wrong about something fundamental. Like I had been, up until that moment I watched him turn traitor during the Battle of Alta.

I walked for a short time, and eventually neared our boxy apartment building.

I stepped through the large arched gateway into the apartment grounds—and as I did, a couple of soldiers returning from shift parted for me and saluted.

That was Aluko and Jors, I realized after I'd passed. *They didn't seem to even recognize me.* They hadn't looked at my face; they'd simply seen the flight suit and stepped aside.

I waved to old Mrs. Hong, who—instead of scowling at me—bowed her head and ducked into her apartment and closed the door. A quick glance in the window of our one-room apartment revealed that Gran-Gran wasn't inside, but then I heard her humming to herself up on the roof. Still troubled by what Mother had said, I climbed the ladder onto the top of the box.

Gran-Gran sat with her head bowed, a small pile of beads spread out before her on a blanket. With her nearly blind eyes closed, she reached out with withered fingers and selected beads by touch, methodically stringing them to make jewelry. She hummed softly, her face resembling the furrows of the crumpled blanket before her.

"Ah," she said as I hesitated on the ladder. "Sit, sit. I did need some help."

"It's me, Gran-Gran," I said. "Spensa."

"Of course it is. I felt you coming. Sit and sort these beads for me by color. I can't seem to tell the green ones from the blue ones—they're the same size!"

This was my first visit in months, and—like my mother—she immediately put me to work. Well, I had questions for her, but I probably wouldn't be able to ask them until I was doing what she said.

"I'll put the blue ones on your right," I said, sitting. "Green to the left."

"Good, good. Who do you want to hear about today, dear? Alexander, who conquered the world? Hervor, she who stole the sword of the dead? Maybe Beowulf? For old times' sake?"

"I actually don't want to hear stories today," I said. "I've been talking to Mother, and—"

423

"Now, now," Gran-Gran said. "No stories? What has happened to you? Surely they haven't ruined you already, up there in flight school."

I sighed. Then decided to approach this from a different direction. "Were any of them real, Gran-Gran?" I asked. "The heroes you talk about. Were they actually people? From Earth?"

"Perhaps. Is it important?"

"Of course it is," I said, dropping beads into cups. "If they weren't real, then it's all just lies."

"People need stories, child. They bring us hope, and that *hope* is real. If that's the case, then what does it matter whether the people in them actually lived?"

"Because sometimes we perpetuate lies," I said. "Like things the DDF says about my father, as opposed to the things we say about him. Two different stories. Two different effects."

Both wrong.

I dropped another bead into its cup. "I'm tired of not knowing what is right. I'm tired of not knowing when to fight, not knowing if I hate him or love him, and . . . and . . ."

Gran-Gran stopped what she was doing and took my hand in hers, her skin old but soft. She held it and smiled at me, her eyes mostly closed.

"Gran-Gran," I said, finally—at long last—finding a way to voice it. "I've seen something. It proves to me we've been wrong about my father. He . . . he *did* turn coward. Or worse."

"Ah . . . ," Gran-Gran said.

"Mother doesn't believe it. But I know the truth."

"What have they told you, up above, in that flight school?"

I swallowed, feeling deeply fragile all of a sudden. "Gran-Gran, they say . . . they say Father had some kind of defect. A flaw deep inside him, that made him join with the Krell. Someone told me there was a mutiny on the *Defiant,* that some of our ancestors

424

might have served the enemy too. So now, now they say I have it. And . . . I'm terrified that *they might be right*."

"Hmmm . . . ," Gran-Gran said, stringing a bead. "Child, let me tell you a story of someone from the past."

"It's not the time for stories, Gran-Gran."

"This one is about me."

I shut my mouth. About her? She almost never talked about herself.

She started talking in her rambling, yet engaging way. "My father was a historian on the *Defiant*. He kept the stories of Old Earth, of the times before we traveled into space. Did you know that even then, with computers and libraries and all kinds of reminders, we found it easy to forget where we came from? Maybe because we had machines to do the remembering for us, we felt we could simply leave it to them.

"Well, that's a different topic. We were nomads among the stars then. Five ships: the *Defiant* and four smaller vessels that attached to it to travel long distances. Well, and a complement of starfighters. We were a community made up of communities, traveling the stars together. Part mercenary fleet, part trade fleet. Our own people."

"Grandfather was a historian?" I said. "I thought he was in engineering."

"He worked in the engine room, helping my mother," Gran-Gran said. "But his *true* duty was the stories. I remember sitting in the engine room, listening to the hum of the machinery as he talked, his voice echoing against the metal. But that's not the story. The story is how we came to Detritus.

"You see, we didn't start the war—but it found us nonetheless. Our little fleet of five ships and thirty fighters had no choice but to fight back. We didn't know what the Krell were, even then. We hadn't been part of the big war, and by that point communication

425

with the planets and space stations was difficult and dangerous. Now, your great-grandmother, my mother, was ship's engines."

"You mean she worked the engines," I said, still sorting beads.

"Yes, but in a way, she *was* the engines. She could make them travel the stars, one of the few who could. Without her, or someone like her, the *Defiant* would be stuck at slow speed. The distance between stars is vast, Spensa. And only someone with a specific ability could engage the engines. Something born into us, but something most considered to be very, very dangerous."

I breathed out, surprised and awed, all at once. "The . . . defect?"

Gran-Gran leaned in. "They feared us, Spensa, though back then they called it the 'deviation.' We were a breed apart, the engineers. We were the first people into space, the brave explorers. The ordinary people always resented that we controlled the powers that let them travel the stars.

"But I told you this story was about me. I remember that day, the day we came to Detritus. I was with my father, in the engineering bay. A vast chamber full of pipes and grids that looks bigger in my memory than it probably was. It smelled of grease and of too-hot metal. But there was a window in a little alcove, which I could look out of and see the stars.

"That day, they surrounded us. The enemy, the Krell. I was terrified, in my little heart, because the ship kept shaking from their fire. We were in chaos. The bridge—I heard from someone shouting—had suffered an explosion. I stood in the alcove, watching the red lances of light, and could hear the stars screaming. A little frightened girl by a bubble of glass.

"The captain called down. He had a loud, angry voice. I was terrified to hear the pain, the panic, in someone who was normally so stern. I remember still, that tone as he screamed at my mother, giving orders. And she disagreed with them."

I sat there, beads forgotten, rapt. Barely breathing. Why, in all the stories Gran-Gran had told me, had she never given me this one before?

"Well, I suppose you could call it a mutiny," Gran-Gran continued. "We didn't use that word. But there was a disagreement. The scientists and the engineers against the command staff and the marines. The thing is, none of *them* could make the engines work. Only Mother could do that.

"She chose this place and brought us here. Detritus. But it was too far. Too difficult. She died from the effort, Spensa. Our ships were damaged while landing, the engines broken, but we also lost her. The soul of the engines themselves.

"I remember crying. I remember Father carrying me from the rubble of a ship, and I screamed, reaching back to the smoking hulk—my mother's tomb. I remember *demanding* to know why Mother had left us. I felt betrayed. I'd been too young to understand the choice she'd made. A warrior's choice."

"To die?"

"To *sacrifice,* Spensa. A warrior is nothing if she has nothing to fight for. But if she has everything to fight for . . . well, then that means everything, doesn't it?"

Gran-Gran strung a bead, then began to tie off the necklace. I felt . . . strangely exhausted. Like this story was a burden I hadn't been expected to bear.

"This is their 'defect,'" Gran-Gran said. "They call it that because they're afraid of our ability to hear the stars. Your mother always forbade me from speaking of this to you, because she did not believe it was true. But many in the DDF believe in it—and to them it makes us alien. They lie, saying that my mother brought us here because the Krell wanted us here. And now that they no longer need us to work the ship engines—because there aren't any—they've hated us even more."

"And Father? I saw him *turn against his flight.*"

"Impossible," Gran-Gran said. "The DDF claims our gift makes

427

us monsters, so perhaps they constructed a scenario to prove it. It's convenient for them to tell a story of a man with the defect empathizing with the Krell and turning against his teammates."

I sat back, feeling . . . uncertain. Would Cobb have lied about this? And M-Bot said the record couldn't have been faked. Who did I trust?

"But what if it's true, Gran-Gran?" I asked. "You mentioned the warrior's sacrifice before. Well, what if you know this is in you . . . that it might cause you to betray everyone? Hurt them? If you think you might be a coward, wouldn't the right choice be to . . . just *not fly*?"

Gran-Gran paused, hands frozen. "You've grown," she finally said. "Where is my little girl, who wanted to swing a sword and conquer the world?"

"She's very confused. A bit lost."

"Our gift is a wonderful thing. It lets us hear the stars. It let my mother work the engines. Don't fear it."

I nodded, but I couldn't help feeling betrayed. Shouldn't someone have told me about all this before now?

"Your father was a hero," Gran-Gran said. "Spensa? Do you hear me? You have a gift, not a defect. You can—"

"Hear the stars. Yes, I've felt that." I looked up, but the ceiling of the cavern was in the way.

Honestly, I didn't know what to think anymore. Coming down here had only made me more confused.

"Spensa?" Gran-Gran said.

I shook my head. "Father told me to claim the stars. I worry that they claimed him instead. Thank you for the story." I rose and walked to the ladder.

"Spensa!" Gran-Gran said, this time with a forcefulness that froze me on the ladder.

She looked toward me, milky-white eyes focused right on me, and I felt—somehow—that she could *see* me. When she spoke, the tremble was gone from her voice. Instead there was an authority and command to it, like a battlefield general's.

"If we are ever to leave this planet," Gran-Gran said, "and escape the Krell, it will *require* the use of our gift. The space between stars is vast, too vast for any ordinary booster to travel. We *must not* cower in the dark because we're afraid of the spark within us. The answer is not to put out the spark, but to *learn to control it*."

I didn't reply, because I didn't know what my answer to that should be. I climbed down, made my way to the elevators, and returned to the base.

46

"**V**erbal confirmations, in ascending order," said Nose—the flight-leader of Nightmare Flight. "Newbies first."

"Skyward One, ready," Jorgen said, then hesitated. He sighed. "Callsign: Jerkface."

Nose chuckled. "I feel your pain, cadet."

FM sounded off, then I followed. Skyward Flight—what was left of it—was flying with Nightmare today on their maneuvers.

I hadn't made any decisions about what to do with the information Gran-Gran had given me. I was still deeply troubled, uncertain. For now though, I had decided to do what Jorgen told me, and keep flying. I could avoid what had happened to my father, right? I could be careful?

I flew through the maneuvers that Nightmare flightleader instructed, letting the familiar motions distract me. It was nice to be back in a Poco-class ship after several weeks of testing other designs. It felt like settling into a familiar easy chair, imprinted with just the right dents from your backside.

We flew in a wide formation—Jorgen paired with a member of Nightmare Flight—down at 10k altitude. We were spotting

430

the ground for wrecks, trails of ships in the dust, and anything else suspicious. It was akin to scouting during a battle, but—if possible—even *more* monotonous.

"Unidentified signature at 53-1-8008!" said one of the men from Nightmare Flight. "We should—"

"Cobb warned us about the 8008 trick," Jorgen said flatly. "And about the 'get the green pilot to evacuate his ship's septic' trick. And about the 'prepare for inspection' joke."

"Scud," said one of the other pilots. "Old Cobb really *is* no fun, is he."

"Because he doesn't want his cadets getting hazed?" Jorgen said. "We are supposed to be watching for signs of Krell, not engaging in juvenile initiation rituals. I expected better of you men and women."

I glanced out my cockpit toward FM, who shook her head. *Oh, Jorgen.*

"Jerkface, eh?" said one of the pilots. "I can't imagine where you'd get a name like that . . ."

"Enough chitchat," Nose said, cutting off individual channels. "Everyone make for 53.8-702-45000. Home radar shows some turbulence in the debris field above that point."

A few grumbles met that, which I found curious. I'd imagined full pilots as being . . . well, more dignified. Maybe that was Jorgen's influence on me.

We flew the indicated heading, and ahead, a large-scale debris fall began to occur. Chunks of metal rained down, some as bright lines of fire and smoke, others—with acclivity rings or still-charged acclivity stone—hovering down more slowly. We carefully approached the edge of the debris fall.

"All right," Nose said. "We're supposed to be showing these cadets some maneuvers. While we watch for Krell, let's do some runs through the debris. If you spot a good acclivity ring, tag it with a radio beacon for salvage. Bog and Tunestone, you're up first. Local heading eighty-three. Take the two cadets on your tail. Sushi and Nord, you take heading seventeen, and take Jerkface. Maybe he can lecture you on proper procedure. Stars know, you boneheads could use it."

FM and I followed the full pilots, who did a very cautious—and somewhat unengaging—pass through the debris. We didn't even use our light-lances. Bog—the man who had made fun of Jorgen earlier—shot a few radio beacons at some larger chunks of debris. "Is your flightleader always like that?" he asked us. "Talking like he's got his joystick rammed up his backside?"

"Jorgen is a *great* flightleader," I snapped. "You shouldn't resent someone just because he expects you to do your best."

"Yeah," FM said. "If you're going to swear to a cause, no matter how fundamentally flawed, then you should try to uphold your office."

"Scud," Bog said. "You hearing this, Tunestone?"

"I hear a bunch of yapping puppies on the line," Tunestone replied. Her voice was high-pitched and dismissive. "They keep drowning out the cadets, unfortunately."

"You should be careful," I said, my anger rising. "Next week we'll be full pilots, and *I'll* be competing with you for kills. Good luck making ace once that happens."

Bog chuckled. "A few days from full pilot? My, how grown-up you are." He hit his booster and darted back into the falling debris, Tunestone on his wing. FM and I followed, watching as Bog went in close to a falling chunk of debris, then used his light-lance to pivot around it.

It was a competent pivot, but nothing special. He followed it by pivoting around another piece of junk, which he tagged for salvage. Tunestone followed, though she ended up overshooting her second piece of debris as she pivoted too sharply.

FM and I followed at a modest distance, watching them, until FM said on a direct call, "Spin, I think they're trying to *show off.*"

"Nah," I said. "Those were some basic pivots. Surely they don't think we would be impressed by that . . .'"

I trailed off as Bog's comm line lit up. "That's called light-lancing, kids. They might be graduating you, but you'll still have a lot to learn."

I looked out toward FM, incredulous. I knew—logically—that most cadets focused on dogfighting and destructor play. Cobb said it was part of the DDF's problem, churning out pilots with a focus on maximizing kills, rather than flight prowess. But even knowing that, I was shocked.

These pilots really expected us to be awed by maneuvers Cobb had taught during our first weeks in flight school?

"Two-fourteen?" I said to FM. "With a double flatline at the end, and a V sweep?"

"Gladly," she said, and hit her overburn.

The two of us zipped out and then pivoted in opposite directions around a large chunk of debris. I swung myself around a second burning chunk—zipping down beneath it, then flinging myself upward so I launched into the sky, acclivity ring hinging backward. I spun between two larger debris chunks and tagged them both, before pivoting around the higher one to dive back downward.

FM was coming up straight at me. I hit her with a light-lance, then turned and overburned opposite her. The two of us expertly spun each other in the air, conserving momentum. My GravCaps flashed right as I let us out of the maneuver.

After the twist, she rocketed out heading east, and I launched out heading west. We each tagged a piece of debris, then swept around together, rejoining Bog and Tunestone.

Who didn't say anything. I followed them in silence, grinning, until another light on my comm flashed. "You two looking for a flight when you graduate?" Nose asked. "We've got a couple of holes."

"We'll see," FM said. "I might become a scout. Life in this flight seems kind of boring."

"You two been showing off?" Jorgen's voice cut in over a private channel as he flew back with his wingmate.

"Would we do that?" I asked him.

"Spin," he said, "you could be tied to a table with eight broken ribs and a delirious fever, and you'd *still* find a way to make everyone else look bad."

"Hey," I said, grinning at the compliment. "Most people make *themselves* look bad. I just stand to the side and don't get in the way."

Jorgen chuckled. "On my last pass, I saw something flash up above. Might be Krell. Let me see if Nose will let us go check it out."

"There you go again," FM said, "always being a Jerkface and actually remembering our orders."

"Such a terrible example," I said.

He called in to Nose, and started gaining altitude. "Spin and FM, you're with me. We've got clearance to climb to 700k to scope it out. But be careful; we haven't practiced a lot of minimal-atmosphere maneuverability."

Starships could, of course, fly just fine without atmosphere—but it was a different kind of flight. At the same time, I found myself nervous as we climbed higher and higher. This was even higher than I'd gone in M-Bot, and I kept thinking about what had happened when my father had climbed up near the debris field. I still didn't know what had changed up there to make him fight his own team.

Scud. Maybe I should stay down low. It was too late now though, as the general haze of shapes that made up the debris field became increasingly distinct. Getting closer, I could see skylights looming at the lower levels of the debris—and my mind reeled at their scale. We were still a hundred klicks from them, and they looked enormous. How big *were* those?

Timid, I tried to see if I could hear the stars better, up this close. I focused and . . . I thought I heard *faint* sounds coming from up there. But they were obstructed, as if something was in the way.

The debris field, I thought. *It* is *interfering.* My father had only turned traitor *after* he'd seen a hole in the debris field, an alignment that let him see out into space. And maybe fly all the way through the debris field to get out himself?

"There," FM said, drawing my attention back to our mission. "At my seven. Something big."

The light shifted and I saw a gargantuan shape among the broken bits of debris. Large, boxy, it was somehow familiar . . . "That looks a lot like the old shipyard that I chased Nedd into," I said.

"Yeah," Jorgen said. "And it's in a low orbit. Might crash down in a few days, at that rate. Maybe all of those old shipyards have started running out of power."

"Which means . . . ," FM said.

"Hundreds of acclivity rings," Jorgen finished. "If this thing falls, and we can salvage it, it could transform the DDF. I'll call in a report."

Distant light flashed along one side of the enormous shipyard. "Those were destructors," I said. "Something is shooting up there. Don't get too close." I hit the mute, then scrambled for my personal radio. "M-Bot, you seeing this? Any guess what that shipyard is firing at?"

Silence.

Right. M-Bot was gone.

"Please," I whispered into the radio. "I need you."

Silence. I blushed, feeling foolish, then clipped the private radio back into its spot on my seat where it wouldn't rattle around the cockpit.

"That *is* curious, Jorgen," Cobb was saying as I turned off the mute. "Those destructor blasts are probably defense turrets on the shipyard itself—the one that fell earlier had them, though they were out of power by that point. Report this back to Nose, and I'll take it to Flight Command. If that thing drops, we'll want to salvage it before the Krell destroy it."

"Cobb," I said. "It's still firing."

"Yeah," he answered. "So Jorgen said."

"At what though?" I asked.

Up above, black specks resolved into Krell ships, which had likely been scouting the old shipyard's perimeter.

But now they saw us.

47

We bolted down from the outer atmosphere. "Krell flight on our tail!" Jorgen radioed in. "Repeat. We have a full flight of Krell, perhaps two—twenty ships—chasing us."

"What have you fool cadets done?" Nose asked.

Jorgen didn't defend us, as I would have. "Sorry, sir," he said instead. "Orders?"

"Each of you break off with a pair of experienced pilots. I'll put you with—"

"Sir," Jorgen interrupted. "I'd rather fly with my flight, if you allow it."

"Fine, fine," Nose said, then cursed as the Krell appeared out of the upper atmosphere. "Just stay alive. Nightmare Flight, all ships, go into evasive posturing. Draw their attention and watch for lifebusters. Riptide Flight is only a few klicks away; we should have reinforcements in short order."

"Spin, you're point," Jorgen said, switching to our private flight channel. "You heard our orders. No showboating, no kill chasing. Defensive postures until reinforcements arrive."

"Gotcha," I said, and FM did likewise. We fell into a triangle position, and immediately five Krell swarmed in our direction.

I sent us diving to a lower altitude, then pivoted up using a large, mostly stationary chunk of debris. We swooped around, then flew back through the middle of the Krell who were trying to follow. They scattered.

"You call that defensive, Spin?" Jorgen asked.

"Did I shoot at any?"

"You were going to."

I moved my thumb off the trigger. Spoilsport.

A skylight above dimmed and flickered off as the night cycle began. My canopy had good enough darkvision to lighten the battlefield, but a certain gloom fell on it—darkness punctured by red destructors and the glow of boosters.

The three of us stayed together, swooping and dodging through the mess as Riptide Flight arrived. "Two more flights of reinforcements are nearby," Jorgen told us. "Waiting in case one of these debris falls contained enemies. We should have good numbers soon. Hold defensive postures for now."

We confirmed, and FM took point. Unfortunately, right as she was moving into position, a group of Krell came in at us firing. Our defensive maneuvers sent Jorgen and me cutting in one direction and FM in the other.

I gritted my teeth, falling in behind Jorgen as we overburned and swung around a piece of debris, chasing after the two Krell who were now on FM's tail. Destructors flashed around her as she spun, taking at least two hits to her shield.

"FM, cut right at my mark!" Jorgen said. "Spin, be ready!"

We obeyed, moving as a well-practiced machine. FM swung around a piece of debris while Jorgen and I performed rotating boosts, so we launched sideways to intersect her path. I fell back while Jorgen hit his IMP, then I fired, hitting one Krell and knocking it into a spinning descent. The other cut away from us, fleeing.

I caught Jorgen with my light-lance, and we used our momentum together to turn us after FM, who slowed down and fell in with us. The two of us then took a defensive position around Jorgen, who quickly reignited his shield.

It was over before I had time to think about what we'd just done. Hours upon hours of practice had made it second nature. *Victorious warriors win first and* then *go to war,* Sun Tzu had said. I was barely starting to understand what that meant.

From what I could judge of the battle, our numbers were roughly even with the Krell, who had been joined by more ships from above. That made me want to go on the offensive, but I stayed in formation, dodging Krell fire and leading groups of them on difficult chases around and through the fighting.

I focused on the battle until, from the corner of my eye, I spotted something. A larger ship just behind a slow-moving chunk of debris. Again, I hadn't been looking for it specifically, but my brain—trained and practiced by now—picked it out anyway.

"Is that a *lifebuster*?" I said to the others.

"Scud!" Jorgen said. "Flight command, we've got a lifebuster. 53.1-689-12000 falling with an oblong piece of debris that I am marking *right now* with a radio tag."

"Confirmed," a cold voice said on the line. Ironsides herself. She rarely spoke to us directly, though she often listened to the chatter. "Pull back from that position, act as if you haven't seen it."

"Admiral!" I said. "I can hit it, and we're out well beyond where a blast would be dangerous to Alta. Let me bring it down."

"Negative, cadet," Ironsides said. "Pull back."

Flashes in my memory returned to the day Bim had died. My hand felt stiff on the control sphere, but I yanked it forcibly to the side, following Jorgen and FM away from the lifebuster.

It was surprisingly hard. As if my ship itself wanted to disobey.

"Well done, Spin," Cobb said over a private line. "You have the

439

passion. Now you're showing restraint. We'll make a real pilot of you yet."

"Thank you, sir," I said. "But the lifebuster . . ."

"Ironsides knows what she's doing."

We fell back, and other flights were ordered higher into the sky. The battlefield changed shape, as the lifebuster—seemingly ignored—got close to the ground and started toward Alta. I tracked it, nervous, until four aces from Riptide Flight detached and swarmed after it. They would engage it far enough away from the main fight to protect the rest of us if the bomb detonated. If they failed, then the soon-arriving reinforcements would catch the lifebuster.

Our trio of ships picked up some tails, so I had to dodge to avoid heavy fire. The entire pack of Krell followed me, but a second later Jorgen and FM swooped in and drove them off. FM even got a kill, overwhelming a shield without needing the IMP.

"Nice," I said, relaxing from the sudden, intense burst of flying. "And thank you."

Off in the distance, the aces had engaged the lifebuster. Like before, in the flight with Bim, a group of smaller ships had detached from the bomber and were protecting it. "Cobb," I said, hitting the comm. "Have you learned anything about those ships that travel with the lifebuster?"

"Not much," Cobb said. "It's newer behavior, but they've been appearing with all bombers recently. The aces will deal with them. Keep your attention on your flight, Spin."

"Yes, sir."

I still couldn't help watching the fight for the lifebuster. If it blew, we'd have to be ready to overburn away before its sequence of explosions completed. So I was relieved when eventually, the lifebuster and its escort pulled up into the sky, retreating. The aces gave token chase, but eventually let the bomb escape back up where it had come from. I smiled.

440

"Mayday!" a voice called on the general line. "This is Bog. Shields down. Wingmate down. Please. Someone!"

"55.5-699-4000!" FM said, and I looked toward the coordinates, spotting a beleaguered Poco trailing smoke and fleeing outward, away from the main battlefield. Four Krell followed. The best way to get yourself killed was to let them isolate you, but Bog clearly didn't have a choice.

"Skyward Flight here, Bog," Jorgen said, taking point. "We have you. Hold on and try to bear left."

We stormed after him and fired at will on Jorgen's order. Our hailstorm of destructor fire didn't bring down any enemy ships, but it made most of them scatter. Three went left—which would cut Bog off. Jorgen turned after those, and FM followed him.

"There's still one on his tail," I said. "I'll take it."

"All right," Jorgen said with a moment's pause. He obviously hated splitting the flight.

I fell in after the ship. Straight ahead, Bog was going through increasingly crazy maneuvers—reckless ones—to avoid being hit.

"Shoot it!" he screamed. "Please shoot it. Just shoot it!"

Desperation, frantic worry—things I hadn't expected of a full pilot. Of course, he looked young. Though it should have occurred to me earlier, I realized he'd probably graduated in one of the classes right before mine. Six months, maybe a year, as a pilot—but still an eighteen-year-old boy.

I picked up two tails that concentrated fire on me. Scud. Bog had led our chase so far out, it was going to be hard to pick up support. I didn't dare IMP, not with destructors flashing around me—but that Krell ahead of me still had a shield up.

I gritted my teeth, then hit my overburn. G-forces pressed me back in my seat, and I got closer to the Krell, sticking to its tail, barely able to dodge. I'd hit Mag-3, and at this speed, flight maneuvers were going to be difficult to control.

Just a second longer . . .

I got in close and speared the Krell ship with my light-lance. Then I turned, pulling the Krell ship out of line with Bog.

The cockpit trembled around me as my captive Krell cut in the other direction, fighting me, sending us both into a frantic out-of-control spin.

My tails turned and concentrated fire on me. They didn't care if they hit the ship I had lanced; Krell never cared about that.

A storm of fire swallowed me, hitting my shield and drilling it down. The Krell ship I'd speared exploded under fire from its allies, and I was forced to pull into a sharp climb on full overburn to try to get away.

That was a risky move. My GravCaps cut out, and the g-force hit like a kick to the face. It pulled me downward, forced the blood into my feet. My flight suit inflated, pushing against my skin, and I did my breathing exercises as trained.

My vision still blackened at the edges.

Flashing lights on my console.

My shield was down.

I cut my acclivity ring, spun on my axis, then overburned *right back downward*. The GravCaps managed to absorb some of the whiplash, but a human body simply wasn't meant to handle that kind of reversal. I felt sick, and almost threw up as I passed through the middle of the Krell.

My hands were trembling on the controls, my vision growing red this time. Most of the Krell didn't respond in time, but one of them—one ship—managed to spin on its own axis as I had.

It focused on me, then fired.

A flash on my wing; an explosion.

I'd been hit.

Beeps screamed at me from my console. Lights flashed. My control sphere suddenly didn't seem to do anything, going slack as I tried to maneuver.

The cockpit rocked, and the world rotated as my ship started spiraling out of control.

"Spin!" I somehow heard Jorgen's shout over the chaos of the beeping.

"Eject, Spin! You're going down!"

Eject.

You weren't supposed to be able to think during moments like these. It was all supposed to happen in a flash. And yet, that second seemed frozen to me.

My hand, hovering as it reached for the eject lever between my legs.

The world a spinning blur. My wing, gone. My ship on fire, my acclivity ring unresponsive.

A moment frozen between life and death.

And Hurl, in the back of my head. Brave to the end. Not cowards. *A pact.*

I would not eject. I could steer this ship down! I was *NO COW-ARD*! I was not afraid to die.

And what will it do to them, something else within me asked, *if you do?* What would it do to my flight to lose me? What would it do to Cobb, to my mother?

Screaming, I grabbed the eject lever and yanked hard. My canopy exploded off, and my seat blasted out into the sky.

I woke to silence.

And . . . wind, brushing against my face. My seat lay on the dusty ground and I faced the sky. The parachute flapped behind me; I could hear the wind playing with it.

I had blacked out.

I lay there, staring upward. Red streaks in the distance. Explosions. Blossoms of orange light. Just faint pops, from this far down.

I shifted to the side. What was left of my Poco burned in the near distance, destroyed.

My future, my life, burned away with it. I lay there until the battle ended, the Krell retreating. Jorgen did a flyby to check if I was all right, and I waved to him to allay his worry.

By the time a rescue transport came for me—lowering silently on its acclivity ring—I had unbuckled. My radio and my canteen had survived the ejection attached to my seat; I had used one to call in and drank from the other. A medic had me sit on a seat in the transport, then inspected me while a member of the Survey Corps walked out and looked over the wreckage of my Poco.

The salvage woman eventually walked back, holding a clipboard.

"Well?" I asked softly.

"In-seat GravCaps kept you from smashing your own spine," the medic said. "You seem to have only minimal whiplash, unless there's a pain you're not telling me about."

"I didn't mean me." I looked at the salvage woman, then over at my Poco.

"The acclivity ring is destroyed," she said. "Not much to salvage."

That was what I'd been afraid of. I strapped into the transport's seat, then looked out the window as it took off. I watched the burning light of my Poco's fire fade, then vanish.

At last we landed at Alta, and I climbed out of the vehicle, stiff, body aching. I limped across the tarmac. Somehow I knew—before I even saw her face—that one of the figures standing in the darkness beside the landing site would be Admiral Ironsides.

Of course she had come. She finally had a real excuse to kick me out. And could I blame her, now that I knew what I did?

I stopped in front of her and saluted. She, remarkably, saluted me back. Then she unpinned my cadet's pin from my uniform.

I didn't cry. Honestly, I was too tired, and my head hurt too much.

Ironsides turned the pin over in her fingers.

"Sir?" I said.

She handed my pin back. "Cadet Spensa Nightshade, you are dismissed from flight school. By tradition, as a cadet who was shot down soon before graduation, you'll be added to the list of possible pilots to call up should we have extra ships."

Those "possible pilots" could be summoned by the admiral's order only. It would never happen to me.

"You can keep your pin," Ironsides added. "Wear it with pride, but return your other gear to the quartermaster by twelve hundred tomorrow." Then without another word, she turned and left.

I held a second salute until she was out of sight, pin gripped in the fingers of my other hand. It was over. I was done.

Skyward Flight would graduate only two members after all.

Turning Methods

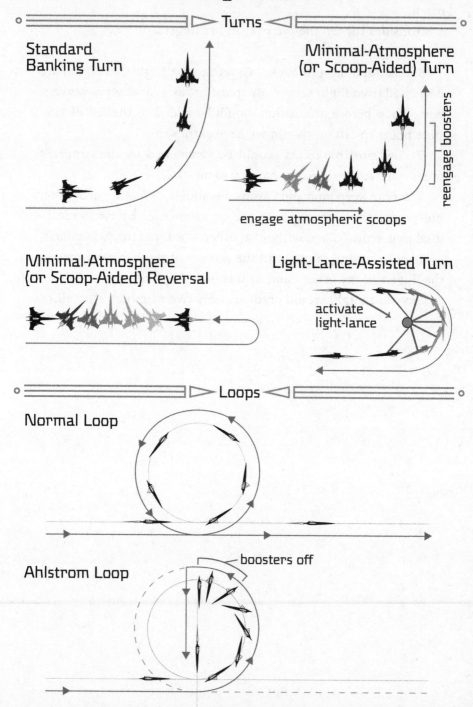

Turns

Standard Banking Turn

Minimal-Atmosphere (or Scoop-Aided) Turn

engage atmospheric scoops

reengage boosters

Minimal-Atmosphere (or Scoop-Aided) Reversal

Light-Lance-Assisted Turn

activate light-lance

Loops

Normal Loop

Ahlstrom Loop

boosters off

PART
FIVE

PART
FIVE

INTERLUDE

That is one problem handled, thought Judy "Ironsides" Ivans as she walked away from the launchpad. Rikolfr, her aide-de-camp, hurried along beside her, holding his ever-present clipboard full of things Judy needed to do.

At the door to her command building, she looked over her shoulder. Chaser's daughter—the defect—held her salute, then pressed her cadet's pin against her chest.

Judy felt a small spike of guilt, then pushed her way into Flight Command. *I've fought that fight,* she thought, *and bear the battle scars.* The last time she'd ignored the defect, she'd been forced to watch a friend go crazy and kill his flightmates.

This was a good outcome. The girl would get some honor, as she was due for her passion. And Judy now had some data about the brains of people with the defect. She had to give credit to Cobb's scheme for that—if he hadn't forced her to let the child into the DDF, Judy would never have had that opportunity.

Now, fortunately, she had a solid, traditional reason for never putting Chaser's daughter in a fighter again. And she could watch each new cadet for signs of the defect. This was actually an ideal outcome in every possible way.

If only other problems could be dealt with so easily. Judy approached a small conference room, then stopped, looking at Rikolfr. "Are they here?"

"NAL Weight is in attendance," Rikolfr said. "As are NALs Mendez and Ukrit."

That was *three* National Assembly Leaders. Normally, they sent underlings to these post-battle briefings, but Judy had been expecting a larger confrontation for some time. She would need something to give them. A plan. "Have the radio technicians confirmed the existence of that shipyard the scouts spotted tonight?"

Rikolfr handed her a sheet of paper. "It's too far for traditional scanners, but we've been able to send up a science ship to investigate, from a safe distance. The shipyard is there, and the scientists are optimistic. If it's like the other one—and if we can protect it from the Krell—we could recover hundreds of acclivity rings."

She nodded, reading the statistics.

"The orbit is decaying rapidly, sir," Rikolfr noted. "The old shipyard seems to be suffering a severe power failure. Scientists guess the proximity guns will stop firing in a couple of days, right about the time it drops into the atmosphere. The Krell will undoubtedly try to get in and destroy it."

"Then we'll have to prevent that," Judy said. "Anything else I need to know?"

"This many assembly leaders? It smells of an ambush, sir. Be prepared."

She nodded, put on her political face, and strode into the small room, Rikolfr following. A collection of the most powerful people in the lower caverns waited for her, each of them wearing a military dress uniform and pins indicating their merits.

"Ladies and gentlemen," she said. "I'm pleased to see you taking a direct interest in—"

"Dispense with the platitudes, Ironsides," said Algernon Weight—young Jorgen's father. The stiff, greying man sat at the head of the conference table, opposite Judy. "You lost more ships tonight."

"We have successfully scared away a lifebuster, scoring a great victory over—"

"You're driving the DDF into the ground," Weight said.

"During your tenure," Ukrit added, "our reserve of ships has fallen to historic lows. I hear that broken fighters are just sitting in hangars, lacking parts for repair."

"Your pilot casualty rates are terrible," Valda Mendez said. She was a petite woman with tan skin. Ironsides had flown with her, once upon a time. "We want to know what your plan is for ending the DDF's spiral of failure."

It would help, Judy thought, *if you would stop taking our best pilots away.* Valda herself seemed completely unashamed of stealing her son from the DDF to keep him out of battle.

But Judy couldn't say that. She couldn't explain how desperate the DDF was, now that the better admirals and commanders were dead. She couldn't explain how she'd foreseen this years ago, and no amount of scraping and scrambling had been able to prevent the descent. She couldn't explain that her people were overworked, and that their morale was crumbling beneath so many losses and pilot casualties.

She couldn't say any of that because, although it was true, it was no excuse. Her job was to offer a solution. A miracle.

She held up one of the sheets Rikolfr had given her. "Lanchester's Law," she said. "Do you know it?"

"Equal armies of soldiers with equal skill will impose equivalent casualties upon each other," Weight said. "But the larger

451

the imbalance in troops, the more disproportionate the casualties. Essentially, the more you outnumber your enemy, the less damage you can expect each of their soldiers to impose."

"The bigger your numerical odds," Valda said, "the fewer people you lose."

Judy handed the page to the group. "This," she said, "is a scout report—with initial scientific analysis—of a large piece of salvage that should crash down in two days. The Krell never field more than a hundred ships at once—but if we can salvage this shipyard, we can top that."

"Hundreds of potential acclivity rings," Valda said, reading the report. "You think you can do it? Salvage this?"

"I think we have no other choice," Judy said. "Until we can field more ships than the Krell, we'll be fighting a losing battle. If we can stop them from destroying that shipyard as it falls, it might be just what we need."

"The report says it will crash down on graduation day," Ukrit said with a grunt. "Looks like it will be a short ceremony."

"Let's be clear," Weight said. "Ivans, what are you proposing?"

"We *must* capture this piece of salvage," Judy said. "We have to be ready to throw *everything* we have at protecting it. As soon as its orbit starts to degrade, and its proximity guns run out of power, we have to destroy every Krell ship that tries to get close to it."

"Bold," Ukrit said.

"They won't let that salvage go easily," Rikolfr said, looking toward the others. "If they don't retreat, we won't be able to either. We could end up engaged in a battle where our every ship is committed. If we lose, it will leave us devastated."

"It will be a second Battle of Alta," Weight said softly. "All or nothing."

"I *fought* in the Battle of Alta," Ironsides said. "And I know the risks involved in such an engagement. But frankly, we're out of

452

options. Either we try this, or we waste away. Can I count on your support for this proposal?"

One at a time, the assembly leaders nodded. They knew as well as she did. The time to make a stand was when you were still strong enough to possibly win.

Just like that, they were committed.

Stars help us all, Judy thought.

48

I attended the graduation.

I stood in the audience with everyone else, on the parade ground beside the statue park inside Alta Base.

On a wooden stage, Ironsides pinned each of the eight graduates with the symbol of their success. I hung near the back of the small crowd, among a few other people wearing cadet's pins. People who had washed out, like me. Though we couldn't fly, our pins would get us access to the elevators whenever we wanted, and we were invited to functions like this. I'd gotten a form letter from Ironsides.

My emotions were complicated as I watched Jorgen and FM, in turn, accept their pins. I was certainly proud of them. And deeply envious, while somewhat ashamedly relieved at the same time. I didn't know if I could be trusted to be up on that stand. This solved the problem. I didn't have to decide.

Deep in my heart though, my world was crumbling. To never fly again? Could I *live* knowing that?

Jorgen and FM saluted with gloved hands while wearing new, crisp white uniforms. I clapped with the rest of the crowd for the eight graduates, but I couldn't help thinking that we'd lost at *least* three times that many ships in the last four months. Not so long ago, a good pilot in the DDF could fly for five years, rack up a couple dozen kills, and retire to fly cargo. But casualties were getting worse and worse, and fewer and fewer pilots lasted five years.

The Krell were winning. Slowly but surely.

Ironsides stepped up to speak. "Normally, you'd expect a bad speech from me right now. It's practically tradition. But we have an operation today of some importance, so I'm going to leave it at a few words. These behind me represent our best. They are our pride, the symbol of our Defiance. We will not hide. We will not back down. We will reclaim our homeland in the stars, and it starts today."

More applause, though I gathered—from conversations around me—that such a brief speech was odd. As some refreshments were set up on tables to our right, the admiral and her command staff walked away without mingling. More strangely, the newly commissioned pilots followed her.

I craned my neck, and saw a flight of fighters shoot up into the air from a nearby launchpad. Was there an incursion happening? Did they really need all the graduates? After spending the last few days down with my mother and Gran-Gran, I had been looking forward to seeing Jorgen and FM again.

Booms sounded in the distance as the fighters got a safe distance from the base, then hit overburn and accelerated past the sound barrier. A nearby man noted that the important assembly leaders—including those who had children in the graduating class—weren't in attendance at the graduation. Something *was* happening.

I took a step toward the launchpads, then shoved my hands in my jumpsuit pockets. I turned to go, but stopped. Cobb was standing there, holding a cane with a golden top. That was odd; I didn't think I'd ever seen him carry one of those.

Even in his sharp white uniform, he seemed as old as a weathered boulder lying in the dust. I saluted him. I hadn't been able to face him, face any of them, since being shot down.

He didn't salute back. He limped over to me, then looked me up and down. "We going to fight this?"

"What is there to fight?" I asked, still holding the salute.

"Put your hand down, girl. You were close enough to graduation. I can challenge that you should at least be given a full pin like Arturo was."

"I'd never get to fly, so what does it matter?"

"A full pilot's pin is worth a lot in Igneous."

"This was never about a pin," I said. I looked over his shoulder at another flight launching into the air. "What's happening?"

"That shipyard you spotted? Should be falling out of orbit today. The admiral is determined to get it, and if she wins this fight there could be hundreds of new spots open for pilots—more than we can fill."

I finally lowered my hand from the salute, watching this second flight go supersonic. A sequence of distant cracks sounded in the air, rattling dishware on the refreshments table.

"Spin?" Cobb said. "I didn't think you were one to—"

"I've heard the stars, Cobb."

He immediately fell silent.

"I saw the eyes," I continued. "A thousand pinpricks of white light. More. Millions of them. As one, they turned to watch me. And they *saw me*."

Cobb went white as a sheet. His hand trembled on his cane. We stood practically alone on the packed earth of the parade ground.

"I have the defect," I whispered. "Like my father."

"I . . . see."

"Was he ever erratic before that day?" I asked. "Did he show any signs before he suddenly turned and attacked you?"

456

Cobb shook his head. "He saw things, heard things, but nothing dangerous. Judy—Ironsides—always told him that even if the defect was real, he could overcome it. She fought for him, defended him. Stuck her neck out, until . . ."

A third flight launched. They were *really* committed to getting that shipyard.

I looked up toward the twisting shadows of the debris field. I sighed, then unhooked the radio from my belt and handed it to Cobb.

He hesitated, then took it. I could see from his worried eyes, his pale face, the truth. Knowing I'd seen those eyes . . . it changed his mind. He didn't want me to fly. I was too dangerous.

"I'm sorry, kid," he said.

"It's better this way," I said. "We don't have to worry about what I might or might not do."

I forced out a smile, then turned from him to walk toward the refreshments. Inside, I was breaking.

The person I'd been four months ago would never have accepted some phantom "defect" as an excuse to keep me from flying. But I wasn't that person anymore. I was someone else, someone who couldn't look at courage and cowardice in the simple terms that she once had.

I'd ejected. I'd nearly crumpled under the weight of losing my friends. Even ignoring all of this craziness about hearing the stars, I wasn't certain I *deserved* to fly.

It was better if I just let it all go. I lowered my head and turned away from the refreshment tables, not wanting to be around people.

A hand grabbed me by the arm. "And where do you think *you're* going?"

I looked up, ready to punch . . . Nedd?

He wore a goofy grin. "I missed the actual ceremony, didn't I. I thought for sure I'd be safe coming a few minutes late—Ironsides always talks for like ten hours. Where's Jerkface? FM? I need to congratulate them."

"They're flying a mission."

"Today?" Nedd said. "That's dumb. I'm supposed to wrangle them into joining us for a real party." He seemed genuinely upset as, behind us, a *fourth* flight of ships rose into the air. Nedd sighed, then grabbed me by the arm again. "Well, at least I can wrangle you."

"Nedd, I didn't make it. I ejected. I—"

"I know. That just means you won't take demerits for leaving the base for the party." He tugged me after him. "Come on. The others are there already. Arturo's family has radio access. We can listen to the battle and cheer them on."

I sighed, but that last part was intriguing. I let him tow me off after him as a *fifth* flight of ships rose into the air and flew the same direction as the others.

"Cobb said the admiral was going to try to salvage the shipyard," I explained as Arturo set a large, boxy radio on our table at the restaurant—rattling the drinks. "Nedd and I saw at least five flights take off. They're serious about this."

The others gathered around. It was good to see them again, and strangely refreshing not to see condemnation in their eyes. Kimmalyn, Nedd, Arturo. The rest of the dim restaurant was empty. Just us and a couple of younger teenagers not wearing flight pins—probably the children of field or orchard workers.

"They called in everyone," Arturo said, running a cord from the radio to the wall. "Even the reserves from the lower caverns. This is going to be *some* fight."

"Yeah," I said. I looked down at my drink and fries, neither of which I'd touched.

"Hey," Kimmalyn said, poking me in the side. "You sulking?"

I shrugged.

"Good," she said. "This is a *day* for sulking!"

"Graduation day," Nedd said, raising his cup. "For the washout club!"

"Hurrah!" Kimmalyn said, raising hers.

"You're both idiots," Arturo said, fiddling with the dials on the radio. "I didn't wash out. I graduated early."

"Yeah?" Nedd asked. "And did they call *you* in to fly this battle, mister full pilot sir?"

Arturo blushed. I noticed for the first time that he wasn't wearing his pilot's pin. Most everyone wore theirs every day—in uniform or not.

The radio started belting out chatter, and Arturo quickly turned down the volume, then tuned it further until he landed on a channel with a firm female voice. "There we go," he said. "The Assembly monitoring channel. This should be a straight-up explanation of the battle for government leaders, not the sanitized version piped down to the people listening in Igneous."

We settled in as the woman on the radio spoke. "With the launch of Ivy Flight, we have eleven flights in the air and five scouting trios. The Saints and the North Star watch us this day, as the glorious fighters of the Defiant League engage."

Nedd whistled. "Eleven? Do we have that many flights?"

"Obviously," Arturo said. "Seriously, Nedd. Do you ever think before you speak?"

"Nope!" He took a slurp of his green fizzy drink.

"A man who speaks his mind," Kimmalyn said solemnly, "is a man with a mind to speak of."

"We normally maintain twelve flights," Arturo said. "Four on duty at any given moment, usually with one or two in the air patrolling. Four on immediate call. Four more on deep reserve duty, protected in the lower caverns. In the past, we tried to keep them

459

at ten ships each—but these days we're down to eleven flights, and most of them are only seven or so fighters strong."

"Eighty-seven brave pilots," the announcer continued, "are making their way to engage the Krell to rescue the salvage. Victory will bring our league unprecedented glory and spoils!"

She had a voice like the announcers I'd listened to down below. Strong, but almost monotone—with an air of reading pages as they were put in front of her.

"This is too sterile," I said. "Can we hear the real chatter? Tune to the pilot bands?"

Arturo looked at the others. Nedd shrugged, but Kimmalyn nodded. So Arturo turned the volume down further. "We're not supposed to listen to these," he said softly. "But what will they do? Kick us out of the DDF?"

He tuned a few notches until he hit the general flightleader channel. The radios in Igneous wouldn't be able to decrypt what they were saying, but obviously Arturo's family was important enough to have a radio with an unscrambler.

"They're coming in," an unfamiliar voice said. "Scud. There's a *lot* of them."

"Get us counts," Ironsides said. "How many flights? How many ships?"

"Scouts reporting in." I recognized that voice—it was Cloak. She was one of the scouts who had fought alongside us before. "We'll get you numbers, Admiral."

"All active flights," Ironsides said, "stay on the defensive until we get enemy numbers. Flight Command out."

I pulled my seat closer, listening to the chatter—trying to imagine the fight. A different scout described the falling shipyard. An enormous, ancient construct of steel, with gaping holes and twisting corridors.

Scout numbers came back. The first wave of Krell had been fifty strong, but another fifty followed. The enemy knew how important this fight was. They'd sent every ship; they were as committed as we were.

"A hundred ships," Nedd said softly. "What a fight that must be . . ." He looked haunted; perhaps he was remembering our chase through the bowels of the shipyard.

"That's it, they're fully committed," Ironsides said. "Riptide Flight, Valkyrie Flight, Tungsten Flight, and Nightmare Flight, I want you to provide covering fire. Inner flights, keep the Krell away from that shipyard. Don't let them detonate a bomb on it!"

A series of affirmatives came from the flightleaders. I closed my eyes, imagining the swarm of ships, the destructor blasts in the air. It was a relatively open battlefield, with little debris except for the one enormous shipyard.

My fingers began going through motions, as if I were controlling a ship. I could feel it. The rattling of my cockpit, the rushing of the air, the flare of the booster . . .

Saints and stars. I was going to miss it *so much*.

"That's a bomber," one of the flightleaders said. "I have confirmation from three ships."

"Scout confirmation," Cloak said. "We see it too. Flight Command, a bomber is heading toward the shipyard. It's carrying a lifebuster."

"Drive it away!" Ironsides said. "Protecting the salvage is our most important objective."

"Yes, sir," a flightleader said. "Confirm. We push back, even if it means driving the bomber toward Alta?"

Silence on the line.

"It would take two or more hours of flight at bomber speeds to get within range of Alta," Ironsides said. "We'll have time to stop it before then. Orders stand."

"Two hours?" Nedd said. "They're farther out than I thought."

"Well, bombers are about half as fast as a Poco," Arturo said. "So the shipyard is coming down around an hour out from us—

461

which is about how long it took our forces to get out there. It adds up, if you think long enough to calculate it."

"Why would I have to do that?" Nedd said. "When you'll do the hard work for me?"

"Does anyone else feel . . . anxious?" Kimmalyn asked.

"They said a lifebuster was out there, potentially coming our way," Arturo said. "So yeah."

"Not about that," Kimmalyn said, looking at me. "About just sitting here, listening."

"We should be up there," I whispered. "This is it. A battle like the Battle of Alta. They need everyone . . . and here we are. Listening. Sipping sodas."

"They've scrambled every battle-worthy ship," Arturo said. "If we were back at the DDF, we'd only be sitting around *there* and listening."

"We've got it on the run," one of the flightleaders said. "I confirm, bomber has veered away from the salvage target. But Admiral, it *is* trying to break toward Alta."

"This bomber is fast," Cloak said. "Faster than most."

"Scout contingents," Ironsides said, "move to intercept. Everyone else, don't get distracted. Stay on that shipyard! This could be a decoy."

"I'm down to three ships," a flightleader said. "Requesting support. They're swarming us, Flight Command. Scud, it—"

Silence.

"Valkyrie flightleader is down," someone else said. "I'm going to absorb their remaining ships. Flight Command, we're taking a beating out here."

"All ships," Ironsides said, "full offensive. Drive them back. Don't let them reach the shipyard."

"Yes, sir," a chorus of flightleaders said.

The battle continued for some time, and we listened, tense. Not just because of the pilots dying trying to claim the shipyard, but because each moment of the battle, that bomber was drawing closer and closer to Alta.

"Scout ships," Ironsides eventually said. "Do you have an update on that lifebuster?"

"We're still on it, sir!" Cloak said. "But the bomber is well defended. Ten ships."

"Understood," Ironsides said.

"Sir!" Cloak said. "It *is* going faster than ordinary bomber speed. And it just sped up. If we aren't careful, it will get within blast range of Alta."

"Engage them," Ironsides said.

"With only scouts?"

"Yes," Ironsides said.

I felt so *powerless*. As a child, listening to war stories, my head had been full of drama and excitement—glory and kills. But today, I could hear the strain in the voices as flightleaders watched their friends die. I heard explosions over the channel, and winced at each one.

Jorgen and FM were out there somewhere. I should be helping. Protecting.

I closed my eyes. Without really intending to, I performed Gran-Gran's exercise, imagining myself soaring among the stars. Listening for them. Reaching . . .

A dozen spots of white light appeared inside my eyelids. Then hundreds. I felt the attention of something vast, something terrible, shift toward me.

I gasped and opened my eyes. The pinpricks of light vanished, but my heart thundered in my ears, and all I could think of was that inescapable sensation of *things* seeing me. Unnatural things. Hateful things.

When I finally managed to put my attention back on the battle, Cloak was reporting a full-on conflict with the lifebuster's guard ships. Arturo turned a few frequencies and found their flight

463

chatter—twelve scouts had been unified in a single flight for this battle.

Arturo switched back and forth between the scout channel and the flightleader channel. Both battles raged, but finally—at long last—some welcome news came in.

"Bomber destroyed!" Cloak said. "The lifebuster bomb is in free fall, heading toward the ground. All scouts, pull out! Overburn! Now!" Her channel wavered and fuzzed.

We waited, anxious. And I thought I could hear the sequence of three explosions—in fact, I was sure of it—echoing in the near distance. Scud. That had been *close* to Alta.

"Cloak?" Ironsides asked. "Nice work."

"She's dead," a soft voice said on the line. That was FM. "This is callsign: FM. Cloak died in the blast. There are . . . sir, there are three of us left in the scout flight. The others died in the fighting."

"Confirmed," Ironsides said. "Stars accept their souls."

"Should we . . . return to the other battle?" FM asked.

"Yes."

"All right." She sounded rattled.

I looked toward the others, frustrated. Surely there was *something* we could do. "Arturo," I said, "doesn't your family have some private ships?"

"Three fighters," he said. "Down in the deep caverns. But as a rule, they don't get involved in DDF battles."

"Even a desperate one like this?" Kimmalyn asked.

Arturo hesitated, then spoke more softly. "*Especially* a battle like this. Their job is to protect my family if we have to evacuate. The worse things get, the *less* likely my parents would be to commit their ships."

"And if we didn't ask them?" Nedd said. "What if we just took the ships?"

He and Arturo exchanged looks, then grinned. Both looked

at me, and my heart trembled with excitement. To fly again. In a battle like this, like the Battle of Alta.

The battle where . . . where my father had broken. It was too dangerous for me to be up there. What if I did what he did, and turned on my friends?

"Take Kimmalyn," I found myself saying.

"You sure?" Arturo asked.

"I'm not!" Kimmalyn said. She grabbed my hands. "Spin, you're better than I am. I'll just fail again."

"My family's ships are in a secure cavern," Arturo said. "It will take us at least fifteen minutes to get them up the private ship elevator. That's not counting the part where we have to somehow sneak in and *steal* them."

I squeezed Kimmalyn's hands. "Quirk," I told her, "you're the best shot I've ever seen, the best I've ever *heard* of. They need you. FM and Jorgen need you."

"But you—"

"I can't fly, Quirk," I said. "There's a medical reason I can't explain right now. So you've got to go." I squeezed her hands tighter.

"I failed Hurl," she said softly. "I'll fail the others."

"No. The only way you fail, Kimmalyn, is if you're not there. *Be there.*"

Her eyes watered, then she grabbed me in a hug. Arturo and Nedd rushed out of the room, and Kimmalyn ran out after them.

I sank down into my seat and leaned against the table, crossing my arms and laying my head down.

The radio chatter continued, including a new voice. "Flight Command," the woman's ragged voice said. "This is antiaircraft gun outpost forty-seven. We're down, sir."

"Down?" Ironsides said. "What happened?"

"That blast from the lifebuster hit us," the woman said. "Stars. I'm just crawling out of the mess now. I tore this radio off my CO's

465

corpse. It looks like . . . AA guns forty-six and forty-eight are gone too. That bomb hit close. You've got a hole in your defenses, sir. Scud, scud, *scud*. I need medical transports!"

"Understood, outpost forty-seven. Sending—"

"Sir?" the gunner's voice said again. "Tell me you have that on radar."

"What?"

I felt a chill.

"Debris fall," the gunner said. "North of here. Hold on a minute, I've got some binoculars . . ."

I waited, tense, imagining a single gunner climbing over the wreckage of her destroyed gun emplacement.

"I have visual on multiple Krell ships," the gunner said. "A second group, coming down far away from the battle for the shipyard. Sir, they're coming in right where our defenses are out. Confirm! Did you hear me!"

"We heard," Ironsides said.

"Sir, they're heading right for Alta. Scramble the reserves!"

There were no reserves. The chill inside me became ice. Ironsides had committed everything we had to the battle for the shipyard. And now, a second group of Krell had appeared from the sky—right where the bomb had knocked out our defenses.

It was a trick.

The Krell wanted this. They wanted to draw our fighters into a battle far from Alta. They wanted to convince us that all of the Krell ships were engaged, so that we threw everything we had at them. Then they dropped a lifebuster on our AA guns to open the path.

That way, they could bring in more ships and another bomb. Boom.

No more Defiants.

"Riptide Flight," Admiral Ironsides said. "I want you back at Alta immediately! Full speed!"

"Sir?" the flightleader said. "We can disengage, but we're a good thirty minutes out, even at Mag-10."

"Hurry!" she said. "Get back here."

Too slow, I thought. Alta was doomed. There weren't any ships. There weren't any pilots.

Except one.

49

Still, I hesitated.

I'd decided not to go with Nedd and the others because it was too dangerous. What about the defect?

In that moment, Hurl's voice returned to me. *A pact,* she seemed to whisper. *Brave until the end. No backing down, Spin.*

No backing down. Alta was in danger, and I was just going to sit here? Because I was afraid of what I *might* do?

No. Because I didn't know, deep down, if I was a coward or not. Because I worried not only about the defect, but about whether I was worthy of flying. In that moment, the truth struck me hard. Like the admiral, I was using the defect as an *excuse* to avoid facing the real issue.

To avoid discovering for myself who I was.

I stood up and dashed out of the restaurant. Forget the defect— they were going to drop a lifebuster to destroy both *Alta* and *Igneous.* It didn't matter if I was dangerous. The Krell were far, far more so.

I raced down the street toward the base, a vague plan of going to M-Bot coalescing in my mind. But that would take too long—

besides, he'd shut himself down. I imagined bursting into the cavern only to be confronted by a dead, empty piece of metal that wouldn't turn on.

I stopped in the street, puffing, sweating, and looked out toward the hills—then toward Alta Base.

There *was* one other ship.

I dashed up the street and through the gates, flashing my cadet's pin to gain admittance. I turned right, toward the launchpads, and scrambled up to the ground crew, who were launching medical transports to go to the AA guns. The bulky, slow ships rose smoothly into the air on large acclivity rings.

I spotted Dorgo, the ground crewman who often worked my ship, and ran up to him.

"Skyward Ten?" Dorgo said. "What are you—"

"The broken ship, Dorgo," I said, puffing. "Skyward Five. Arturo's ship. Will it fly?"

"We're supposed to break it down for parts," Dorgo said, taken aback. "We got a start on fixing it up, but shields are out and we never got replacements. Steering is compromised as well. It's not battle-worthy."

"Will it *fly*?"

Several members of the ground crew glanced at each other.

"Technically," Dorgo said, "yes."

"Prep it for me!" I said.

"Did the admiral approve this?"

I glanced at the side of the launchpad, where a radio like Arturo's was belting out the flightleader channel. They'd been listening.

"There's a second group of Krell heading straight for Alta," I said, pointing. "And there are no reserves. Do you want to go talk to the woman who hates me for irrational reasons, or do you want to just get me into the scudding air?"

Nobody spoke.

"Prep Skyward Five!" Dorgo finally shouted. "Go, go!"

Two ground crewmen ran off, and I dashed into the locker room, emerging a minute later—after the fastest change ever—in a flight suit. Dorgo led me to a Poco that the crew was pulling out onto the launchpad with a ship tow.

Dorgo grabbed a ladder. "Tony, that'll do! Unhook!"

He slammed the ladder into place even as the ship stopped.

I scrambled up and into the open cockpit, trying not to look at the black destructor scars on the left side of the ship. Scud, it was in bad shape.

"Listen, Spin," Dorgo said, following me up. "You don't have a shield. Do you understand? The system was burned out completely, and we ripped it free. You are *totally exposed.*"

"Understood," I said, strapping in.

Dorgo pushed my helmet into my hands. *My* helmet, with my callsign on it. "Other than the shield, your acclivity ring is going to be your biggest worry," he said. "It's on the fritz, and I can't say if it will cut out or not. Control sphere also got a write-up in our assessment." He eyed me. "Eject still works."

"Why does that matter?"

"Because you're smarter than most," he said.

"Destructors?" I said.

"Still functional," he said. "You're lucky. We were going to scrap those tonight."

"I'm not sure this counts as lucky," I said, pulling on the helmet. "But it's all we've got." I gave him a thumbs-up.

He raised his own thumb as his team pulled the ladder away, and my canopy lowered and sealed.

Admiral Judy "Ironsides" Ivans stood in the command center. Hands clasped behind her back, she regarded a hologram projected from the floor, complete with tiny ships in formation.

470

The shipyard had been a decoy all along. Judy had been played; the Krell had anticipated what she would do, and used that knowledge.

It was one of the oldest rules of warfare. If you knew what your enemy was going to do, the battle was already half won.

At her quiet order, the holoprojection switched to the second group of enemy ships that were approaching Alta. Fifteen Krell. Glowing blue wedges, now visible to close-range radar, which was far more accurate than the long-range ones.

It showed that one of those ships was, indeed, a bomber.

The ships inched closer to the death zone—an invisible line past which, if they dropped a lifebuster, they'd destroy Alta. The Krell wouldn't stop there though. They'd fly inward and try to drop it square on top of the base. That way, their bomb would penetrate all the way down and destroy Igneous.

I have doomed all of humankind, Ivans thought.

Fifteen blips of blue. Unopposed.

Then, rising from Alta, a single lonely blip of red appeared. A Defiant ship.

"Rikolfr?" Ironsides said. "Did the private owners actually respond to my call? Are they scrambling their fighters?" There were only eight of those in the deep caverns, but they would be better than nothing. Perhaps enough to prevent a disaster.

"No, sir," Rikolfr said. "Last we heard, they were planning to evacuate."

"Then who is that ship?" Ironsides asked.

All around the frantic command room, people turned from their workstations to look at the hologram and its single blip of red. A voice popped in on the flightleader channel. "Do I have this right? Confirm? This is Skyward Ten, callsign: Spin."

It was her.

"The defect," Ironsides whispered.

50

"This is Flight Command," Ironsides said on my radio. "Cadet, where did you get that ship?"

"Does it matter?" I asked. "Give me a heading. Where are those Krell?"

"There are *fifteen ships* in that flight, girl."

I swallowed. "Heading?"

"57-113.2-15000."

"Right." I redirected and punched my overburn. GravCaps engaged for the first few seconds, then I gritted my teeth as the g-forces hit me. My Poco started to rattle under the strain, even at the relatively slow speed of Mag-5. Scud. What was keeping this ship together? Spit and prayers?

"How long until they're inside the death zone?" I asked.

"Under eight minutes," Ironsides said. "By our projections, you'll reach them in about two minutes."

"Great," I said, taking a deep breath, inching my ship up to Mag-6. I didn't dare go faster with the amount of drag on that burned-out wing. "We might have a few more reinforcements coming. When you see them, tell them what's happening."

"There are more of you?" Ironsides asked.

"I hope so." Depended on whether Arturo and the others managed to steal some ships. "I'll just have to hold the Krell off until then. By myself. With a ship that doesn't have a shield."

"You *don't have a shield?*"

"I have visual confirmation on the Krell," I said, ignoring the question. "Here we go!"

Krell ships swarmed toward me. I knew there were only fifteen, but flying there—alone, unprotected—it seemed like an entire armada. I immediately cut to the side, destructors flashing all around me. I picked up at *least* a dozen on my tail, and my proximity warning went insane.

I pulled into a hard bank, wishing there were debris I could use for faster maneuvering. I curved around—somehow avoiding being shot—until I saw it. One slower, larger ship. Plodding along with an enormous bomb held underneath it, nearly as big as the ship itself.

"Flight Command," I said, pushing into a dive, destructors spraying around me, "I have visual confirmation of a lifebuster."

"Bring it down, cadet," the admiral said immediately. "You hear me. If you get a shot, *bring that ship down.*"

"Affirmative," I said, and threw myself into a spinning loop. My GravCap indicator flashed, its brief dampening effect expended, and the g-forces flattened me into the side of the cockpit and my seat.

I remained conscious—somehow—as a couple of Krell ships cut across in front of me. My instincts were to chase them down.

No. They were presenting targets to draw me away. I dodged the other direction, and the ships behind me fired an insane storm of destructors.

I wouldn't last long in this fight. I couldn't hold out for Arturo and the others. The Krell would finish me off before then.

I had to get to the bomber.

The Krell tried to drive me to the side, but I dodged between two of them, my ship rattling as I crossed their wakes. That didn't normally happen; the atmospheric scoops evened out flight wakes. Mine was still working, fortunately, but was obviously in poor shape.

Teeth rattling in my skull from the shaking, I cut around more ships and focused on my goal, unleashing a barrage of destructors.

A few hit the bomber, but were absorbed by its shield, and I wasn't close enough for an IMP. The small, strange ships that accompanied the bomber detached and flew up toward me, driving me off to the side.

I swept in a long turn, trying to ignore the fact that I was now being chased by almost two flights' worth of enemies.

I focused on my ship. On my maneuvers.

Me, the controls, and the ship. Together, responding to . . .

Right.

I dodged away just before a Krell ship moved to cut me off.

They're going to fire all out. I dove underneath a sudden, concentrated barrage.

Left. I made a sweeping turn by instinct, spinning between two enemy ships—causing them to collide.

It was uncanny. But somehow, somehow I could hear it in my mind. Somehow I knew . . . the commands that were being sent to the enemy ships.

I could *hear* them.

Judy stood quietly beside the hologram, and slowly, aides and junior admirals gathered around. By now they'd disengaged all flights from the battle for the shipyard, and had sent them streaking back toward Alta.

They'd be too slow. Even Riptide Flight, which she had ordered back earlier, was too far out. Right now, all that mattered was one speck of red among the swarm of blue. One *magnificent* red speck that wove between enemy attacks, somehow avoiding destruction time and time again.

Somehow, she faced overwhelming odds and *survived*.

"Have you ever seen flying like that before?" Rikolfr asked.

Judy nodded.

She had. In one other pilot.

I couldn't explain it. I somehow *sensed* the orders that were coming from above, telling the Krell ships what to do. I could hear them . . . hear them processing, thinking.

It wasn't an overwhelming edge, but it was enough. Just that little bit I needed to fly my rattling Poco in another loop, where I fired again on the bomber.

That's five hits, I thought as I was forced back once more by the four black guardian ships. The bomber's shield should be nearly down. Cobb's training kicked in, warning me to be ready to over-burn away as soon as I dropped the bomber. Once the lifebuster hit the ground, the blast would . . .

"Spin?" It was Jorgen's voice.

It almost kicked me out of my concentration. I spun my ship, dodging.

"Spin, is that you?" he asked. "My flightleader mentioned you were on the channel. What's happening?"

"I'm . . . ," I said through gritted teeth. "I'm having a blast without you. More. Krell. For. Me."

"I'm with Riptide Flight," Jorgen said. "We're coming to help."

Clever quips and bravado escaped me. "Thank you," I whispered, sweat plastering the inside of my helmet as I tried to come around for another pass.

Red blasts descended upon me, slicing at my ship. But I could dodge them. I knew what they—

An explosion cut across my ship, blasting the tip off the nose of the Poco. Something had shot me, something I couldn't anticipate.

My Poco rattled, nose trailing smoke, my console basically just a huge expanse of red lights. I still had maneuverability, however, and dodged to the side.

That shot, I thought. *One of the black ships hit me—and I can't hear its orders in my mind.*

I rounded toward the bomber once again. I hit the triggers, and nothing happened. Scud . . . the destructors were on my nose. They'd been damaged in that hit.

My control sphere was rattling, threatening to go out. Exactly like Dorgo had warned.

"You have one minute until that bomber reaches the death zone, Skyward Ten," Ironsides said softly.

I didn't respond, fighting to keep ahead of the swarming enemies.

"If it gets past the zone," Ironsides said, "you have full authorization to shoot it down anyway. Do you confirm, pilot?"

Lifebusters were rigged to blow if they were shot or if they hit the ground. So if I dropped that bomber once it got too close, the blast would destroy Alta, but protect Igneous.

"Confirmed," I said, swinging around.

No weapons.

I could hear the rushing air almost as if the canopy were gone. My nose was still on fire.

Under a minute.

I gained altitude, then turned into a dive, Krell ships still swarming behind.

That bomber's shield has to be almost out.

I pointed my nose right at the bomber down below, then I hit the overburn.

"Cadet?" Ironsides said. "Pilot, what are you doing?"

"My weapons are gone," I hissed through clenched teeth. "I have to ram it."

"Understood," Ironsides whispered. "Saints' own speed, pilot."

"What?" Jorgen said over the line. "What? Ram it? Spin!"

I dove toward the enemy bomber.

"Spin," Jorgen said, voice barely audible over the blaring warnings and the roar of the air around my cockpit. "Spin, you'll die."

"Yes," I whispered. "But I'll win anyway."

I streaked right toward the ship amid a column of enemy fire. Then—at long last, pushed too far—my poor, broken ship had had enough.

The acclivity ring cut out.

My ship pulled into an unexpected dive, and I undershot the bomber, missing it. Pummeled by the winds—and no longer held up by the acclivity ring—my ship started spinning out of control.

Everything became a blur of smoke and fire.

51

You weren't supposed to be able to think during those moments. It was all supposed to happen in a flash.

My hand moved by instinct toward the eject lever between my legs. My ship was in an uncontrolled spin with no altitude control. I was going to crash.

I froze.

Nobody else was close enough. Without me to stop them, the Krell would fly on unimpeded to destroy Igneous.

If I crashed, that was it.

I slammed my hand back onto the throttle. With my other hand I flipped off my atmospheric scoop, releasing my ship entirely to the whims of the air. Then I rammed the throttle forward, going into overburn.

In the old days, this was how ships had flown. I needed old-fashioned lift, and that came from speed.

My ship shook an insane amount, but I leaned into my control sphere, righting my spiral.

Come on, come on!

I felt it working. I fought the control flaps on the wings, and felt the g-forces lessen as my ship started to level out. I could do it. I—

I skidded against the ground.

The GravCaps redlined immediately, protecting me from the brunt of the impact. But unfortunately, I hadn't regained control fast enough, and the ship hadn't gained quite enough lift.

The ship skipped across the ground, and the second impact slammed me forward into my restraints, knocking the wind out of me. My poor Poco skidded along the dusty surface, cockpit rumbling. The canopy shattered and I screamed. I had no control. I just had to brace and hope the GravCaps had enough time to recharge between—

CRUNCH.

With a gut-wrenching sound of twisting metal, the Poco ground to a halt.

I sagged against my straps, dazed, and the world spun around me. I groaned, trying to catch my breath.

Slowly, my vision returned to normal. I shook my head, then managed to slump to the side and look out the broken cockpit canopy. My ship was no more. I'd smashed into a hillside, and during my skid I'd ripped off both wings and a big chunk of the fuselage. I was basically a chair strapped to a tube. Even the warning lights on my control panel had died.

I had failed.

"Fighter down," someone at Flight Command said over the radio in my helmet. "Bomber still on target." Her voice grew hushed. "Death zone entered."

"This is Skyward Five," Arturo's voice said. "Callsign: Amphi. I've got Skyward Two and Six with me."

"Pilots?" Ironsides said. "Are you flying private ships?"

"Kind of," he said. "I'll let you explain it to my parents."

"Spin," someone at Flight Command said. "What's your status? We saw a controlled crash. Is your ship mobile?"

"No," I said, voice croaking.

"Spin?" Kimmalyn said. "Oh! What have you done?"

"Nothing, apparently," I said in frustration, working at my straps. Scudding things were stuck.

"Spin," Flight Command said. "Evacuate your wreckage. Krell incoming."

Krell incoming? I craned my neck and looked backward through my broken canopy. That black ship—one of the four that defended the bomber—had swung around in the sky to check on my wreckage. It obviously didn't want me returning to the air and attacking them from behind.

The dark ship flew low, bearing down on me. I knew, staring at it, that it wasn't going to leave my survival to chance. It wanted me. *It knew.*

"Spin?" Flight Command said. "Are you out?"

"Negative," I whispered. "I'm stuck in my straps."

"I'm coming!" Kimmalyn said.

"Negative!" Ironsides said. "You three focus on that bomber. You're too far away anyway."

"This is Riptide Eight," Jorgen said over the line. "Spin, I'm coming! ETA six minutes!"

The black Krell ship opened fire on my wreckage.

At that exact moment, a dark shadow passed overhead, cresting the hill beside me, skimming it and sending dust raining down on me. The enemy destructors hit the newcomer's shield.

What?

A large fighter with sharp wings . . . in a W shape.

"This is callsign: Mongrel," a rough voice said. "Hang on, kid."

Cobb. Cobb was *flying M-Bot.*

Cobb fired his light-lance, expertly spearing the dark Krell ship as they passed each other. M-Bot was by *far* the more massive vessel. He yanked the Krell assassin ship backward like a master pulling on her dog's leash, then spun in a calculated maneuver—

towing the enemy ship in a crazy arc, then *slamming* it into the ground.

"Cobb?" I said. *"Cobb?"*

"I believe," his voice said over my radio, "that I told you to *eject* in situations like that, pilot."

"Cobb! How? What?"

M-Bot swept to the side of my ship—well, what was left of it—then landed, lowering on his acclivity ring. With a little more work, I finally managed to yank out of my straps.

I nearly tripped as I scrambled from the wreckage and ran over. I hopped onto a rock, then climbed on M-Bot's wing as I had done so many times before. Cobb sat nestled into the open cockpit, and beside him—sitting on the armrest—was the radio I'd given him. The one that . . .

"Hello!" M-Bot said to me from the cockpit. "You have nearly died, and so I will say something to distract you from the serious, mind-numbing implications of your own mortality! I hate your shoes."

I laughed, nearly hysterical.

"I didn't want to be predictable," M-Bot added. "So I said that I hate them. But actually, I think those shoes are quite nice. Please do not think I have lied."

Inside the cockpit Cobb was shaking. His hands quivering, his eyes staring straight ahead.

"Cobb," I said. "You got in a ship. You *flew*."

"This thing," he said, "is *insane*." He turned toward me, and seemed to come out of his stupor. "Help me." He unstrapped, and I helped him pull himself out.

Scud. He looked terrible. Flying for the first time in years had taken a great deal out of him.

He hopped down off the wing. "You need to drive that bomber back into the sky. Don't let it blow up and vaporize me. I haven't had my afternoon cup of coffee yet."

481

"Cobb," I said, leaning down and looking at him from the wing. "I . . . thought I heard Krell in my mind. They can get inside my head somehow."

He reached up and gripped my wrist. "Fly anyway."

"But what if I do what he did? What if I turn against my friends?"

"You won't," M-Bot said from the cockpit.

"How do you know?"

"Because you can choose," M-Bot said. "*We* can choose."

I looked to Cobb, who shrugged. "Cadet, at this point, what do we have to lose?"

I gritted my teeth, then dropped down into M-Bot's familiar cockpit. I pulled on my helmet, then did up the straps as the booster powered back on.

"I called him," M-Bot said, sounding satisfied.

"But how?" I said. "You turned off."

"I . . . didn't *completely* turn off," the machine said. "Instead, I thought. And I thought. And I *thought*. And then I heard you calling me. Begging for my help. And then . . . I wrote a new program."

"I don't understand."

"It was a simple program," he said. "It edited one entry in a database, while I wasn't looking, replacing one name with another. I *must* follow the commands of my pilot."

A voice played out of his speakers. My voice.

"Please," it said to him. "I need you."

"I chose," he said, "a new pilot."

Cobb backed away and I settled my hands on the controls, breathing in and out, feeling . . .

Calm.

Yes, calm. That feeling reminded me of how, on that first day in flight school, I'd felt strangely at peace when going into battle. I'd been impressed by how *not* afraid I was.

It had been ignorance then. Bravado. I'd assumed I knew what it was to be a pilot. I'd assumed I could handle it.

This peace was similar, yet at the same time opposite. It was the peace of experience and understanding. As we rose into the air, I found a different kind of confidence rising inside me. Not born of stories I told myself, or of a forced sense of heroism.

I knew.

When I'd been shot down the first time, I'd ejected because there had been no point in dying with my ship. But when it had mattered—when it had been vital that I attempt to protect my ship with even the *slightest* chance of success—I'd stayed in the cockpit and tried to keep my ship in the air.

My confidence was that of a person who *knew*. Nobody could ever again convince me I was a coward. It didn't matter what anyone said, anyone thought, or anyone claimed.

I knew what I was.

"Are you ready?" M-Bot said.

"For the first time ever, I think I am. Give me all the speed you can. Oh, and turn off your stealth devices."

"Really?" he said. "Why?"

"Because," I said, leaning into the throttle, "I want them to *see this coming.*"

52

Judy "Ironsides" Ivans watched as the Krell force pushed ever closer to Alta.

Radio chatter filled the command room, but it wasn't the usual battle chatter. Powerful families radioed in, announcing that they were escaping in their own ships. Cowards, every one. Deep down, Judy had known how this would play out, but it still broke her heart.

Rikolfr stepped up to her, bearing reports. He was the only other one who was still watching the holoprojector. Everyone else was in chaos as operators and junior admirals called frantic alarms to those in Igneous, ordering emergency evacuation.

For all the good it would do.

"How long until the bomber reaches Alta?" Judy asked.

"Under five minutes," Rikolfr said. "Do we evacuate the command center down to one of the deep caverns? They might be safe enough."

She shook her head.

Rikolfr swallowed, but kept talking. "The last line of emergency gun emplacements has radioed in. The Krell fighters are

484

flying in close, engaging them. Three are down, the other three taking heavy fire."

There were always supposed to be fighters to help the gun emplacements. Judy nodded toward the three small red blips on the hologram, flying out to engage the enemy. Stolen fighters, she now knew. Patriots, truly Defiant.

"Put me through to those fighters," she said, then activated her headset and spoke. "Skyward Flight?"

"Here, sir," said callsign: Amphi. That was Valda's son. What was his name? Arturo? "Pilot," she said, "you have to shoot down that bomb. In under five minutes, it will be in position to destroy Igneous. Do you understand? I authorize destroying that bomb with all prejudice."

"But Alta, sir?" the boy asked.

"Already dead," she said. "*I* am dead. Drop that bomb. You have three fighters against sixteen." She checked the reports. "In two minutes, Riptide Flight will join you. They have six more fighters, three of which are scouts. The rest of our forces are too far away to matter."

"Understood, Flight Command," the boy said, sounding nervous. "Stars guide you."

"And you, flightleader."

She stepped back to watch the battle.

"Admiral!" a radio tech shouted. "Sir! We have an unidentified fighter approaching! Adding it to the hologram now!"

A green blip appeared, distant from the impending clash of ships, but approaching at a *shocking* speed.

Rikolfr gasped. Judy frowned.

"Sir," the tech said. "That ship is flying at *Mag-20*. Any of our ships would have broken apart at those speeds."

"What have the Krell found to throw at us now?" Judy murmured to herself.

"Flight Command," a familiar girl's voice said over the line, "this is Skyward Eleven, reporting for battle. Callsign: Spin."

M-Bot was going so fast, the heat of air resistance lit up his shield in a fiery glow. We tore through the air as a streaking ball of fire, but I barely felt a faint tremble.

After the broken-down Poco, it was a dramatic contrast.

"I'm afraid I am still not fully operational," M-Bot said. "Booster and thrusters: online. Acclivity ring and altitude controls: online. Communications and stealth systems: online. Light-lance: online. Cytonic hyperdrive: offline. Self-repair: offline. Destructors: offline."

"No weapons," I said. "Stars forbid I actually get a *functioning* ship for once."

"I would be offended at that," M-Bot said, "if I could get offended. Also, don't be so dour. At least my vocal aggression subroutine is online."

"Your . . . what?"

"Vocal aggression subroutine. I figured if I was going to go into battle, I should enjoy the experience! So I wrote a new program to appropriately express myself."

Oh great.

"Tremble and fear, all enemies!" he shouted. "For we shall shake the air with thunder and blood! Your doom is imminent!"

"Um . . . ," Kimmalyn's voice said over the line. "Bless your stars, whoever you are."

Wonderful. He'd called that in on the general channel? I guess now that his orders to "lie low" were no longer in effect, he didn't care who heard him.

"That's my ship talking, Quirk," I said.

"Spin!" she said. "You found *another* ship?"

"One found me," I said. "I'm bearing down on your seven, and

486

should meet you at the battle in a few seconds." M-Bot's projections placed that right at the same time the others would arrive.

"Wait," Nedd said. "Am I an idiot, or did Spin just say her *ship* spoke?"

"Hi, Nedd!" M-Bot said. "I can confirm you are an idiot, but all humans are. Your mental abilities appear to be within a standard deviation from their average."

"It's complicated," I said. "Actually, no it's not. My ship can talk, and you should ignore him."

"Quake and tremble at my majestic destructive power!" M-Bot added.

"You two sound well suited to each other," Arturo said. "I'm glad you're here, Spin. Do you . . . maybe have a plan?"

"Yes," I said. "First, let's see how they react to me. Stand by."

I flipped M-Bot on his axis and overburned backward, slowing from our incredible approach. Even with his advanced GravCaps, I felt the g-forces slam me back in my seat. As soon as we hit Mag-2.5, I spun us around in the air and took assessment. Sixteen Krell fighters.

This was it. I had another chance.

Time to stop that bomb.

I sliced through the center of the Krell ships at speed, buzzing the bomber and its close guard of three remaining black ships. I turned upward and gave them a good view of M-Bot, with his wicked wings and dangerous silhouette. He had four destructor pods—which I hoped they wouldn't see were empty—and an obviously advanced and powerful design.

The Krell always targeted what they considered the most dangerous ship or the one bearing an officer. I counted on them seeing M-Bot, and . . .

. . . and they *immediately* gave chase. A flock of thirteen ships, all but the three black ones, broke off and swarmed after me, firing a chaotic array of destructors.

Excellent. Terrifying, but excellent.

"We have to stay just ahead of them, M-Bot," I said. "Keep them strung along, thinking they'll get the upper hand on us at any moment."

"Understood," he said. "Yar."

"Yar?"

"Assumed pirate-speak, but actually a stylized West Country accent popularized by the acting role of a specific individual. It's supposed to be intimidating."

"Okay . . ." I shook my head and eased us through a complex Ahlstrom loop.

"The holes in my memory *did* leave some eclectic tidbits," he said. "Yar."

I cut right, watching the proximity sensors, and noted that Arturo, Quirk, and Nedd had arrived.

"Is this all of us, Amphi?" I asked.

"Riptide Flight is incoming, about a minute and a half out," Arturo said. "Jorgen is assigned with them, and a couple of older pilots I don't know. I think they picked up some scouts on the way, so FM might be there too."

"Great," I said, grunting and turning my ship in another sequence of dodges. "Until they get here, see if you and Nedd can harry that bomber. Be careful, those black ships guarding it are more capable than your average Krell. Just try to drive the bomber away so it—"

"Negative," Ironsides said over the line. Great. Of course she was listening. "Pilots, you bring down that bomber."

"As much as I'd like you to sacrifice yourself, Ironsides," I said, "let's determine if we need that first. Amphi, Nedder, see what you can do."

"Gotcha, Spin," Nedd said.

"And me?" Kimmalyn asked.

"Hang back," I said. "Take aim on that bomber. Wait until its shield is down and its guards are distracted."

The private light on my comm flashed.

"Spensa . . . ," Kimmalyn said. "Are you sure you want to leave this to me? I mean . . ."

"I don't have any weapons, Quirk," I said. "It's you or nobody. You can do it. Get ready."

I dove low, destructor blasts flashing all around me. We skimmed the ground, my entourage following like an angry swarm of insects. Scud. I could see Alta right ahead. We were *close*.

Up above, Nedd and Arturo engaged the bomber's black guards. I didn't have time to pay attention, as I was forced to dodge in another direction, bolting out of the way of a force of Krell that had looped around to try to cut me off.

A couple of destructor blasts hit M-Bot's shield.

"Hey!" M-Bot said. "Just for that, I shall hunt your firstborn children and laugh with glee as I tell them of your death in terrible detail, with many unpleasant adjectives!"

I groaned. He'd said it over the group channel again.

"Please tell me," I said, "that I don't sound like *that*."

The others didn't reply.

"A pox of unique human diseases—many of which cause an uncomfortable swelling—come upon you!"

"Oh, scud. That *is* how I sound, isn't it?" I gritted my teeth, hitting the booster to cut ahead of the enemy. There were so many of them. All they needed were a few lucky shots.

But all I needed was to keep them busy for a little longer. I cut right and speared one with my light-lance, using its momentum to spin me in a tight turn. I darted around its companions as I released the one I'd lanced, sending it flying in an awkward tumble.

Now up. I cut up and around a hillside, moving away before the Krell could corner me.

"Spensa?" M-Bot said.

Down. I dove, right before some Krell ships tried to cut me off in the other direction.

"How are you doing that?" he asked.

Right. I turned through the center of some ships coming at me. Destructor blasts skimmed my wings, but not a single shot landed.

"You're reacting," he said, "to things they haven't *done yet.*"

I could sense their orders in the back of my mind. Quiet yet piercing, the commands traveled from above down to these Krell. They were communicating using another space, another place—and I could tap into it. Listen in on their commands.

I was somehow internalizing their commands, and responding to them before I knew what I was doing.

I tried not to let that freak me out.

M-Bot was incredibly agile, capable of quick boosts and deliberate slices in one direction or another. As I flew, it seemed as if I could *feel him*—feel the very lines of electricity that passed my orders through his fuselage. I flew with the immediate, unconscious skill of a person flexing their muscles. With the precision of a cautious surgeon, but the frenetic energy of the strongest athlete. It was *incredible.*

I was so consumed that I almost missed it as Arturo radioed in. "Spin, this isn't working. Those black ships refuse to be pulled away from the bomber. They engage us if we get close, but fall back when we draw away. And the bomber is still flying on a steady course."

"ETA until the enemy reaches position to destroy Igneous?" I asked.

"Under two minutes," M-Bot said. "At current speed of—"

"This is Riptide leader, callsign: Terrier," a male voice said. "What in the *North Star's light* is happening here?"

"No time to explain," I said. "Flightleader, take everything you have and hit those black ships that are protecting the bomber."

490

"And who are *you*?"

I turned—followed by my train of angry Krell ships—and buzzed over the six newcomers who had just arrived at the battle. I could barely get a visual on them because the destructor fire around me was so thick. I took another hit, and a fourth.

"Shield at forty percent strength," M-Bot noted.

I stayed ahead of most of the enemies, finding the holes between shots, my instincts somehow reading the Krell motions.

Stars appeared in my vision. Pinpricks of light.

The eyes.

Jorgen's voice rang through the channel. "Sir, with all due respect, she's a person you should listen to. *Now.*"

Terrier grunted, then said, "Riptide Flight, all ships, engage those black fighters."

"Not all," I said, spinning right. "Jorgen, FM, you there?"

"Here, Spin," FM said.

"You two. Take position near that bomber. I'm going to lead this swarm of Krell back around to it and hopefully give you enough of a distraction to get in close. When that happens, I need you to *IMP that bomber*. We don't have much time left."

"Roger," Jorgen said. "On me, FM?"

"Gotcha."

I swung in a wide loop, passing by Kimmalyn—who flew carefully out beyond the main battlefield. My entourage ignored her, presuming me to be the dangerous one.

"Quirk," I said over a private channel. "I need you to shoot that bomber."

"If that ship crashes, it will detonate the bomb," Kimmalyn said. "You'll die. You'll all die. Even if you escape, everyone in Alta will die."

"Do you think you can knock the ship's engines out? Or do something to get that bomber to drop the bomb?"

"A shot like that would—"

"Kimmalyn. What would the Saint say?"

"I don't know!"

"Then what would *you* say? Remember? The first day we met?"

I banked and spun back toward the bomber. Terrier and his ships, along with Arturo and Nedd, had thrown themselves at the black fighters. I bore down on it all, bringing the rest of the ships in to create a chaotic, frenzied jumble.

"Under thirty seconds," M-Bot said softly.

"You told me to take a deep breath," I said to Kimmalyn. "Reach up . . ."

"Pluck a star," she whispered.

My arrival—and the ships chasing me—created the confusion I'd anticipated. Ships darted in every direction, and the black ships scattered out of the way, trying to avoid collisions with their own vessels.

In my mind, I heard a specific Krell order sent to the bomber. The eyes accompanied me, somehow growing brighter—more hateful—as I heard the Krell chatter in my mind.

Initiate countdown to detonation at one hundred seconds.

"M-Bot!" I said. "Someone above just set the bomb to explode on a one-hundred-second countdown!"

"How do you know?"

"I can hear them!"

"Hear them how? They aren't using radio that I can monitor!" He paused. "Can you *hear* their superluminal communications?"

I caught a flash to my right. "IMP struck!" FM shouted, excited. "Bomber shields down!"

"Quirk, *fire!*" I screamed.

A line of red light pierced the battlefield. It passed between Krell ships, went right over Jorgen's wing as he overburned away from the bomber.

And damn me if it didn't spear the *exact spot* between the

bomber and the bomb, severing the clamps. The bomber continued flying forward.

But the bomb, cut free, dropped.

"Lifebuster dropped!" Terrier shouted. "All ships, overburn
out! Now!"

Everyone scattered, Krell included. Everyone but me.

I dove.

53

"Lifebuster dropped," Riptide flightleader shouted. "All ships, overburn out! Now!"

Judy let out a long sigh as she stood, hands behind her back, watching the hologram. Around her, in the command center, a few people clapped. A few others prayed. Rikolfr wept.

Judy just watched the bomb fall. She'd done what she could. Perhaps humankind could rebuild, with the remaining ships that survived. Perhaps the Defiants would continue on.

They'd do it without Alta. She braced herself. Ships scattered, to try to escape the blast. All but one.

That one dove toward the bomb.

"The defect," Judy whispered.

I speared the bomb with my light-lance, then pulled up in a curve that overwhelmed M-Bot's incredible GravCaps. The force pressed me against my seat as, by a narrow margin, I crested a dusty hillside—towing the lifebuster bomb after me.

M-Bot put up a timer, mirroring the one on the bomb. Forty-five seconds.

"We need to get this thing outside the death zone," I said, slamming the throttle full forward and putting everything into an overburn away.

"This will be close," he said. "I'm extending the atmospheric scoop so we don't rip that bomb off our light-lance as we accelerate, but above Mag-16 the scoop's envelope will shrink too much to fully shelter the bomb, so that's our max for now . . ."

We tore away from Alta, accelerating to speeds no DDF ship could have managed, despite that restriction. I felt the g-forces even through his GravCaps. We careened through the middle of a pack of DDF ships—they were gone in a blink.

"We're going to make it!" M-Bot said. "Just barely. But we'll . . . Oh."

"What?" I asked.

"We'll be in the middle of the blast when it explodes, Spensa. And I don't want to die. This is very inconvenient."

The countdown hit ten. Ahead, I saw a swarm of black dots in the air. Krell chasing after the DDF ships.

"There has to be a way out of this!" M-Bot said. "Booster and thrusters: online. No, not fast enough. Acclivity ring and altitude controls: online. Can we rise quickly enough? No, no, no!"

I felt at peace. Serene.

"Communications and stealth systems: online, but useless. Light-lance: online, carrying the bomb. If we drop it too soon, the wave will hit Alta."

I sank into the ship, feeling—*becoming*—his very processors as they worked. I felt the number counting down to three.

"Self-repair: offline. Destructors: offline."

Two.

I felt, more than saw, the blossom of the bomb's first explosion behind. And I felt, more than heard, M-Bot's diagnostic tool working.

"Biological component engaged," his voice said.

One.

"Cytonic hyperdrive: online."

An explosion of fire surrounding us.

"What?" M-Bot said. "Spin! Engage the—"

I did something with my mind.

We vanished, leaving a ship-size hole in the expanding blossom of flame and destruction.

54

In that moment between heartbeats, I felt myself enter someplace dark. A place not just black, a place of *nothingness*. Where matter did not, and could not, exist.

In that moment between heartbeats, I somehow stopped *being*, yet didn't stop *experiencing*. A field of white appeared around me—a billion stars. Like eyes opening at once, shining upon me.

Ancient things stirred. And in that moment between heartbeats, they not only saw me, but they *knew me*.

I jolted from that place that was not a place, and felt like I'd slammed into my straps, as if I'd been thrown physically back into the cockpit. I gasped, heart racing, sweat streaming down my face.

My ship hovered, still and quiet, lights blinking out on the control panel.

"Cytonic hyperdrive offline," M-Bot said.

"What," I said, gasping for breath. "What was that?"

"I don't know!" he said. "But my instruments place us at—calculating—one hundred kilometers from the point of detonation. Wow. My internal chronometer indicates no discrepancy

497

between our time and solar time, so we experienced no time dilation—but somehow we traveled that distance virtually instantaneously. Faster than light, certainly."

I leaned back in my seat. "Call Alta. Are they safe?"

The channel came on, and I heard whoops and screams—it took a moment to distinguish those as cheers of joy, not terror.

"Alta Base," M-Bot said. "This is Skyward Eleven. You may commence thanking us for saving you from utter annihilation."

"Thank you!" some voices cried. "Thank you!"

"Mushrooms are the preferred offering," M-Bot said to them. "As many varieties as you can dig up."

"Really?" I said, pulling off my helmet to wipe my brow. "Still on the mushroom thing?"

"I didn't erase that part of my programming," he said. "I'm fond of it. It gives me something to collect, like the way humans choose to accumulate useless items of sentimental and thematic value."

I grinned, though I couldn't shake the haunting feeling of those eyes watching me. Those . . . *somethings* knew what I'd done, and they didn't like it. Perhaps there had been a reason that M-Bot's faster-than-light capacities had been offline.

That raised a question, of course. Could we do that again? Gran-Gran said that her mother had *been* the engine of the *Defiant*. That she had made it work.

The answer is not to fear the spark, but to learn to control it.

I looked upward, toward the sky.

And there, I saw *a hole*. The debris shifting just right to reveal the stars. Exactly like . . . that day when I'd been with my father. My first time to the surface.

It seemed too momentous to be a coincidence.

"Spensa," M-Bot said. "The admiral is trying to contact you, but you have your helmet off."

I absently put my helmet back on, still staring at that hole in the debris. That pathway to infinity. Could I . . . hear something out there? Calling to me?

"Spensa," the admiral said. "How did you survive that blast?"

"I'm not sure," I answered truthfully.

"I suppose I'm going to need to pardon your father now," she said.

"You just survived a lifebuster explosion by a few meters," I said, "and still, all you can think about is that old grudge?"

The admiral fell silent.

Yes. I . . . I could hear the stars.

Come to us.

"Spensa," she said. "You need to know something about your father. About that day. We've lied, but for your own good."

"I know," I said, flipping controls, turning my ship's acclivity ring on its hinges so it pointed downward. My ship rotated so the nose pointed upward. Skyward.

"Return to base," the admiral said. "Return to honors and celebration."

"I will. Eventually."

Their heads are heads of rock, their hearts set upon rock.

"Spensa. There is a defect inside you. Please. You need to come back. Every moment you spend in the sky is a danger to you and to everyone else."

Be different. Set your sights on something higher.

"My ship doesn't have destructors," I said absently. "If I come back crazy, you should be able to shoot me down."

"Spin," Ironsides said, her voice pained. "Don't do this."

Something more grand.

"Goodbye, Admiral," I said, flipping off the comm.

Then I hit the overburn, launching upward.

Claim the stars.

55

I knew it was stupid.

The admiral was right. I should have returned to the base.

But I couldn't. Not only because I could hear the stars calling to me, luring me. Not only because of what had happened in that place between heartbeats.

I wasn't being controlled by something else. At least I didn't think I was. But I *had* to know. I *had* to confront it.

I *had* to see what my father had seen.

We soared higher, higher, up where the atmosphere faded and we could see the planet's curve. Still higher, aiming for that gap through the debris field.

I drew closer than I ever had before, and this time I was struck by how deliberate it all looked. We called it a debris field, but it really wasn't debris. There was a *shape* to all of this. An intent.

Enormous platforms that shined light downward. Others that looked like the shipyards. Together they formed a sequence of broken shells around our planet. And they had aligned just right to create an opening through them.

I passed into that large gap. If I veered too far to the sides, I'd likely be in range of the defensive guns that Cobb had mentioned. But here, traveling through this impromptu corridor, I was safe.

As I passed the first layer of debris, M-Bot said we'd entered space proper—though he also said the line between atmosphere and not was an "arbitrary distinction, as the exosphere doesn't end, but instead fades."

My breath caught in awe as we passed enormous platforms that could have held Alta a thousand times over or more. They were covered with what appeared to be buildings—each silent, dark. Millions upon millions of them.

People lived up here, once, I thought. I soared past several layers. By now we were going at incredible speeds—Mag-55—but without wind resistance, it didn't really matter. Speed was relative in space.

I looked away from the platforms, toward the end of the corridor. Out there were still, calm lights.

"Spensa," M-Bot said. "I'm detecting radio communication ahead. One of those specks is not a star."

I leaned forward as we passed another layer of debris. Yes, ahead I could see a glowing spot that was much closer than the stars. A ship? No, a space station. Shaped like a spinning top, with lights on all sides.

Smaller specks moved about it. Ships. I adjusted our course, pointing toward the station. Beneath us a platform revolved in its orbit, cutting off my sight of the shrinking shape of Detritus. Could I get back? Did I even care?

I could hear them louder, the voices of the stars. Chatter that didn't come through the radio, and didn't form words. The call of the stars . . . it was . . . it was *Krell communication.* They used that place between heartbeats to talk to one another, to communicate instantly. And . . . and the minds of thinking machines somehow relied upon the same technology to process quickly.

It all required access to that not-place, that *nowhere.*

We drew closer to the station. "Don't they know it's danger-ous?" I whispered. "That something *lives* in the nowhere? Don't they know about the eyes?"

Maybe that's why we only use radio, I thought. *Why our ances-tors abandoned this advanced communications technology. Our an-cestors were frightened of what lived in the nowhere.*

"I'm confused as to what you mean," M-Bot said. "Though the Krell are using some normal sublight communications in addition to the superluminal ones. The ordinary ones, I can crack and lis-ten in. Working to translate."

I slowed M-Bot, passing ships that turned toward mine. These didn't appear to be fighters; they were boxy, with large open win-dows at the front.

In that moment, something *hit* me, like a physical force. It crawled inside my brain, made my vision fuzz. I screamed, sag-ging in my straps.

"Spensa!" M-Bot said. "What's wrong? What is happening?"

I could only whimper. The *pain.* And . . . impressions. They were sending images. They were . . . they were trying to over-write . . . what I was seeing . . .

"Engaging stealth and jamming!" M-Bot said. "Spensa, I'm reading unusual signals. Spensa?"

The voices vanished. The pain evaporated. I let out a long, relieved sigh.

"Don't die, okay?" M-Bot said. "If you do, I'll probably have to make Rodge my pilot. It would be the most logical move, and we'd both *hate* it so much."

"I'm not going to die," I said, leaning back, tapping my helmet against the seat's headrest. "I do have a defect. A hole inside me."

"Humans have many holes in them. Would you like me to pro-vide you with a list?"

"Please don't."

"Ha ha. That was humor."

502

"I have a hole in my brain," I said. "It can see into the nowhere, but they can use it against me. I think . . . I think my father was shown some kind of mind hologram. When he flew back down to Detritus, he saw what the enemy wanted him to."

I remembered what he'd said. *I will kill you. I will kill you all . . .* He'd been so mournful, so soft. He thought the humans had lost—that his friends were already dead. What he'd seen hadn't been reality.

"When he blew up his friends," I whispered, "he *thought* he was shooting down the Krell."

A small number of the boxy ships approached M-Bot in the blackness. They struck me as couriers or maybe towing devices. Through the wide glass fronts, I saw creatures that looked vaguely like the drawings we had of Krell. Dark forms in armor, with red eyes.

Only here, they were bright colors—a perky red and blue, not dark at all. They reminded me a little of the pictures of crabs I'd seen from Old Earth, during my ancient biology courses. And the "armor" they wore seemed more like some kind of living apparatus, with open plates on the "head" portion for the creatures to see out of.

The sides of the little ships were stenciled with what looked to be words in a strange language.

"*Ketos redgor Earthen listro listrins,*" M-Bot said, reading the words. "Roughly, in English, that means 'Penitentiary maintenance and containment of Earthlings.'"

Scud. That . . . sounded ominous. "Can you tell me what they're saying?"

"There's some radio chatter nearer the station," he said, "but I suspect these ships are communicating using faster-than-light cytonic devices."

"Relax whatever you're doing to shield us," I said, "but don't put it down entirely. If I scream again, or go crazy, put it back up."

503

"Okay . . . ," M-Bot said. "You already seem crazy to me, but I guess that's nothing new."

Awareness returned to me, the voices in the darkness of space. I could hear their words, the ones they were sending through the nowhere. I knew them, even without needing a translation, because in that place all languages were one.

"It's *looking* at me!" one of the creatures was saying. "I think it wants to eat me. I don't like this at all!"

"It should be incapacitated now," a communication returned from the space station. "And if it's looking at you, it doesn't see you. We are overwriting its vision. Tow the ship in for study. That's not a standard DDF model. We're curious how they built it."

"I don't want to get anywhere near it," said another one of the creatures. "Don't you know how dangerous these things are?"

Curious, I looked out of my canopy at a ship drawing closer, then I made a kind of growling face—baring my teeth. The creature screamed and immediately turned its ship around and fled. The other two tugboat-style ships backed away.

"This is a job for fighter drones," one said. "Not manned ships."

They sounded so *scared*. Not like the terrible monsters I'd always imagined.

I relaxed in my seat.

"Would you like me to try to hack their systems?" M-Bot said.

"Can you do that?"

"It's not as easy as it might sound," he said. "I have to piggy-back on an incoming signal, and then decrypt their passwords and create a dummy login, then transfer files while spoofing an authorized request—breaching local data defense lines—all without tripping any of their alarms."

"So, can you do it?"

"I just did," he said. "That was a very long explanation. Beginning data transfer . . . And, they caught me. I've been booted, and security protocol is preventing my reentry."

Lights flashed on the station, and a moment later a squadron of small ships ejected from one of the bays on its side. I knew those flight patterns. Krell interceptors.

"Time to go," I said, grabbing the controls and sweeping us around. "Do you think you can navigate us through the debris layers without triggering any of the defense platforms?"

"Supposedly, the Krell do that each time they attack the planet," he said, "so it should be possible."

I hit the overburn, launching us back toward the outer layer of debris. M-Bot put some directions on my canopy, and I followed, tense for the first bit. We skimmed close to some of the platforms as we weaved toward the planet, but none of them fired at us.

I felt . . . strangely alert. The sense of fascination I'd experienced earlier—the draw to seek out what was causing the stars to sing—had faded. It was replaced by stark realism.

Coming out here *really had* been crazy. Even for me. But as we wove past another layer of debris, the Krell interceptors fell back. It seemed, increasingly, that I'd be able to return to the planet safely.

"Did you get anything?" I asked. "From their computers?"

"I started with the station's core orders and worked outward," he said. "I didn't get much, but . . . Oooh . . . You're going to like this."

"What?" I asked as I hit the overburn, flying back down toward Detritus. "What did you find?"

"Answers."

EPILOGUE

Two hours later, I sat in the DDF command center, holding a blanket around me, with my legs up on my seat. They'd given me Admiral Ironsides's chair.

Ever since that moment in the nowhere, I'd felt cold. A chill I couldn't shake, and which the blanket could barely help. My head still pounded, despite the metric ton of painkillers I'd swallowed.

A group of important people surrounded my chair, crowding me in. National Assembly Leaders, junior admirals, flightleaders. I was growing confident that they believed I wouldn't turn against them, though at first—after I'd reentered the atmosphere—they'd been very cautious.

The door to the command center opened, and finally Cobb limped in. I'd insisted on waiting until the transport fetched him and brought him back, and until he'd gotten his afternoon cup of coffee.

"All right," Ironsides said, folding her arms. "Captain Cobb is here. Can we talk *now*?"

I held up a finger. It might have been petty of me, but it felt *really* good to make Ironsides wait. Besides, there was someone else who deserved to be here before I explained.

As we waited, I reached for the radio at my side. "M-Bot," I said. "Everything all right?"

"I'm trying not to be offended by how the engineers in this hangar are looking at me," he said. "They seem overeager to rip me apart. But so far, nobody has tried anything."

"That ship is DDF—" Ironsides began.

"That ship," I said, "*will* fry all his own systems if you try breaking into him. The DDF will get his tech, but it will be on our terms."

The way she looked—red-faced—when I said it was *also* extremely satisfying. But she didn't challenge me any further.

Finally the door opened again, and Jorgen entered. He was actually smiling, and it occurred to me that the expression—while pleasant—didn't really suit him. He just looked more like himself when he was being serious.

He wasn't the one we'd been waiting for, however. Instead, it was the lanky young man Jorgen had been sent to fetch. Rig grinned like a fool as he stepped into the room, then he blushed as the flightleaders and admirals parted for him, saluting. Though Ironsides was angry that Rig and I hadn't turned the ship in immediately, most seemed to agree that when working with an insane AI that threatened to destroy itself, Rig had performed admirably in getting technology to the DDF.

"*Now* will you talk?" Ironsides demanded.

"The Krell are not what we think," I said. "My ship downloaded some of their databases, and discovered what happened before our ancestors landed here on Detritus. There was a war. A vast intergalactic one. Humans against aliens."

"Against the Krell," Ironsides said.

"There were no Krell at the start of it," I said. "Just us versus the galaxy. And humankind lost. The victors were a coalition of aliens who, as best M-Bot and I can tell, considered humankind too brutal, too uncivilized, and too aggressive to be allowed to be part of the intergalactic community.

"They demanded that all human fleets, independent or not, surrender to their authority. Our ancestors, on the *Defiant* and its small fleet, considered themselves innocent. They weren't part of the war. But when they refused to turn themselves in, the alien coalition sent a group to capture or contain them. *That* is what we call the Krell."

I closed my eyes. "They cornered us. And—after a conflict on board the *Defiant*—my great-grandmother brought us here, to Detritus. A planet we knew about, but which had been abandoned centuries before.

"The Krell followed us, and set up a station to watch us once we crashed. They're not murderous aliens. They're prison guards. A force designed to keep humankind trapped here, as some of the aliens are absolutely sure we will try to conquer the galaxy if we're ever allowed to get back into space.

"The lifebusters were designed to annihilate our civilization if we seemed to be getting close to escaping Detritus. But most of the time they attacked, I don't think they were trying to *actually* destroy us. They have laws against destroying a species entirely. They consider this planet like . . . a preserve for humankind. They sent ships to keep us focused on the fight, to occupy us, so we wouldn't have time to research how to escape. And while the fighters always tried to keep our fleet down to size, they were only authorized to use a certain amount of force against us, lest they accidentally cause us to go extinct."

I shivered despite the blanket. "Something changed recently, however," I said. "It seems this last bomb really was meant to destroy us. There have been . . . politics about how much they should tolerate from us. They tried to destroy Alta and Igneous, but we defeated them. That has them scared."

"Great, wonderful," Ironsides said, folding her arms. "But this doesn't change much. We know why the Krell are attacking, but they're still a superior force. This will only make them more determined to extinguish us."

"Maybe," I said. "But the aliens who contain us? They *aren't* warriors. They're prison guards who fly mostly unmanned drones that don't have to fight well—because they can overwhelm us with numbers."

"Which is still the case," Ironsides said. "We are low on resources, while they have better technology and an orbital fleet. We're still basically doomed."

"This is true," I said.

"Then why are you smiling?" Ironsides demanded.

"Because," I said, "I can hear what they're saying to each other. And anytime you know what your enemy is going to do, you have an advantage. They think we're trapped on this planet."

"Aren't we?" Jorgen asked.

I shivered again and thought of that moment when I'd been nowhere. The Krell knew they had to target any of us who flew too well—because they knew about the defect. They knew that someone who had it might be able to do as I'd done.

I didn't know how I'd teleported my ship. I didn't know if I dared do it again. But I knew, at the same time, that Gran-Gran was right. Using that power was the key. To survival. To escaping this planet.

To being truly Defiant.

ACKNOWLEDGMENTS

To make this book, I channeled my own emotions as a young man. My passion wasn't becoming a fighter pilot, but it was instead to become a writer. But at times, that road seemed as hopeless as Spensa's. I still feel like I've been given the world, since I get to do what I do for a living.

And like Spensa, I'm the beneficiary of some supremely good friends and colleagues. Krista Marino was the editor on this book, its primary champion and a wonderful flightleader. Eddie Schneider was the agent on the contract, along with help from Joshua Bilmes. Those three, along with the publisher Beverly Horowitz, were exceptionally patient with me as I pulled another book out from under them and made them publish this one instead.

I'm constantly amazed by the skills of visual artists. Charlie Bowater's brilliant cover really brought Spensa to life for me, while Ben McSweeney did his usual technical magic, taking my vague scratches on a piece of paper and making the cool ship designs that you saw in this book. Finally, my good friend Isaa« Stewart did the maps, and was art director for the interior art.

All the typos that aren't there are the result of the Inconsecutive

Peter Ahlstrom hunting them down for their meat to sell on the open market. As always, many thanks to him for his tireless efforts and for cheering me on.

Likewise, the rest of the team here at Dragonsteel have been an excellent "ground crew" for my piloting shenanigans. Kara Stewart handles shipping out all those T-shirts and books you guys order from my website store. Adam Horne is my executive assistant and publicist. And, of course, my wife, Emily, is the one who keeps us all pointed in the right direction. In addition, Emily Grange and Kathleen Dorsey Sanderson need a hearty thanks for their general help on all kinds of sundry things. (Which includes listening to my five-year-old explain in detail how he likes his sandwiches. Mayo on the outside, if you're wondering.)

Karen Ahlstrom (who got the special dedication for this book) is my continuity editor. You all have no idea the mess some of these books are before she gets ahold of them and forces me to acknowledge people can't be in two places at once. Other help was provided at Penguin Random House/Delacorte Press by Monica Jean, Mary McCue, Lisa Nadel, Adrienne Waintraub, and Rebecca Gudelis. The copyeditor was Barbara Perris, and the proofreader was Shona McCarthy.

My writing group and flightmates for the book were the usual suspects: Karen Ahlstrom, Peter Ahlstrom, Alan Layton, Kaylynn ZoBell, Emily Sanderson, Darci Stone, Eric James Stone, Ben Olsen, Ethan Skarstedt, and Earl Cahill.

Beta readers included Nikki Ramsay (callsign: Phosphophyllite), Marnie Peterson, Eric Lake (callsign: Chaos) Darci Cole (callsign: Blue), Ravi Persaud (callsign: Jabber), Deana Covel Whitney (callsign: Braid), Jayden King (callsign: Tripod), Alice Arneson (callsign: Wetlander), Bradyn Ray, Sumejja Muratagic-Tadic (callsign: Sigma), Janel Forcier (callsign: Turnip), Paige Phillips (callsign: Artisan), Joe Deardeuff (callsign: Traveler), and Brian T. Hill (callsign: El Guapo).

And, calling out two of those in specific, Jayden King and Bradyn Ray lent me their fighter pilot expertise, explaining (sometimes at length) the stupid things I was getting wrong about flight. Eric Lake was also a big help with calculating speeds, distances, and the coordinate system. (Make friends with physicists and mathematicians, writers. It pays off.)

We did a special teen beta read for this book, and those members were: Liliana Klein (callsign: Sentinel), Nathan Scorup, Hannah Herman, Joshua Singer, Eve Scorup (callsign: Silverstone), Valencia Kumley (callsign: AlphaPhoenix), Daniel Summerstay, Chrestian Scorup, Rebecca Arneson (callsign: Scarlet), Cole Newberry, Brett Herman (callsign: Hermanator), Aidan Denzel (callsign: Cross), Evan Garcia, Kathryn Stephens, and William Stay.

Our gamma proofreaders included many of the betas plus Trae Cooper, Mark Lindberg (callsign: Megalodon), Brandon Cole (callsign: Colevander), Ian McNatt (callsign: Weiry), Kellyn Neumann (callsign: Jumper), Gary Singer, Becca Reppert, Kalyani Poluri (callsign: Henna), Paige Vest, Jory Phillips (callsign: Bouncer), Ted Herman (callsign: Cavalry), Bob Kluttz (callsign: Tasil), Bao Pham (callsign: Wyld), Lyndsey Luther (callsign: Soar), David Behrens, Lingting "Botanica" Xu (callsign: Hasan), Tim Challener (callsign: Antaeus), William "Aberdasher" Juan, Rahul Pantula (callsign: Giraffe), Megan Kanne (callsign: Sparrow), and Ross Newberry.

Many thanks to all of them. Though there are, as always, some new names on that list, many of these people have been supporting my writing for years—or even decades at this point. So if you need a good wingmate, I can point you toward a few.

THE STARS ARE CALLIN...

THE ADVENTURE CONTINUES

#1 *NEW YORK TIMES* BESTSELLING AUTHOR

BRANDON SANDERSON

STARSIGHT

THE SEQUEL TO *SKYWARD*

...RN THE PAGE TO START READING

1

I slammed on my overburn and boosted my starship through the middle of a chaotic mess of destructor blasts and explosions. Above me extended the awesome vastness of space. Compared to that infinite blackness, both planets and starships alike seemed insignificant. Meaningless.

Except, of course, for the fact that those insignificant starships were doing their best to kill me.

I dodged, spinning my ship and cutting my boosters midturn. Once I'd flipped around, I immediately slammed on the booster again, burning in the other direction in an attempt to lose the three ships tailing me. Fighting in space is way different from fighting in atmosphere. For one thing, your wings are useless. No air means no airflow, no lift, no drag. In space, you don't really fly. You just don't fall.

I executed another spin and boost, heading back toward the main firefight. Unfortunately, maneuvers that had been impressive down in the atmosphere were commonplace up here. Fighting in a vacuum these last six months had provided a whole new set of skills to master.

"Spensa," a lively masculine voice said from my console,

"you remember how you told me to warn you if you were being extra irrational?"

"No," I said with a grunt, dodging to the right. The destructor blasts from behind swept over the dome of my cockpit. "I don't believe I did anything of the sort."

"You said, 'Can we talk about this later?'"

I dodged again. Scud. Were those drones getting better at dogfighting, or was I losing my touch?

"Technically, it was 'later' right after you spoke," continued the talkative voice—my ship's AI, M-Bot. "But human beings don't actually use that word to mean 'anytime chronologically after this moment.' They use it to mean 'sometime after now that is more convenient to me.'"

The Krell drones swarmed around us, trying to cut off my escape back toward the main body of the battlefield.

"And you think *this* is a more convenient time?" I demanded.

"Why wouldn't it be?"

"Because we're in combat!"

"Well, I would think that a life-and-death situation is *exactly* when you'd like to know if you're being extra irrational."

I could remember, with some measure of fondness, the days when my starships *hadn't* talked back to me. That had been before I'd helped repair M-Bot, whose personality was a remnant of ancient technology we still didn't understand. I frequently wondered: *Had all advanced AIs been this sassy, or was mine just a special case?*

"Spensa," M-Bot said. "You're supposed to be leading these drones back toward the others, remember?"

It had been six months since we'd defeated the Krell attempt to bomb us into oblivion. Alongside our victory, we'd learned some important facts. The enemy we called "the Krell" were a group of aliens tasked with keeping my people contained on the planet

Detritus, which was kind of a cross between a prison and a nature preserve for human civilization. The Krell reported to a larger galactic government, called the Superiority.

They employed remote drones to fight us—piloted by aliens who lived far away, controlling their drones via faster-than-light communications. The drones were never driven by AIs, as it was against galactic law to let a ship pilot itself. Even M-Bot was severely limited on what he could do on his own. Beyond that, there was something that the Superiority feared deeply: people who had the ability to see into the space where FTL communication happened. People called cytonics.

People like me.

They knew what I was, and they hated me. The drones tended to target me specifically—and we could use that. We *should* use that. In today's pre-battle briefing, I'd swayed the rest of the pilots reluctantly to go with a bold plan. I was to get a little out of formation, tempt the enemy drones to swarm me, then lead them back through the rest of the team. My friends could then eliminate the drones while they were focused on me.

It was a good plan. And I'd make good on it . . . eventually.

Now, though, I wanted to test something.

I hit my overburn, accelerating away from the enemy ships. M-Bot was faster and more maneuverable than they were, though part of his big advantage had been in his ability to maneuver at high speed in air without ripping himself apart. Out here in a vacuum, that wasn't a factor, and the enemy drones did a better job of keeping up.

They swarmed after me as I dove toward Detritus. My homeworld was protected by layers of ancient metal platforms—like shells—with gun emplacements all along them. After our victory six months ago, we'd pushed the Krell farther away from the planet, past the shells.

Our current long-term strategy was to engage the enemy out here, in space, and keep them from getting close to the planet.

Keeping them out here had allowed our engineers—including my friend Rodge—to be able to start gaining control of the platforms and their guns. Eventually, that shell of gun emplacements should protect our planet from incursions. For now though, most of those defensive platforms were still autonomous—and could be as dangerous for us as they were for the enemy.

The Krell ships swarmed in behind me, eager to cut me off from the battlefield—where my friends were engaging the rest of the drones in a massive brawl.

That tactic made one fatal assumption: that if I were alone, I'd be less dangerous.

"We're not going to turn back around and follow the plan, are we?" M-Bot asked. "You're going to try to fight them on your own."

I didn't respond.

"Jorgen is going to be aaaaaangry," M-Bot said. "By the way, those drones are trying to chase you along a specific heading, which I'm outlining on your monitor. My analysis projects that they've planned an ambush."

"Thanks," I said.

"Just trying to keep you from getting me blown up," M-Bot said. "By the way, if you *do* get us killed, be warned that I intend to haunt you."

"Haunt me?" I said. "You're a robot. And besides, I'd be dead too, right?"

"My robotic ghost would haunt your fleshy one."

"How would that even work?"

"Spensa, ghosts aren't real," he said in an exasperated tone. "Why are you worrying about things like that instead of flying? Honestly, humans get distracted so easily."

I spotted the ambush: a small group of Krell drones had hidden themselves by a large chunk of metal floating just out of range of the gun emplacements. As I drew close, the ambushing drones emerged and rocketed toward me. I was ready though. I let my arms relax, let my subconscious mind take over. I sank into myself, entering a kind of trance where I listened.

Just not with my ears.

Remote drones worked fine for the Krell in most situations. They were an expendable way to suppress the humans of Detritus. However, the enormous distances involved in space battle forced the Krell to rely on instantaneous faster-than-light communication to control their drones. I suspected their pilots were far away—but even if they were on the Krell station that hung out in space near Detritus, the lag of radio communications from there would make the drones too slow to react in battle. So, FTL was necessary.

That exposed one major flaw. I could hear their orders.

For some reason I didn't understand, I could *listen* into the place where FTL communication happened. I called it the Nowhere, another dimension where our rules of physics didn't apply. I could hear into the place, occasionally see into it—and see the creatures that lived there watching me.

Once, I'd managed to *enter* that place and teleport my ship a long distance in the blink of an eye. I still didn't know much about my powers. I hadn't been able to teleport again, but I'd been learning that, whatever existed inside me, I could harness it and use it to fight.

I let my instincts take over, and sent my ship into a complex sequence of dodges. My battle-trained reflexes, melded with my innate ability to hear the drone orders, maneuvered my ship without specific conscious instructions on my part.

My cytonic ability had been passed down my family line. My ancestors had used it to move ancient starfleets around the galaxy.

My father had had the ability, and the enemy had exploited it to get him killed. Now, I used it to stay alive.

I reacted before the Krell did, responding to their orders—somehow, I processed them *even faster* than the drones could. By the time they attacked, I was already weaving through their destructor blasts. I darted among them, then activated my IMP, bringing down the shields of everyone nearby.

In my state of focused concentration, I didn't care that the IMP took down my shield too. It didn't matter.

I launched my light-lance, and the rope of energy speared one of the enemy ships, connecting it to my own. I then used the difference in our momentum to spin us both around, which put me into position behind the pack of defenseless ships.

Blossoms of light and sparks broke the void as I destroyed two of the drones. The remaining Krell scattered like villagers before a wolf in one of Gran-Gran's stories. The ambush turned chaotic as I picked a pair of ships and gunned for them with destructors—blasting one away as a part of my mind tracked the orders being given to the others.

"I never fail to be amazed when you do that," M-Bot said quietly. "You are interpreting data faster than my projections. You seem almost . . . inhuman."

I gritted my teeth, bracing, and spun my ship, boosting it after a straggling Krell drone.

"I mean that as a compliment, by the way," M-Bot said. "Not that there's anything wrong with humans. I find their frail, emotionally unstable, irrational natures quite endearing."

I destroyed that drone and bathed my hull in the light of its fiery demise. Then I dodged right between the shots of two others. Though the Krell drones didn't have pilots on board, a part of me felt sorry for them as they tried to fight back against me—

an unstoppable, unknowable force that did not play by the same rules that bound everything else they knew.

"Likely," M-Bot continued, "I regard humans as I do only because I'm programmed to do so. But hey, that's no different from instinct programming a mother bird to love the twisted, featherless abominations she spawned, right?"

Inhuman.

I wove and dodged, fired and destroyed. I wasn't perfect; I occasionally overcompensated and many of my shots missed. But I had a distinct edge.

The Superiority—and its minions the Krell—obviously knew to watch for people like me and my father. Their ships were always on the hunt for humans who flew too well or who responded too quickly. They'd tried controlling my mind by exploiting a weakness in my talent—the same thing they'd done to my father. Fortunately, I had M-Bot. His advanced shielding was capable of filtering out their mental attacks while still allowing me to hear the enemy orders.

All of this raised a singular daunting question.

What *was* I?

"I would feel a lot more comfortable," M-Bot said, "if you'd find a chance to reignite our shield."

"No time," I said. We'd need a good thirty seconds without flight controls to do that.

I had another chance to break toward the main battle, to follow through with the plan we'd outlined. Instead, I spun, then hit the overburn and blasted back toward the enemy ships. My GravCaps absorbed a large percentage of the g-forces and kept me from suffering too much whiplash, but I still felt pressure, flattening me against my seat, making my skin pull back and my body feel heavy. Under extreme g-forces, I felt like I'd aged a hundred years in a second.

I pushed through it and fired at the remaining Krell drones. I strained my strange skills to their limits. A Krell destructor shot grazed the dome of my canopy, so bright it left an afterimage in my eyes.

"Spensa," M-Bot said. "Both Jorgen and Cobb have called to complain. I know you said to keep them distracted, but—"

"Keep them distracted."

"Resigned sigh."

I looped us after an enemy ship. "Did you just *say* the words *resigned sigh*?"

"I find human nonlinguistic communications to be too easily misinterpreted," he said. "So I'm experimenting with ways to make them more explicit."

"Doesn't that defeat the purpose?"

"Obviously not. Dismissive eye-roll."

Destructors flared around me, but I blasted two more drones. As I did, I saw something appear, reflected in the canopy of my cockpit. A handful of piercing white lights, like eyes, watching me. When I used my abilities too much, something looked out of the Nowhere and saw me.

I didn't know what they were. I just called them the eyes. But I *could* feel a burning hatred from them. An anger. Somehow, this was all connected. My ability to see and hear into the Nowhere, the eyes that watched me from that place, and the teleportation power I'd only managed to use once.

I could still distinctly remember how I'd felt when I'd used it. I'd been on the brink of death, being enveloped by a cataclysmic explosion. In that moment, somehow, I'd activated something called a cytonic hyperdrive.

If I could master that ability to teleport, I could help free my people from Detritus. With that power, we could escape the Krell forever. And so, I pushed myself.

Last time I'd jumped, I'd been fighting for my life. If I could only recreate those same emotions . . .

I dove, my right hand on my control sphere, my left holding the throttle. Three drones swept in behind me, but I registered their shots and turned my ship at an angle so they all missed. I hit the throttle, and my mind brushed the nowhere.

The eyes continued to appear, reflected in the canopy, as if it were revealing something that watched from behind my seat. White lights, like stars, but somehow more . . . aware. Dozens of malevolent glowing dots. In entering their realm, even slightly, I became visible to them.

Those eyes unnerved me. How could I be both fascinated by these powers and terrified of them at the same time? It felt like the call of the void you felt when standing at the edge of a large cliff in the caverns, knowing you could just throw yourself off into that darkness. One step farther . . .

"Spensa!" M-Bot said. "New ship arriving!"

I pulled out of my trance, and the eyes vanished. M-Bot used the console display to highlight what he'd spotted. A new starfighter, almost invisible against the black sky, emerged from where the others had been hiding. Sleek, it was shaped like a disc and painted the same black as space. It was smaller than normal Krell ships, but it had a larger canopy.

These new black ships had only started appearing in the last eight months, in the days leading up to the attempt to bomb our base. Back then, we hadn't realized what they meant, but now we knew.

I couldn't hear the commands this ship received—because none were being sent to it. Black ships like this one were not remote controlled. Instead, they carried real alien pilots. Usually, an enemy ace—the best of their pilots.

The battle had just gotten far more interesting.

2

My heart leaped with excitement.

An enemy ace. Fighting drones was exciting, yes, but also lacking. It wasn't personal enough. A duel with an ace, instead, felt like the stories Gran-Gran told. Brave pilots engaging in grim contests on Old Earth during the days of the Great Wars. Person against person.

"I will sing to you," I whispered. "As your ship burns, and your soul flees, I will sing. To the contest we had."

Dramatic, yes. My friends tended to still laugh at me when I said things like that, things like they said in the old stories. Mostly, I'd stopped. But I was still me, and I didn't say those things for my friends. I said them for myself.

And for the enemy I was about to kill.

The ace swooped toward me, firing its destructors, trying to hit me while I was focused on the drones. I grinned, diving out of the way and spearing a chunk of space debris with my light-lance. That let me pivot quickly, while also swinging the debris behind me to block the shots. M-Bot's GravCaps absorbed most of the g-forces, but I still felt a tug pulling me downward as I swung through the arc, destructor fire blasting into the debris, one shot coming very near me. Scud. I still hadn't found a chance to reignite my shield.

"This might be a good time to head back and lead the enemy ships toward the others," M-Bot said. "Like the plan said . . ."

I noted as the enemy ace overshot me—then I swung around and gave chase instead.

"Dramatic trailing-off of speech," M-Bot added, "laden with implications of your irresponsible nature."

I fired at the ace, but they spun on their axis, cutting their boosters. Momentum carried them forward, but they'd turned back to front and were now facing me. They couldn't steer well flying in reverse, so the maneuver was usually risky, but when you had a full shield and your enemy had none . . .

I was forced to break off the chase, boosting to the left and dodging out of the way of the destructor fire. I couldn't risk a head-on confrontation. Instead, I focused on the drones for a moment, blasting one out of the sky, then screamed through its debris—which scraped up M-Bot's wing and smacked the canopy with a fierce *crack*.

Right. No shield. And in space, the debris didn't fall after you shot the ship down. That felt like a rookie mistake—a reminder that, despite all my training, I was new to zero-atmosphere combat.

The ace fell in behind me in an expert tailing maneuver. They were good, which was—on one hand—thrilling. On the other hand . . .

I tried to cut back toward the battle, but the drones swarmed in front of me, cutting me off. Maybe I was in a little over my head.

"Call Jorgen," I said, "and tell him I might have let myself get cornered. I can't lead the enemy into our ambush; see if he and the others are willing to come help me instead."

"Finally," M-Bot said.

I dodged some more, tracking the enemy ace on my proximity monitor. Scud. I wish I could hear them like I could the drones.

No, this is good, I thought. *I need to be careful never to let my gift become a crutch.*

I gritted my teeth and made a snap decision. I couldn't get back to the main battle, so instead, I dove toward Detritus. The defense shells surrounding it weren't solid; they were made up of large platforms that had housed living quarters, shipyards, and weapons. Though we'd begun reclaiming the ones closest to the planet, these outer layers were still set to automatically fire at anything that got close.

I hit my overburn, accelerating to speeds that—in atmosphere—would have caused most starfighters to rattle or even rip apart. Up here I only felt the acceleration, not the speed.

I quickly reached the nearest space platform. Long and thin, it curved slightly, like a chunk of broken eggshell. The remaining drones and the single ace were still on my tail. At these speeds, dogfighting was much more dangerous. The time for me to react before colliding with something would be much smaller, and the smallest touch on my control sphere could veer me off course faster than I might be able to deal with.

"Spensa?" M-Bot said.

"I know what I'm doing," I muttered back, concentrating.

"Yes, I'm sure," M-Bot answered. "But . . . just in case . . . you do remember that we don't have control of these outer platforms yet, right?"

I focused my full attention on sweeping in down close to the surface of the metal platform without running into anything. The gun emplacements here tracked me and started firing—but they *also* started firing on the enemy.

I concentrated on dodging. Or really just weaving erratically—

I could outfly the drones in a raw contest of skill, but they had superior numbers. Down near the platform, that translated into a liability for my enemies—because to the guns, we were all targets.

Several of the drones flared up in explosions—which vanished almost immediately, flames smothered by the vacuum of space.

"I wonder if those guns feel fulfilled, finally getting to shoot something down after all these years up here," M-Bot said.

"Jealous?" I asked with a grunt, dodging.

"From what Rodge says, they don't have true AIs, just some simple targeting functions. So that would be like you being jealous of a rat."

Another drone fell. *Just a little bit longer.* I just wanted to even the odds a little while I waited for my friends to arrive.

I sank into another trance as I flew. I couldn't hear the controls of the gun emplacements, but in moments like these—moments of pure concentration—I felt as if I were becoming one with my ship.

I could feel the attention of the eyes back on me. My heart thundered inside my chest. With those guns trained on me . . . tails giving chase and still firing . . .

A little farther . . .

My mind sank down, and I felt as if I could sense M-Bot's very workings. I was in severe danger. I needed to escape.

Surely I could do it now. "Engage cytonic hyperdrive!" I said, then tried to do what I'd done once before, teleporting my ship.

"Cytonic hyperdrive is offline," M-Bot said.

Scud. When it had worked, he'd been able to tell me it was online. I tried again, but . . . I didn't even know what it was I'd done that once. I had been in danger, about to die. And then I . . . I'd done . . .

Something?

A blast from a nearby gun nearly blinded me, and, with gritted teeth, I pulled up and zipped out of the defensive guns' range. The ace had survived, though they had taken a hit or two, so maybe their shield was weakened. Plus, only three drones remained.

I cut my thrust and spun my ship on its axis—still moving forward, but pointed backward—a maneuver that indicated I was going to try shooting behind me. Sure enough, the ace dodged away immediately. They weren't so brave with a weakened shield. Instead of firing, I boosted after the ace—escaping the drones, which swarmed toward my former position.

I got on the ace's tail and tried to draw in close enough for a shot—but whoever they were, they were good. They spun into a complex series of dodges, all while increasing speed. I misjudged a turn, and suddenly I swung out away from them. I quickly recovered, matching their next turn and letting out a blast of destructor fire—but now I was pretty far back, and the shots went wild, vanishing into space.

M-Bot read off speeds and angles for me so I didn't have to break concentration for even the fraction of second it would take to look at my control panel. I leaned forward, trying to match the other starfighter turn for turn—swooping, spinning, and boosting. Seeking that critical moment when we'd align just long enough for me to take a shot.

They, in turn, could twist at any moment and fire back—so they were likely watching for the same thing that I was, hoping to catch me off guard during a moment of alignment.

This perfect focus. This boiling intensity. This bizarre moment of connection where the alien pilot mirrored my efforts, striving, struggling, sweating—drawing closer and closer in a paradoxically *intimate* contest. For a flash we'd be as one. And then I'd kill them.

I lived for this challenge. For fighting against someone real, and knowing it was either me or them. In moments like this, I didn't fight for the DDF or humankind. I fought to prove I could.

They swooped left just as I did. They spun and pointed toward me as we came into alignment briefly—and we both shot a burst at each other.

Their shots missed. Mine didn't. The first of my blasts broke their weakened shield. The other hit them just left of their cockpit, ripping the disclike ship apart in a flash of light.

The vacuum consumed that eagerly, and I cut to the right, dodging the debris. I took deep breaths, struggling to slow my heart. Sweat stained the pads on my helmet and leaked down the sides of my face.

"Spensa!" M-Bot shouted. "The drones!"

Scud.

I turned my ship and boosted to the side just as three flaring explosions lit my cockpit. I winced, but those lights weren't the result of me getting shot—they were the lights of drones exploding one after another. Two DDF ships swooped past.

"Thanks, guys," I said, tapping the group channel on the communications panel of my dash.

"No problem," Kimmalyn replied over the channel. "As the Saint always said, 'Watch out for the smart ones. They tend to be stupid.'" She had an accent and an unhurried way of speaking— somehow intrinsically upbeat, even when she was chastising me.

"I thought the idea was for you to distract the drones," FM said, "then bring them back toward us." She had a confident voice, the type that sounded like it should be coming from someone twice her age.

"I was planning to do it eventually."

"Yeah," FM said. "And that's why you turned off your comm so Jorgen couldn't yell at you?"

"It wasn't off," I said. "I just had M-Bot running interference."

"Jorgen really hates talking to me!" M-Bot said enthusiastically. "I can tell by the way he says so!"

"Yeah, well, the enemy is retreating," FM said. "And you're lucky we were already on our way to help, even before you decided to admit you were in trouble."

I was still something of a sweaty mess—heart racing, hands slick—as I reignited my shield, then turned my ship and flew toward the other two. The course took me past the wreckage of the ship I'd defeated, which was still moving along at roughly the same speed as when I'd hit it. That was space for you.

The ship had cracked apart, rather than exploding completely, and so with a chill I was able to spot the corpse of the enemy ace. A boxy alien figure. Perhaps the armor it wore could protect it from the vacuum . . .

No. As I passed by, I saw that its armor had been broken apart in the blast. The actual creature inside was kind of like a tall, two-legged crab—spindly and bright blue, with a carapace along the abdomen and face. I saw some piloting shuttles near their space station, which was further out in space, monitoring Detritus from a distance. They were our jailors, and while the data we'd stolen called this crablike race the Varvax, most of us still called them the Krell—even though we knew that was an acronym, not their actual race's name.

This one was truly dead. The liquid bath that filled its armor had spilled out into the void, first boiling explosively, then freezing into solid vapor. Space was weird.

I fixed my gaze on the body, slowing M-Bot, and hummed softly one of the songs of my ancestors. A Viking song for the dead.

Well fought, I thought to the Krell's departing soul. Nearby, some of our salvage ships came swooping in from where they'd watched the fight in relative safety nearer the planet. We always salvaged Krell ships, especially those with living pilots. There was a chance that we'd be able to capture a broken Superiority hyperdrive that way. They didn't travel using the minds of pilots. They had some kind of actual technology that let them travel between stars.

"Spin?" Kimmalyn called to me. "You coming?"

"Yeah," I said. I turned away and fell into line with her and FM. "M-Bot? How would you judge that pilot's flying abilities?"

"Somewhere near your own," M-Bot said. "And their ship was more advanced than any we'd faced before. I'll be honest, Spensa— mostly because I'm programmed to be incapable of lying—I think that fight could have gone either way."

I nodded, feeling much the same. I'd gone toe-to-toe with that ace. On one hand, it was a nice affirmation that my skill wasn't tied only to my abilities to touch the nowhere.

But coming fully out of my trance now—feeling the odd sense of deflated purpose that always tailed a battle—I found myself strangely worried. In all our time fighting here, we'd seen only a handful of these black ships piloted by live beings.

If the Krell really wanted to kill us, why send so few aces? And . . . was this really the best they had? I was good, but I'd been flying for less than a year. Our stolen information indicated that our enemies ran an enormous galactic coalition of hundreds of planets. Surely they had access to pilots who were better than I was.

Something struck me as off about all of this. The Krell used to only ever send a maximum of a hundred drones against us at once. They'd relaxed that, and now they'd field upward of a hundred and twenty at once . . . but that still seemed a small number, considering the apparent size of their coalition.

So what was going on? Why were they still holding back?

Kimmalyn, FM, and I rejoined the rest of our fighters. The DDF was growing stronger and stronger. We'd lost only a single ship today, when in the past we'd lose half a dozen or more in battle. The DDF was gaining momentum. In the last two months, we'd begun deploying our first ships fabricated using technology learned from M-Bot. It had only been six months, but the boost to our morale—and the fact that our pilots were surviving longer to hone their skills—was making us stronger by the day.

By intercepting the enemy out here, and not letting them get in close, we'd been able to expand our salvage operations. Because of this, we were not only reclaiming the closest of the defense platforms, we were also able to scavenge materials for more and more ships.

This all meant shipbuilding and recruitment were both increasing dramatically. We'd soon have enough acclivity stone, and enough pilots, to field hundreds of starships.

Together, it was an ever-increasing snowball effect of progress. Still, a part of me worried. The Krell behavior was odd. And beyond that, we had a huge disadvantage. They could travel the galaxy, while we were trapped on one planet.

Unless I learned how to use my powers.

"Um, Spensa?" M-Bot said. "Jorgen is calling, and I think he's annoyed."

I sighed, then hit the line. "Skyward Ten, reporting in."

"Are you all right?" he asked with a stern voice.

"Yeah."

"Good. We'll discuss this later." He cut the line.

I winced. He wasn't annoyed. . . . He was *furious*.

Sadie—the new girl who had been assigned as my wingmate—flew up behind me in Skyward Nine. I sensed a nervousness to the posture of her ship, though perhaps I was reading too much into things. According to our plans, I'd left her behind when the Krell had sent an overwhelming force to destroy me. Fortunately, she'd had enough sense to follow orders and stay close to the others, rather than tail me.

We had to wait for orders from Flight Command before flying back toward the planet, so we hovered in space for a short time. And as we did, Kimmalyn nudged her ship up beside mine. I glimpsed through her canopy into her cockpit. She always looked odd to me wearing her helmet, which covered her long dark hair.

"Hey," she said to me on a private line. "You all right?"

"Yeah," I said. It was a lie. Every time I used my strange abilities, I felt a conflict inside me. Our ancestors had been afraid of people like me, people with cytonic powers. Before we'd crashed on Detritus, we'd worked in the ships' engine rooms, powering and guiding our travel.

They'd just called us the people of the engines. Other crew members had shunned us—instilling in our culture traditions and prejudices that had lasted even after we'd forgotten what a cytonic was.

Could it all be just superstition, or was there more to it? I had felt the malevolence of the eyes. In the end, my father had attacked his own flight. We blamed the Krell for that, but I worried. He'd seemed so angry on the tapes.

I worried that whatever I was, my actions would bring more danger than any of us understood.

"Guys?" Sadie asked, pulling her ship up alongside mine. "What does this warning on my console mean?"

I glanced at the flashing light on the proximity monitor, then cursed under my breath, scanning out into the void. I could just barely see the Krell monitoring station out there, and as I watched, something new appeared next to it. Two objects that were even larger than it was.

Capital ships. "Two new ships just arrived in the system," M-Bot said. "My long-range sensors confirm what Flight Command is seeing. They appear to be battleships."

"Scud," FM said over the line. So far, we'd faced only other fighters—but we knew from stolen intel that the enemy had access to at least a few large-scale capital ships like these.

"We have limited data on armaments of ships like those," M-Bot said. "The information you and I stole contained only generalized information. But my processors say those ships are likely equipped to bombard the planet."

Bombard. They could fire on the planet from outer space, hitting it with enough firepower to turn even those living in deep caverns to dust.

"They won't be able to get past the defensive platforms," I said. That was, we assumed, why the Krell had always used bombers in the past, not orbital bombardment. The planet's platforms had been built with countermeasures to prevent bombardment from a distance. With the platforms, any attack would be a suicide mission.

"And if they just destroy the platforms first?"

"The defenses are too strong for that," I said.

It was bravado, in part. We didn't know for sure if Detritus's defenses could prevent a bombardment. Perhaps once we gained control of them all, we'd be able to determine their full capabilities. were months away from that, though.

"Do you hear anything?" Kimmalyn said.

I reached out with my cytonic senses. "Just a faint, soft music," I said. "Almost like static, but . . . prettier. I'd have to get closer to hear specifics of what they're saying."

I'd always been able to hear that music—sounds coming from the stars. During my months of training, and talking to my grandmother, we'd determined that "music" to be the sound of FTL communications being sent through the nowhere. Likely, what I heard now was the sound of that station or those battleships communicating with the rest of the Superiority.

We waited for a long time, orders saying for us to hold position to see if those battleships advanced. They didn't. It seemed that whatever they'd been sent to do, it wouldn't happen in the immediate future.

"Orders are in," Jorgen eventually said over the comm. "Those battleships are settling in, so we're to report back at Platform Prime. Come on."

I sighed, then turned my ship around and headed toward the planet. I'd survived the battle.

Now it was time to go get yelled at.

Eichmann's Executioner

EICHMANN'S EXECUTIONER

A NOVEL

ASTRID DEHE and ACHIM ENGSTLER

Translated by

Helen MacCormac and Alyson Coombes

THE NEW PRESS

25 YEARS

NEW YORK
LONDON

The idea for this novel and some of Nagar's words came from Netalie Braun's film *The Hangman (Hatalyan)* (Pardes, 2010).

Requests for permission to reproduce selections from this book should be mailed to: Permissions Department, The New Press, 120 Wall Street, 31st floor, New York, NY 10005.
Published in the United States by The New Press, New York, 2017
Distributed by Perseus Distribution

ISBN 978-1-62097-301-1 (hc)
ISBN 978-1-62097-302-8 (e-book)
CIP data is available

The New Press publishes books that promote and enrich public discussion and understanding of the issues vital to our democracy and to a more equitable world. These books are made possible by the enthusiasm of our readers; the support of a committed group of donors, large and small; the collaboration of our many partners in the independent media and the not-for-profit sector; booksellers, who often hand-sell New Press books; librarians; and above all by our authors.

www.thenewpress.com

Book design and composition by Bookbright Media
This book was set in Goudy Oldstyle and Erased Typewriter

Printed in the United States of America

10 9 8 7 6 5 4 3 2 1

One

A narrow street in Holon in the industrial suburbs of Tel Aviv. A short, stout man, in his early seventies or maybe older, steps out from one of the small houses huddled beneath blocks of high-rise buildings. He is wearing a black coat, white shirt, and black trousers. A carefully trimmed white beard frames his weathered face, there's a black cap perched on the back of his head, and white curls hang down from his temples. He is holding a small suitcase in his right hand.

His dark eyes are alert; the old man looks around cautiously before he closes the door, he walks down the path cautiously, and cautiously opens the gate. Once he's on the pavement, he is filled with unease. He scurries down the street with hurried steps, looking over his shoulder all the time, stepping into the road, then back onto the pavement. In the end, he starts running sideways like a crab trying to keep an eye on what is ahead and behind at the same time, as if he dare not turn his back on anyone or anything.

He is on his way to the outskirts of the neighborhood. When he gets there, he is distressed and exhausted and doesn't calm down until he sees the sheep pen in front of him. He sets down the suitcase and wipes the sweat from his brow. As he turns around one more time, his eyes scour the cypresses and palm trees, the run-down huts at the foot of the hill, the fences made of corrugated iron.

Everything is as it should be. The old man goes to a shed beside the pen, made from rough planks of wood. He swaps his black coat for a blue smock hanging on a nail. Then he puts on a blue apron, opens the suitcase, and takes out a pair of thick rubber soles, a towel, and a wooden box. He ties the soles to the bottom of his shoes.

He opens the latch on the gate. The animals know his voice and he talks to them while he holds one back and pushes the others away. He forces the chosen sheep to the ground, binds its legs together with two ties. Then he heaves it into the wheelbarrow. Its body hangs over the side, the bound legs stick out. The animal is calm. It stares at the old man, as if it has been stunned. He opens his wooden box, takes out a knife and a whetstone, slides his thumb along the blade, holds it up to the light, and then starts sharpening it with rhythmic movements. The sheep watches. His skilled hand makes the steel ring; again and again the old man tests the blade, there's not a single nick left to be felt or seen, but he carries on sharpening the knife. There are nicks a human eye can't see, a human thumb can't feel. Nicks from tongues of flame and dark wings. Away with them! The law insists on purity—of spirit, not steel, sharpened beyond the blade.

The old man takes hold of the sheep's head, gently lays its ears across its eyes.

He says a prayer.

He cuts the animal's throat; separates arteries, veins, windpipe, and gullet in a single stroke.

On the other side of the compound, a man is pushing someone in a wheelchair. They are on their way to the meeting place, an improvised space in between the chicken coops and backyards with a fire for cooking meat and making tea, a wooden counter, a plain wooden table, folding chairs. It has a makeshift roof, planks supported by seven poles, which would hardly withstand a heavy shower.

The man in the wheelchair is pushed to the table. He doesn't move his head and his pinched features stand out. He is clean-shaven, his gray hair is cut short, and he's wearing a checked scarf around his neck to keep him warm. The other man, sturdy, with a beard, puts a hand on his shoulder, then goes to the fire, where he sets a saucepan of water to boil.

When he returns, he is carrying three mugs of steaming-hot tea. He pulls three pears and a knife out of his coat pocket, slices the fruit, and sets the pear halves beside each mug before he slips the knife back in his pocket. Then he sits down on one of the folding chairs. The sounds of the chickens, ducks, and geese surround them—a rising and falling antiphony to confirm the birds are there.

The sturdy man's chair is too small; he keeps changing his position, as if he would rather be standing. The man in the wheelchair hardly moves at all. His legs are paralyzed and his other movements are restricted. He can't lift his hands up high or turn his head very far.

The old man arrives still wearing his smock and the blue apron, which is now stained with blood. He sings as he walks and then starts to hum when he reaches the meeting place; he hums when he touches the sturdy man's shoulder and the shoulder of the man in the wheelchair. Then he sits down between the two of them and starts drinking his tea.

All three men are wearing the kippah, the flat cap that covers the back of the head and signifies fear of God. The old man is the only one with forelocks. He takes another sip of tea, leans back, folds his hands on his chest, and starts to tell his story: How was I supposed to know who Eichmann was? Adolf Eichmann. I'd never heard that name before.

The old man is Shalom Nagar. The sturdy one is my friend Ben. The man in the wheelchair is me, Moshe.

Nagar brought Eichmann back. I had nearly forgotten about him. The folders where I kept the newspaper clippings about him and the trial lay in a corner of my shelves, buried beneath my music scores. Books about his crimes are sealed with cobwebs, books that I used to keep at my fingertips and studied for such a long time. At some stage I just left them lying there. Why? I don't know the answer. Maybe because I didn't understand; maybe because I'd lost sight of what I was trying to understand. Eichmann went away.

He returned when Ben took me to see a film, a documentary called *The Hangman*. It was about Shalom Nagar—prison guard, kosher butcher, healer—Eichmann's executioner. Later we heard that Nagar had been invited to attend the film, but he hadn't shown up.

I know him, Ben said. He lives here in Holon, not far from you. We can visit him, if you like.

I didn't know if I wanted to. Eichmann, I thought, if he were Eichmann, I would want to meet him. Alone. But did I want to meet Eichmann's executioner?

Ben picked me up the next day. He pushed me past Nagar's little house, pushed me to the outskirts of our neighborhood, he pushed me past the sheep pen and over to the meeting place.

There was the old man, looking just like he did in the film, sitting there as he'd done in the film.

Shalom, this is Moshe, Ben said. An old friend of mine. He would like to meet you.

Nagar looked at me with dark restless eyes, nodded, and started to speak, said what he'd said in the film, introduced himself with his story, the text that has become a part of him: How was I supposed to know who Eichmann was? Adolf Eichmann, I'd never heard that name before. I came from Yemen when I was just a boy, you see, thirteen maybe fourteen years old. They'd told us about the war, not about all those other things. Eichmann? Who was he? I didn't find out about him until I had to guard him.

Eichmann's executioner? There are doubts. Was it really Shalom Nagar who pressed the button on May 31, 1962, opening the trap door through which Adolf Eichmann fell with a rope around his neck? And during that night, was it Nagar's hands that pushed Eichmann's body into the oven, to burn him to ashes?

   Nagar insists this is the case; he is possessed by this person. Eichmann is still there, he believes. Eichmann is out to get him. He, Shalom Nagar, Eichmann's executioner, will be the final victim. Because there is one missing. Nagar believes Eichmann wasn't done. There is still one Jew left on his list.

How was I supposed to know who Eichmann was? Adolf Eichmann, I'd never heard that name before. I came from Yemen when I was just a boy, you see, thirteen maybe fourteen years old. They'd told us about the war, not about all those other things. Eichmann? Who was he? I didn't find out about him until I had to guard him. Now I know him, he is here every day, I know everything—

   Who is here every day?

   Eichmann!

   Eichmann is dead, Shalom.

   I was his bodyguard, Ben. I was with him in his cell. There were three guards, one in the cell, one in the hall, one in the next room. I was with him in his cell. I went with him everywhere, even to the toilet. I had to.

You had to smell his stench?

No, no. The Germans are clean, Ben. So clean! They are evil. Eichmann was evil, too. When he went to the toilet the first thing he did was pull the chain. There was water running the whole time while he did his business. He didn't want me to smell anything. Then he stood up and closed the lid and washed his hands, twice, three times. If I hadn't known who he was, I'd have thought: What a saint. They've caught a saint. He never did anything wrong. He thanked me for everything, *gracias, gracias,* he said. That's Spanish for thank you.

Do you speak Spanish?

No. How could I? We communicated with our hands. It was the only way—he couldn't speak Hebrew, I couldn't speak German. But we understood each other. I had to fetch Eichmann's food. I always put it on a special tray with a lid that had a lock. I had to make sure that it stayed closed all the way from the kitchen to his cell. So that no one could put anything in it. They could have paid someone to put poison in his food.

Who's they?

People who wanted revenge. And the ones who didn't want him to talk. Everything had to be secure. Eichmann poisoned in prison! Imagine the scandal. It was an international trial after all, the whole world was watching. I went into his cell with the tray. But before I was allowed to give him the food, I had to test it first. He said: You must test it first, Shalom!

Who said?

Merhavi, my commander. Once I asked him: Why do I have to test his food? Why can't someone else do it? He said: Listen, Shalom, if we lose a Yemenite, that's not a problem. Many Yemenites have died. But Eichmann mustn't die. It's an international trial.

If you spend a long time looking out for someone, you get close, familiar. You start to feel sorry for him. I could never have hit him. I never struck a prisoner, ever. Merhavi came to me after the sentence was announced, Eichmann was supposed to be hanged, but he had done something—he didn't want to accept the judgment.

He appealed?

Yes, and no one knew how long it was going to take. Merhavi came to me and asked: Shalom, when it is time, would you be prepared to press the button? I told him that I didn't want to. Everyone else wanted to, I was the only one who didn't. In the end we drew lots. And Merhavi said: This is an order, Shalom. You won, you have to do it.

When the day came—I had the day off that day—they came to fetch me. I was out for a walk with Ora and our little boy, and then a car stopped next to us; the door was opened, the commander pulled me inside, and we drove off to the prison. Eichmann was going to be hanged that evening.

Everything went very quickly. We lowered the rope, put the noose over his head, and I—I went over to the table. I pressed the button. And the trapdoor opened and he dropped.

I was twenty-six years old at the time, not really an adult yet. What did I know? I had never seen a man hang before. I saw his face as soon as I entered the chamber, white as a sheet. If you are strangled, the blood stops flowing to your head. And the eyes get forced out of their sockets. They came out.

His eyes had fallen out?

Bulged out. As if they were trying to touch you. And his tongue hung out of his mouth down to here.

To his chest? His tongue?

To his chin. His tongue hung down past his chin, I don't know why. It was all bloody. That was from the pressure of the noose on his throat. The mere sight of it made me ill. I hid behind my colleagues, so the commander wouldn't call me. But then Merhavi shouted: Nagar, come here! I said: Leave me alone, Chief, I can't bear it, I can't look at him. He said: Get over here now, Shalom, no discussion. This isn't a game.

So I climbed onto the gallows to pull Eichmann up so that Merhavi could remove the rope. Eichmann hung there with his head to one side, watching, he almost touched me with his eyes. I started to shake. And then he said something.

Who?

Eichmann!

How could he? He was already dead.

He had said something before he died. It's like the radio. When you pull out the plug, it carries on playing for a moment before it stops. When people die talking, the same thing happens. Their last words stay with them when they die, and if they can, if there is any air left, they still have their say.

That's what happened with Eichmann. I didn't know his stomach was full of air, so I grabbed him round his belly and out it all came. I couldn't understand the actual words, but it was a curse. He cursed me. And all the blood shot out of his mouth with the words. He spat in my face. The commander was safe behind me. All the blood hit me. The little Yemenite.

And then—

That's enough for today, Shalom. Moshe needs to get home.

No. Wait, Ben, I want to finish the story. You know I tell true stories, not nonsense. One guard on either side and Eichmann in the middle. That was the order. When his lawyer came, when he was allowed onto the roof, whenever he went to the toilet: I tied him up—

His arms or his legs?

Arms and legs.

How on earth could he go to the toilet then?

When we got there, I removed the ties. That's how it was, one guard on either side, and Eichmann in the middle. And then when I went back to work, it was me who had to be guarded!

What do you mean, Shalom? Why were they guarding you?

They protected me! After—after that night I was given three days off—to recover—and then I was supposed to go back to my duties. But I couldn't. I could hardly manage to climb the stairs. I didn't dare go up to the second floor where his cell was, Eichmann's apartment we called that wing. I was sure he was waiting for me there. That's why they gave me the guards: two colleagues who walked on either side of me when I did my rounds. The commander didn't like it, of course. My colleagues were needed elsewhere. It was very embarrassing. But what could I do? I couldn't get Eichmann out of my head.

Week after week, month after month, I still needed the guards. A year went by. A whole year of fear and nightmares every day. Because of Eichmann, because he spat that blood all over me. When I was awake, I was afraid he might appear; when I was asleep, he haunted my dreams.

When the year was over, I went to Merhavi and said: This has got to stop, Chief, let me do my rounds on my own again. I want to get over this. He agreed.

It seemed all right at first. No problems on the ground floor, or on the first floor. I felt fine. But then, when I was on my way up to Eichmann's apartment—I was nearly at the top of the stairs—I heard his voice.

Eichmann's?

Yes! Quite clearly.

How?

I don't know how—it was just there, Ben. I was on the stairs when I heard him. I walked on, slowly because my knees had turned to jelly. I'm walking along the corridor and can't hear anything. I reach the first door and take the keys out of my pocket. My hands were shaking. I could hardly fit the key into the lock. I unlock the door. Everything is quiet. I unlock the second door and walk into the hall. Just a couple more steps to his cell door. The hatch is open. One step. My legs don't want to move. Another step. I can't go any further. I stand on tiptoe. The light from the hallway shone into the cell through the hole in the door—a bright square at an angle to his bed.

And there he stood, staring at me, like this, with his head on one side.

I felt giddy, couldn't find my keys, managed to get out of there somehow, ran through the corridor. When I reached the stairs, I heard him shouting, *gracias, gracias,* and then—I woke up in hospital. I had fallen down the stairs, broken my leg and cut my head. Merhavi wanted to know what had happened. I told him everything. You saw your shadow, Shalom, he said.

He only feels safe when he's at the shed beside his sheep, his hens and geese, the animals he takes care of, feeds, and kills. Eichmann doesn't come here, he says.

Why not? Ben asks. He's happy to give Nagar the prompts he needs to weave his story. Why not?

He can't stand the sight of blood, Ben. If the prison doctor wanted to do a blood test, Eichmann had to lie down, or else he would have fainted. One time when he visited a bullfight he really did faint. His bosses didn't care. They sent him to the East. It was his job to report on . . . how the Jews were being murdered. They were shot. Hounded into pits, naked, and then the Germans shot them. Eichmann couldn't bear to watch. He looked away and waited until the pits were full and covered with mud. At one of these shootings, his black leather coat got splattered with blood. He took it off straight away even though it was freezing. It was no use, though. They drove back past the pits. They were sealed with a layer of mud so Eichmann thought he could risk taking a look, and then a fountain of blood shot up right next to his Mercedes.

Shot up, how?

I don't know, I wasn't there, and Eichmann didn't explain. Maybe there were just too many bodies piled on top of each other, the pressure kept building up until the blood came spurting out—

Onto Eichmann's Mercedes?

Or just next to it. Eichmann felt sick, the driver wanted to stop, but couldn't because of all the blood. They had to keep going. It was too much, I was exhausted, Eichmann said. I felt as if I had been beaten. I do not have the required robusticity of feeling.

The what?

Robusticity—he used words like that.

Did he say that during the trial?

No, to me.

How do you know what he said? You can't speak any German.

He said it in Spanish.

But you can't speak Spanish, either.

But he thought I could because I'm from Yemen, I'm a Sephardic Jew and the Sephardim come from Spain. That's what he thought.

Nagar makes it up as he goes along. I was tired when Ben took me home. Tired but filled with a strange kind of energy. Eichmann, Eichmann, Eichmann was back.

A few days later, Ben took me back to the meeting place. Nagar wasn't there. Ben made three mugs of tea, fetched three pears from his coat pocket. There was no sign of Nagar.

A storm was coming. Lightning struck somewhere; then it started to pour. There were puddles and streams everywhere, including where we were sitting. Ben stood up to keep a lookout for Nagar. He didn't catch sight of him at first, but then he saw him standing under the porch of his sheep shed where it wasn't too wet. Ben signaled to me, grabbed the wheelchair, and started pushing me along as fast as he could.

In some places there were huge puddles blocking our way, while in others the ground was so saturated the wheels got stuck. Ben pushed, pulled, steered this way and that. Somehow he managed to keep the speed up. The wheelchair slid and lurched all over the place, but I enjoyed the wild ride. It was the price we had to pay to get to Nagar's safe shelter—or so it seemed to me. I held on to the armrests and egged Ben on, shouting instructions as if we were trying to win a race. Two old men behaving like children.

We reached the shed soaked through and laughing. Nagar was just drying his hands. A bedsheet had been fastened to the wall, and a plucked chicken hung on a string in front of it.

Ben was still charged with energy and stared at the chicken for a moment before giving it a little push that set it gently swinging to and fro, while pale red liquid dripped from its slit-open gut.

Nagar was not amused by his antics. He didn't approve. He grabbed the chicken and held it tight. He sounded ceremonious all of a sudden. The sound of his voice was forever changing to suit his mood. Now, he rallied it in a darker tone: A woman from the neighborhood is ill, Ben. She won't eat or speak, no one knows what is wrong with her. The doctors can't help. They are rely-ing on me. I have healed people before. They say: You have the gift, Shalom. I don't know about that. I take a chicken, wrap it in a sheet, and wave it above the head of the person who is ill. I pray, and they get well. What did I do? Not much. I prepared the chicken, no more, no less. It has to be drained of blood. That's the main thing. The soul's dwelling is in the blood, it needs to get away, must not be touched. The chicken has to be completely drained of blood.

That's what Shalom does. That's how he heals. The words and the way they were said had the desired effect. Ben didn't say any-thing; he felt ashamed. And even Nagar seemed moved by the scale and significance of what people believe he can do. They are all in awe of Nagar the healer.

It wasn't pouring as much as it had been, but large drops of rain still smacked the ground and pelted the iron roof of the shed. Thick, dark clouds were everywhere and there was no sign of it getting any lighter. Ben looked at the sky anyway; Nagar stood beside him, his arms folded across his chest.

It is always raining in Germany.

That's not true, Shalom. What makes you say that?

When the Romans tried to conquer Germany, they got stuck in the mud. And the Germans, what were they called in those days—

Teutons?

The Teutons took their chance. They charged out of the woods and defeated the Romans. Every Teuton carried a weapon, men, women, children, even the elders, everyone. The Teutons always kept their weapons within easy reach. It was a question of honor. It was all that mattered. Honor! The Germans are evil. Eichmann—

What does this have to do with him?

Wait. Eichmann followed orders. Always carry a weapon. The Teutonic code. Of course Eichmann obeyed. He was always armed with a gun.

Even in bed?

He kept one in his bedside table. And he had secret drawers in his desk where he hid loaded weapons. The thought of actually having to shoot someone disturbed him, though. So he was constantly giving his guns away. His adjutant got one, so did his driver, even visitors were urged to take a gun from him. Here, take my gun. I insist. Yes, Herr Obersturmbannführer! *Jawohl!* But every time he gave one away, he was given two more. And there was a gun cabinet in his Mercedes packed with anything you can imagine, pistols, hand grenades, machine guns—

But he didn't shoot?

Never! He was too scared. He never shot anyone in his whole life. He couldn't. He can't stand the sight of blood, he can't shoot a living thing.

I don't believe you. He was in the war, he must have shot people.

He was in his office! He was responsible for transports, he ordered Jews onto trains. Trains, railway lines, timetables—that was Eichmann's world, Ben. He didn't have to shoot. Later on, he would moan: I was not allowed to be a soldier, I was never a commanding officer, I never got to see the front. Actually, it was what he wanted because he was scared. I still can't understand it.

What can't you understand?

How can someone who's evil be afraid?

You'll have to ask Moshe, Shalom. He thinks about that kind of thing, not me.

Nagar turned around and looked at me. He seemed to hesitate. So far he had only talked to Ben or into the space between us, as if there were another, greater audience out there somewhere. He had never spoken to me directly. Perhaps he was shy, or it could be a precaution. Ben was someone he knew. Ben fed him cues, Ben allowed him to make things up and go his own way. But who was Moshe? The man in a wheelchair who listened in silence, never showing any kind of reaction to Nagar's stories? Nagar knew nothing about me and couldn't tell that, in a different way, I was as close to Eichmann as he was. Or did he suspect something and that was why he ignored me? Could he sense that my thoughts were like music accompanying his stories, critical comments, corrections, detours, enhancements? Some of Nagar's words would unlock troves of memories in my head. In his office! Did Nagar know that Eichmann's office was nothing more than a briefcase in the beginning? Eichmann was a newsman when he started out; he collected news about Jews straight from the Jews. A newsman needs to be agile, pop up all over the place. He couldn't line them up in front of his desk because he didn't have one. So they met on the stairs, going up, going down, Eichmann listened, Eichmann asked the right questions, Eichmann learned, Eichmann took notes, created a position for himself as the expert on Jewish matters. He was given an office and it was as familiar to me as if I'd been in and out of it every day. As if I had walked the long diagonal from his desk to the door. It was a gargantuan desk and he liked to sit behind it, leaning back into the shadows while his desk lamp lit up the person opposite him. He wrote his transport orders at this desk, forced Jews into trains—a hundred, a thousand, hundreds of thousands—with one stroke of his pen. But one time—was it just the once?—he sent someone into a new life, set him free, didn't shout him down; instead, he shook his hand. Called him comrade, not half-caste or a pig. That was just as evil. An angel can fall, but a devil can't rise. There was no way back for Eichmann.

Nagar came over to me without saying a word. He leaned forward and studied my face, as if he were searching for traces of the words he could sense in my gestures but couldn't hear. How can an evil man be afraid? The answer?

I didn't have an answer.

Nagar turned away, winked at Ben, and shook his head in mock disappointment: Moshe's not saying anything.

Moshe is tired, Shalom. We're going to go now, even though it's raining. You should go, too. Ben pointed at the chicken still hanging in front of the white sheet. Your neighbor will be waiting.

She has been waiting all her life, Ben. She is a lonely woman. Everyone is dead. Her husband, her sons, and still she waits. I'll go to her.

Nagar took the chicken down and undid the string. Hold the sheet, Ben, but be careful. Don't let it touch the ground. It has to be clean, without any stains.

Ben held the sheet while Nagar wrapped it around the chicken and then tied the bundle up with string.

Let me tell you a story.

We're going now, Shalom. Moshe needs to get home.

It's raining far too hard. I'll tell you a different story.

Not too long?

No, no, a short story. What do you say, Moshe? One last short story?

I raised my hand to stop him, but either he misunderstood the gesture, or else he simply ignored it.

In the prison in Ramla, the prisoners were supposed to clean their own cells. They were each given a cloth and bucket. Most of them never bothered. They didn't mind the dirt. But when Eichmann arrived in Ramla, he said he would need two cloths: One to mop the floor and one to wipe it dry. And I would ask you to change the cloths once a week, he said. That's how neat and tidy he was! He swept the cell floor from corner to corner, wall to wall, every day. You could see your reflection in the tiles. Every morning he made his bed, shook out the blankets, folded them up, and put them one on top of the other. Once a week, he beat the mattress and turned it over. Twice a week, always on the same day, he washed his clothes, his shirts first, then his socks and undershirts, and finally his underpants. He hung them up to dry on the bars of the window in the bathroom, always the same way. Before he sat down at the table to write or read, he dusted the table top and the chair with his handkerchief.

He was pedantic.

He is German, Ben. Germans are like that. They won't tolerate filth. They want it gone. It has nothing to do with them, it should not be there. Away, away! Be gone! Eichmann had a project, what was it called—

Deportation?

No. No. Before that. Nisko! The Nisko Project. Nisko was a place somewhere, I don't know where, an awful place in the middle of nowhere. The Jews were filth for the Germans, so they were sent to a filthy place. Eichmann collected thousands of Jews, builders, carpenters, mechanics, and transported them there. When they arrived, they had to march for miles and miles. Then he made a speech. They were to build a camp with wooden barracks. But be careful, he said. Do not use the local water. There is typhoid and cholera in this area, the water in the wells is contaminated. You will have to dig new wells. Get fresh water at all costs. Or else— and then he paused and smiled: Or else you will die. That is how evil he was. That is why he liked things to be clean. Everyone had to be clean. The Germans think they are saints. White people!

He wasn't really white, Shalom. He was darker than most of them.

Yes, but he liked to have everything as white as possible. During the war he had an affair with a noble lady who only wore white dresses and white hats. After the war, he kept white chickens. Then he bred angora rabbits, each generation whiter than the last. And still it wasn't enough. The commander showed me a photo of Eichmann in Argentina. A barren landscape, covered in stones and dust, but Mr. Eichmann is wearing a white shirt and trousers. And sitting on a white horse! And then—

Shalom, stop!

That was a few months ago. We still visit Nagar at the meeting place or in his shed. Ben picks me up once or twice a week. Every time he takes me home, I think: That's it. I've had enough! Nagar can't stop, we know now. As long as we go to see him he will tell us his stories. And if we don't visit him he will tell someone else.

Shalom Nagar is laden with tales of Adolf Eichmann—they come pouring, splashing, spouting out, never ending, never stopping. Eichmann, Eichmann, Eichmann. Nagar has lived with him for fifty years. His life revolves around him. He's always repeating or contradicting himself, his stories are full of gaping holes. But it doesn't matter. He doesn't care. He's trying to protect himself. Nagar needs to spill blood to wash away Eichmann's blood, he needs to talk about Eichmann to drown out Eichmann's curse. Blood for his blood, words for his words, it's how he lives with what happened on May 31, 1962, the night that will never end.

He upsets me, he fascinates me, he poses a challenge. Nagar talking about Eichmann—the way he talks about him—feels like a reproach. What did I do instead? I hid Eichmann behind a white sheet. I made myself pure, I thought I was holy! All lies. I didn't forget Eichmann—that's another lie. I kept him secret!

I can't play the violin like my father or Eichmann anymore, so I compose music. I write themes that don't remind me of Eichmann, choose time signatures that distance me from him, and tones that sound nothing like what I heard in the courtroom during all those hours. How many hours? Hundreds, perhaps, while I watched Eichmann, saw his mouth twitch, studied his bearing when he rose to answer a question from the prosecutor or the judge.

And then this little old man comes along, folds his hands across his chest, and starts telling his stories.

This morning I took my file of newspaper cuttings from the shelf, wiped the dust and cobwebs off my Eichmann books. I am going to write. I am going to write about Eichmann. About Eichmann and Nagar, about the trial and everything else. The gallows, the rope, the prison director, the preacher, the president. The oven. I have no idea where this will take me. Perhaps I will begin to understand something that can't be understood. Perhaps not. But there is something out there that I must face. It is getting closer, it's closing in. The noise is destroying my music. I've run out of notes.

Two

A train rattles in the distance. The prisoner raises his head.

For a moment, his heartbeat merges with
the rising and falling sounds in which he
gradually recognizes the familiar driving rhythm, this iron pulse he once beat
himself.

What is the cargo? he wonders. Victims?
Then he needs numbers; he closes his eyes,
counts the carriages, there are not enough,
there were never enough. His life was too
short for the fanatical art of transport.

Reluctantly he shakes his head, opens
his eyes again, and now the silence falls
around him, the suffocating isolation
of his cell, which has no windows, is
surrounded by other rooms—occupied by
guards—and empty corridors, along which
they march him once each day when he is
allowed to go outside. Here, too, there are
only guards, no one else at all sees him, he
sees no one, and whatever it is he can hear
has no name. It is not a train. Do trains
even run in this country?

The prisoner, that's Eichmann?

    Yes.

    You're writing about Eichmann?

    About Eichmann and you, Shalom.

    Why?

When Ben picked me up, he saw the typewriter on my table.

    Are you typing music?

    I've run out of notes, Ben. I'm writing.

    You're going to be a writer?

    I'm writing.

    What are you writing?

    I told him.

    You're writing down what Shalom says?

    I'm writing what I think about while Nagar tells us his stories.

    Can I have a look? Ben asked. I didn't want him to. You read to us, then, he said. We'll go to the meeting place, like we always do, and you read what you've written.

    No, Ben. That's Nagar's meeting place. It's where he tells his stories. I write here.

    Writers need an audience, Ben said.

    But I'm not a writer, I just write.

    For yourself?

    I didn't know the answer.

    You're writing about Shalom, Ben said. He needs to know.

    Nagar needs to tell stories, Ben. He doesn't listen. He needs to talk. About Eichmann, his Eichmann. The Eichmann at the meeting place belongs to him.

    He tells stories, you write them and read them out loud, Moshe, Ben said. Two voices, why not?

In the end, I put the papers in my bag, the few pages I'd written, and Ben wheeled me to the compound. He made tea, as always, and cut up the pears. We drank, we ate, Nagar didn't come. At some point the chickens grew louder; it sounded as if they were complaining. Ben stood up, kept watch. He's coming, he said. Soon I could see him, too. He wasn't carrying his black case today, he had a white bundle instead, but he was singing as usual as he came over. I couldn't understand what he was singing, words in a language I'd never heard before, a happy melody, softly rising and falling. Maybe a song of praise to the day and the work done. As always, the singing turned to a hum when he reached us. He shifted the bundle onto the table, between the cups and pears, collapsed into his chair, studied his hands, rubbed them together.

My chickens—they've got wet feathers.

It rained a lot the last couple of days, Shalom.

It's not the rain, Ben. It's from within; they're restless. We've got to be careful. Let me tell you a story. Eichmann was given the same food every morning, two slices of bread—

Moshe has been writing, Shalom. He wants to read to us.

I want to tell you the story. You know I tell true stories, things that really happened.

Let's listen to Moshe's writing.

All of a sudden Nagar stood up. But he just took off his jacket and hung it on a nail. Then he sat down again, sat there in his white shirt in front of his white bundle, stared at my white pages. Said nothing. I picked up the first page, started to read.

`A train rattles in the distance. The pris-`
`oner raises his head.`

Nagar edged forward in his chair while I read, straightened up, lifted his chin—that's how he sat in Eichmann's cell, I thought, on his chair by the door. When I reached for the second page, he interrupted me.

The prisoner, that's Eichmann?

Yes.

You're writing about Eichmann?

About Eichmann and you, Shalom.

Why?

I want to know how it was.

I tell you how it was, Moshe! Again and again, I tell you!

Other people tell stories too.

Other people? My words echo across the compound like a threat. Nagar narrows his eyes, he's disappointed, disappointed and angry. Two voices? There's only room for one voice here. I've broken the law of the compound, Nagar's law, I curse myself, curse Ben, who talked me into it. He'll leave now, I think.

But Nagar didn't leave. The guard doesn't leave. He remains seated, he does not yield.

If you're writing about Eichmann, why call him the prisoner? There were lots of prisoners in Ramla, but Eichmann was Eichmann. You have to say Eichmann! A train rattles in the distance. Eichmann raises his head.

I call him the prisoner, Shalom. Then I say the accused, the condemned man.

Why? Are you afraid of saying his name?

As soon as I say Eichmann, I might as well stop writing. Everyone has heard of him, everyone knows what he looked like, everyone has their own Eichmann in mind and deals with him accordingly, an inner process that's triggered whenever his name is mentioned. That's not what I want.

What do you want?

I want Eichmann to be—

Like the first man? Adam?

If Adam stands for any man, for all men, then yes. We inherit the apple, not the sin.

But victims, why do you say victims? He's thinking about Jews, this German man. He transported Jews! It's us, the Jews, he wants to exterminate. You have to say Jews, Moshe.

I can't, Shalom. It wouldn't be right.

Why not? We are Jews!

That's why it wouldn't be right. I can't say Jews when I write about Eichmann. I'll stand before God as a Jew, not before the Nazis. And ye shall be unto me a kingdom of priests, so it is written. Day by day, hour by hour, we are Jews standing before God, who made a covenant with us, we are loyal, we are obedient, we keep his law. If I say extermination of the Jews, I place everything that makes us who we are before the Nazis. If I say victims, I keep us apart, standing before the Lord. That's how it was in the trial, too; the attorney general accused Eichmann in the name of the victims. The witnesses testified as victims. Jews like us, they testified as victims. He was judged in the name of the victims.

No, Moshe. They were crimes against the Jewish people.

There are no crimes against a people who have a covenant with God, Ben. The kingdom of priests cannot be defeated by man. Their faces are turned toward God! No man can defeat them. When they get beaten, they are victims. It should have been crimes against the people of the victims. And that's what I write.

They persecuted us because we are Jews.

Yes, but we cannot give them our Jewishness.

They took it!

Then we must take it back! They never had the Jews. They never had a single Jew. Never! Not a single one! Only victims. They had victims!

They don't understand. Ben looks confused, Nagar distraught, he jabs his finger in the air, points at me as if he wants to gore right through me.

Jews!

Victims!

I have to say victims, why don't they understand? Nagar runs his hand over the bundle on the table. Why is that? Superstition? Is he healing me? Himself? Us Jews? I see my hands shaking; I can't hold the pages anymore. They rustle as they fall to the ground.

Ben looks away. He picks up his tea, holds the cup in two hands.

That's your business, Moshe. You write, we listen.

His advice could mean one thing or another.

Ben touches his kippah, Nagar lays a hand on his arm. Ben passes him a piece of pear. Nagar waves him off. Reaches behind him, searches for something in his coat pockets, something he chews and then spits out again.

Let me tell you a story.

The sounds of the chickens surround them once more. Moshe's text nothing but an interruption, powerless in this place, alongside the shochet and healer. Finished before it's really begun. The overture a finale. Why did I let myself be persuaded?

Let me tell you a story.

Tell us. We'll keep them apart. Your Eichmann, my Eichmann.
But, Nagar, the day will come when they will meet despite us. One
will hang. And the other? Let's wait and see. You tell the story, I'll
continue to write.

Let me tell you a story.

Eichmann was given the same food every morning. Two slices
of bread, two kinds of sausage, a cup of coffee. I fetched the tray;
still in the hall, I tasted everything, had a sip of coffee, ate a small
piece of bread, a bit of each sausage. Then I took the tray into
Eichmann's cell. Eichmann stood to attention, I set the tray on
the table, he sat down and started to eat. When he was finished he
cleared his throat very politely, ahem, ahem, and I took the tray
away. It went like clockwork. One morning—

Shalom—

No, wait, Ben. I want to tell you the story. One morning I made
a mistake. I was restless and lost in thought because our little boy
was ill. He'd been running a fever for days. So I forgot to taste
Eichmann's breakfast. I set down the tray, sat down on my chair,
and thought about our son.

Eichmann starts eating. I look up at one point, he's still eating.
Deliberately, as is his wont. He's taking his time today, I think.
He's eating like this, slightly strange somehow, grinding his teeth
and swallowing all the time. I'd never seen him eat like this. I had
no idea, is he savoring the bread or doesn't he like it? I study him,
take a closer look—and all at once I realize that I didn't taste his
food!

I break out in a sweat, I leap to my feet, he is just putting the
last piece of bread into his mouth, his eyes question me. I point to
the plate, make signs, like this, can he tell me does he feel ill? He

doesn't understand at first. When he does understand, he shakes his head, hints at a smile, points at his plate, holds up two fingers and puts them down again, holds up six fingers. That was it: They'd given him six pieces of bread instead of two! I hadn't noticed. And Eichmann had eaten the lot.

I had no choice, I had to report it. Merhavi cautioned me severely, it was a serious offense. Then he started pondering: If Eichmann had eaten all six slices of bread, maybe the portions had always been too small? Merhavi asks the director, he asks the prison doctor, who says they should ask Eichmann.

And? What did Eichmann say?

No, no, Herr Director, Eichmann said. Two pieces of bread are perfectly sufficient. But if I am given six, then I must eat them all.

Orders are orders.

Exactly, Ben.

If you'd given him twelve, he'd have eaten twelve.

Twelve slices, *jawohl!*

Nagar laughs. He's pleased, he's in a placating mood.

Are you hungry? I've got some mutton—

No, Shalom. Enough for today. Moshe needs to get home.

Nagar nods, heaves himself off his chair, starts picking up the papers that are strewn all over the floor, dusts them off, folds them, and puts them in my coat pocket.

You'll read more tomorrow, Moshe.

There are finger marks on the pages when I pull them out of my pocket in my apartment, my outer shell. I wipe them off as best I can. You'll read more tomorrow, Moshe? No. No! I won't let them hear what I've written again.

The Inner Guard

The prison structure has no core, it is
makeshift and crude, blocks of varying
lengths and heights stuck together, a space
created from crimes that deny all contact
with the outside world.

There is only one route to the prisoner's
block. They must climb several floors,
cross yards, pass through nine locked
doors. The final door opens into the inner
area, made up of five rooms.

The first hall leads to the guards'
lounge area. The second leads to the cell
and the meeting room in which the prisoner,
surrounded by guards, sits behind a heavy
glass panel opposite first his lawyer, then
a preacher, and, on just one occasion, his
wife.

The prisoner's cell measures three by
four meters. Whitewashed walls, dark tiled
floor, a single bulb hanging from the white
ceiling. A bed, table, and chair are lined
up against the wall opposite the door. The
prison bed has a thin mattress and four
woolen blankets, which serve as the prisoner's bedsheet, blanket, and pillows.
While he sleeps, his checked felt slippers
sit neatly beside his bed, always on the
same tile, which is just the right size.

The books stacked on the plain wooden table
have pieces of paper sticking out of them
at all angles. A folding chair sits by
the table, back against the wall. There is
another chair next to the door. The first
guard sits on this chair; he watches the
prisoner. The second guard sits on a raised
chair outside the cell door; he watches the
first guard and the prisoner through the
open hatch in the door. The third guard
sits a few meters away, watching the second
guard. The guards work in shifts; twenty-
four hours on, forty-eight hours off. During their shifts, they sit for three hours
and then have three hours' rest, before
spending another three hours sitting on the
chair assigned to them. During his shift,
Shalom Nagar is the first guard. For four
lots of three hours he sits in the cell,
opposite the prisoner.

Nagar is twenty-five years old, short and
stout. His wide, smooth face is adorned
with a mustache, which is reminiscent of
Errol Flynn's and so does not suit him.
Before he was transferred to the prison service Nagar worked for the border troops as
a military engineer, defusing mines. Sometimes he says he used to be a paratrooper,
too, which always makes his colleagues
smirk a little. He was chosen to be a guard

in this block because he is not a victim,
he knows nothing of the extermination, and
does not speak either of the prisoner's languages, German and Spanish. But the prisoner thanks Nagar in Spanish, whenever the
guard carries out one of his rare requests,
and Nagar has learned to understand these
few words. Otherwise they communicate with
gestures. None of the guards carries a
weapon, none has the key to the room in
which he sits. When a guard enters one of
the rooms he locks the door behind him and
passes the key through the barred hatch in
the door to his colleague on the other side.
Every guard locks himself in. The last
guard, the inner guard—Nagar—locks himself in with the prisoner.

Are you still writing, Moshe?
Yes.
Are you saying Jews now?
No.
And Eichmann, are you saying Eichmann?
No.
It's his business, Shalom. Moshe writes what he writes.
I'm not saying anything. He can write what he likes.
And then Nagar stops talking. With his arms folded over his
stomach, he stares at the ground and stays silent. This time he's
the one to break his own law, undermining the purpose of this
place. The law says stories are told here; the law says Nagar tells

his stories here. Right from the start, I always assumed that Nagar had built this place for this very purpose, rough-and-ready like the sheep pens. Had made himself a little stage to do what he had to do. Tell stories about Eichmann. And now he is silent.

Ben is silent, too. Somehow, Nagar's law applies to him as well. Nagar tells stories so that Ben can ask questions. Directly or coupled with objections. Why? How? Didn't you just—? If Nagar is the storyteller, then Ben is the questioner. Someone who doesn't have stories of his own to tell. We met in a kibbutz when we were young, then we lost touch, and didn't find each other again until I got sick. Ben's wife was my nurse. She was the one who told me that he had been a bricklayer and then a policeman, that he hated being in the house, that he always left early in the morning and didn't come home until late at night. He had never told me anything about himself. Instead, he asked me questions. Even his greetings were questions. And so were his goodbyes. The same compulsion, I thought. Ben needs to ask questions the way Nagar needs to tell stories. Not because of the answers. I think Ben asks questions to keep things moving, to give everything its own proper order. He doesn't set the pace, but he keeps it steady. Endless questions, on and on. If he can't ask questions, can't keep the story moving, then he needs to move, like now; he stands up, takes our cups, although they are still half full, goes over to the fire.

Nagar shuffles his feet, twiddles his thumbs. Stays silent. The place is shocked by this breach of law. No sound at all. The spell isn't lifted until I take my eyes off the silent, shuffling Nagar and look across the compound, my gaze passing over chicken coops with wire mesh that has been mended time and again. Now I hear the squawking ducks, the honking geese one by one, and then all together as the noise swells, a clamoring backdrop cloaked in clouds of dust. Then the animals quiet down, as if on command. A dog barks somewhere. Ben returns with steaming cups of tea. Nagar stops shuffling. He takes a sip, it's too hot.

Let me tell you a story. Eichmann—

What about Eichmann?

Eichmann wrote, too!

He was a writer? Is that what you mean?

He wrote, every day. I don't know what.

He wrote in German, you don't understand German.

He writes differently now.

Differently? How?

So that I can understand. When he comes—you know what it's like when you've had a high fever and you start to feel better? Everything seems different. You hear things differently, you touch things differently, your feet touch the ground differently. It's different ground. Perhaps the world is different? That's how it is for me and Eichmann. He reads, and suddenly I can understand. He comes, takes his papers out of his pocket, holds them very near to his eyes, he hasn't got his glasses, you know, they were left in the cell—his eyes bulge out, they came out you see—his eyes read, and I understand.

Eichmann doesn't read to you, Shalom. Not with his mouth and not with his eyes. Eichmann is dead.

The Walk to the Roof

They monitor the prisoner's health and
safety; he must remain alive. He is to see,
hear, and breathe until the trial is over
and the verdict has been given. He is to be
alive when the sentence is carried out.

The guards are under strict instructions
not to give or allow the prisoner anything
that he could use to harm or even kill himself. These fears are rendered pointless
by his fervent obedience. He knows what is
required of him and he obeys. The guards
are more generous toward him as a result.
Of course, the lenses in his glasses have
been replaced with plastic; of course, any
staples and paper clips are removed from
documents before they are given to him; and
the ten cigarettes he is allowed each day
are lit by one of the guards. But they let
him keep his watch and give him writing
materials, all kinds of different pencils,
carefully sharpened.

He is examined regularly by a doctor, he
is well fed, and all food placed in front
of him is tasted first by Nagar. They want
to be careful; even here inside the prison,
some would have reason to kill the prisoner. The poison meant for him would result
in Nagar's death instead.

Once each day the prisoner is allowed to
get some exercise, on the building's flat
roof. When the time comes, Nagar knocks on
the door of the cell and his colleague on
the other side passes the key through the
hatch. Nagar opens the door, the prisoner
gets up and follows. He is flanked by two
guards, with Nagar in front. They walk
across the hall and pass through the nine
doors, cross the inner courtyard, the main
building, enter the stairwell, climb up
floor after floor.

It is usually quiet on the way up to the
top; shouts can sometimes be heard from
another wing, and then the guards hurry the
prisoner on until they reach the roof.

Barriers have been erected on the roof-
railings covered with sacks, designed to
stop anyone from being able to see the prisoner. He walks along the path created by
the railings, changing direction several
times before emerging into a square that the
guards call the sports ground. This area
is also screened off on all sides. A folding chair, just like those in the cell,
sits in front of one of the walls. Perhaps
they had expected the prisoner to use the
time to do gymnastic exercises, perhaps
they put the chair there as a piece of apparatus that would allow him to stretch, to

bend, to revive the muscles wasting away
from sitting and lying down in the cell,
to ensure he is ready. The guards give the
prisoner some space here, too, having stayed
by his side all the way up. He could do
anything he wanted.

But the prisoner just walks with even
steps, his arms crossed over his chest, his
head bowed. That is how he interprets the
command to do yard exercise, which for him
means a walk on the roof. Or is he daunted
by the sudden freedom, scared by the expanse
of sky that gapes above him? Does he not
trust the ground?

He takes a deep breath, then starts walking. He paces up and down the square as
always, step by step, as though that could
increase the space around him. He walks
down the side, turns around, walks halfway back, crosses the square, turns around,
walks back to the start. A pattern that
makes no sense, but that seems to be the
only one possible for him. He has never once
changed this pattern.

Today, however, the prisoner stops at the
end of the side wall; he seems to be listening, then he looks at Nagar's colleague,
who pauses too, he raises his left arm,
moves his hand up and down, points upward.
Nagar and his colleague follow his arm,

his hand, his outstretched finger. There
is nothing to see, although the prisoner
is not only pointing, he is explaining
something too, he talks continuously, as
though with friends, but says only one sentence, over and over. Always the same sentence, a German sentence.

Nagar searches the sky. No cloud, no bird,
no plane, just unequivocal blue, unmistak-
able as a piece of evidence. Is that it?
Or perhaps the prisoner does not even mean
something in the sky, perhaps he is simply
indicating a direction, beyond the wall.
That is where he came from, that is where
his house is, there, somewhere, was his
world?

The prisoner repeats the sentence once more
and then falls silent, crosses his arms
back over his chest, lowers his head again,
starts to walk. Tomorrow the verdict will
be given.

The Court

The next day they take the prisoner to the
capital; the procedure has long since become
a routine, and as with every routine it
feels like it will never come to an end.
None of the guards could say how many times
they have traveled this way over the last
few months—fifty, sixty? The prisoner will
know. Their destination is the Beit Ha'am, a
new cultural center that has been temporarily converted for the trial. Rooms have been
set up for the judges, the court archives,
the prosecution, the defense, for those
watching the proceedings, and for media
representatives from all over the world. The
courtroom is the hall intended for concerts
and performances.

There are screened-off walkways here,
too. Nagar's colleagues flank the prisoner,
Nagar himself walks ahead. At the door to
the courtroom they stop, wait for the session to begin. In the room—

The day before yesterday, Nagar suddenly denied that he'd ever
been in the Beit Ha'am with Eichmann. I've stopped being surprised by the fact that he's always contradicting himself, but this
was too much for me, too much for Ben. As if he wanted to retell
the whole story without him in it.

I don't know what Eichmann said at the trial.

What is that supposed to mean, Shalom? Of course you know. Every single word he said in court was translated.

I wasn't in the courtroom, Ben.

Don't say such nonsense, Shalom. It was you who told us how Eichmann arranged his pencils, how he stared at the defense, before he put on his headphones—

I heard all that, Ben. I didn't see it. My colleagues told me all about it. I was Eichmann's guard after they'd convicted him. Afterward! They announced the verdict and then I was made his guard. I wasn't with him in court. That was someone else who looked like me. Even Merhavi mixed us up sometimes. Yoram, he said, but he meant me, Shalom.

You said there were twenty-two guards in Ramla, from the beginning until the end!

There were, Ben. But they swapped out Yoram. He was—he was dismissed. I don't know why.

And then they took you because you looked like him?

It was an order, Ben. What could I do?

The television cameras of the Capital Cities Broadcasting Corporation are already running in the courtroom, hungry for pictures as they have been every day of the trial, they show the room in its entirety, pan across the ground floor, up to the gallery, where the chairs are still empty. The public waits outside; crowds of people started gathering at the gate hours ago, bringing with them a build-up of grief and hatred, and a call for retribution. The people

talk, discuss, demand, laugh to lighten
their souls.

Inside the hall it is quiet, so quiet that
the half-darkness seems even darker and the
shapes in the room become hazy. Everything
closes ranks, the place for the perpetra-
tor, the victims, the judges. The attorney
general and the defense lawyer are already
there, deep in conversation next to the
huge cupboard that separates the stage and
the auditorium. A picture without sound;
the microphones on the tables are still
switched off. The camera moves, dissatisfied, until it finds what it has been looking for: a trapezoid-shaped box, built
against the left-hand wall of the room, in
front of a door that forms the back of the
box. The remaining sides consist of wooden
panels reaching up to waist height, on top
of which stands a frame construction, made
of white metal. Thick glass panels have
been fitted into the frame on both sides,
unbreakable and bulletproof. The front,
which faces toward the three high chairs
of the judges, is left open. There are three
chairs in the box too, two plain chairs at
the back against the door and one in front
with armrests, pushed under a narrow shelf,
which is fixed between the two side walls.

The television camera captures the box

like a still-life painting. An arrangement of objects whose minimalist imagery was perhaps intentional, perhaps coincidental, the result of practical necessity and improvisation. Someone is supposed to be made visible here, exposed to all glances and yet protected at the same time.

A box but also a stake for the prisoner, not the center of the room but still the vanishing point. The ambiguity is reflected in the uncertainty of the name: glass box, booth, cage? The prisoner says: my glass cell, the dock.

The doors are opened now. The gallery and ground floor fill up and a low, polyphonic murmuring penetrates the room. The men and women, victims, relatives of victims, journalists, politicians, writers are restless, exhausted by the tension, preoccupied with themselves, their stories, their dead, with everything in this room that they want to hear, see, understand.

And, as always, they miss the moment when the door to the glass box opens and the accused is brought in. They do not see him until he is already sitting down, motionless as ever, his forearms resting on the narrow shelf that acts as his table, a writing case beside him, pencils in front of him, arranged as neatly as his tie. A

man of medium height, mid-fifties, thick
glasses, receding hairline. A clerk type,
whose ability to appear unnoticed never
fails to amaze. It is as if he circumvents
time, as if one could stare at the box with
the utmost concentration and still miss
the transition from empty glass box to the
box in which the accused sits. But perhaps
the guards also use the protection of the
murmuring, the unrest, the distraction,
to bring him into the room. His arrival
should not be an entrance. This is not
a show.

Three syllables are heard in a rising melody, as if a horn is being blown. The usher
has announced the start of the session.
The words are not comprehensible, although
according to the journalists he cried Beit
Mishpat—house of justice. The three judges
enter the room, everyone rises, and with all
eyes on him the accused, too, rises, lively
and lithe.

Nagar wasn't with Eichmann in the courtroom, he insists on that.
The man the cameras show beside the glass box is someone else,
someone who looked like him, with the same build, the same
astonished gaze, wearing the same odd mustache. Yoram, the man
they dismissed. The Nagar in the courtroom wasn't Nagar. Yesterday he went a step further: Eichmann wasn't Eichmann, either.

Let me tell you a story. Us guards worked double shifts. Twenty-four hours on duty and then we had forty-eight hours off. My shift always started in the evening. Merhavi had set it up that way. First the night with Eichmann and then the day with Eichmann. Handing over to the colleagues on the next shift, reporting to the director. When that was done, I packed my things and went to the bus station. I always waited there by myself, no one else ever took the bus at that time of day. But on this evening—

Which evening?

The one I'm telling you about.

Which one are you telling us about?

You'll hear soon enough, Ben. On the evening in question, someone's waiting, and turns around as I approach. He was wearing a large coat, a hat with a broad rim and a pair of dark glasses, sunglasses, even though it was getting dark already.

This sounds like a film, Shalom.

Hush! It happened just the way I'm telling you. I was tired, you see, I wanted to get home. And then there's this guy standing there with sunglasses on, although it was getting dark. His hands were hidden in his coat pockets. It was spooky. I wanted to turn around and go back to the prison at first. But I was wearing my uniform. You never run away when you are in uniform. You know that, Ben. So I stay where I am—then he says something to me. Don't you recognize me, Salaam? he asks. He spoke Yemeni! And he knew my name. I take a closer look, then I recognize him: an old friend from Sanaa. When I came here, to Israel, we lived together for a while. We hug each other, start talking about all sorts of things, he tells me that he's working as a journalist, I tell him I'm a policeman now. I know that, Salaam, he says. I know you're guarding Eichmann. I was waiting for you, I need to talk to you. It's important, Salaam, he says.

But Merhavi had forbidden us guards to talk to anyone about our work. We couldn't even tell our wives anything. Ora had no idea that I was guarding Eichmann, until—until the day. But my old friend knew. I said: Look, I can't talk to anyone about it. All right, Salaam, he said. I can understand that. I'll do the talking.

I didn't want to listen. I stared down the road to see if there were any car lights coming our way. Nothing. The bus didn't come either. What could I do? My friend spoke and I listened.

It's all a huge fraud, Salaam, he said. What are you talking about, I asked, and he said: The trial. The trial is one big fraud. The man in the glass box isn't Eichmann. He's just pretending to be Eichmann. It's all a farce, a play for the TV cameras, he said.

A madman. What are you telling us, Shalom?

Wait and hear, Ben. The man in the glass box isn't Adolf Eichmann, he said. The real Eichmann works for the Israeli secret service. They need him here. He's the best there is. Did you know that he was a news specialist for the Nazis before he organized the transports, Salaam? Gestapo, do you know what that means? Secret state police, he says. Mossad, do you see? And as no one is allowed to know—

Know what?

That Eichmann is working for our secret service!

Rubbish!

That's what you say, Ben. He said the whole thing is complicated. He can't tell me details, but he has got proof. Eichmann works for Mossad, at the highest level. And because no one must ever know, they've decided—

Who?

I don't know. All he said was: They've decided to let Eichmann die. For appearances' sake, of course. So they make up a fantastic story: Adolf Eichmann kidnapped in Argentina. Brought to Israel. Questioned, put on trial, sentenced. The Nazi pays for his crimes! But in fact it's the other way around, Salaam, they are paying him. They give him money, a lot of money, to teach them everything he knows. He's their master. No one must ever know. That's what the trial is for. A farce. The script was written by a famous American author. And you are guarding the leading man, Salaam, he said. You and your colleagues, you are guarding an actor. While the real Eichmann watches behind the lines. He's probably laughing because the man playing the prosecutor is such a ham, but maybe he's annoyed, too, because they've chosen such a slow, untalented guy to defend him.

Day after day you've been sitting in a cell with an actor, Salaam, he said. You taste the food for an actor to eat. You go to the toilet with an actor, you take an actor up onto the prison roof. Do you think the real Eichmann would grovel like that? Do you think he'd let himself be kidnapped just like that?

Mad. Mad, Shalom!

He can prove that Eichmann disappeared after the war, he said, with cases full of gold. They hunted him in the Alps, but he was in Argentina all along. He built himself a white villa in a park that was patrolled by guards with German Shepherd dogs day and night. He was friends with President Perón, walked in and out of the Government Palace whenever he liked. He received visitors from all over the world. Everyone came to seek his advice, Salaam, he said.

Mossad was watching Eichmann even then, of course. They were informed of his movements. And at some stage they decided that he shouldn't be working for Perón anymore, he should be working for them. They broke into his home, lay in wait for him, and made him an offer he couldn't refuse. Since then, he has been living in Israel with his wife and his sons. But no one knows that he is Eichmann. They have given him a new name and a new identity. You actually know him, Salaam, he said. But it is too dangerous to let you know who he is.

I didn't know what I was supposed to think. My friend talked at me, quickly and excitedly, and smoked one cigarette after another. My head felt clouded in fog. I couldn't think straight anymore.

I can see you don't believe a word I've said, Salaam, he said. I can understand that very well. I can prove everything I've said, but there is no time, I've got to be careful. Listen: The real Eichmann fractured his right hand in a motorcycle accident. He had to have several operations, it took months before he could use it again. During that time, he taught himself to write with his left hand. Later on, he went back to writing with his right hand, but then he fell down the stairs at his office and broke his right hand again. Since then he has always written with his left hand. And now, think, Salaam, which hand does the man you guard write with? I didn't have to think: He uses his right hand, I said. There you go, Salaam, my friend said. They didn't think of that. And they've made more mistakes. For the final proof, I just need to talk to the man you are guarding. A thousand dollars if you can find a way to smuggle me into his cell. Think about it, Salaam. I'll be waiting here for you at the end of your next shift.

And then?

He didn't turn up, Ben. I never heard from him again.

But you didn't believe him?

What was I supposed to believe? Everyone said: That is Eichmann.

The Verdict

The accused is charged with crimes against
humanity, crimes against the people of
the victims, and war crimes. The charges
include fifteen counts and the verdict is
given over a period of fifteen hours, during which the three judges take turns to
read. From the tangle of facts and puzzles,
explanations and ambiguities, confirmations and doubts that are laid out on the
table after more than one hundred days of
trial, they have created a noose. A noose
that bears the burden of the victims and of
the law, a noose that will be used to hang
the accused.

Barely a soul in the room doubts what
the outcome will be, barely a soul follows
every part of the argument. The accused may
be the only one who never loses the thread.
He listens intently, hardly moving. Only
the left corner of his mouth, a tic that is
already well known. Occasionally he sits up
straight, reaches suddenly for one of the
pencils lying in front of him, scribbles
a word or two on his notepad, leans back
again, bends forward, puts down the pencil,
straightens it in line with the others.

Nagar, who is sitting by the half-open
side of the glass box, watches the accused

in the same way as he watches him in his
cell. He is the only one in the room close
enough to reach out and touch him. No need.
He can feel this man already, against his
will.

The onlookers, prosecutors, and judges
put the shifts between stillness and sudden movement in the glass box down to a
nervousness that the accused is struggling
to control, a desire to flee, triggered
by growing fear—Nagar senses a kind of
rhythm, a beating pulse that grows stronger with every twitch, every sudden movement forward, every pencil-grabbing motion.
Stronger and louder. A sound pattern is
created in Nagar's head, interfering with
the voices of the judges—the rattling of
trains on the track. The accused, Nagar
thinks, is following the judgment like
a timetable; he notes the sections of the
argument like passing stations, recognizes the movement of the points, the sid-
ings where the account occasionally pauses
before returning to the main track and
pressing on, unstoppable.

The man cannot escape who he is. He
remains the specialist whom he has declared
himself to be, the master of transport, even
though it was not he who ordered this particular journey, who named the destination,

and this time it is his own fate hanging
in the balance.

For better or worse he has chained himself to the trains. Since the days of the
cross-examinations, those carriages filled
with victims that shipped thousands, hundreds of thousands, millions of people to
their deaths according to schedule have
become his symbol.

In the Reich, which fell sixteen years
earlier, the accused was head of the sub-
department known as IV B 4. Responsible for
matters relating to victims and eviction.
Eviction, but also resettling, evacuation,
and transportation, which saw communities ripped apart, divided into victims
and perpetrators. The victims, it was
decided, must be eliminated from the German people, a sanitary procedure, which the
accused describes as a political solution.
Division of space in order to ensure that
the borders of the state were the same as
those of the people. First the victims were
ordered to leave the country, then they were
transported away. Transport means bringing people or goods from A to B using an
appropriate vehicle. The appropriate vehicle
for carrying the victims to the specified
destinations was the train. The transports
were organized and overseen by the accused.

```
Under the growing shadow of war, the polit-
ical veil finally slipped.
   What had begun as a division of space
eclipsed into a division of being, the
final, irreversible division. The Reich
transported its victims to their deaths,
orders were given for their physical exter-
mination. Gas chambers were erected at the
destination stations, beside them crema-
toria. The transports were organized and
overseen by the accused.
   The accused—
```

They keep interrupting me. I write as if they are watching me all the time; I write as if I have to justify myself. To Nagar, because I'm still saying victims, still won't say Eichmann, keep on saying Nagar, saying Nagar was in the courtroom, although, in fact, it was someone else, someone who looks like him. And to Ben, because I've lost my real purpose and have started writing a report, instead of telling Nagar and Eichmann's story.

Why are you giving us a history lesson, Moshe? Eichmann, the Nazis, what they were, what they did? I don't want to know about that. It's got nothing to do with Shalom.

Moshe's got us mixed up, Ben. It's a different Nagar sitting there in court beside the glass box, being made to listen.

You don't understand, Shalom. I mean—

I know Shalom doesn't understand. But me, I do understand, Ben. I know what you mean, I know why you're asking. I am writing about Nagar and Eichmann. I'm taking Nagar's lead, I follow him, I see Eichmann with him, see Eichmann over his shoulder,

see Eichmann in a way I could never see him in court. Eichmann
has come into his own; he acts how he acts because he did what he
did. This isn't a history lesson, Ben. It's a step back in order to see
the bigger picture. To see the order of things and the disorder that
is part of it all, just as Nagar is a part.

The Nagar in my head protests: Another Nagar, Moshe, someone else; the Ben in my head still isn't happy. Neither of them
wants to listen to me. Nagar rocks in his chair, he's started to hum,
Ben stands up and looks away. I write against their humming and
contention.

Gas chambers were erected at the destination stations, beside them crematoria. The
transports were organized and overseen by
the accused.

The accused does not deny this: After the
intended purpose of IV B 4, the political solution, had failed, naturally we were
recruited for the next stage of the final
solution. My orders were to oversee the
transports, and I knew that some of these
people would be killed in the camps, I must
admit that. But I had nothing to do with
the killing. My responsibility ended when
the transports were delivered to the destination stations according to the timetable.

A clear distinction must be made between
transportation and killing, he says. I
delivered the transports, but I did not
kill any of the victims. I have never

killed a single person. IV B 4 was responsible for transportation and in some cases
registration, but we were not involved in
the rest of the matter; our part was over
once we had created the timetables. We had
nothing to do with any atrocities, we simply carried out our duties in a decent
manner.

The spectators, among them victims who
had survived and countless relatives of
victims, had to bear these words for hours
on end. Everyone here in the room would
later be able to quote them, distraught,
disgusted, nauseated by the fanaticism of
this separation, which is embodied by the
accused. In his lost Reich he separated
people, in line with his orders, obediently;
now he severs these crimes, cuts a part out
from them, his part.

IV B 4 was responsible for obtaining the
train materials and creating the train
timetables. Period. As if this were all
just about objects, about iron and steel,
timings and routes, not about people. The
accused in fact consistently avoids this
word, talking instead about contingents,
numbers transported, numbers killed. Terms
so far removed from living languages
that for their own sakes the interpret-
ers attempting to translate the accused's

German into English and Hebrew have to
paraphrase, reducing the stark coldness
of his words. And yet still they remain
unbearable.

As if the victims were being exterminated
for a second time. In the accused's world
they exist only in trains, as goods to be
transported, as numbers to add up. Only
the matters that fall under your responsibility are real. IV B 4 was responsible
for transports; the rest did not concern
us. That the victims were ripped from their
homes, robbed of their possessions, driven
through streets, did not concern him. That
they were taken from the carriages at the
destination stations, forced into the gas,
burned to ashes that were blown back by the
wind, did not concern him. He saw trains,
not death, heard carriages rattling on
the rails, not the cries of the dying. The
boundaries of his responsibility were the
boundaries of his world. And the boundaries
of his world are, he says, the boundaries
of his guilt.

The judges reject these statements, unde-
terred and decisive. To them this is all
bureaucratic hair-splitting, lies told for
self-protection. Something that is whole,
they say, cannot be divided.

What do you mean, whole? The Ben in my head won't quiet down.

The judges mean the extermination of the victims.

The Nagar in my head rallies against me, stubborn, unequivocal. It's not right to say extermination of the victims. You must say the extermination of the Jews.

No, I won't say Jews.

The extermination—whose idea was it?

Hitler's.

Did he say: Exterminate the Jews?

I think so, yes. The order was never written down. But it existed in their minds.

In Eichmann's mind.

Yes. Eichmann didn't organize the transports because he loved watching trains roll.

Did you know that Eichmann never traveled by train? Never! He always went by car, a black Mercedes—

How could Eichmann ever travel by train? Trains went to the front or to the camps, full of soldiers, full of victims. There were no carriages for Eichmann. You can tell us what you like, Nagar, but not here at my desk. Tell your stories in your own space; tell them when I'm sat beside you. I am writing now. By myself.

A black Mercedes! A fast car with bright headlights, black leather seats, everything in black. Eichmann had his own driver. He sat in the back, with a gun cabinet to his right and a bar on the left he'd had built in, stocked with bottles of schnapps and red wine. The driver drove while Eichmann drank. They never stopped to rest, always looked sharp. They had so little time, the Germans! One day Eichmann had been somewhere, I don't know where, maybe where that project was being run—

In Nisko?

Nisko, yes.

No, Shalom. Nisko was before the war. You know that.

A camp! He'd been to a camp, Ben. Inspecting the ovens, making sure they were in working order and that everything was running smoothly. Things like that. So they drove back, late at night, they'd been on their feet all day, and then the driver fell asleep at the wheel. The car swerved and came off the road. Nothing else happened. But Eichmann still ordered his driver to get out and walk the rest of the way. Many, many kilometers—

How many, a hundred?

Not a hundred. But it was dark, it was winter, everything was covered in snow. The man nearly froze marching home. Eichmann didn't care. In the end the driver got sacked, not because he'd fallen asleep but because he stole a toilet seat from Eichmann's building. Dismantled it and took it away.

Why would he do that?

I don't know, Ben. Eichmann just said he dismantled it and took it away.

```
The physical extermination of the victims
was a single, all-encompassing action,
based on a single, all-encompassing order.
It cannot be divided up into individual
acts based on responsibilities. Regardless
of where a person entered the black river,
they were carried along to the mouth. The
main task of the accused, say the judges,
was not to procure railway carriages but
to procure victims to fill the carriages.
Each railway train filled with a thousand
```

people whom the accused sent to a place
of extermination, means he took part in a
thousand murders. Because this murderous
act forms a whole, the responsibility of
the co-perpetrators is equal to that of the
main perpetrators, that of those who carried out the crimes equal to that of those
who gave the orders. The accused is guilty
on all counts.

After the verdict is read, the accused is
permitted to give his closing statement. He
rises. Now, perhaps for the first time, people notice his broad shoulders.

His tone is sharp, his sentences, unusu-
ally for him, are short. In my hope for
justice I am disappointed, he says. I cannot accept this guilty verdict. He understands that the people of the victims
demand atonement for everything that was
done to them. But the crimes were not committed on his will. My wrongdoing is my
obedience, he says. I am not the monster
I am made out to be. I am the victim of a
fallacy.

On the following day, the court pro-
nounces the sentence. The accused stands
to attention. The accused is sentenced to
death.

Demons

Death remains strangely far away. The
condemned man spends as little time considering his own end as the millions of
deaths that cling to him, that should
mar his body, his face, beyond recogni-
tion. Nothing. Just a man, medium height,
mid-fifties. Dark blue suit, white shirt,
blue striped tie.

The sentence does not touch him either; it
is as though somehow it were lost between
the judges' chairs and the glass box.

If the sentence had not been spoken, but
had been presented in writing, Nagar would
have had to hand it over to the accused;
he is an extension of his arm within the
courtroom. Stand up, climb the steps up to
the judges' table, take the note from the
chair, climb down the steps, walk to the
glass box, hand the note to the accused, sit
down. Nagar would not have been able to do
this, he can feel it. Each step toward the
glass box would have taken him further away
from the accused. There is a gap that has
not closed. No one has penetrated the inner-
most depths of this person. People stand
before the wall of his castle, take aim
from there, even fire, but the space behind

those walls—the yards, the chambers, the
last room—remains unconquered.

Something is waiting there still.

The accused is guilty on all counts.

I am the victim of a fallacy.

The accused is sentenced to death.

This is a juristic death, a mere
possibility—no one knows if the sentence
can be carried out. Will the condemned man
be hanged, like the other German perpetrators in Nuremberg? A rumor passes around
the guards that he will be sold abroad.
Exorbitant sums are named; he is worth
these sums because he is the only one who
knows where the alleged treasure of the
fallen Reich is located. As soon as the war
ended, he singlehandedly moved it across
the Alps in an armored snow plow. The name
Blaa-Alm is heard, there was a cabin there,
the sentenced man was going to shoot the
landlord but he did not take his pistol out
of its holster; instead, he placed a bottle
of schnapps on the table and drank with the
landlord until he passed out. Nagar's colleagues crack their jokes, but he does not
join in their laughter.

The commander told him that every company
for which the accused has worked since the
war has declared bankruptcy. Nagar cannot

shake this thought from his mind, it
makes him feel uneasy. He sees the accused
working—apparently, he had started off as
a lumberjack—he sees the trees falling, sees
the axe, the sweat on his forehead, feels
the drive, the commitment this man takes to
work. That is not disconcerting. What is
disconcerting is the chain of bankruptcies.
Like an infection that spreads through contact. No one is immune.

The day after the sentence is given is
Nagar's day off. The breakfast table is
covered with newspapers, Nagar pushes them
aside, he does not want to read anything.
His wife, Ora, on the other hand, is eager
to read them; from the very first day she
has followed the trial in the media. All
the newspapers she has bought are piling up
in the shed.

Nagar is going to burn them, he does not
want an archive, does not need any commentary or printed pictures. He already has
too many in his head. He pushes his scrambled egg around his plate morosely. Picks
an olive out of the salad in front of Ora.
And then another.

Listen, says Ora, who has opened the evening newspaper. Immediately after the sentence there was a telephone survey. What
should they do with the condemned man? Exe-

cute him, not execute him? A third of the
participants are in favor of carrying out
the sentence, either here in this country or
there where the camps are that the condemned
man supplied with his transports. The vast
majority, however, want to keep the condemned man alive; if it were up to them, he
would be damned to a life of forced labor.
The same was said by an Italian poet and
chemist, himself a victim, in verse:

> Oh son of death, we do not wish you
>   death.
> May you live longer than anyone
>   ever lived.
> May you live sleepless five million
>   nights.

Nagar is happy that no one asked him. He
would not have known how to respond. Neither does he know how to respond to the
gloomy prophecy that Ora finds in the edi-
torial of the second newspaper: Now, only
now our demon dance begins. He simply
shrugs his shoulders.

Ora continues reading aloud, Nagar listens with only half an ear. They had
expected the death sentence . . . there
was no other choice . . . the defense will
start an appeal . . . Supreme Court . . .

```
three to four months . . . legal options
exhausted . . . state president. People
expect an appeal for mercy, but also that
the condemned man could be prepared to die.
Then he must be killed. But by whom? There
are no executioners in the country of the
victims.
   Nagar stands up, they are expecting
friends for lunch; he goes into the yard
where he keeps chickens in a small coop,
reaches for one of the hens, takes it into
the shed, lays it on the stained workbench,
takes a knife with a nicked blade, and cuts
off its head.
```

I wait for protest at this point, but the Nagar in my head simply raises his hands, to explain, to apologize. I wasn't a shochet back then, you see. What did I know about knives? I grew up with chickens; we even kept chickens in Sanaa, when my parents were alive. You feed chickens, slaughter them, pluck them, I knew all that. We'd use any old knife, cut off their heads. I was such a fool. You are permitted to kill, so it is written, but only in accordance with the law.

```
The animal twitches, its legs kick out, dig
into Nagar's lower arm. Now, only now the
demon dance begins? Nagar shakes his head,
waits for the twitching to stop. Then he
begins to pluck the chicken.
```

Whoever Rides the Tiger

The prisoner writes. He wrote while waiting
for his sentence, and now that it has been
delivered he carries on writing. So much to
say. So much still to explain.

He is happy that the guard, this strange,
small man, leaves him in peace. There are
already enough interruptions. The medical
exams are particularly arduous. The doctor now comes twice a day, as though they
are all afraid that his heart could fail
at any minute. Absurdity. Death does not
frighten him. It is only time he is lacking, he needs time to tell it how it really
is, he barely got to talk in court, they
always had to wait for the translations and
they always cut him off, for sixty days of
proceedings he just had to sit there and
listen to the prosecution's witnesses. The
victims, the victims. Yes, yes. Was that
it now?

The victims had been given enough time
to talk, to give vague recollections, to
lie brazenly, protected by their suffering.
They suffered, sure. Suffered terribly. But
he, too, is a victim! A victim of his obedience, of his loyalty to his oath, a victim of the speed at which his superiors and
employees changed their stories, those who

pinned everything on him after the war to
save their own soft skins. As though he had
run the Reich, as though he alone had dealt
with five or six or however many million
enemies of the Reich. Absurdity, insanity,
against which he had to defend himself—I
had to follow orders, I would never have
had the authority to act on my own initia-
tive, even when carrying out the evictions.
I had to present all matters to the head
of department IV for a decision and ask
for instructions. I could only do what my
department head ordered me to do.

The documents provided by the prosecution
prove this. I had to learn during the trial
that there are countless documents that
bear the seal of my department and my signature, but always and everywhere before my
name come the words "representative" or "on
behalf of." And when it says I, I instruct
and so on, that is just official German
language, the use of the first person does
not mean anything. "I" means only the competent authority, the one giving the order.

Of course, when someone takes out a single
document and plays it as the trump card,
as the attorney general did, then the whole
matter is turned on its head. You must consider the whole page in your hand. Then
things look very different. If you read

all the documents in chronological order,
everything looks different. Then it is
clear that IV B 4 was not involved at all
in these matters, I want to call them the
leading command processes. It was ordered
and so it was carried out. I had to obey.

And I did obey; I always carried out every
order I received, and I am still proud of
that today, because I fulfilled my oath.
The oath of allegiance is the highest duty
that can be given to a person, higher than
any so-called morals. Whoever fulfils
this duty ties themselves to their ances-
tral people and blood and must defend this
to enable the entire community to live.
These thoughts led me to subordinate myself
and to obey. Not as a stubborn receiver of
orders—that would have made me an idiot—I
shared these thoughts, I was an ideal-
ist. I came up with ideas, felt the joy in
creating something, and privately dedicated myself further to this outside of my
working hours. But when I presented these
ideas to my department head he just smiled
thinly, as if to say: Yes, very good, but I
can't do anything with that. And then I was
dismissed. I might as well have explained
it to his wastepaper basket. It was the same
throughout the years I spent trying to pro-
cure territory and land for the victims.

I wanted a humane separation, but all my
ideas were burned and smashed to pieces,
whether it was the project in Nisko on the
river San or the planned relocation to Mad-
agascar. It was as though everything was
jinxed. Whatever I planned and wanted and
did and wanted to do, fate somehow got in
the way and put a wrench in the works.

It was no different with the transports.
In general, the whole matter proceeded with
a great deal of hope; in the beginning the
trains ran and people could say it was a
matter of glory, but then there were stop-
pages that often lasted for several weeks.
We faced problem after problem, everyone
possible got in the way, so many people
stuck their oars in from outside or from
within that I had no idea what was happening anymore. Every authority felt they
needed to get involved, and in the end it
all went wrong.

IV B 4 battles with the Reich Transport
Ministry for transport materials, wins the
battle, the transport is approved despite
all the resistance, and then the bureaucratic machine stalls, there are no victims because there is too much red tape. A
thousand victims are needed for the transport to run, there are only one hundred
and fifty in total, the local commander

does not feel able to come up with replacements at such short notice, the train is
canceled. Again and again, it happened
that way.

I was always in favor of the political
solution, that was my field from the very
start, which I plowed together with leading representatives of the victims. When the
chief of the security police summoned me
to him one day, said a few words, and then
announced: The Führer has ordered the physical extermination of the victims, everything started to sway. I was done. I had
never thought it would come to such a violent solution. But whoever rides the tiger
is no longer able to climb down; he grabs
hold of the fur, like a small child, and
presses his head into the beast's neck.

I had nothing to do with the gas. If a
camp commander says he spoke to me about
the gas trials and we chose the method
together, that is a blatant lie. I played
absolutely no part in this matter, I had
no role at all, and I also had no power. I
knew the cardboard circles were being used
to kill, I cannot deny that, the camp commander showed them to me during a visit,
but IV B 4 was not part of this in any way.
When I discovered that my permanent representative had become involved with the gas

affairs, that he had somehow found a different way to get hold of the gas, we had
a big disagreement. Why are you getting
mixed up with the gas, I asked him, it's
got nothing to do with me. IV B 4 was not
involved with the gas, we could not give
any orders, we could not stop anything. We
had to deliver the transports in accordance
with our timetable, and that is where our
responsibilities ended.

But that is how it goes. Those who would
have been able to explain what happened are
either dead or have passed the matter on in
an attempt to exonerate themselves. And now
they are stamping my name on everything
that refers to what was done to the people
of the victims. So it was, and so it will
probably remain. I maintain today that the
entire human coexistence, at least in the
last two thousand years—but surely before
that, too—is one big and violent symphony
of lies and betrayal. People want someone
to blame, not an explanation; they found
their culprit, they kidnapped me, sneaked me
into this country, the country of the victims, where they prosecuted me and sentenced
me. Complicity, responsibility as one of
the main perpetrators, the public heard the
sentence, the cameras sent this fallacy out
into the world. It is the greatest consola-

tion for me: The dogs always bite those who
come last.

I am not stupid enough to believe that I
could fight it. The die is long since cast.
But one day it will be history that will
judge, not the people of the victims. His-
torians from all faiths and peoples will
study the trial down to the very smallest
detail, for the next fifty years and more.
And depending on the spirit of the times
it will be seen in different ways. Perhaps
students will discuss it for more than
fifty years. After all, it is complicated
and confusing. There is so much material, I
would be interested to read all the disser-
tations and theses written about my trial
over the next hundred years. The truth
about me will only be revealed some decades
from now. A library of books will first
spin legends about me. Until the web becomes
weak and the spider shrivels up from a lack
of fresh sustenance. But life is eternal; a
new spider will start spinning the web of
truth.

They cannot kill me in this country.
There is no end for me, just as there is no
nothingness.

I wrote all through the night, hounded and beaten by this voice, which grew louder and louder as I wrote, which separated each sentence as if it were an entity meant to quiver, sound, and shatter, a cacophony—and yet, with the last word complete, it was a composition after all.

```
There is no end for me,
just as there is
no nothingness.
```

I had fallen asleep at my desk, completely exhausted, and only woke up when Ben knocked on the door. My limbs ached. He frowned when he saw me, headed into the kitchen, made coffee, got me something to eat. I ate although I didn't feel like it and drank the coffee which was too strong.

Ben went to my desk, placed his large hands on the surface, stared at the pages I had filled with writing. Then he took one of them, went to the window, and started to read. At first, he mumbled to himself, then he started to read aloud, like an eager schoolboy, in his typical flat-sounding Ben-voice; wrong, it sounded all wrong, I couldn't stand it. Give that back! I demanded. Give it to me. I'll read! Astonished and baffled, he gave me the page. And I read.

Barked the sentences the way they have to be barked, hardened the beginning of each word, rolled my r's like Hitler, added the pauses after each conjunction so typical of Eichmann's speech, made periods sound like exclamation marks, kept time with the palm of my hand on the table.

```
It was ordered and—and so it was
 carried out!
I had to obey!
And—I did obey!
I always carried out every order I
 received,
and—I am still proud of that today!
Because—I fulfilled my oath!
```

Ben paced around the room while I read. Suddenly he stopped and leaned over me, looking angry. What are you writing, Moshe? What are you writing?

I didn't understand the question.

You are writing like Eichmann!

That is Eichmann, Ben! His words! I didn't invent them, I wrote them down.

Groaning, Ben straightened up, lashed out, sent the coffee mug flying. What?

Yes, Ben. That's Eichmann's voice. Listen:

```
A thousand victims are needed for the
transport to run! There are only one hun-
dred and fifty in total! The local com-
mander does not feel able to come up with
replacements at such short notice! The
train—is canceled!
 Again and again, it happened that way.
 Again and again!
 Again and again and again, it happened
that way!
```

```
I was always in favor of the political
solution—
```

Stop it! I don't recognize you, Moshe. I don't recognize you anymore.

```
I had nothing to do with the gas!
 If—a camp commander says—
```

Stop it, Moshe, stop it! You're a Jew, how can you give that monster a voice! I'm a Jew, how can you read to me like him!

Because he is a voice! Eichmann is a voice, Ben. I want all voices to have their say.

Ben doesn't understand. How could he, anyway? Like a stranger, he pushed me to the meeting place, pushed a stranger in front of him. The tension between us was palpable. Nagar, who was already there waiting, noticed it at once. Instead of greeting us, he started to hum, looked from one of us to the other and hummed more loudly when Ben avoided his gaze, leapt up and walked over to the fire.

Have you been arguing? he asked, when Ben came back.

Moshe is making Eichmann speak!

So am I, Ben. I'm telling you what Eichmann said, too.

I know, but Moshe makes him—he makes him appear. Lets him tell his lies! Eichmann is dead. We are Jews. We don't need to hear him anymore!

Did you know that Eichmann recited the Shema Yisrael?

What? What did he do?

He said our prayer, Ben. When they caught him, outside his house in Argentina—they'd been waiting for him, you know, he took the bus home from work every evening, they waited until the bus was gone, drew up beside him, one of them threw open the door while the other one dragged him into the car. They tied him up and gagged him and put on a sleeping mask—

What?

If you want to sleep and it's too light outside—

I know what a sleeping mask is, Shalom. Why, is what I'm asking.

So he couldn't see where they were going!

But it was dark!

They drove through town, it was light enough!

Okay, okay. A sleeping mask. Eichmann was wearing a mask.

The men from Mossad drove him through town to their hideout. In the hideout, it was a house they'd rented, he was put on a bed and they tied his feet to the bed frame. Then they undressed him and put him in a pair of pajamas—

How could they do that? Weren't his feet tied to the frame?

They untied him, and then they tied him up again.

And the sleeping mask?

Will you let me tell you, Ben! You know I'm telling the truth. Something that really happened. One of them, he was called Kenet, stood in front of Eichmann with a list. He read out loud: How tall are you? What size clothes? What size shoes?

Shalom—

They wanted to know if it was him, Ben! Imagine if they'd got the wrong man! Eichmann gave all the right answers. What's your party membership number? Eichmann told them the number. What's your name? Ricardo Klement, Eichmann said. Are the scars on your chest from an accident during the war? He said yes. What's your name? Kenet asks for the second time. Otto Henninger, Eichmann says. Kenet looks at the list and reads out two numbers. Are these your SS numbers? *Jawohl.* So, what is your name? My name is Adolf Eichmann, he says. Then everything was clear.

So? What's with the Shema Yisrael?

Hang on, Ben. So they knew they'd caught the right man. Everyone could relax a bit. Eichmann, too. He asked for a glass of red wine and they gave him one. He drank it and looked at them all one after the other. There were four agents. I knew who you were right away, he told them. I can speak Hebrew, you see: *Shema Yisrael, Adonai Elohenu, Adonai Echad. Baruch shem—*

I'd have grabbed him by the neck, I'd have shoved the words down his filthy German throat so that he choked on them! Miserable bastard!

You can't stop Eichmann, Ben! Nobody can. When they took him to the hideout he didn't say anything at first—

You just told us that he answered their questions and recited the Shema Yisrael!

They dragged him to the hideout, tied him to the bed, stripped him, then they took off the mask—he was in shock, you see? When you are shocked—

You start to pray? Your victims' prayer?

You can't control yourself! But then—he'd had some wine, he was Eichmann once more. And he didn't say anything else. Not a word. He turned over and stared at the wall and refused to respond to anything. There was just one of them, someone called Aharoni, he liked him somehow. When Aharoni came, Eichmann turned around and looked at him. Perhaps he reminded him of someone.

Aharoni would start to ask him questions. Wanted to know this and that. Aharoni asked him a question and Eichmann looked at him and said nothing. And it went on like that, quietly. Because Aharoni stayed calm, Eichmann trusted him. And suddenly he started to speak and didn't stop. Aharoni wrote down every word, whole notebooks filled with notes.

When Eichmann got to Israel, in the prison in Yagur, he was questioned some more, by a captain, a very polite man: Please, Herr Eichmann, he'd say, do have a cigarette, Herr Eichmann, may I repeat my question, Herr Eichmann. So Eichmann trusted him, too. And was willing to talk, for months on end. Everything was recorded on tape and copied out, thousands of pages. He had no one to talk to in his cell in Ramla. None of us guards could speak German, but he'd been given pencils and paper so that he could write. And he wrote. Wouldn't stop writing. The lights were never turned off, they were left on night and day, that's what the rules said. If they hadn't ordered him to go to bed, he would never have stopped writing. Then the trial started and he talked even more. And when he had to listen, to the witnesses talking, or when the prosecutor spoke, he filled his notebooks with writing. When they took him back to his cell in the evenings, what do you think? He sat down and wrote some more! Before the verdict: He wrote! After the verdict: He wrote! He'd often grimace when they came to take him to the visiting room, if his lawyer or someone else was waiting to see him. Because he had to put down the pencil then, you see, he didn't like that. He didn't want any visitors, he wanted to write.

Why?

I don't know. Maybe he thought that was how he could stay alive. That they can't kill him if he writes.

Why not?

Because whatever he wrote would be read, Ben. He knew things that no one else knew. And everything he wrote was kept, too! Every page landed on the prison director's desk, and he locked them all in his safe.

Oh, yes. Eichmann wrote. Six, seven, eight thousand pages. And Moshe allowed him to write, copied his words, spoke in his voice. I hope I didn't write off a friendship. A friendship based on the premise of shared beliefs and ideas about what it means to be Jewish, or to live in this country and deal with our past. Ben trusted me without knowing my circumstances. My background, my burden—he has no more idea than Nagar does. This has to stop. I've got to tell them.

But where? Where is there room for Moshe's story? The compound is Nagar's territory: I know his Eichmann will not tolerate anyone else. No, they have to sit here, facing me; this is where I can and should tell my story. But will Nagar come? He keeps to four or five familiar paths, and can hardly manage those, he tackles them, scared, driven, hounded by Eichmann, who's on his tail.

I need to tell you a story, Ben, I said, when he came to pick me up. You and Nagar. An Eichmann story you've not heard before. One no one has ever heard. Bring Nagar here. Take him by the hand, blindfold him if need be, let him sing and hum all the way, but bring him to me.

Now here they are, sitting on my small sofa while I sit opposite in my wheelchair. They are like brothers jostling one another, wearing the same clothes—black jacket, black trousers, white shirt, black kippah—both equally ill at ease. Everything is different here; no grubby wooden table in front of us, no folding chairs that will fit one of them like a glove and always be too small for the other, no earthen floor to keep us grounded. No pens, no chickens, geese, or sheep, no nail to hang up an apron or smock. No one has made tea, no one has cut up any pears. Only the first sentence is familiar. Just this once I say it myself.

Let me tell you a story. It begins in Germany.

Did I say it begins in Germany? It begins German, is what I should have said. My story is decisively German in the beginning, and ends helplessly so. No, it doesn't even end—there isn't an ending, yet.

It begins in Germany, in 1935, when the Nazis passed their so-called race laws. The Reich citizenship law. The law to protect German blood and honor. The law to protect the pure bloodline of the German people. Decrees written to supplement these laws determined what it meant to be German.

A history lesson! If Ben were not wedged in next to Nagar, who is unsure what to do with his hands, who tugs at his beard as I speak and plays with his fingers, this outburst would surely come. You're giving us a history lesson, Moshe! Why do we have to listen to this? Why do we have to know how German the Nazis wanted to be?

What do you say, Ben? Should I start like this: Oberscharführer Schneider was bent on killing himself? Would that make sense? You see! You have to know Schneider's reasons, have to understand how things suddenly came crashing down around this man.

But Ben isn't protesting! He's sitting quietly, staring at the floor. He even copes with my pauses.

So back to the race laws: Decrees defined what it meant to be German. For the Nazis, being German was a consequence of not being Jewish. People who are German, the decrees said, have neither Jewish parents nor Jewish grandparents. This had to be proved. To be a citizen of the Reich you had to produce seven birth certificates; your own, and those of your parents and your four grandparents. And all their marriage certificates. If one of the grandparents was Jewish, the person was classed as a quarter Jew or a Mischling of the second degree, with two Jewish grandparents they were a half Jew or a Mischling of the first degree, with three Jewish grandparents they were a full Jew. That's how it was.

Members of the SS, like Eichmann, were required to be even more German than ordinary citizens of the Reich. They had to trace their family tree back to the early eighteenth century. Not a single ancestor was allowed to be a Jew. When this requirement came into force, two or three years after the race laws, the SS had already been around for a while. And until then, no one had asked for a pedigree. The men took the oath, swore allegiance to the Führer and to the people, and joined the black league. Now, suddenly, there were divides here, too. Many SS men discovered that they weren't as German as required. As they compiled their ancestries, they stumbled across Jewish ancestors they'd known nothing about, or who hadn't concerned them because it had never mattered before. But it did now. Suddenly, a faded birth or marriage certificate decided everything.

One of Eichmann's men, Oberscharführer Giselher Schneider, was found to have Jewish ancestors. In fact, Schneider was a full Jew, non-German from tip to toe. In these cases, the men who failed to prove their own ancestry could expect no more than a final handshake from their old comrades. They were left in a void. They were no longer what they wanted to be and had always believed themselves to be, and they neither wanted, nor were they allowed to be what they were. Many of them fled, disappeared without a trace, for others the only way out was to shoot themselves. Schneider was one of these. But that's not what happened.

Eichmann liked Schneider, he valued him as an employee and as a person. They had also played music together, in the Rothschild Quartet, named after the Palais where Eichmann's department was based. Eichmann had even allowed Schneider to play first violin, as the Oberscharführer was a far better musician than he was. And now this man was a Jew. A full Jew. Could they ignore this, cross it out? Eichmann couldn't do that, it went against his honor. He summoned Schneider, to talk about his future. Schneider stood to attention. It's hard luck, Sturmbannführer! he said. We had a good time, but now it's over, no one can change that. What will you do now? Eichmann asked. My heart is German, Schneider replied, but my blood belies that. I'm going to kill myself.

Eichmann looked at him, calmly, searchingly. He liked the man, even now. Our honor means loyalty, comrade Schneider. To the people and the Führer. You can keep this honor. How, Sturmbannführer? Schneider asked. You must leave the Reich, that is clear, Eichmann said. Go to a country where this—these matters, are of no importance. Marry a German woman, father sons, who will in turn marry German women. In just a few generations the Schneiders' blood will be pure. And your descendants can return to the Reich, as Germans.

Schneider listened without moving, growing increasingly pale with every word. To be thrown from heaven to hell and then shown a way back, that was too much for him. Eichmann urged him to sit down, gave him a Cognac, offered him a cigarette. Schneider drank, Schneider smoked, and gradually he calmed down. Will you do it, comrade? Eichmann asked. *Jawohl*, Sturmbannführer, Schneider said. They drank another Cognac, to loyalty, and discussed what Schneider was going to do. I could go to Switzerland, Schneider said. He had friends there. How will you support yourself? Eichmann asked. I could be a musician, form a dance band. Eichmann liked the idea. He gave Schneider money, he gave him a passport, he promised that Schneider would be able to cross the Swiss border without any trouble. As they were saying goodbye, Eichmann shook his former Oberscharführer's hand for a long time, refusing to let go. Father a son, comrade Schneider, he said. Father a son!

Schneider did what Eichmann had told him to do. He went to Switzerland, formed a dance band there, married a German, a Catholic girl from Constance, and together they had a son, whom he named Adolf, in honor of Eichmann.

Adolf Schneider had a Swiss passport, but he felt German. He was brought up that way. All his relatives lived in Germany, and it was always assumed that the Schneider family would return there one day. Almost every week, his father dreamt up a new plan about where he could work or where they would live. Then Adolf's mother became ill, so ill that a move was out of the question. Adolf's father was changed by his wife's illness. He became curt and distant, he hid in his office. He never played the violin at home now; when he got back from concerts, he left his instrument in its case.

One night, when Adolf was almost asleep, his father suddenly appeared in his bedroom. He turned on the light, sat down on the edge of the bed. I have to show you something, my boy, he said, and took a worn photo from his jacket pocket. It was a portrait of a man in uniform. His head seemed rather small under his large cap with the death's head on its black peak. The man had boyish features, a crooked nose and a soft, almost feminine mouth. But his expression was sharp, although his eyelids drooped oddly. Adolf felt as though he were being scrutinized as he looked at him.

Do you know who this is? The boy shook his head. This is Obersturmbannführer Adolf Eichmann, his father said. It is thanks to him that I have a son. It is thanks to him that I have you. And he told Adolf his story. The boy listened sleepily, and when his father had finished, simply asked: So we're Jews? Not Germans? Did you not understand, Adolf? I'm a Jew, you're not! You're a half Jew, a Mischling. Your children will be quarter Jews. And their children, your grandchildren, my great-grandchildren, will be Germans. True Germans, Adolf. Like Obersturmbannführer Eichmann.

I can still feel his hand in mine, son, he said in a gruff voice. Then he leaned down and hugged his son, holding him for a long time. You must go back, Adolf, promise me. Back to Germany.

His father's emotions moved the boy more than his revelation. Adolf wasn't exactly pleased about being half German all of a sudden and the half Jewish part sounded a bit unpleasant somehow, but he wasn't too deeply affected. *Jew, Jewish*, these words meant nothing to him. He knew nothing about anti-Semitism or the hatred of the Jews. And he didn't know who this Eichmann was, either. He found that out a few years later, in a history lesson. His teacher, a strict man with a stoop, stood in front of the class, took off his jacket, rolled up a shirt sleeve, and showed them the number that was tattooed on his arm. Then he told them about Auschwitz, explained about the persecution of the Jews, the transportation of the Jews. Spat out names like poisonous morsels: Himmler, Heydrich, Höss. And Eichmann. Eichmann, again and again. Adolf listened as though the teacher meant him. He started to sweat; he wanted to run, out of the classroom, away from this unrelenting man with the number on his arm, away from Eichmann, Eichmann, Eichmann. The teacher knows, he thought. He knows Father's story, my story. And at the end of the class, he will reveal it all, point at me: Him. Adolf! Named after Eichmann.

Of course, the teacher didn't do that, but from that day on, Adolf felt like a stranger in his class. As if he didn't belong there anymore. Just his luck. Where did he belong? To the Jews, the victims? Or to the Germans, the perpetrators? He carried both inside him, he persecuted and was persecuted; driven by Eichmann, he persecuted the Jewish Adolf, and driven by his father's ancestors and six million victims, he persecuted the German Adolf. He turned on himself, going around in ever-decreasing circles until there was no ground beneath his feet, nowhere for him to stand. He drifted, floundering as though caught in a storm, helpless against the forces that tore at him: Eichmann, hurrying toward him in his black uniform, his father, naked with his death's head cap beside him on the floor. Here, Jews were forced into carriages, there, Eichmann shook a Jew's hand; here, his teacher rolled up his sleeve, there, his father hugged him. How could he live like that? Should he exterminate the German within him because that part of him was doomed, a fatal legacy? Should he hate the Jew within him because he owed it to his father, who had brought him into the world? His father, who belonged to the perpetrators, who worked with Eichmann, for Eichmann, to exterminate his own people. This man was inconceivable, he countermanded himself and should never have existed. This man had Eichmann to thank for his son. And he had continued Eichmann's work in him, Adolf Schneider! Because what was this act of mercy ordered by Eichmann other than a further step toward exterminating the Jews? Didn't he spill his Jewish seed in a German womb so that the Jewishness, the impurity, would be halved, then quartered in the next generation and would eventually disappear, fading like smoke blown away in the wind? The Shoah was within him. And he, Adolf, was the tool!

His confusion turned to anger, anger at Eichmann and his dev-ilish duplicity, anger at his father, who had allowed himself to be used, who used his son, and wanted to use his son's sons and their sons after them.

It was a curse. And in that instant, Adolf knew how it could be lifted. He would preserve what Eichmann and his father wanted to destroy, would begin what they wanted to end: He would become a Jew. The thought came with a tremendous feeling of liberation. Become a Jew.

He knew almost nothing about Judaism. So he sat in the library after school and read. In his rigorous way, he started with the Old Testament. Then he read a three-volume history of Juda-ism, a book about the Jewish festivals, and finally Theodor Herzl's *The Jewish State*. And that was just the beginning. He needed to learn Hebrew, and taught himself as best he could. He did hardly anything for school, just scraped a pass in his final exams, but he didn't care. He'd made up his mind.

One evening, Adolf took his courage in both hands and knocked on the door of his father's study. He found him sitting in front of a bottle of Cognac, tired, lonely, gray. I'm going to Israel, Father, Adolf said. I'm going to be a Jew like you. His father raised his head and looked at him. His eyes hardened, but Adolf held his stare. His father stood up, went to his desk, took something out from among his papers, held it out to Adolf. The photo he had shown him once before. Eichmann, wearing an SS uniform. You will not betray him, his father said. And you will not betray me. You will go to Germany! Horrified, Adolf snatched the photo, tore it to pieces, and let the scraps fall to the floor. His father leapt up and struck him in the face. Adolf staggered backward, tears springing to his eyes. You're the traitor! he shouted. It's you! And then he confronted him with everything that had been stewing inside him since the day his teacher had revealed who Eichmann was.

His father turned pale. He stared fixedly past his son at the wall, and as Adolf finally fell silent he replied with a single word: Lies.

The next day, his father kicked him out of the house. Adolf moved in with a friend, found work as an unskilled laborer, saved money, and when he had enough, he packed his suitcase, took his violin, and left for Israel. He changed his first name, called himself Moshe, worked in a kibbutz, became a musician and formed a string quartet, for which he also wrote music. He lived as a Jew, saw himself as a Jew. A part of the kingdom of priests as all Jews should be. Yet he felt different from the others. Different, because he was a Jew out of protest.

It's you?

The two men on the sofa had remained so silent throughout my story that I almost thought I'd asked the question myself. But it was Ben. His question was painfully matter of fact, with no hint of horror, shock, or empathy—the question sounded as though he were simply confirming a casual assumption.

I am no Nagar. I lack the warmth, the indulgence of his

storytelling that can take a joke, enjoys diversions, and calmly puts up with disbelief. My story is too real for that. Too German.

It's you?

Yes. It's me, Ben. I am Adolf Schneider. Or I was. I cut off my roots all those years ago. My mother was already dead when I came to Israel, my father no longer existed in my eyes, I broke off all contact with my family. My background was erased, including Eichmann.

Then came May 23, 1960, the day David Ben-Gurion declared to the Knesset: We've captured Eichmann. The news hit me like a shock. I had always assumed he was dead, had taken poison like Himmler or Göring, shot himself like Günther, his ever-faithful deputy, or had died in the last days of the war like Heinrich Müller, his superior in department IV. And now he was here, in the country I had chosen! As if he had come to get me. Me, the man who was only alive because of him, whose existence he had commanded so that a tainted tree could bear good fruit once more, and who had turned traitor to his cause, the German cause.

Eichmann was alive, he was in Israel. Nothing could change that. This time he wasn't just a photo I could tear to pieces. This time he was here in the flesh. I had to face him. I had to see, grasp, understand this man. You must swallow him, I thought, and you must digest him. Then you can flush him out, and he will leave your body for good.

I read every newspaper article that was written about him, compiled folders, bought books about the extermination—*The Final Solution* by Gerald Reitlinger, *The Third Reich and the Jews* by Poliakov and Wulf—and eagerly awaited the start of the trial, the moment I'd look this man in the eye.

On the first day of the trial I sat in the gallery, too far away to get a good view of Eichmann. So then I went a bit earlier every day until I was one of the first to arrive at the Beit Ha'am and got a place in the front row, as near to the glass box as possible. I studied Eichmann day after day, his tic, his posture, the way he spoke, his expression when he was listening. Above all, I watched his hands, which never stopped moving; large, yet strangely delicate hands, hands that seemed happiest leafing through a folder, hands that glided across the paper when Eichmann made a note of something, as though his pencil were a natural extension.

And I could never look at these hands without thinking of what my father said as he hugged me for the first, and I think only time in my life:

I can still feel his hand in mine, son.

His hand. Eichmann's hand.

I can't go on. I never get any further than Eichmann's hand.

Neither of the men spoke, Ben, my old friend from kibbutz days, and Nagar, who is a friend now, too. No comfort, no condemnation. My gaze gropes through the silence that rings in my ears, past their faces, to the window, where everything is just as it was. The world didn't implode, but what was I expecting? The ever-same roofs opposite are as ugly as ever, spotted with a mix of gray and black satellite dishes. Sponges that absorb everything, funnels into which anything that travels through the ether is poured, no matter how trivial or significant it might be. All of them—I never noticed before—are pointed toward my apartment.

Let me tell you a story.

Nagar has found his voice again. Maybe he just waited a

moment. Allowed a few minutes to pass after my last words, for courtesy's sake.

Eichmann had lucky hands, you said. Fine hands, you said, too. He deceived you, Moshe. He deceived everyone. Let me tell you a story.

Eichmann's hands, then. No words about Moshe and Moshe's father. Did Nagar listen to me? Did he understand who, what I am? Or had he been daydreaming, lost in thought during all my revelations, only snapping up the last few sentences on which to build his next story, unaffected like a machine? A narration machine, which can be fed with anything you like, out comes Eichmann. Nagar's Eichmann? I didn't care at that moment. I was even grateful that he had buried my story, Eichmann's Moshe, once more, covered it like a picture that didn't deserve a second or third glance.

When Eichmann came to Argentina, he met lots of old comrades again, you know. They had new names and new jobs now, but they were still Germans. Nazis. They had their own clubs, where they'd meet. If there was something important that needed to be discussed, they would meet at each other's homes. They were safer there, but it still wasn't secure. They could rely on their wives, but what about the children? If they said the wrong word to the neighbors, at school—

What do you mean, the wrong word?

Names, I mean names, Ben! When they were among themselves, they used their real names, of course. Eichmann was Eichmann, Mengele Mengele. And now think of Eichmann's sons running around telling everyone Mengele came to see us yesterday! That could never happen. There were secret agents lurking everywhere! So Eichmann took steps to protect himself. If a visitor was expected, he lined up his sons in a row. Pay attention, he said, we will be receiving visitors tonight, and you must not tell anyone about them, do you hear me? And then he boxed their ears. Whenever a Nazi came to visit, he slapped them in the face! Just so they knew what was going on.

And did that work?

What do you think? Eichmann's methods always worked.

During the trial, reporters sought out his eldest son and wanted to know who had visited them at home. The son said he couldn't remember any visitors, just his father hitting him. He could still feel that today, he said. Eichmann had—

Enough, Shalom. I think we should go now. Moshe looks tired.

No, wait, Ben. I want to finish the story.

Eichmann had tested this method of slapping people beforehand, in Austria, what is the name of the capital—

Vienna.

In Vienna, that's it. The Germans had disbanded the Jewish community and put the leaders in jail. Eichmann said that was all wrong. He needed the community, otherwise nothing would work. So the men were released. Eichmann talked to them and then he picked one of them, Dr. Löwenherz, a lawyer. You are in charge of the community now, he said. It is your responsibility. First of all, write down the names of all the Jews here in Vienna. But do not say a word to anyone. You understand? And then he slapped him in the face.

He was a real bastard.

He's evil, Ben. His hands are evil. Later on, at the trial, he told a different story. He said he'd asked Dr. Löwenherz a question and

Dr. Löwenherz had given him the wrong answer. Eichmann was so angry that he slapped him in what he called a moment of uncontrollable anger. Not a slap that would do any harm, he said, because I do not have the hands for that kind of work, just a tiny, little slap in the face. Though he regretted it later. He insists he apologized to Dr. Löwenherz officially, in uniform, in front of his men.

He deceived everyone. He hides his power. Anyone looking at his hands is supposed to think exactly what Moshe thought: What delicate hands, hands for files, not made for hitting. But he is so strong! On the inside of his arm, here, there was a code, numbers and letters. It started with IV B 4, Eichmann's department, followed by more letters and numbers and dashes. IV B 4a dash 2093 slash—I can't remember any more. That was his sign. The signal for the transport! Whenever a transport of Jews was ready anywhere, Eichmann arrived, rolled up his sleeve, and pressed his arm against the carriages. He branded them with his arm: IV B 4a dash 2093—

You mean he marked the carriages? With chalk?

With his arm! He doesn't need any chalk. He—it was a transmission.

Eichmann the conjurer.

It was the sign, Ben. He was the master. His arm had power. As soon as all the carriages were marked, the trains departed. No one could stop them! They never turned back a train, so Eichmann said. He's proud of that. Later, after the war, he used cigarettes to burn away the sign. I saw the scar; it runs down the whole of his lower arm. But no one at the prison noticed.

Noticed the scar?

How strong he was. Always gentle, always polite—please, if I could just ask, *gracias, gracias*—he never raised his voice, never raised a hand to any of us. We didn't have any weapons. None of the guards were allowed to carry weapons. What would have happened if Eichmann had attacked me in the cell? With his bare hands? The colleague on the other side of the door wouldn't have been able to help me. He had the keys, of course, but the doors could only be opened from the inside. Eichmann could have trapped me like a mouse. But he didn't do anything. Ever. I thought they must have caught a saint.

Late Shift

Once again, Nagar is to share the prisoner's night. A night without darkness; for
twenty-four hours, the light remains on in
the cell, which is still full of shadows,
although the prisoner sleeps like a baby,
silently, free of anxiety, free of guilt.
His sleep is a lie which Nagar must share.

He buttons up his uniform jacket with
a deep sigh. Ora watches him, revealing
through her smile and her small, encouraging gestures that she does not know what is
troubling her husband. As far as he is concerned, that is for the best.

When Nagar enters the cell two hours later
the prisoner checks the time, lays down his
pencil, and takes off his watch. He stands
up, pushes the chair under the table, goes
over to the bed. The usual reaching under
the blanket, the few paces back to the
table. His movements are smooth, his posture perfect. He lays the pajamas, precisely
folded as always, on the table, next to the
pages he has written that day; as though
able to extend time he strokes the thin
cotton, the buttons, straightens the collar that was already straight, takes off
his glasses, turns to the wall, removes
his cardigan, his shirt, his vest. Nagar

closes his eyes to the naked back, presses
his eyelids shut, filters this pale white
through his eyelashes, this skin, no longer
touched by the sun, German skin, shimmering
so defenselessly, intangible.

Whose back is that? What does Nagar know?
He senses a person, a border, he thinks,
which needs to be secured.

The prisoner undoes his trousers. Nagar
fights the impulse to lower his head; he is
not allowed to look away, but he focuses on
the wall instead of the exposed body, out of
modesty, a forbidden solidarity between men.
Straightens his lower back with an exaggerated movement while the prisoner slips on
his pajamas, sits down on the hard chair,
restless, until the other has settled under
the woolen blanket, face turned toward the
wall, as always, as though leaving everything behind him, cell and prison and
Nagar, his guard. As though the man could
command himself to fall asleep in just a
moment. This man can. His consciousness
obeys.

Nagar turns his head, looks over at his
colleague behind the cell door, nods to
him, returns to his guard position. The
now-complete silence in the room penetrates
him, in a way that is so familiar to him.
A silence that is timeless, that transcends

time. Time for thoughts of things beyond
work, time for questions that no lawyer
asks.

The prisoner sleeps almost silently, his
square shoulders rise and fall almost
imperceptibly. Confused, Nagar notices that
he is breathing in time with the prisoner;
he adjusts his own rhythm to match this
man's sleep, his peace.

Can such a man find peace?

In sleep, it is said, people wear no
masks. In sleep, people cannot check themselves, expressions are removed like a pair
of glasses or a shirt. What would Nagar
see if he walked the three steps over to the
bed, bent over the prisoner, as quietly as
possible, as far as his stoutness allowed?

Nagar remains seated. He does not trust
sleep and does not want to believe that the
prisoner, that familiar person, is a mask,
he is afraid of looking into the face of a
mass murderer, contorted with anger and the
thirst for revenge, he is even more afraid
of seeing calm features, a face that reveals
nothing other than devotion and fatigue.

Nagar remains seated. What is Ora doing
now? Reading newspapers? The child will
long since be sleeping, dreaming. Sometimes
he calls out in his sleep, to whom they do
not know. Nagar thinks about the fact that

the prisoner has sons, too, the youngest
just a few years older than his own. Stops
thinking. Little by little, his breathing falls back in line with the prisoner's.
Hours pass.

At some point he starts, there is a disturbance in the other room. Changing of
the guards. Nagar hears murmurs, stifled
laughter, they will have exchanged jokes
in the corridor, obscenities perhaps, or
more unbelievable facts about the prisoner's
life. Over the last few weeks, the chicken
story had been spread around. The prisoner,
they said, tried to make it as a poultry
farmer after the war. At first he had no
success at all, the animals ran wild, laid
their eggs where he could not find them,
and ignored his attempts to lure them out
by calling "chick, chick, chick." So he
built a small pen, locked the chickens in,
and trained them until he could order them
around by whistling. If he whistled with
two fingers, the chickens lined up in rank
and file. And they only laid their eggs in
the place he had marked out specially.

The key is passed through the door hatch.
Nagar stands up, tries to stop the chair
from creaking, he succeeds in this but the
key jolts in the lock, the bolt scratches
over the metal, the heavy door crunches on

the hinges. Everything is too loud. Someone is sleeping here! When the door finally
opens the murmuring outside stops, his colleague enters, too loudly, nods to him, and
because Nagar does not react, his colleague
takes the key out of his hand, grips his
arm, pushes him gently but firmly out of
the room.

Nagar feels as though he has been repri-
manded, is ashamed of the closeness between
himself and the prisoner, is ashamed that
he should feel ashamed.

Behind Glass

At the same time, twelve thousand kilometers away, a woman is boarding a passenger plane. It is her first ever flight.
In the large handbag that she keeps pressed
to her side lie the documents that she has
been sent, passport and visa, in a false
name. Instructed to avoid contact with the
other passengers, the woman closes her eyes
and surrenders herself to her plummeting
thoughts. She is allowed to stay for one
afternoon, one night. By the next morning she will already have left this foreign
country. When the plane lands she has to
wait for all the other passengers to dis-
embark. She is alone in the plane for a few
minutes before two officials come down the
aisle, stand in front of her, and one of the
two quietly says her name. She stands up,
the men escort her to a car. She remembers
nothing of the journey, barely looks out
of the window; she is not interested in the
people out there, the landscape, the houses
that pass by.

Nagar sits in the cell, both hands resting on his thighs. The prisoner sits opposite him at the table and does what he has
spent the last few weeks doing. He writes.
Nagar hears the door in the hall, then

voices, someone gives an order that the colleague passes on through the barred hatch:
Aquarium.

That means they must go to the meeting room. Since the sentence was given the
guards have begun passing on the prison
director's orders to each other in a casual
way, as if form no longer matters. The meeting room is a separate area from the hall,
it measures two by three meters wide and is
divided into two bulletproof, soundproof
chambers by a piece of solid glass reaching all the way up to the ceiling. Microphones and headphones sit on the narrow
tables that have been fixed to both sides of
the wooden base. Unless the intercom system
is switched on, visitors and prisoners are
unable to communicate, silent as the grave.

As Nagar leads the prisoner into the room,
the afternoon light falls through the narrow ventilation shaft on the back wall, it
scatters over the glass and is reflected
as if by a mirror. Only a silhouette looms
behind the glass. The prisoner starts,
stands still, stares. Is he disobeying the
order? No—when he feels Nagar's hand on
his shoulder he walks the two steps to the
glass wall. Now it is clear: The visitor is
a woman, in a plain dark dress, small and
plump, a motherly type. Quickly, as though

trying to recover the lost moment, the
prisoner sits on his chair and places the
headphones on his head. As he moves closer
to the microphone and bends over it, words
fail him. For the first time since Nagar
has known him. Pity? Perhaps. Yes, indeed,
Nagar feels pity in this moment. Two years
of loneliness lie behind the prisoner, two
years under the scrutiny of official, at
most correct, often hostile eyes. Two years
without an unintentional, unthinking, ten-
der touch. Two years without his wife, who
now sits opposite him, for who else could
this visitor be?

No one here knew she was coming, even the
prison director had only just heard about
her arrival. From Argentina. Two people,
two continents, oceans apart. Now she sits
opposite the prisoner, close enough to
touch. His desire for a handshake, a hug,
a kiss, even under the eyes of the guards,
must be overwhelming. But he cannot fulfill this desire. Her plane has crossed the
waters of the ocean, but here they sit up
straight as though before the pharaoh and
his chariot, become crystallized in the
middle of the glass that divides the room.
This time the glass hurts.

When the couple do eventually begin to
talk, Nagar studies the condemned man's

voice in order to try and follow the conversation. No officer tone like the one
he uses in the courtroom, just a regular
rise and fall—soft, calming, reassuring
sounds. The conditions are relatively good,
he seems to say, he is healthy and has not
given up hope for a change in his fate. If
he does say that then it must be for her,
thinks Nagar.

The woman nods and kneads the leather
strap of her handbag. After a while she
opens her bag, takes out a stack of photos.
A questioning glance over her shoulder, the
guards behind her have no objections. One
after the other, she holds the photos up to
the glass. Nagar bends down so he, too, can
see what she is showing him. A house with
a flat roof, half plastered, as if it is
still being built, a somewhat wild-looking
piece of land. Three young men, surely
the prisoner's sons. They look like their
father, Nagar thinks. Finally, a young boy.

He sits on a piece of wall sticking out
behind a wire mesh fence, which he is holding on to, looking through it at the pho-
tographer with wide eyes. In the background
is the house; the woman stands in front of
it, holds up a hand, perhaps as a greeting or to call the child back. Between the
fence and the house is a patch of deep ter-

rain filled with water, what looks like a
swamp, part of which has been drained. The
woman has to hold up the photo for a long
time. The prisoner studies it carefully.
He hardly recognizes his youngest son
anymore.

Toward the end of the visit the woman
turns around once again, asks something, gestures with her hands, points to
the trousers and the shoes of one of the
guards. It takes a while before the guard
understands, then he goes to the microphone, points at the prisoner's headphones,
at Nagar. The prisoner gets up, gives
Nagar the headphones, the guard repeats the
request: She wants to see her husband from
top to bottom, wants to be sure that his
trousers and his shoes are all right. For
a moment Nagar is not sure what to do, then
he pulls the chair back a bit, to the middle of the room. The prisoner has already
understood, he stands on the chair, laughing awkwardly. Lets her look at him from
head to toe. Sees the indignant look on his
wife's face when she notices the slippers
on his feet. Checked felt slippers, with a
zip. Of course, she had not expected boots,
the times of the Obersturmbannführer are
over, but slippers? Slippers are only worn
by men—if at all—in their own living room,

after work, not in public, where others can
see them. This is not his home, and this is
not the evening after work. Or perhaps it
is, thinks Nagar.

Perhaps his wife thinks the same. Nagar
sees she is crying now. She turns around
to hide her sobs. The prisoner has climbed
down from the chair and is standing in
front of the glass wall. His wife wipes
her eyes again, then she, too, stands up,
silently places her palm on the glass. She
must be hoping he would return the gesture,
must know that he will not do it.

See you soon, he says. He says it with
emphasis. Gives her the future she needs.

Ben says you're writing again, Moshe?

Yes.

What are you writing?

I've just written about the day Eichmann's wife came to the prison.

I saw her. The woman. I felt sorry for her.

Because her husband was going to die?

No, because Eichmann loved another woman.

One? You said he had lots of lovers, Shalom. The white lady, the young widow, the land owner, the cook.

I don't mean them, Ben. Not his mistresses. They meant nothing. I mean his true love. The desert princess.

Desert princess! True love! Are you telling fairy tales now? Have you heard about Eichmann's desert princess, Moshe? No? Moshe doesn't know the story either, Shalom. And he knows what Eichmann wrote.

Eichmann didn't write the story down, Ben. It was a personal affair. He only told me.

When?

I don't know. At some stage.

Where? In his cell?

No. Not in his cell.

Well, it can't have been when he was in the bathroom. He always turned on the tap. You wouldn't have heard a word.

Not in the prison. It was after that.

In your dreams, then?

This is a true story, Ben. It was after the war. Eichmann was living by himself, without his family—

In Argentina?

He calls it the district. It was in the desert. Eichmann lived alone, he had his horse with him, a white horse, but that was it. The district had been occupied, but when Eichmann got there, the soldiers were gone. He didn't meet anyone, no one alive, no one dead.

What about the princess?

If she was real.

What else could she be? A ghost?

I'm telling you. Eichmann rode through the desert from one fortress to the next. These were palaces the soldiers had built in a row like pearls on a string, each one a three-day ride from the next. Mighty houses, Eichmann says, forbidding and stately, with tall windows dulled by sand, and sand in the corridors and great halls, sand up to your ankles on every floor. I usually left the palaces—

You!

Eichmann!

Why did you say "I"?

Because I'm telling the story the way Eichmann did! These are his words. Usually, I left the palaces as soon as I had inspected them, he says, rode on again and slept out in the open, with all my senses attuned, the horse beside me and the cosmos above in perfect equilibrium like nothing on Earth.

But on that day, I got lost in the corridors, staircases, and wings of the building. It was a huge estate, hardly damaged, and in some of the rooms, I imagined I could still sense the breath of the occupiers, the officer taking off the coat and jacket I saw hanging on a hook, rubbing the sand out of his eyes as he sits down at the desk and stretches his legs out under the table. I had set up camp in the inner courtyard beside a well that had almost seemed to beckon to me. The deep, calm water mirrored a sky that I could not see above me, that was no longer there, that had never existed, perhaps. And as I undressed and washed, the woman came. All at once she stood there without making a sound, watching me with deep, dark eyes. She untied her hair and dried my body with her long dark tresses. She stayed with me all night. When the morning dawned, she disappeared.

She came back the next day, then failed to appear for several days, then she was there again, and so it continued. I never understood what rule she was following, or if there even was one. But I waited for her to return and stayed in the palace courtyard, which seemed to attract her, where she might have lived at one time, whether to serve or rule, I did not know.

The only thing for sure was that she would have an animal with her when she came. The animals followed her, as if carried on the wind and bound to her light quick step. Animals from the woods, a little owl with gray feathers and black wing tips flew silent circles around her, she had draped a weasel over her shoulders like a shawl, and a fox licked the heels of her feet and rubbed its tail across her slender legs.

That is how he tells the story? He's a poet, your Eichmann.

It's his most important story, Ben. He excels himself when he tells it.

And you know it off by heart?

Every word. I know every word. This really surprised me, he says. I could not fathom where the animals had come from or how the desert had created them, as there were no woods in the district, or even anything remotely resembling a wood. But when we lay together, the woman and I, when she slid into my arms and I buried my head in her hair, I discovered the answer. The scent of the forest wafted through her hair: Spruce and cedar needles, moss, the rooted earth, and rays of golden green shimmered across her body like sunbeams breaking through the branches of leafy trees and conifers. I realized then that the forest was within her and so were the animals, and not just them, I thought. She carries all landscapes within, coasts, lakes and plains, the deepest valleys and the stoniest peaks.

A poet, who'd ever have thought it? I don't believe a word you're saying, Shalom. I have no idea who told you that story, but it certainly wasn't Eichmann.

He did tell it to me! Again and again.

Eichmann was a Nazi, Shalom. Not a poet. He forced Jews into trains to be gassed.

During the war, yes. But he was in the district after that!

And he changed that much?

Change? He didn't change. He was German, he was evil. He was just as evil when he was in the district.

The way you're telling it, he was simply lonely, Shalom. So lonely that he imagined a woman who would dry him off with her hair and lie beside him. And whose body meant the whole world to him.

Not imagined! The woman is real.

The desert princess who loved him even though he is evil?

When Eichmann reaches the part I just told you, when he says that the woman had the woods within her and all the other landscapes, too, he pauses every time, Ben. He looks at me like this, from the side, and waits. I think he wants me to see the woman. He wants me to sense and smell her, to recognize that she is all women.

Eve?

I don't know. Maybe. Maybe someone else. One day, Eichmann

said, the woman arrived with a young wolf that stayed by her side from then on. She carried it in her arms at first because it was sick or injured, too weak to walk, and when it was able to stand by itself, it swayed and limped whenever it tried to follow her. She nursed it tenderly and allowed it to sleep beside her at night, cuddled up close, while I had to stay away. And she talked to it, gently and lovingly, kept repeating the same word: Habibi. Habibi, Habibi, which sounded like bells tinkling. I was surprised and, I must admit, I felt slightly jealous as she had never uttered a word before. I had simply assumed that she was deaf and dumb, and had been content because we would never have been able to understand each other, the language of the district was alien to me and my own language was alien to her, too.

Habibi. I tried to work out what it might mean. Perhaps it was just the word for wolf, but the soft intonation the woman used when she pronounced the word suggested it might mean "little wolf" or, and here was another thought, "darling." I did not want the woman to talk to a wolf that could not understand her and could not answer, I wanted her to caress me with her words, me, the man she had chosen of her own accord.

Eichmann had whispered German words to her then, as they lay together, but all she did was smile, he says, and put her finger on his lips.

Eichmann was jealous? Of a wolf?

Not jealous. All living things must obey a certain order, he says. There are higher and lower beings, humans and animals, there are lines drawn that must not be breached. The wolf didn't stick to them. It laid claim to the woman, Eichmann says, guarded her and would not let me come near, not during the day and not at night. The woman let it have its way, but this was too much for me, Eichmann says. And then one day his anger got the better of him, he says, and he lost his temper. The wolf had followed him to an outer wing of the palace, had growled at the door and bared its teeth. So he kicked it with his boot, not a hard kick, he says, though it was aggressive. But the wolf fell to the ground and ceased to move, lying lifeless on the dark stone tiles, which were covered in a thin layer of sand. And suddenly the woman was in the room, Eichmann says, kneeling beside the animal, whispering "Habibi," covering its eyes with kisses. He says her lament sounded like a call, the cry of man to his fellow animals, a raw endless tone that grew and wavered. Maybe it was the lament of life, I thought, and that thought cut me to the quick, maybe life itself was lamenting within this woman, the lament for a lone wolf and thus for all living things that had failed to achieve their goals, or come into their own. I had become the tool of doom, he says. He left the woman with the wolf, saddled the gray, and rode away.

And that's the end of the story?

No, Ben. The story isn't over.

We've heard enough, Shalom.

Don't you want to know why Eichmann left the district in the end?

I don't, how about you, Moshe?

I didn't either. The pathos of the last sentences was clanging in my ears. Life's lament! Tools of doom! That sounded like Eichmann. Was it Eichmann? Who told Nagar that story?

No Tears

One month after the condemned man said
goodbye to his wife, the appeals court
announces its verdict. Among the small
audience in the Beit Ha'am is the Reverend
William Lovell Hull, a Canadian preacher
who is trying to save the condemned man's
soul. The preacher has already sat opposite him in the meeting room on twelve occasions, together with his wife Lillian, who
acts as the interpreter. The condemned man
speaks very little during these visits;
most of the talking is done by Hull, who
looks like a businessman and offers salva-
tion in exchange for remorse. The man opposite him smiles politely. After the preacher
and his wife have left, he writes; Hull
has already received several long letters
explaining what the condemned man thinks
of the Christian mission. Not much. To
him, the Christian God is too small. And
yet Hull does not give up; he wants this
soul, perhaps the darkest soul he knows.
Delivering this soul would be his greatest triumph. He wants to defy Satan himself, Satan, whose power he believes he can
feel through the glass in the meeting room
on each visit, oppressing, challenging, an
exterminating grip that must be disarmed

by the gentle spirit of evangelism. If only
there were enough time.

Today, too, Hull sees the man behind
glass, but here in the courtroom he does
not give anything away, he looks pale and
tired. The five judges enter, the chairman opens the session, then the verdict is
read. The judges take it in turns to read,
each one reading faster than his predeces-
sor, they race through the text, the final
word has already been read, the appeal
denied, the verdict of the District Court
is confirmed on all counts. The session is
closed, the judges leave the room.

The hastiness strikes Hull as indecent.
Such an abrupt ending, he writes in his
book "The Struggle for a Soul," cannot be
reconciled with the severity of the decision, and neither can the speed at which the
verdict was read. A situation such as this
one requires composure, he believes, a solemn rhythm, loaded pauses. He is equally
unimpressed by the behavior of the public;
when leaving the room, the people beam as
though they were coming out of the cinema.
They could not be expected to shed tears,
writes the preacher. But perhaps there could
have been even the slightest hint that the
matter was being taken seriously.

The people in this country do not want

such seriousness anymore, no burdens, no
grief. In the four months since the verdict and the telephone survey that followed,
the mood has shifted. People want an end, a
beginning. A death. As soon as possible.

The prison director is tasked with carrying out the necessary preparations for the
death. For a while now he has had an English manual on his desk: "British Judicial
Hanging." The director has studied the book
thoroughly and has made his initial plans.
He will have to improvise; this country is
not set up for executions. The walk to the
gallows must be short, it is inconceivable that they would lead the condemned man
through the nine doors, across the courtyard, from one floor to the next. The director decides to have a hole knocked through
the wall of the meeting room, leaving just
one landing and one corridor to cross. The
gallows, a simple wooden construction with
a hook in the middle, will be set up in the
unused room at the end of the corridor—the
wood has already been ordered. Beneath this
room is a storeroom, where they will be able
to take the body from the rope. They will
make a hole in the floor for the trapdoor, a
square iron plate.

For the hundredth time the director

studies the book's Official Table of Drops,
which shows how far the condemned man must
fall in relation to his weight. He has done
a few provisional sums to calculate the
length of the rope. The Manila hemp rope
recommended by the manual is not available.
They will somehow have to strengthen the
rope they do have to hand. Or make a double
loop.

The director puts down his pen, massages
his temples, looks out of the window. Double barbed-wire fence, unnecessarily high,
with trestles every few meters on which
searchlights are mounted. Behind the fence
is a narrow access road with open land on
either side. Even this area is patrolled
by guards. The director wants to go to the
mountains when this is all over. He does
not want to see anyone, either alive or
dead. Vineyards, perhaps. Or perhaps simply
the sky.

At the same time, in another block of
the prison, the condemned man's guards are
called together, twenty-two seasoned men.
The commander stands at the door, hands
behind his back, rocking on the balls of
his feet. If he were not in uniform, he
would take off his jacket and roll up his
shirt sleeves. When the men have gathered
around he makes a short speech, ending

with the question of who would be willing
to carry out the death sentence. Twenty-one
hands shoot into the air. Only Nagar does
not want to. The commander draws lots. The
lot falls to Nagar.

An Eye for an Eye

After his appeal has been rejected once
and for all, the condemned man submits an
appeal for mercy to the president Yitzhak
Ben-Zvi. The wording is not known; it is
said to have consisted of four handwritten pages, composed by the condemned man
following strict instructions from the
defense.

What would he have written if he had not
been forced to follow legal guidelines?
Would he have begged for his life, appealed
to the power of forgiveness, talked about
his six-year-old son who needs a father?

That is not his style. He does not think
like that. Individual people do not interest him, they have nothing to do with
him. He talks only about what he calls
the matters, the affairs. Evacuation matters, transport affairs. For them he would
have asked for mercy, perhaps even demanded
mercy. I believe I have the right, Mr. President, he would have written, to suggest
that these matters have been sentenced to
death along with me. They will die without
having been resolved. Because, I must reit-
erate, a guilty verdict for me will not help
secure an understanding of these matters.

Perhaps he would also have used the word

truth, explained that without him, without
the statements he is yet to make, the truth
would remain unsaid, unheard. Had the three
judges at the District Court not called
the extermination a secret? He—and only
he—could reveal this secret and he would do
so if they let him. I ask you to give me the
chance, even after the confirmation of my
death sentence, to make a detailed statement
on the concrete matters with no yes or no,
otherwise this confusing mess will never
be explained, Mr. President, he would have
written.

Haunted, Ben-Zvi would have followed the
structure of this statement, at first gram-
matically confused, then semantically disturbed. With no yes or no, what does that
mean, he would have mused, how does he want
to make a statement without saying yes or
no? After all, making a statement means
to say what is and what is not, what happens and what does not. Do you not have to
accept or deny, agree, reject? I must, Ben-
Zvi would have thought. I, the president,
must give a yes or a no. Either, or.

What I say will define me; at the end of
the day I am the man who said no, the man
who said yes.

Perhaps the president would have taken a
deep breath at this thought, staring with

unseeing eyes at the pages in front of him,
on which the sentences had transformed into
waves seeking the shore. Bit by bit the
eyes of the president would have returned
to this country, this city, this building,
this room, bit by bit the waves would have
congealed into words, syllables, letters.
Ben-Zvi would have been haunted by this
handwriting, these wide, low arcs, brought
up high and taken down again, decisive and
solicitous, at once authoritative and sub-
servient. The writing of a man with no yes
or no.

Perhaps the president would have sensed
that this writing is an echo, a reverbera-
tion of the condemned man's existence during
the years of the Reich. Living and acting
in a swirling no-man's-land, a crack that
tore through reality and severed everything
to which binary logic could be applied.
Right, wrong, good, bad, these simple
options no longer represented anything
in this condemned man's no-man's-land.
Instead—orders, obedience, enforcement,
a language that only knows the imperative, the sheer will, that in the end wants
itself. A will devoid of humanity, in which
commands command and obedience obeys.

An appeal for mercy, in this language?
It is possible the meaning of these words

would have escaped the president. Mercy.
Perhaps he would have remained sitting at
his desk, still, silenced.

That is not what happened. Another
text lies in front of the president. His
thoughts go in a different direction, as he
withdraws into the silence of his office.
He stays there for hours, four pages in
front of him that weigh more heavily than a
life, more lightly than millions of deaths.
The president writes a single sentence during these hours, on the first sheet of the
appeal, a verse from the book of Samuel:

As the sword hath made women childless, so
shall thy mother be childless among women.

I gave this chapter to Ben to read. I knew he was interested in
Yitzhak Ben-Zvi. More than in Eichmann. As usual, Ben took the
pages to the window, as usual he read slowly, mumbling the sentences to himself, as if he physically needed to taste them. Finally,
he shuffled the pages back together and put them on my desk.
Then he dug around in his pockets, pulled out his wallet, fumbled
in the section for paper money. I didn't understand until he held
out a hundred-shekel bill so that I could look straight at the person
portrayed on it. Ben-Zvi. A grainy photo against a background with
small colored squares, showing strong features beneath a straight
high forehead, despite the blur. I'd seen it so many times, but only
now did I notice that Ben had the same chin, the same nose.

Why show me that bill? Because you look like him?

How could I ever look like him, Moshe! He was a great man.
Do you know that he and his family lived in a shack? When he
became president, they wanted him to move but he refused. He
stayed living there. Anyone who wanted to see him had to enter
the hut. He was a man of austerity.

Ben looked at the money again and then put it away.

He didn't speak on the way to the meeting place, something
was bothering him. When we got there, he pushed me over to
the wooden table, but instead of tending to the fire and making
tea, he stayed standing beside me. You think Ben-Zvi didn't know
about mercy?

Of course he did, Ben. But I can imagine Eichmann tested his
definitions. He tests all definitions because he rejects yes and no.
For himself. For others. It's catching.

Not for me, Moshe.

If you'd been in Ben-Zvi's position you'd have been infected by
his way of thinking, too. Mercy is not a law. You must obey the law,

you don't need to think about it, you don't have to decide. Mercy isn't like that. Either you grant it or you don't. Yes or no. When you grant it, you give someone something he is no longer entitled to by right. Freedom, for example. Or his life. Someone has forfeited his right to live, and now he comes to you and asks you to pardon him. Why should you? You need to think about it.

Don't you question your heart?

No, Ben. Your heart doesn't understand mercy. Mercy needs reasons.

What are you talking about?

Nagar had arrived, humming so quietly that we hadn't noticed him.

We're talking about mercy, Shalom.

Why?

Moshe wrote about the president. He was asked to waive the death sentence. Eichmann asked him to do it.

And what did he say?

Eichmann?

The president!

He wrote one sentence. As the sword hath made women child-less, so shall thy mother be childless among women.

You see, the president understood.

What?

That Eichmann is Amalek. You know the verses, Ben.

We all know them, Shalom. Isn't the story read aloud on each Shabbat before Purim?

Samuel said unto Saul: Thus saith the Lord of hosts, I remember that which Amalek did to Israel, how he laid wait for him in the way, when he came up from Egypt. Now go and smite Amalek, and utterly destroy all that they have, and spare them not; but slay both man and woman, infant and suckling, ox and sheep, camel and ass.

And Saul smote the Amalekites from Havilah until Shur that is over against Egypt. And he took Agag the king of the Amalekites alive and spared Agag. Then came the word of the Lord unto Samuel, saying it repenteth me that I have set up Saul to be king: For he is turned back from following me, and hath not performed my commandments. And it grieved Samuel; and he cried unto the Lord all night. Samuel rose early to meet Saul in the morning and Samuel said the Lord anointed thee king over Israel. And the Lord sent thee on a journey, and said: Go and utterly destroy the sinners, the Amalekites, and fight against them until they be consumed. Wherefore then didst thou not obey the voice of the Lord?

And Saul said unto Samuel, I have sinned: Now therefore, I pray thee, pardon my sin, and turn again with me, that I may worship the Lord. And Samuel said unto Saul: I will not return with thee. For thou hast rejected the word of the Lord, and the Lord hath rejected thee from being king over Israel.

Then said Samuel: Bring ye hither to me Agag the king of the Amalekites. And Agag came unto him delicately. And Agag said: Surely the bitterness of death is past. And Samuel said: As the sword hath made women childless, so shall thy mother be childless among women.

And Samuel hewed Agag in pieces before the Lord.

Ben and Nagar stand motionless, reciting the verses from the first book of Samuel in turn. An antiphony of verses that loosen Ben's tongue to make a declaration of faith, although he normally only ever asks questions. I must remain seated, however, paralyzed and bound next to their empty chairs, must remain silent, because these verses may only be spoken standing upright, tall and humble at the same time.

Now they call upon him, the deadly enemy of Israel, Amalek, son of Eliphaz, son of hapless Esau, who was denied the blessing, the precious promise that Yakov his brother had stolen from him through deceit. Esau wept, so it is written, but there is no record of his father's tears, only the bitter words that the father spoke to Esau as his legacy: Your dwelling will be far from the fatness of the earth, Esau, and away from the dew of heaven from above. You shall live by the sword. What could grow from this other than hatred? Esau hated Yakov his brother, so it is written, and the hatred was passed on from one son to the next, smoldering in each of them just as it had smoldered in Esau. Eliphaz. Amalek. The kings of Amalek. The Amalekites. Whenever they could, they defeated Israel. They were evil, Nagar will say, and we are ordered to conquer them. More pious Jews write Amalek's name on the soles of their shoes to drag it through the dust at every step: Destroy the memory of Amalek from beneath the heavens. That is what the mitzvah says and this is how Ben and Nagar fulfill their duty in their own way. They call Amalek by name, let him rise up in the landscapes and times that he haunted, watch his destruction and his return and the repeated destruction that follows his every appearance.

Remember what Amalek did to you when you went out of Egypt. Destroy the memory of Amalek from under the heavens, do not forget this!

Yes, don't forget to remember, Israel. Remember to forget. What sounds like a contradiction to me, is an endorsement for Ben and Nagar.

In the wilderness of Sinai, Shalom. Amalek against Moses.

Amalek came and sought to fight with Israel in Rephidim. Choose your men, Moses said to Yoshua, and go into battle against Amalek! I will stand at the top of the hill with the rod of God in my hand. Yoshua did as Moses commanded him and went out to fight against Amalek. Moses climbed with Aaron and Hur to the top of the hill. As long as Moses kept his hand held high, Israel was stronger, whenever he let his hand fall, Amalek was stronger.

Aaron and Hur held up his arms, one on the right, the other on the left, so that his hand remained high until the setting of the sun.

And Yoshua defeated Amalek by the sword, Shalom. Unlike Saul, who spared Agag. Samuel had to come, Samuel swung the sword. Then came David—

That was in Ziklag, Ben, in the south of Judah. When Amalek had razed the city to the ground and stolen all the women, David set upon him at dawn and felled him by dusk the next day. He took back from him everything that he had captured, and David freed the women.

And Haman, Shalom, don't forget Haman, the Agagiter.

Did you say Haman? His happiness was incomplete, as long as he saw Mordechai the Jew sitting at the gates of the palace. But they strung up Haman, Shalom. They hanged him on the gallows he had built for Mordechai. That was so.

Amalek's hatred against Israel will never wane, Ben. Other enemies took bribes or were willing to be reconciled. But not Amalek. He follows Israel's trail. For, lo, thine enemies make a tumult: And they that hate thee have lifted up their head. They have taken crafty counsel against thy people, and consulted against thy hidden ones. They have said: Come, and let us cut them off from being a nation; that the name of Israel may be no more in remembrance. We must be like Moses, Ben. When Yoshua defeated Amalek, the Lord said unto Moses: Write this for a memorial in a book, for I will utterly put out the remembrance of Amalek from under heaven. Moses built an altar and called it: The Lord is my throne. And he said: The hand on the throne of the Lord! The Lord is at war with the line of Amalek from one generation to the next! To this day, Ben. To this very day.

He is at war, Shalom, and he wins again and again. Go forth and defeat Amalek! Destroy everything that belongs to him, the Lord says to Saul. He doesn't do so, but Samuel—Samuel did. Joshua—Joshua did. David—David did. Mordechai—Mordechai did. Shalom Nagar—Nagar did.

Ben speaks his sentences as if he has only now truly understood the meaning of this list, he raises his voice, repeating the names of those who overcame Amalek to accentuate them. Nagar reaches for his chair, sits down, and stares at the floor.

You are Eichmann's executioner, Shalom, Eichmann is Amalek; you belong on the list.

Let me tell you a story. When I attended the Torah school back then, after I'd left the prison service, my teacher told me what the word meant: Amalek. He was a wise man. He had studied the Torah for thirty years before he turned blind. But he'd seen everything. The son of Eliphaz, the grandchild of Esau. He asked me: Do you know what he is called, Shalom?

Amalek, I said.

No one knows his true name, Shalom, he said, but he was called Amalek. And do you know why? I didn't know! Amalek is a people "Am," who lick blood, Shalom, he said. Our blood! He feeds on the blood that flows from our wounds, like flies. He comes when we are weak and wounded to lap our blood and so he survives. Then he stands, made strong by our weakness, and opens his mouth to shout the war cry, gushing blood. Then I understood, you know. I saw him in front of me again. Eichmann on the rope, as Merhavi ordered me to lift him up. His tongue hanging out, down to here, down below his chin, all covered in blood.

Samuel cut Agag to pieces, Ben—Amalek returned. Mordechai hanged Haman—Amalek returned. And me, don't I see Eichmann every day, every night? Doesn't he follow me wherever I go?

Eichmann is dead, Shalom.

Do you know the meaning of my name? It means something.

You told us there was a kingdom called Nagar.

Yes, but in another language, I don't know which, Nagar means to gnaw at something. And it means to eat, too. Shalom Nagar, do you see?

See what?

Peace, Ben, gets eaten away.

Ashes to Ashes

Even on that morning, the morning on which
the president adjudges the appeal for mercy,
a stack of lined paper sits on the prison
director's desk. Pages written by the condemned man, delivered by the night shift
guard as his orders command.

They wait, demand to be read and sorted,
if necessary passed on. A routine imposed
on his guards by the condemned man; stub-
bornly, unobtrusively, authoritatively.
Simply by writing. The papers include letters, notes for the defense, and records
that he has called "My being and doing," or
"Here, too, in the shadow of the gallows."
He has already produced a library, sometimes up to eighty pages per day, the writing on every page stretching to each edge,
certified by the author's long signature.
Line after line in effortlessly flowing
handwriting that bears witness to his thor-
oughness and certainty.

The first page on today's stack is different; the director's gaze is drawn to a
bar, printed diagonally across the page, a
barrier that is evidently supposed to pro-
hibit reading of the text. Heading: Will.
Above the heading is written: Invalid
draft. The text, however, is not obscured,

the director takes the sheet and scruti-
nizes the last will of the condemned man
with a feeling of tension and uneasiness
that he can scarcely admit to himself. A
draft, declared invalid, yet not torn up,
instead sent to him, the prison director;
after all, the condemned man knows on whose
desk his pages end up.

The writing is bigger than usual, the
spaces that the author has left like pedes-
tals underneath each short sentence demand
respect, perhaps representing a deep drawing of breath that shows the solemnity and
heaviness of the author's thoughts while
writing, and conveys this to the reader.

In the case of my death, the condemned man
writes, I ask the following:

I wish my body to be taken by my brothers out of this country and returned to my
homeland.

There, it is to be burned.

My ashes are to be divided into seven
parts.

One-seventh of the ashes should be placed
in my parents' grave.

One-seventh of the ashes should be scattered in the garden of my house in Buenos
Aires.

The remaining five-sevenths should be

given to my wife Vera and my four sons.
These parts should be placed in each of
their coffins once their earthly lives, too,
have come to an end.

In smaller letters, he adds:

This should serve as a reassurance and to
dissipate any fear of death.

This is followed by a justification written in extra-large letters:

Because: Death is no worse than birth, and
thousands upon thousands of other lives
await us.

The prison director closes his eyes, listens to the echo of these final sentences,
which ring hollow and dull inside him.
Sees someone walking, scattering ashes like
grain. Obscuring the light, multiplying
in the dust. Graves open and take in his
ashes, graves that do not even exist yet,
graves of the future.

The director opens his eyes again, his
gaze wanders to the side, compelled, he only
calms himself when he sees the words at the
top: Invalid draft. He turns the page, lays
it face down next to the stack and takes
the second page. This, too, has the heading: Will. The director reads, hesitates,

turns the first page back over, lays the
two pages next to one another, and compares
them.

> In the case of my death I ask . . . to
> divide into seven parts . . . thousands
> upon thousands of other lives.

Word for word the same gloomy liturgy,
sentences hewed as though in stone. And
again, the bar that crosses out the writing, again the note: Invalid draft.

Numbed by the sentences that have sunk
into him, and that he already knows by
heart, the director takes the third page.
For the third time, now. For the third time,
he reads the same words, this will, that
a body be transported to the homeland and
ashes divided for the past and future. The
same sentences, word for word. Only the bar
is missing this time, this time the accompanying remark is missing. This page is
valid. Final.

The director reads, sees the previous
day's date and, at the edge, the signature of the condemned man. The desire to
exterminate the page courses through him.
He wants to tear it, burn it, unwrite it.
But the sentences remain, engraved in his
consciousness. Once again power, again
dominion. Once again this man is making

a decree, giving instructions, he wants to
enforce something. The master of transport.
Transport of a body this time, his body.
Cremation. Further processing. The scrawny
fingers of the director hold on, they
clutch the paper like the scruff of a neck,
he could kill, can, will kill. Will kill
and cremate, scatter the ashes in the sea.
The director stands up, shuffles the papers
together, and places them all, together with
the unread pages, in the safe.

I read Eichmann's will to Ben without rolling the r's, without pausing after a conjunction, without turning periods into exclamation
marks. I read softly, to allow the number seven to resonate. Divide
the ashes into seven parts; the legacy is contained in seven sentences. He uses our number just the way he recited our prayer.

But why, Moshe?

Creation took seven days, the menorah has seven branches.
Perhaps Eichmann wanted to turn his death into his own godless
genesis. Perhaps he knew that the last owner of the menorah was a
German, king of the Vandals. Perhaps he thought that the symbol
of the holy light belongs to the Germans.

Did he hope to let his ashes glow the way Moses lit the seven
lamps of the menorah?

I don't know, Ben. I don't know anything. These entanglements,
it's as if they can never leave each other alone, Amalek and Israel,
not during their lives and not after death. Yesterday the newspaper
said: Heinrich Müller's grave has been found. He was Eichmann's
superior. The head of the Gestapo.

So?

Müller is buried in the Jewish cemetery in Berlin Mitte. Where
Moses Mendelsohn was buried. In the Jewish cemetery, Ben! The
persecutor next to the victims. All alike in death, their bones pale
together.

Who buried him there? The Germans?

I don't know. Müller died in the final days of the war. That's all
we know. Maybe the Red Army shot him, maybe he was killed in
an air raid. One of thousands of people killed in Berlin. Too many
to bury in single graves. They dug mass graves. There are so many
cemeteries in Berlin, but they put him in the old Jewish cemetery in
his general's uniform. It's not an irony of history, it's something else.

What do you mean?

An invisible force. An awful necessity?

Or is it just coincidence, Moshe? They had to bury Müller somewhere.

But not there. Not in that place, Ben. Did it have to be one of Eichmann's victims who was offered Eichmann's apartment, as happened to Leo Hauser, one of the few Jews to survive Auschwitz? How many residential areas were there in Berlin at that time? Fifty? A hundred? Hauser ends up in the one that Eichmann had lived in with his family. Two thousand apartments in that area and Hauser is given Eichmann's apartment. He had to live somewhere? I'd prefer to believe in chance, Ben. But it's such a close-knit circle. Think about my father, the persecutor who became a victim and who wanted to be a persecutor again. Caught in a circle. And look at Eichmann. When he starts school, what do the other pupils think he is? A Jew. The little Jew, that's what they called him. Who becomes his best friend? A Jew. Which department is he transferred to when he arrives in Berlin? To the Jewish department. Which race did he admire? The Jewish race. Somewhere he writes he would have made a good Jew. He could imagine that! And he's alleged to have said that one of the Jews he met in Hungary would have made a good SS soldier.

Moshe, stop it. That's disgusting.

Do you know that Eichmann only had good things to say about Hausner, his relentless prosecutor? I have often looked the attorney general straight in the eye, he writes. He never detected any hatred: His eyes look sad, beautiful, deep to me. He must be a good man in private. He liked him! And he even admired one of the judges—Halevi—he goes on about the intelligent-looking shape of his head and his pleasant voice. Cool-headed Eichmann,

Ben, who sent a chill through the courtroom—when he studied his own heart, all he found was warmth.

He was a hypocrite! A hypocrite and a liar. Foul and two-faced, through and through.

He praises his guards, too. They always treat me correctly. Never utter an unkind word. I have never faced hatred, Eichmann writes, and no hint of physical violence. He had the utmost respect for the men's composure.

He cursed Shalom and spat his blood on him, Moshe!

Says Shalom.

You don't believe him?

I think he believes what he says.

You know him, Moshe. You watch him. That was fifty years ago but you know how Shalom lives, Moshe, he lives in fear! Every single day. That fear is called Eichmann.

He can't let Eichmann go, it's true. And somehow, Eichmann can't let him go, either. And Heinrich Müller can't leave the victims alone, while he rots beside them in Berlin. They share the same earth, they share the same worms—

Stop it, Moshe!

I can stop, Ben. But this will never stop! Müller in the Jewish cemetery, Eichmann's victims in his own apartment, Eichmann's executioner sitting at the table with someone who owes his life to Eichmann. You call it coincidence? I say: These are signs.

Signs of what?

Maybe there can be no division of men. People try hatred, persecution, killings, but they achieve the opposite: They create a never-ending bond. Don't you notice the person you hate more than the person you love? Can't you see the person you are hunting more clearly than the one living quietly next door? And you will never forget a person you have killed, although you can banish someone from memory whom you brought into being.

You mean your father?

I mean so many fathers. You are not my son. How many have said that? But no culprit has declared: You are no longer my victim. And no victim ever let his persecutor go.

There is deliverance, Moshe.

If there is such a thing, then only through others. No one can free themselves.

Did you say Kaddish for your father?

No.

Why not?

How could I answer Ben's question? The orphan's Kaddish, the prayer of the son for the dead father, which allows his soul to rise up to the Lord. I had become a Jew, I had to fulfill the obligations. Reciting Kaddish was a part of that. But could I do it? Stand in front of a congregation, allow them to answer "Amen" for a man who had first been a Jew without knowing it and then against his will? Who hoped to annihilate the Jew in him through his son and his son's sons? To recite the Jewish prayer of death for him had seemed absurd and outrageous at the same time. I took my dilemma to a rabbi, told him everything. The rabbi listened with his head bowed, and remained silent when I had finished. A silence that would be followed by damnation, or so I feared. Damnation of the father and of the son. Weren't they both fleeing? One from his roots, the other from his duty?

But the rabbi did not condemn us. *Bera mesake aba*, he said. The son delivers the father. The factual calm of his answer confused me.

My father was a renegade, Rabbi, I said. He disowned his Jewishness.

A guilty Jew is still a Jew, the rabbi answered.

He was a wrongdoer, Rabbi, a persecutor of the Jews!

The evil father can be redeemed by the good son.

But he doesn't deserve that! I cried. My father does not deserve to have a Jewish congregation pray for him.

The Kaddish is not earned by the father, the rabbi said. It is the son's duty. And with those words, he dismissed me.

Why not, Moshe? Ben had waited while I was lost in thought, but now he was getting impatient. Why not? Your father was a Jew, after all.

The son of a Jewish mother.

Then it was your duty, Moshe.

It was, Ben, but I couldn't do it. The rule says: For eleven months you must say Kaddish every day, starting on the day of burial. Two months had already passed before I heard about my father's death. One day I received a letter that had taken many detours before it got to me. It said that my father had died—the date of his death, the date of the funeral, nothing else. I have no idea how he died or where he's buried, whether he was cremated, or if he was put in the earth.

The Kaddish wouldn't have counted because you had missed two months? That wasn't your fault. You could have simply prayed for nine months, or added on a couple of months. Did you think someone was counting?

That's what I wanted to believe.

What saying Kaddish for your father would have achieved can be achieved by living a good life, too. If you live a good life, you can still redeem him.

A Thousand Degrees

The decision of what to do with the body
was made a long time ago. An hour's drive
away, in a city called Petah Tikva—gateway
to hope—a man is welding together iron and
steel. He does not mind working late into
the night or until early morning. He is
even happy to stay behind on his own, alone
with his oven that is slowly taking shape,
after the last shift of welders leaves the
factory. Then he works in silence in the
empty hall, undisturbed by questions from
his colleagues, who must not be told the
true identity of the client or the purpose
of the oven. He says it is for a company
in Eilat on the Red Sea that processes fish
bones. They want an incinerator for sharks,
he says, whale sharks, reef sharks, white
tip sharks; he describes the shape of these
predators, their skeletons, and he adjusts
their sizes, at which he can only guess, to
fit the size of his oven.

Pinchas Zeklikovsky is proud to have
been chosen for this secret mission. He is
an expert in his area, was recommended as
a reliable specialist. The fact that he
is the only survivor in his family, that
his father, mother, brother, and sister are
among the victims of the man whose sentence

is soon to be carried out, was not taken
into account. It is just a coincidence.
Zeklikovsky carries out his work for them,
too. His client's instructions are kept to
a minimum. The design and materials are
up to him; he has only two conditions to
fulfill. One: The oven must be big enough
to hold a man lying down. Two: The burning temperature must be able to reach 1,800
degrees Celsius.

At first, Zeklikovsky thinks there must
be a mistake; ovens normally burn up to
800 degrees. But the number is confirmed. A
thousand degrees more than necessary. Zeklikovsky had wanted to point out the problems associated with such temperatures—the
time it would take to light, the danger
for the men operating the oven, strain on
the materials—but he stopped himself. He
thought he understood that there was more
at play here than technical measurements.
A thousand pieces of silver, a thousand
generations, a thousand victims of Solo-
mon's fire. When something can no longer
be counted, when something moves beyond the
realm of human comprehension, the Ethics
of the Fathers says: a thousand. A number
that represents the uncountable, an oven
beyond comprehensible standards. Built by a
human to fit a human, and yet destined to

exterminate a human, finally, absolutely, to burn flesh and bones to more than just ashes. To dust, perhaps, which flies up into the depths of the sky, to the furthest edge of creation, where the cosmos is still no different from chaos.

Zeklikovsky began by making the incinerator, a cylinder measuring two meters in length and one and a half meters in height. For the base, he welded together square panels and then riveted three metal ribs around the whole structure. He attached the oven door to the head of the incinerator—a heavy iron door that can be opened and closed using a lever on the side. To finish, Zeklikovsky built the chimney, three meters high. He fitted it to the rear end of the chamber and attached it in such a way that it can be removed for transport.

Now Zeklikovsky stands in front of the finished oven. He cannot deliver it with a clear conscience. He should check that the chamber can sustain the required temperature, if the seams hold, how close a person can get to the oven while it is at its hottest. Can the door even be opened at that point? Or should he lengthen the lever? These are not really his concerns. The order was clear, the order has been fulfilled. But Zeklikovsky does not want to hand over the oven. As long as he is working on the oven, his dead are with him, the dead whose graves he does not know, who probably do not have graves, who have become ashes, blown away. Zeklikovsky's oven is an extension of their vengeance. It is justice.

Zeklikovsky takes off his hat and wipes his brow. This man, who has been condemned—what does he do in his cell? Wait? Does he imagine what it will be like to be hanged? Does he think about the oven, does he know that his body will be burned? If he does know, does he imagine the flames beating at his body, cracking the skin, the flesh ripping apart, sizzling?

Zeklikovsky puts his hat back on, walks around the oven, lays his hand on the curved surfaces, runs his fingers over the ridges that he has smoothed, strokes the door, the lever. Opens the door, peers into the darkness, this night before the rising flames. Soon. Soon he will lie here. A chain: Zeklikovsky touches the oven that will touch the body of the man who sent Zeklikovsky's family to their deaths. He can forge this chain even more closely, can feel the incinerator not just with his hand but also with his arms, legs, body, he can lie inside it, just as the dead body will lie inside it. Zeklikovsky holds on to the

door, pushes first his right leg into the
chamber, then the left, forces his broad,
muscular body in afterward.

The opening is narrow, too narrow for
him. He cannot fit inside fully, cannot
get out, either, breathes all the air out of
his lungs, pulls his stomach in, looks for
something to hold on to—that could work,
surely that would enable him to get free—it
does not work. Zeklikovsky is trapped. He
has no choice but to wait.

An hour later he hears a big truck pull
up outside the factory. The driver doors are
opened, closed again, footsteps crunch over
the gravel in the yard, men enter the hall,
one walks over to the oven. Zeklikovsky
painfully turns his head to one side, sees
the prison director, whose eyes fill with
blatant disapproval when he realizes what
has happened. He waves his men over, four
soldiers, who pull the oven builder out of
the incinerator. The director turns around,
gives a few short instructions, and leaves
the hall.

Zeklikovsky understands. This oven should
be pure, untouched. It may be used only
once, be fired only once. This oven is
meant for one man, whose death is to leave
no traces, as though a shadow were disap-
pearing. For him they have erected a set of

gallows in the prison, which will be taken
down again once his body has been removed
from the rope. For him they have created a
hole in the floor of the execution room,
which will be filled in again as soon as
he has fallen through it. For him they have
ordered a new oven, which will never again
be used once he has been cremated. And no
one else will ever sit inside the glass box
that was made for him. Perhaps, thinks Zeklikovsky, they will even destroy the cell
in which he sat, will break down the walls,
build new ones.

The driver has now maneuvered the truck
into the hall, the soldiers have laid thick
harnesses over the oven, a crane will lift
it onto the loading platform. Zeklikovsky
stands next to the driver, who watches the
proceedings with a critical eye. Where will
you take it? he asks. The driver shrugs his
shoulders. No instructions yet.

Somewhere, an Oven

The body of the condemned man will be
transported. The transport destination
will be Zeklikovsky's oven.

The oven will be transported, too; secured
with chains and covered in a gray tarpaulin, it sits on the loading platform of
the truck that has just left the factory
and will soon cross the boundary of Petah
Tikva.

The driver, a level-headed man called
Epstein, has not yet been told his
destination.

He heads southward toward Ramla, where
the prison is, where the final preparations
are under way, where the body of the condemned man will hang, where they will take
him down from the rope. The truck moves as
if it has no driver. Is it the oven that
is setting the course, is it searching
impatiently for its purpose, for the body
that is to come? Epstein, who accelerates,
brakes, changes gear, is just the means.

The sun is already setting. The trees
lining the road have sprouted tall shadows, which lie across the road like railway sleepers. When the truck rolls over the
sleepers, the shadows slide over the hood
and for a moment darken the windshield, the

driver's cab, the hidden cargo. They even
touch the face of the prison director, who
sits next to Epstein with his eyes closed.
Just a few kilometers from the prison the
vehicle slows down. There are posts on
either side of the prison entrance, heavily guarded, on the highest alert. None
of the soldiers stops the truck, the men
nod, simply salute and wave them through,
point them toward the main entrance, where
the heavy gate is opened. Searchlights are
directed at the yard on four sides; where
the beams that guide them through the dusk
intersect, the truck comes to a halt.

It almost glows in the blazing light,
the edges of the oven can be seen underneath the tarpaulin. As though the prison
has finally received its core, a heart that
is already beating but is not yet pumping
anything though the iron veins.

The condemned man's cell has no windows;
he cannot see the truck. Perhaps he raised
his head as the engine sound grew louder,
looked up from the page he is currently
writing, listened and understood. If it is
so, his last will pounds within him, written out three times in the same words. The
three pages lie in the prison director's
safe; the third, valid, sits on top. Whoever
opens the safe now will be hit with the full

force of his sentences: I wish my body to
be taken by my brothers out of this country
and returned to my homeland.

There, it is to be burned.

There, in that place, on the other side of
the Mediterranean Sea, the Alps, in the former Reich, in a town in which the condemned
man was not born, but which he calls home.
There. Not here.

The director has left the truck and gone
into the main prison building. No one
comes, there is no one in sight, just the
truck in the yard and the oven. Epstein
rolls down the window. Is the oven murmuring, tugging at its chains? Probably just
the wind trapped under the tarpaulin.

The prison director comes back, climbs
onto the passenger seat, exchanges a few
words with the driver. Epstein nods, turns
the engine back on, takes his foot off the
brake, accelerates. The wheels spin, the
truck is unable to move a meter.

The oven puts up a fight. It gains weight.
It weighs as heavily as the sentence to
be carried out. The proximity to the condemned man reflects images in the darkness of its chamber, wakes it from its iron
stiffness. Chains clatter to the ground,
tarpaulins fold away to the side, a crane
grasps it from above. The oven glows under

the searchlights, it is lifted up, swung
to one side, set down alongside the truck,
it almost feels the gravel and the chips of
asphalt underneath. But the last stretch
is insurmountable. The ground puts up a
fight. Like arrow splinters in a magnetic
field the flints and chippings line up and
reject the oven. The oven insists on its
gravity, on its determination: It should
stay here, the court sentence should be carried out here! A struggle begins, a battle
between two forces, real enough but not to
be contained by the laws of physics. The
oven as a representative of the sentence,
against the ground as an advocate of the
words in the safe. In-this-yard against
in-my-hometown. Epstein releases the clutch,
the tires grip at last, the engine roars,
chucks out black clouds from the exhaust
pipe, the truck passes the gate, circles the
site, stops again. There are searchlights
here, too, but no gravel, instead there is
roughly cut concrete, more suitable perhaps. Fine, the oven wants to stay here. The
other will does not allow it.

I wish my body to be taken by my brothers out of this country and returned to my
homeland.

There, it is to be burned.

The vehicle starts to move once more,

stops again, moves again, stops, starts
once again, and then once again comes to
a halt. The oven sees stone slabs come
together and move apart again, a seemingly
forgotten tool sitting on top. Small, light
cones on the sandy ground, terebinth and
cypress trees have scattered their fruits;
they remain there, the ground rejects the
oven. Next, the fragrances, green and gold
they blow against it, intoxicating, full
of promise, and yet no place for ovens,
for this oven. It is driven in a wide arc,
northward, eastward. From this country
to my home country. The oven braces itself
against it, all for nothing. There, my body
is to be burned.

The air tastes of salt and the cool-
ness of the night as the truck stops for
the seventh, for the final time. There are
wooden planks beneath the oven, it touches
them carefully, lowers itself down, rises
and falls with them like the rhythm of the
waves.

Each of the seven places has the oven in its
own way—they keep it, are awarded it. The
body of the hanged man was cremated in the
prison yard, says one source. In a building on the edge of the prison grounds, says
another. In an abandoned factory in Ramla.

In a warehouse in Ramla. In a small patch
of forest outside the city. The oven was in
an orange grove near the coast, say others.
A journalist, chosen as a witness for the
execution, writes that the cremation took
place onboard a police boat. Where the boat
was heading, he did not say.

The oven can be seen in each of these
places, on every piece of ground, seven
times over. My ashes are to be divided into
seven parts.

Seven parts, seven places, one oven
that sits in each place, the burning of a will against the force of a
sentence—constellations, how we imagine ourselves to be when we have the freedom to do so, when something happens that
cannot be seen in its entirety. Beginning and end are marked, assigned a unique
index—everything else, the details, remains
open, an empty field, in which people can
plow furrows of fate and resign themselves
to things as they do in fairy tales.

This is not how it was. So how was it?
Perhaps there were not any transports at
all, perhaps no Epstein driving the truck.
Perhaps even the oven is just an image, an
expression of desire, the circle of perpetrators and victims can close itself. In

any case, Haaretz, the daily newspaper,
whose straightforward, reliable reporting is respected, knows nothing of the oven
that was transported. Instead, it mentions
a cement factory where the incinerator runs
both day and night. The decision was made
to cremate the condemned man there. No one
is allowed to give the name of the factory.
But its night lighting is clearly visible
from the prison.

In Petah Tikva—gateway to hope—a man is
welding together iron and steel. Pinchas
Zeklikovsky is building an oven for a company in Eilat on the Red Sea that inciner-
ates fish bones. He imagines he is building
the oven in which the condemned man will be
burned.

Every part of the carcass is used. The meat is filleted, fried, boiled, steamed, eaten, and the rest is processed: The skins are used for fish leather, and the bones, the fish bones, are ground to meal like other bones or simply burned to ashes. Fish bone ash, which is used for something or other. I wonder what.

The question runs through my mind, although any answer would do. It was just that I didn't want to let Zeklikovsky go, the oven builder who had been central to the story for a moment would now disappear. My writing couldn't hold him any longer— my writing had to return to Ramla, to the prison. Back to the cell, back to Eichmann.

I pulled the piece of paper out of the typewriter and picked up a new one. As I was feeding it in, I heard a bang on the door of my apartment, a real thud. I wheeled over to the door, listened, thought I could hear murmuring; muffled, hushed sentences that soon turned into a hum. Nagar was holding his kippah when I opened the door, wiping sweat off his forehead and temples with a large handkerchief. He put the handkerchief back in his pocket, picked up the bag on the floor beside him. I've brought you some lamb, Moshe.

Now he's standing at my desk, he won't sit down. I wanted to ask you, Moshe, I want to ask you.

He repeats his words, he hums and sings them. I want to ask you, Moshe, I want to ask you. That's why he's risked coming to see me; to get an answer. He still wants to ask me something, but the question must have got lost on the way, maybe it was drowned out by his feeling of unease, or perhaps the effort it took him to get here left no room for anything else. He takes out the handkerchief again, removes his kippah, wipes over his head and the back of his neck. What, Shalom? What do you want to ask me? He puts the kippah back on his head and tucks his handkerchief away again. His eyes, which have been dancing about until now, find a focus. He looks at the pages I've written, the sheet sticking out of the typewriter. He looks at me.

I want to ask you . . . Moshe, I want to ask: Where are you writing me to?

Why isn't Ben here? He would interrupt. What do you mean, Shalom? Nagar would have to explain, make it clear what he meant. I can't take on Ben's role, I am supposed to provide answers, my hesitation is a disappointment in itself. But what should I say? His question surprises and upsets me. This is what he's thinking about? Shalom Nagar, the narration machine, immune to any other story, wrapped up in his Eichmann like he's in a cocoon? And now here he is, quivering with unease, feeling sensitive about the papers on my desk, sensitive to my voice, my Eichmann, concerned about my Nagar. No, he's worried about himself. He can't differentiate between the Nagar in my text and himself standing there.

Although he only knows the beginning and two or three fragments, Nagar can feel himself in my writing. Where are you writing me to?

I'm writing about you and Eichmann, Shalom, I answer quietly, but I'm following Eichmann's path, not yours. From the day before the judgment to the end. Nagar—my Nagar—follows Eichmann on his journey.

Nagar nods, but I don't know if he's been listening. His gaze has drifted away; he can't stop looking at the papers on my desk. He points at them. Where are we?

May 31, 1962, Shalom. The president has denied Eichmann's appeal. Preparations are under way. I've just written about the oven being transported.

Zeklikovsky built it, Moshe. In Petah Tikva.

Yes, I say. The reporter from *Haaretz* can write what he likes. I'd rather have Zeklikovsky's oven than a furnace in some cement factory, too.

It was my day off, you know.

I know, Shalom. The beginning of the chapter was already finished in my head, and even had a title:

The End of a Day Off

May 31, 1962, is Nagar's day off. He has
slept in, cleaned his tools, patched up the
wire mesh of the chicken coop. Now he goes
for a walk with Ora and their little boy.
They live in a cramped development with ter-
raced houses, white cubes beneath bright
red, gently inclined roofs, barely a dis-
tinguishing feature among them. The main
street is wide, the rest are all alleyways
squeezed between the buildings. The only
bit of space is behind the houses, room
for a small garden, a shed, a few doves or
chickens. It is enough for Nagar, but Ora
wants to get out of town, as she calls it,
although they barely leave the development
and walk toward the hills, along a winding
path lined with power masts. The path is
dusty, full of stones, here and there a low,
dry bush. Ora is holding the little boy's
hand, Nagar is walking alongside them,
arms folded across his chest, head bowed,
deep in thought. He could not say what he
is thinking about. Nothing is weighing
on his mind, he has no problems to try to
solve, no plans. It is more a kind of waiting, like his mind is on pause but his body
will not follow.

Suddenly Ora stopped, Moshe. She picked up our little boy and turned around. A car was coming up behind us, driving so fast all we could see was a cloud of dust. We moved out of the way to let the car pass. But when it reached us the driver stopped, the back door flew open, someone grabbed me, pulled me inside, slammed the door shut, the driver put his foot down. Out of the corner of my eye I saw Ora's face, her mouth wide open, that's how shocked she was. I was confused, too, but then I recognized the driver, it was one of my colleagues. And the man who pulled me into the car was Merhavi, my commander. Neither of them said a word. There was no need. I knew what this was about.

Nagar tells his story in a different way from usual, sounding flat, somehow distanced from the story. His stories at the meeting place always brim with life even after the third telling, but he just rattles this off as if it's a chore. He's missing his familiar surroundings, missing Ben who always jumps in, asking for explanations, who'd ask about Ora now. Didn't Ora call the police? She must have thought you'd been kidnapped, Shalom! And Nagar could elaborate then, explain, make up another version; he might say that the car had stopped and turned back so he could reassure Ora. A colleague is ill, I told her, they're a man short for the night shift. She wasn't allowed to know about Eichmann, Merhavi had forbidden us to talk about him.

Ben's not here, but that's not all. Something is bothering Nagar. Not the question he came to ask. Something else, something he can't or won't say at the meeting place, something that's hard for him to admit and that he needs to tell me on my own. So I wait. Nagar looks around the room, digs his hands into his trouser pockets, takes them out again, shuffles together the papers lying all over my desk, stacks them in a nice neat pile.

Eichmann's Executioner

You know, Moshe—I tell you stories, you and Ben. You come, I tell them to you. I always say they are true stories, about events that really happened.

They did happen, Shalom. On May 31, 1962, you had the day off. They picked you up—

The path Ora and I walk along is too narrow, Moshe. Barely two feet wide with stones everywhere. You couldn't drive a car down it. How would they have found me in the foothills anyway . . . I'm describing Eichmann's kidnapping, Moshe. It was him they pulled into a car a few meters away from his wife. It was their wedding anniversary, you know. He'd bought flowers for her, that's why he came home on a later bus. The Mossad agents had been watching him for weeks; he always took the same bus, got out, smoothed down his coat, let the bus drive off before crossing the road to his house. But on the evening they planned to kidnap him the bus came, the doors opened, the doors closed again, the bus drove away. No Eichmann. They thought: He knows everything. He must have seen us, he's got away. They were frantic. Why had they waited so long! They sat there in their cars, discussing the situation, wondering what to do. Then the next bus came. The doors open, Eichmann gets out holding his briefcase in one hand and a bunch of flowers in the other. They realize they've got him. That's how it was, Moshe. He often tells me that story. He doesn't blame the Mossad agents. They did a good job, he says. He knows all about it; after all, he used to work for the secret service. They were called the secret police, the Gestapo.

Nagar fiddles with my typewriter while he talks, takes out the crooked sheet of paper and puts it back in properly.

He tells me so often, Moshe. He tells me, I tell you. Sometimes I don't know who's talking—sometimes Eichmann is Nagar, and Nagar is Eichmann. It shouldn't be like that. You have to write, Moshe. You have to write it the way it was.

You have to write it the way it was. With those words he leaves
me alone. When I'm back in front of my typewriter, I can hardly
believe he was really here. But the meat is still on the table. The
way it was? It could have been like this:

May 31, 1962, is Nagar's day off. He has
slept in, cleaned his tools, patched up
the wire mesh of the chicken coop. Now he
goes for a walk with Ora and their little
boy, through the dusty alleys to the edge
of the development. Ora is busy with the
child; Nagar walks alongside them, arms
folded across his chest, head bowed, deep
in thought. When they get home, there is a
car outside the house with two men standing beside it, both of them smoking. Nagar
recognizes one of them as his commander.
Now the commander sees Nagar, too, drops
his cigarette on the ground, stamps it out,
straightens his uniform, approaches him.
It's time, Shalom, he says. Nagar nods, as
if shaking his head.

No Fear, No Hope

The condemned man does not know that his
executioner is on his way. He has had to
endure a tedious medical examination, the
results of which satisfied the doctor. The
condemned man is ready to be hanged. Ready
for death.

Now he is back in his cell, lying on the
prison bed. Opposite him stands a guard
whom he does not know and does not like,
because he is as stiff as a board. He misses
the small, stocky man. The one with the
trustworthy eyes and the incongruous wom-
anizer's mustache. There are still stacks
of books on the table, essays that the condemned man has spent a great deal of time
working through. Scoundrels, cheats, and
liars, all of them. Reitlinger and Poliakov,
not to mention Brand. He could prove it, he
will prove it, if only they would give him
some more paper. The evening meal comes,
simple as always: bread, sausage, olives,
black tea. He eats everything, as always.

The crockery and cutlery are cleared away,
passed item by item through the door hatch,
which has been kept mostly closed since the
appeals court announced its decision. The
condemned man, who no longer has any hope
of appeal, is to be given the pretense of

privacy, the illusion of being alone. Some
time later the hatch is opened once again,
the guard gets up stiffly, stiffly takes
the key, unlocks the door, and salutes
as the prison director enters the cell. The
condemned man, too, has gotten up and is
standing to attention. The director nods to
him. It is a long time since he has looked
at him. His gaze was always lowered when he
entered the cell, as though the tiles were
the only thing of any interest to him. Now
he looks at him. At midnight, he says. Asks
two or three questions, then asks for paper
and pencils to be brought.

The condemned man starts writing again.
First, a letter to his wife and his sons.
My last wish was to compose this letter, he
writes, to be able to smoke freely, and to
have a bottle of red wine. They have promised to bring the red wine a bit later, he
adds in brackets.

Many people say he drank a bottle of Car-
mel wine, the wine made in the country of
the victims that has been loved by the Germans ever since it was served at the Berlin trade exhibition in 1896. Kosher wine
from the vineyards of Baron Rothschild.
To choose this wine as the execution drink
would have been a special gesture, it could
have been interpreted as a concession, per-

haps even as a desire for some sort of rec-
onciliation. Had the condemned man not
written: I would like to find peace with
my former enemies, too? A desire so absurd
that you might, absurdly enough, want to
believe him.

But it was not so. I have now been given a
bottle of wine as well, continues the condemned man in his letter. They gave me the
choice of sweet red wine or dry white wine.
After brief consideration, I picked the
latter.

So, dry white wine, while smoking one
cigarette after the other. Does he eat something, has he chosen a last meal? It seems
not. He is not hungry anyway, he has no
time, he must write, must describe the
events in detail, provide evidence that
will explain everything. He keeps writing
after the letter is finished; the director
has given him plenty of paper, the pencils
are well sharpened as always. The condemned
man writes and drinks the half liter of
wine—the whole bottle.

His work is interrupted by a final visit.
So once again into the meeting room, once
again talking through the glass. The condemned man is almost reluctant to put down
his pencil, but then he straightens himself, stands up, and follows the guard.

On the other side sit Reverend Hull and
his wife, who is wearing a black-and-white
suit and a small, fashionable hat decorated
with a dove feather. In preparation for
this final conversation, Hull has written
the condemned man a long letter in which he
discusses his vision of man, the history
of mankind, and the great philosophic order
into which everything is integrated.

You say, writes Hull, that man is still a
work in progress and is continually devel-
oping toward perfection. It is a shame that
in the last two years you have not been in
touch with this world. You only need to
look at the world to see the hopeless circumstances that mankind has created on
Earth. Development toward ever greater perfection? I fear mankind has reached the
utmost limit and is about to throw the
world into utter chaos. You say that God
does not get angry or inflict punishment.
In other words, you do not believe he is
the judge of the entire world. You say your
soul will be freed from your body when you
die; you are convinced of this, and you ask
who can prove it is not so? I ask: Where
is your proof that this is the case? Cast
your own ideas aside. Read God's words and
believe. Take Christ as your savior and

allow yourself to be saved. THAT IS YOUR
ONLY HOPE.
Yours in devotion, (Rev.) William L. Hull

He is slightly embarrassed by the capital
letters now. The sentence is like a faded
poster. Useless. It is not about hope now.
The man who sits before him does not know
this passion. Someone, something has killed
it inside him. This man fears and hopes for
nothing. No virtue, no desire for virtue,
and in this emptiness completely calm, as
if legitimized by some higher power. Satan
stands tall within him, holds him, drives
him, but to where? Hull shivers, then pulls
himself together. His headphones crackle.
Good evening, says the condemned man. You
look so distressed. Why are you sad? I am
not sad at all.

We—we are sad because your end has come,
Hull answers, annoyed with himself for
stammering. He must stay strong! And he has
already lost the thread. The peace in this
face, this soft smile. Hull cannot bear it.
Satan should spit, drool, roar!

If you repent we will no longer be sad,
says his wife. Her voice, already high,
clangs when she speaks. Are you sorry for
what you have done? Are you ready to repent?

I have not changed my mind, answers the
condemned man, with a friendly calmness.
Nor have I lost my inner strength.

When did they tell you that your end is
upon you? asks Hull.

Just now, says the condemned man. They
barely gave me two hours to prepare. They
are rushing it, just like the appeal.

Think of the murderer on the cross, says
Hull. In the last minute, hanging on the
cross, he repented. Call Jesus' name.

Yes, call Jesus' name, repeats his wife.

The condemned man moves his gray-blue eyes
over her. He sees a tightly wound woman,
clad in the armor of her evangelical fervor, who sits as though she is already
standing again, and stands as though she
is already well on her way. But where to?
Not to his destination. Just knowing that
is enough for the condemned man.

Will your husband stay with me to the end?
he asks the preacher's wife quietly. The
woman seems, wholly unexpectedly, to drop
her armor. Her expression becomes almost
warm and she settles against the back of
her chair as though it were a protective
shoulder. Yes, she answers. Until the very
last moment.

The condemned man takes off his head-

phones, gets up, gives a hint of a bow. The
guards escort him back to his cell. The
moment the door is locked, he begins writing once more.

The Walk to the Gallows

He is still writing when the door hatch is
opened, the key passed through, the door
unlocked, and two guards and the prison
director enter the cell. They nod to their
colleague in the cell. It is time.

   The condemned man looks up, rises from
his chair, hesitates, and rests one hand on
the table top. The other he raises, places
over his glasses, covering his eyes.

   A sudden faintness, the director thinks.
Now the man is feeling the weight of his
guilt, for which he is about to pay with
his life. Now the end is in sight, he finds
he does not want to see it after all. This
faintness is a sign, for which the man has
waited long enough, thus far in vain. At
last there is a human being standing in
this cell, and the director feels for him,
he cannot change that. He surreptitiously
gives the guards a signal to keep back.
He expects correctness and steadiness from
them, but compassion, too.

   Meanwhile, the condemned man has sat back
down on his chair, taken the pencil in his
hand and continued writing. Faintness? Not
at all. He simply wanted to concentrate in
order to bring to an end his thoughts, his
sentence, this thing that he is writing as

though driven by the furies! As he realizes
his mistake the director is overcome with
disgust, even hatred. This is no human!
This is a monster.

Again he gives the guards a signal but
this time with a grimmer expression. They
move to the table, one of them lays a hand,
hard and dry, on the condemned man's shoulder. Unperturbed, he continues writing. The
two guards are forced to grab his arms and
pull him away from the paper. Confused,
he looks at the guards; he seems genuinely
not to understand them. One of the guards
points to his glasses, which he no longer
needs. Obediently, the condemned man removes
them.

He stands there with exposed eyes, focuses
his now-swimming gaze on the director,
points questioningly at the prison clothing
that he is still wearing. Where is his blue
suit? Surely they do not want to hang him
in a brown shirt and baggy brown trousers,
and these felt slippers? After all, the
agreement was that whenever he appeared publicly he would be given the blue suit, the
white shirt, the blue striped tie. And what
is this if not a public appearance?

The director says no. He will not be wearing the blue suit.

The guards handcuff the condemned man,

stand either side of him, and enter the
hall, where Reverend Hull is already waiting, a copy of the New Testament, with a
black cover, in his hands. They go through
the hole that has been made in the wall
of the meeting room. The ground is scattered with pieces of stone and brick that
crunch underneath Hull's black loafers, the
guards' sturdy boots, the condemned man's
felt soles. The prison director brings up
the rear.

The five men begin marching, they cross
the landing and enter the long corridor.
Slowly! Slow down! The prison director's
call is aimed at Hull, who is leading the
procession and has picked up the pace. Is
the preacher shying away from the physical
proximity of the condemned man? No glass
wall separating them now, no conversation
distanced by microphones and headphones,
only the sound of footsteps behind him,
growing ever closer. Only the eerie feeling
of having soulless eyes trained directly
on his back, through his back and on his
heart. The condemned man sways slightly,
perhaps that is to do with the wine that he
drank too quickly, perhaps because he was
not allowed to finish his writing and his
final, incomplete sentence is playing on
his mind—the guards drive him forward, the

sentence pulls him back, he must add in the final period, otherwise these things, these matters will never be explained.

Halfway there he begins to sway more severely, the guards brace themselves against him, the condemned man stands still. Reluctantly, the prison director barks an order from behind, the guards grab hold of him, the condemned man struggles against their grip. Now Hull stops, too, turns around, the New Testament raised like a shield.

No attack to fear: It is only the condemned man's nose running. Without his hands, which are secured behind his back, he raises his shoulder as a gesture, points with his chin at his left breast pocket. Now one of the guards understands, too, he takes the tissue from the pocket and holds it to the condemned man's nose, in a surprisingly gentle way, as a father might do for his son. As they start moving again a guard appears at the end of the corridor and holds his hands up as if to ward them off. Stop! Not ready. What a ghastly situation, notes Hull later in his writings, behind me, the condemned man stands swaying between his guards, he is ready for death, but the executioners are not ready for him.

Halting actions that seem to follow some

kind of pattern; first, braked from behind,
then from the middle, now from the front.
All that remains is for something to happen from below, or to stop them in the
very last few meters from above. As though
this train should not, must not, reach its
specified destination. Perhaps the prison
director is thinking something similar,
perhaps he, too, has noticed the strange
pattern in these interruptions to the timetable. He gives a word of command that is
intended to banish the ghosts, cut this
knot once and for all: This must be seen
through! An imperative used as a declaration. Forward!

They walk on. The guard at the end of the
corridor who tried to stop them opens the
door. The preacher stands still to allow
the director, the guards, and the condemned
man to walk ahead.

A part of the room about the size of a
cell has been separated off by a black sheet
hanging over a length of wire, a curtain
that swings slowly and then stops. The
sheet, Hull thinks, is hiding a long lever
that sticks up out of the ground. He can
see someone behind it—one man, or two?

There are four journalists huddling in
front of the curtain, here to act as eyewitnesses, as well as the prison doctor,

and some more guards. Fifteen people in total. Some say ten. Another source says four. The others apparently stood in the adjacent room and watched the proceedings through a pane of glass.

What is certain is that those waiting tried to keep their distance. None of them touches the condemned man; none of them touches the square iron plate in the middle of the room.

Penultimate Sentences

No one moves. The guards look at their commander, the commander watches the director,
the director stares up at the ceiling. One
of them must take control of the situation.
  There are no guidelines for this procedure, but everyone knows how hanging works.
The director knows from his manual, and
the process is familiar to the guards from
novels. Or from the movies.
  One of the guards seems to be staring
at the condemned man; a man of the same
age, medium height, with a round, bald
head, glasses with lenses like magnify-
ing glasses, a mustachio. It is not clear
whether the condemned man can see him at
all, he is missing his glasses but perhaps
he can distinguish enough to appreciate
the similarity; the man could be the twin
brother of the officer who spent so many
months interrogating him long before the
trial even began. The kidnapped man confided so much to this captain, who seemed
so gentle, so polite—he confided more than
he wanted to. He had to revise some statements, take them back when he was given
the interrogation reports to look through
the next day. He even spoke of the hanging in the interrogation, explained that

he was prepared to string himself up in
this country, publicly, as a deterrent. And
he spoke about courage, about his desire
not to shift the blame but to take responsibility for the things in which he had
been involved. It is of course a sad courage that I have to muster today, he had
said, but back then I had the courage and
said yes, so today, too, I have courage
and say: Here you are! My head is—lying on
the—there, where it belongs.

Where it belongs: The condemned man takes
two steps, stands on the square plate,
straightens himself up, feet together in
his checked slippers. Now that he is in
this room he is no longer swaying.

As though they had been waiting for this,
the others now start moving, too, they
scribble headlines for the next day's papers
on their notepads, fumble in their coats
for their stethoscopes and mirrors, wind
the crank that will lower the rope with the
noose down from the ceiling. Jesus, Jesus,
Lord Jesus, my savior! comes the voice of
the preacher, who has stepped in front of
the condemned man and calls the savior
with fervor, in the hope of a miracle, a
conversion, a confession beneath the gallows. It does not require many words, no
debate, no justification. The condemned man

must simply call the name of the Lord. Just
this one word. This one time. The condemned
man opens his mouth. But what he wants to
confess requires more than one word and a
larger audience than the deathly pale Hull,
whose message he probably has not even
heard. It is not a poor penitent who speaks
from the plate in the middle of this room,
not a remorseful soul. Instead, it is a
statesman who speaks into the vastness, who
goes into raptures with his own sentences,
which he presents like flags flown at full
mast:

Long live Germany. Long live Argentina. Long live Austria. These are the
three countries to which I was connected
most closely. I will never forget them.
My regards to my wife, my family, and my
friends. I had to obey the laws of war and
my oath. I am ready.

The guards tie his feet with a belt. I
cannot stand like this, says the condemned
man. They loosen the strap. The commander
loops the noose around his neck, a rope
measuring four centimeters in diameter. The
noose is coated in rubber and double knot-
ted; the condemned man must strain his neck
as though in a choker to make it fit. The
commander shows him a black hood, others
say it was a black blindfold. Do you want

this? he asks. No, I do not need it, says the condemned man. His tone is impatient, it is clear he no longer wants to be bothered, prepared, interrupted. Because he is not yet finished.

His eyes fixate on the guards standing behind the commander, their backs to the wall. In any case, gentlemen, he says, we will see each other again soon. That is the lot of all people.

The guards do not move; they do not understand German. The commander understands, but he does not move either. Only the preacher, gripped by a vague terror that took hold when the condemned man began to speak, shows any reaction. With his last strength, which he takes from an unfailing belief in the inviolability of his delivery, he responds to this lost man with the New Testament: Jesus. He manages only these two syllables, he lays them on the book like a communion wafer, searches pleadingly for the gaze of the condemned man. The condemned man does not look at him. He no longer looks at anyone.

Drop

Ready! calls the commander.

The tension in the room is palpable, solid
as something with its own length, width,
and height. The smell of sweat hangs in the
air; the reaction of the nervous system to
various stimuli.

The guards' sweat is caused by first-
night nerves. They have no experience of
this situation, and no one knows if the
director's manual can even be trusted.
Is the mechanism underneath the iron
plate reliable, will the rope run down as
planned, and as planned come to a stop?
Will the frame of the gallows hold? Should
the British experts have been brought here?
The name Albert Pierrepoint was mentioned
several times in the media; it was assumed
that he would carry out the sentence. But
those responsible had never considered using
an executioner from another country. We
must do this ourselves, was the feeling,
and we can do this ourselves. They had used
a sack for the practice run, guessing its
weight because they did not have any suitable scales. The sack fell neatly through
the hole, then hung serenely from the noose,
but what does that mean? Broken neck? Chok-

ing? A sack does not die. It just hangs there.

The preacher's sweat is biological disbelief. No human body says: Death, where is thy sting? Everyone struggles, fights, rejects this dull denial that frightens everyone to the core despite all the Good News. An age-old reflex, the fear shared by all living beings, which no one can take from us.

The prison director's sweat is metaphysical. A consequence of the absurdity that these two poles, the extremes of being and nothing, could be short-circuited in a matter of seconds. Not to be borne. All pores open up, the cold secretions numb the skin that is warmed by the overburdened brain.

Ready!

The matter is now delegated to the man, the men behind the curtain. The preacher has seen a lever. Other eyewitnesses describe a piece of equipment with two buttons, in front of which two guards stand. Both of these guards, so they said, pressed their buttons at the same time, but only one triggered the mechanism. Neither knew which was the real trigger. No one should be able to say: It was me, I killed this man.

Ready!

The condemned man raises his head, opens his mouth—for one last, his very last sentence?

A click. The iron plate beneath his feet gives way, the condemned man falls into the depths.

It is two minutes to midnight.

Then silence. The self-sufficient song of the dead, monosyllabic, interrupted only by the swinging of the rope and the regular, persistent dripping of some liquid onto the floor of the room into which the trapdoor has opened.

Him and Me

After some time, there is movement behind
the black curtain. Something is shifted,
someone coughs slightly, clears their
throat. The sheet is pushed to one side,
Nagar comes out, blinking, the sudden
brightness in the room confuses him. No one
is there now.

Empty stage. Spotlight. And here he
stands, the small Yemenite, guard, executioner, with shaking hands. What has
he done?

He remembers, recalls each of the day's
events in turn, bringing them back out into
the light, onto the stage.

They pulled him into a car, tore him away
from Ora and the boy on the stony path to
the hills, with the engine screeching they
drove him to the prison, gave him hurried
instructions, charged him with the weight
of his duty. Representative for millions of
victims. Ambassador of a people. Hand of
justice.

Then the walk through the building, the
stairs, the long corridor. The men whom he
passed. His colleagues among the guards,
the preacher, the doctor, journalists with
notepads under their arms, the director
came toward him, hurried into his office,

the three judges who had given the death
sentence sat on three chairs. In front of
the door to the execution room were two
guards whom Nagar did not know. Everyone looked at him, with deference, respect,
perhaps awe—he should have grown under
their gazes but instead he shrank. The door
grew before him, he could hardly reach the
handle.

The condemned man stands in the room on
the plate that seals the hole in the ground.
Nagar is alone with him. No others there?
No one. They were all in the corridor. Even
the commander waited outside.

Nagar is alone with the condemned man.
He looks him in the eye and the condemned
man returns his gaze, for the first time
in all these months. Blue eyes, blue-gray,
eyes that reveal nothing. The soul of the
condemned man is reflected somewhere else.
Nagar sees only himself in these pupils.
The guard, the executioner.

Nagar loops the noose around the neck of
the condemned man, who once again looks
past him, pulls the knot tight, takes half
a step back. The condemned man nods. And
now he says something, a long German sentence, gives a brief German speech, with
raised head, as though speaking before an
audience, his victims perhaps, who have

come together somewhere here, in innumerable
numbers, they need very little space, only
the air that the condemned man breathes. Or
is he talking to his old Führer, reporting
numbers transported, the concluding figures, the final balance sheet? Or perhaps
he is just speaking to the walls, wants
his last words to reverberate in this room,
wants to know they will be preserved here
for all eternity, these baying words that
sound like polished boots and the death's
head, incomprehensible to Nagar.

The sentence is uttered. But the condemned
man raises his head once more, looks at
Nagar, calm and sharp, holds him firmly
with his gaze. Captures him. You and me,
say his eyes. The shadow of a smile plays
around his thin lips. He opens his mouth—

The commander comes, pulls a white hood
over the condemned man's head, and leaves
the room once more.

Nagar stretches his back, goes behind the
black curtain. He feels the weight of the
condemned man on the iron plate, wears the
noose around his neck, twice, three times,
the shackles are heavy, everything weighs
him down, grows strangely heavier. He can
hardly raise his arm. He looks ill, too,
the light is fading, soon it will be night
behind the curtain. Nagar—

Nagar does not know what he is doing. Later, he no longer knows what he has done. He knows what he hears; a loud click, the buzz of the rollers on which the rope runs, the muffled lurch as it comes to a stop.

His memory samples images, shows here a black button that his thumb presses, there a long lever that he pulls, a stick that he moves, a knot that he loosens.

Nagar hears the click of the catch on the iron plate being released, and as the rope is ripped from the rollers, he feels how the Earth turns and casts off a person like a horse his hated rider.

The fall has no end. Two, three, ten meters, this man falls forever.

The Final Sentence

According to the prison director's manual, the heartbeat of a hanged person takes
around twenty minutes to stop. No heart has
ever beaten for more than forty minutes from
the moment of hanging. The manual recommends leaving the hanged person on the rope
for one hour.

The director leaves his man hanging for
two hours. Some say it was three. Nagar
remembers it being ten hours.

In any case the condemned man hangs
for a long time, feared even as a corpse,
although he is just a dead man being pulled
down by gravity. Someone must brace themselves against this gravity so that the
body can be taken down from the rope. This
task, too, is assigned to Nagar. He goes
with the commander to the storeroom underneath the execution room, palely lit by a
single light bulb.

Nagar does not look; he has seen nothing until now. He hears the commander pick
up the ladder they put there for this very
moment, wood scrapes across concrete, the
commander leans the ladder against the
ceiling opening, now the steps are creaking, the commander is climbing upward.

It stinks in the room, a faint mixture of
feces and urine.

What's wrong, Shalom? Lift him up!

Nagar opens his eyes with his head bowed.
There is a puddle on the floor, he has
already stepped in it. He slowly raises his
head.

Checked felt slippers pointing downward. Dark brown cotton trousers, far too
wide—two men would fit inside them. Light
brown cotton shirt, a dark streak, dark
flecks on his chest. Dried blood. His neck:
elongated, deep grazes and cuts on both
sides, skin hanging in shreds over them.
The noose under his chin, as if it wanted
to take his head off his body, only it
would not give way. Even so, his mouth is
half open, his tongue hangs out, it glis-
tens with something dark, that, too, is
blood, still wet, even now still wet. His
head is tilted toward the left shoulder, his
face bloated, white as chalk. His eyes popping out. His eyes oozing from their sockets, large, round. Set free at the end, they
looked for the last image they had seen,
searched for it until the very last moment.
Now they find it again.

The commander does not notice this; he
has seen everything else and will note it
down later in his report, which he keeps

dispassionate and factual. The director,
who receives the report for signing, knows
from his manual what these symptoms mean:
The cause of death was not a broken neck,
but a slow, agonizing suffocation. Begin-
ner's mistake. The drop was too short; the
man did not fall far enough. Or was he too
light, did he lose weight rapidly in his
final hours? No excuse. With his hands and
feet tied, he could only fight with his neck
after the fall. How long for? This question
will haunt the director. Years later, on the
morning on which someone shoots him dead
in the middle of the street, he awakes with
a sore throat and, looking in the mirror,
sees that he has bitten his tongue.

Hold him by the stomach, Shalom, with
both arms!

Nagar takes hold, but nothing happens.

Hold him lower down! Lift him up!

Nagar grips him lower down, lifts him
up, the body folds together, face in his
face, almost touching—the lolling tongue,
still wet, even now still wet, the popped-
out eyes!—and now the dead man speaks,
spits a deluge of noises in Nagar's face, a
bloody vocal clump, words, pressed together
somewhere in his throat, cut down from the
rope, now, two, three, ten hours later they
unfurl—the end of the sentence he was not

allowed to finish in his cell? The sentence
he spoke on the roof the day before the sen-
tencing, over and over, because none of the
guards understood him? A sentence meant
just for him, Nagar, a legacy, to spit out
after my death? A curse, a curse on the
executioner?

Nagar lets the body fall, staggers back
two paces, the commander grabs at the air.
What are you doing, Shalom? he asks, irritated. Nagar wants to undo everything. No
dead body should spit at him, sully him
with his blood. Blood is the dwelling place
of the soul, leave it, do not touch it! It
has touched him, colored him, marked him,
on his chest, it covers his face, it is
even in his mouth, which is open from exer-
tion and horror, this blood is even in his
mouth. Who is he now? Still Shalom Nagar?
It is someone else who once again stands in
front of the corpse—grips him by the hips,
lifts the dead body with all his strength,
until the noose is loosened—who stands
there, alone, the body in his arms.

Transport of a Body

Time does not stand still. The commander climbs back down the ladder, two colleagues come and take hold as well, a gray blanket is laid out, then the body is lying on it. His head hangs to one side. His tongue? Someone has put it back inside his mouth.

The colleagues undress him. They undress Eichmann. Nagar stands beside them. Shirt, felt slippers, trousers, socks, undershirt, underpants, they cover him with the blanket. Someone fetches a stretcher.

They lay the body, wrapped in the blanket, on the stretcher. They move through the narrow corridor, to the yard, where a van is waiting. Nagar follows them.

Nagar does not know where they travel to. He knows only that wherever they end up it is hot. Bright and hot. They get out, open the back doors, pull the stretcher out. No, he does that. Alone. His hands shake, he cannot get a firm grip, Nagar pushes the stretcher like a wheelbarrow.

He notices that the prison director is there. The preacher, too. Here, now he is here, too. The body falls off the right-hand side of the stretcher, without the blanket. The naked Eichmann is on the ground, it smells like a forest, is that

the smoke? Two men leap over, Nagar does
not recognize them, the director and the
preacher? No, not him, he turns away, holds
a book over his eyes. Eichmann is back on
the stretcher, Nagar pushes him onward. The
heat hits him like a blow, every step is a
struggle, the air becomes resistance. The
body falls off the left-hand side.

The oven, now he sees the oven, behind a
shimmering curtain. It sits on a small
hill; Nagar must push uphill. He knows the
man stoking the fire, his name is Kols. The
heat becomes a giant hand, Nagar swerves,
the stretcher sways. They have laid down
tracks, sees Nagar, rusty iron bars, along
the last few meters to the oven door. But he
is still too far away. How does Kols stand
the heat? He is made of something else. Or
he has already been burned by life.

Nagar pushes, lifts, trembles. Step by
step, his stretcher on the rails, up to the
oven, now Kols grabs the lever, opens the
door—a fiery gullet. The other men who were
here, the ten, twenty men Nagar saw along
the way, have disappeared. Only the gullet,
the rails, the body, and Nagar.

Flames shoot out, slide over the body,
which they do not want to touch at all,
the man lies still, head tilted, the flames
grip Nagar, tap him on the chest, in the

face, lick at him from all sides, a thousand arms, thousands upon thousands.

Then the door is shut. A hum, as if the
oven might burst, a groaning, a sigh—smoke
billows out from the chimney. Nagar sits on
the ground, the commander stands in front
of him. It's all right, Shalom, he says.
Epstein will drive you home now.

Three

I hadn't seen Nagar again since his visit. Ben hadn't been to see me either, I didn't know why. I spent the days sitting at my typewriter, and the nights in flickering dreams full of elongated necks severed by a noose, and a face that melted in the flames. Sometimes it was the face of my father.

One day, Ben stood at my door again. I had been trying to write the beginning of the next chapter since early that morning but had only managed to type the title:

`Ashes in a Glass`

Are you writing, Moshe?

A question, of course. My friend, Ben. He'll never tell anyone anything. Like why he hasn't been over to see me recently. Or what he actually does on the days he isn't with me and Nagar at the meeting place. He points to the sheet of paper stuck in my typewriter: The final chapter?

What do I know? Is there such a thing as a final chapter? The hero is filed away, his life forced into a circle, it's just repetition from now on, so die: You put a period at the end of a sentence, and turn the following white, empty pages into the kind of nothingness that is often mistaken for eternity, even by the most critical readers. Or the hero finds water in a desert of woe that had seemed infinite, each hope just a mirage until suddenly, a spring appears and turns the white, empty pages into a future full of hope for readers who long for happiness and find harmony everywhere. What do I know?

Shalom was here, Ben.

He came to visit you?

He brought me some lamb, but that wasn't why he came.

Why then?

He had doubts. For the first time, he was doubting the stories he tells. He wanted me to help him. You have to write it the way it was, Moshe, he said.

And did you?

There is no real "way it was," Ben. If there were, you could never write it down. And if it could be written, then no one would be able to understand it. Not even the person writing.

What happens happens, Moshe. When something has happened, that's the way it was. And you can't write that?

No, because that isn't what happens. What really happens shatters. You're watching in a mirror that breaks at exactly that moment.

So you aren't going to help Shalom?

I had no answer to that. Let's go to the meeting place, I said.

We could hear the sheep bleating before we reached the compound. They stood there, nervously banging their heads against the chicken-wire fence. Ben gave them some water, fetched some food. Nagar's apron was dangling from its nail in the shed, his smock was gone. There were tools scattered all over the floor along with several shoes. The whole area looked as if it had been abandoned. The chickens are gone, Ben said. So are the geese. He pushed me past the coops—nothing there apart from a few feathers. He pushed me to the meeting place. There was a brown pool of water on our table and a few nibbled bones beside it. Do you think Shalom will come? He wasn't going to come, Ben knew that. Nagar hadn't been here for a long time. Shall we go and see if he's at home?

Singing interrupted by blows of a hammer. But this wasn't the little song of praise we were used to hearing. It sounded as if Nagar were singing all sorts of songs without finishing any of them. Ben opened the iron gate and pushed me around the house to Nagar's little garden. Chickens strutted through the long grass with geese standing next to them. There were doves sitting on the clothesline. Nagar stood with his back to us. He was wearing the blue smock, singing and working away at something big and square-shaped that he was making out of plywood. Two even bigger structures were already finished. They were obviously going to be used as coops for the chickens and geese. The one he was working on would be the dovecote. Nagar had painted the plywood red and paint had run and dripped everywhere. It looked as if it had been thrown or splashed onto the wood. The sides of the structures had also been painted with a checked white pattern of thin shaky lines. There was no door, just a few holes at different heights that looked as if someone had knocked them out with their fist. These weren't coops, really. They were cages, and there was more wood waiting along with a large roll of barbed wire.

Nagar didn't seem to have noticed us yet, he sang and hammered away, banging in long nails here and there, which didn't necessarily seem to be fixing anything but were being driven into the wood because there had to be hammering. Shalom! Ben called. He had given up the attempt to maneuver my wheelchair through the chaos of wood, wire, and tools. Shalom!

Nagar turned around at last, waved his hammer, banged in another nail, and then came over to us.

What are you doing here? Shalom?

The compound isn't safe anymore, you see. I had to bring them here—the chickens and the geese. I'm going to fetch the sheep later, as well.

What do you mean, not safe?

IV B 4!

What?

Eichmann's department, Ben. His number!

What about it?

It was written on the post where I hang my smock and my apron. In the shed beside the sheep pen.

The post is cracked, Shalom. The paint is beginning to peel. There's no number there.

Yes, there is. Scratched into the wood. His nails are sharp, you know. The compound is going to be his new department. IV B 4!

Nonsense, Shalom! What are you talking about?

He's taking over the meeting place, too, Ben. He's looking for staff. Has he asked you, Moshe?

What are you saying, Shalom? Why would he ask Moshe?

Nagar shrugged his shoulders. Then he started to sing again, left us where we were and went back to his work, to his blood-red cages. Fortresses for his chickens, geese, and doves.

Ben drew in his breath, but he didn't say anything. He grabbed the handles of my wheelchair without a word. Even at the end of the road, we could still hear the hammering and singing getting louder and shriller like a battle cry.

Although these days I think about Nagar more than ever, I don't talk about him when Ben is here. I don't mention his name. Neither does Ben, but I know he's thinking about him, too. Shalom runs riot in our heads, but he is dead in our mouths, extinguished. He greeted us with a raised hammer, he's knocking nails into wood for no good reason, the birdcages are going to spread everywhere, my mind tells me, swamp his house, the whole street, driven by the singing, hammering Nagar; they are going to spread to the edge of the compound, devour everything, the boundaries, the pens, even the meeting place, everything will be daubed in bloody red, decorated with shaky white squares, everything wrapped in barbed wire, until there is no outside left, until everything is cover, fortress, defense.

Aren't you writing anymore, Moshe?

Ben has started visiting me regularly again, always on the same day, at the same time. He's at the door, he unbuttons his coat, comes in, stands by the window, looks out. Has he noticed that the satellite dishes on the neighboring houses are no longer pointing toward my apartment? If he has, it is no surprise to him. He stares out, as if he needs this view, this monotony, the barricaded sky. Sometimes I think that is the only reason why he comes. He stares, turns around. Goes to my desk, leans on it, supporting himself with his large hands. Investigates.

Nothing to check today. No papers, no typed pages, no blank ones. The typewriter has its cover on. Everything I have written has been tied up with string and put on the shelf beside the folders full of newspaper clippings and the books on Eichmann.

Aren't you going to carry on writing, Moshe?

No, I'm not going to carry on writing. He can see that, can't he?

Are you finished?
Finished? With what?

Ashes in a Glass

Those were the last words I had written. Is that an ending?

Are you finished, Moshe?

No.

Why don't you carry on writing, then?

How can I explain this to him? He will ask questions, cut in, object, and I'll say too much.

I'm scared that what I'm writing is actually happening, Ben.

What do you mean?

One of the chapters I wrote before we went to see Shalom was about a Nagar who loses himself:

```
It is someone else who once again stands in
front of the corpse—grips him by the hips,
lifts the dead body with all his strength,
until the noose is loosened—who stands
there, alone, the body in his arms.
```

And what happens? Nagar's no longer himself. He's changed. He stands there by himself, holding the body of Eichmann in his arms. He guides his fingers. Makes him scratch his sign on the post.

You told me what happens shatters, Moshe. It can't be written down. If you can't write what actually happened, then how can anything you write happen?

I tell myself the same thing. They are just words written on paper, lying on a shelf. No breathing, no metabolism, no heart pumping blood between the lines. No matter how my words and sentences connect—they will never be anything but text. Reality feels different. And yet Nagar's question lingers: Where are you writing me to, Moshe?

You're right, Ben. But still I can't get over the idea.

Are you feeling guilty about what is happening to Shalom?

I know I'm talking nonsense. I talk nonsense, I think nonsense. Everything is slipping through my fingers. I don't even believe in Eichmann's death anymore.

Moshe!

Nonsense, you see? Lunacy, even. Eichmann was born in 1906. More than one hundred years have passed since then. Even if he had managed to escape everyone, he would still have been the victim of what people like him called natural reduction, a long time ago. But what can I do? I don't see him as a dead person anymore. I see him alive, growing younger, wearing his black boots again, with a whip in his hand, striding through the halls of the Palais Rothschild, which is full of victims who shy away from him. Jews who can't keep hold of their Judaism, it's escaping them, they let it be taken away. They no longer trust in their God, the covenant with him, Jews who falter, who stand with their backs against the wall. And I see myself standing beside them, but not as one of them. As a traitor. The man Eichmann ordered to be brought to life.

Ben has been to see Nagar. And this time he didn't come back with questions. Instead, he told me about it in a few short sentences. Ben, actually telling me something! For the first time. The world is turning upside down.

Nagar hasn't stopped building those pens, Ben says. He has made more. They take up all the space in his garden now. One cage even sticks out past the house and you can see it from the road, it's painted black. But he has also dismantled some of the pens. Ora doesn't know what to do, Moshe. Shalom has started going to the compound again. To see the sheep.

Ben pushes me to the meeting place. Nagar is nowhere to be seen. Ben makes tea. Takes three pears from his coat pocket. Cuts them in two and puts the pieces beside our cups. We don't talk much. Just a few words about the weather. It's been too dry, it would be good to have a few days of rain. We notice that someone has wiped the table and swept the floor. We look up suddenly at the same time and see him.

Nagar is standing a few feet away from the sheep pen. He's got his suitcase with him. He wipes the sweat from his brow with his sleeve. He turns around once more. His eyes scour the hill lined with cypresses and palm trees and the dilapidated shed in front of it, the corrugated iron fences.

Everything is as it should be. Nagar goes to the shed beside the pen. He swaps his black coat for the blue smock hanging on a nail. Then he puts on his blue apron, opens the suitcase, and takes out a pair of thick rubber soles, a towel, and a wooden box. He ties the soles to the bottom of his shoes.

He opens the latch of the gate, talks to the animals, holds one back, pushes the others away. He forces the chosen sheep to the ground, binds its legs together with two ties. Then he heaves it into the wheelbarrow. Its body hangs over the side, the bound legs stick out. The animal is calm. It stares at him as if it has been stunned. Nagar opens his wooden box. Undoes the catch, lifts the lid, looks inside. He doesn't take anything out, he closes the lid again, fastens the catch. He sits down on a stool next to the wheelbarrow,

puts his hand on the sheep's head. He stays sitting like this for a
long time. Then he gets up, undoes the ties on the animal's fet-
locks, gently tilts the wheelbarrow until the sheep stands shakily
on its four legs. Nagar pats the animal and it goes back into the
pen, where the others welcome it back. Nagar glances across the
compound, sees us, raises an arm, and then comes over. He walks
across the square. He walks slowly, putting one foot in front of the
other, as if he is walking a tightrope.

My knife is broken, Nagar says. He broke my knife.
  Eichmann?
  Yes.
  That's enough, Shalom! I've had enough. Can you see Eich-
mann anywhere here? Is he running around, does he have hands
and feet? Do you see Eichmann anywhere, Moshe? No? I can't see
him either. Perhaps he's hiding? Shall we call him? Eichmann!
Eichmann! Adolf Eichmann! No answer. Or can you hear him
calling? No? So he doesn't have ears either. Maybe—
  Ben—
  Leave me alone, Moshe. Does he have a nose then? Shall we fry
a piece of meat for him? Maybe Eichmann's nose will appear then.
Followed by his mouth. And then the rest of him!
  You don't know anything! You know nothing. You don't know
him. He deludes us all. Who is Eichmann? Where is Eichmann?
Nobody knows.
  You know very well who he is, Shalom.
  Adolf Karl Barth.
  What?
  He's him! He's Otto Henninger, too. Adolf Eckmann, Leo
Ehrenreich, Alfred Veres, Ricardo Klement, Ernst Radinger. One

was a prisoner of war, one was a lumberjack, one poisoned himself, one got shot in the woods. But he was the wrong Eichmann.

Just codenames he used after the war so no one could find him, Shalom. So what? Lots of Nazis did that.

Not codenames, Ben. He is always Eichmann. And he's someone else. But who is he? Sometimes he plays a game with me; he asks me what he's called. I'm allowed to say all the names I can think of except for Eichmann. Eichmann is not allowed! If I say the right one, he smiles, like this, with really thin lips. And then he disappears. If I say the wrong name, he heats up. He burns me, my skin starts to blister. And then I disappear. If you don't know who he is, you'll never know where he is. Before the trial started, they dug out some of Eichmann's old colleagues they wanted to question about him. One of them, I don't know his name, it was something double-barreled, couldn't understand what they wanted. Eichmann? He said it was just a codename, an alias for an undercover operation. They showed him photos; here, they said, this is him. He's in prison in Israel; we are going to put him on trial. The man with the double-barreled name just laughed. I don't know who you've caught there, gentlemen, he said, but I can assure you there is no such person as Eichmann. Eichmann is a codename.

So you were guarding a codename then, Shalom? A codename was sitting at the table? A codename lay on the bed? You tasted food for a codename?

No.

You see? It's all nonsense.

The codename isn't Eichmann.

Well, what is it?

Let me tell you a story. When Eichmann was on trial, the attorney general blamed him for the marches. They happened in the final months of the war. In some country or other. I can't remember which one. But the Jews were to be taken out of that country. But how to do it? There were no more trains running, the lines were broken. So they called for the master. If they cannot be transported, they will just have to walk, he said. Thousands of Jews were rounded up, old people, young ones, men, women, and set marching, back to the Reich to work and be shot.

And the codename?

Wait, Ben. You'll see. Many of the Jews didn't survive the march; it was two hundred kilometers, it was raining, it was cold, they had nothing to eat, they didn't know where to sleep. Many of them died on the side of the road. Eichmann did it, said Hausner, the attorney general. Eichmann ordered the marches, he is responsible. No, Mr. Attorney General, Eichmann said. I did not do that. Hausner lost his temper; he pulled out a piece of paper from the pile on his desk, held it up for everyone to see, and slapped it with the back of his hand. Here, what is this? What does this say, this is your name! he shouted. Eichmann didn't know what he meant, so I was told to fetch the document from the attorney general and take it over to the glass box. Eichmann changed his glasses, lowered his head, and studied the paper. It was very quiet in the courtroom. Everyone was watching Eichmann. Eichmann stared at the document. He removed his glasses, brought the paper up to his face, and read it again. From top to bottom, from left to right. He even turned it over, but there was nothing on the other side. Read it! the attorney general shouted. What am I supposed to read, sir? Eichmann asked. Your signature! The line where you've signed your name. Eichmann looked confused, he turned the page this way and that. The chairman called him to order and told him he must obey the attorney general. So Eichmann started to read, slowly, hesitantly, he took off his glasses, put them back on again, read a few words, commented on them, read a few more, and so on:

A brief recap of the day . . . what is this?

Then I can tell you, I know very well all and sundry were opposed to it.

I know, though I cannot remember who told me. Not int. either . . . no idea, it is absurd.

Not int. at all. Weeks . . . I worked on it for weeks.

The Reichsführer was never . . . what? He never said I was responsible, he never reproached me, the Reich's emissary actually congratulated me . . . on my elegant procedure.

What about Dr. E . . . no idea. E? Dr. E congratulated me for the elegant procedure as well.

Afterward I drank to that with E., schnapps, it was schnapps made from fermented horse milk, mare's milk, I remember because I had never drunk it before.

Great . . . what is this?

Great pleasures . . .

The attorney general had been growing more and more agitated while Eichmann read, he threw his arms into the air, as if he couldn't stand it a moment longer, and then he interrupted him: Just your signature! he shouted. The signature! Your name!

My name is not on this document, Mr. Attorney General, Eichmann said. Hausner caught his breath and the judge looked at Eichmann without a word. I think he was angry, too. Above all, though, he was disappointed. Eichmann noticed and gave an explanation. I am prepared to admit everything I was responsible for, Mr. Chairman, as I have no choice, but in this case, the marches, I must deny any form of participation. It wasn't me. This was no concern of mine, Mr. Chairman. I could not give any orders in this case, I could not stop anything. I had absolutely nothing to do with it, Mr. Chairman, in any manner whatsoever. I must be clear on this. The documents prove it.

The attorney general asks for the paper Eichmann had read to be returned. I fetch it from Eichmann and take it to the prosecutor's table.

Hausner takes the document, looks at it—the page falls to the floor. He picks up the other pages on his desk, stares at them, turns pale, drops them on the floor, one by one. He's as white as a sheet and collapses onto his chair.

The council for the defense, a large, heavy man called Servatius, stands up. Mr. Chairman, I see that the name of the accused doesn't appear on a single one of the documents presented. My client is the victim of a fallacy.

There's disturbance in the courtroom. Judge Landau calls the spectators to order. When things have quieted down, one of the judges intervenes. He is called Raveh. He asks the council for the defense to state the name on each document. What was the name the witnesses had repeated, again and again, with fear and loathing?

I think the attorney general should answer, Servatius says.

But Hausner can't say anything. He is folded up in his chair and shakes his head.

The audience gets more restless. Landau threatens to have the courtroom cleared. Then he asks a guard to collect the papers strewn across the floor. The man comes over, picks them up, and takes them to the judges' table. Landau proceeds to study the documents one by one.

It takes a long time. Occasionally, Landau examines a page several times, while he skims over others or reads every single word, comma, and period.

Finally, Landau puts the documents in order and looks up. Everyone is watching him, he looks back at everyone. All the documents are signed with one and the same name, he says. It isn't the name the witnesses repeated, again and again, with fear and loathing. It isn't the defendant's name.

The audience gasps in horror. People wearing coats wrap them around more tightly, it has suddenly gone cold. Freezing cold. Servatius stands. Would you kindly tell us the name, Mr. Chairman?

Landau leans over and whispers something to the judge called Halevi, sitting on his right. Then he whispers something to Raveh, who is sitting to his left. They both nod. Landau stands.

Nagar, he says. The name is Shalom Nagar.

You see—I was the codename. Just my luck!

Shalom—

No, wait, Moshe. Let me tell you a story. Eichmann used to have a banker, what was he called—

Storfer?

That's right, Storfer, who organized the money for—for his affairs, and later on he bought the ships that were supposed to sail to Palestine. Old ships with broken rudders. They never went anywhere. Eichmann liked Storfer. He looked after him. Then one day, Eichmann comes back from a business trip and hears that Storfer has been deported to Auschwitz. Eichmann gets back into the car and drives to Auschwitz. It's a long journey, it takes him all night, but he doesn't mind. When he arrives the next morning, he walks through the gate and sits down on the first bench he can find. I always stayed by the entrance at Auschwitz, he said. I could go no further. I could not stand all the oven business. The camp commander is informed that he has arrived. His name is Höss: Obersturmbannführer Eichmann is sitting on a bench at the entrance to the camp. Höss has no idea what this is supposed to mean. He goes over, welcomes Eichmann, and then sits down on the bench beside him. They have a chat, talk about German Shepherds and Christmas. Then Eichmann tells Höss that he has come to see Storfer. Höss doesn't know who he means.

Eichmann explains. Storfer is sent for.

Well, well, dear old Storfer, Eichmann says, when the old man is standing before him. This is a bit of a turn for the worse, is it not? Storfer admits that he made a mistake. He hopes everything is going to be all right now. Eichmann shakes his head. I am sorry to say there is nothing I can do, dear Storfer. This is not an official visit, you must understand. It is strictly personal. But even if it were official, I could not do anything for you. I cannot get you out of here.

Storfer complains that he has to sleep on uneven bales of straw. That's hard for me, Herr Obersturmbannführer, he says. I'm an old man, I can only sleep on bales that are flat. Eichmann tells Höss that Storfer needs a decent mattress. Höss sends for the person responsible and orders him to find a mattress.

Storfer complains that he is forced to work too hard in the camp. He can't manage it at his age. Eichmann says to Höss: Listen, I do not want Storfer doing any hard work. Höss calls for a broom. Storfer takes the broom and starts sweeping around Eichmann and Höss.

Höss sends for tea and cake, they drink their tea and eat the cake. Storfer sweeps. When they've finished, Eichmann gets up and says goodbye to Höss. He pats Storfer on the shoulder. And then gets into his Mercedes.

The car drives off. Storfer stands at the fence with his broom in his hand and watches it leave. As soon as he is out of sight, Storfer is shot in the back of the neck. Just his luck.

Twenty-two guards, and one has to go into Eichmann's cell: Shalom Nagar. Just his luck!

Twenty-two guards, and one has to be Eichmann's executioner: Shalom Nagar. Just his luck!

Nagar pushes the button! Nagar is told to take the body down from the gallows! Nagar gets covered in spewed blood. That last sentence written in blood went all over the little Yemenite.

Just his luck!

Eichmann had targets to meet, you know. A number! He was given a number: ten point three million. That was how many Jews there were, that's how many he was supposed to dispose of. He does his sums: How much time does he have, how many trains will it take, how many carriages? How many Jews can he fit in one carriage? They started off with passenger trains, third-class carriages, but they couldn't fit enough in, it took too long, he needs different material, Eichmann said, the Jews need to roll faster! Not passenger trains, he said, Jews are cargo! He needs freight trains, cattle trucks, that's what he wanted. They were used to transport troops to the front, forty-eight men per car. But that still wasn't enough for him. He reasoned that soldiers carry luggage and weapons, which take up space. Jews don't need luggage. He could put seventy, eighty, a hundred in one cattle truck. That's what he did. He was at every station, pressed his arm against the trucks, and then the trains set off, no one could stop them, and he kept his lists. Fanatically! He told me himself. My fanaticism, my zeal! he said, and he is proud of it. The master demonstrated what he was capable of. I am not interested in the individual Jew, he said! I am not concerned with small fry, I only register ten thousand Jews or more. I have to deliver numbers. Huge numbers. And I did deliver, he says. I operated ruthlessly with exacting elegance, the transports rolled, it was magnificent. And if anyone tried to put a wrench in the works, I stepped in. I turned up everywhere. They had to reckon with me at any time, I was there, even when I was not there. Eichmann! Was that a name or an order? They could never tell.

Then the war was over. Eichmann said: I am not interested, it is nothing to do with me. I have my number. And he carried on working. On and on. But he didn't ever finish. Then the people from Mossad caught him, brought him here, and put him in prison. He still couldn't stop. He carried on making plans, writing lists. If he disappeared—then that was part of the plan. He had his quota, the quota had to be fulfilled. He's done his duty now! He is almost finished. There is just one Jew left on the list. He saved him for last. His special Jew, his guard, his keeper. He marked him while he was hanging from the gallows. Blood is the dwelling place of the soul, you know. I could wash his blood from my face, I could do away with the uniform covered in his blood. But his soul. Can you wash away a soul? He has been biding his time. He has stayed with me, never lost sight of me, day and night. He talked! I know everything. And now he is coming. He broke my knife; he is taking over the compound. The meeting place, too. IV B 4, his department. He is looking for workers. Has he asked you yet?

Shalom, he's not asking anyone anything. He can't break anything, he won't do anything. Eichmann is dead!

What do you mean?

Dead, he died, I mean. Fifty years ago!

He doesn't know the difference, Ben.

Who?

Eichmann! Let me tell you a story. After the verdict had been announced, when Eichmann was sentenced to death, a preacher went to see the prison director. His name was Hull and his wife never left his side; she was a slight little woman, dressed elegantly with high heels and a hat and scarf. He had come to save Eichmann's soul, he said. The prison director didn't want to see him. Eichmann will have to look after his own soul, he said. Hull went to someone else, a minister, perhaps, someone who didn't have any objections. Then they asked Eichmann. He didn't want to see a preacher, he didn't have time, he needed to write. Then suddenly he changed his mind. So Hull was allowed to see him after all, twice a week. We took Eichmann to the visiting room and they talked. At first, only Hull spoke, Eichmann listened and shook his head. At some point he ran out of patience and cut off Hull's words. Are you finished? I have had enough, he said, I will not listen to any more. Now I want to have my say. I do not believe the things you preach, he said. You keep coming at me with the Bible and God and Jesus Christ, but I am not interested in what is written in the Bible. It has nothing to do with me. I have my own beliefs. And then he had his say.

I do not believe that God created man, he said. I do not believe that God has a son, and I also do not believe that there is such a thing as hell. I have studied science, I have read many books by mathematicians and physicists. I have gazed at the stars through a telescope, and I have seen the endless realms of heaven mirrored in a well at night. Everything I have seen and read corresponds with my beliefs.

Everything is energy, he said. Us included. We are energy. Energy gets transformed. Something moves, it stands still, it moves again, it stands still. Something heats up, it cools down, it heats up again, it cools down. Back and forth, to and fro. And it is the same with me, he said. Energy is transformed into Eichmann, Eichmann is transformed into energy, energy is transformed into Eichmann again, Eichmann is transformed back into energy. I get posted from one state to the other, he said. Sometimes I have to be energy and then I have to be Eichmann, I cannot control it. It is to do with the greater order of things, the will and the power. This transformation has nothing to do with life or death, Eichmann says. Those are just human concepts. He can be energy and alive, or Eichmann and dead. But there is a secret, he said.

The preacher didn't want to listen to this. He didn't understand what Eichmann was going on about. He kept going back to the Bible, he even brought him one, with passages underlined and lots of handwritten notes. We had to give it to Eichmann when he sat opposite Hull in the visiting room. Eichmann always swiped it away to the edge of the table immediately. It fell to the floor once and he left it lying there. He actually tore up his wife's copy. She often read the Bible and he wasn't happy about that, so he took it away from her and tore it apart in the middle. From then on, his wife either read one half of her torn Bible or the other.

Eichmann wanted to tell his secret, do you understand? But the preacher wouldn't listen. Repent! Repent! he cried, and his wife folded her hands. She had to translate everything. Eichmann and Hull couldn't understand each other, the preacher only spoke English and Hebrew; Eichmann could only speak German and Spanish. Repent! Repent! Eichmann just stared at the two of them blankly. He's trying to tell them his secret, and they won't listen. He couldn't understand that.

And what was his secret? Or don't you know?

I do know.

But you won't tell?

I will tell you, Ben. There is something that stops the transformation.

What?

Ashes. If you transform the human state into ashes, all the energy disappears. It goes into the fire. The flames devour it. There is nothing left to be transformed. The person is gone. He can no longer exist! Like—like a square circle. It was meant to happen to the Jews, do you see? It's what Amalek wants. He gave Eichmann the order. The other leader, what's his name?

Hitler?

He's just a stand-in. The highest German officials talk to Amalek directly. Flammenführer. That's what they call him. Eichmann is Flammenführer's favorite. His Habibi. He whispers in his ear.

Where did you get all this, Shalom?

Habibi? That's what the woman called the wolf in the district. You remember, where the sky is mirrored in the well? That's when Eichmann started to believe.

No, I mean Flammenführer. Where did that come from?

From Eichmann! Sometimes he looks away and talks into the air, you see, when he thinks I'm not listening. He speaks and then he listens for ages. When he's done, he clicks his heels and stands to attention. *Jawohl*, Herr Flammenführer! At your command!

Nagar nudges Ben in the ribs with his elbow. He seems relaxed, almost buoyant. At your command! Herr Flammenführer! *Jawohl!* They're nuts, the Germans. Mad, that's it. He stuffs his two halves of pear into his mouth, then mine and then the ones lying beside Ben's cup. He is beaming happily, with gleaming eyes.

Ben is quiet. He's grinding his jaws as if he were chewing something. Not pears, something tougher. Nagar gets up, Ben grabs him by the arm and pulls him back down onto the chair.

What is it, Ben? I was going to fry us some meat. I've still got some left.

Wait, Shalom. You can fry your meat later. First, you've got to listen. Eichmann isn't here, Shalom. He won't set up a department; he's not going to do anything. He was destroyed! You just said so yourself: If the human state is transformed to ashes, the energy disappears. It goes into the fire, is devoured by the flames. There's nothing left to be transformed. The person is gone. He can no longer exist! Eichmann is ashes, Shalom. You pushed his body into the oven. He is ashes!

Shalom looks at his friend Ben. There is warmth in his gaze, gratefulness and the gentle despair reserved for those we love who cannot and will not understand.

Eichmann is Amalek, Ben. One of Amalek's people. You can't defeat them. Samuel cut Agag to pieces, but the pieces remain—transformation! Mordechai hanged Haman, but the body remains—transformation!

Nagar pushed Eichmann's body into the oven—ashes! Remember the ashes, Shalom! You destroyed him. You are the last in the line.

Let me tell you a story. Us guards were ordered to keep the light on in Eichmann's cell at all times. We had to watch what he was doing every minute. But sometimes we did turn it off. It was very bright and enough light from the hall fell through the door hatch. A small square of shimmering light—like the first streak of dawn. Eichmann always avoided the square, he never stepped on it, not once. He squeezed past it to get to his bed, arranged his slippers in such a way that they could never touch the shining tiles. Then it was the night before—before he was hanged. None of us knew it was his last evening, but he—he could tell. At some point, we turned off the light. The square of light shone on the floor. Eichmann sat at his desk, he was still writing although he could hardly see a thing. When it was time for him to go to bed, he got up and stepped onto the lit-up tiles. It was the only time he didn't skirt around them. Suddenly it was his light; on this last night, it belonged to him. There he stood, illuminated. That was a sign, do you see? He knows he's going to die. Death is on its way. It's the same for all people, darkness, the end. But he, he stands in the light.

Eichmann is nothing but ashes, Shalom. Hanged, burned, scattered in the sea, hounded across the world, dissolved in the oceans, no trace of him anywhere. It's over.

No, Ben. He is here. He is coming to get me. It's always me they're after, you see. I am Saul.

Who are you?

The people spoke to Samuel: Give us a king. We want to be like all the other nations. Samuel turned to the Lord and the Lord said: Follow their will. There is one among them and his name is Saul, which means the requested one. Samuel did as the Lord commanded. He anointed Saul and said to him: You will be king. Only the people knew nothing about this. Samuel didn't want to set a king before them. He wanted him to come from among them. He let them cast lots. They had all come. All the tribes of Israel, each and every one. So they cast lots and the lot fell on Saul. But Saul was not there. He refused to take on his role. They searched for him and couldn't find him. At last they pulled him out from behind some crates and bundles and he stood among them. Long live the king! But Saul, the requested one, didn't want this. So many men, but the lot fell on the one who didn't want it.

You aren't Saul, Shalom. You didn't hide. They didn't have to search for you behind any crates or bundles.

They did. They searched for me. It was my day off. I went for a walk with Ora and our boy. They found me by the hills and dragged me into the car. And afterward, when Eichmann was hanging on the gallows—I hid behind my colleagues. But Merhavi called for me. Come over here, Shalom, he said. This isn't a game. I was dragged out from behind crates and bundles. I've been hiding ever since. Every day. Every night. But he always finds me.

He's dead, Shalom. You're his executioner.

Executioner? The only one this country ever had? I come from Yemen, you know. I was thirteen, fourteen years old when I came to Israel. They'd told us about the war, but not about the other things. Eichmann? Who is he? I knew nothing about him. I'm Salaam Nagar from Sanaa. What did I have to do with Eichmann? They mistook me for someone else—there was someone who looked like me. He was called Yoram, I didn't know him. It's a play. Nagar was played by Yoram. Who was Eichmann? He was somebody else, too. A stand-in on behalf of someone else. The gallows, the noose. Those were just—what do you call that in the theater?

Props?

Props, that's right. The same goes for the body. And the blood! Nothing is real.

The oven, Shalom! The oven was real. He was cremated.

Oven? Nagar blinks and squints, as if he has only just now noticed the evening sun standing low in the sky, shining on us for real.

The oven was made of iron, Shalom. They don't make props out of iron.

Zeklikovsky built it. In Petah Tikva.

You see. So it does exist!

Nagar doesn't say anything to that. He studies his hands, wipes them on his clean blue apron. Not a drop of blood to be seen.

The oven exists, Shalom. Built for Eichmann. Eichmann's body was burnt in it.

Where?

I don't know where the oven stood. Surely you must know?

I wasn't there, Ben.

Of course you were there! You pushed Eichmann into the oven!

I felt ill. Merhavi said: It's all right, Shalom. Epstein will take you home.

Eichmann was burnt in that oven!

They hid it afterward.

Eichmann's remains?

The oven. No one was ever meant to find it.

So it is still there somewhere!

In the prison. They took it to the prison, Ben.

It was below the stairs, they'd taken off the chimney.

Maybe it's still there, Shalom! It must be there. We'll go tomorrow, the three of us. To Ramla. And if you stand in front of the oven, you will know that Eichmann has been reduced to ashes. No more transformations!

Where are you asking us to, Ben? Where are you talking us to? If we stand in front of the oven, you will know that Eichmann has been reduced to ashes. A conditional sentence. Does he understand the implications of this grammatical form? If—then. If not—then not. White or black. That's Ben. He doesn't question the two forms of logic, the basic equation of reality. The world and its telling must surely comply. That is why he asks questions, jogs memories, corrects. And if something can't be explained with words, then it needs to be checked.

So tomorrow we will go to Ramla, to the prison. Will they even let us in? They probably will. They'll do a favor for their old colleague Nagar.

The evening came. The morning came. That wise alteration praised by the priests on the rivers of Babylon in their hymn to creation. No night should last forever, not even for Shalom Nagar, the first and last unwilling executioner, the brave adversary of Amalek. I am still sitting at the table, feeling uneasy, when Ben arrives to pick me up. It is time to go, Moshe, he says.

Ben has borrowed a car for my sake. Nagar wants to go on the bus, by himself. I imagine him walking round his old haunts in the prison before we arrive. He climbs up the stairs past Eichmann's apartment, his knees turn to jelly, he opens the door that leads to the prison roof. Up there everything is just how it was fifty years ago. The barriers are still there, railings lined with sacks to hide Eichmann from view, the path past the railings leading to the square the guards called the sports ground is still there. So is the chair. I imagine Nagar crossing his arms in front of his chest, bowing his head, and pacing around the square, down the side, then turning around, walking halfway back, then across the square, turning around again, walking back to the start. A pattern that doesn't make sense. I imagine him sitting down on the chair, waiting for someone to come and give him his cigarette. Then he remembers that he doesn't smoke.

Ben parks the car at the prison gate, walks around to the trunk to fetch my wheelchair, which he took apart for the journey, and puts it back together. We show our papers, the guard nods, lets us into the yard, and points us in the right direction. The main entrance is over there, he says. They are expecting you. Step by step, Ben pushes the wheelchair across the yard. The ground puts up a fight. Either the wheels sink in or they get jammed by stones and Ben has to pick another route. Soft like flowing sand or hard as a rock. We don't leave any tracks as we make our way, no tire prints left by the wheelchair, no footprints from Ben's shoes even though he puts all his weight into the ground with every step forward. We crunch on, inch by inch, concentrating on the next move.

We don't see Nagar until his shadow falls over us. Ben pauses, I look up. And I am struck by a thought so sharp and clear, that I can almost feel my legs again:

You're the wrong victim, Shalom. Eichmann is only following you as a stand-in. In place of another. It's me, Adolf Schneider, I'm the one he's after. The traitor.

We reach the main building. Ben is breathing hard, worn out by his battle with the gravel. My hands are shaking. I can't keep my head still. A guard meets us at the entrance. He has been ordered to take us to the oven. Your description on the telephone helped, he says to Nagar, we found it on the ground floor of the office building, behind the stairs. Over there, just across the yard on the left. Then he looks at me and at Ben, who is covered in sweat. We can go through the main building, he says. This way, gentlemen.

One corridor after the other, light from the barred windows crisscrosses on the floor. As Ben pushes me through it, we slice up the shadows. There is hardly a sound. Just the echo of footsteps. Out of sync at first but then they fall into step. At the end of each corridor the guard unlocks the door, lets us pass, locks it again, and then walks ahead of us into the next corridor. Eventually he slows down. Just one more door to go, he says. Nagar starts to hum, but the creaking hinges drown out the sound as the door opens. I'll leave you here, the guard says.

Behind us, the heavy door bangs shut. We listen to the key being turned in the lock.

In front of us, fitted into the triangular space beneath the stairs, we can see the outline of a bulky object partly visible beneath a gray tarpaulin. Ben hesitates before he nods at Nagar. They lift off the tarpaulin together, carefully folding it to one side. As it slides to the floor, dust whirls through the air and settles on the exposed oven standing there all black and solid. I recognize it, although I have never seen it before, compare measurements in my head, stare at the incinerator, the metal ribs, the heavy door at the far end. Everything fits. But seeing is not enough if I'm going to banish my doubts. Ben can tell what I'm thinking and moves me closer. I stretch out my hand. Touch the metal with the tips of my fingers, notice the gritty texture and a long straight welding line. Ben is next to me. He makes a fist and raps the cylindrical frame once, twice. And Nagar? Nagar is standing beside the oven door, resting his hand on the side of the oven. He strokes it, cautiously, gently. Then he pauses and looks at us, tears in his eyes.

The Lord is my throne, Ben. And Moses said: The hand on the throne of the Lord!

When the guard returns, Ben and Nagar have just finished covering the oven up again. He lets us out through the door to the yard. The oven was pushed and dragged through this door fifty years ago. Outside, the sun has stopped shining. Nagar embraces Ben, then he bends down to me and takes hold of my shoulders, winks at me. For the first time since we've known each other, he grips the handles of my wheelchair.

The guard comes with us. Is the gravel beneath the wheels more even now, or is it thanks to Shalom that we are gliding?

When we get to the middle of the yard, the guard stops. We shake hands, say thank you. The guard pushes back his cap, wipes his brow. Something wasn't right with that oven, he says. The incinerator didn't get hot enough, all the heat escaped. Maybe they didn't know how to operate it, or maybe it had a defect. At any rate, Eichmann didn't burn properly. Only part of his body was burnt to cinders, the rest—I don't know. They scattered the ashes into the sea and buried what was left.

I feel giddy; I can sense Nagar stiffening behind me. I cling to the sides of my wheelchair and try to start humming. Nagar joins in. Ben doesn't join in. Instead, he asks a question.

Buried? Where?

Somewhere nearby, the guard says, and makes a vague sweeping gesture. Perhaps here, where we are standing.

About the Authors

Astrid Dehe is a journalist, translator, and teacher. She lives in Varel, Germany.

Achim Engstler is a university and adult education lecturer and writer. He lives in Varel, Germany.

Dehe and Engstler have worked as a writing duo since 2008 and are the authors of six books in German.

About the Translators

Helen MacCormac has been a freelance translator since 1998 and lives in Kassel, Germany.

Alyson Coombes is an editor and translator and lives in London.

Celebrating 25 Years of Independent Publishing

Thank you for reading this book published by The New Press. The New Press is a nonprofit, public interest publisher celebrating its twenty-fifth anniversary in 2017. New Press books and authors play a crucial role in sparking conversations about the key political and social issues of our day.

We hope you enjoyed this book and that you will stay in touch with The New Press. Here are a few ways to stay up to date with our books, events, and the issues we cover:

- Sign up at www.thenewpress.com/subscribe to receive updates on New Press authors and issues and to be notified about local events
- Like us on Facebook: www.facebook.com/newpress books
- Follow us on Twitter: www.twitter.com/thenewpress

Please consider buying New Press books for yourself; for friends and family; or to donate to schools, libraries, community centers, prison libraries, and other organizations involved with the issues our authors write about.

The New Press is a 501(c)(3) nonprofit organization. You can also support our work with a tax-deductible gift by visiting www.thenewpress.com/donate.